J-Hawk Nation

Mark Reinsmoen

outskirtspress

DENVER, COLORADO

Outskirts Press, Inc.
http://www.outskirtspress.com

Paperback ISBN: 978-1-4787-0646-5
Hardback ISBN: 978-1-4787-0645-8

Outskirts Press and the "OP" logo are trademarks belonging to Outskirts Press, Inc.

PRINTED IN THE UNITED STATES OF AMERICA

To my mother and in memory of my father who raised our family on a farm and provided us with everything we needed, much love, and room to grow

To my wife, Dianne . . . my soul mate, my partner, and my medical advocate

To the Joice Public School Junior High J-Hawk basketball teams of 1957-1958 and 1958-1959, whose players inspired the creation of the basketball-playing characters in this book and who shared many adventures with me back in those days when we were once young

Foreword

I did not go looking for a book to write . . . the idea for this one found its way to me, came to me . . . like E.T. came to Eliot, . . . and I knew that I was the only person who could write this story and maybe bring a small amount of recognition and honor to my hometown.

As an elementary school teacher I helped develop skills in young students, and I followed their academic successes by searching for their names on the "A" Honor Roll listings in the local newspapers. I also attended their games as they pursued athletic stardom on the soccer and football fields, the hockey rink, and the basketball court during their high school years.

It was while I was watching a basketball game that I thought about my past meager accomplishments when I ran the court in high school. Could I have played with today's young stars? No way. But if . . . and this is the premise for *J-Hawk Nation* . . . if the small school I attended in rural Iowa had remained open, and if the kids with whom I had played basketball on the junior high teams at Joice Public School in 1957-1958 and '58-'59 had all stayed together, then we **might** have had a fantastic high school basketball team in 1961-1962.

All of the basketball action in the book is of course fictional because this season never existed for our high school team. Our school was a victim of consolidation in the fall of 1960, and that caused two of my junior high teammates to move away to other states with their families, eliminating any chance for us to all play together on a high school team.

The characters in this book were pieced together, using my junior high teammates as inspirations. The anecdotal stories that weave in and out through the basketball season are adventures that I remember from my youth, and they are written with as much truth as the fifty to sixty years of passing time has preserved, but I allowed myself to use some literary license to alter them as needed. It has been amazing to me how so many of these incidents came flooding back, sometimes very vividly, and I attempted to give them new life after having buried them in the recesses of my brain for all those years.

As it happens with many teens, it was during my high school years that I fell in love for the first time, and these memories also resurfaced, bringing with them strong emotions of that grand adventure. Having a special friend had been a very important factor in the building of my self- esteem, and I drew upon my own personal experience, as well as years of additional insight about adolescent behavior, (some of which was achieved by raising a son and a daughter), in fabricating the story line of the innocent relationship between the boy who tells this story and the girl he meets during his basketball season.

By including the newspaper columns, I was able to provide a sort of antagonist who drove some of the early action, and it allowed me to write in a second voice, that of a man who saw things from a different viewpoint and who added some maturity and wisdom to complement the narration given by the sixteen-year-old basketball player.

Most of the memories that I revisited were positive, and they brought me contentment, but a couple of them reminded me of a painful experience or two, and I tried to deal with them in my own way through what I wrote.

I am an avid bicyclist, and almost all parts of this story were developed in my mind while I was pedaling my bike on the roads near where I live. While out on my ten and twenty-mile rides I kept repeating dialogue ideas until I felt I had gotten it right, and I retold events of the stories until I thought they made sense. Upon returning from that day's ride, I sat down and wrote as quickly as I could so I would not lose any of what I had mentally written, and I continually revised and rewrote what I had created from the seat of my bike. Since many of my ideas came to me in random order, I had the additional task of working these episodes into the proper sequence in my book.

Writing this book has given me purpose, pleasure, and some peace. I am hopeful that it will bring some enjoyment to past and present residents of my hometown, friends and family members who have waited patiently during the three years of this project, and my former students whom I taught during my forty years as a dedicated teacher.

Prologue

Maybe none of this would have happened had it not been for that one column that appeared in the *Globe* that Saturday in early November. We may still have had a good basketball team at Jeffers High School, but we **were** quite inexperienced, our coach had just a high-school education and was only a few years older than we players were, and he didn't teach at our school. Just a few years back he had centered the only J-Hawk team that had ever made it to "state." Our superintendent asked him to coach our final season, even though he had never coached before, because our previous coach took another job and moved away. Coach did have another job at our school. He drove a school bus, hauling many farm kids to and from the school at Jeffers, so he was connected to many of us.

That column was like an alarm clock going off loudly and directly in our ears. It was a wakeup call: **Get up, you guys! Get going! You've got a lot of work to do. You can't accomplish anything unless you rise up and start moving! Apply yourself! Don't waste this opportunity!**

Perhaps it was like the announcement made over the PA at the Brickyard in Indianapolis every Memorial Day: **"Gentlemen, start your engines!"**

We did wake up, and we did start our engines. That one column fired us up, pushed us to push ourselves, and it is for that reason that I am suggesting that John Garris of the *Globe* was our team's MVP.

Here's the way I see it. Without his printed words maybe we don't wake up. Maybe we let this basketball season happen just like most other seasons have gone in our small town. Play hard, have fun! Win many games, lose some!

Mr. Garris motivated us because we didn't like what he wrote about us.

We're better than that. We want more than this. Let's not be satisfied to just have a good year. Let's make this the best year this town has ever seen.

We didn't exactly see him as a fan of our team. We thought he was an enemy. He did reach us, however, though I don't believe that was his purpose. He had taken his shot at us, and he would move on to other teams, we thought. We figured that all he wanted was an audience for his sarcasm and his wit, and we just happened to be a good target.

As it turned out, his pencil lead was sharp. Though he wasn't a member of our team or even of our community, he was still a big reason for our successful season. He used his powerful pencil well, and because of just a few words he wrote in that preseason newspaper column, our J-Hawk basketball team and our sleepy town became alive.

In the Stands – With John Garris

I'm using my column today to preview the North Central Conference boys' basketball teams. I've talked to coaches and other experts to get a rundown on the teams.

Shelby – The conference championship trophy could find its new home in Shelby at the end of the season. They return six letter winners and a coach who has won over 70% of his games during his 23 years as head coach.

Benson – They reload this year with an upper-class lineup and a strong bench. Rebounding may be their albatross due to the lack of height, so I expect to see them develop as a running squad. I like their chances in the conference.

Mitchell – Every year new shooters step up to make this team competitive, and it appears that this year will not be an exception. Four senior starters return. This team should finish in the upper half of the standings.

Kendall – This team was strengthened with the transfer in of a true center from Troy. With experienced forwards returning, the lineup looks good if the young

guards can push the ball and play good defense. I predict that the Knights will enjoy a successful season.

Ashton – The Cougars may be a strong team this season after taking their lumps last year due to inexperience. They showed steady improvement toward the end of last year, and if they can start where they left off, they will finish in the top five.

Jeffers – It appears that a mediocre season is on the horizon for the J-Hawks. They are an inexperienced bunch with only a single starter returning and a first-year coach. They will need to lean heavily on character to avoid losing more games than they win. Only two seniors will get much time, and it may take several games before the tall sophomores can be counted on to produce in the tough conference.

Morgan – The Mustangs will again be a running team. They have three starters returning, but they are missing their two main scorers from last season. They expect to play ten players and will be counting on lots of fast-break baskets. It could be a long year.

Upton – I expect the Lions to be able to compete with most teams early in the game, but a weak bench will make it difficult to match up with running teams. Two senior shooters will do most of the scoring. Rebounding will depend on positioning due to short baseline players.

Mayville – It's been about a decade since the Eagles have enjoyed a winning season. I don't see it changing this year. Four letter winners return, but individual play has kept them from discovering the value of teamwork. If the shooters are hitting their shots, they could manage some upsets.

Burton – I will be cheering for the Bengal youngsters as they take the court against the more experienced and more skilled teams in the conference. Graduation hit this team hard, and traditionally it takes a couple of years to recover. Two juniors will lead the attack.

Chapter 1
Pickett and the Bus Ride

Tonight's bus ride to Morgan for our first basketball game of the season was nothing like the ride home from my first day of school in first grade. I had never ridden a school bus before that day, as I hadn't gone to kindergarten. When my second-grade sister and I boarded the bus at the end our driveway, beyond the tall maple trees, on that August morning, we were driven directly to the school in Jeffers, as we were the last students to be picked up. I knew the way to town, so I had no problems.

The ride home was a different story, however. The bus driver, a stranger to me, was about a quarter of a mile from our farm on that gravel road when he turned onto another road and headed north.

What's he doing?

Tears started streaming down my face, and I screamed out, "This is not the way to my house!" All the voices on the bus quieted, and everyone stared at me. My sister tried to calm me and explained that since we were the last to get on the bus in the morning, we would be the last to be dropped off in the afternoon. I'm not sure I understood. Why hadn't anyone told me this before? This was very traumatic for me.

I still remember that bus ride, and of course I have laughed about it for years. Often times as I travel by bus to an away basketball game, this memory returns. I don't share it with anyone, and no one has ever teased me about that ride home from school. I think the memory of that ride is lost to everyone but me, and that is good. I just smile, chuckle to myself, shake my head a little, and give a quick thought to my first year in school.

Tonight as I sat with San Juan, heading to Morgan, I asked myself, "What am I feeling tonight?" I'm certainly not afraid. I don't seem nervous. So I'm starting at guard for first time in a high school basketball game? Big deal! I've started before . . . in both seventh and eighth grades. I've started many, many baseball games from ages 8 – 15 . . . even in high school . . . sometimes as the pitcher. There's no nervousness coming from me tonight.

Does Laser appear nervous? I took a good look at him. He is starting at guard in his first game as a senior leader. Like me, he's five feet eight inches tall, but he wears athletic glasses, so no one ever mixes us up. He started only 2 or 3 games last year when injuries forced other players to sit out, but he was a starter in eighth grade, and he's a baseball player too. He's pitched in many games. He has as much or more experience than I do. Laser appears very relaxed. He's always confident in himself.

Then I glanced over at the two tall sophomores, Abe and Captain Hook. They would play the two forward positions for our J-Hawk team, and though they were young, they brought a significant amount of height into the lineup at six feet six and six feet four inches tall, respectively. They certainly weren't looking restless or out of place on the team bus. I think they had discovered in our practices that they belonged in the starting lineup, and all upper classmen had welcomed them. They seemed very comfortable tonight, relaxed, not nervous.

Right now they were talking quietly with Otto and Tucson, laughing frequently. These last two guys were also sophomores, and they would be counted on to make big contributions coming off the bench, giving rest to us starters.

San Juan, another top reserve and a junior like me was sitting next to me. He had started games in junior high and on several baseball teams. He's enjoying the bus ride tonight like the others. Everyone seems loose and relaxed.

When I think about it, everyone who goes to school at Jeffers is counted on to contribute in a variety of ways, whether it involves athletics, music, or drama. Each grade level in high school has only 9 to 13 students, meaning our high school enrollment was under 45 students. We had an uneven split of boys and girls. There were only 18 boys in high school, and a few of the less athletic boys chose to focus on music and drama activities instead of competing in sports. This year we were lucky to fill the twelve uniforms and the twelve spots on the roster. Everyone has numerous chances to be part of something at Jeffers, and many students choose to participate in several activities. All students had performed in the grade-school operettas for several years, and most have sung in concerts, played in the band, acted in plays, delivered speeches in contests, and played on the J-Hawk sports teams. Tonight would not be a new experience for any of us. Our school at Jeffers prepared us for nights like this. We were ready . . . especially Pickett.

When you are the only starter returning from the previous year's team, and you happen to be a senior who is very skilled at shooting, rebounding, passing, and defending . . . you are expected to be a leader, and Pickett did not disappoint.

At six feet three inches tall, he was our center and our lead dog, the player the rest of us could look to for guidance. He was the strongest player by far, and of course he was the most experienced. He had played a lot during his sophomore season as a sixth or seventh man, and last year as a junior he had started every game.

I began calling him "Pickett" last year, and the name caught on with the other players and the students in school. Pickett was famous on our team for setting great screens and "picks" to free up players for open shots whenever our opponents tried to cover us with man-for-man defense. His screens were wide and solid, and they served the purpose of a really tall picket fence: defending players couldn't go through Pickett, they had to go around him. Occasionally a defender was surprised when he ran into the fence called "Pickett." Whenever an opponent ended up on the floor upon impact, Laser and I would shake our heads sympathetically and utter, "Uff da." We enjoyed seeing a player hit the floor because it meant this player might become a little apprehensive about defending so closely and may slow down a little, giving us more of an advantage.

There was a second reason, an even stronger one that supported my choice of the name Pickett. It was based on something that happened last year as our girls' team and boys' team rode the bus to our away games.

Pickett is a gifted musician, a great singer. He has a soft, mellow, bass voice, and on the bus trips to and from the games he sang soft melodies from the back seat of the bus as he used his pick to strum the chords on his ukulele. Most of the time the rest of us relaxed and just listened, but at times a few of us would join in quietly on familiar refrains. Pickett was quite good at playing the uke . . . He could really "pick it."

Setting screens . . . playing the ukulele . . . "Pickett" was the right name for him.

Tonight as we rode the bus for our season's first game, I expected I would again hear a few songs I enjoyed last year: "Michael, Row the Boat Ashore," "We Shall Overcome," "This Land Is Your Land," "Camp-town Races," as well as some Bible Camp favorites.

The music always seemed to calm us. Everyone could relax, enjoy the company of teammates, and think ahead to that night's game. No one ever talked negatively about bus rides to games. For us it was pleasurable. We enjoyed traveling to another school's gym. We didn't see an away game as something to worry about. It was an opportunity.

When we boarded the bus to head to a game there was no anxiety. We all wore confident smiles because an away game was just another game that happened to be in someone else's gym. We had no fear. We had hunger, and we expected to win.

In tonight's first game of the season I think we found out that we will be a tough team to play against this year. Starting two sophomores does make us a young team, but these two guys also make us a tall team. We have good depth, as several bench players showed tonight that they can be plugged into the lineup with no big let downs.

Coach had a great plan for the game tonight, keeping our defense very basic. We didn't use our full-court press that we had worked on in practice. We just played a simple zone, moving our feet quickly and covering the passing lanes with outstretched arms, especially the long arms of our three baseline players.

On offence we moved the ball with sharp passes and took good open shots. All players were encouraged to take their shots when open, even the sophomores. Most of our shots found the hoop, and although we weren't great tonight, we were good, and getting this first win gave us confidence.

Garris had suggested in his article in the Globe that we would be a better team than Morgan. We expected to beat them, but we won't be satisfied just beating the weaker teams. With time we will improve and challenge the top teams. In fact, we expect to become a top team, no matter what Garris had written about us.

We had reached our goal of getting all twelve players into the game tonight, and the bus ride home was as enjoyable as the earlier trip to Morgan had been.

Now Pickett lulled us to sleep with his music.

Tonight was the first step of what we hoped would be an exciting journey for our J-Hawk basketball team and for our small community.

In the Stands – With John Garris

I received some mail from a couple of J-Hawk fans recently. Though it wasn't really nasty, it had some bite to it. One writer took exception to something I had written in my preseason preview of boy's basketball for the North Central Conference about the J-Hawks needing to rely on character to win because of their youth and inexperience. I've been invited to their home opener Friday night (with ticket provided) where I've been told, "Character will be on display."

They are off to a 2-0 start after two road games, defeating Morgan last Friday and then upsetting Kendall on Tuesday. If there are no big games elsewhere on Friday night, I may head to Jeffers with my free ticket in hand for a look and a possible earful.

I was "hand delivered" a second envelope that contained a note about Tuesday's J-Hawk win. It read like this: "

The following characters scored points in the win over Kendall:

Pickett 21
Laser 15
Captain Hook 12
Catcher 14
Abe 10
Otto and Sons 11
Final score: J-Hawks 83 /
Knights 68

I admit my curiosity has been piqued, but I have a question for the J-Hawks. Do you believe that your team has character just because some "characters" scored points? I'll need to see more than this. Stay tuned everyone . . . more to follow.

Chapter 2

Driving the Cows

My quickness was one of my greatest assets in the gym. I had worked on it daily while growing up on the farm. My brother and I shot baskets in the haymow when enough bales had been removed from the south end, and we played baseball every chance we got. Moving quickly was extremely important on our "baseball field" of dandelions, all kinds of other weeds, and a little grass. Whether it was a baseball, softball, rubber ball, or whiffle ball . . . it didn't matter. When an errant throw was heading into the woods that surrounded our small front yard of a playing field, you ran as quickly as you could while you focused your eyes on that exact spot where the ball was last seen entering the dense growth of trees, thorny bushes, and itch weed. How long did you want to stand in that itch weed searching for the ball while mosquitoes were lunching on your arms, legs, face, and the back of your neck? Bobby and I moved quickly. The unwritten rule, and it made sense, was that the thrower was responsible for following the flight of the ball and finding it after it sought refuge in the woods. We learned to judge our throws pretty well, and often times we knew the ball was headed for trouble even before it evaded the intended target, and a mad dash was necessary, or our game might be over.

We played night ball, too, under the one-bulb, yard light pole. Maybe I was even quicker at night when a good hit or bad throw meant my sweaty body would be entering the dark confines of the woods, where the mosquitoes were waiting for fresh meat, and the only sources of light were that distant yard light and whatever fireflies were working the game that evening.

I worked on my long-distance sprinting also. One of my daily chores was to walk down to the far pasture, old beat-up axe handle in hand (no axe head, of course) to "drive" the dairy cows home for Dad's evening milking. These cows knew they would be milked at six o'clock every night, rain or shine, but they always grazed way down by the meandering creek at the far end of our long right-angled pasture, about a quarter-mile away, guaranteeing that I had a job to do every day. Bobby was my assistant, and we both knew I was in charge.

It's kind of funny that my best friend and playing partner, my younger brother by three years, could, in one instant, become a competitor. I "drove" the herd from the rear waving my axe handle in the air for effect while Bobby's job was to walk to the side of the cows, making sure our milk supply stayed next to the fence. Sometimes he lost focus and messed up (It was never my fault.) and allowed a cow or two to turn back, to get between us, and escape in the opposite direction.

When this happened it was as if we had become enemies on opposing track teams. Picture the race starter raising his gun, calling out, "Ready . . . set . . . BANG!" The gun sounded and we runners took off instantly. Bobby ran for his life, diving through the thistles under the barbed-wire fence and sprinting across the fields and down the farm lane, fearful that I would catch him. He was quick and fast, and his head start would maybe be enough of an advantage that he would make it to the safety of the house before I could catch him and teach him a lesson. I also low-crawled under the fence, making sure not to get snagged by the barbs. My motivation for sprinting as fast as I could go was simple: No way was my younger brother going to get by with this mistake again. This was not the first time, and it probably would not be the last. I felt he should learn from his mistakes, and I'd be his teacher. I chased with fire in my eyes, and the cows were left to find their own way home.

Did I know that through this "running and chasing cow chore" I was conditioning my body and spirit for basketball? Probably not, but the skills translated. My first steps were really quick, and my endurance was second to no one. I was an athlete, a good one, because I had spent my childhood playing hard and training.

The cows? They always managed to make it to the barn close to milking time. I asked Dad why we needed to guide the cows home every day if they could find their own way without us. I never did get the answer I wanted to hear, and my training regimen continued with races across the fields on a regular basis.

It really didn't matter if I caught Bobby or not. Eventually I would find him unprotected and punch him a few times as part of the lesson. After supper everything would be forgiven and forgotten, and we would step outside to our ball field to pitch to each other or just play catch.

This season I will need every bit of my good conditioning and quickness because Coach told us we would be a fast-breaking and full-court-pressing team. We will always be moving, and we will play hard. We will not be resting on defense or offence. So far I haven't heard anything from Coach that doesn't please me. I like to play fast. All the players on the team like to run, and we can pull three or four players off the bench to rest us starters. This puts pressure on our opponents to be in really good shape, too, or they won't be able to compete with us. We've only played two games, but we won them both, and the school is starting to buzz because of our winning streak.

Chapter 3

Catcher

I remember that day really well. I was thirteen years old, preparing to play a baseball game in the Midget League on a dirt diamond at an away field in a small town like ours. It was a hot, steamy July afternoon, and our regular catcher had to miss this game because of a family vacation, and we needed a replacement. While I was warming up my arm, playing catch with Laser, I commented to another teammate that, since he'd done a little catching at practice, he'd probably be behind the plate today. Coach heard me and walked over. He wasn't angry, but he tapped me on the chest with his pointing finger and said to me, "You are catcher."

"Coach . . ." I said protesting. "I have no idea what to do back there. I've never caught before."

"Today you will learn," Coach replied. "It's really quite simple. Crouch down behind the plate, far enough back so you don't get hit in the head when the batter swings. Keep your eyes open, and when the ball comes to you, catch it, and toss it back to your pitcher. If you miss the ball, hustle back to the screen, pick up the ball, and then throw it back to your pitcher. If anyone tries to steal, fire the ball to the base in the direction the runner is headed . . . and try not to get your uniform too dirty because we have a makeup game tomorrow."

Those were Coach's instructions. That was it. My lesson for playing catcher had come in "100 words or less," and starting with that game I became "Catcher," just as Coach had named me. Laser was the one mostly responsible for the name sticking that day because all game long he kept saying to me, "You are Catcher," using his best imitation of Coach's voice. Soon the other players were repeating the same phrase.

I remember walking to our bench after our team won that game, wearing a big smile on my face, lots of dirty sweat on all exposed skin, and dirt and grass stains on my faded grey uniform. Of course I was tired. I was really hot because of wearing the mask, chest protector, and shin guards, and I had raced to the backstop several times, though not as many times toward the end of the game as I had at the beginning. During the 5-inning game I had improved my skills . . . a lot, and I felt proud of myself. I had actually enjoyed playing "catcher," and I hoped to get another chance to catch . . . soon . . . maybe tomorrow. I liked all the action.

Coach told me as we picked up the bats and the rest of the gear, "Good job today, Catcher."

After the fall baseball season ended at school this year we started basketball practice in the gym. It was at one of the first practices that Laser explained to me that my name "Catcher" or "Catch" (for short) was a great name for me, and he took total credit for it. He told me it now went beyond baseball. He had an additional reason for the name being appropriate, a reason that he and Pickett had discovered while reading The Catcher in the Rye, a book that was on the reading list for prospective Luther College students. Having an interest in attending Luther next year was not the only reason that Laser and Pickett had read the book. They had heard from older friends that the book was filled with profanity, words and phrases that were not often heard in Jeffers, so they had decided to become "well-read."

Laser said to me after practice one day, "In the book, Holden Caulfield told a friend that he kept picturing a whole bunch of kids playing in a field of rye near a steep cliff, and that he knew that he needed to be responsible for standing near the edge of the cliff and catching any kid who, while running carelessly, started falling off. Holden would be the 'catcher in the rye,' and that's all he wanted to be."

Laser continued as a smile formed on his face, "I see you as "the catcher in the corn" because in your farm chores you have to make sure the cows don't fall into the creek while you guide them to the barn for milking time, and you can't allow them to escape into the corn field either. Save them! Catch them! . . .You are Catcher . . . It's perfect."

As he became more serious, Laser added, "You have become a very good baseball catcher. I like pitching to you. You throw out most of the runners who are trying to steal, and you hardly ever have to visit the backstop any more during our baseball games. 'Catcher . . . The Catcher in the Corn.'"

There's no doubt that Laser was creative. I'm fortunate that my name didn't come from the profanity he had read.

Chapter 4

The Laser Show

Scientists recently, about 1959, conceived the idea of the laser, and they are just beginning to develop its potential. I figured this was the perfect nickname for our senior guard: Laser. It's a good fit. Just as a laser amplifies light, our Laser, the J-Hawk, amplifies our chances of winning because of his leadership and exceptional basketball skills. Scientists have determined that a laser is highly directional. It can be pinpointed, accurately directed to an exact location. Our Laser can do the same thing with his set shots and jump shots. He accurately directs the basketball right through the metal hoop and its attached net. Over the last couple of years he has really been developing his potential. It does really fit him . . . Laser.

No one else on the team could shoot a set shot and a jumper as accurately as Laser. When he was hot he could string together several buckets in a row and really give us a shot in the arm. His strengths on the team were his leadership and his shooting accuracy. It was fortunate for us that we didn't have to rely on his singing ability.

I'm not saying Laser was tone deaf, but neither am I saying he had perfect pitch. Generally he would sing within half an octave of the rest of any group of singers, but it may have been after vocally searching awhile for the correct notes.

I remember a musical event concerning Laser's singing that happened four years ago when I was in seventh grade. For some reason that none of us students could comprehend, the music teacher decided that all twenty of us in Junior High would be required to sing a solo in music class in front of all the other students. When Mrs. Johnson made this announcement in class, all heads turned to look at Laser. We could feel his pain. Later, when he would sing to us, our ears would really feel the pain.

This is how the assignment was laid out. We had two weeks to choose a song, find the music, and "practice singing it until we reached perfection."

Mrs. Johnson would accompany each of us on the piano. Our selection did not have to be approved by her prior to our performance. All soloists would deliver on the same day.

I have no idea, four years later, what song I chose to sing. There were some good soloists in the class, but I do not remember anyone's song or how he sang . . . except for Laser. His solo was very memorable.

When Laser's name was called, he walked up next to the piano and handed Mrs. Johnson his music.

I lowered my head and began to hold my breath as the room became deathly silent. After a couple quick moments I looked up and noticed that there was no sweat on Laser's brow or on his upper lip. What I saw was confidence.

What's going on? Did he take voice lessons during these last two weeks? Is he not aware of his musical limitations? Something is up.

Mrs. Johnson began playing the introduction as Laser calmly stood next to the piano. After a few bars had been played I glanced at the others, a broad smile spreading across my face. Heads began turning everywhere as other classmates awakened.

Mrs. Johnson continued plinking the keys as Laser stood by, waiting for his time to come in. By now everyone in the class was smiling and keeping the beat to the music.

Here it comes!

Laser looked at Mrs. Johnson. He readied himself and leaned forward slightly. She continued playing for a bit, then she paused, nodded to Laser, and he said in a loud monotone, "**Tequila**!"

We all applauded spontaneously as Mrs. Johnson played on, and Laser smiled as he began to sway with the music, awaiting his time to reenter. I believe even Mrs. Johnson was enjoying this performance where her minor role of being the accompanist became the major part of Laser's talent.

Here it comes again!

"**Tequila**!" Laser belted out for the second time of his solo.

Mrs. Johnson really started getting into it on the piano, and the rest of us were kind of doing some sit-down dancing on our seats as Laser continued to swing with the music.

Here comes the last one!

"**Tequila!**" Laser said for the third and final time, and you should have seen the confidence and pride that showed on his face.

When Mrs. Johnson finished on the piano, cheers filled the room. Laser was a hero! His creativity had saved the day . . . for all of us.

This was a great example of Laser's ability to solve problems. He used this skill in our games. He could quickly analyze what was causing problems for us, devise a plan to overcome it, and communicate clearly so we could respond together as one unit. We listened to him during timeouts because we knew he had considered the angles and the consequences. We followed his suggestions because he was creative.

I'm just glad he didn't sing out our instructions.

At the end of warm-ups, Tucson and I introduced Kelly Hallman as our honorary captain for tonight's game. He was chosen because of his great support of community and school sports as well as being one of the early pioneer founders of Jeffers years ago. Tucson and I knew him well, as we often took our lawn mowers to him when we could not get them started. We liked listening to his colorful stories. Kelly received long and loud applause as he stood to be recognized.

Before we headed back to our bench, Tucson announced into the microphone, "After the game, milk and cookies will be available in the lunchroom." His statement received loud applause also.

In tonight's game our press was not very effective. The Lions worked the ball down the floor and made some easy shots. At our first time out Laser told Coach about an observation he had made. "Coach, is it okay with you if we shorten the floor by dropping back a little on defense. If we don't challenge the inbounds pass and instead set up at about half court, we may have a better chance of trapping them and forcing them to make bad passes. Pickett can be our last line of defense under the bucket. Abe and Hook can put their long arms to good use by picking off passes after Catcher and I force them to make some bad decisions. This should slow down their offense and give us a chance for some more fast-break buckets."

"This sounds like something worth trying. They'll have to change their whole approach," Coach responded. "Make sure you are moving your feet. Get into position quickly. All right, let's go."

We broke the huddle with, "We are . . . J-Hawks!"

Laser's suggestion to Coach was perfect. Upton's players relaxed for a time while bringing the ball up court, but they panicked when we trapped them at half court. In this smaller space there was not as much room for their lob passes, and the long arms of Captain Hook and Abe picked off several of them. The Lions became frustrated, and in desperation, threw a few passes that were caught by the fans in the bleachers that surrounded the gym.

While shutting their offence down, we picked up momentum with fast-break layups. By midway in the second quarter we had turned an even game into an eight-point lead for us, and we added on to it, ending the first half up by twelve points.

Laser had been phenomenal. Because of his quickness, he had gotten to the basket often for layups, and his shooting had been right on target whenever he took a jump shot. He had scored almost half our points when we went to the locker room for our half-time break.

In the second half we did not trap or press. Coach wanted us to save energy and work on our zone defense, so we dropped back to defend our basket. Pickett played out high, a few feet short of the free throw line, leaving the baseline for Abe and Hook, our tall sophomore forwards. The Lions had trouble working the ball inside, so they began to shoot from outside. We were on their shooters quickly, so they often rushed their shots and missed badly. Our big guys grabbed almost every rebound, and we hurried the ball to our end, using our quickness to score easy baskets and wear them out.

This definitely was Laser's night. Whenever any of our big guys grabbed a rebound and passed to me as I moved toward the sideline near half court, I looked for Laser heading to the hoop, leading him with passes that took him to the backboard for an easy layup, or allowed him to pull up and take a short jumper. Laser was on fire. The rest of us didn't take many shots because Laser was driving us tonight. With three minutes left in the third quarter, the Lions began covering Laser with two players. Now we really had them. We made an adjustment and started working the ball into Pickett who either took the ball inside himself and shot or fed either Abe or Hook as he moved to the basket.

We kept building our lead, and at the end of the third quarter we led by 21 points. Otto, San Juan, and Tucson started the fourth quarter as our two seniors and Abe took seats on the bench. We played the Lions evenly for the next few minutes, and with three minutes left in the game, both benches were emptied because of the twenty-point difference. We won this home opener by nineteen, and we had played better than we had in our first two games. Laser was certainly "on key" tonight.

After mixing with our parents and friends for a few minutes, we headed for the shower, dressed, and then met in the lunchroom for some milk and a cookie or two.

That's when Captain Hook came up with his good suggestion. "Let's meet in the gym at nine tomorrow morning and do some shooting and run-ning," he said. "It would loosen up our bodies and help us recover from tonight's game. I can get a key to the school from Dad. This may be the only advantage to being the Supe's son."

Laser went a step further. "Let's invite the elementary and junior high kids to join us at 9:30. We'll play with them for an hour, teaching them some of our skills and connecting with them while we also do some good for ourselves."

"Can we offer milk and cookies to the participants after the workout?" asked Tucson.

"I'll check with Coach to see if his dad's dairy might have a donation for us," said Pickett.

"How about this idea?" I asked. "After the snack let's walk the kids to the library on Main Street and read with them for twenty minutes or so until the parents pick them up there at eleven o'clock."

The players all said it sounded like a good plan.

"I'm heading to the microphone for a quick announcement," I said. "I think most of the kids are still here. I think we should open it to girls as well as boys."

Nodding heads gave me the approval I was looking for.

The announcement was met with loud cheering, mostly from the kids, but we did hear some adult voices, too.

Our plan for the Saturday morning clinic was put in place that quickly. It started with a single suggestion . . . additional ideas followed . . . then a couple questions were asked . . . That was it! Teamwork put it together!

We had no idea if any kids would join us at the clinic after we had loosened up with running and shooting, but we were hopeful. We thought some of our older sisters might be interested in helping at the gym or at the library, but we weren't sure about it. Tomorrow would be interesting.

Laser caught up with Pickett and me as we were leaving the gym. Something had been bothering him. He wanted the three of us basketball letter winners to meet with the Supe and convince him to change the policy. "It's not fair," he said to Pickett and me. "Why should our players have to wait until the end of the year, this final year in the history of our school? If we schedule a meeting and share our well-thought-out plan with him maybe he'll see our point."

Pickett and I totally agreed. All we needed to do was defeat our opponents by a sufficient enough score so all players would get to play in the games. We figured that eight of us would get most of the playing time, leaving four to get limited experience at the end of games when we were winning by big margins. We wanted these "bench warmers" to be able to play in eight games by the Christmas break. So far every player has played in all three of our games. "Let's convince the Supe that these players are on track to letter anyway, so please award their letters before Christmas. All players would then be eligible to wear the golden 'J' on the black woolen letter jacket with the white leather sleeves," Laser said.

The timing was crucial. Christmas was coming. Letter jackets would make great gifts from the families.

We would tell the Supe about the pride we felt when we wore the letter jacket to school, to church, around town, to the games. We wanted all players to have this opportunity. This is the last year letters would be awarded in Jeffers. Let's do it right. We needed to get him to understand how great it would look if the entire team entered an opposing gym wearing J-Hawk letter jackets. It may even scare an opponent.

The plan was now worked out. We need to continue to crush our rival teams so coach would use all his players in the game. We want to set up the meeting after our fifth game . . . after the Supe has had a chance to watch a few games.

Chapter 5

Self-Driven

Living on very flat farmland a couple miles outside of town, I didn't get many opportunities to slide down snowy hills on a sled when I was a young kid. This changed one winter when a February blizzard dumped almost a foot of fresh white snow in our area, snowing us in. Luckily, a good-Samaritan neighbor drove over with his tractor and front-end loader to scoop out our driveway. We ended up with a huge hill of snow next to the barn, at the top of a gentle slope right next to our woods. My brother and I grabbed a couple aluminum grain shovels and our metal "no-way-can-you-steer-it" saucer sled, and we proceeded to build a sled run that started at the top of our mountain of snow and snaked down the slope through the trees at the south end of our woods for about forty yards.

We banked up snow around the trees so the rudderless sled would turn and spin around the trees rather than smash directly into them. We worked well into the night, building and rebuilding this run, then took turns enjoying the rush as we sped down on the saucer, snow flying into our faces as we spun around and around, avoiding the trees and having the time of our young lives.

What allowed us to have the most fun with this adventure was that building the sled run was not a task that was assigned to us. Dad didn't tell us to build this. It was our idea. It was a choice that we had made, and we worked passionately. It was all the more enjoyable because we really put our hearts into it. The two of us worked long and hard together to create something fun, and we were both so pleased. Neither of us could have or would have done this alone. It was this teamwork and feeling of accomplishment that magnified the joy.

That's how it was feeling for us basketball players now. Our Saturday clinic definitely was not a chore. It was a pleasure for us because we worked together to create something fun. There wasn't anyone telling us what to do, nor was there a blueprint to follow. We designed our clinic as we went along, listening to anyone's ideas on what to do next. At the same time we were able to celebrate the previous night's victory over Upton while we ran, dribbled, and shot, worked to improve our game, helped our bodies recover, and continued to connect as teammates.

As we loosened up, we began to run at top speed because we understood how important it was to make quick first steps in order to help teammates lead accurately with their passes. The youngsters watched from the bleachers as we warmed up, and they could see how much fun we were having. They heard our laughter and our chatter. Constant applause let us know that we were becoming heroes to this next generation of basketball players.

When these kids were invited onto the floor they were prepared for good exercise, fun activities, and lots of laughter. We taught shooting, passing, dribbling, and rebounding skills, incorporating humor as well as good teaching skills. Then we put the skills to good use in challenges and contests by arranging teams that would compete against each other. Which team can be the first to make twenty bounce passes? Which team can be first to make ten baskets? Which relay team can be the first to dribble down to the other end and back? We dribbled in circles while chanting, "We are . . . J-Hawks! We are . . . J-Hawks!" We went rapidly from one activity to another for about forty-five minutes.

You should have seen the smiles on the faces of the kids. I mean the tall kids, my teammates. I looked at these big guys and saw how involved each one was and how much fun each was having. The smaller players, the youngsters, also were working hard and enjoying every minute.

This clinic was pure genius.

It's a good thing we ended with a cool-down snack of milk and cookies, or we might never have gotten them out of the gym.

A couple sixth graders swept the gym floor while fifth graders policed up milk cartons and wiped the lunchroom tables clean. The junior high kids sat with the younger kids on the wooden bleachers as we players took a quick shower and joined the group for the one-block trek to the library.

We had told the library volunteers after the game last night that we would be visiting with a group when our clinic ended at about 10:30. Now they may have received an additional warning as we shouted repeatedly, "We are . . . J-Hawks! We are . . . J-Hawks!" during our short walk. I think the volume shook nearby windows as we walked past. It was amazing how connected these kids had become to our team in just three games and with one Saturday clinic.

Upon reaching the door of the library the loud chanting stopped. Tucson reviewed some library procedures and expectations: The usual things: No running, only very quiet talking, respect for others, and respect for books. We separated the kids into different age groups. We read some books to them at first, and then we helped them check out books so they could read to us. The half-hour passed so quickly. When moms and dads came to pick them up at eleven many kids complained. They didn't want to leave yet. They had enjoyed their morning so much. Many parents and youngsters asked about next week.

"Absolutely!" we said. "We'll do it again next Saturday morning."

Eventually everyone departed.

We players sat down around a table and just looked at each other.

"Wow! What a morning!" Pickett said.

"Did you see their faces?" Laser asked.

Abe added, "I think they'll all come back next week, and they'll bring friends."

We had a short discussion about the clinic, the snack, and our visit to the library, and we decided to do it the same way next Saturday. The whole team agreed our workout and the clinic had been a great idea.

"Tell your dad 'Thanks' for letting us use the gym, Hook," I said. "Tell him how it went, and ask him to drop in next week and take a look. He'll be amazed. He may begin to look at us differently, see us not just as boys he's had to steer away from trouble," I said with a laugh. "Maybe he'll see we are the future, the leaders of the next generation," I added with dramatic gestures.

Several teammates chuckled.

Laser picked up today's copy of the *Globe* and brought it over to the table. He opened the newspaper and located Garris's latest column, the one written following our win last night over Upton.

We prepared to listen as Laser cleared his throat and waited for silence.

In the Stands – With John Garris

I hinted last week that I would maybe head to Jeffers and use my free ticket to watch the J-Hawks take on Upton if no other game caught my interest. This newspaperman reports that J-Hawk basketball is alive and well. Behind a suffocating half-court trap and Laser's great shooting, the J-Hawks jumped out to a 39-27 first-half lead. The Lions were unable to find a way to stop Laser, and the J-Hawks kept feeding him the ball. All players saw action again in this 81-62 win, their third straight in this young season.

I'm not sure I have the cast of characters correct, but based on the box score I printed last week, I think the scoring goes like this:

Pickett 12
Laser 36
Captain Hook 9
Abe 6
Catcher 10
Otto and Sons 8

The J-Hawk quickness showed, and their passing was sharp. They outrebounded the Lions by about 20 boards and collected over 10 steals. Great job, but I wonder if they have the energy, the juice, to keep the streak going.

I saw a first last night. Prior to the game a couple players announced to the crowd that an elderly town resident had been chosen as an honorary captain for the game. He represented the town's early pioneer spirit. He was a character. I overheard some colorful language after the game as he talked with others in the crowd. He wore his honor well last night.

The J-Hawks are gaining support in the Jeffers community, but they need to understand that it's a very small following, not "an entire nation" that's cheering them on.

I have some questions for the J-Hawks:

1. Do you think you show character by honoring one?
2. Are you trying to add fan support by offering milk and cookies after the game?
3. What's this about a Saturday morning basketball clinic for youngsters?

Chapter 6

First Steps

As soon as Laser finished reading Garris's column, Pickett blurted out, "All right! We are alive and well! Laser, you received some good ink today, and you truly deserved it!"

We all applauded quietly.

"Did he call us a cast of characters?" Otto asked.

"It sounds like we received some compliments. That's better than his previous comments," said Hook.

Tucson added, "I agree, and I think we should continue with the honorary captains. Garris called it 'a first.' It sounds like he liked it. I think it's worth doing again. What has to be done to continue it?"

"I'll be responsible for it," I offered. "I'll bounce my ideas off a few of you guys and ask for some help when I need it. Will that work?"

Everyone agreed to support the plan.

I continued, "Next week I'd like to honor our custodians. They keep our school in great condition, and they never receive any recognition. They're not looking for acknowledgment, but let's give them some anyway."

"Good choice," Pickett stated. "Do it!"

"Three things Garris wrote in today's column struck me," I continued. "He asked some questions that I think we should answer, but I would like us to answer him with actions, not words. I have three suggestions I'd like us to consider. These would be our first steps in responding to his columns."

"Spit them out," Pickett suggested.

"First of all, what do you think of having the announcer use our nicknames, our 'character names' during game action? Garris has already written them twice in his columns. I think most J-Hawk fans know us by these names. Are any parents expressing anything negative about your names? Are you guys okay with it? Otto, it sounds pretty impressive when we can bring **Otto and Sons** into the game from our bench and continue the business of playing basketball. I'm pretty proud of the names I invented for 'Son One' – 'San Juan' . . . and 'Two Son' – 'Tucson.' I'm still working a little on the other four 'Sons.' I'm leaning toward Nicholson for 'Son Five.' Is a nickel still worth five cents? 'Treason is a stretch for 'Three Son,' . . . as is 'Half Dozen' for 'Son Six.' 'Go Forth Son' gets the only biblical sounding name. Are these names okay with you guys? Since Garris gave our names some ink today, let's push it farther by using them in our games. What do you think?"

A two-minute discussion followed. Everyone was on board with this idea.

"I'll talk to Coach, the Supe, and the announcer. This could be fun!" said Laser. "I think they'll go for it because it's unique. Maybe we'll all become famous with these names. I'll call in some of you for reinforcements if I meet resistance."

One idea down . . . two to go.

"Secondly," I said, "Garris wondered if we have the energy, the 'juice' to keep the streak going. I know we definitely do. We're a pretty good team, and we're getting even better. I say we throw these words back in Garris's face, and I think I know how we can do it. Let's call our post-game milk 'J-Hawk Juice.' We can tape this name right on the cartons. The young kids will go crazy when they get 'J-Hawk Juice' after the games. I know it'll be a hit, and it will show Garris that he can't intimidate us. What do you guys think about this idea?"

"We are . . . J-Hawks! We are . . . J-Hawks!" the group said in library-quiet voices.

"And we drink J-Hawk Juice," San Juan added quietly. "Good plan. I'll ask my sister to type out some 'J-Hawk Juice' labels that we can copy and cut up, and on Monday in school we can figure out when and how to dress up the cartons of milk."

Everyone nodded and looked at me, eagerly awaiting my final suggestion.

This is the most I've ever spoken out. I see that my ideas are receiving good support, and I like this new-found feeling of power. This could be dangerous!

"This last one is big," I warned. "Garris made fun of us today. He taunted us about our small town. He said we have small-town support, but we act like it's a whole nation cheering for us. Laser, read Garris's statement again."

" . . . 'they need to understand it's a very small following, not an entire nation that's cheering them on,'" Laser read.

"We never claimed any fan support beyond our own town! These are fighting words to me, so I say we fight back! Let's become our own nation. Let's call ourselves, 'J-Hawk Nation.' We'll spread the name, and people will want to be part of it, and Garris will have to eat his words!" I said with some fire in my voice.

I was on a roll.

"I want to figure out a way to purchase black stocking caps, find a business that can print on them, in white letters, 'J-Hawk Nation,' and make them available for our fans to buy. The kids will beg for them and wear them everywhere. I bet the grownups will wear them too. It will really catch on as a fashion statement. Santa will deliver them as gifts. Friends will . . .

"A couple of you . . . grab Catcher and hold him down. He's starting to foam at the mouth," Laser warned.

Everyone laughed at what Laser had said, but then positive words started reaching my ears.

"I like Catcher's idea," Hook said. "'J-Hawk Nation' sounds impressive. I could use a good stocking cap that would make me feel really proud of our team as well as protect my fragile ears, and my head looks good in black."

I don't consider Hook to be a comedian, but that was funny to me.

"Count me in," added Pickett. "That's a great idea. We'll show Garris not to mess with us. I think we'll need lots of caps. How about giving them to your honorary captains?"

"Yes," Otto and Tucson chimed in. "Do that!"

"The kids will go nuts for stocking caps that connect them to our team," Otto added. "Did you see how they responded today at our clinic?"

"It will be pretty easy to see how many fans we have if they are all wearing black stocking caps," Abe said. "We can sell them at the gym before the games and at our Saturday clinics. Maybe the library would stock them."

"Are you with me then?" I asked.

"We are . . . J-Hawks! We are . . . J-Hawks!"

This time the volunteer behind the checkout desk signaled to us to quiet down.

"My mom knows Mason City pretty well because she works at a radio station there," I said. "I'll ask her for some leads concerning the caps and the printing job. When I'm ready to make a road trip I'll ask a couple of you to go with me. Maybe we can convince someone to give us a really good deal. I'll head right to the bank when we leave here."

"Do you need help? Are you going to rob it?" asked San Juan kiddingly.

"Yeh, right," I responded. "I'm hoping the bankers will give me some seed money, a small loan to fund the first caps. It would be great if the cost came in at or under $1.50 or so per printed cap. Do you think we could sell the caps for two bucks each? This would give us a small profit to help cover the cost of any caps we give away. I was hoping to order 100 of them. If we do this correctly, and it catches on like I think it will, we'll be ordering more right away. I bet that first hundred will move quickly."

Laser seconded my plan, "Yes, order a hundred, and get them printed right away. We need them now!"

"It's really important that we each buy one and wear it," added Pickett. "Make sure your parents, your brothers, and your sisters wear them. That will prime the pump. When we keep winning our games they'll become collector's items. I love this plan. Ask at the bank for a donation to help us cover some costs. Tell them we are getting some milk donations from Coach's dad at the dairy, and tell them Abe's dad has donated cookies for post-game snacks and the clinics. Hey, everybody. Don't overlook anyone. Tucson, will you be our banker?"

"Sure," he replied. "You can count on me," he said laughing. "Do you get it? You can count on me? You know, use my fingers and toes to count?"

"Good choice, Pickett," I said, shaking my head while chuckling.

"We'll need some parent donations for cookies as more people show up at the games," Otto said. "I know my mom will do some baking."

"Mine too," Treason added.

"Great idea," Abe added. "I know my dad would appreciate some help with cookie contributions."

We all took a deep breath and scanned each other's face. Nodding heads and big smiles confirmed how we felt about our team and our new projects.

Laser ended our meeting with, "Play hard! Have Fun!"

We glanced at the library volunteer, smiled, and started chanting quietly as we exited, "We are . . . J-Hawks! We are . . . J-Hawks!"

I headed to The Jeffers Café to see if Dad was still there. I needed to get home because I had work to do.

Chapter 7
Walleye Fishing

Anyone who has played basketball knows it is impossible to play alone against a whole team. A single player can only do so much. Five players playing individually generally cannot match the achievements of a squad that plays together, assisting each other on defense, passing to the open man, taking only good shots when you are not covered closely. It's teamwork like this that has allowed us to win our first three games. If we didn't work together, we would not be nearly as successful as we have been this year.

Two summers ago San Juan and I traveled to the Boundary Waters Canoe Area with my dad and Bethany's pastor for a few days of canoeing, camping, and fishing at the end of the Gunflint Trail. After paddling across Seagull Lake, we located a great campsite near a channel that ran among several small rocky islands. We prepared our site by setting up our two tents and collecting a good supply of firewood which we took turns sawing, splitting and stacking near the cooking grate. Dad organized the cook kit and our food, while San Juan and I moved the picnic table to a better location and leveled it with some flat rocks. We were now ready for a meal of walleye. All we needed was fresh fish.

We prepared the canoes for fishing. San Juan and I walked back into the woods away from the lake, carrying with us our camp saw and our small axe. Our job was to cut down two saplings that each had about a two-inch diameter and from which we could trim off the branches and be left with two straight 10-foot poles. We found a great matching pair among a huge stand of pine trees after a difficult walk.

"These two trees will not be missed," I said, "and by cutting them down, we'll be giving the surrounding trees more room to grow." With those few simple words I had managed to justify a partial destruction of the BWCA.

Using these two poles and several ropes we lashed the two canoes together, effectively making a very stable "pontoon boat" from which we could fish. It was so steady that we could stand up in our two Grumman aluminum canoes without any danger of tipping over. It was a great way to float on the water because only one or two paddlers were needed at a time, leaving the others to daydream or sleep. We each dragged a line in the water, and we agreed that if a fish struck at one line, we other three would reel in quickly to avoid getting our lines tangled due to a desperate fish that was trying to run or spit out the lure and escape.

I was the least accomplished fisherman in the group. My three fishing partners were having average fishing success, occasionally getting a strike, but, so far, I had been shut out. I started dozing off, when suddenly I was awakened from my daydream by my first hit.

"Strike!" I yelled, and I immediately started flexing the rod and winding up the line. I couldn't yet see my fish, but it felt heavy, and I could feel it pulling hard. I had hopes it was a trophy fish or at least "food for four."

When the other three lines were quickly brought in, we discovered that San Juan's line was tangled with mine. Our lines looked like a short braided rope in one area, but I managed to bring the two-pound walleye next to my canoe in about two or three minutes despite the tangled lines, and using a fishing net, San Juan successfully lifted the fish into our canoe. I was exhausted, but I felt pretty proud.

As San Juan carefully retrieved the walleye from the net, a smile began to spread across his face. He looked at me and laughed.

"What?" I asked.

San Juan held up my fish by the line and asked me, "What color is your fishing line?

"I can see it's white," I replied.

"No, it's not. Look at the line on your reel," he suggested. "Your line is black. This fish was caught on a rapala attached to white line."

I looked at my reel and saw the black line that was spooled. Then I studied San Juan's reel and saw his white line. This walleye had struck at his rapala, not mine. Because of the tangled lines I felt the strike, I fought the fish, and I brought it in.

This had been a lesson in teamwork. I never could have caught this walleye without his help. He provided the line and the lure that the fish had struck, I provided the effort of reeling it in, and he handled the net. We had really worked together. Like I said, we had teamed together on this fish.

So . . . who caught the fish? It really didn't matter. We were a team. All four of us would enjoy walleye cooked over an open fire that night.

It's been like this on the basketball team. All of us share in the wins. When someone makes a basket it's great for our whole team. No one worries about who scores the most points. It is your duty as a player to do everything you can to benefit the team. It might mean that you don't shoot very often in one game because your teammates have better scoring opportunities than you do. We don't take turns shooting, we take advantage of the opportunities we are given.

Sometimes it happens like this: Laser defends the player with the ball so well that the opponent panics and puts up a bad shot which Captain Hook rebounds off the rim and passes down court to me. As I dribble toward our basket I see the solid screen that Pickett sets up for Abe who spins into the open under the basket. I toss a high pass up near the rim, Abe catches it, and he drops it softly into the bucket.

So . . . who scored the basket? Who caught the fish? It's flat-out teamwork.

Tonight we would host Ashton in our fourth game of the season, and we expected to have more people in the stands for this Tuesday night game than we did at last Friday night's game. A winning team excites people.

As the girls played their game, I sat with Abe and San Juan on the stage in the student bleachers. We were joking around, talking about everything from sports to cars to music, sharing a lot of laughs. We took time to cheer whenever the girls made good plays, but we didn't watch too intently. When I glanced at the scoreboard, I saw that our girls were down by only three points. Since halftime was approaching, we began to talk about our upcoming game. We would be heading to the locker room soon after the second half started, so we wanted to get our minds ready to play.

Then I remembered that I had forgotten my clean pair of sweat socks in the car, and I needed to retrieve them. As I walked past the locker room I grabbed my warm-up jacket and put it on because it was quite cold outside. As I ran the half-block to the car I stepped on a patch of ice and almost went down, but I recovered my balance and stayed on my feet. I congratulated myself for my grace and nimbleness, but I considered myself to be very fortunate this time. I knew it was stupid to run in icy conditions and risk falling and possibly injuring myself, but I didn't always use common sense. My parents would verify that.

On the way back to the school I slowed down. My breathing rate was back to normal when I reached the lobby, and I walked down to the bathroom to blow my runny nose.

When I returned to the gym entrance I saw a girl I'd never seen before. Her beauty struck me. I couldn't take my eyes off her. I noticed how much her blue eyes sparkled. I don't know how long I stood there staring at her, but I was awakened by a man's voice.

"Young man . . . do you not hear me? I asked you a question. Will you find seats in the gym for my daughter and me?" he asked, somewhat irritated.

I came to, and I was conscious enough to figure out that the girl that had caught my attention was the daughter he referred to, but I did not know what to say. I didn't think it would be appropriate to respond, "Sorry, Mister, but your daughter must have put me in a trance."

Does he think I am an usher?

I was hoping I had not embarrassed myself too much. I decided to help them.

"Sure . . . ," I said politely but hesitantly. "I'll find you some seats in the bleachers. Please follow me." I smiled at them, hoping to repair any bad feelings.

I led them to the bleacher area close to where Coach and our bench players would sit during our game. I recommended that they sit on the second level for a better view. "Will it be a problem for you to sit here in J-Hawk territory?" I asked. "If you root for us you'll be sitting among friends. Otherwise . . ."

I was hoping that my comment would come across as humorous. I didn't dare look at the girl again, but I noticed that her dad smiled a little. He replied to me, "Thank you. This looks like a great area . . . and we did come tonight to watch the J-Hawks."

"I hope you both enjoy the game," I said. Then I walked back to the stage with my socks in my jacket pocket and rejoined San Juan and Abe. They had seen me walk into the gym with the girl and her dad.

Abe asked, "What were you doing? Do you know them?"

"I have no idea who they are," I replied. "The guy asked me if I would find seats for them, so I did. He might have thought I was an usher." I laughed to myself.

When we ran out of the locker room to take the floor for our pregame warm-ups I looked toward the girl. I wanted to see if she would recognize me. Several times I glanced in her direction, and once I saw her dad point at me. They must have figured out by now that I am a J-Hawk player, not an usher, . . . that this is a warm-up jacket I am wearing, not an ushering uniform.

I saw another stranger who was sitting behind and to the right side of this girl. I saw that he was writing in a tablet.

Who brings tablets to games and writes in them? . . . ***WRITERS!***

I wondered if this could be John Garris. I think this man was standing by the ticket table when the first guy asked me to find seats for him, and he must have followed us to the bleachers. If this is Garris . . . I'm glad he's here, but I hope he's not going to be too hard on us if he includes us in his column.

Pickett and Laser introduced our custodians as tonight's honorary captains after we had finished warming up. The spectators stood and applauded, and I could tell the two custodians felt honored.

When the applause died down Pickett again spoke into the microphone, "I have three announcements to make. First of all, J-Hawks, we will be manning the brooms after the game tonight because our honorary captains have been told by Laser and me that they are off duty tonight."

There was lots of applause.

"Secondly . . . after the game, cookies and '**J-Hawk Juice'** will be available in the lunchroom for everyone. Please join us."

There was wild applause and shouting after this announcement.

"And finally . . . young J-Hawks, make sure you join us tomorrow morning at 9:30 for our second Saturday clinic. We guarantee that you will have a really fun time while you improve your basketball skills. See you there."

Wild applause erupted again, and the shouting came from young voices.

We positioned ourselves for the center tipoff. Abe prepared to jump center, having his usual height advantage of four inches or so. Tonight we had a play worked out that we hoped would get us two quick points. Here goes!

The ref tossed the ball straight up between the two jumpers. Abe leaped from his crouch and tapped the ball toward Pickett. Pickett reached out and grabbed the ball, pivoted, and passed firmly to me by the sideline. I quickly bounced a long pass to Laser as he glided to the basket, and he laid the ball softly against the backboard for our first two points. It worked just like Coach had designed. We were off to a great start!

We trapped the Cougars at the half-court line as they dribbled the ball up the floor. Abe, Hook, and Pickett's long arms covered a lot of the area, so there weren't many open spaces to pass into. Hook stretched and picked off a bad throw and passed to Laser, who dribbled toward our basket. We made several quick passes: Laser to Pickett . . . to Abe . . . back to Pickett . . . to me . . . to Hook on the right side . . . back inside to Pickett who was open for a short jumper. The ball dropped silently through the hoop. The game had just begun, and we were up by four due to good teamwork.

We trapped them immediately after their inbound pass, but this time Number 25 threw a long pass that Abe just missed, and Number 20 drove to the basket for a layup.

I hope they keep trying that. That pass will be intercepted every time from now on.

We played our style of pressure defense for the entire first quarter. Most of our points were scored from layups and short jump shots, with Laser and I each getting a few chances. At the end of the quarter I looked at the scoreboard and saw that we had a 19-9 lead. I headed to the bench, and I saw that the girl was clapping.

All right! She is on our side!

Otto took Hook's spot, and San Juan went in for me to start the second quarter. The Cougars kept their regulars in, but they didn't gain any ground on us. We continued to score points off steals, and quick passes found Abe and Pickett open for good shots. San Juan scored on a fast-break pass from Laser, and thirty seconds later Otto drove hard to the basket after a Pickett screen, and he made his layup in spite of being fouled. Then he sank the free throw.

Coach subbed in Tucson, Hook, and me so Pickett, Laser, and Abe could sit and catch their breath, but the Cougars kept their starters in the lineup. I knew we would have a great advantage toward the end of the game because we would wear them down. We continued to hold our lead. Hook hit a short hook shot, San Juan swished a jumper, and Abe put back an offensive rebound. The Cougars weren't shooting well, and Hook and Otto grabbed the missed shots off the rim. I hit an open jump shot, and Hook banked a ten-footer off the backboard. We were playing very well, and our defense did not allow them to get back into the game.

Coach kept rotating our players, putting in fresh runners. At halftime we held a 37-21 lead.

In the second half Laser kept finding Abe open near the rim, and three times he tossed perfect passes that Abe caught just above the rim and dropped through the hoop in a single motion. These were pretty plays, and the fans acknowledged them with loud applause. Hook and Pickett each blocked a shot, Otto and I made a couple steals, Laser hit twice from the top of the key . . . Everything was working for us. Pickett made two turn-around jumpers from the free-throw line, and I made another jump shot from the right side after Hook screened my guy.

Because of our commanding lead with three minutes left in the game, both coaches cleared their benches. It's always nice to see the opposing coach wave "the white flag" and surrender. It was a great victory, with the final score ending at 74-52. Tonight the Cougars were beaten soundly by a better team. Go J-Hawks!

After we lined up and shook hands, we started talking to our school friends and some parents. I tried to position myself so I could see that girl out of the corner of my eye as I talked to some fifth graders. The three boys told me that we had played great tonight, and they all intended to come back to the gym tomorrow morning for our clinic.

The man and his daughter remained in the bleachers, just watching what was going on. I wanted to go talk to them, but I couldn't find the courage to do it.

I noticed that the man with the tablet stepped down to the gym floor and started moving around, listening in on a couple conversations. I decided to check him out.

"Are you John Garris?" I asked boldly.

"Yes, I am," he replied. "How did you know?"

"I think you are the first person I've ever seen taking notes at any of our games. Your tablet gave you away." I continued with a touch of sarcasm. "Please don't be too hard on us," I said. "Remember . . . we are young and inexperienced. Our character is helping us win, however, and we do believe we have the juice to keep it going. Did you stop in the lunchroom for some 'J-Hawk Juice?"

He laughed and said, "I'm heading there now."

I showered quickly, got dressed, and stepped into the lunchroom, hopeful that **she** and her dad might have accepted Pickett's invitation.

I discovered her father talking to Tucson's dad. The two men even shook hands.

That's a good sign.

The girl sat quietly as her dad talked. It didn't appear that she was having much fun.

I should go talk to her . . . but what would I say? If she comes back to another game . . . I'll talk to her for sure. I really will.

Our team's win in the gym tonight was as delicious as our walleye meal had been at the campsite two summers ago.

In the Stands – With John Garris

The Jeffers J-Hawks are not only playing good basketball early in this season, they are apparently offering their services as ushers during the preliminary girls' game. I watched last night in the lobby off the gym as a dad and his daughter approached a young man in a warm-up jacket and asked him if he would help them find a seat in the gym. The young man smiled, hesitated a little, then obliged politely, leading them to a good location on the bleachers behind the home team's bench. Only after the J-Hawk boys took the floor for warm-ups, and this family spotted their "usher" running and shooting in a J-Hawk uniform did they realize their mistake. I observed two very red faces in the crowd when the player made eye contact with them and nodded to them as he headed to his bench after warming up.

Having the custodians serve as honorary captains was a nice gesture, and the players impressed me even more by sweeping the floor and cleaning up the gym after the game, allowing the custodians to enjoy their honors.

The J-Hawks handed Ashton their first defeat of the season 74-52 in a fast-paced game last night. Laser scored 14 points off layups and jump shots, and Pickett had another strong game under the hoop grabbing rebounds as well as leading his team in scoring with 23 points. The young tall guys really helped with defensive pressure, steals, and rebounding, as well as contributing in the scoring department. Catcher played great defense and scored 18 points while directing sharp passes to his teammates that led to some easy baskets.

Let me add it up for you:

*   He directs teammates with good passes.
*   He sweeps the gym floor after the game.
*   He assists people in finding good seats.

It's obvious to me that Catcher **is** an usher.

Chapter 8

Second Chance

I wouldn't exactly call the Wednesday and Thursday practices we had this week easy. We did a lot of running, end to end in our small gym, and there weren't many breaks. I heard no voiced complaints from any teammates, but I detected a facial expression here and there that posed the question, "What's going on?"

Personally, I craved this type of practice. This intense running gave me a sense of freedom and power. I refused to let anyone outrun me. Sweat covered my entire body, and yet, I wanted more. This combination of running, dribbling, and shooting fed my spirit and made me feel invincible. I often felt exhilarated.

Yesterday, when Coach called for our final water break, and we cooled down with some free throw shooting, he explained to us that we needed to be ready to run in Friday night's home game against Benson. The Bulldogs were a running team, and we would teach them how a running game should be played. We would use our full-court press on defense every time we scored, and we would fast break to our basket after every defensive rebound we grabbed. I loved this wide-open style of basketball. I know we will be pumped, and we are in really good shape. We are getting ourselves into better condition every week because of our hard work at practice. Coach knew how hard to work us without wearing us down. He told us that Benson would come into the game with a 3-1 record, their only loss being an away game at Shelby, so we needed to be ready.

I left practice on Thursday really looking forward to Friday night's game for several reasons. First, playing against a good team like Benson would be an exciting challenge for our undefeated team, and we knew that many families from Jeffers would be in our gym cheering loudly for their J-Hawks.

Secondly, Coach's strategy of running against Benson meant the game would be fast and furious. Action would be end-to-end and continuous, and chances are that we all would get to take lots of shots. Playing in our home gym usually gives us a shooting advantage over our opposition, so if everything goes according to form, we expect to win this game.

Thirdly, and this one is a huge stretch, I have hopes that "the girl" whom I "ushered in" to a seat at Tuesday night's game will return, and maybe I'll get a chance to talk to her.

It's kind of funny, but I've thought about her a lot the last couple of days, though I don't even know her name. I can picture her sparkling blue eyes and her beautiful smile, and I really want to see her again . . . talk to her for a while . . . maybe become friends with her.

When I showed up at the gym for Friday night's home game against Benson, I was greeted at the door by five teammates wearing warm-up jackets and huge grins.

"What's going on? What are you guys doing?" I asked.

Hook spoke for the group. "We were feeling a little left out. In his column in the *Globe*, Garris singled you out as 'an usher,' and since we are your faithful teammates, we thought we'd step up and help you out. We want to become ushers too and join you in the fun. We will become 'an official ushering crew.' Swear us in, Catch."

I shook my head and laughed upon hearing Hook's explanation. I couldn't believe it. I shrugged and said to the crew that included Otto, San Juan, Tucson, Captain Hook, and Abe, "Okay, if you want to start an 'official ushering service' as you call it, I will grab my warm-up jacket and join you. But I have one stipulation: If that girl whom I ushered in at last week's game shows up tonight, I own the rights to guide her to the bleachers. Will you agree to that?" They playfully protested, and San Juan called me a dreamer. He told me there was a phone call for me, that Planet Earth was trying to reach me. After a short discussion we agreed to walk people to seats if they wanted our assistance. It might be fun, and it won't interfere with our focus in the game tonight. We also set up a timeline and a procedure to follow when it was time to head to the locker room to dress.

Garris walked in as we finished our talk. He immediately saw our squad and started smiling as he reached for his tablet and pencil and began to scribble down some notes.

What does he have in store for us now? He hasn't been very kind to us. His pencil has been sharp, treating us as if we were wannabees. On the plus side, we are getting newspaper coverage. We are also having a blast on the basketball court, winning all four of our games. The extras we have added have raised our confidence and built camaraderie to a very high level. He certainly can't see it all as bad. Maybe he's finding something that humors him. I am anxious to read his next column.

Who was I kidding about that girl showing up tonight? I really didn't expect she'd show, and even if she did I had no reason to believe she saw me as anything but a smart aleck. In hindsight it might have been better for me, less embarrassing for her dad and her if I had just simply stated the truth. "I'm sorry to have caused you some confusion, but we don't really have any ushers at our games. I'm one of the players on the J-Hawk team, and I had just slipped on my warm-up jacket to make a quick dash out to the car for some clean sweat socks I had forgotten to bring in with me." Yep, that definitely would have been more direct and honest. I pride myself on my honesty, but I was deterred and suffered a brain freeze when I glanced into her sparkling eyes. It was just for a couple of seconds, but I felt the discomfort burn through me, and I could not regain my composure and come up with an adequate response. If I had been thinking at all it was to figure out a way to avoid making these two strangers look too foolish.

And now tonight, if this girl with the dishwater-blond hair does show up, how will she react to seeing the collection of ushers greeting people at the door? Will she think we are mocking her family, or will she possibly find some humor in what we are doing? I'm prepared for a slap across my face.

Garris had made light of my "ushering" in Saturday's column, but maybe this girl does not read the *Globe* and hasn't even heard of Garris.

My freeze is thawing out, and my mind is racing. Is there a chance she even cares? This is just a basketball game, and she doesn't even live here or go to school here. But, I remind myself, I did speak to her at the last game. "Good for you!" my inner voice responds. It sounds like sarcasm again. I think it is sarcasm, but I'm not very good at detecting it, even when the words are pouring forth from **my** own mouth.

I do know that it will be very difficult to dribble, pass, and shoot tonight with my fingers crossed.

I needed to reflect on what we were doing here. Were these actions helping our basketball team? Do we play better because we know how to have a little fun? At practices we have been pretty sharp, and we are improving in our ability to read each other's moves and anticipate cuts into the open or toward the basket. We're not losing any gym time either. In fact, because of our Saturday clinics we are actually spending more time in the gym. Just to have some unstructured, free-shooting time is good for all of us. The haymow in the barn at home can be quite cold at this time of year, and the air is filled with hay dust. There are still many cylinder-shaped bales of hay spread in heaps across the floor, waiting to be tossed down to the cows below at feeding times, so it's difficult for me to work on my shot. I prefer the comfort of the gym.

The community has given us good support. At our last game I saw people in the stands that usually don't attend our games. Something is happening here, and I am glad to be a part of it.

I heard that The Jeffers Café is really busy most mornings serving breakfast and hot coffee while the patrons discuss the success of our team. It's pretty loud at times, some customers say, because of the arguments. "Was Pickett's screen and roll to the basket a more important play than Abe's high altitude catch and soft shot against the backboard?" "Did Laser hit three shots in a row from the top of the key, or was it four?" (Important stuff like that!!) "And how about that 'usher?'" (I imagine there was some laughter after this last quip.)

On mornings that follow a game night it's tough to find room in a booth or a stool at the counter, as the café is packed with critics who are waiting for the early-morning delivery of the _Globe_. Anticipation is as high as the grain elevator down the street. Did Garris include us in today's column? It was a big deal to us to have our small-town team get some ink, to get a little recognition, even if it did have a sting to it. After the last couple columns we've had to lick our wounds.

I walked a couple of junior high girls through the lunchroom to the student bleachers on the stage. They really didn't need an assist from me, but hey, why not join the fun? Then it was Dad's turn. He insisted. He attempted to grab my arm as we walked, but I fought him off as several observers chuckled.

As I arrived back in the lobby I noticed several of my ushering teammates standing at attention. I considered it to be a signal. "Very subtle, guys," I said. "Relax!" Otto pointed toward the door with his head. I now guessed what was going on, so I scanned the lobby doors until I located the mystery girl, her dad, and a woman . . . maybe the mom. My first prayer had been answered. My second prayer was on deck.

I had damage-control duty ahead of me now. Where do I start? I had to get to them before they turned around and headed back out the door.

"Sir, Ma'am," I began. "Miss . . . I'd like to apologize for what might appear to be rude behavior on our parts. We mean no disrespect. I'm hoping that you will listen to my explanation as to what we are doing. Could we please step to the side for some privacy?"

With a slight movement of my arm I indicated an open area away from the ticket table and waited, unsure if they would allow me to speak further. When the man nodded I smiled slightly and moved with them. *So far so good.*

"Again," I continued, "I'm sorry for the way this looks. I unintentionally mislead you last week when you maybe thought I was an usher, and you asked me to help you find some seats in the gym. I was happy to assist you, but I didn't know how to manage the awkward situation so I said nothing. Do you, by any chance, happen to read John Garris's column in the *Globe*?"

All three nodded, smiling, and I could hear my air escaping as I allowed myself to breathe in a normal pattern. *It's not as bad as it might have been.* "Garris poked fun at us, you and me, after our last game," I said. "It didn't bother me, but I felt embarrassment at what I unintentionally did to you. Again, I'm really sorry. As you can see . . . my teammates can be a bunch of clowns . . . but they have good intentions. After a quick huddle tonight we decided, 'Why not? Let's do it. Let's usher people in if they like. We can have a good time, and as they say in basketball, 'No harm, no foul.'"

I continued, "We were really hoping Garris would show up tonight so he could see that we have made good use of his comment about ushers, and maybe he would accept some credit for this new service we are offering, though I'm sure that is not what his intention was. I report happily that he and his tablet are in attendance at tonight's game."

"I want to thank you for coming to Tuesday night's game and returning again tonight. I was hoping you'd had some fun and would return. We need every fan we can get," I said.

The dad said, "We shared some laughs at the dinner table about the newspaper column and our part in it. We decided "unanimously," including Mom, to attend tonight's game.

Good for them . . . Good for me.

"Are you ready to find some seats?" I asked. "I'd like to serve as your usher . . . again. This time I'm 'official.'" All four of us laughed. "Were those seats close to our team bench satisfactory?"

The dad replied, "That's exactly what we had in mind."

Outstanding! Now I'll get to take a quick glance at my mystery girl occasionally as I look to the coach for instructions.

I led them to the bleachers that were behind and off to the side of the team's bench location. I waited until they stepped up to the second row and sat down. Looking right into that girl's eyes, I said in a soft voice, "I'm really glad you came back tonight. I hope you enjoy the game. After the game, J-Hawk Juice and cookies will be served in the lunchroom. Maybe I'll see you then?" My last words were a question, and I hoped for a favorable reply. What I got was a pretty smile.

I am flying high now! She smiled at me. I'll need to get my head out of the clouds and play well tonight. This will be the biggest game I've ever played in. There's a lot on the line . . . and besides, our team needs this win.

Chapter 9
Wild Horses

We ushered until the end of the first quarter of the girls' game. Then we walked as a group to the bleachers on the stage where we sat together and cheered for the girls.

As we sat, Tucson, Abe, and I received lots of thanks from our teammates for all the running around we did in finding black stocking caps, bargaining for a good price, and arranging for having them printed with white lettering. We had even figured out a way for them to be delivered to our school. "J-Hawk Nation" looks pretty good the way it reads, one word above the other. Everyone on the team already bought one, and most of us had worn the caps to school today. They will serve a couple purposes. My head will stay much warmer, and people everywhere will know where I come from. I think "J-Hawk Nation" will rally the entire town to support our basketball team. Many classmates had asked about the caps. I know we'll be selling out soon and ordering more. Two dollars isn't too high a price to pay for warmth and pride.

When a timeout was called with about four minutes left in the third quarter of the girls' game, we players rose from our bleacher seats. We all stood motionless for a few seconds before we softly began our chant: "We are . . . J-Hawks! We are . . . J-Hawks!" The crowd picked up the chant and added some volume as we walked in a very orderly and serious fashion to the locker room with our game faces on. We were now ready to dress for our game and take on the Bulldogs.

Coach joined us in the locker room almost immediately. We hadn't even started putting on our basketball uniforms yet. Usually we had 15-20 minutes alone before he walked in, but tonight it was different.

He began talking about our mission for tonight. "Remember, guys, we want to push the pace tonight. We'll fast break and press so the Bulldogs will have no time to relax or catch their breath. Let's run them into the ground. You are all in great shape, and you are capable of dictating the speed at which this game will be played. I'll give you some time to dress now, but I wanted you to prepare yourselves to run like a herd of wild horses tonight."

What Coach had just said caused me to flash back to a memory from fourth grade, and I started laughing.

Coach turned toward me with a very perturbed look on his face. "Am I humoring you, Catcher?" he asked in a gruff voice.

I quickly glanced at my teammates and saw many stunned faces. "No, Coach," I answered. "I'm sorry I laughed. What you said just made me think of something from several years ago. I'm not laughing at you, Coach, and I'm not trying to disrupt things. I'm ready for this game . . . ready to run hard and play my best. I'm a little surprised no one else reacted to your comment about 'running like a herd of wild horses.'"

I looked around the locker room again and saw only expressionless faces. "Wow!" I said, "Coach, I'm really sorry."

"It's all right, Catch. Forget it. I know you're ready, and I'm not upset. You just surprised me because I didn't think my material was funny enough to draw laughter," Coach said while smiling, and several players laughed in response. We were pretty loose.

"All right! Get yourselves dressed, and then we'll do our best to put on a good show for the J-Hawk faithful tonight," Coach said, and he turned and headed to the door. I heard him say to himself as he walked out, "Wild horses, huh?"

As soon as the door was latched, Tucson said, "Catch, fill us in about 'running like wild horses' while we dress."

"Yeah," said Abe. "Inspire us."

"If we are going to 'run like wild horses' we need to know what tickled your funny bone," Captain Hook added.

I shook my head and laughed to myself. "I'm really astonished that you guys . . . Abe, Hook, Tucson . . . and you . . . San Juan and Otto . . . that you don't remember because you five were all there at the scene of the crime."

"Everyone, get dressed! Catcher, begin the tale," Pickett directed.

I began to put my uniform on as I started telling the story.

"We were all in the same 3rd and 4th grade classroom, and there was some kind of parent meeting or program in our gym on one really hot night in the early fall. Those folding metal chairs had been set up, and they covered the entire gym floor. The gym was packed with people, young and old. I remember I was sitting by myself on the back wooden bleachers, bored as all get out and so hot that sweat was dripping from my face. The meeting went on and on.

"Then I remember hearing a quiet rumbling sound. I sat up and tried to focus my listening on that sound, ignoring all other noises and voices. In a few seconds I realized what that sound was, and I sneaked out the north gym door, exited through the lobby, and raced around the school as fast as I could to the fire escape on the east side. I knew someone was running around on the gym roof, and I wanted to see who it was and join in, because it would definitely be more fun than sitting in that stifling gym.

"I scrambled up the steps of the fire escape, making it about half-way to the top, when Hook's dad came rushing out of the locker room's back door and yelled for all of us . . . and he could only see me at that point . . . to get down immediately. I heard someone say defiantly, 'I'm not going down!' but as I turned around to start walking down the steps I did see you, Abe, and you, Tucson. Then San Juan and Otto appeared and climbed through the metal railing . . . and finally, there you were, Hook, the defiant one. All of you began descending the rickety black iron steps of the fire escape to join me as I reached the ground.

"The Supe was really angry at us, and his face was bright red. He yelled something about all the noise that we had made running around on the roof like a 'herd of wild horses.' I remember that he used those same words that Coach used tonight. That's what made me laugh. This was seven years ago, and I remember it almost like it happened yesterday.

"I never even made it up to the roof, but I was captured with the rest of you, and we were all led into the gym where we were seated on the back bleachers. One-by-one every head in the gym turned around to see who the culprits were. All adult faces, including those of my parents, were stone cold. Several kids smiled, however."

I paused and took a quick look around, saw that my teammates were still engaged, and I continued. "At first I considered proclaiming my innocence to my parents as they gave me the silent treatment on the ride home, but then I realized that you guys were my best friends, and I was honored to be in as much trouble as the rest of you were in. It was very important for me to be part of your group so I said nothing, and I hoped all of you would do the same.

"That's it . . . does this bring back any memories for anyone?" I asked.

"I remember running on the gym roof a few times," said Tucson. "I know the Supe caught us once, but I don't recall what he said to us."

"Same for me," Abe added. "I remember Hook's dad yelling, and I was scared to death. I think I was grounded for a week by my folks."

"You guys had it easy," said Captain Hook. "My dad was pretty tough on me. He was embarrassed by my behavior, and I really heard about it. He said he expected better from me. I was grounded for two weeks."

"Were you pulled into trouble by this group against your wishes, Hook?" I asked.

Hook replied with a laugh, "No, I went very willingly on my own."

"I lost my allowance for two weeks," confessed San Juan, "but I'd do it again in a flash."

All twelve of us laughed at his admission.

"I don't remember anything about it," said Otto. "I don't have enough brain power to recall all the times I have been apprehended by the authorities."

That, too, drew laughter from everyone.

"Does that include the Halloween night when a couple businessmen from Jeffers caught you dragging a post out into Main Street, and you were forced to put back a whole slew of fence posts and poles?" I asked Otto.

"I don't remember anything about that either," answered Otto.

Pickett chimed in, "You are a lousy liar, Otto."

"Great story, Catcher," said Laser. "It is ironic that a group of you got into trouble 'running like a herd of wild horses' on the gym roof a few years back, and tonight all of us will seek glory for the same 'wild horse thing' in the gym directly below."

"That's what I'll be thinking tonight . . . run like wild horses. I'm ready," said Pickett. "Let's give it to 'em tonight! Let's run 'em to death! Saddle up everyone, but let's do it differently than Hook's dad did those many years ago. We'll take no prisoners!"

Everyone howled, especially those of us who had been "captured" that night long ago.

Just then Coach returned. He heard our laughter and looked into our faces. I'm sure he could tell his team was loose and ready to go.

As we rose and prepared to run out to the gym floor for our warm-ups, we began our chant. "We are . . . J-Hawks! We are . . . J-Hawks!"

We were ready!

As I ran out the locker room door, I lifted my head up high and whickered. Then I laughed out loud one more time.

Chapter 10

Jenny

We gathered in a close circle at the free-throw line for a few "We are . . . J-Hawks!" We said these so softly that the sound was unable to drift beyond our group. We broke our huddle and began our warm-up routine with basic right-handed layups, then left-handed. We eased into the running so our bodies could begin to warm up slowly. Next we ran our weaving drill, making easy passes as we cris-crossed the floor. Jump shots followed, with each player shooting from his favorite spots. Then we simulated game action by playing half-court five-on-five, with us starters playing offence first, then switching to defense. Our bodies were warming up. We ended with free throws.

After Laser and I had taken our turns at the free-throw line, we headed toward the microphone to make a couple announcements.

Laser spoke first. "Good evening everyone. Welcome to the game tonight between the Benson Bulldogs and your Jeffers J-Hawks!"

Loud applause filled the small gym.

Laser projected his voice, "I have two announcements I wish to make. First of all I want to remind everyone that J-Hawk Juice and cookies will be available in the lunchroom after the game."

Kids of all ages clapped and cheered.

Laser continued, "Next I want to invite all kids from Grade 1 through Grade 8 to our third basketball clinic which will be held in this gym tomorrow morning starting at 9:30. Come prepared to have fun. After the clinic we will walk to the public library to enjoy some books. Parents can pick up their children from the library at 11:00. All high school students who wish to help out are also invited."

The cheers after this second announcement came from many young voices, as well as the voices of their parents.

Laser then handed the microphone to me. I knew this would be difficult, but I began. "Tonight we have chosen fifth grader Jenny Amundson to be our honorary captain." I waited for the applause to die down. "As many of you know, Jenny is currently battling cancer, and we want to recognize her for her amazing courage and her positive attitude as she continues her fight. We ask all of you to keep her in your prayers and to continue to offer encouragement and support to Jenny and to her family."

I think everyone in the gym stood up and applauded, and my eyes began to water. I hoped my voice would not fail me.

When the crowd quieted again, I added, "Jenny, please accept this J-Hawk Nation cap as a token of tonight's honor."

Laser and I walked over to Jenny and her family. We greeted them as the crowd again erupted in applause, and I handed Jenny the cap. She rose to give Laser and me each a hug and a thank you. She then placed the cap upon her shiny head to even greater applause.

As I headed back to the bench area, I really needed to wipe my eyes. I considered taking a quick glance toward "that girl," but I wasn't sure I wanted her to see my face at this moment.

The whole team greeted Laser and me as we reached the bench, and they patted us on our backs. We only had a couple minutes to get ready for the opening tip.

The opening tip landed in our hands as it usually did. Laser waited for us to reach our positions on the offensive end of the floor, then he dribbled slowly to the top of the key. After a few sharp passes all five of us had touched the ball, and when it reached me for a third time, I was open, and I released a jump shot which hit only net as it dropped through the hoop, giving us our first points of the game. With this first trip down the floor we had met the two requirements we gave ourselves for the start of each game. Before we shifted into a much faster gear two things had to happen. Everyone needed to touch the ball, and we needed to score our first basket.

As I slid into a defensive position for our full-court press, I heard the announcer say into the microphone, "Basket by the usher!"

This totally caught me by surprise. I saw the smiles and back slapping when I turned and looked at Otto and Sons on the bench. There's a really good chance they had twisted the announcer's arm sometime earlier tonight and asked him to call me "the usher," because of Garris's last column. The crowd loved it! They applauded and hooted. I stole a quick glance at "the girl." She was smiling.

Abe knocked the ball out of bounds, and I took that opportunity to find Garris in his spot in the bleachers up and off to the side of our bench. I thought I detected a grin on his face as he wrote something in his notebook.

I repeated these words in my head as I prepared to defend, "Basket by the usher," and I laughed to myself.

Coach was right about the Bulldogs being a running team. Every chance they got they tried to quicken the pace, but they soon discovered that we were doing the same thing to them. Besides moving quickly on offence, they also had to run back to defend. We knew we had the conditioning and the depth to run, and tonight we would find out if they could match us.

During the first quarter we played pretty evenly. Pickett and Abe each picked off a pass, and Hook scored on two short jumpers to get us started. Benson scored on a layup and two long shots. The lead kept changing, and three times we were tied. Both teams were shooting well, so there weren't many rebounds to grab, limiting the number of fast breaks in the game. At the end of the quarter we led by a score of 18-16.

During the break Coach kept everything positive. He said he liked what he saw so far. "Keep running," he said. He looked at me and started laughing. "Wild horses . . . run like wild horses. Keep pressuring them as they bring the ball up the court. Force them to make mistakes. When they start missing their shots we'll grab the rebounds and ---"

"Run like a herd of wild horses!" I interrupted.

"Their tallest guy is only about six feet tall," Coach said. "Block them out when they shoot, and use our height advantage to grab the rebounds, then hurry the ball to the side and down the court."

That was the plan.

The second quarter belonged to us. The Benson players started breathing harder now, and not as many of their shots dropped. The rebounds were ours, and we flew down court. Several times we beat them to the basket for layups, and they began to breathe harder yet. Laser and I each pulled up for short jumpers that swished through the hoop, and we built a lead of ten points. In trying to stop Laser on a drive to the basket, Number 12 picked up his third foul and had to take a seat with three minutes left in the quarter. That put their best shooter on the bench. None of us had more than two fouls, but Coach kept subbing, using eight of us players in a rotation.

In the last two minutes Abe scored twice when high passes from Laser put the ball in Abe's hands right by the rim. There's no Bulldog who can defend Abe at that height. *I bet we will come back to that often in the second half.* Just as the quarter ended I hit a shot from about 15 feet out, and the buzzer ended the half with us leading 35-23. The home fans erupted as we ran to the locker room for our ten-minute break.

Coach had a couple adjustments for us for the second half. He told us, "Keep fast breaking after every defensive rebound. Take the ball all the way in for a layup if it is available, but if they have too many players back on defense, pull the ball back outside and pass it around. Laser, Catcher, . . . find Pickett as he crosses the lane. Then, Hook and Abe, move to the hoop so Pickett can toss you a high soft pass for a bank in, or he can take his own soft shot. Our fast break will make them run, our quick passes will make them constantly shuffle their feet on defense, and the high passes will take advantage of our height. Don't be feeling sorry for them. Any questions?"

"Do you want us to drive on Number 12 and try to foul him out?" Laser asked.

"I don't think we have to target him," Coach replied. "He'll have to defend against your drives to the basket, so he will either commit those last two fouls, or we'll get some easy baskets when he pulls off."

Everyone drank more water before we returned to the floor for warm-ups. We were feeling confident. We knew the second half was generally our better half.

The Bulldogs came at us hard at the beginning of the third quarter. With their tough defending they picked up some quick fouls, but we didn't lose our focus even though they were hacking us hard on our arms as we passed and shot. I wondered what strategy they would try next since their running game was not effective, and fouling us just helped us build our lead. With two minutes left in the quarter our lead stood at 16.

Otto hit a short baseline jumper, and on our next possession Hook rebounded my missed shot and bounced a pass to Pickett who used his left hand to lay the ball against the backboard into the basket. We stopped their efforts to score, so our lead was up to 20 to start the last quarter.

During the fourth quarter we continued to push the ball and play hard. Coach felt this time of the game was useful for sending a message that we will never quit. Since we would be playing Benson in their gym in about a month, we did not want them to gain any confidence. Our goal was to limit the number of positives they could take from this game, and we did that pretty well tonight. If their bus doesn't start after the game tonight, they'll really be down on themselves.

When the Benson coach called for a timeout and put his reserves in for the last two minutes, Coach emptied our bench. Game over! All twelve J-Hawks have now played in all five of our games, so it's probably the right time for Pickett and Laser to schedule that meeting with Hook's dad.

After shaking hands with the Bulldog players, we continued our line over to where Jenny and her family sat, and we shook hands with them. I stood last in line, and I stayed there and talked to Jenny for a short time while my teammates started greeting friends for the few minutes Coach gave us before he called us in for showers. Then I glanced behind our bench and saw that "the girl" and her parents were still seated. They seemed to be talking to each other and observing people moving around on the gym floor. *I hope they stay awhile.*

I saw Coach signal, and I hustled because I had other business to take care of before I could hopefully catch up with "the girl" in the lunchroom. I showered and dressed quickly. I grabbed my J-Hawk Nation stocking cap as I departed the locker room and hurried to the stage bleachers.

My mom met me at the far wing on the stage, past the student bleachers, near an electrical outlet. I grabbed a metal folding chair that I found leaning against the brick wall, set it up, and uncomfortably sat down. I beckoned to Mom to come near and pointed to her bag. She quizzically took out the hair clippers I had asked her to bring to the game. She hadn't asked why I had made this request. There had been a puzzled concern shown on her face then, and it reappeared now.

Laser brought Jennifer and her family up onto the stage as I had asked him to do earlier in the evening, and after Mom surveyed the situation, her light bulb went on. She had figured out the answers to her unasked questions. She smiled at me lovingly, plugged the clippers in, and moved toward the chair where I sat waiting. She touched the switch, and the clippers began buzzing.

She didn't say anything as she carefully glided the clippers, several times, from my forehead to the back of my neck, shearing my blond locks completely off, and my hair piled up on my shoulders, my lap, and the floor.

It didn't take long for a small curious crowd to appear, notice the extremely close-cut haircut I was receiving, and observe Jenny watching intently. After a short time some words of approval and light applause joined the drone of the clippers. My eyes might have been the only dry eyes on the stage. I was more than a little apprehensive about my new appearance. This gesture of support didn't figure to improve my looks much, but it was something my heart told me I needed to do.

It doesn't take too long to get a military-style cut, so the stage party was a short one. As the sound of the electric clippers died out, rumblings of, "We are . . . J-Hawks! We are . . . J-Hawks!" began. I thought of Jenny, her struggles with cancer, and the courage with which she faced her opponent, and my eyes moistened. I felt a little embarrassed, and I blinked my eyes a few times. Jenny quickly stepped forward and gave me the kindest, warmest hug and whispered into one of my exposed ears, "Thank you." She gently rubbed my head for good luck, rescued my black stocking cap from my hands, shook off the loose hair, and then fitted it securely on my almost shiny head. The cap was, of course, identically matched to the J-Hawk Nation cap she was wearing. We were joined in spirit.

As Jenny stepped back she saw the "mystery girl" and asked her, "Who are you? Are you new here?"

"I'm sorry if I shouldn't be here," the girl answered. "I was just curious about what was happening on the stage. I came to the game with my parents tonight, and I had so much fun. I didn't want to leave yet."

"It's okay that you are here. Everyone's invited," Jenny said. Then she asked again, "But what's your name?"

"Oh, I'm sorry," she replied. "My name is Sarah . . . Sarah Jenkins . . . and I guess . . . I'm a new friend of . . . the usher."

Pretty name . . . matches the face. Did she say "friend of the usher?"

"How am I looking now?" I asked no one in particular, a silly grin lighting up my face.

"Hi, Sarah," I said. "My friends call me 'Catch' or 'Catcher.'"

"All right," Sarah replied. "Hi, Catch . . . or Catcher."

"Hey, Jenny," I said respectfully. "Good questions. Way to go. I wish I had your courage, about a lot of things. Then to some chuckling from bystanders I added quietly, "Maybe you could ask Sarah if she has a phone number."

Two other items need mentioning: First, out of the corner of my eye I spied Garris a ways back from the group on the stage, hovering, pencil in hand.

This worries me. Will I somehow be his target in tomorrow's column? Will he see me as weak? What angle will he use if he writes about this"

The second thing that happened almost buckled my knees. As I left the stage and walked toward the lunchroom for some J-Hawk Juice and a cookie, Sarah walked up right beside me and said, "I like your haircut. That was a very kind thing you did for Jenny."

I nodded and said, "Thanks." I looked at her and smiled, and at that exact instant I thought I heard some songbirds calling. *I do hope I have a new friend.*

Sarah and I sat at a table together, along with some of my friends. J-Hawk Juice never tasted so good.

In the Stands – With John Garris

Last night I attended a track meet. It was indoors, and I watched as many fast runners flew by. No batons were passed by either team, but a basketball was . . . often. The Benson Bulldogs used a running game to try to stop the Jeffers winning streak at four games, but the J-Hawks were too tough on their home floor. Both teams ran at every opportunity, but the J-Hawks had many more opportunities because of a huge rebounding advantage and a better shooting percentage. They displayed superior conditioning, and they never let down.

It was another great team effort that resulted in J-Hawk players scoring often on easy layups and short jump shots, leading to a 20-point victory.

Who led the J-Hawks last night? . . . Choose one. They all played well.

I love basketball, but it doesn't make my eyes mist up . . . At least it hadn't until last night. My heart goes out to last night's honorary captain for the J-Hawks, a young girl who is battling cancer. I felt the support for her family pouring out from a newborn "J-Hawk Nation." Those new black stocking caps may catch on and be very worthwhile, especially if you recently received a really short buzz cut. Good for you!

To the J-Hawks: You continue to surprise and impress me. I'll **catch** you at the next game.

Chapter 11
Magic in the Air

Six years ago when San Juan and I were fifth graders, we were chosen to be magician's assistants for a magic show put on one afternoon for the students at our school. The magician had announced to the kindergarten through twelfth-graders, exactly who he was looking for as helpers, then he glanced over all the students who were qualified, were interested, and had raised their hands. There had been four of us . . . all the fifth-grade boys in the school.

"Plaid shirt and green shirt," he announced. "You two come on up on the stage and help me perform some magic."

I was the green shirt. I rose quickly, sprinted forward, jumped up on the stage, and eagerly walked to the magician's side. I had not paid any attention to San Juan, who was now, somehow, right beside me. We looked at each other and grinned. I felt nervously excited and confident. I was prepared for fame and glory, but it didn't turn out anything like I had envisioned.

There were three simple tasks San Juan and I were asked to perform. San Juan always went first, and he always did his work perfectly, with no mistakes. Each time when I tried to duplicate what he had done I failed miserably. The magic wand that San Juan had waved to help the magician with the first trick went as limp as a freshly cooked spaghetti noodle when it was my turn to help. I was stunned! The three large silver metal rings that were individually handed to San Juan were miraculously linked together in a chain when he held them out for the audience to see, but when I was handed the individual rings, they did not connect in my hands, and two fell to the floor and clanged loudly when I tried to hold them up for the audience. *How could this be happening?* I was really embarrassed.

The magician was very irritated that I had messed up his tricks and his equipment, and he told me loudly, for everyone to hear, "There will be severe consequences for you if you continue this type of behavior." I could tell by the tone of his voice that he was very serious.

This magic stuff wasn't as much fun as I had anticipated.

I wanted to make myself disappear.

For the third and final task, San Juan was given a folded-up accordion fan, the kind you can wave next to your face to create a breeze to cool off. He opened it and spread it out for everyone to see. It was beautiful, very colorful, decorative, and in perfect condition.

The magician reclaimed the fan from San Juan, folded it up, looked at me sternly, and handed it to me. I gulped . . . then, slowly and fearfully . . . I opened it. What I saw made me feel sick to my stomach. The fan had fallen completely apart. All the paper was ripped, and the ribs of the fan fell to either side. I had absolutely wrecked it. As the audience howled with laughter at my miserable performance, I knew this was my third strike, and I remembered the warning about consequences.

The magician was angry. He shook his head vigorously and pointed his finger at me. Then he reached into an equipment trunk at the back of the stage and brought out a small guillotine that he placed on a table at the front of the stage and proceeded to do a demonstration of how it worked. He stuck a raw carrot into the opening of the guillotine. When he slammed the handle down, the sharp blade cut the carrot so effectively that part of the carrot flew out to the students who were sitting on the gym floor. Now I was really getting worried.

The gym became totally silent when the magician directed me to place my right arm in the guillotine. I know my eyes were as big as saucers, but I did as he ordered because I didn't think I had a choice. The magician pulled out from his jacket pocket a bloody red handkerchief, held it up for all to see, and handed it to San Juan. He spoke clearly, "You'll need this to help with the cleanup."

As the audience laughed loudly at my misfortune, the magician told me in a soft whisper to raise my arm to the top of the guillotine. I was not sure why, but I trusted his advice. He slammed the handle down. The audience gasped . . . but nothing had happened. Fortunately my hand remained attached to my arm. Whew! I was okay, and I was done with my job as magician's assistant. I knew I would not be volunteering my services again anytime soon.

The students in the audience that day saw a good magician make some wonderful magic, and tonight the fans on the J-Hawk side of the gym saw our basketball team create some great magic of our own as we faced a very good team from Shelby and made their players look as useless as the magician's assistant in the green shirt.

We played a great game. Our full-court press was very effective. In the first quarter we scored ten easy points after stealing five of their passes. Our zone defense forced them to take bad shots because our big guys shifted into defensive positions so quickly, stretching their arms out, closing the passing lanes. As the Jaguars became frustrated they began launching long shots that had little chance of going in, and with our height advantage, we grabbed almost every rebound.

On offense Laser and I tossed high passes into Abe, and on three consecutive possessions he softly banked the ball off the backboard into the bucket. When the Jaguars overplayed Abe to prevent him from getting the ball, I lofted the ball into Hook who scored on four consecutive short hook shots. They couldn't stop us. Our play was magical. It was as if all we had to do was think about making a good play, and it would happen.

Pickett started getting open as he crossed the lane about ten feet from the basket. Laser's passes easily reached Pickett, and his jump shots made the net dance as the ball dropped through the hoop.

This was way too easy. We were up by twenty-one points halfway into the second quarter. The Shelby defenders started sagging on our baseline players, double teaming them and trying to deny them the ball. This meant Laser and I were open for uncontested jumpers, and we were zoned in. Everything kept dropping for us, and the Jaguars began playing with their heads down, defeat written on their faces.

Late in the second quarter a sequence of plays went like this. Laser bounced a perfect pass to Hook who lifted a high arching "gift" to Abe who slammed the ball through the cylinder. It was a pretty play. Number twenty-three for the Jaguars then lost the ball out of bounds when he dribbled it off his own foot. Then on our end I set a screen for Laser who moved toward the foul line where he received a no-look pass from Pickett and swished a jump shot. The Jaguars then threw a pass out of bounds when their two forwards collided head-on as they tried to cross to opposite sides of the lane. It seemed like every time we would make a good play, they followed it by making a mistake. The next time down we made four or five quick passes, forcing Shelby defenders to scramble to cover us, and Pickett found himself free under the basket for a bounce pass and an easy lay in. The Jaguars? . . . Number sixteen happened to be stepping on the end line when he caught a teammate's pass.

We ended the first half with Laser hitting four shots in a row. We had played an amazing half, scoring 58 points, almost balanced evenly among the five of us starters. Our confidence was erupting. I know I could have handled the magic wand, the connecting rings, and the accordion fan with no problems now because our magic was working.

Otto and Sons played a lot during the second half, and we won easily by a score of 87 – 52. Most of our bench players scored points, and we all cheered them on.

This was the best we had played this year. It seemed like we owned their gym because everything went right for us, and they looked pathetic in their efforts.

At the end of the game, as we lined up to shake hands, a feeling I'd experienced a few years back revisited me. I reached out for their hands, and I realized how miserable they were probably feeling. I saw in the Jaguars' faces, disappointment and devastation. They had entered the game with high expectations, with visions of glory, and their dreams had been totally shattered. I remembered that feeling. The same thing had happened to me when I was the magician's assistant a few years ago.

As I continued through the line something funny struck me. The Jaguars were all reaching out with their "guillotine" hands, their right hands, which I checked carefully to make sure they were still intact and not covered in blood, and they were all wearing their green Jaguar game jerseys or warm-up jackets. They had not had a chance tonight against our magic, and they had suffered the consequences.

Though we had played an outstanding game in our big win, this was not the best part of my night. As we started mingling with our friends on our side of the gym after the final buzzer and handshakes, I saw Sarah and her parents step down from the bleachers to the gym floor. She had come to the game!

I just stood there watching as Sarah moved from Laser . . . to Otto . . . from Abe . . . to Pickett . . . to Hook . . . to all the players . . . to San Juan . . . congratulating them on our victory and on playing so well. I think I was her last stop. She looked at me . . . smiled that pretty smile and said, "Catcher, you and the rest of your team played an outstanding game tonight. It seemed like almost all of your shots went in, your passes were perfect, and you didn't make mistakes like the Jaguars did. I don't think the Jaguars had a chance tonight."

I nodded and said, "It was almost magical, don't you think?"

She nodded back and replied, "It almost seemed like it."

"I was surprised when I saw you after the game ended," I said. "I had no idea you would come to an away game on a school night, so I didn't even look for you . . . but I'm really glad you are here."

"I convinced my parents, without much difficulty, that we shouldn't miss any of your games," Sarah said. "I suggested to them that we might be your good-luck charms, and all three of us have become very impressed with you and your friends. We like your exciting style of basketball, and we admire the way you treat and help others. Tonight we made a last-minute decision to come to the game, but I think it will be automatic next time."

"Great!" I said to her. "I'll look for you next time."

Talking to her turned a great night into a fantastic night. This is the third time I've seen her, and each time, I've liked her even more. It sounds like she plans to attend more of our games, so I expect to see more of her pretty smiles.

I looked around the gym and discovered that not a single one of my teammates was still out on the floor. I must have missed Coach's signal. I said to Sarah, "I really need to get to the locker-room now. I think I'm late. Thanks for coming tonight . . . I hope to see you at the next game."

I turned and began sprinting away. Just before reaching the locker room I glanced back to get one more look at her. She appeared to be watching me. I waved to her . . . then I disappeared.

In the Stands – With John Garris

Have you ever had a day when you get to work and notice you are wearing one blue sock and one black sock? Apparently, after washing clothes, "someone" hadn't matched the pairs of socks correctly . . . possibly due to insufficient wattage in his bulb. I call this a mismatch. I saw a mismatch last night, and I wasn't even looking in my sock drawer.

I was sitting in the gym in Shelby, watching the Jaguars get clobbered by a team they were supposed to defeat. This was a reverse mismatch from what I had anticipated. Being a conference power, Shelby was expected to make short work of the J-Hawks from Jeffers, but make no mistake . . . there is nothing short about the J-Hawks, and tonight Shelby had no chance.

It was as if someone had written a script for this game, predetermining how it would play out. All the successful plays . . . the perfect passes . . . the excellent rebounds . . . shots that never missed . . . were given to the J-Hawks, while the Jaguars were assigned the lump of coal . . . all the mistakes. Their players collided . . . they stepped out of bounds with the ball . . . they threw passes to spectators . . . they dribbled the ball out of bounds off their own legs . . . and they took terrible shots that hit nothing but stale air.

The J-Hawks night was built around streaks. Abe hit three shots in-a-row from close in, Captain Hook's hook shots (I think I now understand the origin of his name) found the net on four straight attempts, and Laser ended the first half with three successful jump shots. Their outstanding shooting accuracy continued another streak, a winning streak that has stretched to all six of the games they have played this season.

If I were the Shelby coach I'd ask for a rewrite of the script before I took the floor against Jeffers again next month, and I'd also check my sock drawer ahead of time.

Chapter 12
The Call

If whatever power is in charge of giving away wishes came by today and offered me a chance to trade places with anyone else in the entire world, I would not hesitate a single moment. My response would be an immediate, "No thanks. I'm good." The way I see it, I'm at the top right now. What would I want to change? What could be better than growing up in the Jeffers community, playing basketball as an undefeated J-Hawk, having a great family and wonderful friends, and maybe beginning a friendship with Sarah? "You are wasting your time with me. Move on to someone else who might really need you," I would say. "I am very content with my life."

Now . . . if I were a preacher's son . . . then I might want to make a change. Too much is expected of a preacher's kid. That's not fair to any kid. Preachers should not have children.

Sometimes I think one of my teammates, though not a preacher's kid, is living in a situation that is unfair. Captain Hook's dad is the superintendent of our school. That puts lots of extra pressure on Hook to make sure he stays out of trouble. Maybe that's the reason he's quieter than the rest of us. Preacher's kid . . . superintendent's kid . . . I would want out of both of those families.

Being a farm kid isn't so bad. People don't expect too much of me, either with my studies in school or with my behavior. Living in the country carries its own excuses as well as lower standards.

Captain Hook has always been a winner. In 5th and 6th grades, and again in junior high, I always hoped to be on his side when we played touch football during the noontime recess. Our school's coach had playground duty, and he would always choose the teams. Since Hook and I were the two best passers and the two best receivers, we were almost always on opposing teams, but once a week or so, we got to play together. Even if the rest of our team didn't amount to much, it didn't matter. Hook would pass to me, or I would pass to him, and we would score enough touchdowns to beat the other team every time.

School is pretty easy for Hook because he is very smart. He doesn't waste many words, however, and he only volunteers answers when the questions are too hard for most of the rest of us.

He seems to be serious all the time. While many of us find laughter in a situation, it looks like Hook is lost in another world. Maybe he is thinking about the misfortune of being the Supe's kid.

Captain Hook's name has nothing to do with Peter Pan. You could figure that out easily by watching him shoot a basketball in a practice or in a game. His favorite shot is the hook shot, and he is the best at shooting it. He's the "captain of the hook shot," and he is unstoppable because of his height and wingspan. No one can block that shot, and those that try often catch a left elbow to the nose. We keep a tally sheet in the locker room for how many noses he bloodies during the season. He is already at three this year. These were all opponents in games, because in practices we make sure to give him all the room he needs.

My sister and I drove the two miles to town early enough so she could prepare for her game. That put me at the gym with plenty of time to perform my "ushering duties." I placed the folded United States flag that I had picked up at the Legion on a chair across the floor from the team bench, and headed back to the lobby. I smiled to myself, thinking about that first night when I saw Sarah. I thought about how lucky I was to be standing in the entryway in my warm-up jacket when she and her dad arrived, and I am so thankful that Mr. Jenkins asked me to help them find a seat. Now Sarah and I are getting to be friends . . . and it all started because of a misunderstanding. It's funny how some things happen.

After a few trips into the bleachers with school kids and some adults, I returned to the lobby to find Sarah and her parents waiting for me. I straightened the sleeves on my warm-up jacket and asked politely, "Would you like some assistance finding good seats in the gym?" We all laughed. Then I asked them, "Have any other ushers offered to help you?"

Mr. Jenkins replied, "No. I think we are your personal assignment."

"Good. It's obvious I have intelligent teammates," I said.

I walked them to their usual place on the bleachers, and I sat down next to Sarah for a short time. "It's good to see you again," I said. "I have always loved basketball game nights, but now they are better than ever. Thank you for coming again tonight."

"You are welcome," Sarah replied. "Mom and Dad insist that I go to the games with them," she added with a teasing smile.

"Are you good at keeping secrets?" I asked. "You can't even tell your parents what I am about to tell you. I could get in a lot of trouble."

"Usually I tell them everything, but I'll keep this to myself," Sarah promised.

I leaned over to her ear. *Her hair smells wonderful. I should have thought of this "secret" idea a long time ago.* "We are going to run a very special play for Captain Hook at the end of the first quarter tonight if Coach calls for the last shot. Be ready. You've not seen anything like this before," I whispered, and I wished I would have added more details and taken many more minutes to tell her the secret.

As I leaned away I saw her cover her mouth dramatically. I knew she could be trusted, and I laughed at her. *I really enjoy talking to her. It does seem like we are becoming good friends.*

"I'd like to come back to sit with you after my ushering duties are done," I said hopefully.

"I will save a place for you," she said in reply.

"Mr. and Mrs. Jenkins," I asked, "Will you be able to stay for a while after our game? There will be J-Hawk Juice and cookies, and my mom said that there's been some talk about offering coffee tonight."

"Coffee would be nice," Mrs. Jenkins replied. "We plan to stay. We like meeting your friends and their parents. Maybe we'll get to visit with your parents over coffee."

I wasn't sure what to make of her last statement.

When ushering slowed down, Tucson and Otto told me that I was done because I had started so early. I didn't argue. I headed directly to my reserved place on the bleachers. I did watch some of the girls' game, but mostly I just talked to Sarah and her parents until I needed to get to the locker room and prepare for our game against Mitchell. Tonight's game could be a big challenge because we heard the Wildcat's record was 4-2. We know that they play a very physical game, but we don't plan to back down. I hope we have a good shooting night.

When we completed our warm-ups, Tucson, San Juan, and I headed to the microphone to make the announcements. San Juan gave the usual information about J-Hawk Juice and tomorrow's clinic. Tucson then reached for the mike and spoke, "Tonight we have selected the military veterans from Jeffers and the surrounding communities as our honorary captains. Would all veterans please stand."

I looked around the gym and saw that about fifteen men stood to a round of applause.

I spoke next. "We want to thank these men for their service to our country, for their sacrifices and dedication during wartime and peacetime as they protected us."

All twelve of us players spread out to our assigned areas of the gym to shake hands with the men who were standing. As I headed over toward our bench I saw that Mr. Jenkins was standing, and behind and to his left stood Mr. Garris. *I had no idea either was a veteran.* I shook Mr. Jenkins' hand and said, "Thank you, Mr. Jenkins, for your service to our country." Then I stepped up the bleachers and said to John Garris as I shook his hand, "Thank you, Mr. Garris, for your service to our country."

I noticed many others in the bleachers reaching and shaking hands with the veterans as I walked back to the microphone. I was pleased to see two men standing behind the Mitchell bench also being honored.

Tucson picked up the flag. "This flag honors those veterans who lost their lives in battle as well as those who returned safely.

San Juan completed the announcements. He gestured toward the stage bleachers and said, "Please join these students as they lead us in singing 'God Bless America.'"

I had all I could do to keep tears from streaming down my face as I sang.

I wiped my eyes and headed for the bench. Sarah was smiling at me and clapping, and I saw the sparkle in her eyes.

I had two minutes to prepare for the game.

The first time the Wildcats attempted to bring the ball down court, we used our full-court press. Number 13 received the inbound pass, turned to face us, and started his dribble. He came right at me, then swerved to my left and went around me. I was shocked at the way he carried the ball during his dribble, but neither ref blew his whistle.

Number 13 then continued his dribble down court to his basket and banked a short shot off the backboard that fell through the hoop.

Pickett threw the inbound pass to me, and I took two dribbles before bouncing the ball to Laser. He tossed it into Abe on the left side, and then Abe lobbed a high pass to Hook under the basket for an easy score.

The Wildcats quickly threw the ball in. Number 13 received a pass from a teammate and again dribbled against our press, this time at Laser, and he used the same move, carrying the ball as he made his quick turn. Again no call was made by either ref, and as 13 closed in on the Wildcat basket, he passed off to Number 20 who scored on a ten-foot jump shot.

Coach called a timeout. As we approached the bench, the two refs met at center court for a muffled conversation.

"Coach," Laser complained. "Number 13 is carrying the ball! That's traveling! They've got to call that! There's no way he can get around us that easily with a legal dribble! Can't you complain to the refs about this?"

"Hang on," Coach replied. "They're talking now. Let's see if they do something. Maybe that's what they're discussing. It's better for our team if we don't protest their calls."

After a short discussion the refs moved toward our sideline at half court and called both coaches over. The refs did all the talking while the coaches only listened.

In about a minute or so Coach returned and said to us, "This is pretty unusual. I've not seen this happen in any game I've played. The refs, from now on, are going to make the call. They explained to us that they made a couple mistakes, and from now on they will call Number 13 on the way he is carrying the ball on his dribble. Be warned, as they will call it on you, too. I don't think 13 will be able to break your press with his dribble any longer. Keep playing it really tight. I'm proud of you guys for how you handled this. You played it just right in not complaining to the refs. You showed great restraint and maturity. Let's get out there, force some mistakes, and direct some more shots through our hoop. This game has a new start right now.."

"We are . . . J-Hawks!" the entire team shouted as we broke from the huddle.

The next two times Number 13 tried to dribble around us he was whistled for carrying the ball. Both times we turned his mistakes into baskets, as Laser and Pickett each hit on jump shots, and we began to build a small lead. Number 13 became frustrated, and his anger began showing. He lost his composure and started complaining to the refs. Then he dribbled the ball off his foot and Hook scooped it up, passing it forward to me, and I located Laser on his way to the basket, led him with a bounce pass, and Laser made an easy layup.

The Wildcat's coach quickly called a timeout and sat Number 13.

As the first quarter moved on, both of our teams made some good defensive plays, and few baskets were scored. The Wildcats had played us tough, and it didn't help us that Pickett had picked up his second foul with two minutes left to play in the quarter, forcing Coach to sit him on the bench. Play continued, and we maintained our six-point lead.

Abe grabbed a rebound with about 30 seconds remaining in the quarter, shook off his defender, and passed to Laser, who took his time dribbling toward our basket. Abe and Hook took their positions on the baseline, Otto set up on the left wing, I trotted over to the right side, and Laser stopped at the top of the key with the ball. Laser, Otto, and I had great views of the clock: 20 seconds remained in the quarter. I anticipated that this would be the right time.

Laser looked to the bench and saw Coach make the call. "One shot!"

This is it!

Many of us had watched Hook make this shot so often that we were no longer surprised when it went in. From 5th through 8th grades he had fooled with it during noon recess when he had free gym time, and he took some shots at our junior high practices before our coach entered the gym.

Hook had been smart not to try the shot in front of a coach. He knew any coach would yell at him, tell him to quit wasting his time, and prod him to work on shots he could take in a game.

Abe, Otto, San Juan, Tucson, and I felt that Hook should get a chance to attempt his special shot in a game, when the time was right, of course. We talked about this with Laser and Pickett because we understood that we needed our captains' approval. As the senior leaders, they would get the final say. They agreed with us, and they suggested that Hook should take the last shot of a quarter, in our home gym against Mitchell on Friday night, when Coach made the call. If we had a lead and Coach called for "one shot," we would set it up for Captain Hook.

Yesterday Abe and I discussed the plan with Hook to prepare him. He was excited and eager. Pickett informed all the others on the team so they would not be surprised, but we all agreed that no one would tell Coach. We figured Coach would really get upset, but we were willing to risk his wrath because Hook's shot had a great chance of going in. We also spread the word that no one should celebrate when Hook's shot drops through the net. We knew Hook would be humble, and we would honor his humility.

Twenty seconds left.

Laser passed to Otto. Otto passed it inside to Abe who returned it to Otto immediately. Otto bounced a return to Laser who sent the ball my way. Hook stepped toward me, grabbed my short pass, pivoted toward the basket . . . pivoted again to face me, and passed back to me.

Then I made the call.

"Peter Pan!" I called out with just ten seconds to play, and everyone started moving. Out of the corner of my eye I saw Coach stand up as I dribbled toward the half-court circle. At the same time Otto ran a diagonal route to our right corner to set a screen on Hook's defender. Hook quickly sprinted along the baseline, turned up court at Abe's screen, and moved toward the center circle. Laser raced toward our basket, clearing the area, and his defender followed him.

That left only me out front with the ball. Keeping my dribble alive, I stepped toward the left side, and made a football handoff to Hook who reached the center circle with two short dribbles as I screened his defender. Hook cradled the ball in his right hand, pivoted on his left foot, and launched a high arching hook shot toward our basket from the center circle.

The buzzer sounded as the ball glided silently toward the hoop . . . and swished through the net. The J-Hawk fans went wild, while we players turned and trotted toward the bench very casually. A couple guys told Hook on the way, "Nice shot."

On my way I glanced at Sarah, and we both mouthed the word "Wow!"

"What was that?" Coach yelled at us when we reached the bench. "Last shot means get the best shot you can get! Messing around like that . . . That's how teams lose games!"

Coach was really upset, even though the shot had gone in.

"Coach," I said calmly. "I'm the one that's responsible for this. I made the call. Hook has worked on that shot for several years. He almost never misses it. It's a high-percentage shot, and we knew you wanted us to take a shot that had a good chance of going in. We weren't fooling around. As you could see, we set three screens and cleared the area for him. Every player had confidence in Hook, and he said he was ready. We all felt it was the right time for Hook to get his chance."

Coach looked around at every player in the huddle, saw how calm we were, and settled down . . . "All right," he said. "Good shot, Hook. San Juan, go in for Otto. Trap at half court. Hook and Abe drop back. Let's go!"

We put our hands together in the center of the huddle and shouted, "We are . . . J-Hawks!"

As we broke the huddle and prepared to trot to the center circle for the jump ball, Laser, Abe, San Juan, and I held back after one step, leaving Hook to run alone onto the court . . . to a standing ovation. We joined him as the noise died down. I was feeling really good for the Supe's kid.

Not too bad. I'm glad Hook hit it. Coach did get upset like I thought he would, but he recovered quickly. It's good that he trusts us.

Number 13 tried to break our press with very aggressive dribbling on their first possession of the second quarter. He dribbled directly at Laser, lowered his shoulder, and knocked Laser down as he attempted to drive around him. Laser had held his ground.

The ref blew his whistle and called out, "Number 13 – charging!" While the kid protested the call, Abe and I hustled to Laser and helped him to his feet. Though a little shaken, Laser walked to the foul line and sank two free throws to build our lead to ten points.

Coach subbed us often to keep us fresh, and our press continued to cause the Wildcats to make mistakes. Number 11 threw a couple passes away and traveled once. His coach found a seat for him on the bench. His replacement kicked the ball out of bounds while dribbling, and then Number 13 tried to steamroll around me. I stayed in my defensive stance as he clipped me, and we both fell to the floor as a whistle blew.

"Number 13 – on a charge!" the ref reported to the official scorer as I was helped up by Pickett.

It appeared that the Wildcats were losing it, and we knew that now was the time to pour it on.

We kept our lead at about ten points for most of the quarter. Pickett's return to the floor gave us an advantage in rebounding, and Laser and I were able to find him with our passes when he posted up high. He hit his first two shots. All of us started feeding him the ball, and the Wildcats fouled him often as he shot. Pickett hit 5 of 6 free throws, and we expanded our lead to 15 points.

Number 11 of the Wildcats hit two long shots, but Abe and Hook each hit on jump shots from close in to keep our lead at 15. Mitchell's shooters kept firing up long shots, but we only gave them one chance each time down the floor, because our big guys were hauling in every shot that missed. With less than a minute left in the quarter Laser stole the ball from Number 40 as he tried to dribble to the basket. We sprinted down court, but Laser slowed everything down and looked toward Coach. Coach stood and held up one finger, calling for the last shot.

We spread out on our half, passing the ball around, keeping it away from the Wildcats as they scrambled to follow the ball.

Should we try it again?

I looked over to the bench. I saw Coach nod once in my direction. *I'll take that as a "Yes."*

We made a few more passes, then with about 15 seconds left we moved into our positions. I glanced at the clock and saw that ten seconds remained. "Sam Teng!" I called out.

While Hook made the same run he had made at the end of the first quarter, screens were set, and the area near the center circle was cleared out. Hook approached the center circle, and I bounced the ball on the floor so he could collect it as I moved out of his path.

He made his big pivot, swinging his body around and raising his left arm for balance, and again he lofted his high hook shot toward our basket as I held my breath . . . and again the basketball touched only net as it fell through the hoop . . . and the buzzer sounded. *All right!*

The gym erupted as we trotted off to the locker room with our 17-point lead. This night belonged to the superintendent's kid.

Coach managed to play every player in the second half, and we ended the game winning by 21 points. Our streak had now stretched to seven games.

We stayed on the floor for about 10 minutes after the handshakes. I'd have to say Hook was the most popular player in the gym tonight. You should have seen the way the young kids were crowding around him. I imagine that a few kids will be trying his half-court hook shot. We'll have to discourage that at tomorrow's clinic. We'll tell the kids that none of the rest of us ever attempt that shot. Only Captain Hook can do this. He owns this shot.

It didn't bother me that Sarah again talked to all the other players before she walked over to me. I felt proud of her for doing that.

She touched my arm and said to me, "You made my dad feel really proud tonight when you honored the veterans. Many people talked to him and thanked him at halftime. A couple men invited him to Saturday morning coffee at the café. I think he'll go. Maybe I'll ride along and help at your clinic."

"That would be outstanding! Let me know if I need to give your dad some encouragement," I said. "I guess I need to head to the locker room. I'll hustle, and then I'll meet you in the lunchroom."

As I started to turn away Sarah said, "Thanks for telling me about Hook's special shot. I was ready . . . and it was amazing! I was surprised you tried it again. What did you call it the second time?" Sarah asked.

"I knew the Wildcats would know the play if I called 'Peter Pan' again," I answered, "so I went with 'Sam Teng.' That's our playground slang for 'Same Thing.' The guys in the locker room at halftime thought that was pretty funny. Even Coach had a good laugh."

I was really quick with my shower because I knew Sarah would be in the lunchroom waiting for me. She was sitting with a bunch of my friends when I walked in, but they cleared a space for me. I guess others are noticing that Sarah and I are becoming friends.

"I will be back tomorrow morning," Sarah said to me.

"Good for your dad," I said.

We talked for ten minutes or so, but then her parents came and told her it was time.

Mr. Jenkins looked at me, reached out his hand, and said, "I want to thank you."

I shook his hand for the second time tonight.

"I liked those two calls you made for Captain Hook. He looked really comfortable out there, but it was unbelievable that both shots went in," Mr. Jenkins said.

"This may be hard to believe, but Hook makes those shots so often when he's just fooling around that we don't get too excited any more," I said.

Sarah did come to the clinic the next morning, and she proved to be very helpful. A couple of first grade girls that came with their older brothers didn't really like basketball and decided to sit on the bleachers with Sarah. She talked with them and then read with them at the library.

When all the kids had been picked up by parents at around 11:00, I stayed in the library and looked at some historic photos with Sarah. We laughed at how some of the people were dressed in the photos and how they wore their hair. Mostly I was just glad she had come with her dad today. This was my fifth time seeing her, and I'm getting more confident each time. I had a great time talking to her and laughing with her today.

Her dad walked into the library at about 11:15, and he heard us laughing. He said to me, "Hi, Catcher. We had some differing opinions at the café this morning. Will you clear something up for me? Last night did you tell John Garris that your coach gave the okay for Hook to take his shot again at the end of the second quarter?"

"When I looked toward the bench, Coach nodded to me. I thought he was giving me a signal to call Hook's play again," I replied, "so I did make the second call. Coach wasn't upset with me at halftime. He laughed about Hook making his second shot, so that's why I told Garris that the play had been approved."

"So your coach is not upset with your team?" Mr. Jenkins asked.

"No, he isn't," I answered, "but he did say that Hook won't be trying that shot again. Hook will be retiring his special hook shot with a perfect record. I am glad he had a chance to shoot it, and it was great that he hit on both shots."

"They were great shots," Mr. Jenkins added. "They were fun to watch. Sarah, we need to head home."

"I hope to see you at the next game," I said. "Good-bye."

Sarah waved and smiled as she stepped out the door.

I need to find out what Sarah's phone number is, and when I have figured out a good reason and the time is right . . . I'll make a call.

In the Stands – With John Garris

Last week the Benson Bulldogs fell to defeat as they found out they could not outrun the Jeffers J-Hawks, and last night the Mitchell Wildcats discovered that they could not beat the J-Hawks by running over them. The Wildcats played very aggressively, but at times they were out of control and became unglued when calls did not go their way. Their frequent fouling gave the J-Hawks many opportunities at the foul line, and almost all of these chances were converted. The boys from Jeffers kept their focus, remained positive, and worked the ball inside for high-percentage shots on their way to a 21-point victory on their home court, their seventh win without a loss.

Their "high-percentage shots" included two buzzer-beating hook shots, launched into the air by Captain Hook from the center court. Both shots dropped through the netting as J-Hawk Nation rose to their collective feet and cheered wildly.

I've seen desperation shots before . . . some of which have gone in, but these two quarter-enders were not taken in desperation. They were planned ahead of time by the players and carried out with precision . . . without the knowledge and approval of their coach.

Was this a mutiny?

The J-Hawk coach was irate after Captain Hook's first shot, but his players managed to calm him down. I did a little investigating after the game, and one player did tell me that Coach had called for the same play at the end of the second quarter. Though both shots were successful, I can't say they were well-advised, and I would be surprised to see these shots attempted again.

Last night the J-Hawks honored close to twenty military veterans in a pre-game ceremony. I happened to be one of them. I hadn't given much thought to my Navy days these past ten years, but the players' words made me feel proud and appreciated. The handshakes, the thanks, the display of the American flag, and the singing of "God Bless America" made my eyes well up, and I was humbled at being honored.

I am close to enlisting . . . in J-Hawk Nation, because their actions are having a recruiting effect on me. I could see myself, someday, possibly joining the ranks of those who proudly wear the black stocking cap of J-Hawk Nation.

Chapter 13
The Miraculous Maple Tree

I started calling him Otto a couple of years ago because I heard him repeat, so many times, "My dad is giving me a new auto when I turn sixteen, and I get my license."

"Why doesn't your dad just say 'car?'" I asked. "Everybody says 'car.' Nobody says 'auto.'"

"I don't know," he replied. "He says he's going to buy me a new auto, and I'm hoping for a bright red one."

"Fat chance," I told him. "If you set your hopes too high . . . on a bright red auto . . . prepare for a hard landing. Maybe your dad will get you a bright red Moped." I laughed at my own joke, but Otto didn't.

"No!" he shot back. "It will be a real auto, a bright red one . . . brand new. The day I get it, I'll meet you in Jeffers and take you for a ride. I won't be driving my new auto on your gravel road to pick you up, that's for sure."

"I look forward to the ride, **Auto (Otto)**," I said. "I hope the Moped seat is big enough for both of us."

Otto is a good guy, a good friend, and a good teammate. He knows how to laugh . . . how to joke around. He also knows how to play basketball. He's very valuable as the first player to come off the bench because he can play any position on the floor. He is another sophomore we really count on.

One reason I connect so well with him is that his sister is in my class, and she starts for the girls' team. She's really a good player, as were Otto's two older sisters. Basketball is in Otto's blood.

Tonight we needed to convince Otto that our team would be just as strong as ever with him in the starting lineup replacing Pickett, who had twisted his left ankle. The sprain wasn't too severe, Coach had told us, but Pickett would sit out tonight's game just to be safe. It was an easy decision for Coach because Burton did not have a very strong team. Otto would not come off the bench tonight. His role would be much more significant in this game.

Coach said we would adjust our positioning a little, using three guards and two baseline players. Otto needed to understand that this could be a great advantage for us. We'll be a little quicker, show a different kind of attack, and be less predictable.

The players talked to Otto, built him up, joked with him, and eased his mind. By the time we boarded the bus and headed to the game at Burton, Otto had eliminated almost all of his nervousness, and he was ready to start this game. His perception of himself had changed, and he saw himself as being capable of meeting the challenges that would face him in tonight's game.

Coach had told us at the beginning of our basketball season that "perception," how a person sees something or how something looks to you, can make a huge difference in an outcome. He had said, "If you can't see yourself making a play, you probably won't be able to do it. If you cannot dream and see your difficult shot going into the bucket, it will very likely clang off the rim. You have to believe in order for good things to happen."

It was about five years ago that Abe, Tucson, and I messed with a couple kids' perception of nature as we sat on the top board, the fifth row of the long green bleachers which ran behind the fence from home-plate to the first-base dugout at the softball field. We sat in the shade of a couple maple trees. We were beginning to get stomachaches as we ate lots of sour green apples that we had rescued from an apple tree about a block away. We hadn't considered it stealing when we took the apples because the owner of the tree didn't mind. He didn't eat them, and we were actually saving him the time it would have taken him later to remove them from his lawn before he mowed his grass.

Our stomachs were now as full of sour apples as our jeans pockets had been, and just as we were ready to stop eating the apples, to quit adding to our misery, two young brothers approached us. I guess they were about five and six years old. They asked us where we had gotten the apples. They obviously were hoping to get stomachaches too. Since we had eaten our fill and had several apples left over, Tucson developed a plan concerning our extras. He told the boys we had shaken the apples down from the big tree right behind us.

The older boy looked at the tree and said to us, "This doesn't look much like an apple tree, and I don't see any apples hanging on the branches."

I looked him in the eyes and replied, "If you don't believe there are apples in this tree, then you will be right. There will not be any apples. But if you trust that by shaking the branches fiercely you will cause green apples to fall at your feet, then that will be the truth."

I was impressed with my words. I think I may have sounded like a prophet.

The boys looked at each other questioningly, then raced to the back of the bleachers. They each jumped up and grabbed a low-hanging branch of the maple tree, and they began shaking the branches furiously. As they shook a couple branches, then moved on to a couple others, Abe, Tucson, and I nodded to each other and sneakily started tossing apples over our heads into the branches that were directly behind us, making sure the boys could not see what we were doing.

Sure enough, green apples began dropping to the ground at the boys' feet. They excitedly fought with each other over the prizes, gathered them and set them aside in their two separate piles, and continued attacking the tree's branches. They shook those branches mightily until they were totally exhausted . . . and we were out of apples.

Abe, Tucson, and I were pretty pleased with ourselves over the trick we had played on these unsuspecting kids. We definitely had turned these brothers into believers.

About a month later Abe, Tucson, and I walked the streets of town again looking for a new adventure during another softball game night. Now there were chestnuts ready for harvesting, and we pulled off another rescue operation, saving a second homeowner some yard work.

We sat in our usual places on the top board of the bleachers, under the same maple tree branches, checking out our collection of chestnuts, when the same two brothers of "green-apple fame" saw us and approached.

The older brother asked, "Where did you find the chestnuts?"

With a wink toward Abe and me, Tucson answered, "We shook them down from the tree branches right behind us, but they were really hard to shake loose. It was tough work."

The trusting brothers looked at each other with anticipation in their eyes, then sprinted around to the back of the bleachers, grabbed a couple branches, and shook them with all their might. After we decided their effort was worthy, Abe, Tucson, and I gently and slyly tossed chestnuts over our heads into the tree's branches. The boys dropped to all fours and scrambled on the ground to collect the chestnuts that had arrived at their feet. They were ecstatic.

It was a grand repeat performance.

I don't think these two kids realized how miraculous this maple tree had been, providing them green apples and chestnuts during the same summer. I wonder if they ever went back on their own to see what other prizes they could coax from that tree. They were believers.

Were we doing the same thing to Otto tonight that we had done to these two boys? Was getting him to believe that our team would be just as good with him in the lineup a little bit like convincing the brothers that apples and chestnuts would fall to the ground if they believed it would happen?

It certainly worked on the two youngsters. Tonight we need Otto to be a believer. *Come on Otto! Shake those maple tree branches! You can do it!*

As the team sat together on the bleachers in the Burton gym, watching the girls play and waiting for the half-way point of the third quarter when we would escape to the locker room and dress for our game, the Jenkins family entered the gym. I wasn't surprised to see them because last week Sarah had hinted that they hoped to make it to all our games. I was pleased, though. When I saw them sit on the bleachers on our side, I walked over and greeted them. Since my folks were sitting nearby, I asked Sarah's parents if I could bring Mom and Dad over for introductions.

"Yes, that would be very nice," Mrs. Jenkins said.

I walked Mom and Dad over, and I made formal introductions. I felt a little silly because I think everyone already knew everyone else, but now it was official. I did find out that Sarah's dad was named Andy, and her mom was Carole.

Sarah and I moved off to the side a little, leaving room for my folks to sit down. For the next few minutes we watched as our parents talked and occasionally laughed. It almost felt like I was spying.

After about ten minutes I excused myself and rejoined my teammates.

Abe said, "We were just about to send a posse out to rescue you."

Tucson added, "Do you think it was wise to have your parents sit with Sarah's parents? They'll be trading information now. Forget about keeping any secrets."

"Dumb move, Catcher. If Sarah is looking for a new boyfriend would you give her my number?" Laser asked.

"Thanks for all your advice," I replied sarcastically. "I'd like to start thinking about our game now, if that's all right with the rest of you."

"Good idea," Pickett said. "Prepare yourself. I'll be yelling from the bench tonight, guys. Don't let me down. Let's keep this winning streak alive."

Our game with the Bengels wasn't close to being one of our best of the year. We played well enough to win by 15 points, but we didn't seem to be very inspired. Playing without Pickett's leadership on the floor held us back a little because we didn't have him pushing us to play harder. Otto filled in well, scoring eleven or twelve points and playing good defense. He certainly played like he belonged in the starting lineup.

Abe and Hook each grabbed a mess of rebounds, and their quick passes to the outside gave Laser, Otto, and me several chances to fast break and drive to the basket for layups. In the second half, however, Coach slowed us down and told us to work on our half-court game.

We didn't shoot very well from the outside, so we worked the ball inside, throwing high lobs to Abe. He hit on most of his shots, banking them off the backboard. On the other side of the lane, Hook made a few short hook shots.

The Bengels didn't give up, but they couldn't compete with us because they were quite a bit shorter and not nearly as quick as we were. Maybe we were lucky we weren't playing a better team tonight. By the end of the game we had managed to score 71 points . . . quietly. We didn't have any outstanding plays like the long shots Hook scored on last Friday night, and a couple times I did hear someone on our side of the gym shout, "Peter Pan." I wonder if he was hoping Hook would take some half-court shots.

Coach didn't have us use our full-court press tonight because we were short a player with Pickett out. He wanted us to conserve energy, so we dropped back. Maybe that's why we were a little flat tonight. We never got our motors going. All of us prefer to play a fast-paced running style instead of walking with the ball. I hope Pickett is back on Friday night, and I hope Coach has us running again.

I don't think we were a very exciting team to watch tonight, so we didn't' give J-Hawk Nation much to cheer about . . . except for winning our eighth straight game.

The last two games I was Sarah's last stop on our team, but tonight I was her first stop, and her parents came with her. I just looked at them without saying anything because I wasn't sure what was going on with me. I was afraid that whatever I said would be the wrong thing to say. Finally I just said, "Hi."

"Hi," Sarah said back to me. "Is something wrong?"

"I don't know," I replied. "This game tonight . . . something just didn't feel right. We didn't have any spark, and I don't think we had much fun either. It wasn't like any of our other games. What did it look like to you?"

"It did look a little different," Sarah said.

"At times things looked good," Mr. Jenkins added. "You were a lot better than the other team . . . but I think you are right. It looked more like work than fun tonight."

"I couldn't figure the game out. We didn't talk much . . . we didn't find anything to laugh about . . . we didn't even compliment each other on good plays. It wasn't much fun. This was a strange game. I hope we haven't lost our spirit," I said.

Mrs. Jenkins reassured me, "This was just one game . . . and, besides, you didn't lose . . . you won. That's not bad! I bet your next game will be one of your best."

"Thanks for saying that," I said.

I looked at Sarah, hoping her parents would maybe go talk to someone else. I think she read my mind, and she said, "Come on over here. Let's sit down."

"Sarah," I said, "I'm so glad you came again tonight. I'm sorry I'm not better company, and I'm not really sure what it is. One of my teammates said something to me before the game. I think he was joking, but I let it bother me. I'll say something to him on the bus ride home. Next time I need to laugh it off."

"I've found out that even my best friends can upset me some times," Sarah said.

"It got me down a little. What I need now is a good laugh. Can you help me out?" I asked.

"Maybe . . . I bet I can," Sarah replied. "During the game did you hear someone call out 'Peter Pan?'"

"Yes, I did," I said, " . . . a couple times."

"That was my dad," Sarah said laughing. "He wanted Captain Hook to shoot a long one."

I did laugh, and I felt much better. Maybe that's all I needed. "That's pretty good," I said, still smiling. "I'll be listening for him on Friday night. Will you be coming to our game Friday night?"

Sarah hesitated . . . "Have you ever been to a bad movie?" Sarah asked.

"What? . . . Sure . . . I've been to some that weren't too great," I answered.

"Have you gone to any other movies after that?" Sarah asked.

"Yeah . . . I have," I replied.

"There's your answer," Sarah said. "We'll be at the game Friday night. One 'bad movie' won't keep us from coming back. Movies and basketball games are all different."

"So we were a bad movie tonight?" I asked laughing.

"Not terribly bad . . . You noticed I didn't walk out," she said as she smiled again.

Sarah had pulled me out of a low spot. She was happy and fun . . . just being herself . . . and now I was starting to feel like myself again.

"I think we'll play fast Friday night and put some fun back in the game. I'm already excited! Would you ask your parents ahead of time if maybe you could stay longer after the next game?" I asked. "I like talking to you . . . and you do make me laugh."

"I'll be extra helpful around the house the next couple days," Sarah said in a quiet voice as she looked around from side to side, acting like she was scheming. "I think that will be worth some extra time. I'm getting pretty good at figuring out how to work my parents."

I nodded and smiled at her. Then I saw Coach signaling to us. "Thank you, Sarah . . . for talking to me . . . and for cheering me up," I said. "I'm looking forward to Friday already."

Friday can't get here fast enough.

Chapter 14
The Breakdown

I take no responsibility for naming Abe. I wish I could, but Abe was given this name long ago, probably by his own family. It was as natural a choice for him as it was for Abraham Lincoln. It was a dignified name, a proud name, a name that suggests strength and honesty. I can't do any better than "Abe" for this sophomore who was so important on our team.

Like almost all kids in town, Abe was born here. I knew him from early Sunday-School classes, and in the early elementary school years I discovered that he loved to play sports of all kinds.

There were several important factors that brought us together as friends besides just sports. He lives across the street from my grandma's house, so he was really easy to find. We were close in age, so every-other year, I was in the same classroom as he was in. The fact that we each had a younger brother who liked sports was significant also, because most of the time this meant we had a guaranteed four players for any game we tried to start. Finding just two more players in town would give us a chance for some competition and excitement.

When my brother and I would ride our bikes to town on the two-mile gravel road with the goal of getting a ballgame going, our first stop was at Grandma's house to check in. Then we would see if Abe and Young Abe were available, and most times they were ready, willing, and able. We spent many a summer day playing on his yard, smashing rubber balls across the street with wooden bats.

Our favorite game we called "Fun-ball." It was like baseball on a smaller scale, because we used a smaller field, fewer players, and a plastic, soft-ball-sized hollow ball that had many circular holes cut into it. It was a very fast-paced game. Every play had to be made quickly. The most unique feature of our playing field, besides the several small flower gardens we had to jump over while making fielding plays and the bushes we had to dodge, was the "white monster" that was Henry's house. The house sat in what was deep shortstop and left field, starting behind third base and extending almost to the gap between left and center. It was considered a great hit if you slammed the ball high on the side of the house and slid safely into the dirt spot called second base before the fielder could catch the ball off the house and fire to second for the tag. Old Man Henry never complained about our using his house as part of our playing field, but he never really thanked us either. I wonder if he ever watched from inside? We didn't hurt anything except some grass and a few flowers. Sometimes we used wooden bats, but we preferred hollow plastic ones. Lots of tape extended the useful life of these bats. We never kept track of innings, and the score of the game didn't seem to be important, so we just kept playing until we were worn out.

To help keep the peace in our families Abe had my brother on his team, and I had Young Abe on mine. This eliminated some of the bossing and yelling that probably would have halted some games as younger siblings walked off.

Water breaks meant crossing the street to Grandma's outside water pump with the crank handle. With quick pumping action we could get a steady cold stream of water going, and we took turns cupping our hands under the steady flow while drinking our fill of the cold refreshing water.

If the game was over for the afternoon and we had some money, we headed downtown to the grocery store for our favorite thirst quencher. Fifteen cents would buy a tired, thirsty ballplayer a chilled sixteen-ounce bottle of Coke and a small bag of Planter's Salted Peanuts. Somewhere, somehow, we had discovered that pouring the peanuts into the bottle after a couple of swigs of Coke presented you with a refreshing, delicious combination of a cool drink and a salted chewy snack at the same time. We were inventive kids.

Autumn found us playing tackle or two-hand-touch football. We had no grownups ruining our games by imposing organization and rules. Everything we did was kid-driven so we learned to lead as well as to follow. Bruises were common, and arguments were expected, but another day would bring another attempt at football glory.

In the winter of the elementary and junior high years Abe and his brother would come out to the farm and play ice hockey on our pond if we had been lucky enough to have been hit by a hard freeze after having had heavy autumn rains. If the cold temperatures were somewhat tardy, the water in the pond would follow the stretch of tiles that had been laid several feet deep in the soil and would reach the creek, eventually flowing off the farm. We always prayed that ice-cold temperatures would follow heavy spells of rain.

Using homemade hockey sticks or stick-shaped branches cut from trees in the woods, we slid and slapped the puck across the ice. We spent as much time falling and getting up as we did skating, and sometimes we had to pause the game to search in the snow banks that edged the pond for a puck that had missed the goal.

It was in the haymow, sometime in December or January, after the hay bales in the south end had been fed to the milk cows below, that we refined our dribbling skills and our shooting touch using my dad's old leather basketball. The large wooden panel door that should have been raised vertically to cover the opening on the north wall was stuck in the down position, and the south wall had two high large window openings through which numerous gray pigeons entered and exited at their convenience. The roof itself was missing so many shingles that sunlight poured directly in from above, and we could see the specks of hay dust in the rays of light, just like we had seen in the movie theater when we looked back toward the projector.

Since there was no heat in the barn, room temperature was outdoor temperature, and it was often freezing cold in our second-floor gym above the cows. Sometimes we played so long in the cold air that the ball became rock hard or quite deflated. You learned to focus intently when you shot at the rim, which had been attached to a homemade backboard on the south wall, because there was not much margin for error when you were already saddled with the disadvantages of hats, coats, gloves, and loose floorboards. If my opponent was covering me too closely I would try to shake him by dribbling quickly and closely around the bale-drop chute, making sure not to step on the rotting board that I considered "home-court advantage." I felt quite fortunate to have my own gym, substandard though it was.

Abe really stood out on our team. His ancestry was Mid-eastern, and his skin was a few shades darker than the skin the rest of us wore on our Norwegian-white faces. His last name didn't end in "son" like several of the other players on our team, but that didn't mean anything. If you lived here you were accepted, provided you attended the only church in town, Bethany Lutheran.

Abe also stood out when he stood up. At six-feet, six-inches tall he was quite noticeable. Though only a sophomore, Abe was a starter and a huge contributor with his scoring, rebounding, and defending. His long wingspan was a great advantage in the full-court pressure defense we used. Most opponents struggled with passing the ball around or over Abe. Laser and I were always prepared for easy layups after another steal or a pass that got away. Abe stole so many of our opponents' errant passes that I kidded him that someday his picture would be featured in the post office, next to John Dillinger and other thieves. Every couple of weeks I'd walk Abe into the post office so we could see if he had managed to crack the "wall of shame."

Coach had told us last night in the locker room after our win over Burton that Pickett should be ready to go on Friday, and we would go back to our style of running hard. Everyone cheered and applauded when we heard that news. The bus ride home had given us a chance to relax with Pickett's music, and we had talked about the less-than-satisfying game we had played. We were determined that we would never experience that lousy feeling again. The ride home was much more fun than the game had been.

Tucson didn't get to school until about ten o'clock this morning because of an early dentist appointment in Madison Lake. He had also stopped at The Jeffers Café for a quick breakfast before heading to school.

That's when he found out about the Cade family.

When Tucson arrived at our assembly room between classes, he walked up to Mr. Carter's desk in the front of the room and said, "I need to talk with the basketball team right away. There's a problem."

Mr. Carter sent us all to the two oak library tables at the back of the room. We didn't have much time before our teachers would expect us in class, so Tucson got right to it.

"I heard a tough story at the café this morning," he told us. "A mom and her three young kids . . . last name is 'Cade' . . . are stranded in town because their old Ford broke down a few miles east of here. They caught a ride into town, and the car was towed to Kelly's. He'll be working on it, but he thinks it will take a few days for parts and repairs. Meanwhile this family has no place to go, and it appears that they have very little money for food and a place to stay. Bob was cooking up a hot breakfast for them, but they are going to need some help. I saw four pretty glum faces in that booth. I was wondering if we could do something to help them out?"

"Why not?" Laser asked. "Hook, go get your dad. Maybe he'll excuse us from class for the day."

"All right! I'll be right back," Hook said as he headed out.

"I'll ask my grandmother if this family could stay with her for a few days. They've got to have a place to stay . . . with Christmas coming and everything," I said. "She will probably need some help with feeding them, but she has two spare bedrooms upstairs. I bet she'll do it. Two years ago a teacher stayed with her for a whole year."

"Okay, ask her," San Juan said. "What about food?"

"We'll need some help from our families," Pickett replied.

"I think my dad would donate some food," Abe said. "How old are the kids?"

Tucson answered, "The girl might be five or six, and the two boys look like they are seven, maybe eight. They look like good kids . . . pretty well behaved . . . but they look a little ragged."

Hook returned with his dad.

"I hear you want to be excused from classes," the Supe said. "This better be really good."

"We need to help this family," Otto said. "A mom and her three young kids . . . car broke down . . . stranded here in town . . . no money and no place to stay . . . and Christmas is coming."

"We're trying to come up with ideas to help them, something we could do right away . . . to rescue these kids and their mother," I said. "I'm heading to my grandma's house to see if they could stay with her for a few days, and

Abe is going to check at the grocery store to see if his dad will donate some food so Grandma can feed them"

"We'll enroll them in school today, as soon as you can get them here. That will keep their minds busy, and their mom won't have to worry about them," the Supe said. "They will also get a hot school lunch every day. That will help."

I couldn't believe how he jumped right in with his suggestion about school. Everyone else looked shocked.

"I'll give you one excused hour, then you are all back in class," the Supe said.

We left immediately. San Juan drove Abe, Tucson, and me to my grandmother's house. My request caught her by surprise, but she said the Cades were welcome to stay as long as they needed to. "We'll be back with them soon," I said. "Thanks, Grandma. We're working on getting help with food."

Abe told his dad a quick version of what was going on, and his dad said the grocery store will be glad to help.

Now we were ready to meet the family and get this rescue operation rolling. Pickett, Laser, Otto, and Hook were waiting for us outside The Jeffers Café.

Tucson led us into the café and to the booth where the family was sitting. Then he introduced all eight of us, and we found out who they were -----Mom (Martha), David, Billy, and Susan Cade. Mrs. Cade told us their car had broken down on their way to go live with her sister in Colorado, and that they've been on the road for a couple days.

"Tucson told us about your car, and we are here to help," Pickett said to Mrs. Cade. "We have to be back in class in about 40 minutes, but I think we can get everything done. Tucson checked with Kelly about your car. It's being worked on, but it will probably take a few days to get the parts and make the repairs, so here's the plan, Mrs. Cade. Catch, you go first."

"You'll be staying at my grandmother's house. She has two bedrooms upstairs, and she's always home. She lives alone, so she will appreciate some company," I said. I looked at Mrs. Cade. Her eyes were misty. "Abe, you're up."

My family lives across the street from where you'll be staying. My brother, Young Abe, and I will be checking in on you. My family has a grocery store in Jeffers. Dad is happy to be able to provide food for your family," Abe said. "San Juan, what about their things?"

"As soon as we drive you to the house, a couple of us will go get the things from your car," San Juan said.

"There's not much, just a couple old suitcases and a couple boxes," Mrs. Cade said. "We couldn't take much in the car."

"We'll get everything for you." San Juan repeated. "Hook . . . what about the kids?"

"As soon as you meet Catcher's grandmother and see where you'll be staying, we'll walk David, Billy, and Susan to the school. My dad is the superintendent, and he said your children need to be in school while you are waiting for your car. They'll make some new friends and have fun learning. It's a great school. We need to know what grades your kids are in so the teachers can be told," Hook said.

Mrs. Cade buried her head in her hands. She broke down. We could all see the tears.

"What's wrong, Mom?" David asked. "Are you okay?"

She recovered and managed to say, "Nothing . . . nothing's wrong. I didn't know what we were going to do . . . and now I think we'll be okay until I can figure some things out. Kids, we'll be okay. I was really worried and . . . now it looks like we have been rescued by . . . " she looked at all eight of us in our black stocking caps, " . . . J-Hawk Nation."

We all looked at each other's caps and started laughing. It released us from our sadness.

"What's J-Hawk Nation?" Billy asked.

Laser replied, "It's our whole community. It's everyone who cheers for our school and our basketball team. We all play on the J-Hawk basketball team, and . . . I know this sounds like bragging . . . but . . . we are pretty good."

"We are . . . J-Hawks!" we all responded.

"What grade are you in, Billy?" Hook asked.

"Second," Billy replied.

"I'm in third grade," David said, "and Susan is in kindergarten."

"Perfect," Hook said. "A few of us will head to school so teachers can get things ready for you. I'll tell them you will be there in about half an hour. Mrs. Cade, my dad would like for you to stop by and see him at school later today."

"I will," Mrs. Cade said. "Thank you. Thank all of you."

"Abe, will Young Abe walk David, Billy, and Susan home from school today?" I asked.

"Good idea," Abe replied. "He'll pick them up in the morning, too. As soon as we walk these kids to school, we'll pull my brother out of class, introduce everybody, tell him about his important new job, and show him their classrooms. He'll be feeling really important. My brother is very responsible, kids, but don't tell him I said that. I know you'll like him . . . . he'll be a big brother to you. Maybe instead of calling him 'Young Abe,' you could call him 'Big Brother Abe.'"

Everyone thought that was quite funny.

It's good to see these kids and their mom laugh. I bet there hasn't been much to laugh about lately. I think they all trust us already.

"Let's go everyone," Pickett said. "We have a deadline."

Mrs. Cade walked over and thanked Bob for breakfast. "Thank you for being so kind to my family."

"It was my pleasure, Ma'am," he replied. "As long as you are going to be stuck in town for a few days, would you think about working here each day for a few hours. We've been really busy lately, mostly because people come in for early breakfast and coffee. They all want to hear the latest about the J-Hawks. I could use some help."

"I'll come back later today and talk to you," Mrs. Cade said.

In the next thirty minutes we hustled to get everything done. San Juan had the only car, so sometimes it took two trips, and sometimes some of us had to walk. We got the kids settled at school and reported to the Supe just in time.

"Good work, J-Hawks," was all he said, and he chased us off to class.

I think Tucson's back was feeling a little sore when he walked into his English class. A bunch of us had patted him on his back for his efforts this morning. He was the one mostly responsible for the rescue operation.

"Good save, Tucson," I said. "It's lucky you had that dentist appointment this morning, otherwise we might not have heard about this family. They might still be sitting there, not knowing what to do."

"Dentist appointment? Oh . . . that," Tucson said as he looked around to see if anyone else was listening in. In a much quieter voice he continued, "My appointment is sometime next week. This morning I just overslept."

I laughed hard and hit him a good one on his back. Like with my sweat socks, sometimes things just happen. This was another case of an accident with a positive twist.

Chapter 15
Regular Seats

Friday, the last day before Christmas vacation started, was movie day at school. All the students from Kindergarten through 12th grade sat in chairs or on the gym floor to watch the movie the Supe had selected for this year: *The Long Trailer* starring Lucille Ball. There was one misadventure after another while this mobile home on wheels was being pulled on narrow roads, up hills, and around sharp turns. All of us in the audience found lots to laugh at while we ate popcorn and drank from the bottles of pop the Supe had given each of us. It was a very good day.

School was dismissed early, and almost everyone walked the single block to Main Street where the merchants' two-o'clock drawing was held, and several lucky families heard their names announced and were given a certificate for a frozen turkey that could be picked up at the grocery store.

This main intersection on Main Street was packed with adults and children, and all the parking spots were filled with cars and pickups. Everyone was awaiting the arrival of Santa Claus. As he had done each of the past several years, Santa arrived with a huge bag and several boxes, and he handed out to all the children, brown paper bags that were filled with peanuts and hard Christmas candy. For most of us, this was our first Christmas gift of the year. I made sure that David, Billy, and Susan got in line with me, and we filed by Santa, received his gift, and thanked him.

The Cade kids were pretty excited to receive the gift bag and see all the people walking around in the downtown area. After about a half-hour, Abe and I checked in with the three kids at The Jeffers Café where Mrs. Cade was still helping out as a waitress.

"Mom!" Susan said excitedly as she held up her brown bag, "Look what Santa gave us!"

Mrs. Cade hugged her kids and shared in their excitement. "You can eat some now, but don't ruin your supper," Mrs. Cade said.

"School was great again today, Mom. We saw a movie and had popcorn and pop," David said.

"Mrs. Cade," I said, "we have a basketball game at our gym tonight, and we'd really like you to be there. It will help you and your children experience J-Hawk Nation. You'll find most of the café's customers sitting in the bleachers, cheering at the girls' game and at our game that follows. Abe and I will be among the ushers tonight, and we'll guide you to good seats. You don't even have to worry about tickets because they've already been set-aside for you. Will your family come?"

Mrs. Cade looked at her children's smiles and said, "Of course we will. We would not want to miss your game and miss seeing our new friends."

"Great!" Abe said. "It's best to arrive before seven. One more thing," he continued. "Tucson, Catcher, and I will be making a few announcements right before our game. At that time we'll be introducing you as the newest family in town, and we want you to be our honorary captains for tonight's game. People will cheer for you when we announce your names, and all you have to do is smile, wave to the crowd, and help cheer our team to victory. How does this sound to you?"

"What do you think, kids? Honorary captains? Can we do this?" Mrs. Cade asked her children.

"Really?" Billy asked.

"Why us?" David asked.

"Lots of reasons," I replied. "We choose special people like you . . . people who, we think, will bring us good luck . . . people who have good spirit like the players on our team. We believe that your car breaking down near Jeffers may have happened for a reason. Maybe you are supposed to be here for Christmas. Can you see why we chose you?"

David and Billy both nodded and said, "Yes."

"Good," Abe said. "When you are walking to the gym tonight, practice saying this: 'We are . . . J-Hawks!' You'll hear it and get to shout it at our game. It fires up the team, and we play even harder and better. We'll see you at the game tonight."

At about six-thirty people started arriving for the girls' game. I'm not putting down the girls' team, but I think these early birds just want to get good seats for the boys' game. If you wait until seven o'clock, you may end up with standing-room-only. There might still be some empty seats on the bleachers, but bigger and bigger crowds are starting to show up. At one game soon I bet the gym will fill, and it will be SRO.

I stood in the lobby after I had made a few trips into the gym guiding school kids and families. I looked at the frosted glass on the outside doors. There I was, somewhat reflected on the glass, and I walked toward the doors, noticing for the first time what I looked like in my "ushering uniform." Together with my black pants and black shoes, the black and gold shiny jacket which had "J-Hawks" lettered on the back panel did make me look a little like an usher.

I could see why Mr. Jenkins could mistake me for an usher that first night. He had never been in our gym before. Maybe he thought that, because the gym was so small, it was unsafe to walk into the gym on your own, especially if the clock was running. Some of the chairs on the far side are just a couple inches outside the line, and the spectators' legs and feet are actually on the court. I understand! It wasn't unreasonable to ask for help, though John Garris made it sound that way in his column. I think what Garris wrote was unfair to Sarah and her dad . . . but I am very grateful that Garris wrote what he did, and that the Jenkins family found humor in the column, and that they returned to our gym for the next game. That column gave me my connection to Sarah.

I continued to look at my reflection in the glass, and I began to think about all my good fortune. 1) I had taken a risk in explaining our "ushering service" to Sarah's family . . . and they had listened to me and accepted what I said. 2) I invited this "mystery girl" to stay for J-Hawk Juice and cookies after the game . . . and she stayed. 3) I sat with her on the bleachers . . . and we became friends. Wow! All of these things had worked for me.

The next thing I knew, my reflection disappeared as someone opened the door and walked into the gym. My mind was now reconnected to my body.

I walked some junior high kids to the bleachers on the stage, and on the way back I noticed the full-length mirror hanging on the stage wall, partially hidden by one of the huge maroon curtains. Actors in school plays used this mirror for one final glance at themselves to make sure they looked good before they walked onto the stage for their performance. I stopped and looked into this mirror. It offered a clearer reflection than the door in the lobby had.

Is this what Sarah sees when she looks at me? Not exactly, I decided, because Sarah sees me as right-handed, and my reflection suggests that I am left-handed. But what does she see on the inside? How does she really feel about me? What am I to her? Is it just about basketball? What will happen when our season is over? I have fallen for her . . . but what if she decides to just move on when the games have ended?

These questions scared me. I turned away from that mirror and quickly walked away. I didn't like where these questions were taking me.

"Do you realize what you are doing?" I asked myself. "Quit digging this hole! Quit putting yourself in a bad place. Set the shovel down immediately . . . no, throw that shovel as far as you can, and never pick it up again! Nothing good happens when you think like this. Give it up! Keep it positive! No more digging!"

*After a couple of minutes I felt much better. I started looking at the positives again. Sarah and I always have fun together. She's always been kind and friendly to me. We are able to laugh at lots of things, and we don't take things too seriously. Why should I worry about something over which I have no control? I'm not going to worry about tomorrow. I'll put my energy into enjoying today and let tomorrow take care of itself. Sarah is **now**! Focus on **now**! The best thing I can do is to bury the shovel!*

It's a happy, loud crowd entering, buying tickets, and noticing the crew of ushers. Many people good-naturedly ask for assistance in finding a seat in the yet nearly empty gym. Others just head for their "self-assigned" seats. These are the regulars. They have had the same seats for years, and no one else would dare sit in their spots.

A good usher knows who the regulars are and where they sit. You can't usher anyone else to a "regular's seat." You do not want to mess up a system that works.

My dad is a regular, having attended J-Hawk basketball games for years. The only seat I've ever seen him occupy is one of the metal folding chairs placed on the gym floor, right outside the sideline on the south wall, fifth chair from the east end. It's Dad's seat. If you sit in his chair you'll be asked to move . . . by lots of people. Regulars protect the seats of other regulars. If you mess up and try to sit in a "reserved" seat it means you have not been paying attention at previous games, or you are a new fan this year. We ushers perform an important service in steering unsuspecting fans away from big trouble.

If Garris ever asked me to usher him in, I was considering directing him to my dad's chair if Dad had not yet arrived to the game. The consequent assault and battery on Garris, delivered by a bunch of Dad's friends would have been a good column topic for the next day, if Garris were still able to write.

I may have figured out why Dad sat in this exact location. First of all, it was right next to the action. It was very possible that in that location he would have sweat dripped on him from a player at some time during the game. He also may end up catching an errant pass. Sitting courtside is the next best thing to actually playing in the game. A second reason involves a rumor that had begun to spread when Dad played for the J-Hawks twenty-some years earlier.

According to Dad's own assessment, he was a pretty decent starting guard at the time. His coach had heard a rumor that, though he was only sixteen, Dad was experimenting with smoking cigarettes.

In those days the girls did not have a team. The evening's games consisted of a preliminary JV game, followed by the varsity contest. Though Dad started on the varsity team, Coach put him into the starting lineup for the JV game and played him the whole game at a forward position, meaning he had to run from baseline to baseline every trip up and down the floor. After a brief intermission between games, so varsity players could warm up, Dad again started at forward in the varsity game. Again he played the entire game. The coach was checking Dad's wind, and Dad passed the test. For the remainder of that season and for the next season Dad started only the varsity games and he always played guard from then on.

I think the real reason Dad chose to sit in this location in the gym was because it allowed him a quick and convenient escape route to the boiler room, where the smokers would light them up during half-times and betweens games. Dad enjoyed his cigarettes.

I'm guessing the coach was right in suspecting Dad some twenty years ago.

Sarah and her parents arrived just after the girls' game had started, and my heart started beating faster as I directed them to the bleachers near our bench where they liked to sit. I wanted to sit down with Sarah right away, but I knew I should help usher for a while longer. I did stare at her sparkling eyes for a few moments, and I smiled, but I didn't say much.

The Cade family walked in a little before seven, and Abe took them to the bleachers on the stage. I watched as the family looked around and saw some familiar faces. Several kids and some customers from The Jeffers Café walked over to greet them.

After ushering I sat next to Sarah while waiting to dress for my game. I found that I'm more relaxed around her than I used to be, but my heart still gets a good workout. I tried to think of a secret I could whisper into her ear so I could get really close to her, but I didn't want to risk Sarah pulling away, so I held back. Just being friends would have to be enough for me until I gained more confidence. I knew how I felt about her, but I didn't know what she thought of me. I would keep looking for signs.

At the end of warm-ups, Abe, Tucson, and I made the announcements. I reminded everyone in the gym about J-Hawk Juice and coffee after the game, and I also mentioned the 9:30 basketball clinic that would be held tomorrow and the two following Saturdays, even though we would be on Christmas vacation. I could tell the kids loved that.

Tucson spoke second. "Tonight we are honoring a new family in Jeffers, the Cades, who are staying with us while their car is being repaired. I want to thank all of the families who have provided food, friendship, and shelter to them, and I hope you will continue to welcome them. I know many of you have already met Martha Cade at the café earlier this week, and David, Billy, and Susan have already made many new friends while attending school."

Abe took the microphone and spoke to the Cade family. "I now officially welcome you to J-Hawk Nation." He handed black stocking caps to all four

Cades as the spectators applauded. "We hope you will help cheer us on to victory tonight."

Early in the game the Eagles from Mayville shot very well from long range, but any misses were grabbed by Pickett, Hook, and Abe, and we used our fast break to score some easy layups. The score stayed close during the first quarter.

We had passed the ball quickly on our offensive end, and I saw that the Eagles weren't very interested in shifting positions in their zone defense. It was just like Coach had told us. The Eagles like to shoot, but they don't play tough defense or pass the ball around much.

We met by the bench at the end of the first quarter. "All right," Coach said. "Keep using the fast break after every defensive rebound. Let's see what kind of shape they are in. I expect them to get a little discouraged before this half ends. Tighten up on your half-court defense. They aren't passing, so step up and put your hand in the shooter's face. I think they'll start missing more shots. Move your press back to half-court. Pickett, stay behind Laser and Catcher, supporting them in the middle. Abe and Hook . . . keep your hands up. On offence, pass quickly and watch for Pickett on the high post. Abe and Hook . . . keep crossing the lane down low. The Eagles are standing still, so quick passes will get you open right at the basket. If they sag back . . . loosen them up with jump shots from out. Let's go!"

"We are . . . J-Hawks!"

Coach had the Eagles figured out. Everything he had said happened. Their shooting fell way off, and we were able to get good shots by passing the ball around, creating openings. Abe and Hook scored several baskets, Pickett hit three turn-around jump shots from just inside the foul line, and Laser and I continued scoring on layups as well as hitting a few long jump shots. By halftime we were up by a score of 43-28.

The third and fourth quarters were repeats of the second quarter, except that Coach subbed in our entire bench, and we still extended our lead. When the final buzzer sounded, the score on the scoreboard showed another J-Hawk win by a score of 82-58. We had played well in winning our 9th straight game.

Chapter 16

Putting It in Motion

As soon as the buzzer signaled the end of the game we lined up to shake hands with our opponents. Then we all headed over to the Cade family.

"Thanks for coming to the game tonight and serving as our honorary captains, Mrs. Cade, David, Billy, and Susan. You really brought us good luck tonight. The Eagles didn't have a chance with your family cheering us on," Laser said.

"Way to go kids!" Captain Hook added.

"We were lucky to have you here tonight," said Nicholson.

"Thanks, Mrs. Cade, for bringing your family and letting us show you what J-Hawk Nation is about. We don't get new families in town very often," I said.

Mrs. Cade replied, "**We** thank **you**! The people in your town have been really good to us. We are feeling very fortunate right now."

Pickett looked at the three kids in their black J-Hawk Nation stocking caps and said, "You look good in those caps."

"Do we get to keep them?" Billy asked hopefully.

"Of course you do!" San Juan said. "We expect you'll keep bringing us good luck by wearing them to school every day. There's a tag inside each hat where you can write your name. You don't want to get them mixed up, and there are getting to be a lot of them around."

"They'll probably want to wear them to bed," Mrs. Cade said as she laughed, "but I think we'll give the caps a rest each night and put them in a safe place. I appreciate the kindness you have shown my family."

"Are you excited that Christmas is almost here?" Otto asked the three children.

The kids lowered their heads a little and didn't reply.

Mrs. Cade explained, "Christmas will have to be delayed this year because of our circumstances. With the car breaking down, it looks like we aren't going to make it to my sister's place in Colorado for a few days. When we eventually get there we hope to stay for awhile until we can sort some things out."

"It's just like last year," Billy said sadly.

"I'm sorry, Billy, but we talked about this," Mrs. Cade said. "We just need to get back on our feet, and then we'll have Christmas," she added.

I looked around at the rest of the players, searching for a sign. I saw several faces that I thought were expressing a feeling that we needed to do something . . . so I decided to take a chance. I hesitated just a moment . . . then I asked the kids, "Haven't you heard?"

Tucson jumped right in, "I bet they don't know!"

"They've only been here three days. How could they know?" Laser asked.

"Know what?" Billy asked.

"Yeah! What are you talking about? David asked curiously.

"Mrs. Cade, may we explain to them?" I asked. "It's pretty important stuff for your kids to hear. It'll be okay."

She nodded, but she didn't show a lot of confidence.

Pickett said to me, "Go ahead. Tell them."

Laser also nodded for me to continue.

"All right," I began. "Kids, Mrs. Cade, . . . you are really lucky that your car decided to break down here in Jeffers and that you'll be spending Christmas here because . . ."

"Tell them!" several players urged me on.

" . . . because Santa really loves our town and all the kids that live here, and each year he visits every house on Christmas Eve and leaves gifts for the children," I continued, as I looked into the eyes of my teammates.

"He never forgets any of us!" Laser said.

"That's right!" several voices chimed in.

"How will he know where we live?" Susan asked worriedly.

"Oh, he will know, Susan! Don't worry," I said. "He'll know you are at my grandma's house. Mrs. Cade, he **will** find your family."

Several players nodded assurance.

When I looked at Mrs. Cade I could tell she was hopeful that somehow Christmas would find her children.

That's how we committed ourselves to bringing Christmas to the Cade children. We hadn't worked out any details, but I was confident we could do it. I'm glad my team was with me on this.

Captain Hook asked, "Mrs. Cade, kids, . . . are you ready for J-Hawk Juice and cookies in the lunch room? I think you may find that some of your new school friends are already in there. We'll join you after we get showered."

"Let's go, guys," Pickett suggested. "Shower up, drink up, and meet up at our place on the stage in about 20 minutes."

I turned and found Sarah standing nearby. "I'm disappointed that I haven't even gotten a chance to talk to you," I said. "Will you please stay awhile? I'll be out to join you for J-Hawk Juice in ten minutes. Will your parents be willing to stay a little longer tonight? It's really important. We're going to brainstorm ideas at our meeting."

"I asked them earlier. They'll give me some extra time tonight," Sarah replied.

"Could I have everyone's attention, please?" It was the Supe, speaking into the microphone. He waited patiently as the gym quieted, and everyone turned to see what was going on.

"It was brought to my attention by the leadership of this J-Hawk basketball team that one of our school's policies is unfair and needs to be changed," the Supe announced. "I listened to them, I have considered their case, and I find myself in agreement. The policy is unfair, and tonight we will fix it. Because all twelve of the J-Hawks have appeared in a minimum of seven games so far in this basketball season, and their prospects for playing in several more games appear to be very good, Coach and I have determined that all twelve of these players will be honored as letter winners immediately. Since this is the final year of J-Hawk basketball, waiting until the end of the season to award letters would be an injustice.

"The ceremony will begin now," the Supe continued. "As your name is called, please step forward to receive your letter and certificate, and know that you are officially a 'J-Hawk Letter Winner.'"

There was loud applause as, one-by-one, players stepped up to receive their awards. When my name was called I walked up and said quietly to the Supe, "Thank you very much for making this decision. It is good for our team, and it is right for my teammates."

We were a happy team. Only three of us had previously won a basketball letter, and five players were receiving their first letter, not having lettered in baseball. I don't know who was the most excited, first-time winners, or the senior captains and me. All the players were shaking hands with each other, and then the parents and the townspeople joined in. It was a great ceremony and a great honor for us.

As I headed for the showers I wondered how many of my teammates might be receiving new letter jackets for Christmas.

The Cades stayed in the lunchroom only a few minutes after I sat down next to Sarah. Mrs. Cade told us her children were tired out from that evening's excitement, so they needed to walk back to my grandma's house where the beds were waiting.

"Thanks again for the J-Hawk Nation caps and all you have done for us," Mrs. Cade said as they headed for their coats.

"Good night, kids," Sarah and I said together.

"David, Billy," I added, "Young Abe will stop at your place at 9:15 tomorrow morning to walk with you to the gym for our basketball clinic. It's your turn for basketball tomorrow."

"Mrs. Cade, are you helping at the café tomorrow morning?" I asked.

"Yes, I'm in charge of the coffee," she replied.

"Then Susan should come to the clinic, too," Sarah said. "She can keep me company on the bleachers."

"That would be really nice," Mrs. Cade said. "How about that, Susan?"

"Goody!" Susan shouted.

It was while we drank J-Hawk Juice and ate a couple cookies in the lunchroom that we began the discussion about Christmas for the Cades. We all agreed that we needed to make this a special holiday for this unfortunate family whose car broke down, landing them with complete strangers in Jeffers over Christmas, and we decided to change their misfortune into fortune. Now we needed some privacy and some good ideas, so we moved out to our corner at the back of the bleachers on the stage. We knew that we had a tough job ahead of us, and we only had two days in which to pull everything together.

All of the basketball players were there, and a few of us had sisters who wanted to help. Several other friends of ours had joined in, and Sarah wanted to be part of the plan also.

"I guess I got us into something," I said. "How are we going to do this?" I asked as I looked around at everyone.

"Let's start by making a list of gifts for the kids and jobs that we will each do," Laser said to start the discussion.

"We'll need some money," San Juan added. "How about we see if we can each come up with a couple dollars to contribute to a Christmas fund? We can collect the money after our clinic tomorrow. I'll throw in the two dollars I would have spent on Catcher's gift," San Juan said laughing.

"Great idea, San Juan!" Abe added, also laughing. "I'll give the money I would have spent on Catcher, too."

"That's sounds good. I'm in," Laser said. "Sorry, Catch, but—"

"Don't leave me out!" Otto interrupted. "My apologies, Catcher, but you won't be getting a gift from me either."

It was contagious. Many two-dollar pledges were given by players, friends, and sisters. Almost everyone said the same thing, "Sorry, Catcher. I'm donating the money I would have spent on you."

"Time out!" I shouted. "Maybe we should rethink this money fund. Maybe it's not such a good idea."

I got several laughs when I made that comment.

I turned toward Sarah. "Sarah," I said, "I need you to know that not a single one of my generous friends had any intention of getting me a gift for Christmas this year. I'm just the butt of their jokes, but I am impressed with their Christmas spirit."

Sarah laughed, and I knew she had figured this out. Besides being very pretty, she is also very smart.

"I would have been spending ten cents on penny candy for each of my twenty closest friends," I continued, "but I've changed my mind. Now I also will have two dollars to contribute to the fund tomorrow . . . and don't bother asking me if I had counted you among my top twenty. It's a secret that I won't reveal to anyone, . . . except that, Sarah, you were on my list," I said with a smile.

Sarah smiled and clapped.

"All right! We'll have a fund to work with," Pickett said. "How about a list?"

"I've visited these kids at Grandma's. They don't have much," my sister offered. "Their clothes are a little ragged. Can we find some 'like-new' coats, mittens, and boots that have been outgrown? What about socks, shirts, jeans, and maybe a sweater . . . a dress or two for Susan?"

"Check at home tonight, everyone. Check with neighbors," San Juan said.

Tucson said, "I think that David must be about nine and Billy must be eight. Susan is probably six."

"Good job! Great ideas!" San Juan's sister added. Let's use the fund to buy the kids some socks and new underwear, everyone's favorite Christmas gifts."

Her suggestion was met with laughter and approval.

"We need some games," Captain Hook said. "What are the favorites for kids at that age? In my family we play Monopoly often."

"Yeah," Laser said. "Check tonight to see if you have a 'like-new' Monopoly game you want to donate."

"Don't forget Sorry and Candy Land, "Sarah said.

"Sarah, you're not still playing Candy Land are you?" Abe teased. He looked at me. "I don't know, Catch."

"It happens to be one of my personal favorites, Abe," I joked.

"I might still have both those games," Sarah said. "I'll check tonight to see what kind of shape they're in."

"Guys . . . girls," I said seriously. "I'd like to explore the possibility of using most of the fund to buy new bicycles for all three kids. Can you imagine their faces on Christmas morning if new bikes are standing by the tree? Never mind that they don't really have a home. Kids shouldn't have to worry about that, but every child should have a bike. It would give them something really positive to look forward to. Their spirits would soar! There's no gift better than a new bike."

There was some silence as everyone looked at each other. There were some murmurs and nodding heads, and soon there was an avalanche of support.

"Where will you find bikes at this time of year, and what would they cost?" San Juan asked.

"I don't know," I replied, "but will you go with me to Madison Lake after our meeting tomorrow morning, San Juan? We'll go to the big hardware store where they might sell bikes, and we'll get some information. Sarah, does your dad know if bikes are sold at that store?"

"I'm not sure. May I bring him over?" Sarah asked. "You can check with him."

"Sure, Sarah," I replied. "Bring your mom, too."

When Sarah returned with her parents, Mr. Jenkins said, "Sarah told us you are looking to buy some bikes for the Cades. I think the hardware store on Main Street usually has a few bikes on hand. Would you like some help there? I've done business there, and I know the owner. I could meet you there tomorrow afternoon if you like."

"That would be great!" I said. "San Juan and I can be there at one o'clock with our fund. Will that work for you?"

"I'll see you then," Mr. Jenkins said. "Are you ready to go, Sarah?"

"I need a few more minutes, Dad," Sarah answered.

Mr. and Mrs. Jenkins left the area, and our group continued our discussion.

"Let your parents in on our plans," Laser said. "They may have ideas and might know others who can help. We need to put this together tomorrow after the clinic, so come prepared. Any other questions?"

"I'd really like to get Christmas stockings for the three kids, decorate them, and put their names on them so they have something to hang up for Christmas Eve," Sarah said. "I know where I can find the socks. I've helped my mom design many Christmas stockings, and we already have materials at home. Please, may I be part of this?"

Several nodding heads gave approval. "That's a great idea," San Juan's sister suggested. "Thanks for offering to do this.

"I'll need to find out the exact names and the correct spellings," Sarah added.

I jumped in quickly. "I'll help you with that," I said eagerly. "I'll stop at my grandma's house on Saturday and talk to Mrs. Cade privately about our plan to have special Christmas stockings made for the children. I'll ask her what names the kids would like on them and make sure of the spellings. I'll tell her that the stockings will be delivered on Christmas Eve before bedtime, so the kids will have time to hang them up for Santa. I'll also explain that a group of us from the community are arranging for some gifts that Santa will be dropping off later that night, because all children in our town deserve (and receive) a visit from Santa. This way she won't have to worry about not having anything to put into the stockings. I'll thank her for giving us this opportunity to help her family celebrate Christmas this year."

"That sounds great!" Pickett replied.

"Good job, Catch," said Tucson.

"Sarah, I'll call you Saturday night with the names and the spellings," I said.

"Good . . . and thank you," Sarah said.

Then I added sheepishly, "I'll need to know your phone number."

Laser burst out laughing. "Wow, Catcher! That was really a smooth move," he said sarcastically. Then he altered his voice to a mocking tone and repeated, "I'll help you with all that, but I need to know your phone number." Then he laughed again.

"I'll need to remember this idea," Tucson added. "Especially if it works."

"Me too," added Otto. "I hope that someday I too can be this smooth."

"You guys aren't helping me much," I said. Then I turned to Sarah. "Sarah, I apologize if my friends have caused you some embarrassment. Sometimes they are just too funny."

"I'm not embarrassed at all," Sarah replied. "I actually think your friends **are** quite funny. As to the question of whether or not you are 'smooth,' . . . I'm not sure. I'll need to check with my mom on that," she said as she turned and walked toward her mom.

Everyone looked at me with shocked expressions.

I panicked and called out after her, "Sarah . . . "

Sarah turned back and walked up next to me. Then she said quietly while the others listened in, "I'm sorry I said that last comment. I meant it to be funny, but it didn't sound very funny after the words came out. I didn't mean to be unkind. I was headed to Mom for paper and a pencil so I could write down my phone number for you, that's all."

I breathed a sigh of relief. "I did think you were pretty funny myself, Sarah, but I admit it did catch me off guard a little," I said to her. "I accept your unnecessary apology."

While Sarah was talking with her mother, Laser addressed me as the others stood by. "Heads up, Catcher! She may be way out of your league. She's certainly bolder than you are, and she's obviously a lot smarter too," he chuckled. "I think we can all agree that she's much funnier than you are also."

"I'm willing to accept all that without an argument . . . and she no doubt is a lot better looking than I am," I added to the conversation as I enjoyed all the laughter.

"Agreed!" several others responded.

We were all laughing when Sarah returned, and I could see by her expression that she was wondering about all the laughter. "What did I miss?" she asked as she handed me a small folded piece of paper.

"My friends just paid you several compliments . . . many at my expense," I replied. "It was all friendly and positive about you. I'll tell you about the conversation when I call you on Saturday night," I continued as I held up the piece of paper with Sarah's number on it and showed the paper . . . but not the number . . . to everyone nearby.

"You **are** smooth!" San Juan said.

I know I was gloating, and it felt really good. I didn't do too badly. I now have Sarah's number and a reason to call her.

Then we got back to the task of planning for the Cades' special Christmas.

"Abe, can we store things at your house?" I asked. "It would really be convenient for Santa on Christmas Eve."

"I'm sure that will be fine," Abe replied.

"We can assign jobs tomorrow, figure out what else we need to get, organize the wrapping of the gifts . . . I think we have done well putting things in motion so quickly," Pickett said. "I'm very impressed with you guys, and I look forward to tomorrow. See you at the clinic . . . 8:45 . . . and good game tonight J-Hawks."

"We are . . . J-Hawks. We are . . . J-Hawks." This time it was said quietly, but it came from everyone in the group, and I could sense the determination. These are great friends, and I'm glad to be part of this Christmas rescue.

As our group began to disband, I noticed John Garris standing nearby, scribbling furiously in his notebook. I knew I needed to talk to him. "Sarah, will you come with me for a minute?" I asked.

We stepped over to Garris, and I confronted him. "Mr. Garris," I said, "I don't know what your intentions are, but I am asking you to please not write about our Christmas plans for the Cade family." Any gifts that these kids receive need to come from Santa. They can't know anything about what we are doing."

"You are exactly right," Garris replied. "I see a great story here, but Santa will be receiving due credit. I have an idea how I can write this without compromising your efforts."

"Thanks," I said.

"Merry Christmas, Sarah . . . Catcher. I'll see you in the new year," Garris said.

"Merry Christmas," Sarah and I both replied.

I walked with Sarah to her parents. "Thanks for the extra time and your help," I said to her parents. "We've taken on a project, and it feels good. Tomorrow will be a big day."

"Yes, it will be," Mrs. Jenkins said smiling. "It feels good to us, too."

"Thanks for your offer to help with Susan," I said to Sarah. "Now I know for sure that you'll be here tomorrow for our clinic. Good night. I'm really glad you came to the game again tonight." I felt awkward just saying good-bye that way, but her parents were standing right there.

At nine we took the floor for some shooting and running. At first we moved slowly, but as we loosened up we regained our rhythm and felt good.

We were finding our Saturday routine to be very valuable.

Over twenty-five kids attended the basketball clinic. David and Billy joined right in with the others. The smiles on their faces really stood out, making me even more excited about our plans for their Christmas.

At the library the kids received small brown paper bags that had been filled with Christmas candy and peanuts by the library volunteers. That was a nice surprise . . . for all of us. Today most of the kids chose Christmas books. I watched as Susan held Sarah's hand and sat with her. All those little things . . . they mattered to the kids.

When parents came to pick up their children, many told us "Thank you," . . . and "Merry Christmas." That mattered to us big kids.

Sarah and I walked for a while until her dad stepped out of the café. *I'm glad he is a regular for coffee because this means I get to see Sarah every Saturday.*

"One o'clock?" Mr. Jenkins asked.

"One o'clock," I replied.

San Juan drove the two of us to the hardware store in Madison Lake, where Mr. Jenkins was waiting for us. I had the Christmas fund in an envelope in my letter jacket pocket.

Mr. Jenkins greeted both of us. "Hi, Catcher . . . San Juan. I want to introduce you to my friend, Bob Hanson. He owns this store."

"Hi, Guys. J-Hawks, huh?" Mr. Hanson said. "I've been reading Garris's columns about your team. I've heard from other customers that you have a pretty good squad. Andy tells me you are looking for bicycles for three youngsters. I have several in the back. Follow me."

We walked with him to the back of the store where we saw several shiny new bikes. San Juan and I picked out the perfect three right away. The two boy's bikes weren't fancy, but they were shiny-new, and they would be the right size . . . the red one for David . . . the blue one for Billy. The shorter girl's bike was pink, and it came with training wheels. *Wow! I hope we can do this.*

"We're on a pretty limited budget," I said to Mr. Hanson as I handed him our envelope of money. "I'm not sure we can afford three bikes."

"Your fund is actually greater than that," Mr. Jenkins said as he pulled another envelope out of his pocket. "At the café this morning, we sent Mrs. Cade on an errand to the grocery store, and I quickly told the customers about your bicycle plans for the Cade children. We took up a collection. The coffee drinkers were feeling the Christmas spirit today, so maybe you **can** buy all three bikes." He handed me the envelope. I was stunned for a moment. Then I looked at San Juan. He also looked quite shocked. We both thanked Mr. Jenkins, and I passed the envelope on to Mr. Hanson.

"Thank you!" I said again to Mr. Jenkins. "I guess I won't be complaining any more about not being allowed in the café on Saturday mornings. This is very kind of you and your coffee-drinking friends. Wow!"

"Yeah, thanks, Mr. Jenkins," San Juan said. "Will you tell them at the café how much we appreciate their help? This is great!"

"I will . . . but I think they already understand," Mr. Jenkins replied.

Bob Hanson grabbed a tablet and a pencil and did some figuring. He counted the money from both the envelopes as San Juan and I continued to check out the bikes. Hanson walked over to the bikes, then back to the tablet and pencil for more calculating. He was really giving the pencil a workout. In a couple more minutes he approached the three of us with a big smile on his face.

"All right!" he said to San Juan and me as Mr. Jenkins listened in. "I have a suggestion. These kids need something for winter fun, too, so here's my idea. With my Christmas discount, you have just enough money for those three bikes, this sled (He picked up a wooden sled which had metal runners and an attached rope.) . . . and two snow shovels. (He pointed to his collection of shovels hanging on the wall.) How does that sound?"

"We really do?" I asked. "The bikes . . . the sled . . . and the shovels?"

Hanson nodded, and I saw him smile at Sarah's dad. I was pretty sure we had just gotten a really good deal.

"That's fantastic!" San Juan said. "Catcher, let's shake on the deal before he changes his mind!"

We all laughed . . . and we did shake hands . . . all of us. I said to Mr. Hanson, "Thank you for your generosity. Santa will be very pleased. If you get a chance," I added, "come to Jeffers and catch one of our games. Our teammates should get a chance to shake your hand. Mr. Jenkins knows our schedule."

I turned to Mr. Jenkins. "I don't know what to say. We couldn't have done this without your help."

"You are welcome," he replied. "I think you are doing a wonderful thing for that family, and I'm very pleased that Sarah has joined your group on this. I will borrow a pick-up and deliver these Christmas gifts to Jeffers later this afternoon . . . at about five o'clock. Where would you like them?"

"We are storing things at Abe's house," I answered. "San Juan and I, and maybe a couple others, will meet you at the library at five, and we'll sneak everything into Abe's house without the Cades seeing us. Maybe I can keep the kids occupied at Grandma's house while the rest of you move the things."

"That should work," San Juan said. "Leave it to you to find a way to avoid the heavy lifting."

"Mr. Jenkins," I said. "I'd like to ask one more favor of you. I have a Christmas gift for Sarah, in the car. Would you please hide it under your Christmas tree. I want Sarah to be surprised when your family opens your gifts."

"I can do that," Mr. Jenkins said, smiling.

As we three left the store, I ran to San Juan's car to get the gift, and I carefully handed it to Mr. Jenkins. "Thanks," I said. "I'm really hoping she will like it."

I visited Grandma and the Cades while the bikes, the sled, and the shovels were being hidden at Abe's. I had found out at school earlier in the afternoon that we had successfully completed our lists, and everything was in the process of being wrapped up. Many families had given clothing items that looked as good as new for the kids, and there were some things for Mrs. Cade and my grandma as well.

Everything would be ready for Santa to make a quick delivery on Christmas Eve, and he would only have to carry the gifts across the street, not all the way from the North Pole.

I couldn't wait for Christmas Eve to arrive.

In the Stands – With John Garris

The Jeffers J-Hawks didn't face much of a challenge in their two basketball games this week . . . from either the Burton Bengals last Tuesday night or from the Mayville Eagles at home on Friday night, but in the time between these two games, the J-Hawks challenged themselves, coming out big winners in my opinion, in what might be their most impressive accomplishment of their season.

For the record . . . there was no big crowd applauding their efforts in this challenge, and the J-Hawk winning streak did not increase even by one. Their terrific foot speed and accurate shooting touch did not help them at all in their quest, and their height granted them no special advantage. Their outstanding full-court press was not even a factor, and their unmerciful fast break meant nothing.

So . . . how did the J-Hawks do it? They used initiative, teamwork, solid organization, and great problem-solving skills . . . and what they did was not about basketball. It was about life.

A reliable source alerted me to this story . . . this rescue operation that the J-Hawks pulled off on Wednesday when they heard about a family whose car had broken down near Jeffers. These basketball players took immediate action, finding a place where this family of four could stay, arranging for prepared food as well as groceries to sustain them, enrolling the three children in school, and helping in many other ways to make the situation bearable for this unfortunate family.

Don't forget that these J-Hawks are teen-agers. They are not part of a governmental social organization that assists families in times of hardship. They are students . . . athletes . . . regular kids who chose not to act like regular kids . . . and through their leadership and great effort, engaged others in being part of something good, something significant, something right and just and powerful.

To make this rescue operation complete, the J-Hawks vowed to communicate with the North Pole, in order to guarantee that Santa would find this family that is now sheltered in

Jeffers and would deliver gifts on Christmas Eve that, in the eyes of these children, will rank right up there with gold, frankincense, and myrrh.

I believe it was a "columnist" from a much earlier time . . . possibly it was Paul, who wrote, "And the children will lead them."

The J-Hawk winning streak now stands at nine, plus one for J-Hawk Nation.

Chapter 17
Up on the Housetop

Saturday night, right after supper, I called Sarah for the first time ever. I was nervous. She surprised me when she answered the phone, as I was expecting to hear her dad's or her mom's voice.

"Hi, Sarah," I said. "This is Catcher. I'm calling you about the names for the stockings." *I bet she thinks I sound like an idiot.*

"Hi, Catcher. I've been expecting your call," Sarah said. *She sounds so poised.*

"There aren't any surprises," I continued. "David, Billy, and Susan are the names the kids go by," and I spelled them out to make sure we didn't have mistakes and to make the call last longer.

"Thanks," Sarah said. "Dad told me you did great on the bikes. Those kids will be so excited!"

"Yeah, I bet they will," I replied. "Your dad made it possible with that donation from the Saturday morning regulars at The Jeffers Café. We had no chance without it. I bet your dad thinks we had a pretty stupid plan."

"No, not at all," Sarah answered. "Mom and Dad are both impressed with what you and your friends have done, coming up with ideas so quickly and pulling everything together."

"That's good to hear," I said, feeling more reassured. "Many families have been very generous. Are you going any place over vacation?"

"We're driving to my grandparent's place in South Dakota for two days next week," Sarah said. "Otherwise we'll be at home."

"Last night when you came back from talking to your mom and we were all laughing . . . the guys and girls were giving me a hard time, pointing out that you were much bolder than me, much smarter, much funnier . . . and I threw in 'much better looking.' That's why everyone was laughing, and it was directed at me, not you. I'm sorry if you felt uncomfortable," I said.

"Thanks for your explanation. Only good friends can get by saying things like that. I wish I had been there to hear them," Sarah said, chuckling.

"Is it okay if I come by to pick up the stockings at about seven tomorrow night?" I asked.

"Sure," Sarah answered. "They'll be ready. Our house is three blocks north of the school." Then she told me her street name and house number, things we don't have in Jeffers.

'I'll see you then," I said. "I've enjoyed talking to you tonight. Good-bye." *Now she'll know for sure that I'm not "smooth." I bet I did sound like an idiot.*

A group of about twenty of us had decided to walk the town at seven-thirty on Christmas Eve night singing Christmas carols. We had earlier brainstormed a list of songs we knew and wanted to sing. We chose the usual Christmas standards: "Silent Night," "Joy to the World," "Hark! The Herald Angels Sing," "Oh Little Town of Bethlehem," and "We Wish You a Merry Christmas." Our main caroler was Pickett because of his mellow voice and his ukulele. As a junior last year he had received the highest rating, a "one," in the state music contest for soloists. He could probably help us stay somewhat in tune. We were a group of several basketball players, some sisters, and some friends . . . including Sarah.

When I had driven to Sarah's house to pick up the three Christmas stockings she had designed for the Cade kids, I had politely asked if she would like to go back with me to sing carols with a bunch of us and work as one of Santa's agents by delivering some gifts. She would then be able to personally deliver the stockings to the kids. I told her with a smile that if that job fell to someone else it might be messed up. We needed her. It only took three or four minutes for her to convince her parents to let her escape from their family Christmas for a short time. I assured her parents I should be able to return Sarah to them by ten-thirty. Their response: "Absolutely home by ten-thirty!"

I asked myself, "Does this count as a date?" Since we'll be with a large group, and in light of our Christmas duties, I'm just considering it "community service." If all goes well we can meet her parents' deadline, and that will be very important to my future because I'm not sure Sarah's parents appreciated the fact that I invited her out on this night to be part of our group.

We sang at several houses and received warm welcomes. Our mission included singing for Grandma and her houseguests. It felt really good to see the faces of the Cades on Christmas Eve, especially because we knew what surprises awaited them on Christmas morning. As we raised our voices in song I thought about all the joy I felt on this night, the silence and the peace that surrounded us, and the people living in our little town who also shared hopes and dreams. When we neared the time to depart for the next house, we took a break from the singing, and Sarah walked up to the door to present the stockings.

"David . . . Billy . . . and Susan. These stockings are for you," Sarah said as she held out the three Christmas stockings. All three kids looked toward Mom to receive permission to accept Sarah's gift. Mom's nod produced huge smiles, and the three kids reached for the gifts.

"Thank you!" Billy and David said.

"Thank you, Sarah," Susan added.

Sarah nodded, and I could see her eyes sparkle as she walked back toward me.

My sister provided some advice to the three youngsters. "Lay those stockings on a chair near the tree, and make sure you are in bed **and asleep** by nine o'clock. Santa is on a tight schedule. He often doesn't have time to return later if someone is still up and awake."

Tucson added, "It probably wouldn't hurt if you set out a carton of J-Hawk Juice. I hear Santa loves the stuff. Do you happen to have one here?"

Three bowed heads shook sadly.

"Did you know that I am a Boy Scout?" Tucson asked. "I am always prepared." He produced a carton of J-Hawk Juice from his coat pocket. Everyone applauded, and the children sighed with relief.

"Maybe you should set out one of Grandma's sugar cookies next to the 'Juice,'" I quickly added. This comment was met with additional applause and a few quiet "Ahahs" from my friends as they read my shallow mind and figured out I was positioning myself for a cookie snack later tonight.

We were having so much enjoyment that it was difficult to leave, but we took our cue when Pickett plucked the chords of "We Wish You a Merry Christmas." With misty eyes clouding the vision of many, we singers turned toward the one last house where we would sing carols tonight.

I quickly trotted up to Grandma's door before she closed it to privately wish her a Merry Christmas and thank her for housing the Cade family, for feeding them, and lifting their spirits. I reminded her to please leave the front door unlocked because "Santa" would be dropping by at about 9:30 with some gifts and stocking stuffers.

After having walked, laughed, and sung for about an hour, we warmed ourselves at Pickett's house and drank some delicious hot chocolate while eating freshly baked cookies. There we finalized "Operation Claus."

Many carolers stayed at Pickett's or retreated to their own homes at 9:15 as a few of us escaped to our present-storage headquarters at Abe's house, right across the street from my grandma's. We removed the sheets that covered the three bikes and the wrapped boxes of other gifts that were for Mrs. Cade, her children, and a couple for my grandma. I'm thinking they will all really surprised, especially Grandma.

Abe, Tucson, and Otto each grabbed a bike, and my sister moved forward to manage Grandma's door. Several of the rest of us grabbed gifts and joined the parade. I couldn't help myself, and I whisper sang, "Over the river and through the wood to Grandmother's house we go." I was shushed by a thousand quiet voices as we neared the house.

There was no singing now, no talking either, and as we stealthily sneaked across the snow-covered street I reminded myself of how this felt like doing Halloween pranks, in some regards. It was secretive, fast paced, and as anonymous as we could make it.

Cat burglars could not have done it any better. The bikes were stood up next to the tree with care, the gift boxes were stacked under the tree, and the stockings were generously filled. I could imagine this room tomorrow morning as the children discovered all the gifts. New-found hope and cheer would cause the retreat of sadness and despair.

We weren't finished. Tucson drank his J-Hawk Juice, and I devoured Grandma's sugar cookie. No one challenged my right to enjoy the cookie so I did not have to invoke my "relative clause." Now we were done. We were in and out in three minutes.

Someone started humming "Silent Night" as we walked back toward Main Street to reclaim our cars. I read the faces of those who participated in "Operation Claus." Smiles . . . some happiness tears . . . a few hugs. Several voices offered thanks.

"Thanks for all your help."

"Thank you, everyone, for letting me be part of this."

"Great job buying the bikes, and the stockings looked terrific."

"Everyone, . . . thank your parents for all their generosity."

"This is the best Christmas ever."

"I guess I'm not getting three new bikes from Santa after all." That was Abe feigning alligator tears. He drew laughs, backslaps, and loads of fake sympathy.

Happiness is a great feeling. The Cades will no doubt be really surprised and appreciate the many gifts, but I was standing with the people who were receiving the most from this event. This night had really connected all of us. It definitely is as the saying goes, "It is better to give than to receive." No one here would disagree. We have lived it tonight. We have felt it, and we believed it.

It was now just past ten. Cinderella had an early curfew so we headed out. This had been my best Christmas Eve ever!

Chapter 18
Glad Tidings

Sarah had been pleasantly surprised last night when I invited her to join me for the ten o'clock Christmas service at Bethany, and her parents had approved. We figured the Cades would be there, and we wanted to hear about their visit from Santa and look into their faces. As we walked in and sat in a pew next to my family, I spotted Abe and Tucson sitting with their families. They both yawned and rubbed their eyes when we made eye contact. I couldn't help but smile, thinking how great last night had been.

The Christmas service had always been special to me because I loved the familiar Christmas songs and the reading of the Christmas story from Luke. Today I let my mind wander during the service. When the preacher spoke about Mary and Joseph traveling by donkey, I thought of the Cades' travels and their broken-down car. I heard the part about not having a place to stay, and I thought about the Cades spending Christmas in the home of a stranger. The Christmas story was hitting home today.

At the end of the hour we were ushered out, and I turned to Sarah and whispered, "I could do this job. I have experience."

I introduced my friend to the preacher, and he shook our hands firmly, smiled, and said, "I understand you did some caroling last night and spread some Christmas cheer. Good for you and your group. You have certainly honored Christmas well. You may want to seek out the Cade family in the parish hall. I spoke with them prior to the service and found them to be quite excited about some gifts Santa had left them last night, including bicycles. May God bless you. Merry Christmas."

"To the parish hall," I said to Sarah, and we almost ran. It wasn't difficult to find Billy, David, and Susan. We merely guided on the noise. Were they excited!

"Santa brought us bicycles!" David said quite loudly.

"No kidding?" I replied. "We told you he visits all the children's houses in our town, remember? But bicycles! Really? Outstanding! Good for Santa, and good for you kids."

David also told about getting some new shirts, a sweater, and some pants.

Susan added, "Don't forget about the boots and socks and underwear!"

Everyone around the kids laughed at Susan's reminder, and David looked at her with some embarrassment on his face, but he recovered quickly and blurted out, "Santa brought us Monopoly and Sorry!"

Sarah and I noticed Mrs. Cade standing nearby, speechless as she watched her children in their glory. She stayed back, allowing them to be "kids on Christmas Day" as well as the most important people in the room. Her moist eyes and huge smile gave evidence to all the love she felt for her children.

Now it was Billy's turn, and his words came rapidly. "This is the best Christmas ever! We got winter coats and mittens! There's a sled so we can pull Susan on the street! And David and I each got snow shovels!"

I couldn't resist. "Shovels? Santa gave you shovels?"

"Yah!" David replied. "Now we can shovel Grandma's sidewalk!"

*Wow! Smart boy. I bet that's exactly what Santa had in mind. Now these two boys will also be able to feel the spirit of giving as they help out. Good job, Santa. Then it struck me. Did he say "**Grandma's** sidewalk?"*

Sarah was staring right at me. We both silently lipped the words **"Grandma's sidewalk"** and smiled in wonder. Our town had adopted this family for Christmas, and now these kids had "stolen" my grandma. I chuckled to myself. I guess I had received new relatives for Christmas.

"Santa drank the J-Hawk Juice and ate the cookie, too!" Susan said excitedly.

Susan wildly told more about other new clothes and things Santa had left for her mom and Grandma. She paid no attention to whom she was speaking. It didn't matter. Her eyes saw only best friends.

Seeing this excited family and listening to them tell their story made a huge impact on Sarah and me. I could see it in Sarah's eyes and feel it in my tightly squeezed hand. I could feel my heart pound. How could this not be considered the best Christmas ever? That's what Billy had called it, and

David and Susan agreed. Their mom confirmed it with the happiness expressed on her face.

Susan noticed that Sarah had a J-Hawk Nation black stocking cap hanging part way out of her coat pocket. "Is that new? Did you get it for Christmas?" Susan asked.

"Yes, it was a Christmas gift from a special friend," Sarah replied, and she pointed at me.

Susan's eyes and mouth opened wide, then her hands moved to cover her mouth. She was in awe, just as I always am when I am in Sarah's company.

I felt so proud of J-Hawk Nation. Many moms had organized so quickly after the team decided something needed to be done for this family. They had properly guessed the correct sizes for the clothing that was needed, and because money is tight, "just-like-new" hand-me-downs were cleaned, collected, and wrapped beautifully. The Cades would never have seen these clothes worn before by others so they **were** new to them. The kids would be just like most of us now, just like me, because I wore clothes handed down to me from an older cousin. Everything had been done to perfection. This seemed like another "win" for the J-Hawks.

It was obvious to me that many parents had talked to their children about the Cade family having so little. Not one child appeared jealous at hearing about the bikes, the sled, and the games. They all celebrated with these new friends they had made this last week in school.

When the excitement died down a little, Sarah and I approached Mrs. Cade and wished her a Merry Christmas. "I'm glad you and your family landed in our town," I told her.

"I thank you so much for all the attention you have given my children," Mrs. Cade said humbly. "You saved us. Your grandmother has been wonderful. All three kids love going to your school, and they can't wait for the next basketball game and reading at the library. This week has been so uplifting for us.

Uplifting is the right word. Uplifting for all of us who welcomed this family.

One church service down and one to go. I had told Sarah I would gladly attend her church's service at twelve . . . "to reward her for attending mine,"

I said with a smile. In reality, I would have sat in church all day if it meant I could spend the day with her. She was growing on me.

As we walked into her church I figured a few pairs of eyes would be staring at me because of my really short hair and the fact that this was my first visit to this church. Then I came to my senses. **No one** will be wasting time watching **me** when I am walking with **her**. She'll be everyone's focus. My confidence returned as we slid into a pew next to her parents.

Maybe Lutheran churches have a mandatory format they must follow for their services on Christmas Day. This service was a repeat of the earlier one. We sang most of the same songs and read the same Christmas story, just as I expected. Again I heard elements of the Luke story that connected so well with what had been happening to the Cades. I let my mind wander again.

I came to as I heard the minister ask, "How many of you have read the last couple columns written by John Garris in the *Globe*? Heads nodded and hands were raised everywhere, including in the balcony and in the choir.

Wow, John! You should see this! You would be impressed with yourself!

The minister continued, "In reading the Christmas story I was drawn to how the story parallels what has been happening in our neighboring community where they call themselves J-Hawk Nation. I've heard the boys have a very good basketball team, but I've been hearing even more about what they are achieving with their good will in the community. Garris wrote about the family they adopted last week. According to Garris the players on the basketball team were directly responsible for finding a place for the family to stay, getting the three children enrolled in school while they are stranded in town, and arranging for food for the family. The family was even chosen to be honorary captains for the game last Friday night. The entire community is rallying around this family because of the leadership of the players, and everyone is talking about how good it feels to help.

"Garris kept the privacy about what Santa's plans were, but I found out with a quick call to my preacher friend at Bethany. The report is that Santa did it just right with clothing necessities, a couple games, bicycles, some school supplies, and some candy. God bless Santa. May there be more of him."

Who would have thought you would ever hear a preacher promoting Santa like this?

Of course we were ushered out at the end of the service, and Sarah sent me a beautiful smile as we headed toward the traditional handshake with the minister. Sarah didn't even have time to introduce me before the minister reached out and grabbed Sarah's hand, then mine, in firm handshakes. "God bless you, Sarah . . . and Catcher . . . and your friends for what you have done. Mr. and Mrs. Jenkins, I bet you are proud of these kids," he said.

The minister leaned forward and whispered, "I received a J-Hawk Nation cap for Christmas. It was a special request I made to my wife. For now I'll just wear it in the house, but I didn't want to be left behind on your great journey."

I thanked the preacher for his kind words, and we walked down the steps toward the doors. Sarah and I both donned our black stocking caps and stepped out into the crisp December air. I noticed it didn't feel very cold. I was warmed from the inside out.

Church was over for the day, but I had been invited to join the Jenkins family for Christmas dinner. What was it that Billy had said? Yes, indeed, this was the best Christmas ever.

After Sarah and I cleared the table and washed and dried the dishes, we went for a walk. Though the frozen ground was covered with white snow everywhere, it wasn't too cold. We walked to the school playground and sat on the swings, slowly gliding freely back and forth.

"Sarah," I said to her, "this has been the most fun weekend I can ever remember. Winning our game Friday night . . . planning for the Cades' Christmas . . . singing carols and assisting Santa with a delivery . . . sitting through two church services . . . and feasting at your house with your family. Every one of these events was outstanding! I know why, too. You were there, at each of these."

"I have enjoyed these days, too," Sarah said. "While sitting in church I was trying to decide what made these days so great, and I came up with two reasons."

We walked back toward her house in silence for a few moments.

"Will you tell me?" I asked.

"All of the days in this weekend have been about Christmas, and I really love Christmas," she answered.

I waited for her to continue . . . but she didn't add anything else.

"By my count . . . that's only one thing," I said.

"Yes, you count well," Sarah said as she looked at me and smiled. "My other reason will be kept in secret for now and shared at another time."

I was disappointed. I was hoping to hear her say that she liked being with me. *She does seem happy, and we did hold hands during our walk . . . I think she's had fun . . . Maybe that has to be enough for now.*

We returned to her house where I thanked Sarah's mom and dad again for the great dinner.

"Merry Christmas, Sarah," I said. "I have really enjoyed this day. When will I see you again?" I asked.

"Dad is planning to go to The Jeffers Café for Saturday morning coffee," Sarah answered, "so I'll come to your basketball clinic."

"That'll be great!" I replied. "I usually really look forward to Christmas vacation, but this year seems different. I'll miss seeing you."

"Next week, on Wednesday, I plan to walk up to the library at 1:00 to work on a project for English class," Sarah hinted.

"Next Wednesday, 1:00, huh," I replied. "It's funny, but I need to do some library research myself. I think my teacher said that it would be best done on a Wednesday, so I'll work on meeting you there."

We both laughed.

"I'll miss seeing you, too," Sarah said, and she reached out and hugged me.

That's a good sign.

I almost skipped down the sidewalk to my car.

"We are . . . J-Hawks!" I shouted out into the crisp air of a wonderful Christmas Day. "Merry Christmas to all!"

Chapter 19

Time Out

All twelve of us on the basketball team showed up at 8:30 for our Saturday morning clinic on the 30th. We wanted to have a full hour of running, dribbling, and shooting. Since we had already practiced on three mornings this week, we had already shed most of the rust from our layoff. We had a good workout.

We started with easy layups to get some sweat going, not even letting the ball touch the floor as we shot, rebounded, and passed. This was one of my favorite drills because we kept an easy constant pace, almost like a machine. We also dribbled in at top speed from half-court, just like we do on our fast break in games. Since we've scored many points in games on our fast break, we really concentrated on this skill. We chattered and cheered for each other, building our spirit and making sure every player knew he was an important part of our team.

For about twenty minutes we worked on our favorite shots, with three shooters and three rebounders at each basket. Our goal was for each player to take at least 100 shots. Whenever a shooter made three shots in-a-row, his rebounder would shout out loudly, **"HOT STREAK!"** After more running we ended our practice with free throw contests.

Twenty-six kids showed up for the 9:30 clinic and rushed to the gym floor when we waved them on. They all seemed to enjoy gym time. Today we worked on shooting and dribbling skills, pivoting, passing, and sliding our feet while on defense. Every chance we got we complimented the kids for their good play and great effort.

Sometimes we big guys got a little silly and tried to amaze the youngsters with some no-look or trick passes. Laughter was definitely a big part of the clinic.

We concluded the morning with some contests we had invented. They were a hit again as they have been every time. Today's clinic highlight was when Sarah put on gym shoes and took a few shots. Every time she made a basket she received the greatest applause of the day, especially from me.

After snacks, showers, and cleanup we visited the library. I played teacher's aide today, working with Sarah and four second graders. Mostly I just watched her and admired how everything was so easy and natural for her. She captivated four students and one assistant today.

It was after library time, as Sarah and I were walking near the park, hoping her dad would drink coffee forever, that this stranger approached us.

"Are you Catcher?" he asked.

"Yes, I am," I replied, "and this is my friend, Sarah Jenkins."

"Nice to meet you. I've been hearing about you at The Jeffers Café, how your J-Hawk team helped that family that was stranded in town. I've been staying in town for about two weeks, and I have had lots of coffee and most meals at the café. This is a friendly town. I think I met your dad today, Sarah, and I know who your parents are, Catcher," the man said.

"My first day in town was on Friday, the fifteenth of December, and I went to your game that night because that's what all the talk was about at the café. You honored veterans that night. Since I'm an Army veteran I stood with the others, and one of your players shook my hand. I wanted to thank you for that," he said.

"I remember you," I said. "You were sitting behind the scorer's bench."

"Yes, I was. My brother, Sam, was a veteran, too, but he was killed in Europe during the war. I've been angry at the world ever since. He was a year older than me, and we were really good friends as well as brothers, and I've had a hard time moving on. That Friday night in your gym helped bring me some peace."

The man continued, "When Sam died I ended up with a small house that our parents had lived in many years ago, here in town. I live up in Minnesota, and I hardly ever get down here any more. Over the years, and up until about a year ago, I've had renters living in my house, but now it sits empty. I came here to fix some things and freshen it up a little so I can rent it out again."

"I watched you play again last night, and your excellent teamwork, along with your J-Hawk Juice, cookies, and coffee are good enough that I plan to continue to attend your games while I am in town," he said with a smile.

Sarah and I both smiled back.

"The real reason I looked for you today is about my house," he continued. "I'm almost done with my work. I just need to paint the inside walls and have some new flooring installed, then it's ready to be lived in. I figure $25 a month will cover my taxes as well as some other expenses. I don't need any more than that. Do you think you know a family that might like living in my place?" he asked.

Sarah and I both understood where he was going.

"I think you should talk to Martha Cade," I suggested. "The whole family seems to like being in Jeffers. Mrs. Cade is still working at the café, and the kids have made several new friends. I don't think their car is fixed yet either. Maybe they would stay here if they could afford a place to live in. That's a great idea, Mr. . . ."

"Olson," he said. "My name is Bill Olson."

Sarah and I shook his hand again.

"You said you had some painting to do. I bet I know a bunch of kids who would love to have a 'painting party,'" I said as I looked at Sarah again. "Do you have the paint, Mr. Olson?"

"I pick it up today," Olson replied.

"Monday is New Year's Day," I said thinking aloud. "Tuesday . . . afternoon . . . Would you be willing to take a chance on a bunch of high school kids bringing brushes to your house on Tuesday afternoon at about one o'clock to paint your walls? We're pretty bored because of no school right now, and if there is a chance the Cades would stay in town and live in your house . . ."

"Let's go talk to Martha Cade at the café right now," Olson said.

Sarah and I waited outside while Bill Olson went in. After a few minutes we heard some applause, and the door was opened to us. The café's owner invited us in.

"Are you sure?" I asked. "It's Saturday morning, and I know the rules."

"It's okay. I'm making an exception for you two today. Come on in. How about some hot chocolate? We're celebrating. Martha and her family are going to stay in Jeffers in the Olson house," Bob said.

Everyone cheered, and Mrs. Cade wiped her eyes and smiled.

I didn't care if people were watching. I reached out and gave Sarah a hug.

Everyone cheered again. I turned to face everyone, smiled, and nodded. I did see a smile on Sarah's dad's face. I turned back to the counter and began enjoying my hot chocolate with my favorite friend. I knew I would sip this drink slowly, making this morning last as long as possible.

As far as parties go, this was one of the best. Over fifteen kids had responded to phone calls and were here stirring paint, taping woodwork to protect against mistakes, and preparing to slap paint on the walls with wide brushes.

We split into groups of three or four and headed into the different rooms. Besides the living room, there were three bedrooms, a parlor, an eating area, a bathroom, and an inside porch. Mr. Olson had already painted the walls in the kitchen. Abe and Captain Hook, with the aid of step stools, were in charge of painting near the ceilings. They had such a long reach that ladders were unnecessary for them.

The Cades had visited the house last Saturday, so Olson knew which bedroom the boys would share, which would be Susan's, and which one Mrs. Cade would have. They had been so excited when they saw the house. They couldn't wait to move in.

"Mr. Olson," my sister asked, "may we paint the kids' names above the doorway on the inside of their bedrooms? We'll use an artist's touch, and it will look professional."

"Of course," he said. "That will make their rooms very special."

San Juan's sister left for her house to pick up a couple smaller brushes, and Otto's sister and my sister headed to the hardware store to see if they could talk their way into receiving a donation of one quart of paint that they could use for the names.

I was working in the boys' bedroom when I heard a few people call out,

"Catcher, you have company!"

When I walked out to the kitchen I was surprised to see Sarah and her mother standing there. They were delivering some milk and a big pan of brownies for the painters.

Sarah looked at me and laughed. She said, "I'm just guessing . . . but based on what I see on your face and your shirt, are you putting light blue paint on a wall somewhere? I'm glad I wore old clothes today because you look dangerous."

Sarah's mom and I laughed. "Are you here to help?" I asked hopefully. "We do have some extra brushes."

"Mom thought you might need a snack this afternoon so we decided to drive over," Sarah answered. "Mom loves to paint. She's very artistic. We are here to help."

Sarah's mom added, "We would love to help."

"Mr. Olson!" I called out. "Two more artists have just arrived, and I have a couple of really, really good ideas," I announced. "What do you think about having the words 'There's no place like home' painted somewhere on a kitchen wall?"

Olson laughed and nodded his head.

"I also think that a painting of a J-Hawk Nation stocking cap should be hidden behind one of the cabinet doors and a painting of their clunker car should be behind another, so that whenever someone opens the door to get a glass or a plate they'll be reminded of the spirit of J-Hawk Nation," I said seriously.

"We are . . . J-Hawks!" several painters said loudly.

"Mr. Olson replied, "I like that. The Cades will be living in the town's only art gallery."

Everyone started laughing and headed back to work.

"I'm really glad you joined us, Mrs. Jenkins . . . Sarah, and thanks for bringing the snacks. Will you choose a good place and paint those words on a kitchen wall for us?" I asked. "Those walls were painted a couple days ago, so they are ready for you."

At about three o'clock Olson called for a break, and Sarah and her mom served us the brownies and milk. Everyone raved about the delicious brownies. We all sat on the kitchen floor and admired the perfect work Mrs. Jenkins had done. Sarah had completed the stocking cap and would write "J-Hawk Nation" on it when the paint was a little drier. It looked great. She had also painted an old beat-up car with its hood open based on a quick sketch by Tucson. It was also done very well. My sister and San Juan's sister were almost finished with the kids' names in their bedrooms. We figured we would be cleaning up in about another hour.

Mr. Olson raised his glass of milk and said, "To J-Hawk Nation!"

The reply came from everyone. "We are . . . J-Hawks!"

Tucson added, "To Bill Olson . . . and the Cade family."

Everyone repeated, "To Bill Olson . . . and the Cade family."

At about 4:30, when all the painters and the artists had completed their work, we started packing up to leave.

"We have another home game next Tuesday, Mr. Olson. Will you still be in town?" I asked.

"If I am still here, then I will be there," he said with a laugh. "The Cades and I thank you for all of your help."

"Thanks for hosting the party, Mr. Olson," a couple painters said as they left.

"I'm sure the Cade family will like their new home," Mrs. Jenkins offered.

"Will you make it to the clinic on Saturday? I asked Sarah. "Maybe we could get another exception and have hot chocolate at the café."

"I think Dad will need coffee on Saturday morning. I'll come to your clinic if get my research completed at the library," Sarah said with a wink.

I winked back at her, and we both smiled.

Sarah was already working when I arrived at the library. I located a couple books I needed, sat down at a small wooden library table across from Sarah, and began reading. I wasn't entirely focused on the books. I did look up from time to time, just to look at Sarah, and I did have to read some paragraphs several times since I wasn't always concentrating on the words and the ideas, but I kept at it.

We didn't talk even once until about an hour had passed. Then we moved to a sitting area where we sat in comfortable stuffed chairs and talked quietly. Yesterday's painting party was the first thing I brought up.

"It looked like you mom had fun yesterday. I'd never seen her laugh so much," I said.

"She said she felt like a kid again," Sarah said. "She's really glad we helped, and she did enjoy all the laughter."

"Both of you are very artistic. The lettering, the J-Hawk Nation cap, and the clunker car were beautifully done. I bet the kids will be impressed," I said. "To go from 'no home' to having their names on the walls in their own rooms is quite a step up."

"It was fun," Sarah said, "and I could tell Mr. Olson really appreciated the help. The painting party was a great idea."

"The home-made brownies and the milk you brought for us were a big hit. Is there any chance the talented Sarah Jenkins assisted in the baking?" I asked.

Sarah laughed. "Mom was busy with school reports so I did the baking. Did I do okay?"

"You went far beyond 'okay,'" I answered. "You can bake for me anytime. You have amazed me again."

"Would you like to know about a secret plan we've worked on in practice over the last month or so?" I asked.

"Yeah," Sarah replied. "Is this another long shot like Captain Hook made?"

"No," I answered. "This is a lot trickier. You can't tell anyone . . . not your parents or your friends. If we use this in a game, and it does not work, we may lose the game. No one can know about it, but I do trust you. I want you to be ready for it if it happens."

"I won't tell a soul," Sarah promised, as she smiled and crossed her heart.

I know Coach wouldn't want me to tell Sarah, but I can't help it. She comes to all our games and cheers for us, and I really like her. I'm hoping we'll become even better friends.

"Nicholson is the key," I whispered, moving closer to Sarah and enjoying every second of this. "First of all, you have to understand that we may never use this secret plan. Coach will call for it only if the game is really close at the end and we need some sure points. I will give you a signal if Coach makes the call. First I'll make eye contact with you. That part will be really easy for me because I've had lots of practice. If I hold my hand in front of my face, palm out, five fingers extended, it means 'Fifth Son,' Nicholson, will enter the game and the plan is on. There are two things to watch for. First of all, Nicholson's shoestring will be untied, and hopefully a ref will say something to him or Coach will have to yell to him to tie his shoe. The second thing that will happen is that Nicholson will trip over his own two feet as he crosses the gym floor to his position as a forward. We expect everyone in the gym will laugh at Nicholson, especially the other team. That's all I can say for sure. We are baiting a trap, and everything else depends on how the other team responds. If I give you the signal, then you can tell your parents to watch and try figure out what the secret plan is. Make sure you mention the shoestring and the trip at that time before those things happen, then your parents will be really impressed with you when they do happen. Remember, we may never use this, but we are ready if we need it."

"Wow!" Sarah responded. "I like knowing about this. Thanks. It almost feels like I am a special agent or something."

I just laughed at her and shook my head. "Are you teasing me?" I asked.

She just smiled that innocent smile and shrugged her shoulders.

After studying and researching for about another hour I walked Sarah home. I could have driven. I had parked the car at The Grill nearby, but I knew that walking would take longer. As we talked and laughed on our way, I wished that her house had been further away. I would not see her again until Saturday's clinic, but I do have a telephone at home.

On the drive home I thought about my afternoon and all I had learned today while doing library research: 1) Sarah and her mom both had a great time at the painting party. 2) Sarah can make a "mean" pan of chocolate frosted brownies. Delicious! 3) Sarah is a very serious student. 4) Sarah loves knowing about special plays our basketball team has planned. 5) Oh, yeah . . . William Shakespeare wrote 38 plays . . . divided among histories, tragedies, and comedies. 6) I think I might be falling in love . . . and I'm not talking about Shakespeare.

This had been a great afternoon. I decided that I should have been visiting the library to do research a long time ago, and that the Madison Lake library was the best one for me. I am going to consider becoming a more serious student. Maybe I should get glasses.

This had turned out to be the best school vacation I could remember. Our time out of school is now over, and next week we would be back in our usual routines of school, basketball practice, homework, and the big games. Did I forget to include phone calls?

I'm looking forward to the next part of our season, and to spending more time with Sarah.

Chapter 20
Bad Timing

The Madison Lake High School principal visited school today, our first day back from Christmas vacation, to give us our first official welcome for next year. Because the seniors will graduate from Jeffers in May, they were excused from the assembly that was held in the high school's main classroom. Eighth graders sat in the seniors' desks, eyes wide because of their new status and new surroundings. They all looked really small in my eyes.

As the principal, Mr. Weston, introduced himself and began his welcome speech, I was sure he could tell he was looking into the faces of a hostile group of J-Hawks. Maybe our Supe had even warned him that we weren't going willingly to MLHS. I wanted to walk out in protest, and I made eye contact with a few others who shared my feelings, but the Supe was observing us closely, and he gave us the "stare and glare," slightly shaking his head and lipping, "NO." We backed down. I would have followed Captain Hook out the door for sure because he would have needed company if he had opposed his dad on this issue.

Though I had trouble listening because of my negative frame of mind I heard something about a greater variety of course offerings, excellent teachers, wonderful facilities, and many activities in which to participate. Then he tossed out the carrot to the boys. "We have a football team."

I could not understand how he could come to our school and not say anything about the good things that were happening here. He didn't even mention our boys' basketball team and our winning streak of nine games. *He talks like we have nothing positive at our school. How about at least waiting until our season is over? Why did you have to come today?*

By this time I was getting angry. I should know myself by now, that my mouth often speaks without the help of a fully functioning brain when I'm upset, but that did not stop me. I casually raised my hand, interrupting the principal's speech. Out of the corner of my eye I saw the Supe lower his head when I was acknowledged.

I spoke politely. "Sir, we already have excellent teachers in **this** school, loads of activities in which we all participate, enough courses to guarantee that we have more than enough homework, fall and spring seasons of base-ball for the boys as well as fall and spring softball for the girls, and a gym in which visiting basketball teams have little chance of defeating us. I think we are perfectly satisfied with the way things are here."

The assembly erupted in applause, and a bunch of kids stood and nod-ded their heads vigorously.

Then I took my best shot. "How is your girl's basketball team doing this year?" I asked. The room was dead silent, except for the Supe's cough. It seemed like time stopped for a long moment as the principal looked down, collecting his thoughts. We all knew that no girls' sports, not softball, not basketball, were offered at Madison Lake, and this fact alone was enough to rally all of us to despise Madison Lake's takeover of our school.

I took a quick glance at the Supe, and I noticed that there was a slight grin on his face, and I detected a nod or two. Though he expected his stu-dents to show courtesy and respect, he understood our feelings because he was being pushed out of a job by this consolidation, and his family was already making plans to move away. I realized that he was really part of us. I now saw him through different eyes.

There was no way to turn back next year's plan. Our school board had made its decision because of budget problems. Jeffers could no longer afford to have a high school or junior high. As students, we knew this, but we had a very difficult time accepting the consequence. Today all of us wanted to be heard. Today we stood together, united. If anyone in this assembly was look-ing forward to experiencing the bigger school next year . . . he was silent.

The principal never answered my question. He understood my defiance and decided to move on to other positives he had listed on his cheat sheet. No one listened, so he excused himself because of "pressing matters at his school," and his welcome speech ended up being ineffectively short. This guy was lucky we hadn't recently plucked chickens and heated up the vat of tar.

After allowing time for our "guest's" escape, several quiet conversations began. Soon the volume picked up, and the Supe called for order. I was certain he was going to put a stop to this and send us back to class, but instead he suggested that we continue this meeting, this discussion. He insisted, however, that we conduct ourselves civilly and allow all to speak and to be heard. Then he left the room.

This was exactly what we needed. We came together. Several questions were raised, and answers were offered. "How can we stop this?" ("We can't.") "Why is Madison Lake doing this?" ("Our school board asked them to educate us because we don't have the money to fund our own school.") "Why next year?" ("Again, no money.") "What if we don't want to go to school in Madison Lake?" ("Move . . . or drop out.")

Eventually the well of questions ran dry, and no satisfactory answers had been given. "What's next?" Someone suggested we find the seniors and ask them to join us. We excused the eighth graders after ordering them to locate the seniors. "Don't stop looking until you find all thirteen of them. Tell them it's us, not the teachers, asking them to return. We need their help to move forward together."

It started softly at first but gained momentum. "We are . . . J-Hawks! We are . . . J-Hawks! We are . . . J-Hawks!"

What came out of this meeting? We dedicated the rest of this final year to each other. To the seniors: Leave a lasting legacy, and graduate with glory. To the underclassmen: Make this final year memorable. Do everything you possibly can do to make sure "the world" remembers us. Sing, speak, write, act, play music and sports as if this is your last opportunity . . . because it may be your last opportunity.

It was at this "dedication ceremony" that we boys on the basketball team stated for the first time in public, "We **will win** Iowa's small-school state basketball championship this year! **We are . . . J-Hawks!** We **will crush** our opponents and take no prisoners! **We are . . . J-Hawks!** People **will remember** our school and our town! **We are . . . J-Hawks! We are . . . J-Hawks!"**

Chapter 21
Lost and Found

I arrived at the gym at about 6:15 and joined the "ushering squad." We had continued to enjoy doing this service, and I looked forward to it for each of our home games. Nicholson and Treason joined us regulars for tonight, so we now numbered eight. As more people were attending the games, the extra help was appreciated.

Each time I returned to the lobby after guiding someone to a seat I looked for Sarah and her parents, as I expected them to appear at any time now. Every time I was disappointed. At 6:45 I started getting worried.

They've never been this late before. I hope nothing has happened. What if they decided not to come to the games anymore? What if Sarah has lost interest? Did I say or do something that upset Sarah, her dad, or her mom?

Like a steel ball that is bouncing around in a fast pinball machine, my mind kept racing from one thought to another as I continued helping people find seats in the bleachers, and none of my thoughts was positive. I really started getting anxious. My heart was pounding like a drum, and I could hear it quite clearly.

I was glad I was able to sit down on the bleachers, where the Jenkins family usually sat, when we stopped ushering at the end of the first quarter of the girls' game, but I was still very worried by Sarah's absence. I kept looking toward the gym door.

When it was time for our boys' team to head to the locker room to dress for our game, Sarah still had not arrived.

What's going on? This is not good.

I had a difficult time during warm-ups because I could not get thoughts of Sarah out of my head. I was really bothered, and I could not focus. Almost none of my shots went in, I dropped several passes, and it seemed like I was lost in a fog during the entire 15 minutes we warmed up.

Right before the game was set to start, Laser and Pickett grabbed the microphone and introduced several library volunteers who had been chosen to be our honorary captains for tonight's game, but I didn't hear much of what either player said, as I kept looking toward the entrance to the gym, hoping the Jenkins family would suddenly walk in. I was beginning to get really scared.

When we met in the huddle for Coach's final instructions, I tried to snap out of it, to collect myself, to get ready to play hard, but my head kept turning toward the door. Twice Coach yelled at me to pay attention, and I wasn't really sure I heard what our plan was for offence or defense for the start of the game. I really felt "out of it."

Abe tapped the opening tip-off to Hook. He shook off his defender and passed to Laser at the left sideline. Laser dribbled slowly toward our end and bounced a pass in my direction, but I had not been watching for the pass, and the ball hit my left arm and trickled out of bounds. Groans filled the gym. I had made a terrible mistake. Junior high players don't even mess up like I just had.

I've got to wake up and get my head straight!

In the next 2 – 3 minutes of clock time I made one basket out of the four shots I took, I threw the ball away twice, and I wasn't much help with our full-court press because I was often out of position. I just didn't seem to have it tonight. This game appeared to be too difficult, too fast for me. My mind wasn't right, I wasn't able to concentrate, and my eyes kept looking toward the gym lobby.

Coach called a timeout at the halfway point of the first quarter and re-moved me from the lineup, putting Otto in to take my place. As the timeout ended Coach glared at me, shook his head pathetically from side to side, and pointed to a spot at the end of the bench. I was now in Coach's doghouse, and unfortunately I deserved it. I couldn't get focused on the game. I almost felt like walking right out of the gym. I was miserable, and I had played miserably.

At the end of the first quarter, despite all of my mistakes, my team was only down by four points.

As we prepared to begin the second quarter, Coach stared at me in the huddle and said in a gruff voice, "Catcher, go in for Otto. This time try to play with us, not against us!"

I only lasted for a couple of minutes before Coach yanked me again and put San Juan in. I had missed both shots I had attempted, passed badly to Laser on a fast break, and dribbled a ball off Hook's foot and lost it out of bounds. This was like a bad dream, and I couldn't wake myself up. I felt that negative things were going to happen whenever I touched the ball, and I was generally right.

I was really upset at myself. Now we were down by six points, and no one was taking charge. Where was the leadership?

I had a towel draped over my lowered head and was staring at the floor as I sat at the end of the bench. I figured I had used up all my chances for playing time tonight. Coach wasn't even talking to me. There were just a couple minutes left in the quarter, and we had played evenly with the Knights during most of the quarter, but we still trailed by five points. We needed a spark, or we might lose for the first time this season.

As Kendall's Number 20 was getting ready to shoot a free throw, I saw three sets of legs pass in front of me, heading for seats, and I heard Sarah's voice ask, "What's wrong? Are you okay? Why aren't you playing?"

I looked up from under the towel, and there she was . . . a concerned smile spreading across her face, her eyes sparkling as always. Upon hearing her voice, a huge weight lifted from my shoulders, from my back, my legs . . . and my mind. I exhaled slowly and drew in a long slow breath.

I replied quietly to Sarah, "I'm not hurt. I'll be okay now." I removed the towel from my head and sat up straight. After clearing my head, I glanced at the scoreboard. There was just about half-a-minute to go in the quarter, and we were down by six points.

Maybe I can be the spark we need . . . from the bench.

As Laser dribbled the ball toward our basket, I stood and started clapping. The other bench players looked at me, then one-by-one, they stood and joined in. Soon school kids in the stands, then the adults, rose to their feet and added to the noise.

If we can score the last basket of this half we'll only be behind by four. There's a lot of the game left to play. We're not out of it. We still have a good chance to pull this game out.

After holding the ball for a few seconds, Laser threw a pass to San Juan who found Hook open near the baseline. Hook glanced at the clock, and passed the ball back to San Juan.

Fifteen seconds left. It's too early for a last shot.

They kept moving the ball: San Juan to Laser . . . to Pickett . . . back to Laser. Laser looked up at the clock. Only a few seconds remained before the buzzer would signal the end of the quarter. Laser nodded toward Abe. Abe faked his defender to the outside, rushed to the basket, jumped up with his arms extended just above the rim, and received a perfectly timed pass from Laser. Abe dropped it into the cylinder just before the buzzer sounded.

I rushed onto the floor along with the rest of the bench, and we celebrated the basket that had brought us within four points of the Knights. It was almost as if we had won the game. This last-second basket was huge. It was a spark. Everyone was cheering wildly, and we regained our spirit.

As I trotted toward the locker room I heard Coach say, "I'm glad to see that Catcher is alive after all. That's good because we'll need him in the second half."

In the locker room all the conversation was positive. Everyone knew we could handle this team. Several guys came over to give me some encouragement. Both seniors made sure I would be ready. They made it clear that I needed to lift my game.

Pickett said to me, "The first half is done. Forget about it. This game begins for you now. Don't let yourself down. When you get the open shot take it. They'll start falling for you. Keep working. We need your spirit out there."

"I'll get you some open shots early," Laser said. "Focus on the rim, and get your shooting rhythm. You are due. Just play hard . . . have fun. When you get your confidence back, we'll get ours. This half will be a pleasure."

Coach looked at me and nodded. "We start the second half with our full-court press." Laser, you and Catcher support Pickett's in-bound challenge with pressure after every bucket we make. Abe and Hook . . . set up just beyond the half-line and pick off their long passes. On offence . . . work quickly. Move the ball around. Find each other, and don't be afraid to take your open shots. Keep crossing the lane, high and low. Confidence is the name of the game. No one came here to see us lose tonight, and no one goes home disappointed . . . except for the Knights and their fans. Starters, don't forget to report to the scorer's table. Let's go!"

"We are . . . J-Hawks!" filled the locker room as we ran onto the floor to take a few warm-up shots.

I could feel my focus returning. I only had to think about basketball now. Sarah was fine, and she had come to the game after all. My worries were gone, and I could enjoy playing again. This was a much better feeling.

I was a different player in the second half. I felt relaxed, and I played without any pressure. Laser and Pickett made sure I was given the ball when I was open, and I was not afraid to shoot. Our first three shots of the third quarter were taken by me, and all three jump shots dropped quietly through the hoop, tickling the net, giving us our first lead of the game. The crowd went wild after the third shot, shouting, standing up, clapping, and stomping their feet.

Laser hit his first two shots, and after our backcourt had scored those ten points on 5 of 5 shooting, Kendall's defenders had to move further out, giving Abe and Hook more territory in which to work. It was now easier to pass the ball inside, and Abe, Hook, and Pickett had their own three-way passing game working, allowing them to keep moving closer and closer to the basket for easier shots which they did not miss.

Our defense was superb. Laser stole a pass, Abe grabbed one, and I captured two. The Knight guards also panicked and threw two passes out of bounds. They didn't have much to show for their first ten possessions of the quarter. They began to get frustrated, and they started to yell at each other. They also took some really poor shots that missed, and we rebounded. I seemed to be standing in the right places, and several long rebounds came to me. We had them on the ropes, and we had no intention of letting them get away.

Since we were now scoring easily from inside, the Knight guards started falling back closer to the basket to help. That left me open again, and I hit three more jump shots in a row. I was feeling it. In the first half I couldn't hit anything, but now in this quarter I couldn't miss. What changed?

By the end of the quarter we had scored 30 points, and we now led by 16. This was more like it.

We kept up the pressure in the fourth quarter, using several bench players, and we continued to score on layups, jump shots, and a couple short hook shots by Captain Hook. I played the entire quarter, missing only one of my four shots. I had never shot as well as I did in the second half tonight. I had jumped from the freezer in the first half to the furnace in the second. Is this what happens when you play with confidence and play relaxed?

With the big turn-around in the second half we were able to defeat the Knights by 21 points: 76 – 55. They didn't know what hit them. It was another great victory for us. Hopefully we learned a lesson or two playing this game: Don't get down on ourselves . . . don't give up . . . and don't lose focus. (The focus part . . . that was all me.)

After the final buzzer sounded, and we had lined up to shake hands with our opponent, many parents and friends began approaching us near the team bench. Sarah was one of the first to arrive, and she was very excited as she hurried toward me and exclaimed, "Wow, Catcher! You played an outstanding game! You were on fire with your jump shot! I can only remember you missing one shot!"

"Thanks, Sarah," I replied. "You only saw the second half, however. I was terrible during the first half, and I rode the bench most of the time."

My dad walked up to us and said, "Hi, Sarah. It's good to see you again. Son . . . I just enjoyed watching the best half of basketball I've ever seen you play. Congratulations on your hot shooting. You also played great defense . . . . However, this great half followed on the heels of the worst half of a game I've ever seen you play. I'm sorry to say this, but you didn't do much right in the first half. You were pretty bad. What was going on?"

"I just had a tough time focusing, Dad," I answered. I think that's mainly what it was. I just couldn't concentrate."

Dad continued, "I saw you look toward the lobby a lot before the game and while you were playing, and I noticed that Sarah and her parents didn't arrive until just before the end of the first half. Was that the reason for your lack of focus . . . that Sarah wasn't here?" Dad asked.

I was a little embarrassed. I lowered my eyes toward the floor, and I didn't answer his question. We both knew he had it figured out.

Sarah reached for my arm, and I raised my eyes and looked at her. "Was it because we were late tonight?" she asked. "Were you looking for us? Were you worried we weren't coming? Oh, Catcher! I thought I had told you that I had a band concert at school tonight! I'm so sorry! We rushed here as quickly as we could. We escaped and ran to the car right after the band's last selection. We were laughing so hard at what people might be thinking. We didn't want to miss any of your game, but I had to play in the concert."

I spoke quietly, "It's okay, Sarah. It's not your fault I played so poorly. I was worried that something had happened to you on the way to the game, or that maybe you had found something better to replace the basketball games. I thought I might have upset you in some way. I just couldn't shake these negative thoughts," I admitted. "Then you walked in . . . and I was able to get my mind back on the game."

Moving closer and speaking almost in a whisper, Sarah said, "You never should have let yourself get worried like that. My parents and I plan to attend all your games. I love watching your team play . . . and if you do upset me in some way, I'll talk to you about it. You can count on that. For now, just trust me to be your good friend, and understand that I'm not looking to replace you anytime soon." Then she smiled at me.

Relief . . . that's what I was feeling now.

I didn't care who was standing nearby or who might be watching. I gently put my arms around Sarah and held her for a moment. "Thank you, Sarah," I whispered into her ear.

This was our tenth win in a row. Though the first half didn't look so good, we did recover and played very well.

We were getting more and more attention by people in town, area farmers, and the local papers. Garris had continued to watch our games, and he was writing more positive stuff about the J-Hawks now.

Hey! Was he here tonight? . . . I didn't even notice . . . I was too busy with other things. Maybe he went elsewhere to watch a game tonight. I hope he didn't see the way I played in the first half, and then left at halftime. Anyway, it doesn't matter how I played tonight, because the J-Hawks collected another win. That's what really counts.

In the Stands – With John Garris

Charles Dickens wrote *The Tale of Two Cities.* I am reporting on "The Tale of Two Halves." Last night I watched from the bleachers in Jeffers as the J-Hawks played a pretty dismal first half and fell behind the boys from Kendall by as many as eight points. The J-Hawks showed little spirit. Nothing seemed to work for them, and they didn't seem to be expending much effort. Catcher looked lost on the floor as he missed some easy shots, threw the ball away a few times, and often was out of position on defense. Because Catcher was way off his game, Coach sat him on the bench for the majority of the half. The J-Hawks did not look at all like the team that had won its first nine games.

Then, with about two minutes left in the first half, the cavalry arrived. The regiment was not in uniform and numbered only three, but it seemed to be enough, as one of the three, in particular, seemed to inspire one of the J-Hawks, in particular, to elevate his game in the second half. Somehow Catcher found himself after the intermission.

His shooting was spectacular as he hit on 9 of his 10 shots. He played excellent defense in the second half, and his leadership gave new life to his team.

The J-Hawks erupted with outstanding shooting accuracy, precise passing, and a pressure defense that forced the Knights into making bad passes and taking poor shots. The J-Hawks outscored the Knights by 25 points in the second half. They looked completely different . . . much stronger, better skilled, much more spirited . . . like a team that deserved to be sitting with a 10-0 record.

It was "the worst of halves" followed by "the best of halves" for the J-Hawks.

I was there "in the stands." I witnessed this outstanding second-half performance, and I found it absolutely amazing that one person could have such a great impact in the turnabout of a team and the outcome of the game . . . and **she** isn't even on the basketball team.

Three cheers for the cavalry . . . but next time, try to get to the game on time.

Chapter 22

J-Hawk Retaliation

On the bus ride to Upton, the whole team was very relaxed. Pickett's music was soothing, and our conversations were quiet. I expected that we would win this game if we played well because the Lions did not have enough depth to run with us, and we would run. When we played against Upton in our first home game, we took advantage of Laser's hot shooting from outside and scored on several fast breaks in winning by about twenty points. We all figured that the Lions would cover Laser closely tonight. They probably would not want him scoring thirty-six points like he did against them in the last game. That might work to our advantage if they overplay Laser. We are able to score points in many different ways. Abe is great at soft shots off the backboard and slams, Captain Hook has been hitting his hook shots, and Pickett has been deadly on his jump shots from ten feet. My long jump shots have been falling, and Otto and Sons have been contributing about ten points in each game, coming off the bench. Our fast break and full-court press have been good for many easy baskets. I don't think the Lions will be ready for us.

During the first two quarters we ran at every opportunity and built up a lead of ten points. We would have been leading by more except that Number 30 and Number 22 were hitting their shots well, keeping the Lions in the game. When we couldn't run the ball down court, we lobbed it into Abe. They had no one tall enough to cover him so we kept tossing him the ball, taking advantage of his superior height. He banked in several shots.

At the end of the third quarter we led by twelve, and we felt that we were in control of the game. We were working hard and playing well.

Early in the fourth quarter Hook started getting open near the basket. He scored twice on short hook shots and passed off to Pickett for two more scores. Lions guard Number 30 hit on two long shots to cut our lead to 15 points with about four minutes left in the game.

The Lions' coach called for a timeout.

Coach told us in the huddle that we were playing well. "It's time to finish them off," he said. "Start trapping again after they throw the ball in. There's no way they can stay with us. I can see they are wearing down. Give me two more minutes of fast action. That should build the lead by a few more points, and then I can empty the bench."

What happened next scared some fans in the bleachers, but it caused our team to toughen up, connect solidly as a team, and play some of our best basketball of the year.

We let them inbound their short pass. Then Laser and Pickett quickly moved in and trapped the guard who held the ball. He had no time nor space for dribbling out of trouble. His only chance was to try a desperation pass. I anticipated its direction and timed it well, stepping in to intercept the ball. With two dribbles I reached the basket and stretched up with the basketball in my left hand to lay a soft kiss against the backboard as the defender closed in.

Then my lights were dimmed. I heard the Jeffers fans as they protested angrily and jumped to their feet. Number 31 had clobbered me, using his elbow against my head to keep me from scoring. He was called for the obvious foul so I would be getting two free throws, but I needed to stay seated on the floor for a moment . . . to let the dust settle, to allow those flying bluebirds time to finish their circular flight pattern, to let the stars I was seeing align themselves into some kind of constellation. Meanwhile the fans remained standing, not yet willing to let this intentional mugging be easily forgotten.

I heard one of the refs yell to our bench, and Otto came rushing out with a towel. Only some of the moisture that I felt on my face was sweat, the rest was blood that was oozing from a cut that had opened when the sharp elbow connected with my face just above my left eye. I was allowed to sit there for a few moments to collect my bearings while pressure was placed on my forehead. Coach told me that the cut was not very deep or long, but that it had found the blood supply route.

The ref said to Coach, "You have three minutes to stop the bleeding, patch him up, and leave him in the game, or take him out and the opposing coach will select another of your players to take the foul shots."

Tucson and San Juan helped me up, and I walked to the bench under my own power. My head was beginning to clear.

I looked at my teammates gathered around me, and I noticed all the serious, angry faces. *This could get ugly.* "I'm okay," I told them. "Just cover the cut, and I'm ready to go.

"This could have been much worse," Otto said with sympathetic innocence. "What if it had happened to one of us good-looking players?" The huddle became deathly silent as everyone stared at Otto. Suddenly spontaneous laughter erupted, and I tossed a towel at Otto and joined in with the others. Otto had changed the mood of the team completely, and we would be able to regain our focus. As the laughter continued I glanced at Sarah and her parents on the bleachers behind our bench. I caught them all enjoying Otto's humor, and I pretended I was astonished. When Sarah saw the look on my face she covered her mouth and stopped laughing . . . but only for a second. Then she shrugged her shoulders and sent me a warm smile. I chuckled a little and smiled back. The Jenkins family liked being close to the action that surrounded our team, and I liked that Sarah was nearby.

As my cleanup job continued I told Coach that I was fine and that I needed to stay in the game. "We can't let them or anyone else think they can beat us this way, Coach. Let's not allow them to gain confidence through intimidation. I have an idea. May I speak?"

"All right, everyone, listen up. Catcher, go ahead," Coach said.

"I suggest retaliation . . . J-Hawk style," I began. "We will not foul, we'll draw no blood, and we'll not even say a single word while we victimize Number 31, by each scoring a basket while he defends against us. Since he's covering me in their man-to-man defense, we'll need to set picks so he switches to each of you in turn. Seniors go first. Pickett, when I receive a pass, set up a hard pick for me, then roll to the hoop. Number 31 should switch to try cover you. I'll send you a bounce pass as you go hard to the basket. You may have to run over him a little, but you'll get the layup and probably a free throw. How's that sound?"

"I'm there," replied Pickett.

"Laser, you're next. When Hook has the ball I'll screen your defender. Move to my open side, receive the pass from Hook, and take your jumper as Hook screens Number 31. You should have an open shot."

Laser nodded assent.

"Hook, I think your patented short hook shot over 31 after I set a pick on your man would be a good call. Whoever has the ball, look to the Hook. Be sure to keep your left elbow in, Hook. We don't want to bloody someone's nose."

"Got it," Hook said confidently.

"Okay, Abe. Are you ready to throw one down into the cylinder?"

"Can't wait," answered Abe.

"I'll bring Number 31 in to you and screen your guy. Laser, how about tossing a high pass to Abe right at the basket. Don't hold back, Abe. Slam it down."

As Abe and Laser made eye contact I knew this would be effective.

"That only leaves me, but you guys will probably have already destroyed 31's self-esteem. I'd appreciate a two-man senior screen on 31, and with a give-and-go with Hook or Abe I'll take a jumper from the top of the key," I continued.

"Remember to keep your game faces on, and don't say anything or celebrate our successes. This message is being delivered with action only. Let's run all five plays quickly but precisely. If we miss a shot, just run the same play again," I suggested.

"When we break the huddle I'm going to walk directly toward Number 31 . . . to extend my hand for a handshake. You know . . . no hard feelings. He won't be expecting this, so I'll probably catch him off-guard. Then . . . we'll unleash 'J-Hawk Retaliation,'" I concluded with somewhat of a sneer.

The bleeding had now been stopped, and a couple band-aids protected the wound.

The ref came to our huddle. "Coach, what's it going to be?"

Coach replied, " He's fine. He's staying in. We're ready."

Pickett brought us together. "All right. Let's do it."

We broke the huddle with, "We are . . . J-Hawks!"

In just over two minutes we scored five baskets and made one free throw. All five shots had gone in, and five doses of humility had been delivered to Number 31. He had not been given much defensive help from his team-mates. Perhaps they also were sending him a message. On the defensive end we had made two steals, and they had misfired on two terrible shots. Their only open shot hit the rim, and Abe grabbed the rebound. Coach called a timeout after my shot went in, and we walked toward the bench with a little pride showing and loud applause filling our side of the gym.

Our fifteen-point lead had been extended to twenty-six, and this game was basically over with just two minutes to play. Both benches were emptied by the coaches, and we starters were given cheering duty for the rest of the game.

This game was a huge confidence builder for us. We had not backed down one inch. We had kept our focus and had used our brains and skills well. Our determination had allowed us to do exactly what we had planned.

At the end of the game we quickly dried off and lined up to shake hands with the Lions. We generally told the opponents, "Good game."

When I extended my hand to Number 31, I didn't say anything, but when I heard a weak "Sorry" from him I nodded back. It was over and forgotten.

I really appreciate Coach letting us mix with our friends and parents after our games for five or ten minutes before we are sent to the showers. That's good connecting time for us, and we are able to thank people for coming.

Mom and Dad came over to see how I was doing, then walked around and talked to other players and their parents. They knew I was more inter-ested in talking with Sarah now, them later. Sarah's parents went around to talk to players and other parents, while Sarah sought out each of my team-mates, one-by-one, to say something to him. She talked to Tucson and shook Laser's hand . . . she smiled and said something to San Juan . . . I saw her talking to Abe and Pickett and Treason . . . she laughed with Otto . . . she patted Captain Hook on his back . . . she even spoke with the bench guys who didn't play much tonight. Finally Sarah walked over to me.

She kissed her index finger and then gently touched my band-aids. I had forgotten about my cut, but now I felt better immediately. She definitely possessed some magic, some power over me.

Sarah's parents approached. Mr. Jenkins apologized. "I'm sorry I laughed at Otto's comment in the huddle. Mostly I got caught up in how your teammates reacted."

"That's all right," I said. "My feelings weren't hurt. Otto was hilarious. We were all laughing. That was exactly what we needed."

Sarah jumped in, "You guys really humbled 31. It was fun to watch you carry out your plan so seriously. Is your eye okay? I was worried by all the blood, and then you stayed down so long."

"My eye seems to be okay. It doesn't hurt," I answered.

"What did the ref say to you after the game?" Sarah asked.

"He told me it was classy that I sought out 31 to shake his hand as play resumed. He also said he was impressed at our play during the next two minutes," I answered. "He may have lost his impartiality for a short time."

"You had a great plan, Catcher," added Mr. Jenkins. "I was as impressed as the ref. In those two minutes everything seemed to happen just as you hoped it would."

"Yeah," I replied. "Everything worked exactly right. We were lucky, but we were also very determined. I have great teammates, don't I?"

"I enjoyed this game, but I didn't appreciate the scare. I'm glad you are okay," said Sarah. "Please don't let this happen again."

"I'll do my best," I replied with a smile. "It really helps me that you come to the games." I reached for her hand though her mom and dad were standing there watching. "I'm glad all of you come to the games."

"I had to beg Sarah to come with me to the first game we saw," Mr. Jenkins said. "I wanted company because I was sure I wouldn't know anyone else there. Now I'd be in trouble with Sarah and her mother if I didn't take them to your games. I honestly think we are three of your best fans. We plan to continue to attend all games, home and away. Basketball hasn't been this exciting for me since I played in high school, and your team is very entertaining.

"Dad has become a Saturday-morning regular for coffee at The Jeffers

Café, so I'll be at the clinics if you like," said Sarah.

"That's great!" I replied. "You are invited every Saturday. The young kids and my teammates really like seeing you there . . . and I don't mind it much either."

Sarah smiled sweetly.

I stared into Sarah's sparkling blue eyes for a couple moments. Then I called upon all the courage I could gather as I turned to face Sarah's parents.

"Mr. Jenkins . . . Mrs. Jenkins," I said quietly, "I intend to ask Sarah out on a real date one day very soon. This would be something different than a church service, a basketball game, or a clinic. I'd like to take her to a movie, then maybe get something to eat."

Sarah stood by, listening intently.

I looked into Sarah's eyes again.

"I hope that you will say 'yes,' Sarah," I continued. Then I focused again on Sarah's parents. "And I hope you will allow her to go with me."

This seemed like a dress rehearsal to me. Maybe now I'd know how to ask her. Maybe now I'd know what to say. I was afraid Mr. Jenkins would tell me that Sarah wasn't allowed to date yet. I also feared a possible negative response from Sarah's mother, and maybe Sarah has no interest in going to a movie with me. No one said anything, but all three smiled. I did not know what they were thinking, and they didn't give me any clues.

"It looks like we're heading to the showers. Thanks again for coming. I'll see you at the clinic tomorrow, Sarah. Could I get one more healing finger kiss? I teased.

This time the kiss was flavored with light laughter. I don't know if life can get any better than this.

Chapter 23

The Chosen One

I was quite tired and a little banged up from the game against Upton so I slumped down in my seat on the bus, closed my eyes, and listened to the chords Pickett was strumming on his ukulele. My thoughts drifted to Sarah. I'm just getting to know her . . . but I've never felt this way about anyone else before. I was really close to letting my soul float away on puffy white clouds when the music stopped and the conversation began.

"I think I'm in love," Tucson said.

"Really? Who's the unlucky girl?" Captain Hook asked.

"That new blond girl, Sarah," Tucson replied. "Did you guys see . . . she headed straight toward **me** after the game . . . like an arrow shot from Cupid's bow . . . straight for my heart."

"You . . . are an idiot," Laser said. "She was walking toward **me**, and you just happened to back up and get in her path just as she was about to pass you by. Cupid's arrow was directed at **me**. Sarah had her eyes focused on **me**. She looked really embarrassed when she got stuck talking to you . . . Sarah told **me** I played really well."

"She told **me** I played really, really well for the two minutes that I was in the game," Go Forth Son said. "I can tell Sarah likes sitting kind of close to me on the bench at our games. I think she likes **me** the best because she spends so much of the game sitting near me."

"I think Sarah loves **me**," Otto said. "When she was talking to me she touched **me** on the arm. It was a very special moment."

"Hey, Otto," Pickett said. "I happened to be watching you at that time. You were picking your nose, and Sarah was pulling at your arm trying to get you to stop. Believe me . . . the moment was not that special."

I couldn't control my laughter. I kept it quiet, but my body started shaking.

"Sorry, guys, but I think **I** am her favorite," said Treason. "Sarah was really smiling when she came to **me** and told **me** I played a great game, even though I wasn't in the lineup very long."

"You, too, are an idiot, Treason," Laser stated. "Is it possible that the reason Sarah was smiling was because you played tonight with your jersey on 'inside out?' You're lucky she didn't laugh in your face when she talked to you."

"You guys are all wrong. Sarah actually **ran** over to see **me** and tell **me** how well I played. **I'm** the one she loves," San Juan said, stating his case.

"You've got to be kidding, San Juan!" Pickett said, shaking his head. "You didn't notice that **everyone** was running at that time . . . away from Nicholson? You didn't **smell** it? Everyone else in a five-mile radius did!"

By now I had almost lost it. I started shaking like crazy, but I was hoping to hear more. I kept my head down and continued to pretend I was asleep.

"Sorry, everyone," Abe said as he joined in. "Sarah not only smiled and said **I** played really well, she touched my arm, too, and her eyes were filled with love."

"You were picking your nose, too? I'm glad I was not the only one," said Otto.

"There's a good chance that Sarah's eyes were watering because of Nicholson's 'tear gas,'" Laser explained.

I was definitely losing it. I tried to maintain control of myself. *Go on! Continue! . . . Sorry, Sarah. I'm not laughing at you. I'm not making fun of you. Honest.*

"I think Sarah talked with **me** the longest," said Half-Dozen. "That's a sure sign that she likes **me** the best."

"Good try," Captain Hook said as he jumped in. "Sarah probably spent more time with you because she wanted to make sure she wasn't using any words that had more than two syllables . . . hopefully giving you a chance to understand what she was saying."

"Hey, everyone. These are all powerful bits of evidence concerning who Sarah loves the most," Pickett said dramatically. "It's too close to call. We have a dilemma. I think we should wake Catcher up and seek out his thoughts on this matter. He's part of this team, too. He also will probably want to try on the glass slipper . . . though, in my opinion, he has no chance."

San Juan reached over and poked me. "Hey, Catcher . . . wake up! We need some help!"

I pretended to be groggy, but everyone knew that I had been awake and had been listening during the entire conversation. I stood up, though the bus was rolling along, and I burst out laughing.

"You guys are a pathetic bunch of morons!" I said laughing, and tears started rolling down my face. I could not stop my laughter.

Everyone started applauding and joining me in gut-busting laughter. Several of the boys reached over and shook hands with others.

"You were great, Laser," said San Juan.

"Good job, Otto," said Hook as he mimicked picking his nose.

Then everyone quickly scattered into new seats away from Nicholson.

Coach, our bus driver, yelled to us in the back of the bus, "Settle down back there! Stay in your seats!"

"Pickett, you were outstanding," Abe said.

I regained control of myself and said, "I am ready to share my thoughts. I think all of you tie in the 'Sarah Sweepstakes.' It is my belief that she loves you all the same, much like a mother loves all her children the same, no matter how immature they might act. However, I'm sure you all understand, unless you have had blinders on these last few weeks, that it's not a first-place tie . . . it is for second place. I am light-years ahead of all of you, and . . . seriously . . . I hope Sarah and I will be friends forever."

All laughter had stopped, and light applause filled the back of the bus.

"You guys need to know that Sarah thinks all of you are great," I continued. "She doesn't come to our games just to watch me. She has told me that she likes seeing the way we work together, the way we care about each other, and the way we make our own fun. She and her parents think we are a special group of 'young men,' . . . and I believe that all three members of the Jenkins family are quite intelligent. I totally agree with their opinion."

There was more light applause, but this time there were also rumblings of "We are . . . J-Hawks! We are . . . J-Hawks! We are . . . J-Hawks!"

It became very quiet for a few moments . . . then Pickett, from his seat in the back of the bus, picked up his ukulele and strummed a few bars . . . then paused . . . and, speaking in a mellow voice that was nearly as polished as that of an experienced radio announcer, said, "And now . . . for your listening pleasure . . . I will play some quiet-time music dedicated to the morons in the back of the bus."

Everyone burst out laughing again.

Pickett began strumming chords and singing about a girl named Marianne, who spent her days on the beach, playing in the sand, and all the children loved her. It was a great song, but the girl in my thoughts right now was not named Marianne. Based on the recent dramatic performance given by my teammates on the bus, it appeared to me that all the "children" love Sarah, too. I listened as Pickett continued singing about this young girl who sat by the water and built castles. *I'll have to ask Sarah if she likes building sand castles at the beach.*

It was a great bus-ride home to Jeffers, except that my quiet time was often interrupted by my own loud outbursts of laughter as I thought about my moron friends in the back of the bus.

My eye felt good as I arrived at the gym at about a quarter-to-nine the next morning. There was only a hint of a black eye. By nine o'clock all twelve of us players were dressed for our workout and the clinic, and we began with some easy running and layups. We transitioned smoothly to taking jump shots from the free-throw line, then followed that with full-court grapevine weaving, running at good speed and making crisp passes, not allowing the ball to touch the floor. Our groups of three ran continuously with little rest. Though this drill really tired us, we knew it was very beneficial for conditioning.

We did a cool-down shooting drill with partners. Each of the six shooters had a rebounder who kept feeding the ball to the shooter as he moved to new locations, faced up to the basket, and took several quick shots. Partners switched jobs often as we did several repetitions. After our quick-paced half-hour, we were ready to work with the kids.

Today there were twenty-five kids from 1st through 8th grade on the bleachers waiting for their turn for fun on the gym floor, and they hustled to the center circle when we called for the clinic to begin. We ran the clinic just like we did the previous weeks, and everything went well. We made sure all our comments were positive, and we laughed and joked as we taught and demonstrated. Each of us moved from group to group, so we all worked with every kid. We gave them a good workout before we concluded with J-Hawk Juice and cookies.

The kids volunteered that they'd be back again next Saturday, so we knew we were doing things the right way. Several other high school kids, some of them our sisters, joined us at snack time and helped with sweeping and cleanup while we twelve players quickly showered and prepared for our trek to the library.

Today the first graders led us in marching as we shouted out, "We are . . . J-Hawks!" I enjoyed seeing these young kids act as our leaders, and I understood the power we older kids had as role models.

We had so many reading tutors today that I spent some of the time just watching Sarah, admiring how well she related to the students and how easily she held their attention. I could see the admiration in the kids' eyes, and I figured my eyes probably looked like theirs.

The half-hour passed quickly, and after all the kids had either been picked up or had walked home, I finally felt I had a chance to speak with Sarah privately. I approached her to help her with her coat. Before I could utter a single word, Sarah blurted out, "My dad and I looked in the newspaper after getting home from the game last night, and we discovered that the Saturday night movie begins at seven."

I smiled and took this as a very encouraging sign. "That's very ironic," I said while looking directly into Sarah's sparkling eyes. "Last night I asked my dad if I could use a car tonight to go see a movie. It appears that we both have an interest in seeing a movie tonight. Would you consider going with me?" I asked.

Sarah smiled and nodded yes . . . and I didn't know what else to say.

We just stood there for a silent moment, smiling to each other.

"Did you read Garris's column today?" Sarah asked. "He was quite impressed by the way your team responded after you were hurt. Based on today's column, it sounds like Garris has almost become a member of J-Hawk Nation."

"The paper hadn't arrived yet when I left for the clinic, but Mom will probably have it sitting on the table for me when I get home," I said.

"I'm really glad you asked me to go to a movie with you tonight. I don't know how my dad would have handled the disappointment if you hadn't asked," she added with a laugh.

I thought her comment was quite funny. "Will your dad be going with us?" I asked, only half joking.

Sarah burst out with laughter. "No! Definitely no! But I will tell him that you asked.

Very smooth! Now I've insulted her dad. I'll no doubt spend the entire afternoon thinking about my first date tonight. This is new territory for me. I won't know what to do, how to act. The only thing I know for sure is that I've chosen the right girl. I really hope we both have fun.

We stepped outside and began walking down Main Street toward The Jeffers Café. Just as we reached the café, Sarah's dad walked out the door.

"Dad," Sarah said, "Catcher has asked me to go to a movie with him tonight."

Mr. Jenkins looked at me and nodded. "Then we'll see you tonight, Catcher," he said.

"Bye," Sarah said as she smiled shyly.

"I'll pick you up at 6:45," I said quietly. "See you then."

I stood there, watching and waving as their car headed west on Main Street toward the turn that would take them home to Madison Lake.

I did it . . . I asked her out . . . and she accepted . . . and her dad approved. Wow! I'm going on my first date tonight . . . and it's with Sarah! How great is that?

Saturday, January 13th

In the Stands – With John Garris

During my lifetime I have delivered thousands of verbal messages to people while standing face-to-face with them. I have written numerous letters and posted countless notes on bulletin boards. I have phoned messages too often to count. During my Navy years I signaled messages with semaphores and Morse code, and I've even sent copious numbers of telegrams. STOP!

But I've never sent a message like the Jeffers J-Hawks did last night in their game against the Upton Lions. It wasn't in code . . . and not a single word was spoken . . . and nothing was written. It was all action . . . and this was their message: We will not be intimidated by physical play.

Upton was down by 15 points in the fourth quarter when an aggressive Lion defender hammered the J-Hawk, Catcher, with an intentional elbow to the face as he drove to the basket for a layup. Blood was drawn, a timeout was called, and medical attention was administered. During the three-minute intermission, a plan dubbed "J-Hawk Retaliation" was hatched by the Jeffers players as they kept their composure and met at the bench. Their retaliation involved no fouls and no blood, no words, no taunts, no celebrations, and no attempts to seek revenge . . . unless you call scoring 11 straight points on the offensive end while suffocating the Lions with pressure and allowing them not a single good shot and no points on the defensive end . . . "revenge."

In a very methodical two minutes, the J-Hawks ran five choreographed plays, setting up each J-Hawk on the floor to go up against the hard-fouling Lion, and let him know, by each scoring a basket while he attempted to defend, that what he had done was unacceptable. **Message delivered! Special Delivery!**

Everyone on the Jeffers side watched admiringly, as did the two zebras. It was quite impressive. When a timeout was called after the fifth J-Hawk scorer ended the restitution, and the lead had been stretched to 26, the J-Hawks trotted to their bench with just a little smugness showing on their faces, and the entire "J-Hawk Nation" rose to their

164

feet and applauded their messengers loudly . . . with hands and voices.

In a reversal of "Don't shoot the messenger," I observed how well these messengers could shoot.

The J-Hawk winning streak now stands at eleven.

Chapter 24

Firsts

I felt a little nervous as I drove to pick up Sarah for our first date, but I considered myself to be very lucky because her parents already knew me. I expected that there wouldn't be an interview or a test I had to pass before we would be allowed to leave. That helped give me some confidence, and I had already talked to Sarah at basketball games, Saturday clinics, church services, libraries, and even at a painting party. I should not be nervous at all.

I guess some kids, when they go on a first date, might not even know each other. In my case, I not only know Sarah, I already like her a lot. My hope is that she also likes me.

Mr. Jenkins answered the door when I knocked. "Come on in, Catcher," he said. He was smiling, and I wondered why. *Did Sarah tell him that I asked if he was going with us?* "Garris wrote another very positive column about your basketball team. I think he said it perfectly. I agree with everything he wrote. You were tough last night."

"Thank you," I replied. "We really pulled together in the fourth quarter."

"Sarah will be down in a minute," Mr. Jenkins said. "She's pretty excited about the movie because she has already read the book. She also is pleased that she's going with you instead of with her mom and me."

I didn't know what to say so I just smiled.

Sarah's mom came to the entryway with Sarah. "Hi, Catcher," she said. "I hope you enjoy the movie. I'll get Andy to take me on a movie date soon I hope. Maybe I'll get to see *Swiss Family Robinson*, too."

"Hi, Sarah. You look great!" I said.

"Thank you," Sarah replied. She put on her coat, then held out her J-Hawk Nation stocking cap for me to see before she walked to a nearby wall mirror. She made sure the cap looked just right when she put it on. Now she looked even better to me. "Good-bye Mom and Dad," Sarah said. "We're leaving now."

"You two have a good time," Sarah's mom said.

Be home by eleven," Sarah's dad said. "First date and all . . . "

"Good night," I said as we turned to walk out the door.

The first thing I did was to reach for Sarah's hand as we walked to the car. *Wow! We are dating!*

The movie was perfect. There were many funny parts and lots of action. The Robinson family members were so creative in solving their problems, and life looked so good for them that I wished I were on that island and that Sarah was with me. Often during the movie I turned my head slightly and glanced at Sarah to see if she was having fun, but I looked straight ahead at the big screen during any scenes where kissing was involved.

We held hands during the entire two-hour movie, even during the wild pirate attack. I was in heaven.

At the conclusion of the movie we both stood and applauded. I asked Sarah if she thought it was good enough to watch again another night. She said, "Definitely! Are you asking me out on another date to see *Swiss Family Robinson* again?"

I smiled and replied, "I will definitely ask you to go with me to another movie very soon. I wouldn't mind seeing this again, but maybe we will find another good one to watch."

We drove to The Grill for sodas and hamburgers. I could now tell by Sarah's smile and her excitement in talking about the movie that she was having fun tonight.

I thought about my night. This was the first time I had sat down with Sarah and ordered something to eat at The Grill. I noticed other kids walking by, looking at us, and I wanted to stand up and announce to them, "This is my first date with Sarah Jenkins, and I'm having a great time!" I decided that I probably didn't need to say these words out loud. There's a good chance observers could just read my thoughts by looking at my eyes and seeing the smile on my face. I'm sure my feelings were pretty obvious. I made up my mind right then that I would ask her out again for next Saturday night when I said "Good night" at her door.

We made it back to her house right at eleven. Then we sat inside near the entryway for a while longer. I did not want to leave, but I also wanted to be able to see her again. We knew her parents were still up, sitting in the nearby living room so we talked very quietly, but it was difficult to turn the volume down on our laughter.

Eventually I knew it was time to leave, so I stood. "Sarah, I've had a great time tonight," I said, "and I know that *Swiss Family Robinson* will be my favorite movie forever."

She smiled and replied, "I had a great time, too. Thanks for taking me to the movie."

"You don't have to answer tonight," I continued, "but I'm asking you if you would go to another movie with me next Saturday night. You could tell me your answer at my Friday night game."

She smiled warmly and asked me, "Would you like to know my other reason?"

"What? . . . Oh, yeah . . . from Christmas," I replied. "If you think this is the right time, then I'd like to hear it."

Sarah looked at me quite seriously. She hesitated for a moment . . . then she said, "My other best thing about that Christmas weekend was just like what you had said to me. I was very happy to be able to spend that time with you at your game, during Christmas Eve caroling, going to the two church services, eating dinner on Christmas Day at my house, and walking to the park. I should have told you how I felt on Christmas Day, but sometimes I like keeping things a mystery. Will you forgive me?"

I smiled, looked into her eyes for a moment, and nodded. "Wow!" I said. "The first two times I saw you and did not even know your name I called you 'my mystery girl.' You still continue to be a mystery to me, but I am learning more and more about you."

I looked into her sparkling blue eyes and tried to build up my courage. *Do I take a chance? What if . . . ?*

I continued to look deeply into her eyes, and very tenderly I placed my hands on her shoulders. I slowly moved my face toward hers, closed my eyes . . . and, for the first time ever, kissed her softly on the lips. When I moved back slightly, I studied her eyes again and gently wrapped my arms around her.

"Thank you, Sarah, for the best night of my entire life," I whispered. I reached for her hands and stood there smiling. "I won't get to see you again until Friday night, but I do know your phone number." *I knew that I would call her during the week.*

Sarah smiled, and we both stood there, almost frozen. I wanted to kiss her again, but I didn't dare. Maybe a second attempt would be turned away. I nodded, smiled, and said as warmly as I could, "Good night, Sarah Jenkins."

I took a deep breath as I walked toward the car. I looked up and saw that thousands of bright stars filled the sky above me, and I felt wonderful. They were smiling at me, and I smiled back at them.

I raised both arms toward the sky in a salute, and I called out to all of the shining stars, "We are . . . J-Hawks!"

Chapter 25

Fouls

I think I had just finished second grade when I tried it for the first time. I felt ready because I had watched the older boys for a couple summers, and I had learned from them . . . now it was my time to start chasing and capturing foul balls. Even though I would be competing against some older kids, I knew I had a chance to earn a few nickels, so I rode with Dad to the Sunday afternoon baseball games, knowing I wouldn't be sitting in the bleachers with him. I would be standing on the street near the cornfield by myself or maybe near other foul-ball chasers.

The manager and coaches of the Jeffers town team tried to keep their costs down, and since new baseballs cost money, they relied on us kids to chase down each foul ball and get it back into the game as soon as possible. That way only three or four new balls were needed for each game. One man with a pocketful of nickels would sit near the tall screen behind home plate, waiting for one of us to run in at top speed to trade one retrieved foul ball for a silver nickel. Any time I ran in with a ball, I also sprinted back to my area after getting my reward, because I didn't want to miss a single chance.

I learned to run toward the baseball field between batters so I could check to see if the on-deck hitter would bat left or right handed, then move to a new location if I needed to. Since I couldn't run as fast as the bigger kids, I needed to be smarter, use better judgment about where to stand, and be better at anticipating where a foul ball might end up. My skills also included being able to turn quickly and run close to the ground between the cornrows so the sharp leaves of the stalks would not cut my arms so badly. I was good in the corn. At some games I earned thirty-five cents or more.

There wasn't much game-time traffic on the street that ran next to the baseball diamond, but sometimes screeching brakes would cause people in the bleachers to turn quickly toward the noise to see if one of us foul chasers had darted into the street without looking for cars and had become a hood ornament. During the four or five summers I chased fouls, I don't recall anyone colliding with a car. We led charmed lives.

The farmer who owned that field west of the bleachers on the first-base side of the ball field rotated his crops each year between corn and soybeans. In a bean year I stood right in the beanfield, next to the end rows, where I could follow the flight of a baseball and determine the rows I needed to run between to claim my prize. More than once I had to dive for the ball to reach it first, and I came up with the ball and a face full of dirt. Though I found it easier to chase foul balls during a bean year, I was more successful during a season of corn.

Since the town team played five or six Sunday-afternoon home games each summer, and I worked every game, I was able to earn around $2 chasing fouls in a summer, but it was the chase, rather than the money, that drove me. The competition inspired me, the sprints and quick turns excited me, and the capture of a foul ball really satisfied me. It was a great new "sport," and I was rewarded both physically and financially.

Sometimes as I race down the basketball court in a practice or a game, and I make a quick turn, or I dive for the ball . . . I get that same excited rush, and I think about chasing those foul balls. I realize that I still need to play smarter than my opponent, I need to use better judgment than he does, and I need to be able to anticipate what might happen next, just like those days when I sprinted around the ballpark, on the streets and in the corn and the beans. Those foul-chasing days helped me become a better athlete, and I am thankful for town-team baseball. I'm also glad that many of those kids I raced against for fouls over the years are now my J-Hawk teammates. We were "in training" way back in second and third grade. Who knew?

Just like those summer baseball games, tonight's away game against the Benson Bulldogs was all about fouls.

After Pickett grabbed the opening tip from Abe, we dribbled the ball down the court and passed it around until all five of us had touched the ball. When we spread out on the big floor to open up the middle area, Laser saw an opening down the lane, and he drove to the basket. A Bulldog player stepped right in front of him at the last second, and Laser and the other player collided. The refs blew their whistles. I figured Laser would shoot a free throw and get a second one if he made it, but one of the refs pointed at Laser and called him for a charge.

What? The guy was moving. He was never set. There was no charge. That was a blocking foul!

Number 22 made two free throws so we started the game from behind.

Laser dribbled the ball to our end. He passed to Pickett who had cut to the foul line. Pickett passed the ball to me. I saw Abe move quickly toward the basket, and I threw a high two-handed pass in his direction. He jumped straight up, grabbed the ball, and shot it softly against the backboard into the basket. A whistle blew, and a ref called out, "Number 33 . . . white . . . over the back . . . no basket."

It was on Abe. I couldn't believe it. He had gone straight up, and his man had backed into him. *That was a really terrible call.* We already had two fouls against us, and we had not yet gotten off a single shot.

Number 15 made his first free throw, but he missed his second one, and Pickett grabbed the rebound. Coach called a timeout. "All right," he said to us as we met at our bench. "It appears that we can't even breathe on them tonight. Do you guys all have bad breath?" He looked around at the five of us who started the game.

We just stared at Coach, not knowing if he was being serious. When he smiled at us, we knew he was just joking, and we all started laughing. He was trying to get our heads back in the game, hoping we would forget about the bad calls.

"We'll still break out fast every chance we get, and I want you to trap at half-court," Coach instructed. "The refs are calling them close tonight, so be smart out there. Give the Bulldogs some room. We'll still play our brand of ball, but we may have to back off a little. Let's go."

"We are . . . J-Hawks!" everyone responded.

Laser passed the ball in to me, and I dribbled down court. Hook stepped toward me by the right sideline, and I threw him a chest-high pass. He pivoted and faced his defender, then made a spin move and dribbled toward the basket. When he was about ten feet from the hoop, Hook stopped, jumped up, and lofted a shot that dropped cleanly through the rim.

All right! Now we're on the board!

Neither Laser nor I challenged their inbound pass, but we put pressure on Number 22 as he dribbled his way toward his basket. He dribbled mostly with his left hand, moving quickly toward the left sideline after crossing the line at half-court. Laser held his position, using the sideline to attempt to stop Number 22, but the Bulldog dribbler pushed his way past, knocking Laser down.

The ref that was standing nearby blew his whistle. "Number 20 . . . white . . . blocking!"

What? Laser was not moving! Number 22 charged! How can you call it that way? That's two bad calls on Laser. First charging . . . now blocking. Get it right! Is this your first game?

Coach was out of his seat in a hurry. "Call it both ways!" he shouted out to the refs.

As one ref headed toward the foul line, the other ref trotted over to Coach. "Sit down, Coach," he said. "You coach . . . we'll ref."

Tucson went in for Laser.

Abe picked up his second foul about a minute later while pulling in a rebound. Two Bulldogs had clearly pushed Abe under the basket, but the call went against Abe. *This is ridiculous!*

Coach sat Abe and brought in Otto. We had played only about three minutes, and we already had two starters on the bench with two fouls each. It was looking to me like these two refs had it out for us. I'd never been in a game like this before.

At the end of the first quarter we were down by a score of 18-14, and we had been whistled for eight fouls, while Benson had been called for only one.

Coach pulled us in closely. "We've got our hands full tonight, guys," he said quietly. "We have a couple choices here. Listen carefully. You are playing like you expect to lose tonight because all the calls are going against you. If you play that way . . . you will lose this game. It will happen. Another choice is to pull it together . . . forget the calls . . . focus on your shots . . . push the ball hard . . . and turn this game around. You are the better team. You can win this game if you make the correct choice."

"Catcher, take some shots from out . . . loosen them up. Hook, you've got room for that soft hook from seven / eight feet out, and Pickett . . . start hitting your signature jump shot from the lane. We've got to make our shots count tonight. Forget the refs! This game is in our hands. Play hard . . . have fun," Coach said as we ended our huddle.

In the second quarter our shots started dropping. Pickett and Hook each scored three buckets, and I hit on two long jump shots. San Juan and Tucson each made a fast-break layup, but the foul calls against us continued to pile up. Abe, Tucson, and Laser all had three fouls by halftime, and we trotted off to the locker room leading by a score of 34-32.

When we started the 3rd quarter Coach kept Laser and Abe on the bench. Though we really needed Laser's jump shots and Abe's soft touch near the basket and his rebounding, the refs had basically taken them out of the game with their terrible calls. Coach was saving them for later.

We played the Bulldogs evenly in the 3rd quarter. Otto picked up a couple early buckets from in close, but he also picked up two quick fouls. Pickett was our main scorer as he found the range on his jump shot, and Captain Hook grabbed almost every rebound when the Bulldogs missed their shots. Hook was tough! Our fast break led to layups for both San Juan and me, but the refs' whistles kept sounding, and we were called for more fouls.

J-Hawk Nation was getting restless in the bleachers. Some adults yelled out at the refs to call it fair. Some started booing. This was not the kind of game they were used to seeing.

Midway into the quarter Laser and Abe reentered the game. Laser picked us up when he made two long jump shots, and Abe banked in a short shot after receiving a great pass from Hook. It looked to me like we were ready to start putting it together, but in the next four minutes Abe and Laser each picked up another foul and were called to the bench. We were in trouble. We had a quarter left to play, and two of our best players were sitting with four fouls.

What bothered me the most was the inconsistency of the refs' calls. It was as if the refs were guessing, instead of calling what they were seeing, and all the bad guesses went against us. The Bulldogs were only whistled a few times, for really obvious fouls. It was very one-sided. I had a feeling that the refs wanted us to lose, and I did not like this feeling. I had never looked at a ref as an enemy before, but tonight that's how I saw it.

Tucson fouled out early in the final quarter, and Abe followed shortly after. We kept the lead between four and eight points, but it was a struggle. Laser scored on another jump shot, then I made a steal and drove for a layup.

I know we can do this, but we need Laser to stay in the game.

The Bulldogs hit on a few close-in shots as our defenders pulled away, afraid of fouling. Tonight we had to play softer defense and much stronger offence. Captain Hook hit on two easy shots after grabbing offensive re-bounds, and Pickett found the range again from inside the lane. San Juan threw me a great fast-break pass, and I scored on a left-handed layup.

The Bulldogs hit on their next two attempts.

Laser scored again the next time down. Our lead was up to ten. Hook made a beautiful block of Number 15's shot, but Hook was called unfairly for a foul. *He never touched the guy. Terrible call!* Now Hook had three fouls.

Luckily the shooter missed both free throws so we kept our lead at ten points.

I dribbled slowly toward our basket, using up some of the clock, then passed to Laser on the left. He saw another opening in the middle and drove down the lane. As he went up for his shot a whistle blew, and we all held our breath.

The ref called out, "Number 20 . . . in the white . . . charging . . . no basket!"

Laser had just fouled out. Three times he had been called for charging tonight. In all our previous games he had been called for only one charge . . . . total. These refs were bad.

Coach called for a timeout.

"It's time to make that choice again," Coach told us in our huddle. "If you focus on the refs you cannot focus on your game. Forget the refs! We can do this. Slow the game down a little. We're short three players now . . . so you guys are it. Work the ball inside. On defense keep your hands straight up. Don't touch them, and don't breathe on them." Then Coach smiled at all of us. He wasn't panicking, that's for sure. He was calm, and he kept us calm.

"You've got to fight through four more minutes. Let's build some character out there tonight," Coach said. "Let's do it!"

"We are . . . J-Hawks!"

The next two minutes didn't go well. We were called for two more fouls, and the Bulldogs scored six points on two free throws and two shots from close range, while we missed on two attempts and threw the ball away once.

Our lead stood at four, and there was about two minutes left to play.

San Juan dribbled twice, then passed to me near midcourt. I pivoted and tossed a sharp pass to Hook by the right sideline, and he quickly turned and dribbled toward the baseline. Finding his path to the basket closed off, Hook brought the ball outside again and fired it back to me.

Pickett then crossed the lane in my direction near the foul line, and I bounced a pass to him. He took a single dribble, jumped high into the air as he turned toward the basket, and tossed a soft shot which hit the rim on its way down and bounced off to the side where Number 22 of the Bulldogs reached high to grab it. He swung his elbows wildly while protecting the ball, and his coach yelled loudly for a timeout.

One minute and thirty-five seconds remained in the game.

"Listen up," Coach said as we huddled by the bench. "I think this is the right time. If the Bulldogs don't score on this possession, they will probably foul, so . . . Nicholson . . . go in for San Juan and play forward. Otto . . . move out to a guard spot with Catcher. Remember how we need to play this. Nicholson, you have to sell it . . . shoestring . . . and the trip. Make the bait so enticing that the 'Dogs' can't resist. The rest of you . . . do your jobs. Let's see if we can get three fouls out of this."

Before we broke the huddle I made eye contact with Sarah, then held my hand in front of my face, palm out, all five fingers extended as I wiped sweat off my face with the back of my hand. I saw Sarah's mouth open as she realized I had sent her our signal, then she turned to her mom and dad and appeared to quietly begin explaining what would be happening next. I watched as John Garris, sitting behind Sarah and a little to her left, leaned in toward the Jenkins family to listen in.

"Here we go J-Hawks. Let's pull this one out and enjoy the bus ride home," Coach said.

"We are . . . J-Hawks!" we all shouted.

Four of us trotted out onto the floor while Nicholson checked in at the scorer's table. When Nicholson left the sideline to walk across the floor his right shoestring was untied, dragging on the gym floor. One of the refs stopped him and pointed to his shoestring.

Coach yelled in an agitated voice, "Nicholson, tie your shoestring! Come on! Be ready!"

Nicholson knelt down, tied it up, then rose to his feet and began to trot into position. As he crossed the floor his feet got tangled up, and he tripped himself, falling flat on the gym floor as everyone looked on. On the J-Hawk side of the gym, fans groaned, and from the Bulldog bleachers much laughter erupted. Even the Bulldog players on the floor laughed at Nicholson. Otto, Pickett, Hook, and I lowered our heads. This was embarrassing.

The Bulldog coach yelled to his players as they were setting up to throw the ball into play, "Number 40!"

No team has 40 plays for inbounding the ball. Hey! Nicholson is wearing Number 40. I hope their coach just picked out Nicholson as the player to foul if they miss their next shot.

The Bulldogs inbounded the ball from the sideline near our end of the floor. Otto and I pressed loosely, trying to slow them down a little, making them use up some of the clock. We knew we could not foul anyone. We needed the clock to keep running. They could not be allowed to score any points on a stopped clock.

Number 33 dribbled across the centerline and passed to Number 12 who was standing near the right sideline. He dribbled three times, then launched a long jump shot which hit the far side of the rim and shot almost straight up into the air. Nicholson was in great position. He timed his jump perfectly, grabbed the ball with both hands, landed and pivoted toward the outside, and started his dribble. Immediately Number 11 hacked him on the arm and was whistled for a foul.

J-Hawk Nation applauded and appeared shocked.

Pickett and I approached Nicholson. Pickett said to him in a voice loud enough for the Bulldogs to hear, "Make sure you stay behind the line. Take deep breaths before you shoot."

I added, "Relax, and make sure you bend your knees. Let your legs help lift the ball."

Nicholson took his stance behind the free-throw line, and a ref bounced him the basketball. Both refs extended their arms, showing one finger on each hand. If Nicholson made the first shot he would get a second one. We needed these points to extend our four-point lead. I held my breath. The shot went up . . . and dropped through the exact center of the net.

All right!

Nicholson prepared for the bonus. He bounced the ball three times and stared at the rim. He crouched slightly and lifted his shot toward the rim. The ball skimmed the rim as it fell through the hoop. J-Hawk Nation stood and applauded loudly

The lead was up to six.

The Bulldogs rushed the ball down the floor as the clock ticked past the forty-five second mark. The Benson guards looked for an opening as they passed the ball back and forth. Number 22 received a pass and took two dribbles, then fired a jump shot from the free-throw line. It was good.

Pickett threw the ball in to me quickly. Immediately two players sur-rounded me, but they were careful not to foul me. I jumped and passed to Nicholson who was standing near the sideline. After he caught the ball he dribbled once before Number 15 caught up to him, reached for the ball, and slapped Nicholson on his arm. The ref blew his whistle sharply and extended both arms, signaling another one-and-one.

So far . . . so good. We really need two from Nicholson here. We need to act like we are worried, but he knows we have confidence in him.

I walked to the free-throw line and told Nicholson to relax and take deep breaths.

Nicholson caught the pass from the ref. After bouncing the ball three times and taking a deep breath, he shot the ball just over the front edge of the rim with perfect backspin on the ball, and the net twitched as the ball dropped through. Nicholson had earned the bonus shot.

"You can do it," Hook said.

"It's automatic," Otto added.

The second shot hit only net as Nicholson converted on his fourth straight attempt.

The Bulldogs hustled the ball into play and worked it toward their bas-ket as we tried to slow them down. They crossed the centerline with 25 seconds to go in the game, down by six points. We knew they would take a quick shot so we all kept our hands up.

"No fouls!" I called out.

Number 15 was covered well by Otto, but he fired a jump shot anyway that clanged off the rim, and Pickett leaped high and grabbed the rebound. He passed to me at the side, and I dropped the ball off to Nicholson as he crossed the court toward me. Two Bulldogs ran toward Nicholson who shielded the ball as he pivoted. The whistle blew, and the ref called out to-ward the scorer's table, "Number 22 . . . on the arm . . . one-and-one!"

So far this had worked just like we had hoped. Coach was hoping for three fouls out of this, and Nicholson had now been fouled for the third time.

Two more points would definitely put this game out of reach.

"Relax, then focus," Pickett said.

"Just over the front of the rim," Otto added. "Two more."

Nicholson was handed the ball. He now wore the look of confidence on his face as he eyed the basket. He crouched, raised his body slightly as he ex-tended his arms, and shot the basketball right through the center of the net. Bulldog players couldn't believe it. Nicholson had now hit five-in-a-row.

At the bench, Coach quickly got San Juan up to report in.

I walked over to the foul line. "Tie your shoestring again. It looks a little loose," I said to Nicholson. He bent to the floor. "It looks like San Juan will be coming in for you after you make this next one. Your six points will have been huge in this game. Be ready for loud applause when you head to the bench. You . . . are a hero."

Nicholson looked up at me and smiled.

I continued, "Remember what I told you before . . . 'trip in, trip out.' It will add to all the stories people will tell about this game, and it will be good for your image."

"One shot," the ref said as he bounced the ball to Nicholson. There was no doubt about his shot . . . straight through the net and the hearts of the

Bulldog players, their coach, and their fans.

The buzzer sounded, indicating a substitution would be made. San Juan headed from the scorer's table toward the center of the floor where he stopped and waited. The bench players stood and joined the four of us on the floor in our applause as Nicholson trotted toward the center circle on his way to our bench. As he closed in on San Juan, his right foot caught on his left heel, and down he went again, sprawled out on the gym floor. This time J-Hawk Nation did not groan . . . they applauded, and this time the Bulldogs and their fans did not laugh . . . they were too stunned. They were probably wondering how this clumsy player who couldn't even run without tripping could have made six straight free throws and put the game out of reach with only 15 seconds left.

San Juan helped Nicholson to his feet, and Nicholson trotted the rest of the way to our bench where he was mobbed by his teammates.

I could see the huge smile on Nicholson's face from where I stood on the court. I looked at Sarah in the distance. I showed five fingers extended, palm out, in front of my face. I nodded to her and clapped my hands again. The plan had worked perfectly. The 'Dogs' had gone for the bait.

Bulldog player Number 33 scored on a jump shot just as the buzzer sounded to end the game, leaving our victory margin at six points . . . Nicholson's six free throws.

It was a great win . . . against a tough team . . . and two refs.

Coach called us over before we lined up to shake hands. "Not a single word about the refs or bad calls!" he said seriously.

As we shook hands with the Benson players, I heard the Benson coach say to Coach, "You were really lucky tonight, your player hitting all those free throws."

Coach responded, "Yes, we were fortunate."

As we turned toward our bench I asked Coach, "Didn't you think Nicholson would make them?"

"I knew he would make them," he replied.

"Then why did you say we were fortunate?" I asked.

"We were fortunate that the Bulldogs took the bait and fell into the trap," Coach said with a big smile.

I caught up with the others as we reached our bench. Everyone was slapping Nicholson on the back.

Sarah and her parents were among the first to reach our bench area. Sarah walked directly to Nicholson and said, "You were fantastic!"

Sarah's parents shook his hand.

I was drying off when Sarah and her parents reached me. Sarah asked, "Did your signal at the end of the game mean everything worked exactly as you hoped it would?"

"Just like we planned," I replied with a grin.

John Garris stepped right into the middle of our conversation. "I have some questions," he said. "Did Nicholson trip on purpose?"

I nodded to Sarah. "Go ahead," I said. "I'll help if you need it."

Sarah smiled and began her explanation. "I heard from a very reliable source that Nicholson actually works on his tripping skills at practice. Nicholson did trip on purpose so the Bulldogs would think he was clumsy and maybe not a very good player. That's also why his shoestring was not tied. Both of these were part of the bait used to set a trap for the Bulldogs. If they needed to foul someone, they would probably choose someone that hadn't made a very good impression when he entered the game, and Nicholson was that guy. However, they didn't know that Nicholson is the best free-throw shooter on the team." She turned to me. "Sorry, Catch. I didn't mean to hurt your feelings."

I laughed.

"Was Coach angry at Nicholson? He yelled at him loudly," Garris said.

"That sounded pretty serious, but it was all part of the plan," Sarah said. It showed the Benson Bulldogs that even Coach had no confidence in Nicholson. Did you see the players put their heads down when Nicholson tripped? They looked really embarrassed. It was a great act."

"Great job, Sarah! You understood everything," I said proudly.

"Were you expecting the ref to notice the shoestring?" Sarah asked me.

"We hoped he would see it and stop the game, bringing a little attention to Nicholson, but Coach was all set to yell," I answered. "We got both."

"That was quite effective," Sarah's mom said. "I was embarrassed for the poor kid."

"Most of J-Hawk Nation groaned when Nicholson tripped the first time," I said. "They did their job well, and they didn't even know they were part of it."

"What about Nicholson's trip on the way back to the bench?" Garris asked. "Was that one an accident?"

Sarah looked at me for help.

"That was just for show," I answered. "I told Nicholson a couple of weeks ago that I had an idea that would really add to his image. I called it 'trip in - trip out.' Tonight it was a way to reveal to the other team, the ones who had laughed, that they had unknowingly been the victims of a trap that had been set for them and that they had fallen into. Did you notice the four of us on the floor watching Nicholson as he trotted to the center circle on the way to the bench? Did you see that instead of having our heads down, we smiled and clapped when he tripped? We were ready for his curtain call, and he did it well. He has worked on that trip in practice for a few weeks now. He's the best we have at both free throws and trips."

"What if Benson had fouled another player instead of Nicholson?" Garris asked.

Sarah jumped right in. "Then that player would have made the shots. They are all good shooters." She almost sounded upset at the question.

Way to defend us, Sarah!

I have a question for you, Mr. Garris. "Did it look to you like we played a lot rougher than the Bulldogs did tonight? We were called for a lot of fouls, and they had just a few called against them until they fouled Nicholson at the end."

"No, you weren't any rougher," he answered without hesitation. "There were many bad calls made against you. This game was called very poorly. It was not right. It was unfair."

"One more thing, Mr. Garris," I said. Don't make us out to be a bunch of complainers if you write about the game, and make sure you give Nicholson credit with his heroics without making the Bulldogs look too bad."

"I'm always fair and very careful," he replied as he headed to the scorer's table.

"I'm really glad you came tonight," I said to Sarah and her parents, "but this had to be a tough game to watch."

"These refs were quite biased, in my opinion," Mr. Jenkins said.

"I was so excited when I saw your signal," Sarah said to me. "I knew what was going to happen. Thanks for telling me about the plan." Sarah said.

"Shh," I said quietly. "Coach can't know that I told you about it."

"You would have beaten them badly if it hadn't been for all the fouls called on your team," Mrs. Jenkins said.

"Only two guys, Abe and Pickett, had fouled out once each in this whole season, and tonight three guys fouled out in one game. The refs called it very differently tonight," I said.

"You won, and you deserved to win," Mrs. Jenkins said. "That's what matters."

Sarah and I walked away from the bench so we could talk privately.

"It's good to see you again," I said. It's been almost a whole week. I've missed you, and I thought about *Swiss Family Robinson* all week."

"Me too," Sarah said. "That was a special night. I will see you tomorrow morning at the gym . . . and what time will you pick me up for the movie tomorrow night?"

"How about 6:30? If your dad is going to shorten our evening at the end, I'll just have to extend it at the beginning," I said as I laughed.

"That's a great plan!" Sarah said.

We held hands for a few moments, and then Coach began to round us up for the trip to the locker room.

"Tomorrow," I said as I smiled.

In the Stands – With John Garris

The Jeffers J-Hawks are well known in their conference for their trapping defense, whether it be of the full-court or half-court variety. Last night at Benson the J-Hawks went on the offensive with a trap that helped them secure a six-point victory in a hard-fought game with the Bulldogs. It was drama . . . live drama, and the creatively-designed trap was carried out excellently by the cast of J-Hawk Nation, most of whom had no idea they were playing a supporting role.

It all began with only a min-ute-and-a-half left on the game clock when seldom-used substi-tute, Nicholson, Number 40, en-tered the game for the J-Hawks with **an untied shoestring**. The plot thickens! . . . A ref points to the hazardous shoestring, holds up play while the shoestring is tied, and the J-Hawk coach **yells** at his player for not be-ing prepared. Number 40 then trots toward his position on the floor and **trips** on his own feet, **falling flat on his face** in the center of the floor. There was **much groaning** from J-Hawk Nation (You played your part

well.) and **much laughter** from Bulldog fans. (Realize it or not, you may also have influenced the outcome.) The four supporting J-Hawk actors on the floor low-ered their heads in embarrass-ment and defeat.

If you are the coach of the Benson Bulldogs, and your team needs to foul a J-Hawk with hopes of getting the ball back after missed free throws, whom would you foul? Choose from the three starters and the sixth man who have all played and shot well, or the clumsy kid who just entered the game and fell on his face. It would have been an easy decision for me to make.

In about one minute's time, Nicholson was fouled three times . . . and he buried six free throws into the center of the net, provid-ing the winning margin.

The plan worked perfectly.

I heard from a reliable source after the game that Nicholson is the best free-throw shooter on the team and that he works diligently on this skill at every practice. All the J-Hawks had to do was to get him to the foul line. That's why the trap was set. My reliable source also told me that Nicholson can perform a "self-trip" better than any other J-Hawk and that he works on this skill at practices, too.

The J-Hawks did not complain last night about how the refs called the game, but I am voicing a complaint in this column. These two young refs called 25 fouls on the J-Hawks while calling only 8 on the Bulldogs. These refs couldn't have been watching the same game I was. Both teams were engaged in a similar style of play, but the fouls were called with total inconsistency, and the J-Hawks were on the short end of the stick. I have no idea what was going on, but it was not right.

Only because the J-Hawks kept their poise and their focus, got great contributions from their bench players, and set out some great bait did the J-Hawks pull this game out, and they were, by far, the superior team.

The winning streak for the boys from Jeffers has now reached 12.

Chapter 26
Family Time

I had called Sarah twice during the week just to talk to her and hear her wonderful voice. I also had tried to be funny during the calls because I love hearing her laughter. On my Monday night call Sarah told me that *Blue Hawaii*, an Elvis movie, was playing, and she accepted my Saturday night movie invitation. I had been pretty sure she would say "yes." I was counting on it. She asked me if I was okay with going back to her house after the movie instead of stopping at The Grill. That was fine with me.

It was another great movie night. I would never forget *Blue Hawaii* either, though I am not a great fan of Elvis. I am, however, a great fan of Sarah. I know that it's not the movie that makes the night so much fun for me. It definitely is the company. I think I love that girl.

After the movie we did go back to Sarah's house. Her dad had a fire going in the fireplace, and Sarah and I sat on the carpet in front of the hearth and watched the yellow and red flames dance above the logs as we listened to Johnny Mathis and The Fleetwoods on Sarah's stereo. Though Sarah's parents were in the room with us, I was not bothered at all. I like her parents, and I feel very comfortable with them. I really didn't care who was with us as long as Sarah and I could talk and laugh together, and the music and the fire really added to the atmosphere.

At about ten Sarah took me to the kitchen where she brought out a pan of freshly baked chocolate-frosted brownies, just like the ones she had baked for "Painting Day." She dished up four brownies, putting them in bowls, then added vanilla ice cream as I watched helplessly. My job, and I did it well, was to carry the bowls to the table while Sarah grabbed forks, spoons, and napkins. All four of us sat at the table together and enjoyed the delicious dessert.

I told Sarah for the second time, "You can bake for me anytime. These brownies are fantastic again."

Maybe it sounds strange that Sarah and I spent time with her parents while we were on a date, but I didn't have a problem with it. I don't think Sarah did either. I just hope it was Sarah's idea, not her parents'. Like I said before, I'm just happy to be able to spend time with her, even if it's at a game, a clinic, the library, or even church. Being with her parents is a lot better than not being able to see Sarah at all. What if they had told me she was too young to date, or if they didn't trust me? *I hope we aren't here tonight because they don't feel they can trust me.*

Several times at Sarah's house I referred to Sarah as "a reliable source." All four of us laughed about that because it's possible that only Sarah, her parents, and I knew that Garris's "reliable source" was not me or any other J-Hawk basketball player, but instead a J-Hawk Nation special friend of mine who happened to know all about the trap that we set for the Bulldogs because I had told her some secret information.

Sarah likes knowing secrets, and she has fun being mysterious.

The two of us sat by the fire again after we cleared the table, and Sarah's parents wanted to hear more about the trap we had set for the Bulldogs last night.

Sarah's dad asked, "Was Nicholson okay with everything that happened when he went into the game . . . the groaning and the laughter when he tripped . . . the coach yelling?"

"He knew how it would probably go," I answered. "We had explained to him that everything our team did was part of the act, that we had to make it look good, or it would not work. We had shown total confidence in him while he shot free throws in practice. We kept telling him, 'Don't take it personally when we do any of the bad stuff. It's all an act.' Because everything worked perfectly last night, and he was treated like a hero, I think he was not bothered. He was extremely pleased with his trip on the way back to the bench, and he appreciated all the applause. We won because of his free throws, and we made sure he understood that. Sarah, your comment to him after the game made him feel very proud."

"Do you have any other special plays or tricks that you can tell us about?" Mrs. Jenkins asked.

"No, we don't," I replied. "We're down to playing regular basketball the rest of the way unless Coach comes up with something else. Will this be enough to keep you coming to our games?"

The whole Jenkins family laughed at my question.

"I can't speak for Sarah, but her mother and I will attend every game we possibly can. Your 'regular basketball' is good enough for us."

Sarah looked at me and laughed again. "Catcher," she said, "you know I'll be there. I won't miss a single game. I may have to sneak onto your bus to get there, but I won't let you down. I'll be in every gym cheering for all of you J-Hawks."

"You have true J-Hawk spirit, Sarah," I said.

At about eleven o'clock I told Sarah and her parents that I needed to leave. "Coach asked all of us to make sure we get enough sleep," I explained. "All twelve of us made a commitment to be in bed and asleep by midnight on weekends during the rest of our basketball season."

I turned to Mr. Jenkins, smiled, and asked, "I was wondering if you made this curfew suggestion to Coach?"

Sarah's dad laughed loudly. "You give me too much credit," he replied.

"I'm glad you two came back here tonight after your movie," Sarah's mom said to Sarah and me. "You are always welcome here, Catcher."

"Thank you," I replied. "I've had a great time tonight."

Sarah walked me to the door where we stood for awhile. I was glad her parents hadn't followed us. Sarah and I held hands and talked about next week's games, figuring out when we would see each other again. I was starting to figure out that maybe she liked being with me.

"I have had a wonderful time again tonight. This was my best night ever for sitting by a fire," I said. "I'm glad we came back to your house after the movie."

Sarah smiled and said, "I had a great time, too, and I'm glad I could be part of another 'best night' for you."

I held her in my arms, and I did not want to let go, but I figured her dad was watching the clock in the next room, wondering if I would make it home on time.

"Sarah, every time I see you I have a great time. You are a very 'reliable source' of fun for me," I said as I smiled and looked into her eyes.

She laughed and moved closer to me.

Our voices were silent now, but our eyes and smiles spoke quite clearly.

I kissed her . . . and I was not afraid. I kissed her a second time.

I very slowly pulled my hand away from her hand, reached for the doorknob, stepped out into the frozen night, and walked toward my car.

"We are . . . J-Hawks!" I yelled out. "Coach, I'm heading home right now!"

Chapter 27
The Post

Halloween was a very important holiday in Jeffers. As the young kids did the usual "trick or treating," the older boys would run through the town doing mischief. Any green John Deere, orange Allis Chalmers, or red Farmall tractor awaiting service at the implement shop would be pushed out onto Main Street. Empty chicken cages from the egg and poultry business would be carried out to the street and spread around to block cars from being able to drive through the town. All the fence posts and telephone poles from the outside storage area at the lumber yard would be rolled or carried by teams of boys and scattered as barriers.

We were not vandals . . . We were mischief-makers. We were careful not to damage anything. The purpose of all this hard work was to offer some disruption to ordinary life. Our souls needed some adventure, so we found our excitement by slightly stepping across the line that separated right from wrong.

This last Halloween several of the business people in town served as our opposition. They patrolled in their cars and guarded the four-block business section and the back alleys. We ran and hid, using hand signals instead of talking or shouting, moving in small groups to any unprotected area where we would locate other objects that we could push, pull, roll, or carry out into the street. We felt the adrenalin rush as we ran through the streets and across the dark backyards, dodging the authorities.

At one point a whole bunch of us escaped toward the school playground, but the cars followed us, with their headlights and spotlights lighting us up as we jumped the four-foot wire fence that served as the playground's boundary, and we ran into the cornfield and hid. The yet-to-be-harvested tall dry cornstalks provided good cover. We crouched silently and listened as the mayor shouted into his megaphone, "Come on out! We know who you are!"

We almost lost it. We couldn't control our laughter. We definitely were not coming out from the cornfield, and as for knowing who we were . . . of course they knew who we were. We were every boy (ages 13 – 17) who lived in town plus most of the country boys. This was a real adventure, something that wasn't found often in Jeffers, except for Halloween night. It was a delicious wicked feeling to be part of this Halloween "strike and run" squad.

On our basketball team this year I've experienced this same sense of adventure. I've felt the adrenalin rushes during the fast-paced action as we worked together toward a common goal, often using hand signals to communicate, uniting against the opposition. Does this sound like Halloween adventures? Sometimes it seems like it, except for the wicked part. It's kind of funny to think that our Halloween activities may have indirectly been part of our training, one of the reasons that we have achieved some success as a basketball team this year.

Three years ago I did something during Halloween mischief that I still regret. Otto had seen one single fence post at the lumberyard still in its place in the rack, so he decided to carry it out into the street. The officials caught him in the act, and his punishment was to put all the other posts that had been scattered in the street back where they belonged. I was hiding nearby . . . and I observed this, and I remained hidden. Because of moving one stinkin' post, Otto had to pick up and return over 50 fence posts . . . and I stayed in hiding and watched him carry every single one.

I regret that I did not have the courage to come out from hiding and assist Otto. Sadly, all I did was watch him as he dutifully returned the posts to their storage location.

I talked to Otto about that night a couple weeks after it happened. I apologized for not helping him. Otto just laughed and said it was no big deal. He said he deserved to be caught for making such a stupid move, and he told me he would have done the same thing I had done. I'm not sure I believe that.

I've thought about that night, and I think about that single post. It still bothers me. If someone does something to me and they apologize, I forgive them. After a while I forget and forgive even if there is no apology, but I have a hard time forgiving myself for something I have done. I'm still carrying guilt from that Halloween night.

I'm older now, and hopefully smarter now, and I would not make that Halloween mistake again. I would stand up for any of my teammates, my family, my friends, and especially for Sarah. I wish I had helped Otto. I will next time.

The only negative about our Halloween fun was that Main Street was perfectly clean the next morning when we arrived at school. It was as if nothing had happened, and no adult ever said anything about it. Maybe the authorities enjoyed the rush as much as we kids did. No one got hurt, no damage was done, the streets were cleaned up, and the game was over . . . until next year. We kids understood that we could get away with this behavior only on Halloween night. If we tried this on any other night we would be in serious trouble, and everyone would know about it. It was an unwritten rule in our small town.

I've noticed that most of the town officials who tried to limit the amount of mischief we did last Halloween night attend our games, and they cheer for us. As the mayor said, they know who we are.

Pickett's music settled both the girls' team and our team on our bus ride to Mayville. We didn't expect a tough game tonight because we had beaten the Eagles by over twenty points back in December, but we still wanted to play well. We were hoping that when we stepped on the floor for warm-ups, we wouldn't see the refs who had called our last game. It seemed like it had been awhile since we had played really well. We were due for a good game.

We got off to a fast start, breaking out quickly after every defensive rebound. Abe, Hook, and Pickett were monsters on the boards, snatching every rebound and firing the ball down-court. Laser and I scored often on fast-break layups. Our running game was outstanding. San Juan and Tucson took over at guard late in the quarter, giving Laser and me some rest, and we continued to score some easy baskets. Almost all our points were coming from fast breaks, and we were looking good.

We held a twelve-point lead at the end of the first quarter. Coach called us together at the bench. "Okay, guys. Great job so far," he said. "The first quarter was dedicated to our fast break. The second quarter belongs to the post. I want everything to go through the post. Find Pickett at the high post, and feed Abe and Hook at the low post. I want the guards to slow the ball down so we can get set on our offensive end, then use sharp passes to move the ball quickly on our half. Pass around their zone defense, and feed the ball inside. The big guys will be scoring the points during this quarter."

Our second quarter matched our first. Pickett scored on a few shots from ten feet out, Captain Hook was hitting his specialty, and Abe cleaned up and put back the garbage. Our lead was up to twenty at halftime.

We didn't use our press when we started the 3rd quarter because it was too easy. Coach wanted us to have to work harder for our points. He subbed often, mixing up our lineup, but we continued to run whenever we grabbed the Eagles' missed shots, and we extended our lead to twenty-six.

With three minutes left in the 3rd quarter, Captain Hook grabbed a rebound with both hands, slapping the ball loudly. He pivoted in my direction toward the left sideline as I started running down the floor. He led me with a perfect pass, and after one dribble, I passed ahead to Otto who went strong to the basket for a right-handed layup, and I followed him in for a possible rebound.

While Otto was still in the air, Eagle guard Number 24 cut in front of him, taking Otto's legs out from under him, and Otto fell hard to the floor on his back as the ball dropped silently through the net. He groaned as he lay there, and I hurried over to check him out and help him up.

That's when I saw the anger in his eyes as he quickly rose to his feet, neglecting any pain he was feeling. I stepped right in front of him, nose to nose, and I put my open hands on his chest and prepared to brace my legs. I sensed that Otto was getting ready to go after Number 24.

"Are you okay, Otto? . . . Hey . . . Otto!" I spoke quickly but calmly. "Do you remember that Halloween night and that one stupid fence post? Do you remember what you said to me? . . . You told me you should have left it alone . . . just walked away . . . ignored it. You admitted that you brought trouble on yourself because you didn't just leave it where it was. That's what you told me . . ."

The refs motioned for all other players from both teams to move away.

I continued, "Tonight we are going to just walk away . . . you and me . . . walk away from that fence post and all the trouble that comes with it. This time I'm here to help you, Otto. I'm sorry about that other time when I should have helped you, but I messed up. Tonight I'll get it right."

"We need a timeout," I said to the ref who was standing nearby, and he blew his whistle.

"C'mon," I said to Otto as I led him over to our bench. "Let's catch our breath and get some water. You've got a free throw coming to complete your three-point play."

During the timeout Otto calmed down. He drank some water and wiped some sweat off his face and his arms, then he told Coach he was fine. He turned to me and started laughing. "So you still remember that Halloween fence post, huh?" he asked. "You can probably let that go now. I think we left that post behind tonight, thanks to your help out there. You kept me from going after that guy. I was pretty angry at him. You saved me some trouble. I owe you. I'm not sure I would have had the energy it would have taken to complete my punishment of carrying 50 posts back to the rack tonight, even with your help."

Everyone, including Coach, laughed. It was a relief that Otto was okay.

I took a couple deep breaths, and it felt like a huge burden had been lifted from me. Laser and San Juan and Abe all came over to me and told me I had done a great job in protecting Otto. I looked at them and said, "We are . . . J-Hawks."

"You got that right!" San Juan replied.

Otto made his free throw and played out the third quarter. Then Coach sat him for the rest of the game as a precaution.

Our starting lineup played for the first four minutes of the final quarter, and we ran hard. We did everything at top speed. We worked our fast breaks, and we fed the ball into the post. The Eagles couldn't compete with us. Our lead stood at 31 points when Coach emptied the bench for the last four minutes of the game. We had needed a good game, and we had played one. It felt good.

When we shook hands with the Eagles, Number 24 told Otto he was sorry, and he asked if he was okay. That was a good move on his part.

As we headed back to the bench, Coach stopped me. "You may have saved the rest of Otto's season for him tonight," he told me. "He probably would have gotten suspended if he had gone after that guy. I wouldn't have gotten out there in time to stop him before the damage was done. You possibly saved our season, too, because refs don't take kindly to teams that fight. That was very 'heads-up' on your part. Good work. I'll let you go now because I see you have someone waiting for you."

I looked toward our bench.

Sarah had come down to the gym floor, and she was standing by patiently. She didn't say anything . . . she just stood there and smiled at me. Her dad arrived, and he spoke first.

"Stopping Otto might have been your best play of the season, Catcher," he said. "Your team could have been in big trouble. You did well."

"Thanks," I said. "Otto's my teammate. The other guys would have done the same."

Sarah still didn't say anything, but she moved closer. She reached out with her arms and gave me a hug. "You were fantastic!" she said.

"Now I'm not jealous of Nicholson any more," I said, and we both laughed.

"What did you say to Otto?" Sarah asked.

"There's a long story behind what I told him," I replied. "Are you okay if I tell you on the phone tomorrow night?"

"Sure," she replied. She handed me a small piece of paper. "Here's Becky's number for San Juan. I hope you can convince him to call her."

"I think he's ready," I said. "Hey, thanks for being here tonight, Sarah. I really like that you come to our games. It means a lot to me. Wish me luck with San Juan. I've got to go. It looks like I'm the last one out here again. Good night."

After showering, packing up my sweaty uniform and gym shoes in my duffle bag, and dressing for the bus ride back to school, I approached San Juan.

"Would you like to go to a movie Saturday night in Madison Lake?" I asked. "I think there's a Western playing."

"Sure," answered San Juan, "but aren't you planning to go out with Sarah again on Saturday?"

"Yes, I am, but I was hoping for some company. Can you get the car? We'd pick Sarah up at 6:45, then she would show us how to get to Becky's house. Then we'll go see the movie. After the movie we could get some burgers and sodas at the grill. Here's Becky's number. You'll need to call her tomorrow night. I'll know when you make the call because Becky will call Sarah for sure, and then Sarah will call me. Will you do it?" I asked.

"Are you saying . . . a date?" San Juan was more than a little hesitant. "I don't even know her."

"Have you forgotten about our game against Kendall two weeks ago?" I asked. "Sarah brought a friend to the game, remember? That friend was Becky. She knows who you are. She has asked Sarah about you, and Sarah and I both know that Becky would be pleased to be invited by you to go to a movie. Tell her in your call that you will be doubling with Sarah and me. We'll have a great time. There's safety in numbers, San Juan. As an added benefit for me . . . since it will be your hands on the steering wheel, I will be free to hold hands with Sarah or put my arm around her while you drive. Will you do it?" I asked again.

San Juan didn't look too sure of himself, but he answered weakly, "I guess I will. Okay."

"Great!" I said. "Good decision! I'm really glad because Sarah has kind of arranged it already. She's been talking to Becky, and Becky is actually expecting a call from you tomorrow night. When you ask her if she'd like to go to a movie with you, she will definitely say, "Yes," and I think you will like her and have a great time. Be sure to call early in the evening, or she might think you are a little afraid."

"I'll do it," San Juan replied with some newfound confidence. "I'm ready. Please don't say anything to Sarah about this until she calls you tomorrow night. Then you can thank her from me for the little push."

"So, do you think you'll enjoy the bus ride home tonight, San Juan?" I asked. "With our big win tonight . . . your great shooting on the fast break .

. . Pickett's mellow music from the back of the bus . . . your thinking ahead to the movie on Saturday night . . . ?

San Juan answered only with a smile.

When I stepped out of the locker room with my duffle bag, I saw John Garris still standing near the scorer's table. I approached Garris with a J-Hawk Nation stocking cap in my hand. "Mr. Garris," I said, "it's pretty cold out there tonight. I'd like to offer you some J-Hawk protection for your ears." I handed him the black cap.

He actually grinned and put it on, pulling it down over his ears.

"Just be careful," I warned. "Wearing this may turn you into a J-Hawk fan."

He nodded thanks, and I'm thinking that was for the cap and the warning.

As he turned to walk away I asked him, "Do you have a family? It's none of my business, but I'm just curious."

He shook his head slowly. "Nope," he said. "I'm by myself just hoping to find my way."

We both snickered at his attempt at humor.

I stammered, " . . . My teammates and I . . . the town . . . we all appreciate the ink you've given us in your column this season. You've got some fans in town. At first we considered you an enemy, but it appears that you have softened a little. You have even given us a compliment or two. We've been getting some of our momentum and many of our ideas from your early-season columns. It was as if you were challenging us to prove ourselves. We decided that our team would not only accept your challenges, we would aim to go way beyond them and prove to you and others that we could not only play basketball, but that we could play better than all the rest of the teams. You've already noticed that we have implemented some of 'your ideas' with our J-Hawk Juice, the ushering squad, and our J-Hawk Nation stocking caps. We like our chances in the gym this year, and we have been having a blast with our games and all the other activities.

"To change the subject . . . have you ever had lunch downtown at The Jeffers Café? I hear they serve a great soup-and-sandwich special on week-days over the noon hour. You'll find great food, small-town atmosphere, and wonderful service. You might even have an opportunity to discuss hog prices with some local farmers. When you do visit, if you plan to be critical of our basketball team while you're in the café, you'll need to have some bodyguards with you. We definitely own home-court advantage there. Think about it. It will be worth your time.

"I hope you'll keep coming back to catch more games. We want to make this the longest season in school history, and we'd like to see you putting lots of miles on your car as you travel to our games and write your columns and your stories."

"I wish you continued luck with your season," Garris replied. "I think I might check out that lunch special this week, and thanks for the stocking cap."

Chapter 28
Taking Charge

Sarah called me on Wednesday night before I had a chance to call her. Time had gotten away from me after supper as I sat at the dining room table, reading my Shakespeare assignment and completing my proofs for geometry. Lately I had become a more serious student, and there were times I actually found doing schoolwork somewhat entertaining. It's an understatement to say that this new behavior really surprised me. That time I studied with Sarah at the Madison Lake Library had influenced me. I had seen how focused she was on her assignment, and I was impressed. It caused me to look at my attitude about schoolwork. I decided that I needed to make a change because, compared to Sarah, my effort was pretty weak, and I wanted to be worthy of Sarah. I figured a little improvement on my part wouldn't hurt my chances with her. Now I was beginning to feel some pride in my work. *I wonder if she has cast a spell on me.*

Sarah told me that Becky had called her to report that San Juan had made his call, and we were on for a double-date movie for Saturday Night. *Good for San Juan. His courage had held up.*

I told Sarah what I had said to Otto at last night's game, and I explained the story behind it. She told me that she was very impressed at how I had helped Otto and had calmed him down. "That's what good teammates do for each other," I said.

Thursday was a tough day at school. Six high school students went home because of symptoms of the flu bug, and two of them were very important members of our basketball team: Laser and Pickett. They both were absent on Friday, so we will be playing Friday night's game without them.

Ten of us formed the ushering squad on Friday night. We didn't just represent the basketball team, tonight we ten were the whole team. J-Hawk Nation showed up early to make sure they got good seats, so we were busy walking people in. I was pretty sure that all the seats would be filled for this Friday night game, unless people knew that we would be playing without our two senior captains. Then some might choose to stay away and avoid seeing "the first loss of the season." Our long winning streak had created lots of interest. Even John Garris arrived early, found his usual seat, took out his tablet, and started writing. He probably hadn't heard that we would be playing short-handed. *I wonder why he never uses our ushering service? Maybe he doesn't trust us.*

The Jenkins family arrived and waited for me in the lobby, even though San Juan and Captain Hook were standing right there.

"May I help your family find some good seats, Sir?" I asked. "I know a great location behind the J-Hawk bench."

"Yes, young man," Mr. Jenkins answered. "That would be very kind of you."

Then we all shared a good laugh. I was thinking back to that first time when Sarah and her dad mistook me for an usher.

I feel honored that they always wait for me to take them to their seats. Every time I walk them into the gym I think about that first night and how lucky I was to be standing in the perfect spot when Sarah and her dad walked in. That was such a chance meeting, and it all happened because I had forgotten my sweat socks in the car. Then Garris had made fun of us in his column, and maybe, because of his words, this had turned into the best friendship I have ever had. That amazes me . . . everything happening because of a forgotten pair of sweat socks. What if I hadn't forgotten my sweat socks in the car that night? Would I have missed out on meeting Sarah?

Every time I put on a clean pair of socks for a game I think of Sarah and that first night, and every time I put my warm-up jacket on I smile to myself, and I remember my first "ushering" experience. I still melt whenever she smiles, and holding her hand always causes my heart to beat faster and stronger. I worry that one day, someone standing near me when I am touching Sarah's hand will ask, "What is that sound? Everyone, listen! It sounds like a drum." I think Sarah controls the volume for my heart, and she turns it way up just to tease me. Maybe that's why she smiles at me so often . . .

because she realizes how much power she has over me.

I stopped ushering when the second quarter of the girls' game started, and I sat with Sarah and her parents. The bleachers were quite packed, not leaving much room for me, so I had to sit really close to Sarah. I appreciate big crowds in our gym.

We talked about our movie date for tomorrow night. Sarah told me that Becky was very excited and almost came to the game tonight, but she wondered how San Juan would have felt about that. She told me that Becky plans to make it to the next game. Sarah talked about her biology class at school, a writing project she was working on, songs her choir was preparing for her upcoming concert, band rehearsals, and questions her friends and a couple teachers had been asking her about J-Hawk basketball. Everything she said was interesting, and I listened to every word. Sarah did most of the talking tonight, and I was glad.

Sarah wanted to know about tonight's game. "Will you be running?" she asked. "Games in which you run your fast break and use your press seem to be your best games."

"You need to share your opinion with Coach," I replied. "Sometimes he slows us down, but we would rather play fast. We expect to fast break and press tonight, so hang on, and prepare for action. Also, please give me a little time to towel off after the game before you come to the bench area."

Sarah laughed and said, "I've watched how hard you play, and I've always been proud of your great effort . . . and I will give you some time to dry off after the game."

Sarah also asked about Laser and Pickett, because I had told her on the phone last night that they were ill.

"We won't have either of them tonight," I said. "This could be a very tough game. Both San Juan and Otto will start, leaving Tucson as our sixth man. None of us will get much rest tonight, but we are prepared to play hard and play well. Our starting lineup tonight is the exact same starting lineup we used just three years ago when we were all in junior high. We definitely are on the young side tonight."

I told Sarah about Coach's plan. "Otto will play a guard position with me on defense, because he and I are the best combination to run the fast break.

On offence, Otto will play center so Abe and Captain Hook can play their normal forward positions. That puts San Juan at guard with me on offence and at forward on defense, because Abe will move to defend at the center position."

I noticed Sarah's puzzled expression, and I laughed. "You don't have to understand this," I said. "I just wanted you to know about our lineup, but all you have to do is watch us and cheer when we do well."

"Don't get into foul trouble," Sarah advised, "and pace yourself so you can play the whole game."

I smiled at her and said, "I am very lucky to have you as my coach and advisor. Honestly, Sarah, I'm so glad you come to watch us play and are so interested in our team."

"I hope you understand that there is one special J-Hawk that I cheer for even more than the others," Sarah said while looking at me seriously. "You do realize that, don't you?"

"That's what some people tell me," I replied as I flashed her a smile, "and that makes me feel pretty good.

"By the way," I continued, "Coach told me at practice yesterday that I'll be our captain for the game tonight if Pickett and Laser can't play, so I guess I'm it. I'm not really surprised . . . I kind of expected it . . . I am the logical choice . . . but it hit me that I will need to be a leader, that I'll have to take more responsibility than I usually take in just playing. The first thing I told Coach was that I wanted San Juan to be a captain, too. I explained that being a captain will help San Juan feel he belongs in the lineup, and Coach agreed.

"You've already shown leadership," Sarah said. "Haven't you been the captain of the ushering squad?"

I had to laugh at that. I figured she was just teasing me.

"Next year I'll be sure to include that information on my college applications," I replied. "May I list you as a reference?"

Now I had her laughing, and I loved it. Whenever I am with her I feel like I am important. That's what she does to me. I think I walk taller, and I know I smile more. I might even feel smarter, and I do try to behave myself. Her innocence and playfulness make a huge difference in how I feel.

As I got up to walk to the locker room I almost felt the same as I do when I say goodnight at her house after a date. I didn't want to leave, but I did have a game to play, and if the captain doesn't show up on time it doesn't show much responsibility or leadership.

Before we headed out to the floor to warm up, Coach had a few things he wanted to tell us. "We are in a tough position tonight, playing without our senior leaders. I don't believe anyone except the J-Hawk Nation faithful will expect us to win this game because Morgan will run at us with ten players. We've got an excuse . . . we're short-handed because of the flu bug. Is there anyone here who thinks we should use that excuse?" he asked.

"No, Coach!" we all replied.

"Winners don't need excuses, Coach," I added. "We're going to beat these guys because we are better than they are, and we don't know how to lose. Coach, do you want me to go out and explain to the Mustangs that they can only play five guys at a time?"

Coach looked at me and started laughing. My teammates joined in.

"I can tell you are fired up tonight, Catcher," Coach replied. "We'll follow your lead out there."

"One more thing, Coach," I said. "I've really grown to like that zero in our loss column. I think we should keep it."

"We are . . . J-Hawks!" everyone shouted as we exited the locker room.

Abe and Tucson handled the duties at the microphone tonight, singling out the business owners of Jeffers for honors, thanking them for their great support for both of our basketball teams this season. As Abe named some of the stores, my mind took some short side-trips as memories surfaced. He listed the people who ran the three gas stations on Main Street, the Farmers Savings Bank, and the barber shop with its huge glass windows in front, so everyone who walked by could see who was sitting in the chair, being clipped. When he mentioned the lumberyard, I thought back to Otto and the Halloween post. Abe thanked my uncle who owned the hardware store, and I remembered all the Saturday baseball games and football games I watched on the TV that attracted customers into his store. Next was the pool hall where my dad shot pool with his friends, and I sat in a chair along the wall and watched and waited for countless hours.

Tucson thanked Bob and his family at The Jeffers Café, and I could see, plain as day, members of J-Hawk Nation sitting for hours on the stools at the counter, drinking coffee and discussing basketball. Next was the butcher shop and meat locker, and I thought about the narrow brick ledge around the building where Tucson, Abe, and I, and many other young kids, would test our skills as we clung to the bricks and saw how far we could walk on the ledge before falling four feet to the ground.

Abe thanked his family at the grocery store, where many times I had picked up things for Grandma and had asked them to please write it on her account. He listed the egg and chicken business, and I laughed to myself as I tried to figure out which came first.

Tucson received big applause from young kids when he mentioned the dry goods store, every kid's favorite because of the "penny candy." Then there were the three shops where engines of all sizes were repaired, including the two places where I often took my grandma's lawn mower when I couldn't get it started.

Next Abe listed the tavern that I'd never set foot in, the beauty salon, the grain elevator where our burlap bags full of oats were ground into chicken feed, and the creamery where butter was made with the cream from our dairy cows. He thanked the drug store, where many kids had read comic books without buying them, and where we would sit on the stools at the soda fountain if we had a nickel to spend.

Tucson ended with thanks for the post office, the flooring store, the watch-repair shop, the Legion, and even the library and the fire department. It was a great tribute to the entire Jeffers' business community.

Everyone applauded loudly.

The announcements about J-Hawk Juice after the game and tomorrow's clinic drew additional applause, especially from the kids.

I motioned to San Juan, and he and I took a couple steps out onto the floor to shake hands with Abe and Tucson when they arrived back to the bench. Several others patted them on the back, and we all told them that they had done a great job.

We had just two or three minutes before the game would begin.

"Well, guys, here we go," Coach said. "Play smart."

"May I say something, Coach?" I asked.

"Go ahead," Coach replied.

"During warm-ups I noticed that the Mustangs were yucking it up when they saw that Laser and Pickett were not with our team tonight. That really upset me. You don't do that to other teams, and you definitely don't come into our gym and treat us like that.

"I decided to look at their team to see who they didn't have available to play for them tonight," I continued. "Here's what I observed. They don't have the tall, mean and lean Abe with the long wingspan . . . owner of a really sweet soft shot and a hard slam. He's with us, and San Juan has big plans for Abe tonight because the tallest Mustang standing next to Abe looks like a pony. They don't have Captain Hook either. Have you looked into Hook's eyes tonight? I'd hate to be the guy who has to guard him and fight against him to try score and rebound, but that's okay, because Hook is a J-Hawk, and he is playing with us tonight. Watch out! I figure at least one Mustang will have his nose bloodied in this game.

"I didn't see the kid who can play anywhere, Otto, shooting on their end either. He'll be scoring fast-break baskets and hitting jump shots for us . . . and he can run forever. The Mustangs don't have San Juan either, and tonight is his 'coming out party.' They may not know him well yet, but they'll wish they had never met him by the time the game has ended.

"And don't forget about our good bench players. You guys work so hard in practice, pushing all of us to improve, and the Mustangs don't have any of you guys on their team tonight.

"You are all J-Hawks! Our five will outplay any five that the Mustangs dare put on the floor tonight."

"Hey, Catcher, you forgot someone," San Juan said. "They don't have you. One-by-one they'll be tiring and dropping out, and at the end of the game I bet you'll still run to the bench, big smile on your ugly mug, sweat dripping from everywhere, and you'll have another victory in your hands. Like Coach said, we'll follow you tonight."

I nodded to him. "Are we ready?"

Everyone nodded once, and we all shouted, "We are . . . J-Hawks!" and the volume almost knocked me over.

As we prepared for the opening tip, people who had arrived late were searching to find a place to stand on the stage at the side of the bleachers or on the steps leading from the lobby. The gym was absolutely packed.

Abe's job was to tap the ball to either Hook or Otto, but if the Mustangs covered each with two players, then Abe would send the ball back toward San Juan or me. Tonight the ball was directed to San Juan, who took a few dribbles, then passed to me. I found Hook on the right sideline. He faked a drive toward the basket, pivoted, and bounced the ball back to me. I passed quickly to Otto in the lane. He fired the ball back outside to San Juan. He held the ball for a couple seconds, then lobbed a high pass to Abe who reached up by the rim, caught the ball, and dropped it through the hoop.

We were off to a good start. All of us had been involved already, and we had scored on our first shot. Now we would quicken the pace.

We dropped back near half-court to trap. Otto and I doubled on the dribbler, keeping our hands moving, while Hook and Abe covered the area behind us, ready to pick off passes. San Juan defended the lane.

Because of our pressure, Number 12 tried a long pass down court, but the pass did not clear Abe's outstretched arms. After snatching the ball out of the air, Abe passed to Otto, and Otto tossed the ball to me. Because two defenders blocked my path to the basket, I slowed down and waited for the big guys to arrive on our end. San Juan and I passed to each other a couple of times, then San Juan threw another pass toward the rim when he saw Abe break toward the basket. This time Abe was fouled as he scored, and his free throw was good. We had jumped out to a five-point lead, and our confidence was growing.

"Way to take charge out there!" I shouted to San Juan and Abe.

Since we had scored both times, the Mustangs couldn't get their running game going. We moved back to half-court, but this time Number 20 was able to dribble into his own end, and the Mustangs passed the ball around while we kept shifting positions and defending with our arms raised. Number 32 was open for a split second, and he launched a jump shot from just beyond the key. The ball hit the back of the rim and bounced up and out toward Abe who had blocked out his man in the lane. Abe leaped high and grabbed the ball. After securing it and making a quick pivot, he threw the ball to Otto near the left sideline. After two dribbles Otto led me with a pass that sent me to the hoop for a right-handed layup, and our lead reached seven.

The Mustang coach called for a timeout, and J-Hawk Nation stood and applauded.

"That's a good way to start this game," Coach said to us in our huddle. "Those were great passes, San Juan. Keep looking to Abe, but I think the Mustang game plan will change now. I expect them to double-cover Abe, front and back, so Otto and Hook will become better options now. Catcher, work it in to these guys. Otto, you have a couple good choices. Either pass to Hook as he moves to the basket, or take the shot if it's there. Hook, same for you. Look for Otto, or take your shot. When they start sagging back, Catcher, heat up that jump shot. When we start hitting, they'll leave Abe alone, and then we'll go back to him with the high pass. This game is going to be fun as long as we can figure out how to stay a step ahead of them. The Mustangs will discover we have several ways to score, and when they take one away, we have to be smart enough to take advantage of the others. We're going to save some energy for a short time by not trapping at half-court. Drop back. I'll give you a signal, Catch, when I want you guys to start the trap again. Keep it up out there, and let me know when you need a breather. Tucson is getting restless. Let's go!"

"We are . . . J-Hawks!"

During the remainder of the first quarter both teams ran hard, and some easy baskets were scored. Coach rotated Tucson with Otto and San Juan so they could get a couple minutes to catch their breath, and we continued to maintain our lead. At the end of the quarter we led by a score of 18-13.

In the second quarter Captain Hook got hot and scored on three short hooks, only one of which bloodied a nose. When the Mustangs overplayed him, San Juan found Abe at the rim again for another short bank shot, and Otto scored twice on jump shots from near the foul line. We had a good variety going, and we kept the Mustangs off balance on defense, but we had trouble stopping their offence. They began to substitute often, and they kept running, making us work hard on defense. I scored on a ten-foot jump shot just before the quarter ended when I pulled up on a fast break, and we trotted off to the locker room leading by eight. We were pleased with our effort, but we knew that we were working really hard. I wondered if we could keep this up.

Coach told us in the locker room at half-time that he would spread out our timeouts in the second half so we could get a short breather once in a while. "I'll get Abe and Hook a short rest once or twice in this half, but, Catcher, I'll need you to stay out there to lead us. Let me know if you need a break, but I may choose to ignore your request," Coach said as he looked in my direction.

"May I say something, Coach?" I asked.

"Captains always gets a chance to speak," Coach answered. "Go ahead."

"If I were the Mustangs, I would be expecting us to wear out tonight," I said, "but it's not going to happen. Let's not give them even a glimmer of hope. When a timeout is called we all need to run to the bench. When we leave the locker room, we run out together. Show them that we can run all night. They are probably waiting for their chance to pick up the pace when we tire, but that won't be until the final buzzer sounds. The longer we run, the more demoralized they will become. I'm very proud of the way you guys have played tonight. You are unbelievable! I think our team is even better than it was in junior high. Let's win this game for our seniors, and show everyone that J-Hawks will rise to any challenge. Thanks, Coach."

"We are . . . J-Hawks!" everyone shouted, and we ran out to the court for a short warm-up.

The third quarter was wild. We broke out fast every time we collected a defensive rebound, and the Mustangs also ran at every opportunity. We realized that the best way to slow them down was to hit our shots, and when we couldn't take it all the way to the hoop on a fast break, we slowed it down and passed the ball around while we caught our breath, and we worked the ball inside to Otto, Abe, and Hook. I could see that it bugged the Mustangs when we slowed the pace down. Both teams preferred to run, but tonight it was better for us to rest occasionally when we had the ball, so we put Abe near the basket and Hook at the high post. I set up at the top of the key, and Otto and San Juan played the wings on my left and right. Whenever the Mustangs used two players to cover Abe, we knew we could play "keep away" out front because they could not cover four of us with three players. We were careful with our passes, but we were quick so the Mustangs always had to keep moving, and we turned their defenders into "chasers." Whenever they brought a fourth defender out to us, we threw Abe a high pass near the rim, and he usually was able to convert his shot into two more points for us. Coach had certainly figured the Mustangs out, and he made all the right moves.

At the end of the third quarter we held on to a 51-47 lead.

As I reached the bench for our short break, I took a quick glance at Sarah. She smiled and nodded to me. I read her lips. "You can do it!"

I nodded back to her.

We drank water and talked strategy. Coach said, "Catcher and Otto, run our break every time, but don't expect the big guys to run with you. Take it all the way in whenever possible, but if you can't get a layup, pull it back outside and wait for your friends instead of shooting a jump shot without having rebounders in place. Then make lots of quick passes until you can get a good shot from in close. You have played a great game, adjusting to their defensive changes. J-Hawk Nation has watched you play courageously tonight, and I sense they'd like to see one more quarter that matches the other three. Play hard . . . have fun! Let's go!"

"This is the quarter where we show character," I added.

"We are . . . J-Hawks!" we all shouted.

We ran onto the floor to begin the final quarter.

Abe won the tip against his much shorter opponent, sending it toward the long arms of Captain Hook. He handed the ball to me, and I dribbled deliberately to our end. I bounced a pass to Otto who was standing near the free-throw line. Otto threw the ball to San Juan who surprised everyone and faked a high pass to Abe. Three Mustangs immediately surrounded Abe, leaving only two players to cover four of us as we passed the basketball out front. After several passes San Juan again faked a pass toward Abe, and the Mustangs again responded by surrounding Abe near the basket. It was almost comical, and it ate some more time off the clock.

As the defenders moved to cover the rest of us again, I passed to Hook at the high post. He pump-faked, drawing his defender off his feet, then drove to the basket for a layup.

"Great play, Captain Hook!" I shouted as we move back down the floor.

Our lead was now six, and we had burned another minute off the clock.

Mustang player Number 42 dribbled toward the half-line and passed through our trap to Number 50. He held the ball briefly, pivoted toward the basket, and dropped the ball back to Number 42 on the right side. After looking to his left, he put the ball on the floor and dribbled to the basket at top speed, crashing into Captain Hook right before laying the ball off the backboard into the basket.

The ref blew his whistle sharply and called out toward the scorers' bench while displaying the number with his fingers, "Number 42 . . . charging . . . no basket."

Otto assisted Hook to his feet, and we all ran to the other end of the floor for Hook's one-and-one. After making the first shot, Hook got the bonus, and he swished that one also.

"Way to take the charge!" I said to Hook. "That was worth four points. Great job taking one for the team!"

In the next three minutes each team scored twice and each missed on a couple shots, so the lead stood at eight with four minutes left in the game.

As I dribbled the ball toward our basket, Coach called for a timeout. "All right, guys," he said, "drink some water, catch your breath, and listen up. I think we'll need six more points to pull this game out. I've got four of the points figured out. San Juan, you have made several great passes to Abe tonight, and you have fooled the Mustangs with all those fake passes. Outstanding work! I need you to make three more plays. I've watched the defenders become very frustrated as they hustled to sandwich Abe, only to find out you had just faked them out again. They are almost getting angry. They think you are toying with them. I want you to fake that pass two more times. I think they'll be slower and slower with their defensive shift and more upset each time when they see it's just another fake, and they wasted energy again. That will work for us, because on the third play you need to throw that pass to Abe at the rim. That one will fake them out. I think they'll hang back, expecting that it is just another attempt to fool them, and they won't cover him very well, and Abe will catch your pass and drop it into the cylinder for two more points."

Coach continued, "On our next possession after you score, Abe, I want you to move quickly to the outside and look for a pass from Catcher. They'll probably send two guys to cover you, so I think Hook can spin around his guy at the high post and find a clear path to the basket, receive a lob from Catcher, and make a layup. That's four points worth. I'll call our last timeout with a minute or two left to play. Keep moving your feet on defense, and raise those arms. I know you should be getting tired, but you still look fresh to me. Let's go get 'em!"

"We are . . . J-Hawks!"

We didn't follow Coach's plan exactly. San Juan didn't throw the ball on the third attempt because he saw two defenders move early, so he ended up faking the pass for a third straight time. It was a good decision. I began to see the anger in the faces of the Mustangs. San Juan passed to me . . . I threw the ball to Hook, and he passed to Otto on my right . . . Otto bounced it back to me . . . I shoveled it off to San Juan. San Juan looked at me, and without even glancing in Abe's direction, tossed a perfect pass to the rim. Abe caught the ball and dropped it into the bucket without a single defender there trying to stop him. San Juan had fooled them again. The Mustangs were caught flat-footed.

"Wow, San Juan, that was pretty, but don't you try driving without looking tomorrow night," I said as we moved into defensive positions.

He looked at me with a huge grin on his face.

Number 32 brought the ball down-court quickly, shot a jumper from the right side, and scored off the backboard. The lead was again down to eight. *We've got to slow them down a little. That was way too easy for them.*

San Juan and I traded passes as we moved into our end. I set up at the top with the basketball. I slapped the ball once, and Abe sprinted to the outside. I looked directly at Abe, but I saw Hook spin toward the basket out of the corner of my eye. Then I lobbed the ball just over his head, and Hook caught it, stepped once, and laid the ball against the backboard for two points.

"Nice move, Hook! Great pass, Catcher!" Otto shouted.

"Pick 'em up!" I shouted to my teammates, and we trapped at half-court. This slowed them down and burned off more time. The Mustangs started scrambling, running around instead of setting up for shots. They made several passes as we covered closely, and eventually a player took a shot from outside. The ball hit the front of the rim and dropped into Abe's outstretched arms as he leaped high. He fired the ball to Otto on the outside, and I moved toward the center and received Otto's pass. I took three dribbles toward the basket, then turned back to the outside because I didn't think I could beat the two defenders to the hoop. I kept my dribble alive as I waited for my teammates.

The clock was winding down to the last two minutes. Hook stepped out in my direction, and I threw him the ball. He returned it, and I fired it off to Otto. The three of us on the right side passed quickly. Otto . . . to Hook . . . back to Otto . . . to me. Hook turned and headed for the rim, and Otto circled around to the left side. Their defenders went with them. I looked left and prepared to pass to San Juan, but when my man slid over to try to pick off my pass, I dribbled around to the right and found myself open from fifteen feet out. I jumped up, lifted the ball above and to the front of my head, and directed my shot toward the rim. It dropped through the center of the net, and our lead was built to twelve.

"Beautiful!" Abe shouted.

Again we trapped near mid-court, and the second hand continued to circle the face on the clock as the Mustangs began to panic, realizing the game was slipping out of their reach. After a few passes, Number 33 thought he was within his shooting range, and he went up for a shot that Hook reached with his long right arm and slammed toward the bleachers. "Wow! Head for cover!" San Juan yelled.

We were all wound up, playing on adrenaline.

Only about thirty seconds remained, and we were playing our toughest defense of the night. J-Hawk Nation fans stood and started applauding, and I rallied my teammates to try to stop the Mustangs from making even one more bucket.

"Hands up!" I called out. "No more shots! Shut them down!"

The volume in the gym rose to a high level.

"Stay with them!" I said, "Man on man!"

All five of us matched up with a Mustang and stuck like glue as the red-faced clock, in its final moments, wound down to about ten seconds. We shut down their passes, and I could see the life drain out of their bodies. Only five seconds now remained, and they didn't even attempt a last shot. They were done. The buzzer sounded, and we trotted to the bench, having earned a great short-handed victory, and J-Hawk Nation continued their loud applause.

I grabbed a towel and tried to dry off before I would join my teammates to shake hands with the players from Morgan. I saw that no one was lining up.

"What's up?" I asked.

They all stood there looking at me.

"Like I said earlier, we'll follow you," San Juan replied.

I looked at each player and nodded. Then I led them through the line. As we returned to our bench, fans remained standing and applauding.

Coach said, "Okay, guys, they are calling for you. Take a couple steps out, and wave to the crowd."

We all hesitated.

"Catcher . . . San Juan . . . take your iron-men . . . step out and wave! It's what they are waiting for . . . and the noise is hurting my ears. Get out there," Coach encouraged.

We stepped out and acknowledged the crowd by waving. I could feel my eyes begin to mist up. As I turned back toward the bench, I looked at Sarah and her parents, and I saw Sarah and her mother dry their eyes. That was it for me. I smiled at them and used my towel to wipe my face.

I've never seen or felt anything like this. J-Hawk Nation must have really appreciated our effort tonight, and I have nothing left.

Sarah didn't give me much time before she stepped down from the bleachers. I was relieved when I saw her walk first to Abe and Hook. Then she talked to Otto, San Juan, and Tucson while I dried off some more and put on my warm-up jacket.

Several people came by and told me I had played well. I thanked them as I looked through the crowd for Sarah. I turned my head, and there she was, just standing right there, watching me, and waiting quietly. I smiled to her, wiped my face one last time, and tossed my towel onto the bench. Sarah returned my smile and walked toward me.

"You were fantastic, Catcher!" she said to me.

"That's my second 'fantastic' in-a-row!" I said. "I should tell Nicholson."

We both laughed, and I reached for her hand.

"Wasn't that something the way the crowd responded at the end of the game?" I said. "It blew me away."

"It gave me goose-bumps," Sarah replied.

"I saw that in your eyes," I said tenderly. "Let's walk the floor a little. I need to cool down, and I need to drink some more water."

While we wandered in a circle on the gym floor I received a few back slaps and some more congratulations, but I wasn't paying much attention to any of the people. My focus was on Sarah, and I remained quiet as we walked. I was too tired to say much. I don't know how long we walked, but after a while I headed to the locker room for a shower, leaving Sarah in the crowded gym. I would see her in the lunchroom soon.

Coach was brief in the locker room. "You played inspired ball tonight. I am very proud of the way you faced the challenge. This game showed your character, and you certainly fired up J-Hawk Nation. Great job! Maybe we'll have Catch give another speech before the next game."

Everyone clapped and laughed.

"Rest your legs over the weekend, and I'll see you on Monday. Hopefully we'll have everyone back for the next game., but if we don't, just like to-night, we'll manage. Hey, Catch . . . I like that zero, too."

I headed right to the lunchroom after I showered. Sarah was sitting at a table with her parents and some friends when I walked in.

"Who did you see tonight?" I asked Sarah as I sat down next to her and began drinking my first of two cartons of J-Hawk Juice.

"I talked with Jenny. She looks really good, and her hair is starting to grow back," Sarah said. "She told me she looks for me at every game and that she's glad that you and I have become good friends."

"Me too," I said. "I see Jenny often in school, and she has said the same thing to me. I'm glad she's getting better."

"Susan ran up to me, almost knocked me over, and we walked in the gym, holding hands, for a couple minutes," Sarah continued. "She said she really likes her house, especially her name in her bedroom and the paintings of the J-Hawk Nation stocking cap and the old car behind the cabinet doors."

"I really like those paintings, too," I said. "I'm a good friend of the artist. Sometimes we hold hands."

Sarah could probably tell I was in a silly mood and really tired. She shook her head and smiled at me. "John Garris had a couple questions for me, so I talked with him for a short time," Sarah added. "Then both Coach and Hook's dad told me that they were glad that my parents and I keep coming to the games. I talked with your mom and Abe's mom. I saw quite a few people."

"You are getting to be pretty popular around here," I said.

"Several kids and grownups told me that you had played a **great** game tonight. I wonder why they told **me** this? Do you think they know about us?" Sarah asked as she smiled that beautiful smile.

"I hope they have figured it out. I think I make it pretty obvious," I replied.

I saw San Juan walk in. "San Juan, sit here with us for a minute," I said. "I need to tell you what I was thinking about at the end of the game."

"I'll grab a carton of J-Hawk Juice and be right there," he replied.

"First of all," I said, "You played an outstanding game tonight. Your passes and your fakes made a huge difference."

"Thanks," he replied.

"I want to tell you about something that happened late in the game. I couldn't get it out of my head," I began. "Some teacher had read us this story a few years back. Every time you faked that pass to Abe, and the Mustangs rushed to cover him . . . I thought about that book, *The Boy Who Cried Wolf*. Every time the boy shouted out that a wolf was threatening the sheep, and it was a false alarm, the townspeople became very angry. Every time the Mustangs quickly moved to cover Abe and found out that it was another faked pass, they became more and more upset. Nobody liked being fooled and being made to look foolish, but that boy . . . and you . . . kept at it. Eventually, when the townspeople heard the cry again, they ignored it because they did not believe it was a serious cry for help, and the wolf killed all the sheep. Tonight, at the end of the game, after being fooled by you many times, the Mustangs saw you preparing to pass to Abe, and they ignored it because they believed that you were going to fake them out again, and they did not cover Abe, and your perfect pass earned us two points. You had cried 'wolf' so often that they didn't believe you any more. They didn't think you would throw the ball, so you were really able to fake them out that last time.

I continued, "I wanted you to yell '**WOLF**' every time you faked the pass to Abe. That's what kept going on in my head. It was driving me crazy that the Mustangs didn't know the story. I almost felt sorry for them. I thought about calling a timeout and explaining everything to them."

"Wow, Catch!" Sarah said. "You played too long and too hard tonight. I hope you don't fall asleep during the movie tomorrow night, then wake up and cry '**WOLF**.' You'll empty the theater, at least the first couple of times."

San Juan and I really laughed at what Sarah had said. *Maybe I had played too hard tonight.*

"Becky almost came with me tonight," Sarah said to San Juan. "She should have been here. She missed seeing you play a great game! I know she's excited about our movie night."

"I'm looking forward to the movie, too, though I'm a little nervous," San Juan replied. "I'm glad we're doubling."

"Sarah, are you ready?" her dad asked. "Let me rephrase that. Sarah, we really should be heading home now. I've got to get up early tomorrow for my Saturday coffee at The Jeffers Café, you know. Catcher, you guys played exciting basketball tonight. I think all the J-Hawk fans are worn out from watching how hard you played. We'll all sleep well tonight, especially you."

"Will I see you tomorrow morning, Sarah?" I asked.

"Yes, I'll be there," she replied. "Dad always wants company on his drive to and from coffee, so I'll be a good daughter and ride along."

Sarah and I both laughed.

"Good night, Jenkins family," I said.

After taking just a couple steps toward the door, Sarah turned around and smiled at me. "Great game, Captain," she said, and then she saluted.

I smiled back and gazed into her sparkling eyes until she turned around again and walked away with her parents.

I had played well. I felt good about that . . . and Sarah's playful salute and beautiful smile . . . that's the picture that I want to freeze in my mind until I see her again tomorrow morning.

In the Stands – With John Garris

Last night the Jeffers J-Hawks may have faced their toughest adversary of the season, and they still came away with a hard-fought victory. A flu virus had struck at Jeffers High late this week, and it claimed the two senior captains among its victims, making them unavailable for the Friday night home game with Morgan. Because Laser and Pickett were resting at home in their sickbeds, the J-Hawks found themselves short-handed against the Mustangs.

As I observed the warm-ups, I noticed that neither senior captain was on the floor, and I almost left the gym before the game started. So far this season I've watched the J-Hawks put together an impressive winning streak, and I was not prepared to see the streak broken because of the absence of two key players.

I gathered my courage and stayed, however, and I'm glad I did. I'm eating some "crow" here, but I saw great character on display last night. I was impressed by the play of sophomores who played like upperclassmen, and I watched as a young inexperienced coach devised great strategies for a short-handed squad of J-Hawks and urged them on to victory.

The J-Hawks used an ironman lineup, giving four starters very limited rest by rotating the sixth man, but leaving Catcher and his leadership on the floor for the duration of the game. Though young, this lineup looked very capable. The two juniors and three sophomores played like veterans . . . and this shouldn't surprise us. According to a reliable source, last night's starting lineup was exactly the same as the lineup that the **junior high team** had put on the floor only three years ago.

Both teams scored often on fast-break baskets, but the J-Hawks also took advantage of their height, working the ball inside to the tall sophomores for some easy scores. On defense they trapped the Mustangs at mid-court, forcing many bad passes as well as a few violations. Both teams played well, but the J-Hawks played with such great determination, never allowing the Mustangs to gain the lead, and the Jeffers boys held on at the end and sprinted off the court with another victory when the final buzzer sounded.

The J-Hawk winning streak has now stretched to fourteen games with this improbable short-handed upset over the Mustangs and the flu bug.

Chapter 29

Double Date

San Juan drove out to the farm to pick me up at about 6:15 for our Saturday night double date. When I jumped into the front seat of his family's blue and white Ford, I noticed we were dressed like twins. We both were wearing black pants, our Jeffers letter jackets . . . black wool body with white leather sleeves, and black J-Hawk Nation stocking caps. We both thought we looked pretty sharp.

San Juan and I were really proud of our letter jackets with the big gold "J" attached on the left side, chest high. On our left sleeve, at the top, were sewn the gold numerals six and three to indicate that we would graduate in '63. Our jackets were identical except that "San Juan" was stitched in white script across the chest on the right side of his jacket, and mine said "Catcher."

It bothered him, as it did me, that we would graduate from Madison Lake High School, not Jeffers, and next year it would not be acceptable for us to wear our Jeffers jackets to our new school. That's why it had been important that all players were awarded their basketball letters early for this season . . . by Christmas. This meant Otto, and four "Sons" became first time lettermen at Jeffers. Four others, Abe, Captain Hook, San Juan, and Tucson had previously lettered in baseball, but this was their first award in basketball. Now all twelve of us have jackets and are able to wear them for the remainder of our basketball season and the rest of the winter. I'm very thankful that the Supe listened to Laser, Pickett, and me when we delivered our proposal to him in private. His decision to present the newly earned basketball letters right after the home game on December 22nd in a special ceremony was perfect.

As San Juan and I drove to Madison Lake to pick up Sarah and Becky, we mostly talked about last night's game against Morgan. We had worked hard because of missing both seniors. Our teamwork had really stood out, and so had the Mustangs' individual play. We both concluded that they had two or three good players, but they didn't help each other much.

"I'm so glad I'm a J-Hawk," I said. "We know how to play together, and that has made our season so successful and so much fun."

"I totally agree," San Juan added. "Our team is solid. Everything we have done with the clinics, J-Hawk Juice, stocking caps, Christmas for the Cades . . . all that stuff has brought us together."

When we arrived at Sarah's house San Juan parked at the curb, and I hopped out of the car. "Come on," I said. "Walk up to the door with me. Sarah's parents have adopted our whole team. They'll want to see you."

San Juan saw that I was right. Mr. Jenkins answered the door and invited us in, as Sarah and her mom entered from the kitchen. "Good evening, Catcher . . . San Juan. Great game last night." He extended his hand to us. "It's good to see you both. Sarah tells me that her friend, Becky, is joining you for a movie tonight. I hope you have a really good time."

San Juan and I both nodded thanks, but we didn't say anything.

Mrs. Jenkins added, "Your team played really hard last night, and neither of you got much rest. If I'm counting correctly that's fourteen straight wins. I've enjoyed watching your games tremendously, and I'm always looking forward to the next one. It's also been fun having a special connection to your team and your community through you, Catcher."

I smiled again and said, "Thanks. I've really enjoyed everything, too."

"It's good to see you here tonight, San Juan," Mrs. Jenkins continued. "I've known Becky for a long time, and I expect you will find her to be a lot of fun."

"Mom, Dad . . . we need to get going. Becky's expecting us in a couple of minutes," Sarah said.

"Of course," Mrs. Jenkins replied.

Sarah received hugs from both her parents.

"Have a fun time everyone. Enjoy your 'Western,'" Mr. Jenkins said as we started out the door. "And, Catcher . . . not too late tonight."

"No, Sir," I replied. "Does 11:30 sound all right?"

"The early side of 11:30 would be fine," Mr. Jenkins answered. "Drive safely, and enjoy the movie."

As we stepped into the cold air I said to Sarah, "You look really great again tonight. I especially like your beautiful smile and your special stocking cap."

"Why thank you," Sarah replied as she stopped to curtsey.

As we walked swiftly to the car, I asked San Juan, "Is there room for all three of us in the front seat? As navigator, Sarah should sit up there, and as co-pilot, I should really ride shotgun."

"Sure," San Juan replied. He wasn't very talkative right now.

After we were all seated and the engine was started, I added, "When we pick up Becky . . . she can just sit in the back."

I was hoping to get a reaction from San Juan. Sarah nudged me in the ribs with her elbow and smiled, but San Juan said nothing.

"I have a suggestion for tonight," I offered. "All three of us are wearing J-Hawk Nation stocking caps, and I don't want Becky to feel left out. I brought an extra cap along tonight, and I think we should give it to Becky if she would like to wear it. Sarah could say it's from her, or it could be from all three of us, or it could be from you, San Juan. What do you think?"

San Juan didn't wait long. He asked me, "Did Sarah get her cap from you?"

"Yes," I replied. "I gave it to her as a Christmas gift."

"Then Becky should get her cap from me," San Juan stated. "I'll offer it to her, and I'll pay you for it later."

"Good choice," I said, and Sarah nodded in agreement.

Because of Sarah's good guidance it only took a couple minutes to drive to Becky's house. As San Juan got out, I opened my door, stepped out, and assisted Sarah. Instead of opening a door to the back seat, I turned to Sarah and said, "Let's walk up to the door with San Juan. That way we can be there to tackle Becky if she turns to run away."

I don't think San Juan appreciated my comment or gained any confidence from it, but I was feeling funny tonight.

Sarah frowned and scolded me, "Becky won't be running away, Catcher! San Juan, don't pay any attention to him."

"I really do think we should walk with San Juan to the door, though. Seeing you, Sarah, will put an immediate smile on Becky's face, and I want to see what Becky does when San Juan offers her the cap. I missed seeing your reaction when you opened my gift. Seeing what Becky does might have to be the next best thing," I said.

Sarah quickly called to San Juan who was halfway to the house, "Are you okay if we join you at the door?"

"Sure," San Juan replied as he slowed down. "I appreciate the company, but, Catcher, . . . no more jokes."

Becky answered the doorbell, and her parents walked into the entryway to meet and greet the three of us. I thought they appeared to be very nice people. Becky's dad said to San Juan and me, "I'm going to have to attend your next game. I've been hearing and reading a lot about your team. Congratulations on your season so far."

"Thank you," we both said.

Becky's mom hugged Sarah, and then said to all of us, "You have a good time at the movie."

Becky said good-bye to her parents and added, "Don't wait up for me."

"Right," her dad replied with a laugh.

As Becky's parents walked away, San Juan held out the J-Hawk Nation stocking cap and said, "Becky, I would be honored if you would accept this cap and wear it tonight because it's part of the official uniform for our movie double date."

I was shocked and really impressed with what San Juan had said. I looked at Sarah and read her expression to mean the same.

It was great to see Becky's big smile as she accepted the cap, walked over to the big wall mirror, carefully put it on, and pulled it down over her hair and ears. Then she called out, "Mom, please come in here a minute."

Her mom returned, noticed Becky's cap and big smile, and said, "You are looking good, Honey! All of you are! Here's to J-Hawk Nation!" Then she clapped for us. She gave her daughter another hug.

As we headed back to the car, I said to Sarah, "Now that was worth seeing! What did you do or say when you received the cap from me, Sarah? Were you surprised? . . . excited? Will you please tell me? I really need to know. How about at the end of the evening when we get back to your house, you re-enact the Christmas morning event when you opened my gift? I would be extremely grateful to you, Sarah."

"You are quite the funny guy tonight, Catcher. I will think about it during the movie, but I know my answer will be 'yes.' I will re enact the scene for you. We will end the evening with drama," she said, and then she laughed dramatically.

I felt so lucky to have Sarah as a special friend. I loved her smile and her laughter, and she was so good at making me laugh and feel good about myself. I just liked being around her. I knew this would be a wonderful night because Sarah had really captured my heart.

The movie was filled with action, but the actors were not great, only decent. I expected I would see a better performance at the end of the evening.

We walked one block east to get to The Grill. This seemed to be the place to hang out if you were in junior high or high school. The four of us sat in a booth away from the huge frosty windows. After we waited a few minutes, a waitress took our order: hamburgers, sodas, and one order of fries that we would share.

As we sat talking about the movie, several kids came over to greet Sarah and Becky. Many had also been to the movie, but some were at The Grill just to hang out. One girl who knew Sarah well asked her, "Who are your friends?"

"This is Catcher, . . . and this is San Juan," replied Sarah as she introduced each of us. They are both basketball players on Jeffers' undefeated team."

Leave it to Sarah to mention we were undefeated. She is really proud to be a part of J-Hawk Nation.

"Are these your real names?" the curious girl asked.

"These are our real nicknames," I answered, "and it's part of a long story which I don't have time to tell tonight."

"Another friend asked, "Where did you get the J-Hawk Nation stocking caps?"

"San Juan and I had to buy ours at school," I said, "but these lucky girls knew someone on our team that gave them the caps as gifts." Out of the corner of my eye I saw Becky and Sarah smile to each other.

A couple guys with Madison Lake letter jackets came over to talk basketball. "Are you still undefeated?" One guy asked.

"Yeah," I answered. "We've been lucky a couple times, but we've won them all.

"Next year you'll join us," said the other kid. "That should make our team a lot stronger because we'll have several good players."

"We're going to have to finish this season first," I replied, trying not to sound snobby.

"Before we look at next year we want to make some history at Jeffers this year," San Juan added.

I'm glad he said something to back me up. Our "friends" in the booth appeared to appreciate our comments. All four of us are members of J-Hawk Nation, so we stick together.

"It was good to talk with you guys," said the first kid. "Good luck with the rest of your season."

"Thanks," San Juan and I replied. I thought I heard Sarah say "Thanks," too.

I turned to my three friends and said, "I have a riddle for you. See if you can get this. How was the 'cowboy movie' we just saw like the basketball game we played last night?"

"There was a lot of shooting!" Sarah answered quickly.

I laughed spontaneously. "Good one, Sarah, but that's not it," I said.

"The cowboys and the basketball players all worked really hard!" San Juan offered.

"True," I replied, "but that answer is so lame, San Juan."

We all laughed.

"I wasn't at the game so this is just a guess," Becky said. "The horses and the players all ran really fast."

"Another true response, also a little weak, . . . but a lot better than San Juan's," I said dramatically to more laughter.

"Do you give up?" I asked.

"We give," answered Sarah. "Tell us."

I started drumming on the table . . . then stopped and said, "The good guys won!"

The three of them sat in silence for a couple moments.

"Come on! That's a great answer!" I protested.

Sarah looked at me and admitted, "That's true. It is good, but I like my answer, too."

I grabbed a spoon from the table and spoke into it like it was a microphone. "Ladies and gentlemen!" I said in my best imitation of an announcer's voice. "The judges have made a ruling on my riddle, and I accept their decision. To honor my very special friend, Sarah Jenkins, the pride of J-Hawk Nation, the new and correct answer to my riddle . . . 'How was the cowboy movie we saw tonight similar to the basketball game we played last night?' . . . will be, from this night forward . . . 'There was a lot of shooting, and the good guys won.'"

Sarah laughed, clapped loudly, and hugged me. *Wow!* Becky and San Juan also offered applause and smiles.

We were a little loud, but we were having so much fun.

Our food was delivered to our table. The burgers were good, but the fries in the center of the table ended up being the main attraction. Sarah started it when she attacked my hand with a fry after I reached for a fry of my own. I feigned grave injury to my hand and rushed it to the blood-red ketchup. Soon we all were "sword fighting with fries" and laughing quite loudly.

The waitress came over to see if everything was all right. I think she was really sent over to quiet us down.

I did see several of the younger kids in the grill watching us and smiling. I don't believe we were bothering anyone, but we sure had fun, and they noticed.

None of us wanted the night to end, but soon it was already eleven, so we walked back to the car.

San Juan didn't stay long at Becky's door after walking her up to the house. I considered this a private moment for them so I did not spy on them.

When we reached Sarah's, I told San Juan, "I'll be a few minutes. I've been promised drama."

Sarah laughed and leaned her head on my shoulder as we walked up the sidewalk to her house. The lights were still on in the entry and the living room. At the door I gently put my arms around Sarah. I kissed her on the forehead and said, "Thank you for sharing this night with me. I've had so much fun. I'll remember this forever."

I kissed her again. This time it was a real kiss.

Sarah grabbed my hand and led me into her house. She called softly to see if her parents were still up. They were in the living room. "Mom . . . Dad," Sarah asked, "is it okay if Catcher and I come into the living room for a couple minutes? He asked me to re-enact the scene when I opened his gift on Christmas morning and discovered my black J-Hawk Nation stocking cap."

"Sure." Sarah's mom said, "Come on in here, but I'd like to stay and watch if that's okay."

"Me too," Mr. Jenkins said. "I've watched Sarah perform quite often. She's good, especially around her mom and me when she wants something."

Sarah and I entered the living room, and I quietly laughed at her father's last comment.

What I saw was amazing. First Sarah performed a silent version, using exaggerated expressions and actions. I watched in wonder as she mimed opening the gift and showed her surprise at what she found. I almost choked up when she hugged her own cap and cried tears of happiness into it before putting it on and running to the mirror, . . . and my heart surrendered. I had my answer. I had found out everything I needed to know from that one performance, but now she wanted to do a second version with words. She said this one would be a "talkie."

"What's this?" she asked as she pretended a gift had been delivered to her. "The tag says, 'To Sarah . . . From Catcher.' Do you know anything about this, Mom? . . . Dad?" Neither responded, and I suspected it had happened exactly the same on Christmas morning.

"I'm going to open it right now," Sarah said. She pretended to open the gift very carefully, saw what was in the box, and then she put her hands to her face in awe and happiness. She showed the cap to her parents. "Catcher gave me a J-Hawk Nation stocking cap!" she shouted to her parents who were sitting nearby. "I know he likes me! We've got to keep going to all his games, Dad . . . Mom! I now am truly a part of J-Hawk Nation! I'm going to call Grandpa and Grandma right away!" Then Sarah put on her cap and ran to the mirror, as real tears began to stream down her beautiful face.

When I saw her tears, I moved my hand to my face to wipe my own eyes. As I stood and applauded, Sarah's parents shouted, "Bravo! Bravo!" Sarah bowed like the star that she was. She was a magnificent actor, but that was only part of the reason I was cheering. I was overcome by her reaction when she opened my gift. I was more focused on "what" she felt and "what" she said than "how" she said it, but I was very pleased and impressed with everything she had done. I loved this girl.

I glanced at a clock.

Oops. I forgot about San Juan in the car.

"I'm sorry, but I need to run," I said to Sarah's mom and dad. "San Juan's waiting for me in the car. Good night."

Should I have been surprised that they didn't ask me to stay longer?

Sarah walked me to the door.

"You are really something, Sarah," I said to her. "You took my breath away tonight. Thank you for the wonderful drama. I will never forget this night."

I received a warm smile and a wonderful kiss.

"Before I go," I said, "I want to apologize for 'showing off' in front of San Juan tonight. I wanted him to see how much I like being with you, and how comfortable I feel with you, and maybe I got a little goofy. I'll probably hear it from him on our drive home."

"Catcher, you were very funny tonight and great company, and I loved every minute of our date. Remember, this was drama night, for you as well as for me. San Juan won't be upset with you. He'll be so thankful for the night you have given him and for the great fun he had with Becky. I bet they'll want to try another double date very soon," Sarah said.

I reached for her again and held her in my arms. I hated leaving her at the end of a date.

One more . . . two more kisses, then I'll have to go.

"Good night, Sarah Jenkins. "I'll call you tomorrow," I said tenderly with a smile.

After Sarah closed her door I walked down the sidewalk toward the car. "We are . . . J-Hawks!" I shouted out into the darkness of the night.

San Juan was not upset at me for anything, not even for making him wait in the car during drama time. He kept thanking me over and over.

"I really had fun tonight," he declared. "You were right about everything . . . Becky is a lot of fun. She told me she really had a good time. We need to double date again very soon. Want to go to a movie with me Saturday night?"

We both laughed, . . . and I noticed again that we really did look like twins.

Chapter 30

The Question

The bus ride to Ashton on Tuesday night felt great. Besides the girls' team sitting in the front of the bus and the three cheer leaders, there were twelve of us guys wearing letter jackets, sitting in the back of the bus, listening to Pickett strum chords on his ukulele. We were back at full strength for tonight's game. The flu bug had moved on.

Coach had told us that the Cougars had won almost half of their games, and that they had won most of their games on their home floor, so we would go into the game expecting a tough battle. Coach also had told us at yesterday's practice that we would come out running and try to wear them down. We would put pressure on their guards by picking them up right after their inbound pass, and we would hound them constantly and substitute often. It sounded like a great plan to me.

For now, we were relaxing with soft music and light laughter. We'd be ready by game-time, and tonight we'd use at least eight players, maybe nine, so each of us would get some rest during the game. I was looking forward to this. With only four conference games left, we felt we had a chance to win the conference championship without losing a single game. That wasn't our only goal this year, but it was one of them. It wasn't even the most important goal, but still, we wanted to be undefeated in the conference if it were possible. We wanted to do this for our school and our community. We wanted to give J-Hawk Nation something they could talk about for years to come.

My mind wandered from one idea to another during the bus ride. I felt like I was a water bug, racing on the surface water of a pond, going first one direction, then another, with no rhyme or reason for where I was heading. I thought about my basketball team. I knew I would really miss the adventure of this season and all the fun I've had with these guys when our season ended, and the end was not that far away. We were only guaranteed five more games this year. Any additional games would have to be earned by winning in the playoffs. I did not want this season to end.

What would happen to Sarah and me when basketball was over? I hope we are friends for life, but is it basketball that is creating the interest for her right now? What can I do so she will continue to like me?

Next year I'll be a senior at Madison Lake High School. What activities and sports should I sign up for? Should I try football? I catch passes really well. That might be fun. How about chorus? Sarah sings in the chorus.

Where can I get a summer job? I need to earn some spending money. Maybe I can stack hay bales like I did last summer, but that job doesn't last very long. What else can I do? Is there anything in Jeffers? Maybe I'll talk to my uncle about delivering propane tanks for the hardware store. I have to find something besides cleaning bean fields.

What about baseball? Does Madison Lake have a summer team? Could I play for them this summer?

I need to start looking at colleges. Do I want to follow Laser and Pickett to Luther? What do I want to do with my life?

I kept jumping from one topic to another. Nothing kept my focus very long. *I better be able to concentrate better than this in the game.*

When I sat in the bleachers during the girls' game, I moved around to talk to San Juan and the sophomores. I had a suggestion.

"Abe . . . Hook," I said, "I think it's really important that we get Laser and Pickett involved right away tonight so they can see again how valuable they are to our team. Let's make sure they get lots of opportunities to score. They need to see that we really need them . . . that we really missed them at the last game. Let's build them up tonight. Let's make it 'Senior Night.'"

The players I talked to thought it was a good idea. We agreed not to make it look too obvious.

I saw Sarah enter the gym with her parents early in the third quarter of the girls' game. Becky and her dad were right behind them. I waved to Sarah when she looked my way, but I didn't walk over to talk to her because we were just getting ready to head to the locker room. I really wanted to play well tonight so I could feel good about myself when I talked to Sarah after the game. I noticed how pretty she was, even from a distance. She has definitely captured my heart. I think of her very often, and I have so much fun when I am with her. Last Saturday night was great!

After the opening tip we didn't get off to a great start. During the first quarter both teams played pretty evenly. We stole the ball a couple times with our full-court press, but we missed on several shots. The Cougars didn't take as many shots, but they made most of them. At the end of the quarter the score was tied. We felt we could have done a lot better, so Coach told us to increase the pressure on the Cougars and relax as we took our shots.

Laser hit on two jump shots to open the second quarter, and Pickett scored on three straight jump shots from inside the lane. Now we started to put it together, and it was the two seniors who were leading us. Abe and Hook kept clearing the rebounds, and we rushed the ball down-court as quickly as possible. I finally scored on a fast-break layup. Then I picked off a pass and immediately hit a ten-foot jump shot. That gave me four points in about five seconds.

We started to build a lead. Our fast break was working well, and Laser and San Juan both drove to the hoop for layups. When the second quarter ended we were up by ten.

The second half started out with Laser hitting a long jump shot. The Cougars panicked when Laser and I pressured the ball handler, and Number 12 threw the ball away. I passed to Captain Hook, and he threw it to Abe who had sneaked behind his man at the basket and laid the ball against the backboard for two points.

The Cougars had difficulty getting the ball into their own end of the court. Abe deflected a pass that Pickett grabbed up and tossed to Laser. Laser found me on the way to the basket and hit me with a perfect pass, and I laid the ball into the bucket. That increased our lead to sixteen points, and the Cougar coach called a timeout.

During the rest of the third quarter, Coach subbed often so all of us got a breather, and we held the lead at about fifteen points. Everyone was shooting well now, and we didn't make many mistakes. We had the game under control.

Not much changed in the fourth quarter except that we pulled back to the half to trap the guards. Pickett kept hitting his shots from near the free-throw line, and Abe cashed in on a couple short attempts. We limited the Cougars to one shot each time down the floor because our big guys attacked the boards and collected all the defensive rebounds, and we increased our lead to twenty points.

With three minutes left in the game, Coach pulled all of us starters, and he put in the reserves. We starters felt really good about that because it was a goal of ours that everyone would get to play in each game. It was a good reward for working hard at practice.

At the final buzzer we walked off the floor with our fifteenth-straight win without a loss, and we had made sure that our seniors had gotten a chance to shine. It was another successful game.

I toweled off, then greeted a few people including Becky and her dad. I'm glad for San Juan that they both came. Mom and Dad both told me I had played well. (They are my parents, after all.) Then they moved off to talk to the other players, their parents, and Coach. They under-stood that I wanted these ten minutes or so to visit with Sarah and her parents, and they mostly honored that. I always looked forward to my time with Sarah, even if it was only for a few minutes.

Tonight Mr. and Mrs. Jenkins hardly even stopped. They both said, "Good game, Catcher," and walked over to some of my teammates, leaving only Sarah standing there by me. This was kind of unusual. I didn't know what to make of it.

I smiled at Sarah, but she didn't exactly smile back. She didn't even say anything to me. I could tell something was bothering her. I wondered what I had done now. *What's going on?* I said a very quick prayer.

"Sarah, is something wrong?" I asked very seriously.

"I'm okay. I'm not upset," Sarah replied, "but I have a question I need to ask you. When you asked me out on our first date you called me 'your special friend,' and last Saturday night at The Grill you called me 'your very good friend.' Is this the way you see it? Is this what I am to you?

She continued, "It's been a little uncomfortable for me when your teammates have referred to me as your 'girlfriend,' and then last week your brother asked me at a game if I was your 'girlfriend,' and I didn't know how to answer his question because I've never heard you say that I am your 'girlfriend.' So I'm going to ask you . . . right now . . . Catcher, am I your girlfriend? Will you please tell me? I really need to know."

She is upset. What have I done?

I reached out for Sarah's hand. I knew I needed to choose my words carefully, so I was very deliberate. "First of all, Sarah," I said. "Do you remember when I told you last week that I would never forget 'drama night?'"

"Yes," was all Sarah replied.

"Do you realize you just used the same words I used when I asked you how you reacted when you opened my Christmas gift?" I asked.

"Yes, I do," Sarah answered again. "I was touched by your words Saturday night, and I want you to know that I'll not forget that night either."

I smiled, hoping to reassure her.

I spoke as tenderly as I could. "I don't have your acting skills, so I will just tell you in a direct way, like I wish I had done before tonight. Sarah, I consider you to be not only my very special friend . . . and my best friend . . . but also my girlfriend. To me, these all mean the same thing. That first night I saw you and helped you find a seat in the gym, I started falling for you, and I didn't even know your name. You are the only girl I've ever been interested in, and I want our friendship to last forever. I've been hesitant to use the word 'girlfriend' with you because I wasn't sure how you would take it. I worried about that. What if you weren't looking to be someone's 'girlfriend?' What if you thought that I was rushing things? What if you wanted to be 'just plain friends?' I didn't want to give you any reason for walking away."

I looked deeply into her eyes and said, "Did you know that one of my teammates told me you were 'way out of my league,' that I had no chance for a friendship with you? I've thought about what he said, and I can't shake his comment because I've worried that it might be true."

I continued. "Sarah, while doing my chores on the farm I have told all the cows, most of the pigs, and about half of the chickens on the farm that I feel so lucky to have you as a girlfriend. I've whispered it outdoors in the quiet of nature, and I've shouted it to faraway trees in the woods, but I've not yet had enough courage to say it to you when we've stood face-to-face. I wish I had said something before tonight . . . before you asked me. I'm very sorry, Sarah. I didn't know you felt this way, but now I can tell this has bothered you. I had hoped you knew how I felt about you by the way I talk to you and how I act when I am with you. I'm sorry I did not make this clear to you."

Sarah's face had now regained its beautiful smile, and I couldn't resist putting my arms around her. *Maybe I'll hear about it from Coach or my parents, but, hey . . . Sarah **is** my girlfriend.*

"I'm glad I asked," Sarah said, "and I do understand your explanation. I should not have let this little thing bother me."

"I think you did it just right by asking me about this tonight. I think it's really important to talk and understand each other. I am so sorry I put you in uncomfortable situations," I said. "I did not mean to do that, but I should have done better, because I really care for you Sarah, You mean everything to me."

Sarah's smile warmed my heart. "You mean everything to me, too," she said sweetly.

*I'm not sure what it's like to be in love, but it must be something like how I feel right now. All right . . . be smart . . . don't say anything more . . . and **don't** kiss her here.*

Sarah continued, "I have a little confession to make to you about tonight. The reason my parents didn't stop to talk with you was because I told them I needed all your time. When I said I had something important to say to you, they appeared to be a little shocked."

"Then I'd like to greet your mom and dad again," I suggested.

"That's a good idea," Sarah replied. "That might help eliminate some of their questions on the ride home."

I was only able to talk with Sarah's parents briefly before Coach gave the signal, but I think they could tell that everything seemed good between

Sarah and me. I said to Sarah as I turned toward the locker room, "I'll call you tomorrow night."

As I walked away I asked myself, "How in the world did I get so lucky that I found Sarah?"

I looked around for him as I headed to the showers. I spotted him, and quickly hurried over because I had something I needed to ask of him, and I didn't have much time.

In the Stands – With John Garris

Though the Ashton Cougars played on their home court last night, they could not match the hot-shooting Jeffers J-Hawks, falling by a score of 74-58. After ending the first quarter tied, the J-Hawks used their full-court press to great advantage in the second quarter, forcing Cougar errors and stealing passes which the J-Hawks converted into easy layups and wide-open shots, resulting in a ten-point half-time lead. With their accurate shooting in the second half, the J-Hawks maintained their comfortable lead and won the game without much of a challenge. Laser and Pickett led the scoring attack, but it was another solid team effort, with contributions from all starters and several players off the bench.

This win improves the J-Hawk record to 15-0 . . . and I had them picked to be a middle-of-the-pack team. My sources must have given me faulty pre-season information.

At last night's game I was asked by one of my readers if I would include in my next column a special message. It may appear that in doing this I am crossing the line from being a sports columnist to being an advice columnist. I am unsure if this is a higher or lower calling, but since I have written about this young man a few times previously, I felt compelled to honor his request.

This young man told me that if the following words were included in my column, it might raise him to "hero status" with a special friend. I'm all for that. I was young once.

Dear Sarah,
Catcher wants to make it very clear to you, your parents, your friends, and everyone else that he wants you to be his girl-friend . . . forever.
Sincerely,
John Garris – Special Correspondent for the Teen-age Heart

Chapter 31
"Billy Johnson"

The next night, after eating supper and completing my homework, I called Sarah. Her dad answered.

"Hello, Mr. Jenkins," I said. "May I please speak to Sarah?"

"Hi, Catcher. I read Garris's column today," Mr. Jenkins replied, then he started to laugh. "You made a nice recovery. What did that cost you?"

I just laughed back.

"Carole and I both got a kick out of your message. We remember when we were kids," Mr. Jenkins added. "I'll get Sarah for you. By the way, you played very well again last night. I would have talked with you longer after last night's game, but Sarah seems to be the boss in this family. She's right here."

"Hi," Sarah said sweetly. "I read the column today. Several kids in school told me about it, and three of my teachers mentioned it, too. You are making me famous. How did you get Garris to write that?"

"I just asked him courteously and respectfully," I answered, acting like it was nothing special. "I explained my situation briefly and asked if he would please include my message in his next column. He laughed a little when I told him the words, but he did write them down. I had hopes he would print my message, but I had my doubts. Maybe he felt he owed it to me because of earlier things he had written, or maybe he considered the J-Hawk Nation stocking cap I gave him last week was an acceptable bribe."

"You have certainly answered the question I asked you last night," Sarah said, "and I'm very happy . . . and very proud of you. I cut the column out of today's paper, and I taped it to the mirror in my room so I can read those words every day. Thank you, Catcher. You have made things very clear for me.

"Oh, I almost forgot," Sarah continued, "I heard from Becky at school today that we are double dating again with San Juan and her on Saturday for another movie night. When were you going to ask me?" Sarah asked with a quiet laugh.

"Tonight!" I replied, a little panicky. "San Juan must have talked to Becky after the game last night. On our drive home last Saturday night San Juan said something about wanting to double again soon. I guess he meant this weekend. Are you okay with that? Will you go to a movie with me Saturday night?"

"Yes, I will," Sarah answered. "I think San Juan and Becky will appreciate our company again."

"I didn't ask you last night because I wanted you to have time to think about what I had said to you, to make sure that I had given you enough of an explanation. Thanks for understanding. Am I doing okay with your parents?" I asked.

"Yes, you are," Sarah replied. "They both care a lot about you, but still, they are very protective of me."

"I have seen that," I said, "and I think that's good."

"Did you know that someone from my school asked me if I would go to a movie with him? It was over Christmas vacation, about a month after I met you," Sarah said.

"No, I didn't," I answered as I started to get worried again.

"You don't need to know who it was, but he's popular . . . a junior, and he's a football player. I'm going to call him 'Billy Johnson'. I told him I needed to check with my parents," Sarah continued.

"When I talked to Dad about it, we had a good conversation, and I learned a lot," Sarah said. "It went something like this."

"I said, 'Dad, Billy Johnson has asked me to go to a movie with him. If I wanted to go, would you let me?'

"Dad answered immediately, 'No, your mother and I have discussed this, and we both feel that you are too young to date.'

"Then I asked him, 'What if Catcher asked me to go to a movie? Would I still be too young?'

"Dad wanted to know if you **had** asked me.

"I told him, 'No, but maybe he will. What if he does?'

"Dad thought about this for a while. Then he told me, 'That might be different. Catcher has passed my test.'

"I asked him, 'Test? What test, Dad?'

"He answered, 'The character test. I know quite a bit about Catcher from watching him play basketball. I've seen the way he treats people, and I've noticed all the things he's done to help others. I've heard him speak respectfully to his family and friends, and I've observed him act kindly toward young kids as well as older people. I've talked with him. I believe he's smart, and I feel he has a good heart. Yeah . . . he's passed my test. I would trust him to treat you with respect and keep you safe. If Catcher asks you to go to a movie . . . I think that might be different.'"

"Your dad said all that?" I asked incredulously.

"Yes," Sarah said, "and you are the first and the only boy who has passed Dad's test."

"Wow! I'm really liking your dad!" I said. "So you didn't go with 'Billy Johnson'?"

"No, my first date ever was with you . . . on January 13th," Sarah said. "I told 'Billy' that I couldn't go on a date with him. That's all I said. I did not give him a reason."

"I am learning so much about you and your family every time I talk to you. You absolutely amaze me. Sarah, I don't want this conversation to end," I said, "but I'm getting a signal from my sister that she needs to use the phone. I'll call you again tomorrow night."

"All right," Sarah said. "Tomorrow night I'll have to watch the time more carefully, however. Can you believe my parents want me to limit calls to ten minutes?"

"Good night, Girlfriend," I said warmly.

I sensed her smile, and I heard light laughter.

"Good night, my hero," she replied.

I will fall asleep tonight with Sarah's laughter in my head.

Chapter 32
Play Hard? . . . Have Fun?

I took swimming lessons with my friends for a few summers. Soon after school was out at the end of May, but before the water had warmed up much in any lakes, the lessons began. The school bus would make the trip from our school in Jeffers to Clear Lake twice a week, loaded with kids whose parents had signed them up for swimming lessons. Almost every kid took lessons. Why not? What else were you going to do?

For seven or eight weeks covering most of June and July, we boarded that bus pretty early in the morning, dressed in shorts and T-shirts over our swim suits, with maybe a sweat shirt for warmth, carrying a paper bag that contained a towel and probably some snacks for the ride home.

Generally the bus was quiet for the first few miles but became noisier as most kids awakened and began engaging in conversations that were spread across the bus. When we were just a few miles from arriving at the lake, we reached an old farmstead where a rickety old windmill stood as a landmark and served as our signal for us to start getting ourselves ready for our lesson. We focused on two things: 1) We stripped down to our swimsuits and carefully placed our clothes in our paper bags after pulling out the towel. 2) We looked toward the lake in the distance when the bus reached its highest point on the road, and we checked for whitecaps on the water. We hated whitecaps. If we saw them it meant the wind was blowing hard enough to make the lake surface pretty rough and the air a little chilly to a wet body. It seemed to me that every time there were whitecaps it was "back-float day," and that made my lesson at Red Cross Beach more difficult and a lot less fun.

Most of us did learn to swim, and I really enjoyed the last few minutes of each lesson when we were given free swimming time and were allowed to climb the metal ladder up out of the water to the long wooden dock, and we could practice diving into deeper water. There was something adventurous about diving headfirst, even if I wasn't particularly graceful. Diving made me feel brave, and it added speed to my swimming strokes. I challenged myself to dive out farther and swim for greater distances under water before coming up for air.

When our neighboring town of Madison Lake put in a new community pool, it was more convenient for our family to swim there instead of driving all the way to Clear Lake. Here there were diving boards, and I worked on improving my diving style. I also challenged myself to see how far I could swim underwater before coming up to take a breath. At first I could only manage one width of the pool, but with practice and determination I extended that to a second width, and eventually I pushed myself to my personal record of three widths, though I came up gasping for air after touching the side of the pool. The third width was achieved through determination alone, as I had no air left in the tank, and I credit this training for giving me extra stamina on the basketball court. Maybe my lungs have a greater capacity than the lungs of others because of this under-water swimming. I don't know for sure, but even thinking that it's true gives me a mental edge.

When I was eleven or twelve I did learn something about how swimming affected me. I discovered that after a day of swimming I had terrible control as a baseball pitcher if we played a game under the lights that night. My pitching speed was just as good, but I had trouble throwing strikes. Did this knowledge keep me from swimming on a game night? No, but I decided I would be smart about it. I conserved my energy while in the pool. I did more diving and less actual swimming. Diving was smart, I thought, though I'm not sure it made a big difference in the number of strikes I threw that night. These were just baseball games, after all. They were not "life and death." I was okay with the combination of swimming and baseball. If the games had been really important I hope I would have been smart enough to figure out that I should even stop diving if it would help my team.

We expected the Shelby Jaguars to come into our gym and try to prove something tonight. Back in December we had clobbered them on their court when we played our best game of the season. We knew they'd put up more of a challenge tonight, but we were confident. All of us were healthy and prepared, and we would play hard.

The gym filled early tonight, because at last Tuesday night's game, many spectators could not find seats and had to stand in the wings and look over the heads of other people. Standing during the entire game was a tough way to watch the action. When all seats were taken, my ushering duties were over for the evening, so I headed for my reserved seat.

I sat with Sarah and her parents for about thirty minutes while the girls were playing. I found this time to be a great way for me to relax before my game. I certainly didn't think about the Jaguars when Sarah was right next to me. I asked Sarah about her hobbies and her friends, and then she wanted to know what it was like growing up on a farm. I saw Sarah's mom glance over at us a couple times and smile. *I wonder what she was thinking.*

Even though a basketball game was being played directly in front of us, neither of us paid any attention to it, and those thirty minutes zoomed by. *I've got to figure out a way to slow time down.*

When Coach joined us in the locker room he didn't have much to say to us. He just looked around and asked, "Are you ready?"

Pickett spoke for all of us. "We're ready to go, Coach."

That was it. There was no motivational speech, no laughter, and no game plan. On his way out Coach said, "I'll knock on the door when it's time to warm up."

We all looked at Pickett and Laser after Coach closed the door. Laser said, "It looks like we need to come up with our own strategy for tonight. Let's run our fast break on offense and press full-court."

Pickett added, "Hit the boards hard, and if they play a zone, make quick passes, and find the soft spots. We need to hit our shots and force them into man-to-man coverage, and then we can take advantage of our height under the basket."

"If Coach gives different instructions," Laser continued. "we go with what he says. He doesn't seem like himself tonight, so give him some space."

Laser and Otto headed to the microphone to make tonight's announcements. Otto started with a reminder about J-Hawk Juice after the game and the 9:30 clinic tomorrow morning.

Then Laser spoke, "Tonight we are honoring the 'clinic-kids,' the young J-Hawk boys and girls who have been attending our Saturday morning basketball clinics, learning skills, having fun, and inspiring our team to play our best. I'd like to invite all of the 'clinic-kids' to step out onto the gym floor so J-Hawk Nation can see who you are."

There was loud applause as kids raced onto the floor and raised their arms toward the roof as champions often do, and J-Hawk Nation stood and acknowledged these future basketball stars. It seemed as if the gym had been turned into a circus.

Otto continued, "We'd like our teammates and the other high school students who have assisted us in the gym and the library to please join us out here on the floor."

The ten of us who were standing by the bench hustled out and started shaking hands with the kids and patting them on their backs. I looked at Sarah in the bleachers and gestured to her to join us. Soon some of our older sisters stepped out also, and we all waved to the applauding crowd. It was loud, and it felt great.

Laser concluded, "Saturday clinics will continue until our basketball season has ended. Our goal is to be playing well into March."

The gym erupted. The young kids on the gym floor were jumping and yelling like crazy. Laser and I saw that the refs were getting a little impatient so we started corralling the kids and chasing them back to the bleachers.

We passed the ball around their zone after we retrieved the opening tip. Abe and Captain Hook stretched toward the sidelines, and Pickett took up his station just above the foul line. We made several quick passes so we could figure out how they were going to play us, and we would know where to begin our attack. Whenever I touched the ball, the Jaguar guard on my side moved out on me, but the guard on Laser's side sagged back into the lane. When I passed to Hook on my sideline, Abe's defender slid into the lane close to the basket. I could see that they were going to give us opportunities to shoot from outside. All we had to do was make our open shots.

The next time Laser caught a pass he took one quick dribble to get his rhythm, then guided a jump shot that swished through the net. *Good start!*

We set up our full-court press with Pickett challenging their inbound pass. Our small gym gave them trouble. Their third pass was too long, and it slammed into the wall on the far end. That mistake cost them when Pickett hit a turn-around jumper from near the free-throw line. We were up by four, and they had not yet taken a shot.

The first quarter settled into a shooting contest. Whenever a Jaguar player shot, both of their guards immediately turned and hustled back to their defensive end, leaving their three baseline players alone to rebound against all five of us. This took away our fast break for now, but we grabbed every rebound, limiting them to one shot on each of their possessions. We needed to make sure the Jaguars didn't get open shots, and we also knew we needed to pass until one of us had a good opportunity to score.

At the end of the first quarter we led by a score of 21-16.

In the second quarter the Jaguars closed to within three points a couple times, but we extended the lead to eight by halftime. We went into the locker room at halftime feeling pretty good, but I was concerned about Coach. He hadn't done much coaching tonight. His mind didn't seem to be on the game. He didn't say much to anyone. The only thing he did was make a substitution once in a while.

We just sat quietly on the benches in the locker room, looking at each other, waiting for some instructions. All Coach said was, "Good job out there."

He kept looking at the floor, and I had a hard time not staring at him. I wanted to ask him, "What's wrong, Coach?" but I didn't.

"What do you want us to do in the third quarter?" Laser asked.

It took a few seconds before Coach replied, "Um . . . just do what you have been doing. It's working."

I don't think Coach even knows what we have been doing. He's not in this game at all. Something is really bothering him.

In the 3rd Quarter the pace quickened. The Jaguars started keeping one guard in to help rebound, so we took advantage of that by hitting them with our fast break. This forced all of their players to run harder. This is the style game we liked playing, so we fired up, and we built our lead to twelve points by the end of the quarter. I felt that we had control of this game. No one was in foul trouble, and all of our scoring options had earned points tonight, so all we had to do was keep playing the way we were, and we would be okay.

Not much changed at the beginning of the 4th Quarter. We tossed the ball in to Abe and Hook whenever we slowed down, and they each scored twice on close-in shots. We played tough defense, making the Jaguars work hard to get open shots, but they had the touch tonight, and many of their shots hit the target, so our lead remained at about twelve.

It was with less than four minutes left in the game, that everything began to fall apart, and J-Hawk Nation began to collapse. There was no warning. It appeared to be just like a lot of other plays we had made this season, but this time the results were very extreme.

Number 22's shot went up and bounced off the rim and the backboard. Pickett grabbed it, landed, pivoted to the outside, and threw the ball down-court. His pass led me by too much. I raced after it with three or four quick steps, but I saw the ball heading toward the sideline near our bench. I took two additional powerful steps and extended my body low to the floor and dove as far as I could with all my strength, and I reached for the ball with my left hand. I swatted the ball toward Laser, who was heading down the floor ahead of me, and my sweaty body slid several feet into the bench area. Laser stretched his arms toward the floor while running at top speed, grabbed the ball, dribbled twice, and laid the ball against the backboard into our basket.

When San Juan and Otto saw me sliding toward them, they stepped out and used their bodies to slow me down, to keep me from sliding hard into the feet of the bench players and the hard wooden bleachers. They softened what could have been a hard crash.

I was just a little dazed, but I had seen Laser score, and I listened as the crowd applauded our effort. It was a good play, and that basket increased our lead to fifteen points.

San Juan stood up, called to the refs, and motioned toward the floor in front of our bench, "Wet floor here!"

A ref blew the whistle to stop play and directed the two sixth-grade sweepers to get towels and wipe up the sweat I had spread across the floor when I slid to save the ball.

San Juan and Otto grabbed their own towels and stepped out in front of our bench, out of the way of the two kids who were working on the floor. In cushioning my slide into the bench area, they had gotten a little wet from my sweat, and they were not happy about it. They started drying off their hands, arms, and legs. They kept shaking their heads in disgust, not even cracking a smile, and they made a big production of wiping themselves off.

Then Tucson, Nicholson, and Treason, with the assistance of the other bench players, reached for other towels and jumped out toward me and started drying me off by wiping me down, head to toe, and fanning me off with their waving towels. They worked quickly like a pit crew in a big race, and the spectators applauded and laughed hard.

I just stood there expressionless. I didn't do anything except put up with my teammates' actions as the crowd continued to enjoy the humor they saw.

Coach walked over to me and got right in my face. "What do you think you are doing out there?" he yelled.

I answered innocently, "Helping us get two more points, Coach. Laser scored a layup on that play."

Coach's face was red. "I told you to play smart! Look at the scoreboard! We're up by fifteen points! Diving across the floor . . . that was a dumb play! You could've gotten hurt! Would that have helped your team? Take a seat, and think about it!" Coach yelled. He was fuming.

I sat down at the far end of the bench, and I did think about it. *Coach is being unfair. He always wants us to play hard. That's what I do! That's what I did!*

Coach shouted at the rest of my bench teammates, all of whom were still holding towels in their hands, "So this is funny to you clowns? Sit down . . . Now!" He was in a rage.

The ref blew the whistle to resume play.

"Am I still in, Coach?" I asked. "We need another player."

"No! You are done!" he replied angrily.

Laser called to the bench from the center of the court, "Coach, we need another guard out here."

Coach didn't even respond.

One of the refs trotted over and said something to Coach. Coach shook his head, and the ref blew his whistle to signal that play could begin.

The Jaguars inbounded the ball, and my **four** J-Hawk teammates, one player short, moved back into defensive positions.

In about a minute's time, the atmosphere in the gym had gone from enjoyable laughter to stunned silence.

It was deathly quiet in the gym. You could hear every bounce of the ball, and I saw many people turn to their neighbors on their left and right. It appeared that everyone wondered what was going on.

The Jaguars passed the ball around our four-person zone, working the ball closer and closer to the basket. Number 22 found an opening and passed inside to Number 50 who laid the ball off the board into the basket. With about three-and-a-half minutes left to play, the lead was down to thirteen points.

Coach knew he had only four players on the floor, and he made no effort to correct that. *What's going on?*

I leaned forward from my position at the end of the bench. "Coach, you've got to put someone in," I said. "They need some help out there."

Coach ignored me, and all the players on the bench stared in my direction.

Play went on. Laser missed on a jump shot, and the Jaguars collected the rebound and hustled down the floor. After a few passes Number 11 was open inside, and he scored on a soft bank shot. Now the lead was down to eleven.

Pickett threw the ball in to Laser, but he had difficulty dribbling the ball down to our end because he didn't get much help. He could pass to the big guys, but he was the only dribbler out there, so the Jaguars put two guys on him. After Hook caught a high pass from Laser, Hook tried to lead Laser with a pass as Laser ran by, but the timing was off, and the pass sailed out of bounds.

The Jaguars set up their offence. I could see Laser and Pickett start to get frustrated as they tried to cover five opponents with only four players. The Jaguars were playing smart. They passed quickly, moving the ball inside . . . and back out, from the left side . . . to the right. Again they found Number 50 open in the lane near the basket, and he caught a bounce pass and scored. Now we only led by nine with two minutes to go.

Pickett called for a timeout. The four guys walked to our bench.

"Coach, we need some help. You need to put someone in, or we may lose this game," Pickett said. "We're one player short. All you have to do is put in our fifth player."

Coach just stood there for a few moments. Then he turned his back on the eight of us who had been sitting on the bench, and he replied to Pickett, Laser, Abe, and Hook, "There's no one here ready to help you. All I have on the bench are a bunch of amateur comedians and a reckless daredevil. They are all done for the night. They are not thinking basketball. You are much better off without them. Get back out there."

Everyone was stunned.

Abe helped Laser get the ball to our end. This time Pickett was able to sneak inside and score on a short jump shot, increasing the lead to eleven, but no one in the gym applauded or stood. Everyone remained silent. There was no cheering. These four guys were on their own. Coach did nothing.

Number 20 for the Jaguars dribbled all the way to his basket and scored with little resistance. It almost appeared that we were giving up. Our four needed help and support. The lead was again down to nine.

I got San Juan's and Otto's attention on the bench, and I motioned for them to stand up with me. They hesitated, but they stood. We began to clap. The rest of the bench stood and joined in. We looked out and made eye contact with our guys. *Don't give up! We are with you! You can do this!*

We didn't signal to anyone in the bleachers to stand up. If others wanted to join us . . . that was up to them. The young clinic-kids were the first to stand and start clapping. There were no voices . . . just hands making noise. Then high school and junior high kids stood and applauded. I watched as my dad and his friends on the far side of the gym rose out of their chairs.

The clock kept winding down. At one minute to go in the game Jaguar Number 21 scored on a jump shot from the free-throw line, and our lead was down to seven.

I looked at Coach. He was sitting quietly, just looking out at the floor, saying nothing. He looked lost.

*What is wrong with him? Does he **want** us to lose this game? I've never seen him* *do anything like this. Has he turned against us?*

The four J-Hawks on the floor began working even harder. They did not quit. Soon all of J-Hawk Nation was standing, and the noise of clapping hands was getting louder. Captain Hook rebounded a missed shot, passed to Laser, and Laser dribbled toward our end and went up for the layup. He was fouled hard, and the ball was hammered into the wall.

Laser hit his first free throw, but the second one rattled off the rim, and the Jaguars hustled down-court with the ball.

Only forty-five seconds remained. Number 11 hit a lucky shot from way out bringing the Jaguars within six points, and I felt the tension take over my body. I didn't even bother looking at Coach. Right at this moment I hated him. I could not understand why he was doing this.

Those last forty-five seconds counted off so slowly as J-Hawk fans remained standing and kept clapping. Hook found the range from about eight feet out, but Number 20 answered quickly with his own twelve-foot jump shot. Pickett was open for an easy shot, but the ball hit the back of the rim and bounced out into the hands of Number 20. He dribbled twice and passed sharply to a teammate under the bucket. His basket brought the Jaguars to within four points, but Laser's long pass to Abe got us out of trouble as the clock wound down and the horn sounded. The game was finally over.

The four tired J-Hawks walked to our bench. I could see how worn out and how upset they were. Laser said to the eight of us, "Line up for the handshake. Let's go!" I could tell he was angry, but I didn't know if it was directed at the eight of us who were riding the bench.

As I went through the line I didn't say anything to any players. All I did was shake hands. Then I walked directly toward the locker room without talking to anyone. I was seething. Anything I said now would land me in further trouble, so I figured my best option was to make my retreat.

I undressed, threw my wet uniform into the laundry basket, and showered as quickly as I could because I wanted to get out of there. When I was clean, dry, and dressed, I put away the rest of my stuff and hung up my warm-up jacket. Just as I was ready to exit the locker room, Laser walked in.

"How are you doing?" he asked.

"I don't know," I replied. "I just need to get out of here."

"It's not your fault, you know," he continued. "Coach just lost it. I have no idea why he yelled at you and made us play a man short. You had made a great play, and we had scored. Something must have gotten to him. He almost lost this game. Everyone will be here at 8:30 tomorrow so we can talk this over before we work out. Hopefully we'll figure this out."

"Right now I don't know if I want to play ball again, especially for Coach," I said, "but I'll be here tomorrow."

"You better get going. The other guys are coming in soon, and they'll all want to know how you are doing," Laser said. "Besides, there's a very cute J-Hawk Nation fan waiting for you under the basket on this end. She asked me to check on you. She wants to talk to you."

"I wonder if she'll yell at me, too," I said.

Laser laughed and replied, "That's pretty unlikely. It wasn't anger I saw in her eyes. She'll treat you better than Coach did, that's for sure. She's waiting. Get out of here."

When I walked up to Sarah we both spoke at the exact same time, and we said the same words, "I'm sorry."

I went first. "I'm sorry you were there to see and hear that, Sarah," I said. "I think everyone in the gym heard Coach yell at me, but unfortunately for you . . . and for me . . . you had front-row seats. I felt really embarrassed for you."

"I'm sorry your coach was so rude to you," Sarah said. "I wasn't embarrassed. I was shocked . . . and angry . . . at your coach. He was an embarrassment to himself."

"What did your folks think?" I asked.

"They were both quite upset at Coach. I was afraid Dad was going to step down to the floor to say something to him, but I think Mom held him back," Sarah replied. "They could not understand why your coach was so hard on you. They thought he was way out of line. All you had done was make a great play that resulted in two more points for your team. No one blames you for what happened."

"Would you like to sit with me and drink some J-Hawk Juice?" I asked. "I understand it's powerful stuff, and I've heard that even Santa loves it."

Sarah laughed, and her laughter chased my anger away.

While we sat at one of the long tables, a few people came by and patted me on the back. Others told me I had played well and that I had made a great play. I started feeling better.

As Sarah and I talked, some teammates and friends joined us, and eventually I almost forgot about how the game had ended. When Tucson started talking about my slide into the bench area and the antics of Otto and Sons, I took a quick look around the lunchroom, hoping I wouldn't see Coach sitting or standing anywhere. I didn't need him yelling at me any more tonight.

"That was a great comedy performance you guys put on," Sarah said. "I was laughing so hard about all the action you did with the towels, but then Coach started yelling, and all the fun ended. Several people I talked with tonight mentioned how entertaining you guys were. I really like watching how hard your team plays and all the fun you have, and I've heard your coach say many times, 'Play hard . . . have fun' . . . except he didn't seem to mean that tonight."

When Sarah's parents found us in the lunchroom, I asked them if they would like to join us and stay for a few minutes longer. They surprised me when they said they would because I think they were wanting to leave once they found Sarah.

"What happened to your coach tonight?" Mr. Jenkins asked.

"I have no idea," I answered. "He has yelled at me before, but he's never let it affect his coaching like it did tonight."

"I heard a couple people suggest that he be invited in for coffee at the café tomorrow morning. Maybe he'll show up and explain himself," Mr. Jenkins added.

"Or maybe he'll quit coaching," I said. "He's been a great coach except for tonight. I must have really set him off."

"There had to more to it than that," Mrs. Jenkins said. "You made a great play. It must have been something else. I really hope he's okay."

Then Mom and Dad got up from another table where they had been drinking coffee, and when they spotted us, they walked over.

Now it was Sarah's turn. "Would you like to join us?" she asked.

This was great! Getting our parents talking would give Sarah and me more time together. Though I listened in to some of our parents' conversation, most of the time I looked at Sarah and wondered at my good fortune.

After a few minutes I said to her, "I think I have just come up with the perfect name for you, Sarah, but I'm going to keep it to myself until I know for sure that it's right. Besides, it's my turn to own a secret."

By the time both of our families left for our homes, I had forgotten all about the game. Tomorrow I would see Sarah twice: at the morning clinic and on our evening movie date. By Sunday I figured I would be able to forgive Coach and become excited about playing basketball again.

I had no idea that the next two days would bring even more difficulties and more trouble.

In the Stands – With John Garris

It was one of the most bizarre endings I've ever seen in a basketball game. I have no idea what was going on. It didn't make any sense, and it almost led to the first loss of the season for the Jeffers J-Hawks.

Last night the Shelby Jaguars traveled to Jeffers for their second attempt in trying to knock off the undefeated J-Hawks. After several lead changes during the first two quarters, the J-Hawks picked up their intensity in the second half and, capitalizing on their great stamina, built a ten-point lead behind the trapping defense of the guards. The Jaguars were forced into making wild passes which often sailed out-of-bounds or were picked off by the long arms of Abe and Captain Hook. On offence Pickett led the charge, supported by the sophomores and the hot shooting from out front by Laser and Catcher. Everyone was playing well. The machine was cruising along smoothly.

Then, with only four minutes left in the game, and with the J-Hawks owning a 15-point lead, the wheels came off. No . . . that's not exactly right. The coach yanked out a spark plug, limiting the effectiveness of the engine. It was nearly a disaster.

The J-Hawks had been playing hard, as they always do. They had just scored on a layup after a great dive and slide across the floor kept the ball from reaching the bleachers. The crowd stood and applauded loudly, showing appreciation for a great effort, but the coach became furious at some of his players. Catcher took the brunt of the coach's anger, but all players who were on the sideline at that time suffered the coach's wrath. He berated them loudly for reckless play and for not taking the game seriously enough. Catcher and the seven reserves were benched for the remainder of the game, leaving only four J-Hawks on the floor, and the Jaguars began chipping away at the fifteen-point deficit.

I looked into the faces of J-Hawk Nation, and I saw disbelief . . . confusion . . . anger.

Only in the final minute did the fans rally themselves and offer support to the undermanned J-Hawks who held on by a wing-and-a-prayer for a four-point win, their sixteenth straight victory.

With sectional play beginning in a couple weeks, this is not the time for a team to fall apart. The J-Hawks had been a team on the rise all season, and now they appear destined to crash.

At this time I have more questions than I have answers or opinions. Will the coach get a second chance? Will the legacy that this team wanted to leave behind for their school and community burst like a punctured balloon?

I have watched the J-Hawks play several times this year, and I have always been impressed with their fast style of play . . . their teamwork . . . their positive attitude . . . their enjoyment quotient. They have entertained me, and I have slowly been drawn in as a J-Hawk supporter.

Instead of my opinions, today the J-Hawks get my advice. **FIX THIS NOW!** Take a few deep breaths . . . then resolve to put everything back together again . . . the way it was . . . the way it should be. You have a chance to be special, a chance to become champions, a chance to leave your school and community something of which everyone will be extremely proud.

You are . . . J-Hawks! You can do this . . . and it won't take "all the king's horses and all the king's men." It will only take the same high level of effort and positive attitude that you have given all season in your games, your activities, and your fun.

Repair this, and move on. You play again on Friday night. J-Hawk Nation is counting on you!

Chapter 33

Searching for Answers

Eleven teammates were sitting on the bleachers when I walked into the gym just before 8:30. I wasn't late, but I was the last one to arrive. As soon as I sat down next to San Juan on the dark-stained wood, close to where Sarah and her parents sat when they watched our home games, Pickett said, "All right, let's get started. We've got to figure this out . . . see where we are . . . decide what to do."

"Here's what we know," Laser said. "Coach quit on us last night. We don't know why, but he did nothing in the way of coaching us. In benching eight of you, he almost cost us the game. That's not acceptable."

"We haven't had a chance to talk to Coach yet, but I know he's expected at the café this morning," Pickett added. "Laser and I plan to walk right in and sit down at about 9:30 to listen to any explanation he offers. Before we go we need to know from you guys what your thoughts are."

Everyone just sat there quietly, looking at each other. Since no one else offered anything, I decided to speak up. "Last night Coach made me so angry I could spit," I said, "but before I give an opinion about what should happen, I want to hear from Coach. I need him to tell me what was going on."

Abe, Otto, and San Juan nodded in agreement, and others joined in.

"Does anyone else want to say anything?" Laser asked as he looked at each of us.

"We need to know Coach's story," Captain Hook added. "I agree with Catcher. I'll say more when I know more."

"All right," Pickett said. "We'll leave it there. Laser and I will walk to the café when our practice ends. Are you okay without our help at the clinic today?"

"We'll handle it," San Juan replied.

"We'll catch up with you at the library at about eleven and tell you everything we find out," Laser said.

Our important meeting had lasted only a few minutes, and nothing had been solved. I was not feeling very patient today, but I accepted the fact that this was going to take some time. We drifted over to the locker room and began dressing for our practice.

I had hopes that we would find some spirit and have a good workout this morning, but everyone seemed to hold back. The gym itself was too quiet. It was very evident that we had other things on our minds.

During the clinic we picked it up a couple of notches, and the kids were treated to their usual good time. Their laughter and great effort helped us get going. It was what we really needed. Sometimes when you think you are doing someone else a favor, you discover that the roles are reversed and you are the one getting the help. That's what today was like. These kids probably had no idea that we were suffering a little and that they were the medicine that would help us recover. I figured Sarah could tell, but she didn't say anything about it to me. I did notice that she watched me quite closely, however.

As eleven o'clock approached, Laser and Pickett walked into the library to join us. Coach followed them in, his head down. I can't say I was glad to see Coach. Last night had put a bad taste in my mouth, and I hadn't yet gotten rid of it. I turned back to the four young kids that were reading with Sarah and me. *Why is he here?*

"Coach would like to talk to the team," Laser announced.

I glanced at the clock. "I need these last five minutes to finish this story," I said without even turning around.

Exactly at eleven I got up and said to Sarah, "I'm sorry about this. I was expecting to have some time to talk to you today. I don't know if I will be back before your dad comes for you. If I'm not, I'll call you as soon as I can."

"It's okay," Sarah replied. "I'll stay with these kids until they are picked up. Then I'll read until you return or Dad stops in for me. We can talk later."

I could see in her eyes that she cared.

"We're going back to the gym where we won't have any distractions," Pickett announced as we all stepped out from the library into the cold February wind and blowing snow.

I looked at Laser and tried to read his face for clues about what he knew. He showed nothing. Coach didn't utter a single word, letting Pickett and Laser do the talking and the directing. It almost felt like the same attitude Coach had shown during the game last night. Coach also didn't smile or make eye contact with a single one of us. I didn't like any of what I saw. Coach looked defeated.

I need to know what caused him to act like that during our game. Last night I hated him, and now I'm feeling a little bit sorry for him.

Laser led us to our team bench area, the same location where Coach had yelled at me just a few hours before, and where he had sat me on the bench with seven others as the rest of our team fought hard to hang on and not lose the game . . . one player short.

Forget about feeling sorry for him. I remember exactly what he did last night, and now I'm upset again.

I could feel my teeth clenching together, and my fingers began to curl and form into fists.

Pickett spoke first. "Coach asked to meet with us so he could explain about last night. He has already spoken and answered questions at the café earlier this morning. He's our coach. Listen to him," Pickett said.

Coach stood and faced us. He studied us for a few moments. I could tell this was difficult for him, and we all waited patiently. There was no movement from anyone in the bleachers.

"I wish more than anything that I could erase what happened last night," Coach said, speaking softly. "What I did to you may be hard for you to forget . . . and maybe even harder to forgive. What I tell you now is not offered as an excuse. This is an explanation. I have no excuse for what I did. I'm not going to tell you details, but yesterday, early in the day, my family had a very close call on the farm. One careless action nearly caused a disaster, and it put me in shock. It bothered me all day. At last night's game I kept thinking about what had happened . . . and what the consequences might have been. I couldn't get it out of my head, and I couldn't get my mind on your game.

Then, Catcher, you dove and slid into the bench area, and I saw that as another careless action, and it triggered my memory of the farm incident, and I over-reacted and came down very hard on you guys. When I saw several of you clowning around I lost it. I saw nothing funny, and yet I noticed many of you making light of something that to me was totally serious . . . and I thought again of the near disaster earlier that morning. This doesn't excuse what I said or what I did, but maybe it will help you understand. I'm sorry for the way I handled things. I was very harsh and unfair with you. That's all I have to say."

Coach hesitated for a moment, then slowly turned and walked toward the door.

We all sat there, stunned. After a short time we began to search each other's faces for some help in trying to understand what we had just heard.

After a few moments in which the only sounds heard were some sighs and bodies beginning to squirm on the wooden bleachers, San Juan asked, "Now what? What do we do?"

"I don't know," Laser replied, shaking his head slowly from side to side as he looked down at the gym floor. "Hook's dad is going to meet with Coach first thing on Monday morning, but maybe we have a chance to influence what happens. We need to talk about what we think the Supe should do."

"Do you have any idea what your dad is thinking, Hook?" Tucson asked.

"Nope," Hook responded. "He doesn't share things like this with me."

"Coach has given me something to think about," Otto said. "I need some time."

"Me too," Abe added.

"Yeah, let's take some time," Pickett said. "Think about it today. Talk to each other. Then come hungry to my place tonight at 6:30. My mom has offered to cook up some spaghetti for a captains' dinner. We need everyone there. After we chow down we'll talk . . . listen to everyone . . . agree on a plan. We've got two games left before sections start, and we've got to get everything straightened out. We're in the middle of a very serious situation. Whatever we decide to do, we all have to work together. We have a chance to really do something special this year."

"Anybody have questions?" Laser asked.

No one said anything, but I saw a question forming on San Juan's face. I knew what he was thinking, and I shook my head slightly. *Don't even ask.We all need to be at the dinner and meeting.*

I knew that I had to call Sarah and break our movie date, but it was not a call I wanted to make, so I kept putting it off. Finally at 1:30 I realized that I was not being fair to Sarah. She should be given time to make new plans for tonight if she wants to do that. I was very disappointed about not getting to see Sarah tonight, but I needed to be responsible to my team. I felt caught between "a rock and a hard place."

When I dialed, Mrs. Jenkins answered.

"Hello, Mrs. Jenkins," I said. "May I please talk to Sarah?"

"Hi, Catcher," she replied. "Hang on. She's in her room. I'll call her."

I didn't have to wait long.

"Hi," Sarah said. "Did you figure things out this morning?"

"No, we didn't, but we raised some questions," I replied. " I really don't have anything I can share yet. We have no idea what's going to happen, but I can tell you that the whole team is going to talk things over tonight. Sarah, I have to break our movie date because everyone on the team is expected to attend a captains' dinner at Pickett's house tonight. After we eat, each player will offer his opinion about what he thinks should happen with Coach. I have to go to this. It's very important. I hope you understand how disappointed I am about not seeing a movie with you."

"I understand," Sarah replied. "Becky already called me after she heard from San Juan. We both know that you two need to be there. We'll have plenty of other chances for movies."

"You were supposed to hear about this team event from me," I said. "I should have called as soon as I heard about it, but I was hoping something would change. I was trying to figure out how to go to the dinner and see you."

"It's okay," Sarah said. "Becky is coming over here tonight so we'll still have fun. It will be just half of a double date. Only you, San Juan, and the movie will be missing."

When I heard Sarah's laughter I knew things would be okay.

The spaghetti dinner was delicious, though I'd rather have been some-place else. Laser's parents helped Pickett's mom and dad, and we twelve players cleaned our plates, only to have them covered again by more pasta, meatballs, and tomato sauce. These parents were intent on feeding us well, that's for sure.

I noticed that our laughter increased as the dinner moved along, and conversations became louder. It seemed like our team spirit was making a comeback, as evidenced by our good appetites and the volume in the room, and uncertainty was being shoved into a back seat. I sensed our strong J-Hawk connection returning. I started feeling confident that we could fig-ure out what to do by working together.

Pickett announced to us after our two tables had been cleared that he hoped we wouldn't be too disappointed, but he would not be singing to-night and playing his ukulele. Tucson and Treason applauded, and everyone laughed. Pickett then called us all to the TV set at 8:00 and told us he had lined up some other entertainment. He turned the tube on, and when it warmed up, we saw on the screen briefly, " . . . starring W.C. Fields." It was a hilarious comedy of Fields having all kinds of trouble trying to control his cue while shooting pool. Laugher filled the room as we watched, and I forgot all about the mess at our game last night. The pool hall episode lasted less than 30 minutes, and then Pickett turned off the TV, and everyone gradually quieted down.

I knew what was coming next and, because I had thought about our di-lemma and had talked to Dad about it while helping him with some chores in the barn that afternoon, I knew how I felt, and I was ready to share my thoughts when it was my turn to speak. I had decided that there was only one right way for the team to get back on track. I held out hope that my teammates had come to the same conclusion.

Laser led the meeting. "We will hear from all of you . . . no exceptions, and we won't leave tonight until we have reached agreement on how we want this resolved," he said.

It took about an hour, but everyone agreed that the best possible out-come was that Coach would continue being in charge of the team. After some statements, questions, and clarifications, there was no dissent. We vowed to back Coach 100%, and we would do our best to forget the ugliness that was Friday night. There had been several statements made to support Coach and the outstanding job he had done:

1) He had guided us to a perfect season so far.
2) He had listened to us, allowing us to make suggestions about changing things during games.
3) He had supported our community projects.
4) He never complained when we made announcements before the start of our home games.
5) He had made basketball practices fun for all of us.
6) He treated everyone fairly.
7) He understood us, and he liked coaching us.
8) He knew from his playing days how we needed to play.

The only negative mentioned was last night's game, and as a team, we were willing to chalk that off for Coach as "a bad night." We felt he should get a second chance (and a third and fourth if he needed it). *I certainly had been given second chances this season. It should be the same for Coach.*

Since we had reached agreement on what we wanted, now we needed to figure out how to convince the Supe that letting Coach continue was the only good solution. Captain Hook was given the job of finding out what time his dad planned to meet with Coach on Monday morning because all twelve of us intended to walk into the office right behind Coach and stand with him, showing Hook's dad how we felt. When Hook found out about the meeting time, he would spread the word. If the Supe allowed Coach to continue on with us, then we would really put out with a spirited practice after school on Monday. Hopefully that would heal everything. If that meeting concluded with a different result . . . then we would move on to Plan B.

We felt we were ready for anything.

Chapter 34

Brothers and Sisters

O tto's sister came up with the movie idea while we were all at church on Sunday morning. "Let's go to a movie this afternoon in Madison Lake. We'll have a brother-sister adventure. We'll have no arguments . . . no fights . . . no ridicule. We'll just have fun seeing a good movie. *Gidget Goes Hawaiian* is playing."

Her plan involved six of us: Otto, San Juan, and me . . . along with our three basketball-playing big sisters. We would meet at San Juan's and his sister's house, and San Juan would drive. It was such a simple plan that we didn't even check with our parents first. How could they say "no" if brothers and sisters wanted to do something together. Usually we argued, complained about not getting to use the phone, competed for the car, and seldom minded our own business.

The movie wasn't too bad. All of us thought it was pretty funny, but we guys didn't laugh at the same things our sisters did. We had different opinions about that. The girls focused on the romance, and they were moved to tears a couple of times. That brought even more laughter from us boys. The agreement about no fighting or arguing was thrown out early in the movie, and we were asked to quiet down a couple times by others in the theater.

After leaving the theater, we all put on our J-Hawk Nation stocking caps and walked to The Grill for sodas since we all agreed that it was way too early to go home. I wondered if people who saw us were curious about our group of six because all of us were wearing identical stocking caps.

When we set foot in The Grill, the first thing I saw was Sarah sitting in a booth with a couple girls and three boys. I tried not to let it bother me because it was almost the same thing as what I was doing . . . except that Sarah doesn't have a brother.

"Hi, Sarah," I said quietly as I walked by. I may have startled her. She turned toward me, smiled slightly, then looked away. I wondered if she was upset at me because I had canceled our movie date last night. I continued walking with the others to the tables in the back room, and I began to let it bother me that Sarah was sitting with some boys.

After a few minutes of arguing with the girls, I overheard Sarah say from the other room, "Stop that!"

I didn't know what was going on out there, but it got my attention, so I stood up and said to the others at the table, "I need to go out there. You guys stay here. I'll be back soon."

When I reached the booth I just stood there at first and looked things over. The boy next to Sarah had his arm around her. She said to him quietly, "Please remove your arm."

He just sat there with a big smirk on his face.

I kept my composure, took a deep breath, and spoke in a steady voice, trying not to show either the fear or the anger I was feeling, "I'm pretty sure that you heard what Sarah said, so I'm guessing that your problem is that you don't understand what she means. I'm willing to translate for you if you like."

The kid looked at me for a moment, then slowly removed his arm from her shoulders and the smile from his face.

"Sarah, would you like me to walk you home?" I asked politely.

She said to the two boys on her side of the booth, "Excuse me, I would like to get out."

Sarah didn't say anything to me as she put on her coat, J-Hawk Nation stocking cap, and her black mittens.

We walked the first block in silence. I had no idea what to say to her because I didn't know what to think. What had been going on?

Finally I said, "Sarah, I'm sorry if I embarrassed you back at The Grill, but I don't understand. I thought you and I were doing quite well . . . becoming good friends . . . and then this . . . Now I don't know what to think. Please help me understand. Talk to me. Is this about last night?"

That's it! That's all I said . . . Sarah said absolutely nothing . . . so I bit my lip and did not speak again during the rest of the three-block walk to her house. Besides the day being cold, it was icy between us.

When we reached her house she started crying, and my heart started breaking. "Please don't cry," I pleaded. Sarah quickly opened the door and rushed in. I stood there for a moment, speechless, not knowing what to do. Finally I closed the door, turned, walked down the steps and the sidewalk, and started trudging back to The Grill, weighed down by sadness. I was worried that I had wrecked things with Sarah. I felt lost.

I heard someone call to me.

"Catcher, I need you to come back here! I have some questions!" It was Mr. Jenkins. He had come out onto the steps and had yelled to me. I had never heard him speak like this before. He sounded angry.

"Yes, Sir," I said as I hustled back to the house.

"What's going on?" he asked. "Sarah ran to her room crying, and she won't tell her mother or me anything. What happened?"

"It's my fault," I said. "Sarah didn't do anything."

I explained about seeing her at The Grill after the brother-sister movie, about the six of us sitting in the back room at a table while Sarah's group stayed in the booth, and about hearing Sarah sounding upset.

"Mr. Jenkins," I said. "I was worried about her. She sounded angry, or maybe a little scared, or unsure, so I went out to her booth. She wouldn't look at me, and I saw that this kid had his arm around her shoulders. I heard Sarah tell him to stop.

"That's when I butted in and said something to him. I also offered to walk Sarah home. Maybe she thought I was angry. It was my fault. If I hadn't been at The Grill, I don't think any of this would have happened. I think this kid was hoping I would do something stupid and maybe upset Sarah . . . and it looks like that's exactly what I did," I said sadly.

"Sarah didn't even talk to me on the walk here, and then she started crying when we reached your house. She didn't say anything to me, and she didn't even look at me. I'm really sorry, Mr. Jenkins," I said sincerely. "I never meant to hurt her. I feel terrible. Would you please tell Sarah that I'm really sorry?"

"That's it? . . . There's nothing else? . . . Nothing else happened?" Mr. Jenkins asked.

"No," I replied as I shook my head slowly. "That's everything I know."

"All right," Mr. Jenkins said. "Thanks for explaining this. We'll talk to Sarah. I'm sure she'll be fine. Maybe you should call her tonight."

"I don't think calling her tonight is such a good idea. I'm not sure she will ever want to speak to me again," I said sadly.

Mr. Jenkins looked at me very seriously. "I really think you should call her tonight," he said again.

When I returned to The Grill, I explained to Otto, San Juan, and our sisters everything that had happened.

"I really did it this time," I said sadly.

Otto and San Juan were both sympathetic. Our sisters just looked at each other and shook their heads.

"Don't you get it?" my sister asked me, sounding a little irritated.

"Get what?" I asked her.

"Don't you even have a clue about what happened?" she asked again.

"I told you what happened!" I almost shouted back.

"It's probably not what you think," San Juan's sister said calmly. "It sounds like you handled things well."

"You are just like my little brother here," Otto's sister said to me.

" . . . Blind . . . deaf . . . and dumb, in the stupid sense."

"Hey!" Otto protested.

"You should call Sarah tonight," my sister said. "You need to talk to her."

"That's just what Mr. Jenkins told me," I said, "but I don't know."

"**CALL HER!**" our three sisters yelled.

I dialed Sarah's number. Sarah's dad answered.

"Hello, Mr. Jenkins," I said. "May I please speak to Sarah?"

"Hello, Catcher. It's good that you called," Mr. Jenkins said.

I heard a quiet voice on the other end. "Is that for me, Dad?" It was Sarah's voice.

"She's right here . . . and thanks for calling," Sarah's dad said.

"Hello," Sarah said.

"Hi, Sarah. I am really sorry about this afternoon," I said. "I wish the whole thing had never happened. It was my fault. If I hadn't gone into The Grill, this kid never would have bothered you."

"It's okay, Catcher. You didn't do anything wrong," Sarah replied, "and neither did I. It wasn't what it maybe looked like. My two girl friends and I were just sitting in the booth talking when these three boys came along and sat down. We were kind of trapped. We were just talking. None of us even like these guys, but when you came into The Grill, Joe put his arm around me. I think he was trying to bug you, and it really upset me."

"It was none of my business, and I should not have stepped in," I explained. "I'm sorry. I was worried about you. I thought you looked a little scared, and it didn't feel right to me. That's why I said something."

"I'm glad you did. Thanks for walking me home. That was very kind of you. I'm sorry I didn't talk to you. That was mean of me. I wasn't angry with you. I was embarrassed at what I had let happen to me. I was worried about what you had seen and what you might think. What if you didn't believe me? I'm glad you were there to rescue me," Sarah said.

"Sarah . . . I do believe you," I said. "It really saddened me to see you cry. I was afraid I caused that, and that you were really angry with me. I promise I will never, ever make you cry, Sarah. I wasn't sure you would speak with me, but I but I decided to call anyway. Did you know that your dad suggested that I call you tonight?"

"He did tell me that, and I was hoping you would follow his advice. He's a very smart dad, you know. I think he probably would like you to call me often," Sarah said.

I laughed. "I think you are absolutely right. Out of respect for your dad that will be my plan," I said.

What had started out as a serious situation turned into a great conversation. Sarah and I talked for several minutes, and we laughed about things that other kids probably wouldn't even think were funny. Sarah thought it was hilarious when I told her what Otto's sister had said about Otto . . . and me. I wanted to stay on the phone all night.

"After talking with you tonight, it sounds to me like we are doing okay," I said. "My heart feels good again. Does everything feel okay to you?"

"Yes," Sarah said. "Talking with you has made me feel much better. I wish I would have explained things on the walk home, but I was afraid you might not understand. I know I should have trusted you to believe me."

"Yeah . . . I think we both were a little worried, and not talking and not trusting made it a lot worse for me. Please don't ever give up on me. Promise me that you will talk to me if something like this happens.

"I do promise to talk to you, and I won't ever give up on you," Sarah replied.

"I want you to know that if I ever go into The Grill and see you are there with friends, I'll immediately turn around and walk out," I said. "I won't interfere from now on."

"No, Catch, I think I have a better idea," Sarah said. "I want you to walk over to us boldly and say in your best John Wayne voice, 'Howdy, everyone. Some of you will need to move so I can sit next to my girl.'"

"My John Wayne voice, huh?" I said. "I'll start working on that right away, and I repeated Sarah's words using a tough-guy voice . . . 'so I can sit next to my girl.'"

We both laughed, and I knew I had some voice work to do.

"Since you don't have a game Tuesday night, could you come to my choir concert at school?" Sarah asked. "It starts at seven o'clock."

"I'll see if I can use the car. It's probably about time I started adding some culture to my life," I replied.

Sarah ended our call by saying, "Thanks for calling me and for understanding."

"You are welcome. Thank you for taking my call. I hope to see you at your concert on Tuesday," I replied. Then I tried my John Wayne voice for a second time. "Good night, Pardner!"

I could hear Sarah's laughter as she hung up the phone, and I breathed a big sigh of relief.

Chapter 35

Recovery

Coach had been surprised when he saw all twelve of us players standing outside the Supe's office on Monday morning when he reported immediately after completing his bus route. He had looked at each of us as we stood tall in our black-and-white letter jackets, and each of us had nodded to him, letting him know that we were there for him. When we started filing into the Supe's office behind Coach, the Supe had said in an irritated voice, "This is a private meeting. Get to class!"

Pickett and Laser had refused to leave. Laser said to the Supe, "The decision you make today affects all of us. We need to represent our team."

The Supe had hesitated . . . then said, "Oh, all right. You will not say anything unless I ask you to speak. The rest of you . . . OUT!"

Like I said, we had felt we were ready. We had discussed the possibility that the Supe would kick us out, and we were prepared for it. We considered it to be a good compromise for us if Laser and Pickett were allowed to stay for the meeting.

In about thirty minutes Pickett and Laser made the rounds to our classes, got our attention, and shook their heads without saying a word.

It hadn't gone the way we wanted. Now we would have to move on to Plan B.

Our Tuesday practice at the end of the school day may have been our best of the season. Everyone felt energized. We all ran hard, and there was constant chatter and laughter. Laser and I were hitting our jump shots from the top of the key like well-oiled machines, and teammates were whooping loudly every time the ball made the net dance as it dropped through the hoop. The louder the gym became . . . the hotter we shot.

Captain Hook was almost perfect with his short hook shots from the right side of the lane, left arm extended, left elbow searching for unsuspecting noses to bloody . . . and Pickett never missed on his fade-away jump shots from near the foul line. Abe's long springy legs lifted him high off the floor as he caught passes above the rim and slammed them through the hoop, showing the knotted net no mercy. Otto and Sons played their hearts out, pushing all of us starters to keep working harder and aiming higher.

Everything seemed so good and so easy. Our spirit was outstanding, and we kept glancing at Coach, who often ran the floor with us, encouraging us and firing us up. I knew that our team was back. We had climbed up out of the deep hole we had fallen into at our game last Friday night, and we were preparing ourselves to show J-Hawk Nation and any upcoming opponents that we J-Hawks again deserved to be feared.

Our coach was definitely back. The way he blew his whistle told us that he was again in charge, and all twelve of us were glad for that.

I hadn't gotten a favorable response when I asked to use a car Tuesday night in order to attend Sarah's choir concert. Dad had a seed-corn meeting about an hour away, and Mom had a planning meeting at the church in town, so it looked like I would be shut out. It caught me by surprise when Mom said she would catch a ride home if Dad would drop her off at the church. That freed up a car for me to drive to MLHS to hear some choral music. I didn't even have a chance to tell Sarah that I was coming, but this would help balance out the crummy weekend that had just passed. I know that Mom likes Sarah, and she probably sees Sarah as a good influence on me. Maybe that's why I'm getting more opportunities to use a car.

Since I had never before been to Sarah's school, I allowed myself plenty of time for the drive. If I happened to arrive too early, I decided I could sit in the car and work on my math assignment. Prior to meeting Sarah I never would have carried homework with me when I went out. *What had she done to me?* Now I make better use of my time, and my teachers have commented on the improvement in the quality of my completed assignments.

When I saw other people start entering the school at about a quarter to seven, I decided to follow them in. Upon setting foot just inside the doorway, I dropped my jaw. There stood Sarah, off to the side, dressed in a royal purple choir gown that was accented by a shiny gold "collar" that was draped over her shoulders and extended down to her waist in the front of her gown. She looked radiant. I made eye contact with her, surprising her, and we both smiled.

"You came to my concert," Sarah said, a big smile decorating her beautiful face.

"Yes, I did," I replied, and I smiled again. "I am grateful that you have met me at the door to usher me in. By the way, your ushering uniforms are much classier than ours at Jeffers."

Sarah knew I was teasing. She looked at her reflection in the glass door, turned to me, and burst out laughing. "Yes, they are," she said, nodding as she reached for my arm and started walking me to the auditorium. "You may have trouble believing this, but I left some music at home, and Dad ran home to get it for me. I was just waiting for him at the door. He should be back any minute."

I studied her face for a moment, then nodded slightly. "Sure, Sarah. Good story," I said.

Sarah found a good seat for me right next to her mother. I told Mrs. Jenkins about meeting Sarah at the door in her choir gown. I could tell Mrs. Jenkins appreciated my sense of humor as I related the conversation that Sarah and I had shared.

Sarah's choir was about twice as large as my choir at Jeffers, and the singers were really good. I was impressed. As soon as the concert ended, Sarah's parents and I left the auditorium and walked down the hall to her rehearsal room.

"Wow, Sarah!" I said when I spied her hanging up her gown. "That performance was at least as good as one of Captain Hook's half-court swish shots plus three or four of Nicholson's clutch free throws!"

"That good, huh?" she laughed.

"Maybe I should have offered you a 'fantastic,'" I added.

This time she hugged me, and her parents both laughed at us.

"Could I meet your director?" I asked. "I have a question about next year."

"Miss Taylor," Sarah said, "this is my friend, Catcher, from Jeffers. Catch . . . this is Miss Taylor, my choir director. Catcher has a question he'd like to ask you."

"Hi," we both said as we shook hands.

"You have a great choir. I sing in the choir at Jeffers," I said. "I was wondering if there might be a chance to be in choir here next year during my senior year."

"I will be talking to Mrs. Johnson in a couple months to ask about recommendations and possible tryouts," Miss Taylor replied. "I expect there will be several from your school who might be interested in joining us. We will certainly welcome you."

As we walked down the hall, heading for the exit, Mrs. Jenkins said, "We have dessert waiting at home. Do you have time to join us, Catcher?"

"I can do that," I replied. "Thanks. I'd be willing to give Sarah a ride home if you don't mind."

"And I want to hear about your basketball team," Mr. Jenkins added.

I thought about taking the long way to Sarah's house because I hadn't been alone with Sarah for a long time, but I also felt a little unsure because of last weekend, so I drove straight there. As I turned to open the door after parking at the curb, Sarah reached for my arm. I stopped, turned back toward her, and looked into her sparkling eyes. I listened to them, and I surrendered.

I've missed you, "I said. I kissed her tenderly, and I no longer felt unsure about anything.

Sarah's smile melted me. "Why don't you bring this geometry book inside with you. Let's see about extending your visit with a study session after we eat."

While we ate apple crisp at the kitchen table, I told the Jenkins family what had happened since Saturday morning. "Everything looks good again," I began, "but it took a while to put everything back together. At our captains' dinner all twelve players spoke in favor of supporting Coach. On Monday we sat in the Supe's outer office waiting for the meeting between the Supe and Coach. We wanted Coach to see that we stood behind him. The Supe chased us all back to class except for Pickett and Laser, who refused to leave. They stood up to the Supe, and I think that was very important in how things turned out. That showed how determined our team was.

"We found out shortly after that meeting that the Supe had decided to delay his decision. He wanted more time to think things over. He said **he** would run the practice after school."

I took a bite of my dessert.

"What happened at your practice?" Mrs. Jenkins asked.

"First of all we needed to know how Hook felt about having his dad take over as our coach," I continued. "Hook explained, without any hesitation, that he was totally against it. He said he couldn't play for his dad. He said we needed Coach back, so we proceeded with Plan B."

I slowly took another bite of my apple crisp.

"Tell us about Plan B," Sarah insisted. "What was Plan B?"

I paused for a second and looked at Mrs. Jenkins. "This apple crisp is delicious," I said, and I slowly wiped my mouth with my napkin.

"Catcher!" Sarah sounded a little irritated. "Finish your story!"

I was kind of enjoying this. I looked at Sarah for a moment . . . then I continued. "When practice time arrived, we all reported to the locker room with all our stuff . . . like we do every day, but this time we carried our homework and our jackets, and we walked straight through the locker room and out the back door to the great outdoors, and we escaped to our homes . . . except for Captain Hook. He knew he couldn't go home, so Otto took him in. Otto said he had always wanted a little brother, but he had never gotten his wish. Now he said he was willing to lower his standards and accept Hook."

All of us laughed.

"So we all skipped practice, knowing the Supe wouldn't be too pleased, but we were hoping he would understand our motives and allow Coach to come back. Hook knew that his dad had a meeting out of town with other superintendents at seven o'clock last night, so we returned to the gym at 7:15 for a make-up, hour-long practice after talking our custodian into opening the gym for us. We had no intention of letting our basketball skills slide, so we ran drills and practiced our shooting.

"Then this morning the Supe announced at our morning assembly that Coach would be returning and running the practice today and that it was important for us to finish the season strong. He told us to put last Friday night behind us and only look forward. That's what we're gonna do . . . look forward . . . one game at a time . . . until someone tells us that we have no more games . . . that our season is over."

"I love happy endings," Sarah said as she applauded.

"But we don't see this as an ending, Sarah," I explained. "This is a new beginning. We are starting over, and we have big dreams."

"I also love happy beginnings," Sarah said smiling.

I stared at her . . . without saying anything . . . and I thought of the first time I saw her . . . and that I, too, love happy beginnings. I nodded in agreement.

Sarah asked her parents, "Is it okay with you if Catch stays for a while and we work on our math assignments at the table?"

"I will need to leave by 9:30 for sure," I added.

Sarah's mom nodded approval, and Sarah's dad said, "This kitchen table looks like a great study area for a couple of serious students."

Sarah and I cleared the table and began our homework. I completed my geometry problems while Sarah finished her algebra assignment. We only worked for about thirty minutes. Since it was not yet nine o'clock, Sarah told her parents we were going for a short walk.

The sky was so clear that the stars shone brightly in the cold air. I pointed out the big dipper and showed Sarah how to use the two "pointer" stars on the front of the dipper to find the North Star. "Now you will never be lost," I said. We listened to the snow crunch beneath our shoes as we walked around the block holding hands.

"This has been a great night," I said. "I'm really glad I came to your concert. This has been my best night ever for listening to a choir concert."

"It was nice to have you watching me for a change, even though it was just singing," Sarah said. Then she added, "I think we should study together more often."

"Yeah, I agree with that," I said. "Maybe I could become an 'A Honor

Roll' student like you are."

We walked in silence. After a couple minutes, I stopped and held Sarah in my arms. "This feels a lot better than Sunday," I said. "I don't want Sunday to ever happen again. I was afraid that I had lost you. Please remind me, Sarah, that any time we go to The Grill . . . I should never order a sundae . . . not even hot fudge."

Sarah put her arms around my neck and smiled that perfect smile. "No sundaes," she said.

I kissed her forehead.

We held each other in the cold February air . . . and I felt so warm inside. I knew for sure that I had fallen in love.

Just before 9:30 I thanked Sarah's parents for inviting me for dessert, and I walked down the sidewalk to the car.

I stood next to the car and searched the sky . . . found the North Star again . . . and shouted out, "We are . . . J-Hawks! . . . and we are no longer lost!"

Chapter 36

Homecoming

Immediately after Coach was given back his coaching position on Tuesday morning, some high school seniors started the ball rolling. They proposed that Jeffers hold its first ever Homecoming, and that it be centered around our final high school basketball game ever to be played in our Jeffers gym.

First ever Homecoming . . . last ever home basketball game in Jeffers. The irony of this didn't escape me. I thought it was a great idea, but I figured it had no chance to be a start of a new tradition.

During the school day on Tuesday, some students started making signs to put in the windows of Main Street businesses. The signs gave information about the upcoming Homecoming event on Friday night, February 9th. I saw signs that read, "Former J-Hawk letter winners will be honored," and "Tell your grown-up children about this event."

We had no idea what to expect, but we guessed that the gym bleachers would be crowded. I made sure I told Sarah and her parents to arrive early on Friday night. I wanted to be able to usher them in to their usual seats.

When the gym doors were opened at six o'clock, there were already close to a hundred people waiting. My family and Sarah and her parents were among them. Our squad was swamped as we worked hard to clear the lobby area. This was the earliest I had ever seen our gym fill up. When all the seats had been taken and most of the standing room spots had been grabbed, I was free to watch the girls play. However, there was a problem. Sarah had not been able to save a place for me. That's how packed the bleachers were. Now I needed a Plan B.

Pickett and Laser were sitting at a card table in the lobby selling J-Hawk Nation stocking caps. They motioned me over.

"About ten people have bought caps so far tonight, but we have some things to go over for the introductions and announcements," Laser told me.

"Could you take over for us here? You only need to stay until half-time ends. Then secure everything in the concession stand. You can ask one of the guys to help you."

"Hey . . . Plan B!" I replied. "Perfect!"

"What?" Pickett asked.

"I'll do it," I said. "I'll take over for you. I'll be right back."

I worked my way through the people that were standing by the entrance to the gym and waited for a stoppage in play. Then I quickly stepped over to where Sarah was sitting.

"Sarah, I could really use your help," I said. "I'm taking over for Laser and Pickett, selling caps at a table in the lobby. If you sat at the table with me . . . I bet we would have a lot of people interested . . . me for sure." I grinned. "I'll bring you back for the start of the 3rd Quarter, right before I head to the locker room."

Sarah looked at her parents and said, "Please save this space for me. I need to help Catcher." She then stepped down to the floor, and we headed to the lobby.

I heard a voice from the bleachers say, "That was done very well, Catcher." I did not turn around, but I felt a smile build on my face as I turned and looked at Sarah. *That wasn't John Garris's voice, was it?*

The area around our table was really busy during halftime, and five or six kids bought caps before we closed up. Quite a few of the young kids had talked with me, but most of them had been more interested in Sarah. I actually had felt a little jealous, but I kind of understood. After watching her for a short time I remembered that I had seen, a few weeks back, that she was like a magnet. She was an attraction. She drew people . . . like me. I wanted to be around her because she was fun, and she made everything fun. She was always the center of smiles and laughter.

Though I had a game coming up tonight, I knew it would be difficult for me to take Sarah back to her seat on the bleachers and walk to the locker room. I felt like a small piece of iron filing that had no chance against the pull of the magnet called Sarah. Maybe my teammates would have to scrape me away.

Before we returned to the gym, I guided Sarah to a private corner in the lobby. "I want to tell you about a special play for tonight," I said quietly. "We're hoping to pull this off at the end of the game . . . the final play of an official game in this gym. Coach told us we **might** get to run it, but he said it depends on how the game goes."

"What is it?" Sarah asked with great interest.

"First of all . . . don't be fooled by how it starts," I explained. "It will look like we are repeating Hook's 'Peter Pan' shot, but we tinkered with it. Instead of shooting, Hook will send a high arching hook pass to Abe by the rim, and Abe will use his length to attempt to catch the ball and slam it through the hoop. Our final play . . . an exclamation point!"

"I hope you get to do it, and I hope it works," Sarah said.

"Me too. Don't tell anyone about it, even your dad," I continued. "When your dad watches it unfold . . . if he says something about 'Peter Pan,' then you can tell him right away that he's wrong, that it's going to be 'Tinker Bell,' because we tinkered with it. Maybe he'll get a laugh out of that, and if the play works, you'll have everyone around you knowing you are a witty basketball genius."

Sarah laughed. We talked for a couple more minutes, and then I knew it was time for me to start getting dressed for my game and for my good friend to reclaim her place in the bleachers. It felt good knowing that Sarah would be watching the game, anticipating a spectacular ending.

The locker room was pretty loud as we dressed in our gold uniforms with the T-shirt style jersey and talked about the Bengals. We had been watching how people had packed into our gym tonight, wondering if they had come because of our trouble at our last game or if they were here because it was indeed our last game in our Jeffers gym. We were fired up, and we wanted tonight's game to be among the best ever played here.

I walked over to Abe, Hook, and Pickett to do a quick review of our signals for the set plays that Coach wanted us to try out tonight. These weren't really new plays. We had scored many points doing these same things in several games, but in those previous games, things had just happened . . . they weren't planned ahead of time. Tonight I would give a signal that called for a certain play for Captain Hook, or for Pickett, or for Abe.

I said to Captain Hook, "Watch my right hand. If I curl it up like a hook, you need to set a screen for Pickett . . . then roll back to the left. I'll bounce you a pass, and you should be free for one of your special eight-to-ten foot sweeping hook shots. You've made so many of these this year . . . I expect you'll make some more tonight. If I see you curl your hand, I'll know you are begging for me to call your play."

"Okay, Pickett, you know the signal for your play," I said. "Move toward Laser . . . then break back quickly for my pass. You'll be shooting your fade-away jumper from your sweet spot near the free-throw line."

Abe's play would take precise timing and location. Pickett would move out to the free-throw line and prepare for a high pass from me. He and I each had to be standing in an exact location, because the high, hard pass that I would throw above Pickett's head was intended to reach Abe by the rim, and hopefully Abe would catch it and slam it through the hoop in one motion. Pickett's job was to draw defenders as he moved and jumped for the ball, but he would allow the basketball to pass over him without even touching it. I really liked the possibilities of this play. It had a chance of fooling (and impressing) a lot of people.

"Good luck, Abe," I said as I shook his hand.

Laser talked with these same three guys because he had a play for each of them that he would run from his side of the floor.

We were ready. Tonight would find us using our full-court press, running our fast break, and calling planned plays, and we expected to tame these Bengals. We needed to show J-Hawk Nation that what had happened to us a week ago had been repaired, and we were a good team again.

Laser and Pickett handled all the announcements and Homecoming introductions. Besides the usual information about refreshments in the kitchen after the game and tomorrow's clinic, they asked all former and present Jeffers J-Hawks to stand. I looked at my mom and dad, my brother and my sisters, and all the others who stood. J-Hawk Nation had swelled its ranks tonight.

Former letter winners in softball, baseball, and basketball were invited to step out onto the gym floor, and special recognition was given to the boys' J-Hawk basketball team from '57-'58, the only team from Jeffers that had ever made it to the state tournament. Eight players from that team walked to the center circle and waved to the crowd, and my teammates and I walked over to them and exchanged handshakes. I heard several of them tell us, "You can do it. Go for it all." That certainly was our goal. We wanted to feel their success and then some.

When the ref tossed the ball up for the center jump to start the game, Abe reached high and tapped the ball to Pickett. He secured the ball and pivoted to face our basket, and the rest of us moved into our positions and began to organize on our end, making quick passes inside and around the perimeter. When Hook returned a pass to me and I was not covered closely, I jumped up and shot the ball cleanly through the hoop for the game's first points. Immediately we set up our full-court press. The Bengals struggled while trying to move the ball up court. Their second pass overshot its target and was grabbed by Abe. He relayed the ball to Laser and he bounced it to Pickett for an easy layup.

As the Bengals passed the ball in for a second time, we dropped back to the half and put pressure on as soon as they crossed the line. We covered them tightly and didn't allow them much room in which to dribble or pass. Number 31 caught a pass and took a quick shot over Laser's hands, and the ball barely reached the rim. Abe grabbled the rebound, swung around, and passed to Laser as I sprinted up court. Laser threw the ball to me, leaving just enough room for me to take one dribble before I laid the ball against the backboard for our third basket of the game.

The Bengals again inbounded the ball, and while bringing the ball up the court, Bengal player Number 20 threw a pass out of bounds while trying to pass around the press. Laser put the ball in play, and Pickett found an opening and took a short jump shot that bounced off the rim. Abe was there to grab it and drop it through the netting. On the Bengal's next possession Number 20 took a wild shot that missed, and Pickett collected the rebound and passed to Laser on the right sideline. Again I sprinted toward the basket, grabbed Laser's pass, and softly shot the ball into the basket with my left hand.

We were up by ten points after only three minutes, and the Bengals took a timeout.

Otto, San Juan, Tucson, and Treason all got playing time in the first quarter, and we continued to score easily and run at every opportunity. At the end of the first quarter we held an 18-8 lead.

We met at the bench after the buzzer signaled the end of the 1st Quarter. "Great job pressing, running, and defending," Coach told us. "We'll come back to this in the 3rd Quarter, but we're going to run set plays in the 2nd. That means you five starters are playing until I change the plans. Let's build a big lead so the rest of the guys get some good playing minutes in the second half."

"We are . . . J-Hawks!" we all shouted, and five of us headed to the center circle.

I grabbed the ball that Abe tapped my way, and I dribbled into our end. I curled my right hand as I dribbled with my left, and Hook made his move . . . just as we had set it up. His defender followed him to Pickett, and Hook broke free as he moved back to my side. I bounced him a pass. Hook grabbed the ball, stretched out, and gently tossed his hook shot cleanly through the hoop.

"Great job, Captain Hook!" I shouted as we ran back to defend.

The next time down Laser called a play for Abe. The play worked well, but Abe's shot bounced up off the rim. Hook was in a perfect position, and he tapped the ball into the basket. So far . . . so good.

All of us slid our feet quickly on defense, not allowing the Bengals to pass the ball inside or get good shots from the perimeter. We owned the rebounds. Laser and I continued to call plays without making too many extra passes. Pickett hit a jump shot, and Hook was perfect on a ten-footer. I had signaled for both of these plays.

Laser called Pickett's play, and the result was two more points for us after Pickett banked in a soft shot from about six feet away. The Bengals scored on a jump shot, but our lead now stood at 14 points.

It was time for Abe's special play. I dribbled over to my spot and gave the signal by lifting my chin upward. Pickett moved out toward the free-throw line, lining himself up with the basket, and I passed the ball high in his direction. He jumped up and reached for the ball, but he let it fly between his hands as two defenders moved in to cover him. Abe timed his break to the basket perfectly, and he caught the pass close to the rim and threw it down inside the netting. Wow! It was outstanding, and the crowd loved it.

Laser and I kept signaling plays, and Abe, Pickett, and Hook kept getting open for scoring opportunities. Many of the shots were successful, and when halftime arrived, we led by nineteen.

"Nice work, men," Coach said in the locker room. "On Tuesday night we'll run these plays again, but tonight in the second half, we'll just run. Everything will be wide open. I'll be making lots of substitutions, but I intend to keep either Laser or Catcher on the floor to control things out front, and I plan to keep one of the big guys underneath for rebounding. Take your open shots. Let's see if we can get a basket from each of you tonight."

During the 3rd Quarter we built our lead to 26, as Tucson, Go Forth Son, and Nicholson scored their first points of the game. I could tell by the noise level in the gym that J-Hawk Nation was enjoying this.

During most of the 4th Quarter our bench players took all the shots. I felt that my job was to give them good chances to score. Our shooting percentage wasn't great, but we kept shooting, and eventually we led by thirty with about a minute to go.

When Nicholson grabbed the rebound on a Bengal miss, Coach stood and called for a timeout.

I hope he gives us a chance.

"All right, J-Hawks," Coach said, "you've earned this opportunity. Starters are back in. Milk the clock down by making quick passes, and set up for your final shot. Good luck. Let's give J-Hawk Nation something to remember."

"We are . . . J-Hawks!"

The crowd stood and applauded when we starters took the floor. Pickett passed the ball in to Captain Hook. He pivoted left and right before he passed the ball to me. I passed to Laser. We swung it around quickly . . . to Abe . . . Laser . . . inside to Pickett . . . back to Laser . . . to me . . . Hook

. . . me . . . back to Hook . . .

Twenty seconds remained in the game, and the volume kept increasing.

Laser took a couple of dribbles, then he held the ball while we other four met at the free-throw line.

The clock kept winding down.

"Let's go!" Pickett yelled, and we ran back to our positions.

Then we ran the play.

Laser passed the basketball to me, and Pickett set a screen for Hook. Hook ran the baseline under our bucket and turned up-court after running by Abe's screen. Laser cleared out his area by running a diagonal to Hook's corner, and Laser's defender followed him. When Hook met me at the top of the key, he took over my dribble in a nifty exchange of the ball, and I stepped in front of his defender as he set up for his "shot."

With his left arm extended for balance and the basketball cradled in his right hand, Hook extended and launched a high arching pass toward the left side of the rim. In one motion, Abe leaped high, grabbed the ball out of the air, and slammed it through the hoop. *Outstanding!*

I raised my arms toward the rafters in celebration as the buzzer sounded . . . and I held them there as the buzzer continued to blare for about five seconds because the guy running the clock chose to add another exclamation point to the final play in the gym.

Our entire team ran to the center circle and huddled closely. "We are . . . J-Hawks! . . . We are . . . J-Hawks! We are . . . J-Hawks!" we shouted loudly before lining up to shake hands with the Bengals.

As I passed through the line saying, "Good game," I heard my guy, Number 30, say to me, "Win it all. You guys are tough."

We stayed in our line and walked the perimeter of the gym, shaking hands and slapping hands of young and old members of J-Hawk Nation as everyone stood in place and kept applauding. When we had completed our lap, we walked to the center circle, looked outward to the crowd, and applauded them in appreciation of their great support. Soon the gym floor was completely covered with people.

It was a great ending to an outstanding game. I felt it.

This was our 17th straight win tonight and a great way to celebrate the final game that would ever be played by J-Hawks in our gym. Tonight almost felt like a festival because of the return of former J-Hawk players. Honoring the players who had played basketball on previous teams had increased our motivation in tonight's game, and we had been determined that all twelve of us would have opportunities to score points.

I found Sarah and her parents waiting next to our team bench area. I grabbed a towel and quickly dried off. While I was playing I knew I had to keep my focus on basketball, but now I could relax. I would not want Sarah to know this, but while I ran the floor, I tried to forget she was here watching. Now she was all I focused on.

Tonight Mr. Jenkins did a lot of talking. He was so excited about our win, about how well we had played, and about how many former players had returned for tonight's game. He had compliments and praise for every player. Sarah, her mom, and I just looked at each other and smiled, adding to the conversation only occasionally.

"Did your dad think he was seeing 'Peter Pan' again?" I asked.

"When he saw Captain Hook with the ball at the top of the circle he said, 'Peter Pan,' so I did just as you said and explained that this time it was 'Tinker Bell,'" Sarah replied. "I amazed him, just like you predicted."

"Did you like the plays we ran, Sarah?" I asked.

"Yeah, I did, especially the pass over Pickett to Abe, or was that a mistake?" Sarah asked.

"No, it was planned. Didn't you see my signal?"

"I didn't see any signals," Sarah replied. "Did you really give signals?"

"Both Laser and I called the plays with signals. I'll tell you about them later," I said.

After a few more minutes of mixing with parents and friends on the gym floor we players headed for the showers. We would be back out for a snack shortly.

I grabbed a couple cartons of J-Hawk Juice and a couple cookies and sat down with Sarah at a lunchroom table next to some other players and friends. I was pumped. I had so much I wanted to say to Sarah, to tell her how glad I was that she had come to the game, how pretty she looked again tonight, how much I enjoyed her smile and her humor, how nice I think her parents are . . . I just didn't know where to start.

I decided to skip all the small talk. "Sarah," I said, "would you like to go to a movie with me tomorrow night? I don't know what's playing, but I don't think it really matters what the movie is about. I just want to sit next to you in the theater."

By the look on her face I could tell she was going to turn me down. I wondered if I had said or done something to upset her.

"I'm sorry, Catcher," she replied. "Tomorrow night is family night at my house, and I'm staying home with Mom and Dad to play cards. Would you like to come over to play "Hearts" with us? We have a lot of fun. Usually I invite a girlfriend to join us, but Mom suggested I ask you this time. She and Dad would love it if you said yes . . . and I wouldn't mind it much either."

What a relief! I was really worried I had messed up somehow. Playing cards with Sarah's family does sound like it could be fun. What Sarah said last . . . I've heard that before . . . No . . . I've said that before. I said it to her. She just got me back.

I'd love to join your family tomorrow night," I replied. "Thanks for asking me. I look forward to playing cards with you."

"The card game starts at seven," she said. "Come prepared. Mom and Dad both play for blood, and **they** taught me."

I grinned. *I'm not going to tell her that my friends and I play Hearts often, and I'm pretty good at it. I hope I don't get too intense. It's important to me that her whole family likes me. I'll be on my best behavior.*

"By the way, Sarah," I continued. "You look very pretty tonight, and I really enjoy seeing your smile and hearing your laughter. I'm so glad you and your parents come to the games. I think your parents are great."

Our hands met in the center of the table, and neither of us spoke.

Tonight's Homecoming event had turned out great, and now Sarah has invited me to come to her home to play cards tomorrow night. I guess that the whole weekend is a "Homecoming" for me.

In the Stands – With John Garris

Darkness! That's how the J-Hawk game had ended on that Friday night, one week ago. The coach had been seriously angry at eight of his players, shouting at them near the bench . . . and all players had been upset with their coach who had placed the game in jeopardy by putting only four players on the floor for the last few minutes of the game as the lead dwindled. That kind of darkness.

I thought it would have been fitting for the lights to be off or maybe turned way down low for the start of the home game last night against Burton because most people expected that the dark cloud might still be hovering. No one knew how the J-Hawks would respond to their recent turmoil.

Maybe the ushering squad knew. Their heads were not down. They wore the look of confidence as they walked fans to seats while smiling and joking around. I studied the cavalry regiment . . . the family that had arrived near halftime of one game and appeared to rescue the J-Hawks from a certain loss . . . and they,

too, looked as if they knew that J-Hawk Nation would be pleased by tonight's game. (Maybe they had inside information.)

It only took about a minute of the game clock for me to know how this game would turn out. "Let there be light!" The J-Hawks were light footed and fast as they sprinted to three early fast-break baskets. They knew the spotlight was on them, yet they played as if they carried no extra burden . . . as if their hearts were light, and they made the game fun again. After three minutes of play, a timeout was called, and I saw the lightness of their spirit. Two J-Hawk benchwarmers stood up and held up a hand-lettered cardboard sign that they had been sitting upon. It read:

COUNT THEM!
NO MORE . . .
PLAYING JUST 4.
WE'LL STAY ALIVE
BY PLAYING ALL 5.

J-Hawk Nation rose, laughed, and applauded as the sign was turned and shown to all in the gym. The lights were back on! Light feet . . . light hearts . . . light verse. That kind of light . . . and for the Bengals who came into the J-Hawk gym tonight . . . it quickly was lights out.

The fast-breaking guards, the high-jumping forwards, and the sharp-shooting center played extremely well, and the J-Hawks subbed often and scored easily . . . and yes, I did count them. I needed to be sure.

The Homecoming crowd was treated to a great display of skill, effort, and teamwork . . . and J-Hawk Nation will remember this final game in their small gym as being one of the best ever, resulting in a 32-point victory over the hapless Bengals, extending the J-Hawk winning streak to 17 games.

The final play, a resounding dunk by Abe, set up by several screens and a precise "hook pass" from Captain Hook, was an excellent final tribute to this gym that has treated the home team so well over the years, as well as to all the J-Hawks who have run this floor and contributed their sweat to the floor boards and this gym's history.

With one final conference game to be played and play-offs just ahead, the J-Hawks appear to be ready to begin their march toward March.

Chapter 37

A Game of Hearts

After another energetic Saturday-morning practice, followed by an inspiring clinic that was attended by the usual 25 or so kids, and ending with a great trip to the library, Sarah and I went for a walk. It was cold on this February morning. We didn't stray too far because of the cold air and because Sarah said her dad would be stopping at the library for her at 11:20.

Twenty minutes! I have twenty minutes to walk, talk, and laugh with Sarah without having to share her with anyone else. I really look forward to Saturday mornings.

It didn't take long before we felt the cold, so we stepped back inside the library. It would have been nice to have some hot chocolate while we talked, but this was not The Jeffers Café. The twenty minutes passed too quickly, and we said our good-byes when her dad showed up.

"I'll see you tonight," I said.

As soon as I got home, I found the *Globe* and read Garris's column. I thought it was good. I laughed at a couple things he had written, and I decided that Garris is pulling for us to do well.

While looking in the paper I saw an ad that caught my attention . . . because of a picture. It was a heart. With Valentine's Day coming up . . . and having just spent some time with Sarah . . . and with an evening ahead of playing "Hearts" . . . I noticed the heart. I had been wondering about what I could get Sarah as a special gift for Valentine's Day, and now I thought I had found my answer. I read about this silver heart that was called a "Forever Heart." The ad read, "The Forever Heart is made from a high quality metal. The satin-silver, simple, smooth heart is the size of a dime, and it will last a lifetime."

It was the "lifetime" phrase that grabbed me. I wanted our friendship to last a lifetime. Maybe this was a sign. The ad said that the heart came with a matching beautiful necklace chain. I was sold.

I found Mom and showed her the ad. "Could you lend me a little money so I could get this 'Forever Heart' for Sarah?" I asked.

"Are you sure about getting this?" Mom asked. "You've only been friends with Sarah for a few months, and it's pretty expensive for a kid who doesn't have much money."

"I know it's expensive," I replied, "but it will last a lifetime, and that's what I'm hoping for. It's exactly right for Sarah. I think she'll love it and wear it. I really want to get this. Can we go today? I'll pay you back with my hay-baling money this summer."

She didn't hesitate long. "We'll leave in an hour," Mom said. "I have a couple errands to run, so it won't be an extra trip. Make sure you bring the ad . . . and I think you are right. Sarah will love it."

It hadn't taken much to convince Mom about the necklace. That kind of surprised me, but lately I've noticed that both Mom and Dad seem to be more open-minded about things that I ask about. Maybe they are rewarding me because my basketball team has done so well, or maybe it's because meeting Sarah has changed me, and they like the changes. Anyway, now I'm set for Valentine's Day except for a card and a plan about how to give the heart to Sarah. I need to think of a special surprise . . . because Sarah likes surprises and mystery.

At seven o'clock I knocked on the Jenkins's door. All three members of Sarah's family were standing at the door to greet me.

"Come on in," Sarah's mom said. "We're so glad you chose to join us tonight."

I asked Mr. Jenkins how coffee was at The Jeffers Café this morning. "Is there anything that we players should know about?" I inquired.

He smiled at me and said, "The coffee was hot and plentiful, the place was packed with regulars, and the conversation was lively but friendly. That's all I'm able to share with you."

I moved on to Sarah. "Great job with the kids again this morning," I said. "You are a natural when you read to them. I find that I'm not much help at the library anymore because I just want to watch you and listen to you read. It's kind of funny that our library time was just a last-minute idea we threw on at the end of the clinic, and it's become a very important part of our Saturday morning. You've been a great help. Have you ever thought about becoming a teacher some day like your mom?" I asked. I can tell you'd be great at it. I know I'd pay attention and learn a lot as one of your students."

"I have thought about it," Sarah replied. "I especially like the youngest kids."

We sat down at the dining-room table. I was across from Sarah, who reached for the cards, shuffled them expertly, and dealt. We agreed to follow the usual "Hearts" routine of passing three cards left, then right, then across, and then, on the fourth hand, holding the cards we were dealt. I looked into the faces of my competition, and I knew I would have to protect myself from each of these three trying to collect all the point cards, giving the rest of us 26 points each.

The games were very quiet but fiercely competitive. There wasn't much conversation as everyone was concentrating on the game. Each of us played some good hands, but occasionally someone suffered from some "bad luck." We were all quite evenly matched, and I really enjoyed the games with Sarah and her parents, but it wasn't the actual card game that was the highlight of my evening.

A couple hours into the card game Mrs. Jenkins asked for some help bringing in some snacks from the kitchen. Mr. Jenkins was busy shuffling the cards, and Sarah said that she needed to recheck her addition on the scorecard, so I volunteered to help.

On the way to the kitchen I asked Mrs. Jenkins, "Do you think we can trust them?"

She burst out laughing.

The homemade apple pie alamode was delicious. When everyone was finished Sarah and I cleared the table and took the dishes to the kitchen while Mr. Jenkins dealt the next hand.

When we returned to the table, I picked up my cards and started fanning them out, sorting them by suits, while everyone else seemed to be just sitting there watching me. I was a little concerned, but then I saw the special card in my hand. It wasn't part of the regular deck. Delicately written on this card was a question: "Will you please go with me to my school's Sweetheart Dance next Saturday night?" Next to Sarah's name was a small red heart.

I smiled across the table to her and said, "Yes, I will go with you to your dance. Do your parents know about this?"

"My parents know about everything," Sarah replied.

"So, Mrs. Jenkins," I said looking directly at her, "they couldn't be trusted after all."

"That's why I laughed at your suspicion. I knew they were stacking the deck for you," she added. "Sarah came up with this idea a couple of weeks ago. We all figured you would like her special invitation."

"Sarah, I admire your creativity. During a game of "Hearts" you have invited me to your Sweetheart Dance. You are something special," I said.

I hesitated a little, and then I continued. "There may be a problem though. I was a little rude to your principal, Mr. Weston, when he visited our school about a month ago. Here we were, in the middle of the last basketball season at our school, having won all our games so far, and he came to talk to us about our school being closed next year. His visit hit me the wrong way, and I made a couple smart-aleck comments. I don't think he appreciated what I said, and he'll remember me for sure."

"Bob Weston is a friend of ours," Mr. Jenkins said. "He told me about his less-than-friendly reception at your school. He said one kid in particular created some issues. That was you?" he asked, looking surprised.

I nodded sheepishly.

We all just sat there looking at each other for a few moments.

"I'm certainly willing to apologize to him, but he might not let me attend your dance anyway, since I am an outsider. I admit that I didn't make a very good impression," I said. "I'm sorry, Sarah."

"How about I give him a call at school on Monday to smooth things over? He knows our family. I'm sure he'll understand," Mr. Jenkins suggested.

"Thank you, Mr. Jenkins, but I think that I should make my own call. Since I caused this problem, I think I need to be the one to fix it," I replied.

"I'll call Mr. Weston at school after lunch or during my study hall and apologize for my impolite behavior during his visit. I'll explain that Sarah has invited me to the dance, and I'll ask him if he would be willing to give me a second chance. Do you think my apology will help?"

"I think it will," offered Mrs. Jenkins.

"Do you think I should grovel? I asked.

Mr. Jenkins laughed loudly. "You might want to give it a try," he said jokingly.

I like Sarah's dad. He's easy to talk to, and I think he understands me.

Sarah asked her mom, "What does it mean to 'grovel?'"

Mrs. Jenkins explained, "It means to be very humble, to act like you are almost unworthy, and that you have little self-respect."

"I don't want you to have to do this, Catcher," said Sarah. "This dance is not worth it. We can do something else next Saturday night. Let's go to a movie."

I replied to Sarah very respectfully and honestly, "Sarah, . . . this dance **is** very important. I've just been invited to my first dance ever by my girlfriend, and I don't want to miss it. I don't want you to miss it either . . . because of me. I'll be all right with Mr. Weston. This time I'll be more respectful."

I could see in Sarah's parents' faces that they expected Mr. Weston to accept my apology, especially since it was Sarah who had extended the invitation. I'm hopeful that things will work out, and I will be welcome.

I went to the office right after I finished eating my lunch on Monday, and I received permission from the secretary to use the phone to call Mr. Weston at Madison Lake High School. There wasn't any privacy in the office so I felt very uncomfortable. I wasn't eager to share my predicament with another pair of ears so I asked if there was another phone I might be able to use. I was really surprised when Mrs. Halden directed me to the Supe's office and closed the door as she returned to her desk. Now I was out of excuses, and soon I would be out of lunch-time, too.

I took out from my pocket the paper on which I had written the phone number for MLHS. I then took a couple deep breaths and prepared to dial.

Part of me hoped the phone wouldn't work, that I had written down the wrong number, or that no one would answer, but that certainly wouldn't solve my problem. No . . . I needed to talk to Mr. Weston . . . respectfully . . . apologetically . . . and, I told myself . . . I cannot react negatively to anything he tells me. I repeated it to myself again: "RESPECTFUL . . . APOLOGETIC!"

I took two more deep breaths . . . Then I dialed. After three rings a voice answered. "Madison Lake High School. My name is Marilyn. How may I help you?"

"Hi, I'm a student at Jeffers High School," I replied. "My friends call me Catcher, and I would like to talk to Mr. Weston if possible. He's not expecting my call, however."

"Just a moment," she said. "I'll see if he's available to take your call."

"Thank you," I replied.

It seemed like I waited for an eternity, but it may have been only for a minute or two.

"This is Mr. Weston. How may I help you?"

"My friends call me Catcher," I said for the second time in this call. "I'm a junior at Jeffers, a basketball player, and I was present in the assembly room when you visited our school about a month ago. I'm sure you remember me because I'm afraid I was the student who made comments and asked questions during your talk. I would like to apologize for how I acted and for what I said.

"Yes," Mr. Weston said. "I certainly recall that visit . . . and I do remember you."

This may not turn out well.

I continued respectfully, "I'm sorry for how I spoke to you and what I said that day. I was wrong in how I acted. I'm hoping that you will accept my apology and give me another chance."

"I appreciate your call, Catcher," Mr. Weston said. "I do accept your apology. At Madison Lake we believe in second chances. I'll be back at Jeffers in a few weeks for another try at a welcome, and I hope you students will give me a second chance."

"The students often listen to me," I added. "I'll do what I can to help make your next visit go better."

I went on. "There is a second reason for my call."

"I'm listening," Mr. Weston stated.

"One of your students, Sarah Jenkins, a sophomore, has recently invited me to Saturday's Sweetheart Dance at your high school. I gladly accepted Sarah's invitation, but then I explained to Sarah and her parents that it's possible I will not be welcome to attend the dance because of my behavior on your visit to Jeffers. Mr. Jenkins told me he's a friend of yours, and he offered to call you on my behalf, but I knew this was a call I needed to make myself.

"You said you believe in second chances. Does that mean you would allow me to attend the dance with Sarah? This event is very important to her and to me," I added.

"I've learned a lot about you from our conversation today, Catcher, and I have no problems with you attending the dance with Sarah Jenkins. In fact, I'll be the one welcoming you at the door on Saturday night," Mr. Weston concluded.

"Thank you, and thank you for taking my call," I said. "I know that Sarah will be as pleased as I am. Good-bye, Mr. Weston."

I breathed a big sigh of relief as I hung up the phone.

With chores done, supper eaten, and homework completed . . . now I had some time to think about a valentine card. I had no money to spend on a card, so I expected I would have to make one. I sat down at the dining room table near where my younger sister was working. A sixth-grader, she was surrounded at the table by crayons, pencils, scissors, paste, and paper . . . all kinds of art supplies. I watched her for a couple minutes as she cut out some paper hearts and designed a valentine, and I knew what my next move would be.

"You are a talented artist," I said. "Would you please help me make a valentine that I could write in and give to Sarah? It would really help me out."

"It's for Sarah?" she asked.

"Yah," I replied. I opened the small wooden box that was sitting on the table. "This is the heart necklace I'm giving her, and I need a good card. I'm planning to write a poem. When I finish it, I'll type it and give it to you, and you can paste the poem inside and decorate around it with hearts. I'll tell Sarah that you made the card, and she'll be grateful to you."

"Okay," she replied.

"I'm going to write my poem now because I need to get the necklace and the card to Sarah's parents somehow at the game tomorrow night. It will be a Valentine's Day surprise for Sarah. You can't say anything," I told her.

"Do you want me to seal my lips with paste?" she asked with a grin.

I just raised my eyebrows and smiled back at her.

The words came easily once I decided what direction to take. I focused on the fun times Sarah and I had enjoyed together. My plan was to remind her of those times and tell her that I really liked her. I thought that should work for a valentine.

In a little over an hour I had finished it. It took another half hour to type it without mistakes. After checking it one more time for errors, I set it on the table in front of my sister who was still making valentines.

She picked it up and read it aloud while I stood watching and listening.

"Through basketball games and J-Hawk Juice
And Saturday clinics, too,
With movie dates and phone calls
I've come to cherish you.

Our walks on snowy evenings,
Talks . . . and swinging in the park,
Searching for the North Star
On that chilly night so dark,

A Christmas Eve of caroling,
Twice in church on Christmas Day,
A time or two things fell apart,
And we had to find our way."

MARK REINSMOEN

"Did you really write this? You have good rhymes. I bet Sarah will like it. I hope I get one like this someday," my little sister said, and then she continued reading.

"A pan of home-made brownies
On that day I painted blue,
And every single moment
I was thinking just of you.

An evening of soft music
As we sat next to the fire,
And I visited your high school
Where I listened to your choir,

A game of 'Hearts' . . . an invite,
All these things I won't forget,
My life has changed to wonderful
Since that first night we met.

Your sparkling eyes and laughter,
Our great friendship from the start,
Through all of these, Sweet Sarah,
I have given you my heart.

Please Be My Valentine! Forever!

"I'll start working on your card right away. It needs to be my best one. I'll show it to you when I am done. Do you want me to show Mom your poem?" my sister asked.

"That won't be necessary," I said, and I winked at her.

It was about nine o'clock when I called Sarah to tell her about my phone conversation with her principal. I told her everything I could remember . . . what Mr. Weston said . . . how he sounded . . . .second chances . . . welcome at the door . . .

"Your call is the second one we have received tonight about the dance," Sarah said. "Mr. Weston called Dad about an hour ago, and they talked for about ten minutes. Dad wouldn't tell me much. He said I needed to hear about everything from you, but I could tell the conversation was very positive, and I could see satisfaction on Dad's face. Thanks for making that tough call today. I hope you didn't have to grovel."

We both chuckled.

"I'll call you later this week after I get more information about the dance. I'm so glad everything worked out," Sarah said.

"Me too," I replied. "Thanks for inviting me to your dance and standing by me. It means a lot to me. Please tell your parents that my call to Mr. Weston went well. Good night, Sarah."

My sister and I both stayed up a little later than usual, but the envelope and the finished card were outstanding.

As I headed to bed I reflected on my day. Maybe I grew up a little today. I think I learned a lot about myself. If I'm smart I'll pay more attention to what I'm doing from now on.

Now . . . if I only knew something about dancing.

Chapter 38
King of the Hill

The fluffy white snow had just begun falling when we boarded the school bus that would take us to Mitchell for our final conference basketball game of the season. I sat alone, quietly, talking to no one, looking out the partially frosted window toward the school, thinking about my valentine plan, when my eyes were drawn to the seldom-used road which ran east of the two-story, brick school building. This gravel path of a road was at the edge of the school property, next to a farm field, and as I gazed out the window, I thought about the shallow ditch that dropped from the road to the wire fence that surrounded the field. Fresh, soft whiteness was now blanketing the ditch.

I remembered our winter recesses the year when I was in fourth grade, when we fourth-grade boys took on the third-grade boys in friendly games of "King of the Hill," trying to be the "kings" by pushing the third graders back until their feet gave way, and they slid down to the bottom of the ditch. Oh, I loved that game! It was constant action, and you needed to be ready at all times. Staking your territory . . . pushing out with strong arms . . . spreading your legs and digging in to maintain good balance . . . watching for any advances by the "enemy" and alerting your teammates . . . This was a great team sport.

Working alone didn't accomplish much. You had to work together, covering your zone and quickly going to the aid of someone in trouble. If you found yourself at the bottom of the ditch, you organized a group assault, because an entire team working together had a much better chance for success.

Working together . . . that's what we would be doing against the Wildcats tonight, and I had a feeling that the Wildcats would find themselves at the bottom of the ditch for most of the game.

Pickett's soft music really relaxed me tonight. It struck me that he seemed to be singing mostly love songs while strumming on his ukulele, and that made it hard for me to focus on the upcoming game. I had other things on my mind. All my teammates knew that we had the conference championship sewn up, even if we lost tonight, but we weren't traveling all the way to Mitchell to lose. We had won all seventeen previous games, and we wanted to claim the conference title with a perfect record: eighteen wins . . . followed by a goose egg in the loss column.

I felt confident, but I knew we needed to play a solid game. The Wildcats had lost only five times, and most of those were on the road. Besides having a better team, we had another advantage tonight. While the Wildcats would miss one of their top scorers who was sitting out with an ankle sprain, we were all healthy . . . at full strength, and we were ready to run them to death. We planned to use our outstanding fast break and several different presses to force them into making mistakes. Our goal was to score early and score often.

While sitting on the bleachers watching the girls play, I saw Sarah and her parents come into the gym. As soon as they sat down, I walked over, carrying my letter jacket carefully over my left arm. In the left pocket of my jacket I had hidden the small wooden box that contained the silver heart, and I had carefully placed the Valentine's Day card inside the folds of the jacket. In the back right pocket of my pants I had concealed the note that I would secretly pass to Sarah's mom or dad at a time when Sarah was not watching me. It contained my request:

Dear Mr. and Mrs. Jenkins,
    Would you please do me a big favor? In the left side pocket of my jacket is a small wooden box. It contains a Valentine's Day gift for Sarah. Hidden inside my jacket is a card I wrote for Sarah. When I walk with Sarah out to the lobby, would you please remove these two things, keep them hidden from Sarah tonight, and put them on your table at home tomorrow morning so Sarah can find my Valentine's Day surprise at breakfast?
    Thank you . . . and Happy Valentine's Day.
Catcher

I was prepared.

"Hi, Jenkins family," I said as I sat down next to Sarah and set my jacket on the bleachers beside me. "Thanks for coming to our game again tonight. We're expecting to play well and win this final conference game. We had a great practice yesterday."

"I'm glad to hear that," Mr. Jenkins said. "We're hoping to see another good J-Hawk win tonight."

"Hi, Catch," Sarah said. "I heard at school today that the boys are expected to wear ties to the dance on Saturday night. Girls will wear party dresses."

"Great! I'll wear my Sunday clothes," I said, "and I know I'll be with the prettiest girl at the dance. Don't laugh, Sarah, but I've been practicing with my sister."

Sarah and her parents smiled.

"I don't expect I'll have many friends at the dance," I added. "I'll need to keep my eye out for Billy Johnson and Joe."

Sarah gave me a reassuring smile and replied, "I know we'll have a really good time."

"Let's go out to the lobby, Sarah," I suggested. "I want to look in the Mitchell trophy case to see what a conference championship trophy looks like."

As Sarah stepped down the bleachers toward the floor, I quickly pulled the note from my pocket and made a quiet sign in Mrs. Jenkins's direction as I quickly handed the paper to her when Sarah turned her back. Then I followed Sarah. As we headed toward the lobby, I turned back to look at Sarah's parents, smiled, and nodded. I had done well.

We didn't find the trophy I was looking for, but that was okay. That's not really why I walked Sarah out of the gym. When we returned to the bleachers, Sarah's mom smiled at me and nodded. I lipped the words "Thank you" to her.

After a couple more minutes I saw San Juan motion for me to rejoin the guys, so I wandered back.

When the game started, we played really solid defense. Each of us covered our area of the zone, and we were quick to slide over when teammates needed help. Our great teamwork limited the Wildcats from getting any open shots. It definitely was a team effort. As Number 12 tried to drive around me on my left, near the sideline, I slid over and stepped in front of him, stopping him in his tracks.

Then it hit me. This was just like "King of the Hill." For a split second I was tempted to put my arms out, brace my legs, and give him a hard push with my hands. It's good I held back because the refs wouldn't have liked it much, but the feeling was so real. I could almost taste the cold air and the snow.

Though I was playing basketball inside in a gym, for a brief time my mind carried me to the ditch and the snow and bracing my legs and pushing and using all my strength and effort to defend the hill. I was in two places at one time.

"Watch the guy on the left side," I shouted out, and we shifted over to help cover that area. I kept turning my head, looking both left and right, watching to make sure that no one was trying to sneak up on me. When the third graders made a run at us, I raised my arms in front of me and stood in a defensive stance. I was ready for anything, and I met those snow-covered challengers right at the edge of the road, pushed at them quickly and pulled my arms back again so they could not grab me and pull me with them as they slid down into the ditch.

The first quarter belonged to us because of our defense and our fast break. When the buzzer sounded to end the quarter, we were up by six points.

The Wildcats came out more aggressively to start the 2nd quarter. They kept trying to sneak players in to set screens on us, but we kept talking to each other, warning our teammates. Laser and I kept turning our heads to check around us and behind us, and we kept our bodies balanced so we could move quickly.

On offence we passed the ball around the perimeter, and we watched how they shifted their defense. We were looking for their weaknesses. Laser was able to pass inside to Pickett, and he scored on a bank shot from close in. I found Abe open close to the basket, and when I tossed him a high pass he dropped it softly through the hoop.

My brain was messing with me tonight.

We huddled up. "Here's what we're gonna do," I said confidently. "We'll spread out and let them think we intend to rush them straight ahead, but then we'll all shift to the right side and attack, because that looks like their weakness."

I took the lead as we ran forward, knowing that I probably would not make it because I would draw at least two defenders, but I knew this would give us the best chance to regain the road and win the game today. I would be willing to sacrifice myself for the good of my teammates, and I kept that thought in my head as I was pushed down the side of the ditch and collected a mouthful of dirty snow.

Coach made sure all of us starters got a short rest on the bench in the second quarter because we all had been running hard and working really hard on defense. Tucson came into the game to play guard alongside me, and Otto was sent in to give Pickett a breather.

Wildcat player Number 15 became frustrated by our press, and he barreled into Tucson as he attempted to dribble around him. An elbow caught Tucson squarely on his nose, and he went flying. Otto and I hustled over to help him up after the foul was called, and I saw the blood dripping from his nose.

"Are you all right?" Otto asked him.

"Yeah," Tucson replied casually as he wiped his face with the back of his hand and noticed the blood. "When you play a game like this you have to expect to get banged up once in a while."

Coach called a timeout, and we gathered at the bench.

As Tucson's nose received some medical help, I watched, and it triggered another memory that seemed so similar to what had just happened, except that tonight, Tucson's bloody nose was not caused by San Juan and me. That day on the "hill" we had pushed Tucson backward and, instead of sliding down, he had tumbled roughly and smacked his head on the snow. I knew we were in big trouble when I saw the blood on his face . . . San Juan and I would probably lose some recess over this. Everyone rushed to him, and I was ready for Tucson's anger and tears. When someone asked him if he was all right, he nodded and said something like, "Yeah. When you play a tough game like this . . . sometimes you get bumped around."

That was it. He didn't cry, and he wasn't angry, and he never even told on us. I remember admiring him for his toughness, and I felt proud to be one of that group of kids that could play so hard and have so much fun and still be friends if someone got hurt. I also remember that day because with that bloodstained face, Tucson became our inspiration for toughness. He wore the "Red Badge of Courage," but unlike Henry Fleming in the novel we had read earlier this year, Tucson's courage was real.

Tonight felt like a replay of that day on the hill, and Tucson's badge shown brightly. This was who we were . . . a bunch of kids who could play hard, play together, stay focused, and remember that above all else, we were all friends. This was "King of the Hill."

"This is just like 'King of the Hill,'" I said aloud in the huddle.

"Is this another story from the past?" Abe asked.

I laughed. "It's the game we played during recess on that road with the ditch when snow covered the ground. Doesn't anyone else remember?"

"I do," Tucson said as he pointed to the blood on his hand.

"Me, too," both San Juan and Otto answered.

"That game made us all tough," I said. "Look at us now! We're still play- ing hard, and we get hammered and knocked down once in a while, but we always get back up. We didn't quit seven years ago . . . and we'll never quit now. Tucson impressed us with his toughness on that hill, and tonight he shows us again."

"'King of the Hill!'" Captain Hook said. "That's still what we're playing for. After tonight our perfect record will really make us 'King of the Hill,' and then we'll keep working and stay there until we can stake our claim on the 'hill' in Des Moines."

"All right," Coach said. "Here we go. Same lineup. Run on every defen- sive rebound you grab, and pick them up immediately after they inbound the ball. Don't let down. I'll send in fresh legs in a couple minutes."

"We are . . . J-Hawks!" we shouted as we broke the huddle.

"Kings of the Hill!" Captain Hook added.

We gathered in the locker room for a short rest during halftime, holding a lead of eleven points. No one said much, but everyone was looking into the eyes of everyone else. I could see determination and pride . . . respect and trust . . . caring and confidence. Our team was in a good place. Play hard . . . have fun.

In the third quarter Captain Hook and I had a little fun with our passing. Whenever I passed the ball to him when he was standing about halfway between the lane and the sideline, my guy would sag back on Hook to help double cover him. Hook would then just pass it back to me. I passed it right back to Hook . . . he passed back to me. We did this several times. We could have done this all night. Since we had a big lead, we didn't need to score as long as we kept the ball away from them. Twice Hook bounced a pass to Pickett as he ran toward the basket, and Pickett laid the ball in for easy points. The Wildcats had no luck finding a way to take advantage of us.

Laser and I both were able to get open for jump shots whenever we passed to Pickett at the free-throw line. The Mitchell guards always dropped back to try double team our three big men whenever we sent the ball inside, so that left us open when the ball was quickly returned to us. We both hit about half of our shots, and with our fast break going well, Laser and I got a lot of opportunities to score.

We gradually built up our lead until it stood at twenty-one points when the buzzer signaled the end of the game. Tonight we had played very well against a strong team. This might have been our best defensive game. Our fast break had been very effective, and we had been able to find several ways to score against a good defense.

Tucson had played very well. At least six of our points and a whole lot of our toughness were scored by Tucson. This was his night.

Coach told us we would only have a few minutes before heading to the locker room so I found Sarah right after I toweled off.

"Good game tonight, Catcher! All of you played well," Sarah said, "and you completed your conference schedule without losing a single game. Congratulations!"

"Thanks," I replied. "It felt really good tonight. I thought we played great on defense, and everyone worked hard. This is a lot of fun. I really like our team."

"Do you play again on Friday night?" Sarah asked.

"I think we do," I replied. "Coach will find out tomorrow about who we play, where we play, and what time the game will start. I'll call you tomorrow night and tell you the details. It looks like I have to go, Sarah. Thanks for coming and cheering for us. I hope you have a Happy Valentine's Day tomorrow."

"Happy Valentine's Day to you, too, Catcher," Sarah replied.

I bet she'll be surprised tomorrow at breakfast.

In the Stands – With John Garris

"Bloody, but unbowed" . . . that's the way I saw it. Last night was the second time this season that I watched as a Jeffers J-Hawk caught an elbow to the face and blood was drawn, and this was also the second time this season that the result was not anger and retaliation, but instead, increased determination and greater focus.

I could see it in Tucson's face behind the streaks of red. It was not smugness or defiance, but instead . . . resolve. "You can try to hurt me . . . but you can't defeat me (and it didn't hurt)."

The J-Hawks not only showed a physical toughness, they wore a mental toughness, and these two together translate into a team that's tough to defeat. What more evidence do you want besides a winning streak of 18 straight games in the tough North Central Conference? The Wildcats probably didn't get the result they were hoping for. The J-Hawks don't overreact and fall apart at the sight of their own blood . . . they "fall" together.

The J-Hawks wrapped up the conference championship by four games. How did they do that? They surpassed my preseason prediction by several wins. I'd like to revise my prediction if that's okay. "The J-Hawks are a young but talented team that follows the leadership of a proven coach who understands the game and his players, and their unselfish play, their great effort, their high level of skills, and their determination will enable them to win many games this season."

The J-Hawks defeated the Wildcats by 21 points last night by using a suffocating pressure defense, running a well-oiled fast break, and playing with a lot of heart.

HEART! It's Valentine's Day! Here's a chance to honor that special friend in your life. Take a risk. Open up your heart. That's going to be my plan.

Chapter 39
Mail Call

I had a tough time concentrating in Math and English on Wednesday morning. Valentine's Day had caused a lot of excitement for me even in my first years of school as I wondered what treats might be attached to the valentines that had been dropped through the slot of my homemade, decorated shoebox, but this year went far beyond that. My mind was stuck on Sarah. I needed to know if she liked the heart necklace and the card.

I knew I would be thinking about her all day . . . kind of worrying. I was fighting this confidence thing again.

Mr. Carter brought me back to earth a couple times when he asked me questions about geometry proofs. I recovered and did okay, but my classmates gave me a hard time, and I heard San Juan say in a quiet voice, "I wonder just how many valentines Sarah will get today." They knew where my head was.

In English class we were told to read the first two scenes of Act I of *Twelfth Night*, and after reading the first scene, I had no idea what it was about. As soon as I had read the word "love" in the first line, I ditched Shakespeare for Sarah. I read the same lines over and over, but they could just as well have been written in a foreign language, because I couldn't understand anything. I reread and reread, but it was wasted effort . . . I just couldn't concentrate.

While I was eating a hamburger in the lunchroom, the Supe walked in waving a red-and-white envelope. "Mail call," he announced to everyone in the room as he approached the table where a bunch of us guys from the basketball team were sitting. "Letter for Catcher," he said as he grinned and handed me the envelope. Then he walked out.

I saw that the envelope had Sarah's name written in the corner. I quickly slid it under my tray and continued to eat, though at a much faster pace. With one hand on my burger and the other slapping at hands that were trying to grab the envelope, I quickly finished my lunch and fled the lunchroom for a private spot on the bleachers in the gym. After sitting down, I took a deep breath and examined the envelope. I was hoping it was a valentine.

It was! It was a homemade card! Sarah had printed on the front, "Valentine's Day: A Day for Hearts," and she had decorated it with many red and pink hearts. I don't know how long I stared at the hearts and the words on the front of the card, but I woke up when a few of my friends joined me on the bleachers and moved in very close to me.

"What do we have here?" San Juan asked as he reached for my card.

"Looks like Catcher has a sweetheart," Tucson offered.

"Read it to us," Abe said. "I want to be in love, too."

"I haven't even read it **myself** yet," I replied. "Give me some space, let me read it, and then **maybe** I'll show it to you."

They slid down the bleachers about ten feet, then faced me and acted like a litter of begging puppies, sitting up with paws extended, their tongues hanging out as they panted.

They were quite comical, and I knew I wanted to share the card with them if it weren't too embarrassing.

I opened the card . . . and I was amazed. There had to be about twenty hearts pasted inside, and each one had drawn on it a miniature colorful picture. After a quick glance at a few, I figured out these were memories of something for Sarah and me. I studied every single one while smiling to myself and wiping away a tear or two. Then I took a few deep breaths and waved the "puppies" over.

I opened the card and listened as Otto read out loud, "Memories That Warm My Heart. Be My Valentine! Love, Sarah."

"These pictures that Sarah drew all represent a special time she and I shared," I explained.

"Hey . . . the warm-up jacket and the socks . . . I remember that first night when Sarah and her dad thought you were an usher," Hook said excitedly.

Abe jumped in next. "The basketball . . . for all the games she has watched us play . . . and the three Christmas stockings . . . for Christmas Eve when we went caroling and gave the Cade kids the bikes . . . and the paint brush and brownies . . . for the day we had our painting party!"

"Hey, Abe," I said smiling, "don't get carried away. These are Sarah's memories with me, not with you."

"San Juan, do you see the one about our movie double date?" I asked.

"The French fries . . . We had duels with French fries at The Grill," he answered. "That was a fun night."

"Hey, San Juan," Abe said, "don't go claiming Catcher's memories."

"Is that you getting your head shaved?" Hook asked.

"I learned Sarah's name that night after my haircut," I answered.

"Explain the rest of the hearts," Tucson said.

"All right," I said as I reclaimed my card.

"For Christmas I gave Sarah a J-Hawk Nation stocking cap . . . We went to *Swiss Family Robinson* on our first date . . . A couple times we've walked to the park to swing," I explained as I pointed to hearts that contained drawings of a cap, an elaborate tree-house, and two swings.

I continued, "We've taken several walks in the snow . . . and studied together at the library at Madison Lake . . . One night I showed Sarah how to use the Big Dipper to find the North Star . . . And this is for the time I went to her choir concert. When I walked in she was standing by the door in her purple choir gown. I told her I liked her ushering uniform, and I thanked her for being there to usher me to a seat. She told me she was waiting for some sheet music her dad was bringing to her, but I didn't buy that story." I touched the drawings of the footprints in the snow, the library building, the Big Dipper and the North Star, and the purple choir gown with the page of music.

"Is the phone and piece of paper for when you asked her for her phone number?" San Juan asked.

"I think so," I replied, "but Sarah and I have had fun talking to each other on the phone many times. The deck of cards showing the 'Ace of Hearts' is for when I played 'Hearts' with her family, and she invited me to her Sweetheart Dance that is coming up on Saturday night. This picture of a fire is for the night Sarah's dad built a fire in the fireplace at their house, and Sarah and I watched the flames while we listened to music. This one looks like cups of hot chocolate sitting on a counter. See the stools? That's when Mr. Hanson walked us to the café to see if Mrs. Cade was interested in renting his house. Bob gave us hot chocolate, and we sat there, even though it was Saturday morning, and customers clapped for us."

"What do you think this bigger heart, the picture that looks like a whole bunch of calendars means?" Otto asked.

"I have my fingers crossed that Sarah is saying we'll be friends for a long time," I replied. "That's what I hope it means."

"Wow! That's a great card!" Otto said. "Ask Sarah if she'll make one for me."

We all looked at each other, laughed loudly, and shook our heads.

"We're late! We've got to get back!" San Juan said, and we jumped down and hurried to the assembly room.

After I sat down at my desk and put my card away, Laser walked over.

"You know you didn't have to show those knuckleheads your card," he said.

I laughed. "Yeah," I said, "but they are really good basketball players, and we can't win without them.

"You're right," Laser replied. We do need them. Keep them humored . . . Keep them happy."

"Yes, Sir, Captain!" I said with a grin and a weak salute.

"You are pretty lucky, Catcher," Laser added, " . . . about Sarah. You've found yourself a good one. Don't mess it up."

"Yeah," I said again, and my one-word response was for all three things he had said.

We had a very good practice after school ended for the day. All of us were focused and serious. Coach told us we would be playing the Mayville Eagles at the new gym in Conrad on Friday night. We had drawn the early game for the start of the playoffs. If we win, we play again next Tuesday, but if we lose . . . we are done . . . the season's over.

I will not allow us to lose. We have to keep winning.

I did my chores when I got home, then I sat down at the dining room table to work on my homework. I looked at the phone hanging on the wall, and I studied the clock positioned above it. I needed to talk to Sarah, to thank her for the great card she had made for me, but I knew I should wait until after supper.

At six-thirty, after I had eaten my second hamburger of the day, I asked Mom, "Do you think this would be a good time for me to call Sarah?"

"Wait a few more minutes," she said. "They might still be eating."

Five minutes . . . I watched the clock for five more minutes before I reached for the phone and dialed Sarah's number. It rang only once, and then I heard Sarah's voice say, "Hello."

"Hi, Sarah," I said. "Happy Valentine's Day. I want to thank you for that wonderful valentine you made for me. The Supe delivered it to me while I was eating lunch. He announced it to everyone like an Army 'Mail Call.' The guys surrounded me in the gym bleachers when I tried to read it, and I liked your card so much that I showed all of your drawings to them, and I told them about all of the memories. I hope you don't mind that I did that. By the way, Otto wants you to make a card like this for him."

Sarah and I both laughed.

"You are welcome. I'm really glad you like it," Sarah replied. "I had fun making it and thinking about the great times we have shared together. I was reading by the phone tonight because I knew you would call.

"This morning when I went downstairs, both Mom and Dad were sitting at the table drinking coffee," Sarah continued. "When I grabbed toast and orange juice and sat down with them they both stared at me. I wondered what was going on . . . then I saw the card and the wooden box. Thank you so much! Your card is wonderful, and I love the beautiful silver heart necklace. What a great surprise! Thank you, Catcher. How did you do this without me knowing about it?"

"I know how you like mysteries, so that's all I'm going to say," I replied.

"I wore the heart to school today and showed all my friends, and I read your card over and over," Sarah continued. "Shakespeare has been a good influence on you."

"Yeah, he's given me some help," I said laughing. "I have to ask you about the calendar drawing in the largest heart. I told the guys that I hope you meant that you and I will be friends for many, many years. Is that what you were thinking?"

"Just like the 'Forever Heart' you gave to me . . . That's a 'Forever Calendar,'" Sarah answered.

"That's perfect," I said. "I'll keep your valentine forever. Thank you, Sarah. Yours is the best valentine I have ever received, and this has been my best Valentine's Day ever."

"Mine too . . . best ever," Sarah added, "but you may have gotten my dad in a little trouble with my mom. He **bought** a Valentine's Day card for her, and she had really been impressed with the card you had **made** for me," Sarah said. "Next year you might have to help Dad write a poem."

"Maybe your dad and I can sit down and write poems together next year. Can you picture that?" I asked.

Sarah just laughed. "It's very interesting to me that both of our cards were about memories we've shared. I like that," she added.

After talking for a few more minutes, Sarah said that her ten minutes were up. "I'm sorry, but I have to hang up now. Call me tomorrow about your Friday game, and you can talk to my dad about it, too. I'll ask at school about the dance so I can tell you more," Sarah said.

"Sounds good," I replied. "Thanks again for the great card. Good night, Valentine. This has been a great day for hearts."

Chapter 40
The Teen Center

A s the bus headed for our playoff game against Mayville, I thought about what Coach had told us yesterday. "Don't be feeling sorry for them," he warned. "Forget that we've beaten them before. You need to play as if this is the best team you have ever gone against. If you play your best I think you will bury them. If you think you won't have to work hard, that they'll just roll over for you . . . then you'll have a tough game on your hands, and in the playoffs, if you have one bad game, your season could be over."

I don't want our season to end . . . no one does. We made a pledge to each other back in early January that we would do everything possible to make it to the state tournament, and once there, we would work even harder so we could play for the small school state championship. That's still our goal. Winning the conference was nice, but that's not enough, and tonight is our first step in this second part of our basketball season.

We went right to the locker room when we reached the school because we were playing in tonight's opening game. We wouldn't be watching the girls play first as we had in all eighteen of our previous games. Coach had told us to prepare ourselves during the bus ride, because game time would arrive about 45 minutes after we reached the gym.

During warm-ups I tried to keep from looking in the bleachers for Sarah. I wanted to concentrate on my shooting and passing, and I did not want any distractions. This was the most important game of our season. I told myself that Sarah didn't matter right now, but I didn't feel that this was totally true. She did matter to me . . . all the time . . . every day . . . but tonight I was trying to set aside any thoughts of her while I played. I only searched the bleachers twice, very quickly, and I did not find Sarah. That was okay . . . she really didn't matter tonight.

Coach gave us our final instructions at the bench. "It all starts with great pressure defense. Make it hard for them to get the ball into their own end, and don't give the Eagles any open shots. Keep your arms up. When you big guys grab the rebounds, hustle the ball to the outside and get it down the floor. Let's get all the fast-break baskets we can. Play hard . . . have fun."

"We are . . . J-Hawks!" we all shouted.

Just as we broke from the huddle, my eyes spotted Sarah, and we both smiled.

"*Okay! She's here! Now forget about her!*" I told myself. Immediately I was sorry that I had thought that. It felt cruel and unkind. *This isn't working.* I tried to send Sarah a mental message with my eyes. "*I'm sorry, Sarah. I'll never forget about you. I can't. It's just that, right now, I need all of my focus to be on basketball. I know you understand. We can talk about this later.*"

Coach should not have worried about how much effort we would give against Mayville. We did not take them lightly. We threw everything we had at them: aggressive defense, great rebounding, quick passes, an outstanding fast break, accurate shooting . . . We played really well, and the Eagles had no chance.

Whenever we slowed the game down, Laser and I were able to pass the ball inside to Abe and Hook, and they hit their open shots on almost every try. Pickett caught our passes when he set up on the free-throw line, and he either took his jump shot or used a pump fake to get his defender up in the air so he could dribble around him and score on a layup.

At the end of the first half we led by eighteen points.

In the second half Coach mixed up the lineup, giving Otto, San Juan, and Tucson lots of time, and we continued running and pressuring the Eagles. Even though we had never played in this new gym, we shot really well. All parts of our game were good, and we made this game look easy in defeating the Eagles by a score of 76-49.

This was a great way to start: **One playoff game down, several**

more to go.

I found Sarah as soon as I returned to the bench after shaking hands with the other team. "Sarah," I said, "I'm really glad you came tonight. Coach said we had to clear out of here right away because another team needs the bench for the second game. Will you walk with me?"

We walked along the sideline to the locker room.

"You played really well tonight, but you looked so serious," Sarah said. "What was going on?"

"I wanted to play my best game of the year since it's the playoffs," I replied, "so I tried to be more focused, but it backfired on me. It took some of the fun out of it. I'll try to explain it to you later, but I know you'll laugh at me. I used a plan I know I won't try again."

When we reached the locker room Coach told me to get showered.

"Can you stay for a little while?" I asked Sarah. "I'll hurry."

"I'll check with Dad, and I'll watch for you," she replied.

While we showered, Coach told us about "Hamburger Night at The Jeffers Café." He said, "Bob is inviting all the high school kids to stop in for ten-cent burgers, fries, sodas, and milk. Tonight, The Jeffers Café will be your new Teen Center. The kids in the bleachers have just been told about this, too. The café will only be open until 11:00, and then you guys need to be home by 11:30 as we agreed earlier in the season. I understand your parents have been invited to Abe's for coffee and dessert, so it looks like everyone will have fun tonight."

"Do our parents have an 11:30 curfew, too?" Tucson asked.

"They'll be parking on Main Street at 11:00 and will be your rides home," Coach said with a smile.

It didn't take me long to shower, dress, and pack my stuff in my duffle bag.

"I'll be right back, Coach," I said as I hurried out the door.

I almost ran over Sarah as I turned the corner. "You're still here . . . Good!" I said catching my breath. "Did you . . ."

"Mom and Dad have been invited to Abe's house for coffee, and I've been invited to The Jeffers Café with all the high school kids," Sarah interrupted. "I have to go now, but I'll see you at the café."

When the team walked into the café, everyone shouted out, "We are . . . J-Hawks!" It felt good. Sarah was already there, talking to some of her new friends. We found an empty booth and sat down with San Juan, Otto, and two girls from my class, and we placed our order with Mrs. Cade, who was helping Bob tonight along with two other women.

The two girls asked Sarah about her heart necklace and looked at me and nodded their approval. "That's a nice looking heart," Otto said to me.

Otto and San Juan thanked Sarah for the valentine she had sent to me. San Juan said, "Catcher shared it with a bunch of us guys, and we had fun talking about the memories." All I could do was smile at Sarah.

Someone put money in the jukebox, and the music filled the café. Several kids were singing along, and most of us were laughing and talking quite loudly.

I hadn't ever been in a teen center. In fact, I didn't know there was such a thing in any rural parts of Iowa, but now I know exactly what every teen center should be like. It should be just like ours.

There should be a jukebox that has all the best and latest popular 45s, and on the counter should be one of Bob's coffee cups containing a whole bunch of nickels that kids could use to pay for their song selections. One good pinball machine should be standing near the door where kids could use their own nickels to challenge their reflexes and their luck. The center should admit high school kids only, with a few adults present to cook and serve food. There should be lots of laughter, loud talking, and some singing along with the music from the jukebox.

I could tell everyone was having a great time. I treated Sarah to a hamburger, soda, and fries that we shared, and I ate two burgers and drank a glass of cold chocolate milk. I spent just over half of my dollar.

At 10:30 some kids started carrying dishes to the counter, and others started wiping down the booths and tables. Four of the senior girls went back to the sink and washed and dried the plates and glasses. Otto's sister went around to everyone suggesting we leave a nickel, dime, or quarter for the cooks and servers on the napkin she had set on the counter. San Juan and I grabbed brooms and swept near the booths, then Tucson and Abe took them from us and worked their way to the stools at the counter. It seemed like everyone found something to do to help out.

At a few minutes to eleven, Pickett stood and asked for everyone's attention. "We want to thank you, Bob and your workers, for welcoming us tonight to The Jeffers Teen Center Café. The food was fantastic! Thanks for the music, for letting us be a little loud, and for giving us a place to have a good time with our friends. We won't forget this," Pickett said.

Every kid stood and said, "Thank you." I don't know who started it, but we all shouted, "Hip, hip, hooray! Hip, hip, hooray! Hip, hip, hooray!" and then we applauded until our hands began to get hot and sore.

Sarah and I said good-bye to our friends and stepped outside to look for our parents' cars. When we saw the two cars parked next to each other half-way down the street, engines running, we decided to take the long way.

"I've really had fun tonight, Sarah," I said. "This was my best night ever at The Jeffers Teen Center Café."

She smiled that beautiful smile.

When we had almost reached the cars, I gently pulled Sarah into the darkened entryway of the drug store, and I put my arms around her and kissed her. I knew our parents would know what we were doing, and I was okay with that. Sarah and I both laughed at our sneakiness.

I started moving my feet like I had just struck gold in the Sierra Madres, and I said, "I'm really looking forward to the dance tomorrow night."

Sarah laughed and replied, "Me, too. I know it will be my best dance ever."

She was beginning to sound like me.

I heard cars start pulling out of their parking spaces so Sarah and I stepped back out onto the sidewalk, and I opened her car door. I hugged her one more time.

As her dad backed up the car, I waved to the Jenkins family and stepped over toward our old Ford and yelled out, "We are . . . J-Hawks!"

This had been another great night of basketball that was made even greater with the "grand opening" of The Jeffers Teen Center Café!

Chapter 41
At the Hop

It was quite cold out, so after the clinic and library time, Sarah and I decided to stay inside the library to talk and look at old books until her dad came for her.

"Are you going to teach me your special dance tonight?" Sarah asked.

I could tell by her smile that she was teasing me. "It's not really a couple's dance," I replied seriously. "It's more of a man's celebration dance. I saw an actor, playing the part of an old prospector, do this dance in the movie *The Treasure of the Sierra Madre* when he discovered gold in Mexico. I hope you won't be too embarrassed tonight if I do this dance to celebrate finding my own treasure when I met you."

Sarah's laughter sounded musical.

I stood up and started shuffling my feet quickly and swinging my arms wildly, back and forth. "I found the treasure! . . . I found the treasure!" I tried to shout in a quiet voice. I quickly sat down when I noticed that a library volunteer had been watching me.

This time Sarah laughed out loud. "You'll get everyone's attention if you do that dance tonight," she warned.

I think she was beginning to get a little worried.

"Do you think Joe will ask you to dance with him? What do you think you would do?" I asked.

"I don't know," Sarah replied.

"I might get a little upset if you dance with him more than once or twice. I don't have a very good opinion of him because of that Sunday in The Grill," I said. "I won't let him give you a hard time or bother me tonight."

"He's not such a bad guy, but I don't particularly like him," Sarah replied. "I might dance with him or one of his friends once just so he doesn't think I'm a snob."

"Good idea, Sarah. You don't want to be snobby," I said teasingly. "No one likes 'snobby.'"

I had become much more relaxed around Sarah lately. We had become good friends, and I felt much more confident and sure about her. Laughing together was easy for us, and we both were into friendly teasing.

At 11:15 Sarah's dad walked in.

"Hi, Mr. Jenkins," I said. "How was coffee at The Jeffers Teen Center Café today?"

"Bob had plenty of stories to tell this morning. He said his ears were still ringing, but he had enjoyed hearing all the singing, the laughter, and the talking last night. He said he plans to do that again," Sarah's dad said as he turned back to the door. "Let's go, Sarah. I guess I'll see you tonight, Catcher."

"I'll be at your house a little before seven," I said to Sarah.

We said good-bye with big smiles.

I felt the butterflies in my stomach as I rang the doorbell. There were several reasons for this. This was my first dance ever, and I wasn't feeling exactly comfortable in a coat and tie. Also, this dance was in a school that was not familiar to me, and I knew that I wouldn't have many friends there. I was going to be depending on Sarah tonight.

When Sarah descended the stairs to where I was standing, her beauty took my breath away. She absolutely sparkled. She wore a beautiful valentine-red dress and a radiant smile. She looked so poised, so perfect. Around her neck hung the silver heart necklace I had given her just three days ago.

I couldn't take my eyes off her. All I could do was stand there, silently, and remind myself to breathe once in a while.

Sarah's mom walked over with a camera. "Catcher, why don't you take off your overcoat so I can get a picture of the two of you," she said. She directed us toward some empty wall space in the living room.

"Mrs. Jenkins," I said, "could you also take a picture of just Sarah? She hasn't given me a picture of herself yet, and she looks even prettier than usual tonight."

Mr. Jenkins joined us. "Would you be more comfortable if I found an old basketball for you to hold?" he asked as he smiled at me.

I guess it was obvious how I was feeling. I figured I would be more re-laxed once we left their house.

"All right, kids . . . big smiles," Mrs. Jenkins said, and the camera flashed.

She took several more pictures, including a couple of Sarah and me each standing alone. Eventually Sarah told her mom that we needed to leave.

"We're going to have a fire blazing in the fireplace this evening," Sarah's dad told us. "You two are welcome to join us when the dancing wears you out. Catcher, you've got to save those legs for your next game."

"Yes, I do," I said. "I'll have to pace myself."

When Sarah and I stepped out the door, Sarah's mom said, "You two have a great time. I'll have a dessert ready for later, and then I'll want to hear about the dance."

Mr. Weston was standing at the door to greet kids, just like he had told me he would be when I called him, and he did welcome Sarah and me.

"Hi Sarah . . . and Catcher. Welcome to the Sweetheart Dance," Mr. Weston said to us. "You look lovely tonight, Sarah."

"Thank you," Sarah replied, and I reached out my hand to Mr. Weston and nodded a thank you.

"There's a place for your coats on the hooks and tables by the gym, and there's plenty of room in the gym for dancing or sitting," Mr. Weston added. "I hope you both have a great time tonight."

When we walked into the dimly-lit gym, Sarah spied some of her friends, and she walked me over for introductions. Becky was there with a date, and she appeared to be a little uncomfortable when she saw me. Maybe she was reminded of our double date with San Juan.

I was introduced to several kids, including Joe and his friend, Marcia. I made sure I looked right into Joe's eyes so he could see I was not afraid of him, and I did not smile.

Sarah and I sat at a small table in a corner of the gym. Neither of us seemed to know what to do. After looking around and talking for a few minutes, I heard a song that I really liked.

"Sarah," I said as I stood, "would you like to dance? When I heard this

Johnny Mathis song at your house the other night as we sat by the fire, I felt like this should be our song, and I would like it if our first dance was to this song."

I extended my hand to Sarah. She stood, and we walked together out toward the middle of the gym floor, away from the kids who were sitting and standing at the gym's edges. I felt that everyone was watching us. When I found an open area, I faced Sarah and smiled. With my left hand holding her right hand, and my right arm around her waist, we started moving our feet slowly, and I listened to the words of "Chances Are."

I didn't know what to expect. I was sort of afraid I would step on her toes, and I was worried that I would start sweating because of nervousness, but we glided slowly in our small space, enjoying our song. I felt relieved when the music stopped because I hadn't tripped or even stepped on Sarah's toes one time during the entire song.

Sarah was smiling when I looked into her eyes, and I knew she could tell how I was feeling.

"Did I do okay?" I asked.

"That was my best dance ever," she replied.

I smiled at her, but I didn't say anything because I was unsure if she meant that or if she was teasing me again. "You really look beautiful again tonight," I said.

We sat and talked more than we danced, but we had a great time. Joe did come over to us once and asked me, "Can I dance with Sarah?"

I didn't correct his grammar, but I did answer him. "You'll have to ask her," I said. "Sarah thinks for herself."

Sarah danced one time with Joe, and I didn't watch. I stepped out of the gym until the song ended because I thought watching Sarah with Joe might really bother me. It doesn't take much for me to start worrying about her, and I didn't want this perfect night to have a bad ending.

When Sarah walked back alone after that dance, we went to get some punch. She looked at me and said, "I know that bothered you," she said. "I'm sorry about that, but it was important that I dance with Joe. He won't be asking me to dance again tonight . . . or any other night. He knows that I'm

your girlfriend, and don't forget . . . I have a 'Forever Heart.'"

I tried not to show that I was relieved. I put my hands on her shoulders, looked into her sparkling blue eyes, and smiled at her. "I'll be right back," I said as I turned and walked across the gym floor.

In less than a minute I was back, and I stood silently next to Sarah. Then I heard it.

"They're playing our song," I said, and I walked Sarah out to the middle of the gym.

"Did you request this?" Sarah asked, smiling.

"Is that what you think?" I asked. "Your chances are . . . awfully good . . . that you are right," I replied.

We danced several more times, and we sat in the chairs at the edge of the gym, talking about school and basketball. "Remember, Sarah, that your dad suggested that I save my legs for basketball," I said. "Would you be okay with going back to your house and sitting by the fire? Your parents invited us. I think they will want to hear about your night."

Sarah replied, "I don't really want this night to end, but I'm okay to go home after a couple more dances with you."

We sat together, talking and laughing, having a really great time. When we heard another Johnny Mathis song, "The Twelfth of Never" begin playing, we both stood and walked over to the gym floor. As I listened to the words, I was hoping that the song meant as much to Sarah as it did to me.

We stayed at the dance for another fifteen minutes or so, dancing one more time, and during that last dance I kissed her softly on her forehead. As we walked out of the gym and found our coats, I knew I wouldn't be nervous about school dances anymore.

I heard classical music playing on the stereo when we reached the Jenkins house, and Mr. Jenkins had a good fire going. Both of Sarah's parents seemed glad that we had decided to come home a little early.

"Well . . . how was it?" Sarah's mom asked. "Did you have fun?"

Sarah and I looked at each other and smiled, but neither of us said anything at first.

After a few uncomfortable seconds . . . I spoke up. "I had a great time, and I don't think I stepped on Sarah's toes even once," I answered.

"We really had fun, Mom and Dad," Sarah said "Catch was a little nervous at first, and so was I, but after we had been there a while, he confidently walked over to the stereo and requested a song by Johnny Mathis so we could dance to our favorite music."

"So you're not just a basketball player?" Sarah's dad said as he nodded in my direction.

I removed my coat and loosened my tie, and for the rest of the night we watched the flames as they danced in the fireplace, and we laughed and told Sarah's parents about our first dance experience. I know they could tell that we had enjoyed the evening.

"This was my best night ever at a school dance," I told Sarah as we said goodnight at the door. Her smile melted me, and I held her in my arms and did not want to let her go. "I'm glad you invited me."

"This has been a great week," Sarah said. "It was as good as the Christmas weekend, and I really like my necklace."

"That's good. It's supposed to last forever," I said, and after kissing Sarah once more, I stepped outside and walked toward my car.

Halfway down the sidewalk I turned and saw Sarah standing at the door, looking out at me and waving. I couldn't resist. I started moving my legs really quickly and swung my arms wildly, back and forth, doing my celebration dance. She started laughing, and I knew that she really was my sweetheart.

I blew her a final kiss and walked the rest of the way to the car. "We are . . . J-Hawks!" I shouted into the cold February air. "And if we play well . . . our chances are awfully good!"

Chapter 42
Officer Milton

It started out as a pretty ordinary bus ride to an away game on a Tuesday night, though this was a playoff game . . . meaning that if we lost it would be the end of our season. There were only thirteen of us on the bus: our twelve players . . . and Coach, who was also our bus driver. From one of the back seats Pickett was plucking the strings of his ukulele and quietly singing ballads and camp songs. I was tempted to ask him if he knew "Chances Are," but I decided that it was important to keep that song private for Sarah and me.

Pickett's music soothed me as I thought about our basketball team. We were going for Number 20 tonight . . . our twentieth win without a loss this season . . . and I knew that every game from here on out could be tough. After the first playoff round had been completed, half of the teams were done for the season, and after tonight, only one-fourth of the small-school teams in the state of Iowa would remain alive, and most likely, these would all be good teams. We wouldn't be playing against any more "cupcakes" that might roll over and play dead if the game didn't go their way. Thinking about this scared me a little, but then I thought about the other teams. Are they worried about the J-Hawks? They should be! I would be!

Everything had come together for us this year. Our two senior captains had given us great leadership and excellent play. Four sophomores had stepped right in and had never shown any signs of feeling overwhelmed, and San Juan and I, both juniors, had worked hard and had done our part, too. We had stayed quite healthy, and all twelve of us had treated practices as a great opportunity to improve our skills. Coach had given us great guidance, and he had allowed us to play a running style that best fit our skills. That made practices and games a lot of fun for us. I don't think I ever thought that basketball had been work this season.

In all of our previous games we had used our speed well in rushing the ball down-court after grabbing defensive rebounds, and we had applied our quickness in pressuring our opponents when we were defending. No teams had matched the height of our frontcourt players who stood 6'3", 6'4", and 6'6", and these guys generally played taller than they stood, giving us a huge edge in rebounding.

All five of us starters were good shooters when we focused on our specialties. It was tough for opponents to stop Pickett's fade-away jumper from the free-throw line or Captain Hook's soft, high-arching hook shots from about ten feet out. When Abe wasn't double covered we threw high passes to him, and he grabbed the ball up by the rim and either dropped or slammed the ball through the center of the hoop. How do you stop that? Both Laser and I could consistently score on jump shots from the top of the key, and Otto, San Juan, and Tucson filled in well when they came off the bench to give the starters some rest. We had a lot of ways we could score, so our opponents couldn't target one or two of us defensively. They had to cover all five of us . . . play us honestly.

The bus rolled along, and I lost myself in the music.

After a few minutes I turned around to see what Laser was up to. I was pretty sure that I wouldn't see him singing along with Pickett. Nope, he was talking to Abe, who was parked in the seat in front of him. I could only hear part of their conversation, but I picked up something about watching for a signal, then faking to the outside, and quickly turning and rushing to the basket and jumping as high as he could with his hands up by the rim. I expected I'd see that play a few times tonight. Abe has gotten really good at scoring that way.

I saw that both Otto and San Juan had their eyes closed, and Captain Hook and Nicholson, eyes open, were staring blankly out the windows. I chuckled when I saw Treason drawing pictures in the condensation he made when he "huffed and puffed" on his window. He was not very artistic, but he seemed to be entertaining himself.

We were closing in on Mason City when I heard an explosion that came from the front of the bus. All of us looked toward Coach who was sitting in the driver's seat.

"Hang on, everyone," he called out. "I'm going to pull over as close as I can get to the edge of the highway. We might have a fire under the hood. Be ready to evacuate out the back if I give the word, and take everything with you. Don't leave anything behind."

Coach opened the door, stepped out, and then hurried to the front of the bus and raised the hood. After a few moments he stepped back inside and said, "There's no fire. It looks like the radiator hose burst, and we've got spurting water and lots of steam. Pickett, come out and hold a flashlight for me so I can get a better look." Laser followed Pickett outside.

In a couple minutes Laser came on again and walked to the back where the ten of us were sitting. "We've got a problem," he said seriously. "If this bus were a horse we'd have to shoot it."

"What?" Go Forth Son asked loudly. "What's this about shooting a horse?"

"The bus has broken down. It won't be taking us the rest of the way to our game in Conrad," Laser explained.

Otto pulled an imaginary six-shooter from inside his jacket and fired one shot in the direction of the engine. "BANG!" he shouted.

"Now what?" I asked. "How will we get to our game?"

"Someone will come along," Laser replied. "Don't forget, we've got J-Hawk Nation."

"Yeah," Captain Hook grumbled, "and we also have only about 45 minutes before our game is supposed to start.

I saw the headlights of a car approaching from the rear, and I watched as it slowed down and pulled in behind us. It was a highway patrol car, and its lights were now flashing.

We all jumped to our feet and ran up the aisle to the front of the bus so we could find out what was going on.

The patrolman approached Coach with his shining flashlight and said, "Hi, I'm Officer Milton. It appears that you have a bus problem."

Coach replied, "The radiator hose just burst, and we've lost all the coolant. My basketball team has a 6:45 playoff game in Conrad against Fraser, and we're not going to get there in this bus."

"Can you start it up and pull it into that driveway about 200 yards ahead? It needs to be off the road," Officer Milton added.

The engine barely turned over, but Coach coaxed it to kick in, and in a couple of minutes he was able to drive the bus slowly to the driveway ahead.

The officer drove his squad car forward and parked it behind the bus. "A tow truck will be coming out here to haul your bus to a garage near our headquarters. A mechanic there will make your necessary repairs," Officer Milton explained. "I've called for two other squad cars to come out. They'll be arriving in two or three minutes. Tonight your team will be riding with the highway patrol."

All thirteen of us looked at each other and started laughing and cheering. "We are . . . J-Hawks!" we shouted loudly.

"I see on your stocking caps . . . 'J-Hawk Nation.' I've been hearing and reading about your team," the officer continued. "I've read John Garris's columns. I know him."

"Do you know him as a friend or some bad guy you've had to arrest?" Otto asked.

A few of us exploded with laughter.

Officer Milton studied Otto.

The two squad cars pulled up beside us, and two patrolmen stepped out.

"All right, J-Hawks, put your gear in the trunks," Officer Milton said. Then he turned to the two other patrolmen. "Let's get this team to Conrad."

We packed into the three vehicles . . . Abe, Hook, Otto, and I jumped in with Officer Milton. The patrolman turned and looked at the four of us in his car, switched on his flashing lights, and said, "Hang on, boys. We're going for a ride." Then we sped off.

Officer Milton drove a lot faster than Coach had driven the bus. "We're not used to this fast a ride," I said. "Generally we travel a little slower and listen to Pickett play his ukulele and sing mellow music. Tonight I guess we'll have to get mentally prepared for our game by hanging on and listening to your police radio."

"Listening to my radio is a much better alternative than listening to me sing," Officer Milton replied.

We laughed at his admission. I knew my perception of highway patrol officers would never be the same after tonight.

When the three patrol cars pulled up right in front of the school, Officer Milton said, "Grab your stuff. I'll walk in with you to make sure they understand why you are late."

As soon as we entered the gym behind the patrolman, a school official rushed to meet us. "We wondered what was up. Is everyone okay?" he asked.

"Their bus broke down. Everyone is okay, and the whole team is now here. They'll need some time to dress and warm up," Officer Milton explained.

"All right," the school official said. He asked Coach, "How about if we push the game time back twenty minutes? Will that be enough time for you?"

Coach looked at a clock hanging on a gym wall. "Yeah," he replied. "That would be great."

"Thanks for the ride, Officer Milton," I said. Then I added, "Is it possible that you could walk us through the gym to our locker room?" And then I continued in a quieter voice, "And would you make it look really good?"

He winked at me and addressed the team loudly, "Shape up those lines! Let's go! You are coming with me!" Then he marched us down the sideline of the gym toward our locker room as everyone in the bleachers stared at us and gasped.

This is kind of fun. I bet everyone wonders what kind of trouble we have gotten ourselves into now.

John Garris arrived at the locker room door at the same time we did. He was writing hurriedly in his tablet as he took his last few steps to reach us.

"Are **you** writing **me** a ticket?" Officer Milton asked incredulously. Then he smiled and said in a much friendlier tone of voice, "Hi, John. Are you working on another story?"

"Hey, Mike," Garris replied. "I am working on a column. Do you have time to sit with me and answer a few questions?"

"I think I do," the officer said. "I need to stay for this game because I feel it's my responsibility to make sure these boys have a way to get home." Then as our team filed into the locker room he called out to us, "Have a good game, J-Hawks."

We dressed quickly, but we weren't feeling panicked. Coach had told us that we'd have time for our regular warm-up routine.

Warm-ups went well. Our spirit was good, and we quickly fell into our usual rhythm. My jump shot was falling, and as I ran I felt the sweat coming. The guys were fired up, and I heard lots of chatter and a little laughter. We were preparing to have some fun.

I sneaked a peek into the bleachers behind our bench, and I did see Sarah. She smiled and gave me a slight wave. I nodded to her, turned back toward our bucket, caught a bounce pass from San Juan, and swished a 15-foot jumper. *Yeah! Let's get this game going!*

We met at the bench for final instructions.

"We've had an exciting night so far," Coach said to us. "Officer Milton and the two other patrolmen used speed to get us here tonight, and I think we should honor them by showing them that we have some speed of our own. We're going to run on every chance we get. Let's show J-Hawk Nation that we are deserving of the Highway Patrol's flashing lights. On defense, challenge them with pressure . . . force mistakes. Let's play our best game and keep this streak alive."

"We are . . . J-Hawks!" we shouted as we put our hands together in the huddle.

From the student section in the bleachers echoed a reply that was even louder. "We are . . . J-Hawks!"

I could sense our high energy level, and I was glad that Coach was going to let us run. This was our best strength, and tonight we would dare the Falcons to try to keep up with us.

I smiled toward Sarah in the bleachers, and I saw that John Garris was sitting two rows behind her. Next to him sat Officer Milton.

As I took up a position at the center circle, I laughed to myself, thinking about Otto's question about "friend or bad guy." *I sure hope Otto doesn't make siren noises when we start running.*

Abe stretched high and directed the opening tip to Pickett. Pickett reached in, grabbed the basketball, pivoted toward me, and snapped me a pass. I took two quick dribbles as I ran down the floor, and then I tossed the ball toward our basket, ahead of Laser. Without breaking his stride, Laser caught the ball, took a high running step, and laid the ball off the backboard and through the hoop for our first points of the game.

Before the ball had time to fall through the net to the floor, Abe and Hook sprinted for the center of the gym. Pickett challenged the inbound pass while Laser and I set up to pressure the Falcons as they attempted to move the basketball toward their own basket. Number 21 dribbled toward Laser's sideline, but Laser stepped in front of him and stopped him in his tracks. Pickett closed in from behind, and now the dribbler found himself boxed in by two defenders. I slid to the center circle, and Abe and Hook backed off a few steps. There was no way for Number 21 to make a good pass. He tried to pivot as he protected the ball, but he ran out of time, and a ref blew his whistle for a five-second violation.

After being handed the ball by the ref, Pickett threw the inbound pass up by the rim, and Abe collected it and dropped it through the hoop. It was that easy!

Again we set up our press.

This time Number 10 tried to make an immediate long pass toward the far end after catching the throw-in, but Captain Hook sprinted back and intercepted it. He dribbled toward me and passed me a bullet. I grabbed it, turned, and passed off to Laser who found Pickett in the lane for a short jump shot that dropped cleanly through the net, and we were off to a 6-0 start.

The Falcon coach called for a timeout.

At the bench we drank water as we listened to Coach. "Do not let up! They haven't figured out how to break our press so keep up the intensity. Set it up the same way, but if they work through the press twice-in-a-row, drop back the next time and trap them at half-court. My scouting report says the Falcons like playing a slow game, a half-court game. Let's not give them a chance to do that. Keep it at a fast pace. Let's go!"

"We are . . . J-Hawks!" we shouted, and the bleachers behind our bench echoed again, "We are . . . J-Hawks! We are . . . J-Hawks!"

I like that.

I smiled in Sarah's direction.

The game was less than two minutes old, and already we had shown a spirited, aggressive style of play.

Coach turned the first quarter into a chess match: The Falcons changed the way they brought the ball up the floor . . . We changed to a half-court trap. They switched to a three-guard offence . . . We adjusted our defense. The Falcons tried to slow the game down . . . We sped it up. When the Falcon guards sagged back on Abe, Hook, and Pickett . . . Laser and I started shooting (and hitting) open jump shots. When we were covered more closely out front . . . We passed the ball inside. It was a great game of "cat and mouse," and we J-Hawks were the cat, and we held "the upper paw." At the end of the first quarter, we held a nine-point lead.

To start the second quarter, Otto came in for Pickett and covered the center of the gym behind Laser and me as we continued to pressure the Falcons. Abe and Hook covered the back half. This slight change gave us more speed on the floor and took away the Falcons' passes in the middle.

It did cause them problems. In the next four attempts to get the ball to their basket, we stole the ball twice, and they threw the ball away another time. We picked up four more points when Captain Hook banked in a short hook shot and I hit on a short jumper, while Number 50 for the Falcons missed their only shot.

Halfway through the quarter Coach gave us a rest by calling a timeout. Pickett, San Juan, and Tucson checked into the game as Otto, Abe, and I sat out. Coach turned San Juan and Tucson loose with their fresh legs to harass the dribblers, and Laser covered the center of the floor. Tucson dived and stole the ball as a player tried to dribble around him, and San Juan scored on a layup after a great pass led him to our basket.

Coach kept rotating players. Abe, Otto, and I reentered, and Laser, Tucson and Hook took a seat.

Frustration was beginning to set in for the Falcons. This was not how they wanted to play. Their two good shooters weren't getting any chances. They hardly touched the ball on their own end, and they started yelling at their own teammates to get them the ball.

We've got to keep this up. They are losing their confidence.

At the end of the second quarter, Pickett's last-second shot bounced off the rim, but we ran to the locker room with a twelve-point lead.

"Wow!" Coach said in the locker room. "Officer Milton must have inspired you tonight. If you can keep this up for the rest of the game I'll have to talk to the Supe about getting flashing lights for your shoes."

"Otto was hoping for a siren," I said.

"Catch your breath, everyone," Coach suggested. "When we go back out we'll go with the starting five and our 1-2-2 press. Pickett, switch to a 2-1-2 if the Falcons use the center of the floor to bring the ball up. Laser and Hook . . . you each have two fouls . . . everyone else is okay. You are playing this game perfectly, guys. Play the second half like you played the first, and we'll adapt to their adjustments. Play hard . . . have fun! Get out there and warm your bodies up again. Tipoff is in about five minutes.

We kept running, but the Falcons made sure two guys were back at all times, so if the layup wasn't there for us, we passed the ball until we had open shots. Pickett outmuscled his defender to establish good position in the lane, and Laser and I were quick to deliver him the ball. Abe and Hook broke to the basket, giving Pickett options to shoot or pass off to either guy. Besides running time off the clock, we were adding to our lead, a couple points at a time. We continued to guard the two main scorers for the Falcons closely, and they could not get into a shooting rhythm.

The buzzer sounded to end the third quarter, and we trotted to the bench leading by a score of 55-38, and I watched the Falcons trudge off the court with their heads down.

Do not feel sorry for them! Do not let up!

The Falcons played the last quarter in desperation. As the time ran down I could see the fear and sadness in the eyes of their leaders as they realized that they could not match our play tonight, and this would be the final game of high school basketball for their seniors.

We J-Hawks, on the other hand, would get to play again Friday night because of our 18-point victory.

We shook hands at center court, and two Falcons told me that they hoped we could make it to the state tournament this year. Number 20 said,

"Go, J-Hawks! We'll be cheering for you guys."

Number 44 walked to our bench after shaking hands, and he said to Coach, "You are the best team we have faced this year. We could not keep up with you. Good luck the rest of the way, and keep running."

Again we had to clear the bench area immediately because another game followed ours. I did not have a chance to talk to Sarah because Coach hustled us out of there.

As we showered, Coach told us we had ten minutes to get dressed and packed up because Officer Milton was coming in to walk us out to the lobby. It was the patrolman's request this time.

"All right!" Tucson shouted. "Can we get him to come back Friday night?"

"I've got an extra J-Hawk Nation stocking cap with me tonight," I announced. "What do you guys think?"

"Yeah!" Laser answered, speaking for the team. "He rescued us! Sign him up for J-Hawk Nation, but wait until we get to the lobby and have a big crowd around us."

As we exited the locker room, we stood face-to-face with Officer Milton. "Good game, J-Hawks!" he said excitedly. "All right. We're otta here. Stay together."

Although we were not "in step," we walked as a group out to the lobby where most of J-Hawk Nation was waiting for us. As soon as we reached them, the applause started. I looked around . . . found my folks talking with Sarah's family . . . and walked over.

"It looks like you have earned another game for Friday night," Mom said.

"Congratulations on winning Number 20!" Sarah said enthusiastically. "You guys really had your running legs tonight."

"We did run well, didn't we," I replied, "and our shots were falling, too. We must have been inspired by Officer Milton's ride to the gym," I added with a smile. "I think the Supe should hire the patrolman to drive the bus to our next game."

"When the officer walked you into the gym it looked like you were in trouble," Mrs. Jenkins said. "What was going on?"

"We were just having some fun," I answered. Then I turned toward Sarah. "Will you come with me? I'm going to offer Officer Milton a stocking cap because of the help he gave us tonight."

We started walking across the lobby.

"I heard some of the conversation between Garris and the patrolman during the game," Sarah said. "I couldn't help listening in. Garris was really complimenting your team, and he said he felt like he was a part of J-Hawk Nation now. The two of them laughed a lot about something Otto had said earlier. So now you might have a writer and a patrolman in your corner?"

"Yeah, and that would be good," I replied, "but it can't compete with having 'the mystery girl' as one of our best fans."

Sarah gave me a one-arm hug as we reached Officer Milton.

"Could I have everyone's attention please?" Laser asked loudly. Then he waited until the conversations slowly died out. "The J-Hawks would like to thank Officer Milton for his rescue tonight from what could have been a big disaster for us. Maybe you noticed that we seemed to play in a higher gear than usual tonight. That was probably a result of our faster than usual ride to our game."

I saw nodding heads, and I heard soft laughter as Laser looked to me.

"Officer Milton, we would be honored if you would accept this J-Hawk Nation cap. Now you'll have a prop to use when you tell your story about how you saved the J-Hawks," I said as I handed him the cap.

"Thank you," he replied as he took the cap. "I appreciate this, and I hope you continue to play well. I just heard on my radio that your bus has been repaired and is waiting for you at the garage. I have the only squad car here, however, but I am heading back to headquarters. Coach, I can offer you and two or three of your players a ride."

"That would be great," Coach replied. "Is there anyone who does not have a ride back to school where we can hang up our things? All twelve of you need to check in with me now."

Everyone had a ride back, but Pickett and Laser chose to go in the squad car with Officer Milton so they could keep Coach company as he drove the bus back to Jeffers. I had two possibilities for rides. I accepted the offer from the Jenkins family to give me a ride to the locker room and then to my house. It did not appear that I hurt Mom and Dad's feelings when I didn't go with them.

I sat in the back seat with Sarah, and I was smart enough to keep some space between us. I was able to reach out and secretly hold hands with her though. Mr. Jenkins asked about our bus problems and our ride with the Highway Patrol. I told them the whole story, and then we talked about how we had played tonight. After that, when the conversation slowed down, Sarah and I took a few minutes to discuss school and our other activities.

"Mr. Jenkins," I said, "I really appreciate the ride from your family. And I'm glad you're not driving as fast as Officer Milton did. He drove well, but it was too fast for me. Do you know that I'm a careful driver, and I don't speed?"

"Yes, I do know that," Mr. Jenkins replied.

"Sarah told us that you are a good driver," Mrs. Jenkins added.

*They **do** know everything.*

"Usually I get to hear live music on the way home from a game, Sarah," I said. "Do you know the words to 'Michael, Row the boat Ashore?'"

We sang together the rest of the way to the Jeffers gym, often even messing around with attempts at harmony. Because of Sarah's encouragement, her parents even joined in on some songs. It was another of those great nights.

After a quick stop at the school, I directed Mr. Jenkins to my house in the country. When we pulled up by the garage, Sarah got out with me and walked me up the short sidewalk to the porch door. We laughed about this reversal.

We stood at the door under the bright yard-light, and I guessed that her parents were watching us. I said to Sarah, "This was my best ever ride home from a basketball game." We held hands, and I looked into her eyes.

I know they are watching . . . but I don't care right now. I put my hands on Sarah's shoulders, and I gave her a quick kiss. "Good night, Sarah."

"Good night, Catch," she replied.

As Sarah turned and walked back to her car, she raised her arms toward the sky and shouted, "We are . . . J-Hawks!"

I started laughing, and Sarah turned back to look at me, and I could see the beautiful smile on her face. *I love this girl.*

I stood watching and smiling as Sarah's dad backed the car up and drove down the driveway. I kept waving, and my eyes kept following the car until it completely disappeared from my view.

As I stepped into the porch I thought about Officer Milton's rescue. I was feeling proud of the Highway Patrol. I removed my J-Hawk Nation stocking cap from my head, held it in the air as a kind of salute, and said, "To the Iowa Highway Patrol. Thank you, Officer Milton."

I entered the kitchen, and I thought about how fortunate my team was tonight. This could have ended very differently for us. Were we lucky . . . or are we a team of destiny?

In the Stands – With John Garris

I can't sugarcoat it. They were speeding.

In last night's sectional playoff game against the Fraser Falcons, the J-Hawks from Jeffers ran at speeds that deserved a reading from a radar gun, and the man who sat next to me in the bleachers had the equipment and the know-how to use it. That man was Officer Milton of the Highway Patrol, and he may have been the person who was mostly responsible for the relentless fast break that the J-Hawks unleashed against the Falcons last night.

Officer Milton had been on patrol in his squad car when he came upon the broken down school bus of the Jeffers J-Hawk basketball team that was on its way to Conrad for its game. The patrolman made a call on his radio to arrange for a tow truck to haul the bus in for repairs, and he summoned assistance from two additional officers who had just completed their shifts so the J-Hawks could get a ride the rest of the way to their game.

According to a couple players I talked to, the speed at which they ran during the game may well have been directly attributed to the fast speed (and occasional flashing lights) that the patrolmen used while transporting the J-Hawks to Conrad. One of the players said, "That ride got my motor going," and a second player reported, "Officer Milton's thrill ride must have kicked in extra adrenaline for me tonight." The ride in the squad cars had inspired them.

The boys from Jeffers won the game by eighteen points and will play again Friday night. In the meantime . . . if I were a parent of a J-Hawk . . . I might hide the car keys for a few days . . . until the emotional experience and memory of riding with the Highway Patrol has worn off and the J-Hawks are again content with life's normal speed.

Chapter 43

Expectations

It surprised us a little, but maybe it shouldn't have. He's been doing this type of thing since the beginning of our basketball season, so the unexpected isn't so unexpected any more.

Suggesting that the Cade kids be enrolled in our school while they were stranded in Jeffers . . . changing the school policy so athletic letters would be awarded to basketball players before Christmas vacation . . . allowing us students to discuss our feelings and frustrations after Mr. Weston visited and riled us up about having to attend school at Madison Lake next year . . . all of these things showed that the Supe was changing, and I didn't see him as someone to be feared as much anymore. He appeared to be on our side.

I thought about these things on Thursday night at dusk as I was in the haymow of our barn, dropping hay bales down the chute to the dairy cows below. I could almost understand it. The Supe was caught up in the closing of the Jeffers school, too. He would lose his job at the end of the school year, and he would be moving his family to a new town, but for the rest of this year, and especially for as long as our basketball team kept winning, he was possibly the most important member of J-Hawk Nation.

This morning, after attendance had been taken in the assembly room, the Supe had called all twelve of us players outside to the hallway for a private meeting. He told us he had a proposition to offer, and that he had already discussed this with Coach, but it was totally up to us. He tossed it out and said he'd be back in about ten minutes. Our job was to talk it over and make a decision.

It took us by surprise, but it did make sense. Pickett led the discussion.

"What do you guys think?" Pickett asked as he looked around at all of us. "There's plenty of room in the bus, and it won't cost the school any extra money."

"Will it interfere with your music?" Laser asked. "I really like the music . . . It helps me relax."

"It will be a lot noisier," Go Forth Son added. "We may not be able to prepare for the game like we usually do."

I looked at the others, trying to guess who might speak up next, but there was silence for the next five to ten seconds.

Tucson stepped up. "Except for the last two games, we've shared the bus all year with the girls' team," he said. "I think the bus has been too quiet and too empty with just us sitting in the back of the bus."

"A little extra noise won't bother me," Abe offered. "I've got a loud brother."

"He is pretty loud," San Juan agreed. "You need to work on that."

"How about just telling the others that we'd like them to keep the noise level down?" Treason suggested. "They'd do that for us, I think."

I thought the time was right for me to share my thoughts. "I'm in favor of letting our classmates ride with us on the bus to the game," I said. "They've been cheering for us all year, and we really need them. They are J-Hawk Nation. Like Treason said, ask for some quiet on the way to the game, and then, after we demolish Benson they can turn the volume up for the ride home. Besides, I think Pickett could use some new voices singing backup."

Several guys laughed at my comment.

"If the students ride our bus they'll be there during our warm-ups," San Juan added. "That will help fire us up. It will seem just like a home game."

"Anyone else?" Pickett asked.

Heads shook, and everyone was silent.

"So we are all in agreement?" Laser asked.

The heads changed direction, and a few "yups" were said.

"Okay then," Pickett concluded. "I think it's a good idea, too. You guys go back in and sit down. Laser and I will wait here for the Supe and let him know what we decided."

Though it had seemed like something very minor, it had felt quite positive to me . . . one more example of us figuring things out by ourselves and knowing that we did have some say in how things were done. I recalled that the Supe had said, "It's totally up to you," and I sat on a hay bale and watched my breath in the dusty cold air as I thought about his words.

He was right . . . about everything. Friday night's game **was** totally up to us. Coach will guide us, for sure, but our season depends on how the twelve of us play in that game. If we play well we have a good chance of winning, but if we don't . . . our dreams may be shattered. I didn't even like thinking about that possibility. Too often my thoughts of basketball were mixed with thoughts of Sarah. Would the end of one lead to the end . . .

I yelled at myself silently and stopped that thought from going any farther.

I looked at the hoop and the attached net that hung on the south wall of the haymow, exactly ten feet above the dusty, weathered wooden floor-boards below. I pictured myself in a real gym, sprinting toward our basket, catching a quick pass from Laser, turning to face the rim, and lifting myself into the air as I fired a perfect jump shot. As many times as I ran this mental movie through my head, my shot never missed. This was my dream . . . that I would never miss.

When I felt the chill get to me, I scrambled down the six worn rungs of the vertical wooden ladder, walked over and around the bales of hay that the cows on the north side were feeding on as they stood in their assigned stalls, and I followed the path through the snow to the house.

I didn't call every night, but I knew Sarah expected me to call once or twice during the week. Talking to her was something I really looked forward to, and I tried to choose nights that helped bridge the gap between those times when I saw her in person. By now we were really good friends, and I couldn't see myself ever caring about someone else as much as I cared for Sarah. She was the best thing that had ever happened to me, and I thought of her often. Working on ideas that I hoped would keep her liking me took a lot of my free time in school.

I dialed.

Sarah answered, as she usually does now. "Hello," she said, and my heart skipped a beat when I heard the sweetness in her voice.

"Hi, Sarah," I replied. "It's Catcher. How are you?"

"I'm good," she said through light laughter. "Don't you think I will recognize your voice? Sorry for laughing, but you said your name as if you were calling a stranger."

"How do you know that I didn't do that just to make you laugh?" I asked. "You have the sweetest laugh that I have ever heard in my life. Maybe I call just to hear you laugh?"

She laughed again.

"See! This really works. Don't be expecting me to change anything," I added. "I'm tempted to hang up, call back, and do this again."

Now we were both laughing.

"Are you ready for tomorrow night's game against Benson?" Sarah asked.

"Yeah, we are really looking forward to it," I answered. "We think they might try to run against us again, but that just plays into our best strength. We played really well against them at home. Do you remember that game?"

"Yes, I do," Sarah replied. "We learned each other's name at that game . . . and your mom cut your hair . . . and we sat together in the lunchroom for the first time and drank J-Hawk Juice. I remember that game well."

"That was one of my best nights ever," I said.

"There were a lot of fouls called against your team in your game at Benson, right?" Sarah asked. "Nicholson was the hero when he made all six of his free throws?"

"Wow, Sarah!" I said, "I am very impressed. Do you remember all our games?"

"You can test me some time," Sarah said. "I think I would do quite well."

"We think the Bulldogs will be expecting to play us close, maybe even think they can beat us tomorrow night, but I think we'll do all right. We want to crush them this time," I continued. "Will you be able to come to the game?"

"Of course I'll be there," Sarah replied. "Whenever you play . . . I will come to watch and cheer for you."

"There's something new for tomorrow, Sarah," I said. "The other high school kids have been invited to ride our team bus to the game with us. I'll tell you about it at the game."

"What about for the games after that?" Sarah asked.

"I like your positive attitude," I replied, "but first we need to take care of business on Friday night."

We talked for about ten minutes. The conversation was so easy that it felt like I had known Sarah for several years, but that didn't make it any easier to say "good-bye." It would be another whole day until I would get to see her again.

When we arrived early at the gym in Conrad, it was empty and eerily quiet, unlike last Tuesday night when we were given a ride by the Highway Patrol, and we were escorted into a noisy gym just a few minutes before game time. Tonight we were a little more relaxed.

The bus ride had felt good. Pickett provided the music, and the conversations were quite hushed. Having other kids in the bus was a great idea because we could see that we weren't going alone into the game against Benson.

During warm-ups I noticed several of the Bulldogs watching us as their teammates were shooting. This was something we never did . . . watch the other team warm up. We focused on our own shots and cheered for each other. Any time the other team watched us during warm-ups . . . we called it "admiration," and it gave us even more confidence. We figured that meant that they were a little afraid of us.

After passing the ball off to San Juan, I took a quick glance into the bleacher area behind our bench. I was able to find Sarah's parents, but Sarah was not with them. *She said she would be here.* I didn't want to lose my focus so I turned away quickly and tried to get Sarah out of my mind. After a few seconds passed I glanced again toward the bleachers at a bunch of kids standing and waving. There she was . . . in the student section. *I knew she would be here. I wonder why she is not sitting with her parents?*

Very early in the game both teams established that they would be using a running game again tonight. That probably didn't surprise anyone. The ability to run had accounted for most of our victories, and we had heard that it was the same for the Bulldogs. Way back in December Garris had written in his column, after watching our first game against Benson, that he had attended a "track meet." That's what it felt like again tonight.

The Bulldogs could match our speed, and they could shoot, but we could shoot well, too. Where we had a big advantage was in rebounding, because each of the J-Hawk front-court players stood four or five inches taller than the Bulldogs that were covering them, and Coach had drilled into all of us the importance of blocking out and getting ourselves into good rebounding position.

In the first quarter it was our rebounding edge that helped us build a small lead. After Laser missed his jump shot on our first possession, Abe jumped up and grabbed the rebound as it bounced off the rim, and he put it back against the board into the bucket before his feet had returned to the floor. Though it had taken us two shots, we had gotten the basket, and anytime we scored, the Bulldogs couldn't run their fast break to the other end. The best way to slow them down was to make baskets, and grabbing rebounds gave us many more chances to score.

Every defensive rebound by both teams led to fast breaks, and both teams had to hustle back in order to try to prevent an easy score. Benson pushed every opportunity all the way to the hoop, because if they missed their shot, they had a chance to grab the rebound if our big guys had not yet arrived at the basket. It was a good strategy for them. Sometimes it worked.

We, on the other hand, pulled up on our fast break if we felt we did not have the advantage on the play. Slowing it down meant our rebounders could take up their positions, and if we missed our shot, there was a really good chance we would get a second or maybe even a third opportunity to score if we needed it. This was a great strategy for us, and it often led to points.

That's how the first quarter went. Because of our second and third shots we pulled out to a six-point lead, and Coach managed to give all five of us starters a short rest on the bench by putting in Otto, San Juan, and Tucson. The Bulldogs only played their starting five.

In the second quarter Benson switched to a man-to-man defense so they had more of a chance to block our guys out on rebound opportunities. That's a good idea, except that meant that Number 15, who stood about 5 feet ten, had to cover Captain Hook by himself, and Hook had six inches on him. Several times Hook drew his defender toward the lane, and I bounced a pass outside toward Hook's left, where he grabbed the ball and stepped right into a very short hook shot, his specialty. Being in a better position to block out on rebounds didn't do the Bulldogs much good when we didn't miss very many of our shots.

On the left side of the court, Laser and Abe had their own little game going. Abe stood about six inches taller than his defender, too, and Laser's passes gave Abe several opportunities for close-in shots, and again there were very few rebounds for the Bulldogs to grab.

I thought it was kind of funny that Pickett, our big horse, didn't get to do much except for setting picks and screens, but I could see the smile on his face, and I knew he was enjoying this.

The Bulldogs kept playing just five guys while we rotated eight players, and at the half-time buzzer we had increased the lead to thirteen points. As we headed to the locker room, J-Hawk Nation stood and applauded. This was exactly the kind of game they were hoping for and expecting to see.

"Benson will probably come out in their zone again in the second half," Coach told us. "That will give them a chance to double-cover Abe and Hook, but it means that Pickett should be open at the free-throw line. Let's ride him for a while. We shouldn't need to take many long jump shots tonight. Our rebounding advantage has made a huge difference. It forced the Bulldogs into making changes that gave us several easy baskets. Let's use this second half to build our confidence even higher. J-Hawk Nation came here tonight expecting a victory. Let's give them a big one."

"We are . . . J-Hawks!"

Five new Bulldogs started the second half. Though they had fresh legs, it was obvious to me that they were second-stringers. They ran and scored occasionally, while we played really smart basketball, choosing to fast break sometimes and slow it down other times. Our rebounding edge continued to give us many chances for second shots, and our lead grew.

I try to never feel sorry for the other team, but tonight I couldn't help it. The Bulldogs were good players and nice guys, but their season would end tonight. I looked into their faces and saw sadness that I did not want to experience myself. I watched as their seniors took seats on the bench toward the end of the fourth quarter when the game was no longer winnable for them, and I felt a little guilty that I was partly responsible for that sadness. Twice I shook hands with players as they reached out to me when they walked by on the way to their bench, while everyone in the gym applauded what had been their final effort of the season. It didn't feel very good.

Here we were . . . winning the section championship . . . and I felt the Bulldog loss more than I felt our big win. I decided I would talk to Laser and Pickett on the ride home to find out if they have ever experienced this.

Coach had been able to get all twelve of us into the game, and two players who don't often score made baskets. Nicholson scored on a perfect jump shot, and Half-Dozen made a fast-break basket and a free throw. All the rest of us celebrated with them at the bench as the game ended, then we joined into a line to shake hands with the Bulldogs.

By now some of the sadness on their faces had disappeared, and as we told them "good game," a few players complimented us on our game and our season.

"Good luck the rest of the way," Number 12 said. "Make our conference proud."

Since ours was the only game in the gym tonight, Coach gave us a chance to talk with our families and friends before we showered. While I was talking to a couple young boys, I watched Sarah go around to the other players. I could understand why everyone liked her, and why a few of the guys on the team seemed to envy me. Mom and Dad stopped briefly, and then Sarah's parents came over. Then the four of them moved off and started talking.

I'm glad they are friendly to each other. It would be pretty awkward if they weren't.

"Good game, Catcher," Abe's dad said to me.

"Thanks," I replied, "But I think that most of the credit tonight goes to Abe and Hook. Their rebounding and shooting carried us. They were both really tough."

"You guys played really well tonight!" Sarah said as she approached and reached for my hand. "Congratulations on winning the section championship."

"Thank you, Sarah," I replied. "I thought you might want to see at least one more game."

"At least one more," Sarah said laughing. "Maybe several more."

"I noticed you sat with the students," I said. "Problems with your parents?" I smiled so she would know that I was not being serious.

"A couple kids came over right after we arrived and told Mom and Dad that it was time for me to sit in the student section. They explained that they needed my voice for extra volume," Sarah added. "Mom and Dad told me to go ahead, but I think they maybe were a little disappointed when I moved. I'll ask them about this on the ride home."

"I'm glad you came tonight. I was worried for a moment when I saw your parents, and you weren't with them," I admitted.

Sarah smiled at me. "I suppose you know that we won't be seeing a movie tomorrow night," she said.

"Why not?" I asked.

"The Jenkins family has been invited out for dinner tomorrow night," she replied.

I just stood there, because I didn't know how to respond to what she had just told me. I didn't think a dinner invitation was a very good reason for breaking a movie date.

She looked at me quizzically. "You don't know about this?" she asked.

I shook my head.

"Your mom invited us to your house for dinner," Sarah said. "We'll be spending the evening at your house . . . with our parents."

"That sounds like fun," I said as I recovered. "We'll save the movie for another time. I have an idea about what we can do after eating. Bring boots, and wear a warm coat. If it's not too cold I'll take you on a nature hike down to the creek. This could possibly be an outdoor adventure you will remember forever . . . and we won't be inviting our parents to walk with us."

"I look forward to the nature hike." Sarah said, smiling.

"Will your dad be going for coffee tomorrow morning?" I asked.

"That's a very important Saturday routine for him," Sarah answered, "and I expect to ride along to keep him company."

"That's great," I said. "Then I'll see you at our clinic and talk to you after our trip to the library. It's funny how Saturday morning has turned out to be the best morning of the week, and it's not just because there's no school."

As Coach started chasing all of us players to the locker room, he announced to everyone still in the gym, "Our next game is not until Friday, in Stallworth. I should know by Monday who our opponent will be.

Not until Friday. Maybe I'll need to work on a project at Madison Lake Library on Tuesday or Wednesday. I better start planting the seed.

The bus ride home was pretty noisy, but it was fun. Pickett encouraged others to sing with him, and it sounded almost like our school choir. J-Hawk Nation was content for now, but I expected that the only way to keep it that way was to continue winning. That would be our plan for Friday night.

Chapter 44
A Different Kind of Winning

Dad had agreed to drive to The Jeffers Café a little earlier today because I wanted to get a few extra shots in before our short practice started. He diagonal parked the old Ford in front of the café, and I hopped out and walked the single block to the school.

The temperature wasn't bad for February, but the sky had chosen to wear kind of a dark gray today. Just as I reached the school property, I heard the honk of a car horn, and I turned around to see Sarah's dad pull up. The passenger side door opened, and Sarah stepped out. *Maybe seats are filling even earlier than usual at the café these mornings.*

"Good morning, Sarah," I said. "Thanks for coming to help with the kids."

"Good morning to you," she replied. "I look forward to this every week. Susan and others count on my being here."

"You are absolutely right," I said. "I am one of the 'others.'"

The gym door was not yet unlocked, so I knew we were the first ones here. We continued our conversation.

"It's not supposed to be too cold tonight," Sarah continued, "but I hear it might snow a little today. Will you still take me on the nature hike?"

"A blanket of fresh white snow will make the nature hike even more fun for the city girl from Madison Lake," I answered as I smiled and stared into her blue eyes.

We had a good practice. It was just enough to help us loosen up but not wear us down. All the regular kids showed up for the clinic, and there was one new kid. His mom introduced him to me.

"This is Larry," she said. "We're from Madison Lake where Larry is in fourth grade. It's his birthday tomorrow, and instead of having a party, he asked me if I would bring him here so he could play basketball with your team this morning."

I held out my hand and said, "Welcome, Larry . . . and Happy Birthday. You chose **us** instead of having a party. Wow!"

"I turn ten tomorrow," Larry explained.

"How did you know about our basketball clinic?" I asked.

"I live just a few houses down from Sarah Jenkins," he said. "She told me about it."

I looked at Sarah in the bleachers and nodded. "Good for Sarah," I said.

"Meet Larry," I announced to everyone as we were getting ready to start the clinic. "Larry is a fourth grader in Madison Lake. It's his birthday tomorrow, and his mom brought him here today as his present. What do you think of that?"

Several kids responded, "Hi, Larry. Happy Birthday!"

Larry and the other kids played hard today, running, dribbling, passing, and shooting baskets. We set up a few passing and shooting contests, hoping everyone would win at something. During a short break, Abe treated the kids to a couple dunks, and Captain Hook really stretched out his long arms as he banked a few short hook shots off the backboard and into the basket. Laser, San Juan, Otto, Tucson, and I had a quick competition shooting rapid-fire jump shots from the top of the key. Today I had the hot hand. Pickett staged a pick on Treason that knocked him down, and everyone laughed and applauded. It appeared that the kids were impressed with everything we did today.

When we took the kids into the lunchroom for J-Hawk Juice and cookies after the workout, my brother, Bobby, came up to me and said quietly, "Larry said he really had fun today. I found out in talking to him that his dad is living away from home. I think that coming here today might be the only birthday present that Larry will get. Do you have an extra J-Hawk Nation stocking cap you could give him?"

"Great idea," I replied. "Why don't you go into the locker room and find my bag in the far corner. I have one extra cap in there. Why don't **you** give it to Larry, and just say **we** want you to have this as a birthday present."

That's what Bobby did, and I noticed that Sarah was watching when the cap was given to Larry, and he put it on immediately. A huge smile lit up his face, and everyone cheered and sang "Happy Birthday" to him.

Sarah looked at me from across the room and lipped "Thank you."

I smiled back and felt good for Larry . . . and for me.

My younger sister had the game all set up on the coffee table before the Jenkins family arrived. I knew she and Bobby would both be willing to play <u>Careers</u> with Sarah and me. I had a special reason for choosing that game. I wanted to learn more about Sarah, about what kinds of things were important to her, and I thought that playing this game might give me some clues.

I stepped outside just before six-thirty to shovel the fresh snow off the steps and the sidewalk. It had been just a light dusting, only about an inch, but I also tidied up the path to the yard-light pole, near where Mr. Jenkins would be parking his car. I took a couple deep breaths, hoping that the smells of the farm would not be too strong tonight, because I was just a little worried that Sarah would notice them. It didn't bother me . . . living on a farm . . . living with the smells of the hog yard and the cattle barn . . . because I was used to it, but it would be a new experience for Sarah, and I figured it would not be a positive one. *What if it bothered her so much that she wouldn't want to be friends with "a farm kid from Jeffers" anymore?* It was for this reason that I was a little troubled that Mom had invited the Jenkins family for dinner. I was afraid of the way that Sarah might look at me from now on. *I hope this fresh snow will settle things down . . . and at least there's very little wind tonight. That's good.*

Since Mom had extended the invitation, she was the one who went to the door when Sarah's family arrived. Dad and I backed her up. I hustled their coats upstairs to lay them on my bed, and when I came downstairs again I saw that Sarah's eyes were wide open as she looked around the kitchen at everything. She was smiling, and her eyes sparkled like the freshly fallen snow that quietly covered everything outside.

"I really like your house," she told Mom. "It feels so warm and homey, and it smells so good."

Her last statement was music to my ears, and I allowed myself to begin to relax. I led Sarah through the dining room into the living room to sit down, and the first thing she did was to walk over to the square display of four baby pictures that hung on the wall above the sofa. She smiled when she saw them. She studied the pictures, turning her head this way and that, and then she looked at me. I figured she wanted some help in finding out which baby I was, but I just shrugged my shoulders and offered nothing. I considered it a kind of test for her.

Sarah stared at Bobby and Debbie as they stood next to me, but neither said anything. Finally Sarah pointed to one, and after a couple seconds of suspense, Bobby raised his arm up into the air and smiled to her. Sarah shook her head and chose a second one, and this time my arm reached up.

"I would have been pretty disappointed if you had chosen either Debbie or Maggie," I said as I began to laugh.

Sarah's attention was then drawn to the two big oval golden frames that held curved glass and very serious-looking photos of four of my great-grandparents. She pointed to my dad's grandpa and said, "I think I see a resemblance."

"Please, no!" I protested. "I've always considered him to be kind of scary looking. Tell me you are kidding."

This time it was Sarah's shoulders that shrugged.

All four of us kids sat on the floor around the coffee table looking at the Careers game board.

Mom stepped in from the dining room and said to us, "We'll start eating in just a few minutes."

"Maybe we have time to discuss how to play," I said. "Do you know this game, Sarah?"

"I've heard of it, but I've never played it," she replied.

"You'll like it," Debbie said. "It's fun and kind of easy."

"Remember the number 60," I said. "The formula you decide on needs to be some combination of fame, fortune, and happiness that totals 60. You could choose 20 points for fortune, 20 for fame, and 20 for happiness, or you can choose any combination you want. The first person to collect the points and money that equals his secret formula wins the game.

"You write your numbers down on a small piece of paper and keep them secret during the game," I continued. "I'm sure you are excited about this 'secret' part. While you are collecting and recording your points on your score sheet, no one else will know what your formula is or if you are close to winning. It would be a good idea to look at the board now to see where the best places are for collecting points for each of the three categories."

"Time to eat!" Mom called from the dining room.

"Think about the numbers you will choose for your formula while we are eating," I advised Sarah, "but don't' tell us."

I watched as Sarah reached for her heart necklace.

"I already know mine," Sarah replied. "I'm choosing . . ."

"Don't tell!" Bobby and Debbie both yelled as they cut in.

Sarah just laughed. "I was just messing with you," she said. "I wasn't going to tell you."

Sarah was getting to be more playful as I got to know her better. This was one of the things that made me like her so much. She always seemed to be so happy, and nothing seemed to ever bother her. It felt good just being around her.

Mom had made a thick beef stew, a fruit salad with whipped cream, and fresh homemade buns for our meal. Everything tasted great, and Sarah's mom was especially impressed. Much of the talk at the table was about the J-Hawk basketball team.

"So your next game starts the districts?" Mr. Jenkins asked me.

"Yes," I answered. "Our next game will probably be the toughest game we've had all year. Coach told us that there are only about 60 teams left in our class in the tournament."

"You've had a great season," Mrs. Jenkins added. "We've enjoyed watching your team play. I hope you can keep winning."

"Thanks," I replied. "If we continue to play our best . . . I think we have a chance in any game we play. Abe and Hook have really improved since the beginning of the year, and Laser has really played well. Pickett gives us power in the middle, and Otto and Sons have done well coming off the bench. We've gotten great coaching, and the seniors have given us great leadership. We've played well together . . . That's a big part of how we win."

"You've played just as well as the others," Sarah said. "You forgot to say that. In some games you have been the best player on the floor."

"You have done well," Dad added, "except for the first half in that one game when Sarah arrived a little late."

Everyone laughed. Now it was funny, but it hadn't been on the night that it happened. I still remembered that game. I had been so worried that Sarah might have lost interest in watching me play.

"I don't know what we'll do for entertainment when your season ends," said Mr. Jenkins. "You J-Hawks have been the highlight of our winter."

Mr. Jenkins turned to his daughter. "Do you remember that first game we went to, Sarah?" he asked. "You did not want to go with me, but you said you would go if your mom and I reconsidered on something. What was it I had to promise you in order to get you to go that game with me?"

Sarah looked embarrassed and said nothing.

"I remember what it was. Are you okay if I answer for you, Dear?" Sarah's mom asked.

Sarah looked at me, then nodded slightly toward her mother.

"Your father and I agreed to **consider** letting you go out on a first date before you turned sixteen," Mrs. Jenkins said, "and that's the night you met the young man who ended up taking you on your first movie date . . . at age fifteen. Isn't is amazing how life sometimes writes its stories?"

Sarah's eyes met mine, and I smiled at her and said, "I'm really glad you drove a hard bargain with your parents. I think I was the big winner that night."

After we finished eating, we kids headed for Careers. I had a great time watching Sarah play, but Bobby was lucky and made the right moves, so he ended up winning quickly with his chosen formula.

Each of us pulled our piece of paper out from under the game board and showed our numbers to the other players. I noticed that Sarah and I had chosen similar numbers. She had written on her paper: 10 fortune, 5 fame, and 45 happiness. Mine had 15 fortune, 5 fame, and 40 happiness. I was hoping that our similar formulas for winning meant something.

"That was so quick," I said. "Let's play one more. I need one more game."

Each of us wrote on another paper and concealed it under the board. Again the game moved quickly, and again Bobby won.

When we revealed our formulas, Bobby said to me, "I clobbered you. You weren't even close to winning."

I looked at Sarah's numbers, then at her beautiful smile. She had kept her numbers the same, and I had not changed mine either. "No, Bobby," I said confidently, "tonight I won."

He looked at me like I was nuts and shook his head.

"I think I know what you mean," Debbie said to me.

I motioned for her to come over and whisper her idea to me.

"Very good!" I told her. "You do understand. While Sarah and I are on our winter nature hike, maybe you can educate your brother. Understanding this might be very valuable information for him someday."

The moon was close to full, and the clouds had moved on after dropping the snow, so after our eyes adjusted to the darkness, we could see quite clearly without the use of the two flashlights we carried.

"It is so quiet out here!" Sarah said as we walked down the farm lane in the direction of the creek. "All I hear is our footsteps in the snow. This is spectacular! The moonlight on the snow makes it look like there are diamonds everywhere, and everything I see is in black and white! There are no other colors. This is a wonderful winter hike!"

"Let's stop for a moment," I said. "I think I heard something."

We stood perfectly still. The only sound I could hear was our quiet breathing. Then, in the distance over by Moss's Woods, I heard the faint sound again.

"What's that?" Sarah asked excitedly.

"It's an owl," I answered. "Since it wasn't invited for beef stew, it's probably out hunting for mice. Once I was so close to an owl that flew over that I felt the air move when I heard the swishing of its wings."

We continued walking, hand-in-hand. I shined my flashlight toward the snow-covered field of alfalfa and saw some rabbit tracks.

"We've got company out here," I said. "This field provides cover and food under the snow for mice and rabbits. They, in turn, draw owls, hawks, and foxes that are looking for their next meal. Let's look for more tracks."

We left the lane and searched the field with our flashlights.

"What's this?" Sarah asked.

I could tell by the change in the tone of her voice that she was upset. I shined my light around where she was looking, and I found bloodied and disturbed snow with a small amount of fur left behind.

"That's part of nature," I answered calmly. "These look like fox tracks. I think a fox caught a rabbit here. Sometimes it's sad, but that's how nature works. I've seen all kinds of young rabbits and pheasant chicks run freely out here on summer days, and I've laughed at how much fun they seemed to have. Other times I'm reminded that animals need to eat in order to survive."

I wrapped my arms around Sarah to comfort her.

"It's okay," I assured her. "It's the way of things out here, but I'm sorry you happened to see this."

"I'm all right," Sarah whispered. "I understand. I've heard about animals in the wild, but I haven't experienced it before. I'm glad you showed me."

"Do you know your directions out here?" I asked.

Sarah shook her head.

I turned her and said, "North is this way. Can you find the 'big dipper' in all of these stars?"

She searched the sky for a few seconds.

"Is that it?" she asked as she pointed to the northern sky.

I stepped behind her and my eyes followed the direction of her arm.

"Good work," I said. Can you locate the North Star by using the two pointer stars?"

"There's the brightest star in the line," she replied. "That must be it. Hooray! We're not lost!"

Her laughter suggested to me that she had recovered from nature's lesson.

"If we stayed out here several hours," I continued, "we would see the 'big dipper' seem to change its location in the sky, turning around the North Star. Don't be fooled, though. It's not the stars that are moving. It's the earth spinning. You better hold on tightly to me, or we could be in trouble."

We did hold on to each other, fighting the coldness of the air as we stood under the star-filled sky, standing almost knee-deep in an alfalfa field that was covered with fresh whiteness, and I felt wonderful.

"Sarah," I said tenderly, "I want you to know that I love you, and I hope you will be my best friend forever."

I don't know how many rabbits and foxes were watching as Sarah and I kissed, but I was glad to be able to share this night with them.

"I don't want to go back. I'd like to stay out here all night, but I'm starting to feel a little cold," Sarah said. "Promise me you'll bring me out here again, spring and summer and fall, too, and I'll be your friend for life."

"You drive a hard bargain, Sarah, but I already knew you were capable of doing that . . . from something I heard earlier tonight," I replied. "We'll come here often . . . anytime you like. I know you and I both enjoy the outdoors . . . and I think I discovered something else about you tonight."

"What's that?" Sarah asked warmly.

"Careers," I answered. "You chose happiness over riches and fame. You did this in both games, so I think you see happiness as being the most important thing in life. It **was** more that just a game to you. Am I right?"

Sarah nodded her head.

"You did the same thing," she said. "I almost reached over the table to hug you when I saw that your numbers were almost identical to mine. I wonder what your brother and sister would have thought? It reminded me about our valentines . . . how our ideas were the same."

"You make me very happy, Sarah. My life is so good. I don't ever want it to change," I said.

"Me, too," Sarah replied. "This is my best night ever for Careers and my best winter nature hike ever."

I smiled at her and said with a touch of disappointment in my voice, "That's exactly what I was going to say to you. You beat me to it. I'll be quicker next time."

Hot chocolate and freshly baked chocolate chip cookies were awaiting us when we returned to the house. We removed our boots and warm clothing and sat down at the table with our parents.

"My, you two certainly have rosy cheeks. How was the nature hike?" Mrs. Jenkins asked.

"It was wonderful out there, Mom," Sarah answered. "It was so quiet and beautiful. We saw animal tracks in the soft snow, and we heard an owl hooting in a far away woods. We looked at the stars . . . and we talked. It was so much fun. Catcher promised to take me on more hikes in the different seasons."

"We've had fun, too," my mom added. "This has been my best night ever for having the Jenkins family over for dinner."

I just sat there. I was dumbfounded. What she said kind of struck me. It sounded just like something I would have said. I looked at Mom, then at Sarah's mom. I saw kind-looking smiles appear on both faces. When I looked at Sarah I thought I saw a touch of guilt showing on her face.

"Do you tell your parents everything?" I asked. "Everything?"

For the second time tonight Sarah shrugged her shoulders, and I started laughing and shaking my head. I loved everything about her.

They stayed until almost eleven. When I walked Sarah to the car, following a few steps behind her parents, I whispered to her, " . . . my best night ever on the farm."

The yard light shined on her beautiful face as I opened the car door for her. After giving Sarah a quick hug, I said to her, "This was really fun tonight. Thank you for hiking with me, for playing the game, and for making me a winner."

I stood under the light as Mr. Jenkins backed up the car and turned it toward the driveway. Sarah rolled down her window in the back and waved. When the car was halfway down the driveway, I raised both arms in a salute to the stars and yelled out, "We are . . . J-Hawks . . . and we are . . . winners!"

Chapter 45
Cat-Quick

Just as I was set to call Sarah on Thursday night, I noticed the picture of Geronimo on the desk, and I set the receiver down. I missed him. It had been several years now, but sometimes there was an empty feeling inside me when I thought about him. My thoughts drifted back to a few years ago, when twice a day at milking time, the cats on the farm would meet in the barn for a feeding of fresh warm milk, compliments of my dad. At times there were fifteen cats or more, ranging in size from kittens to moms and "toms" and in colors that included white, black, gray, orange, and all kinds of calico mixtures of these colors.

There was one cat on the farm, however, that did not join the other cats for the warm milk. He was not an ordinary mouser. He was privileged, and he was afforded the run of the house. His name was Geronimo, and he knew he was a special cat.

When he wanted outside he sat on the kitchen floor and scratched on the heavy wooden door, and when he wanted to come back inside, he pawed on the screen door of the porch, banging the door loudly enough that we could hear it from inside. He acted like he was the master of the house.

Geronimo was powerful and quick, and everything he did was done confidently. When he was just a little orange and white kitten, we kids liked how brave and fierce he was, and we felt he deserved a name that fit his character. That's why the name "Geronimo" was chosen.

Though I never saw him catch a mouse or a bird, I knew he was a great hunter. I watched him often as he crept so quietly across the living room carpet on his soft padded paws, stalking a restless foot whose owner was unaware that Geronimo was hunting in the neighborhood. A twitching or bouncing foot was an enticing target, and Geronimo's quick attack often brought screams of fright that were followed by fits of laughter, and with the hunt completed, Geronimo tip-toed silently to another area of the house.

I know Sarah would have liked Geronimo. I wondered to myself if I would have formally introduced her to him or if I would have allowed her to become "a victim of the hunt." *Tough call.* It might have been pretty funny, but it also might have been too big a risk for me to take.

When I dialed Sarah's number, she picked up the phone and immediately explained to me that she couldn't talk very long tonight. We had cheated a little on the two previous calls this week, talking for about fifteen minutes each time, and Sarah said she was paying the penalty for that tonight.

"I'm sorry about that," I said. "I'll be sharing in your penalty."

We talked briefly about tomorrow night's game.

"The high school kids are riding our bus again," I informed her. "I wish you were a student at Jeffers so you could ride the bus with us."

"Next year you'll be in school with me at Madison Lake," Sarah replied. "Maybe we'll get to ride a bus together then. Are you guys ready for your game?"

"I think so," I said. "No one is sick or hurt, and we had a great practice today, so we expect to play well. Coach told us we'll need to be at the top of our game and not to get discouraged if the game doesn't start out the way we want it to. We know that Alcorn is a good team. Coach said that the Alcorn Cougars and our team are considered to be the best of the eight teams playing in our district."

"I'm sure you'll play well," Sarah said, "and I'll be there cheering for you. I have to hang up now."

"Good night," I said. "See you tomorrow night."

"Good-bye. We are . . . J-Hawks!" Sarah replied. Then she hung up the phone.

This had seemed like a long week because of not having had a game on Tuesday. I hadn't seen Sarah since Saturday night. I had asked Dad if I could use a car on Wednesday night to drive to the library at Madison Lake to study and work on my homework, but he shook his head and pointed to the dining room table. He left no room for discussion so I dropped it. I wondered if Sarah's parents and mine had talked about limiting the number of times we got to see each other during the week. Maybe the nature hike hadn't been such a good idea. It may have given our parents an opportunity to discuss our friendship and set restrictions on us. They didn't need to worry about anything. We were just really good friends who liked spending time together.

Talking to Sarah on the phone three times this week had helped, but I felt that up to this point my week had just been okay. I couldn't wait until tomorrow night's game.

The bus rolled along, and Pickett's soft music reached the seat that San Juan and I shared. I was glad our game was the early game of the two tonight. Last night's winners, Murdock and Payton, would meet in the early game on Tuesday night, and if we managed a win tonight, we would be playing in the second game on Tuesday . . . but I knew better than to look that far ahead. *One-at-a-time . . . Get this one first.*

I closed my eyes for a moment and pictured myself scoring on perfect jump shots. My confidence was good. *We have to win. We have to reach our goal. Everyone is counting on us. This is our chance to do something . . . to be somebody.*

During the entire ride to the game I thought of nothing but basketball. I visualized accurate passes and soft layups against the backboard. I saw myself with knees bent, legs spread shoulder-width apart, and arms up, sliding quickly from side to side as I defended . . . and I never once got winded.

Everything was on the line again tonight, and I wanted to play my best game and help my team win its 22nd straight. When we reached the gym and walked to the locker room, I didn't even glance into the bleachers. I was focused on the game.

It's always fun warming up when your classmates are sitting in the bleachers, making noise and cheering. I think the sweat appeared a little earlier than usual tonight, and I felt ready.

I did find Sarah sitting in the student section when I took a break from shooting, and she gave me a slight wave and smiled. I nodded once, knowing that the only person in the gym who would probably notice my response was Sarah. It was like a secret code just between us that meant, "I'm here to cheer for you. Good luck in your game," and "I'm glad you came to the game, Sarah. I'll play hard."

That's all I needed from Sarah. I had my confidence, and I would give all my attention to my teammates and the game. Sarah understood.

We met at the center circle and shook each other's hands. I saw that two Cougars stood just as tall as Pickett, and another player, Number 44, though a couple of inches shorter, was wide and appeared to be very solidly built. *This could be a tough one.*

Abe tapped the ball to Pickett, and he grabbed it and protected it as Number 44 immediately closed in on Pickett and started bumping him, pushing him with his chest and hacking him hard several times on his arms as he tried to knock the ball loose. A ref's whistle stopped play, and I listened to his call.

"Number 44, black," the ref announced toward the scorer's table as he held up four fingers on each hand and gestured a pushing motion. "One-and-one."

Wow! Right off the bat they are trying to intimidate us. Is this their plan to try to get us off our game? I'm glad the refs didn't let him get by with that.

We walked to our basket where Abe and Hook took up positions on the lane as Pickett toed the foul line. Laser and I stood at center court.

After Pickett was handed the ball, he bounced it three times, gazed at the hoop, and softly tossed it through the air. With perfect backspin, the basketball dropped through the center of the net without threatening any part of the rim. Pickett's second shot did the same.

We set up our full-court press to test their ball handlers. The two tallest players took up positions just beyond the center-court stripe as Number 44 tossed the ball to one of the guards. I could see right away that the Cougars had set up a plan for how to break our press. They looked confident.

Number 15 began to dribble, and Laser and I moved closer to the left sideline. Number 44 slid in our direction and received a return pass. He picked up steam as he dribbled toward the opening between the sideline and me. I had plenty of time, and I shifted further to my left and took a defensive stance as I completely blocked the lane next to the sideline, and Number 44 took two more clumsy dribbles and plowed into me, knocking me backward to the floor. He tripped, and his momentum carried him forward where he partially landed on me. I really felt the impact, and I struggled to regain my breath. I hurt all over.

Though I heard the whistle, I didn't hear the ref's call because my focus was on catching my breath. A second whistle sounded as a timeout was called. Coach hustled onto the floor to check on me, and my teammates gathered around.

It took awhile for my head to clear. I could feel some pain on the left side of my ribs, and when I glanced at the Cougar's bench, I saw Number 44 smiling as his teammates were patting him on the back. I began to get angry. *Twice he has tried to hurt us. That's not basketball!*

"I'll be okay, Coach," I said. "Just let me catch my breath. I've been run over harder by young calves trying to escape from the barn."

Coach and my teammates thought this was funny.

"It appears that Number 44 is on a mission to do some damage tonight," Coach said. "I don't like the looks of this. According to my scouting report, he usually doesn't get much playing time. Watch out for him. I'll register a complaint with the refs."

I missed the front end of my one-and-one, and the Cougars grabbed the rebound and brought the ball down the floor. They passed around the perimeter until they sneaked Number 20 inside Abe, and he scored on a short bank shot.

Pickett posted up at the free-throw line as Laser dribbled the ball down the court, and Number 44 kept leaning on Pickett and bumping him, but this time no foul was called. We passed the ball around quickly. When I saw Pickett set a screen on Hook's man, I fired the ball to Laser. Hook turned inside toward the basket and caught Laser's pass and went in for the layup, but Number 44 had switched to cover Hook, and he hammered him to the floor as Hook jumped up and attempted his shot.

This time all of J-Hawk Nation stood and protested as the whistle blew, and Number 44 was called for his third foul in about two minutes.

This is ridiculous! One of us is going to get hurt. It looks like the Cougar plan is to hit us hard and knock us out of the game.

There was an official timeout as Coach and the refs checked on Hook. He had hit his left elbow and his head on the floor when he fell, but there was no blood. "I'm staying in the game, Coach," he said, and I could see in Captain Hook's eyes that the Cougars would be paying for this one.

I watched as both refs walked over to the Cougar bench. I couldn't hear anything, but it looked like the Cougar coach was really upset. He kept waving his arms around, and he was very animated, but the refs finally turned their backs and walked away. One headed to the scorer's table, and the other approached our bench and pulled Coach aside.

After a short conversation, Coach returned to our huddle. "All right," he said. "Number 44 has been disqualified for excessively rough play. You have to put those fouls behind you now, and concentrate on playing J-Hawk ball. Pickett . . . Catcher . . . Hook . . . are you guys okay? We need you out there."

"Yeah," all three of us replied.

"Sounds good. We've only played two minutes, so we've got almost a whole game ahead of us," Coach said. "Let's start this one over. Clear your heads. Number 44 is gone. Concentrate on playing good defense and running your fast break. It's pretty obvious that Alcorn knew they couldn't beat you straight up, so they've tried to bang you up a little. Let's show them how J-Hawk basketball is played. Be focused, and play smart. That's our style. We run hard, play hard, play tough, and play together. Have fun out there."

"We are . . . J-Hawks!" we shouted, and the student section echoed our cry.

There were no more hard fouls during the rest of the first quarter as play went back and forth. We worked the ball inside to Pickett, and he dished off to Abe and Captain Hook for three easy baskets. Our offence was clicking. Laser hit on three straight jump shots, but the Cougars were shooting well, too. When the quarter ended, the score was tied at fourteen.

During the second quarter the lead exchanged hands a couple times, but neither team ever led by more than four. I missed the one jump shot I attempted early in the quarter, and since I felt it a little in the ribs, I was hesitant to shoot again. Abe banked in two short-range shots, and Hook tossed in a perfect hook shot. Pickett found the net on two fade-away jumpers, and Laser was deadly on two more shots from the top of the key. He was hot tonight. I added one fast-break layup and a free throw.

The Cougars moved the ball well. They were disciplined and took only good shots, finding the range on many of them, and by making their last shot as time expired in the quarter, they pulled within two points of us at halftime.

We drank water and had a few quick conversations with each other about adjustments we needed to make in the second half. Then we sat down and waited for Coach to analyze our first half.

"I am very proud of you guys tonight," Coach began. "You've played well on both ends of the court, and you kept it together when that goon tried to rough you up."

Everyone laughed at Coach's description of Number 44.

"Let's go out there in the second half and tighten the defense just a little. Put a hand up high in the shooter's face so he doesn't get a good look at the basket," Coach continued. "Keep running the fast break so we can wear them down and get a few easy baskets. The Cougars are a good team, but I think we are better. Play hard . . . have fun. Let's go!"

I sprinted the width of the court a couple times as we were warming up so I could check out how my ribs felt after sitting and resting for a few minutes. *Not too bad. I can do this. No one will even know I'm a little sore.*

When I shot a few jump shots I felt a little pain, but many of my shots went in. I decided that I would shoot in the second half when I was left open. I looked around and saw that not one of us had our head down. We had lots of energy, and we would give the Cougars all we had for the rest of the game.

We had not played against a team this year that matched our skills so evenly. During the 3rd Quarter both teams played well, and neither team could gain an advantage of more than five points. When the quarter ended, we were down by one basket. This was not a situation that we were very familiar with.

When we met at the bench prior to the start of the final eight minutes of play, Coach looked at each of us and said, "Now is the time to show what champions are made of. Keep plugging away. Do not panic. If each of you can give just a little extra . . . to grab that rebound . . . block that shot . . .

collect that loose ball . . . that might make the difference in the game. Your teamwork has been your strength all year, so help each other out. Fourth Quarter belongs to us."

"We are . . . J-Hawks!" we shouted as we left the huddle, and the echo sounded twice from the student section.

I glanced at Sarah before I walked onto the court. She had her hands clasped, and she smiled confidently. I could see the hope and encouragement in her eyes.

Abe reached high and tapped the opening tip to Captain Hook, and after three or four passes, Laser was wide open for a twelve-foot jump shot, and he buried it to tie the score. J-Hawk Nation erupted.

The Cougars threw the ball in, and Laser and I applied pressure near the centerline, while Pickett patrolled the middle of the floor right behind us. This time Number 12 tossed a long pass over all five of us, but it missed its target and hit the wall under our basket.

This will be huge if we can score on this possession.

Laser dribbled the ball toward our end and passed to Abe by the left sideline. Abe looked to Pickett, but the Cougars had two guys covering him. Abe returned the ball to Laser, and Laser swung the ball over to me. I quickly bounced it to Hook who took a couple of dribbles toward the lane, stopped, and fired the ball back to me.

I had room. I bounced the ball once and stepped into my shot. I grunted just a little as I launched the ball, and I watched as it dropped cleanly through the net, giving us a two-point lead, and J-Hawk Nation went wild.

The Cougars called a timeout.

"Thanks!" Coach said to us and smiled as we reached the bench for instructions. "I prefer having the lead. Otto, I want you to go in to give Pickett a short breather. Support the press by covering the middle of the floor. Let's see if we can steal a couple buckets in the next minute or so."

The Cougars beat our press this time down, and after a few passes around the perimeter, Number 20 scored on a shot from the corner. Now the game was tied again.

Laser walked the ball to our end and passed to me on the right side. I bounced it inside to Otto, and the Cougars looked a little confused. Hook's defender left Hook to double on Otto, but he was late getting there, and Otto found Hook with a soft lob as he ran to the basket, and he scored on an easy layup.

We set up our trap near the centerline. This time Otto played in front of Laser and me. He followed the ball and put pressure on the ball handler as Laser and I covered our areas and prepared to move in quickly when we saw a Cougar was having trouble. We were careful not to foul. Otto and I trapped Number 25 at the sideline just after he had crossed the center stripe with the ball. He picked up his dribble and looked to pass, but his options were limited. He pivoted, trying to create some space, but we kept the pressure on. As he was running out of time, he lofted a cross-court pass that was picked off by Abe, and Abe bounced a long pass ahead to Laser. Laser took one dribble to draw the last defender, then he bounced a short pass to the left in front of Otto, and he went in for an uncontested layup. The entire sequence had been run perfectly, and our lead was up to four.

At the next stoppage of play Pickett returned to the lineup, and Otto took a seat.

The four-point lead did not last long. Number 25 threw up a long shot that bounced in off the backboard, and after my poorly thrown pass to Pickett was picked off, Number 15 worked his way into the lane for a jump shot that tied the score.

Only two minutes remained in the game.

When we brought the ball down court I could see in Captain Hook's eyes that he wanted the ball. He faked inside, then turned and moved outside two steps and caught my bounce pass. With perfect rhythm, Hook reached high and tossed the basketball quietly through the hoop, giving us another lead of two points.

Now we needed to stop them from scoring.

We backed off our press to the centerline again where Laser and I challenged the ball handlers, Abe and Hook took positions behind us, and Pickett stayed near our basket as our last line of defense. Captain Hook anticipated a pass to his man and stepped in front to pick it off. Now we had the ball and a two-point lead.

I dribbled toward my favorite shooting spot on the right side. Hook stepped out toward me, and we passed to each other a couple times. Then Hook spun around his defender and headed for the basket. I lobbed the ball over his head, and with one dribble, Hook reached the basket and laid the ball against the backboard. All of J-Hawk Nation stood and clapped as the ball dropped through the netting.

Our lead had now reached four points, and the clock showed about a minute-and-a-half to go. It was time to shut them down.

The Cougars called for their final timeout.

"No fouls," Coach reminded us at the bench. "We want that clock running. I do expect the Cougars to foul us as time runs down. You need to be focused and alert to everything. We have only one timeout remaining. Let's go."

This time the student section stood up and joined in as we shouted, "We are . . . J-Hawks!" and the volume rocked the bleachers.

Laser and I applied a little pressure in order to slow the Cougar ball handlers down and burn some time off the clock. We kept giving ground, however, until we reached our normal half-court defensive positions.

The Cougars snapped off quick passes, and we shifted our zone to cover the most dangerous areas, raising and waving our arms, hoping to deflect or pick off a pass. Number 22 took a risky shot, almost getting it blocked by Abe, but it bounced off the backboard into the basket.

I can't believe that shot went in!

With less than a minute to go Pickett tossed the ball in to me, and I took a couple dribbles before passing to Laser. He took it slowly into our end, and we spread out to keep the ball away from the Cougars. We had no intention of shooting another shot, unless it was a sure basket. We were good at this keep-away game. We had fun at practice, doing this almost every day for one fast minute.

Laser, Abe, Hook, and I were the corners of our box, and Pickett kept rotating and moving toward us from the inside. We made quick passes, but we were really careful to protect the ball and maintain possession of it.

With about thirty seconds left in the game, Number 10 reached in and fouled Abe by hacking him on his arms while going for a steal, sending Abe to the line for a "one-and-one."

We needed at least one point here, and the only way go get it was for Abe to make his first shot. During the season he had made about "two of every three." I hoped that this would be one of the "two."

Although our team was pretty relaxed, I could sense tenseness in the bleachers. Both teams were leaning on hope.

As players took positions on the lane, Abe stared at the rim. He was focused. Upon receiving the ball, he bent his knees and bounced the ball twice. Then he lifted the basketball over his head and softly shot it in a perfect arch toward the rim. I was sure it would be good, but it hit the back of the rim and bounced out. When Number 10 of the Cougars grabbed it, we hustled down court to defend our two-point lead.

The Cougars wasted no time. After only two passes around the perimeter, one of their guards tossed a long jump shot toward the hoop. It was an ill-advised shot, but it hit the backboard . . . then the rim . . . the backboard again . . . then dropped through the hoop. I couldn't believe it. Now the game was tied.

We had the ball and about 15 seconds in which to score a basket and extend our season to another game.

Coach called our final timeout.

"Our whole season has come down to one possession, guys," Coach said calmly as he looked at us in the huddle. "I need to know from each of you if you are confident that you can make your next shot."

"I can do it," Pickett replied immediately.

"Me, too," Laser added. "I'll make it."

Captain Hook, Abe, and I all repeated Laser's confident reply, "I'll make it."

Even four of the bench players said they could make the last shot.

Coach grinned and said to us, "All right, let's get this one. Work the ball inside. Pickett, if your shot is there, take it with a few seconds left, just in case Abe or Hook need to help it in. If you are covered, pass it off, and someone else can hit the winning basket."

I thought the students had yelled loudly last time, but this time it was even more deafening. **"We are . . . J-Hawks!"**

All of J-Hawk Nation stood.

Laser passed the ball in to me, and I returned it to him. We moved quickly toward our basket, realizing that we had less than ten seconds to get off a good shot.

Laser found Pickett open at the free-throw line and bounced a pass to him. Pickett brought the ball into his body and pivoted. He found he had room and, with one dribble, stepped into a fade-away jumper, and Abe and Hook turned and ran toward the basket . . . just in case.

It was a clean shot . . . straight through the net without touching the backboard or any iron, and J-Hawk Nation began yelling and clapping.

Number 20 for the Cougars grabbed the ball, stepped outside the line, and threw a long pass down the court. I knew there were just three-or-four seconds left, but Number 15 caught the ball with a couple steps on me at the centerline. I leaned forward as I took two strong strides, cried "Geronimo," and laid my body out as far as I could reach, and with my right hand, I swatted at the ball as it touched the floor at the bottom of a dribble, tapping it toward the far left corner of the gym. Then I hit the floor, and while sliding several feet, ribs aching, I watched every revolution of the ball as it rolled in what seemed to be slow motion . . . and I saw the Cougar guard run to the corner after the ball with everything he had . . . and stretch out his arms to reach for it . . . but as his fingers touched the leather, the buzzer sounded to end the game . . . and I saw him raise his head toward the rafters . . . and he shouted **"NO!"**

It was over. We had squeaked out a two-point victory. J-Hawk Nation rushed onto the floor. There was no way to hold them back. The two refs hurried to their dressing room as the announcer called into the microphone several times, "You need to clear the floor! You need to clear the floor."

San Juan was the first person to get to me, and he helped me up. "That probably didn't help your ribs much, did it?" he said as he patted me lightly on the back. That was a great play, and we live to play another day."

We lined up to shake hands, and I didn't see any happy Cougar faces. Though they told us "Good game," I could see the obvious disappointment and sadness they felt, but I had no feelings of sorrow for them. I looked Number 44 directly in his eyes when I touched his hand, but I kept my mouth shut, saying nothing. I had no respect for him.

Coach hustled us to the locker room, where we congratulated each other and whooped it up a little.

"That was a great shot, Pickett!" I yelled out.

"Thanks," he replied, "but a lot of you guys could have made your own shot."

That's the way it was on our team. We played together, and no one got too much credit or too much blame. We had said earlier in the season that we would win and lose as a team, and so far we had won every time we played.

"Great job, J-Hawks!" Coach said when some order had been restored. "Next time . . . do me a favor . . . don't make it such a close game."

It was a very happy and loud locker room. All of us walked around, shook hands, patted backs, and tousled hair. The victory felt really sweet, especially because of the hard fouls against us early in the game.

"Watch out when you leave the locker room," I warned my teammates with a smile, "Number 44 still has two more fouls coming."

Laughter filled the room.

Coach came over and put his hand on my shoulder. "How are the ribs?" he asked.

"I'll be all right," I replied. "Thanks for letting me stay in the game."

"Your play at the end . . . I'd call that giving a little extra . . . and it made the difference," Coach continued. "You were as quick as a cat going after a mouse. I've seen that dive before. Both times . . . great plays. Get your rest this weekend. Take it easy at the practice and clinic tomorrow."

The lobby was so packed it was difficult to move around. Everyone was so excited for us. Many parents and kids said they were very proud of us.

Bobby and Sarah reached me at the same time, and Sarah gave me a big hug.

I groaned just a little.

"Oh, I'm sorry," she said. "I didn't realize . . ."

"No," I said to her, "don't be sorry. I will gladly accept a hug from you anytime. I'm all right . . . just a little sore."

Bobby butted right in. "Before you dove and knocked that ball away at the end of the game . . . did you really cry 'Geronimo?'" he asked.

My smile was my answer.

"Geronimo . . . " Bobby repeated. " . . . just like the old days." He smiled and walked away, shaking his head.

"You need to tell me about 'Geronimo,'" Sarah insisted, and she flashed me that beautiful smile.

"How about tomorrow?" I asked.

"Tomorrow's good," Sarah replied, "and tomorrow night we are having a game night at Becky's house. San Juan and you are invited."

"Sounds like fun," I said. "Does San Juan know about it?"

"He will as soon as you tell him," Sarah replied, smiling.

"Clinic tomorrow?" I asked.

"Only if it's Saturday," Sarah answered, and her smile warmed my heart again.

"It looks like Coach is wanting us to get on the bus," I said. "Thanks for coming to the game and cheering for us tonight. I look forward to seeing you tomorrow morning and tomorrow night, and I'll see if I can come up with something for tomorrow afternoon, too. Does your dad need some help around the house?"

Sarah and I both laughed, and I stood there and kept looking into her eyes.

There was one more smile, and Sarah touched her shiny silver heart.

"Tomorrow," I said as I turned toward the door.

On the bus ride home all my thoughts would be about Sarah . . . and maybe . . . I would give a little time to Geronimo.

In the Stands – With John Garris

In their toughest test of the basketball season, the J-Hawks of Jeffers withstood an opening barrage of bruising fouls as well as pin-point shooting from their opponents and squeaked out a two-point victory over the Alcorn Cougars in the opening round of the district tournament. In this game of evenly matched teams, neither the J-Hawks nor the Cougars could build a lead of more than five points, and the game went down to the wire.

It was a very tense ending to a hard-fought contest.

With the score knotted at 66 and with only fifteen seconds left on the game clock, the J-Hawks went to senior captain, Pickett, for the final shot, and he delivered cleanly on a ten-foot fadeaway jumper from near the lane, as he has done so often this year. With no timeouts remaining, the Cougars immediately threw a long inbound pass that found its target at center court, and it appeared that, as the last few seconds ticked off the clock, the Cougars had a chance at a layup that would tie the game and send it into overtime, but in a play that won't show up in the score sheet, Jeffers guard, Catcher, dove to knock the ball away toward the corner at the last second. This secured the J-Hawk victory and preserved their winning streak that now stands at 22 games.

Alcorn's rough stuff in the opening two minutes was not enough to disrupt the play of the determined J-Hawks, who with their trademark teamwork and unselfish play, kept their dreams alive.

Tuesday's games at Stallworth match Payton against Murdock in the early game, followed by Jeffers versus Chambers in the nightcap.

Chapter 46
Game Night

When I woke up Saturday morning I didn't feel very rested. I hadn't slept very well because every time I rolled from my back to my side I felt some pain in my ribs and woke up. While lying there staring at the deep crack that ran across the ceiling, I decided that I should take it easy at practice and the clinic. I would work on my shooting and run just enough to loosen the muscles in my legs. During the clinic I would do what I could, but I was thinking that Coach would probably want me to sit in the bleachers . . . by Sarah. Hopefully my teammates will agree to that, but I expect them to give me a hard time, to "rib me a little."

Last night on the bus ride home I told San Juan about game night at Becky's. He wasn't hesitant at all. "Good," he had said. "I'll drive. I bet we'll have fun. I was thinking about calling her tomorrow . . . I really was. What kind of games are we playing?"

"I have no idea," I had told him, "but we can ask Sarah at the clinic. Maybe we'll play 'Hearts.' You should call Becky to tell her you are coming. She needs to know."

I talked Dad into going in early for coffee because I wanted as much time as possible to try to loosen up in the gym, and I was the first one there. San Juan arrived after a couple minutes, and he and I were talking about "game night" at the door when Captain Hook walked over with the key.

Before I dressed for practice I stood under hot water in the shower for a few minutes to warm my body up. I think this really helped because my rib cage felt better when I took the floor and shot a few layups and short jump shots. I still decided I wouldn't push too hard in practice. It made more sense to me to just loosen up and let my body heal up a little.

We split the 30-minute practice into thirds, with layups, favorite shots, and easy grapevine weaving getting equal attention. Since I felt pretty good, I ran with the others, only holding back a little by not shooting as many long jump shots.

Our practice was very spirited. We felt relieved to have won last night's game, and we began to prepare for Tuesday night's game against Chambers. Much of the laughter during the practice was attributed to just one word: "goon." If you happened to bump into someone while going for a ball, one or more teammates would say, "Watch it, 'goon.'" If you touched someone while rebounding . . . you were a "goon." Even if you put your arms out to keep from running into another player, someone labeled you as a "goon." That one word kept us laughing for thirty minutes, and we made sure that the kids understood why we were laughing before we started the clinic. The laughter washed away any tension we were feeling from last night's game, and it felt good to awaken the J-Hawk spirit that had carried us all season long.

We ran the entire clinic as contests today. The youngest kids worked on the east end of the gym, and the oldest kids were sent to the west end. We kept mixing up the teams and challenging them on dribbling relays, shooting contests, passing drills, and running races. One J-Hawk big kid was on each team to provide leadership, but I sat on the bleachers with Sarah, dreaming up the next contest. I had a great, creative assistant. A couple of times my teammates asked her to step onto the floor to demonstrate what the kids needed to do for that particular contest, and she got good applause from everyone both times. When I stepped onto the floor once to demonstrate, only one kid clapped, and he stopped immediately when Laser shook his head at him. When I dramatically lowered my head and sulked as I walked back to the bench, everyone laughed and then began clapping. Sarah even stood. Not taking things too seriously was a standard behavior of our team. All season long we had been having fun . . . and playing hard.

After library time, Sarah and I walked Main Street and watched several high school kids as they painted slogans and drew pictures on the big store windows. We critiqued the designs, and the "artists" laughed at us and told us to move on down the street. Only once did we find a word misspelled: "J-Haks."

I asked my sister, "Who are the J-Haks?"

Maggie checked her work. I can't believe I did that," she said. "Thanks for editing for me. It won't be hard to fix that."

"Maybe you need to concentrate a little more," I advised her. "I know I play better basketball when I focus."

All three of us laughed, and Sarah and I waved "good-bye" and continued down the street, reading the windows as we walked.

Fresh black paint at the hardware store read "Home of J-Hawk Nation," and the drug store had a picture of an almost round basketball dropping through a hoop and net. The words "Go J-Hawks!" were printed below the picture. The huge barber shop window had the names of all twelve of us players painted in black, surrounding a J-Hawk Nation stocking cap, and our jersey numbers were painted in gold paint beneath our names. San Juan's sister was just finishing her work here when we walked by.

At The Jeffers Café, now renamed "The Jeffers Teen Center Café" with a freshly painted sign on the window, Otto's sister had written "J-Hawks – winners of 22 straight games! Almost every store window on both sides of Main Street had some kind of J-Hawk message, and many adults and kids were on the street watching and offering suggestions, and it felt to me to be as busy and exciting as it usually was around Christmas time.

Sarah's dad must have been looking out the windows of The Jeffers Café to watch for us, and he stepped outside to call to Sarah as we walked by.

"We better get going. Mom will be worried about us," he told Sarah.

"You've got to see the windows, Mr. Jenkins," I said. "J-Hawk Nation is everywhere."

"We can take a few minutes to look," he replied, and we walked across to the north side, and headed down toward the grocery store. We passed the butcher shop and gas station, then crossed back to the lumber yard where my sister was cleaning up. In about two more minutes we had returned to the café where Mr. Jenkins had found a good parking spot earlier this morning.

"Your basketball team has awakened this town," Mr. Jenkins said. "All the talk at the café was about the J-Hawks."

"It is pretty exciting," I said, "and we aren't done yet. We plan to play well on Tuesday, so I think we have a chance to win another game."

"Sarah," Mr. Jenkins said as he opened his door. "Let's go."

"I'll see you tonight, Catch," Sarah said sweetly. "We should arrive at Becky's at about seven."

I opened her car door, touched her hand, and whispered, "Did you notice how I talked your dad into giving me five more minutes with you?" Then I added for Mr. Jenkins to hear, "We'll aim to be at your house at 6:45. It was really good to see you this morning. Thanks again for helping at the clinic and the library."

The three of us reached Becky's house right at seven, and she invited us down to the lowest level of her split-level house. The first thing I noticed was two full-sized pinball machines.

"What are these?" I asked excitedly.

"Dad's prized possessions," Becky replied. "He buys old machines and fixes them up as a hobby. He's working on several others in his shop in the next room. Would you like to play?"

"Yeah, but I'd like to hear from your dad that it's okay," San Juan answered.

I didn't know if he was kidding or not, but I decided to have some fun, so I jumped right in. "We don't want any trouble," I said, trying to sound really serious. "You didn't invite us here just to land us in trouble I hope. You aren't trying to get us kicked off the team because you have relatives in Chambers or something like that, are you?"

Becky and Sarah looked at each other and shook their heads. They both sprouted huge smiles.

"As a matter of fact I do have a few kin in Chambers," Becky declared. "Uncle Billy Bob is the mayor and Cousin Festus is the police chief."

San Juan and I quickly and dramatically removed our hands from the machines and stepped back.

Sarah and Becky began laughing out loud, and San Juan and I joined in. The evening was already off to a great start.

Becky's dad appeared at the top of the steps and said, "You boys are welcome to play those pinball machines . . . and what's that nonsense about an Uncle Billy Bob and Festus?"

"Dad!" Becky admonished her father. "We were just having some fun, and remember what you promised . . . You said we could have some privacy down here. No more listening in."

"Let's play," I suggested. "San Juan . . . I don't have any nickels. Could you lend me one?"

San Juan checked his pockets. "Sorry . . . I don't have any change."

"Well, I have one nickel," Becky said, "so I guess I'll be the one playing."

San Juan, Sarah, and I stepped to the sides of one machine, and Becky fed it the nickel and activated the lights and sounds. She shot the first ball into play and started racking up points, using the flippers really well to score bonus points by hitting the main targets when they were lit up. I was impressed. She started winning free games while only on her fourth ball, and then she added several more free games while playing the final ball.

"You've won 13 free games!" San Juan said. "Good playing!"

"Thank you," Becky said politely. "Now it's your turn."

She pressed the button to cash in one of her free games, and San Juan stepped to the machine and tested the flippers.

The machine was not kind to San Juan. He couldn't keep the steel balls in play very long, and his score was much lower than Becky's. He fell short of winning any free games.

Sarah looked at me and said, "You try it."

"Okay," I replied, and I walked confidently to the end of the machine as Becky activated a second game.

I tried my hardest, but two of the balls retreated quickly between the flippers, and I had no chance to save them. The whole game lasted just a couple minutes, and I had scored no better than San Juan. This stung because I expected to do better than this.

"Sarah, you are next," Becky said.

"No, I can't," Sarah said as she put up her hands and stepped away.

"Come on, Sarah, give it a try," I encouraged. "You'll do fine."

All three of us started saying, "Sarah . . . Sarah . . . Sarah . . ."

"All right, but don't laugh at me," Sarah said as she approached the machine and located the flipper buttons.

Sarah shot the first ball and kept it in play for a long time, and her score kept climbing. I looked over at San Juan. We were both feeling a little embarrassed. Sarah surpassed my score while she was playing just the third ball, and she won two free games while playing the fourth ball. On the final ball Sarah played the flippers expertly to hit the main targets and score extra points, and she earned four more free games before the ball dived down between the flippers.

"Wow, Sarah! That was outstanding!" I said.

Becky was beaming. "Nice job, Sarah. I guess we were a little luckier than the boys were."

"San Juan . . . you and I have been humbled. These girls have crushed us. We have tasted defeat at the hands of experts, and my pride is wounded," I said. "I hope I can recover by Tuesday night's basketball game."

"Same for me," San Juan added.

"Oh you poor guys," Sarah said. "Becky, can they have a couple more tries at this? I don't want to feel responsible if they give a poor effort on Tuesday night."

"Sure," Becky replied. "Let's use both machines so they can have twice as many chances to recover their pride."

Becky grabbed several nickels from a glass on a bookshelf and placed them on the second machine.

San Juan and I each stepped forward.

"Do you know what this reminds me of?" I asked San Juan.

San Juan looked straight ahead and continued playing. "Confirmation class?" he answered as a question.

"Yeah," I said. "That's it exactly. Boy did we get into trouble that day . . . because of you."

"Tell us," Becky said. "What kind of trouble?"

San Juan and I both kept focusing on our games, touching the flipper buttons often to direct the ball up to the bumpers.

I began. "San Juan was a big winner that day, but his timing was bad."

"Really bad," San Juan agreed, as he shot another ball into play.

"The pastor gave us a 15-minute break after we had sat in confirmation class at the church for an hour because he needed a cigarette," I continued. "All we had left to do after the short break was fold bulletins for Sunday's church service, but we were late getting back. The pastor sent a couple girls to go find us."

"What were you doing?" Sarah asked.

"We had walked over to The Jeffers Café, and we were playing the pinball machine," San Juan replied. "I was really good that day. I had won several free games, and we couldn't just leave them on the machine, so we kept playing, not paying any attention to the time."

"Wasn't it fifteen games you won?" I asked.

"Or sixteen," San Juan corrected. "I just know it was more than Becky won tonight."

Both of the girls laughed.

"When we got back to the church we got a stern talking to, and for the last month of class, we didn't get any more 15-minute breaks," I admitted. "It was all because of San Juan's great skill at pinball."

"It looks like your pride has found its way home," Sarah said as she smiled at me.

We had a great time, playing for another half-hour or so, and I did manage to win a couple free games. Becky brought some pop and chips downstairs, and we snacked and played "Hearts" for an hour. Then Becky suggested that we walk to the park.

She lived three blocks from the park, just like Sarah, but their houses were in opposite directions. It wasn't very cold out, and there wasn't much snow on the ground, so we decided to walk to the swings. There were only two good swings, so we shared. The girls sat and glided while San Juan and I gently pushed, and we talked and laughed about everything. I could tell that San Juan and Becky were both enjoying the night.

Becky turned on the stereo when we returned to her house, and San Juan and I walked back over to the pinball machines.

"Go ahead," Becky said. "It's 'game night.'"

San Juan and I played several more games, switching to each other's machine a couple of times. Sarah and Becky were content to just watch us. Maybe they were worried that they wouldn't play quite as well as they had played earlier. We kept talking while we played, and the conversation turned to basketball.

"The Alcorn team was pretty good last night," Sarah said, "but I didn't have any respect for them because Number 44 tried to hurt you. If Pickett or Captain Hook or you had been knocked out of the game . . . that might have changed how the game turned out."

"Don't forget that we have San Juan and others that come off the bench every game, and they all play well," I replied. "We'd have been okay."

"It was a really good game . . . very exciting," Becky said. "I hope you win Tuesday night. Maybe I'll get to go if you play on Friday."

"We'll play hard, and I think we have a good chance if we play well," San Juan said.

I looked at the clock and noticed it was 11:15.

"We have to get going, San Juan," I said almost in a panic. "We'll be cutting it close tonight. Sarah and I will wait for you in the car. Thanks for inviting me tonight, Becky, and please thank your dad for letting us use the pinball machines. This was a fun night."

I didn't figure we'd be waiting long for San Juan, so I kissed Sarah as soon as we sat down in the back seat.

"I've really had a good time again tonight. Every time I'm with you it's like this," I said. "You have made this my best winter ever."

"It's been my best winter, too," Sarah replied. "I've enjoyed sharing all the adventures with you."

"It looked like Becky and San Juan hit it off tonight," I said.

"Yes, it did. Becky didn't know if San Juan would ask her out again, so she decided this was a way to ask him," Sarah added.

"Every time I see a pinball machine now I will think of you," I said. "This was my best night ever for playing pinball, though I didn't do very well. The best part was watching you play. You were really good at it. I don't think you were just lucky. You seem to be good at everything . . . school, painting, baking, singing, drawing, reading, smiling, laughing . . ."

"How about basketball?" Sarah asked with a smile.

"You are just fair at basketball," I admitted honestly as I smiled and looked through the darkness into her beautiful eyes. "But I think I play better when you are watching me, so I'll give you credit for that, too."

Sarah laughed and leaned against my shoulder. "What will happen when basketball is over?" she asked quietly.

"We'll have more movie nights and game nights . . . nature hikes and walks to the park . . . studying at the library . . . sitting by the fire . . . phone calls . . . We can go on bicycle rides . . ," I answered quickly. " . . . maybe I can mow your yard and wash your cars . . . help your mom around the house . . . ."

Sarah raised her head, smiled the most beautiful smile I've ever seen in my life, and fell into my arms. I held her warmly. She had just asked the question I had worried about often, and now I felt a little better because now I understood that she had been worrying about it, too.

"I love you, Sarah," I whispered.

San Juan pulled his car door open and got in. I almost told him that his timing was really bad again, but I held back.

It was a quick "good night" at Sarah's door. Halfway down the sidewalk I turned and looked at Sarah standing behind the glass. She touched her necklace, smiled, and raised her arms into the air.

As I looked at her I raised my arms and cried out to the surrounding houses. "We are J-Hawks! Chambers . . . We'll see you on Tuesday night's game night!"

Chapter 47
Dizzy's Train

On a really still day at the farm or when a soft breeze blows from the southwest, I can often hear when a freight train rolls through town and sounds its whistle at the crossing. It was early March now, and warm enough that I could smell just a hint of an arriving spring, and on Monday I was finishing my chores as darkness was approaching, and a train going through Jeffers blew its whistle so clearly it sounded like it was passing by the woods just beyond the tractor shed. It seemed so close, and the train's warning whistle was so distinct in the crisp spring-like air, that it really caught my attention. It was as if the train was calling to me. Generally I don't even notice the sound, but today I did.

My mind jumped to the Major League Baseball Game of the Week. I loved listening to Peewee Reese and Dizzy Dean give the play-by-play and commentary for the Saturday afternoon televised games that I watched as I was growing up. Dizzy Dean had been an outstanding pitcher, years back, for the St. Louis Cardinals, my favorite team. Dean's brother Paul, who was nicknamed Daffy, pitched for the Cardinals, too. I thought it was hilarious: brothers named Dizzy and Daffy.

Dizzy Dean often fractured the English language using words like "slud" instead of "slid," "brung," and "ain't." Some teachers around the country complained that he was a terrible role model for youngsters, and he should be relieved of his broadcasting duties. To me he was a colorful character. He was "country," and I liked that.

Sometimes Dizzy even sang during the telecast. My favorite among the songs he sang was "The Wabash Cannonball," a song about the sound of a train as it "rolls along the woodland, through the hills, and by the shore." Today's train . . . maybe it was the Wabash Cannonball.

With my chores about done, and the train whistle causing me to think about baseball and warmer weather, I was feeling good.

I stood, leaning against the aluminum grain shovel, listening to the cry of the whistle. Again it seemed to be calling out to me, trying to get my attention. I held my breath, stood perfectly still, and tried to shut out all other sounds.

Wait! It is calling to me! I threw the shovel down and began sprinting for the house as fast as I could go. *I should have been more alert, more focused! Why didn't I clue in on that whistle? What if it's too late?* I rounded the corner by the chicken house and eyed the front door of the house about forty yards away. *That train whistle was calling for me to do something, and I let my stupid mind wander to Dizzy Dean! Run faster!*

I passed the yard-light pole . . . covered the length of the sidewalk in two long strides . . . and ripped open the porch's screen door. As I pushed against the heavy wooden kitchen door and turned the knob, I yelled out, "I need to use the phone!"

Without removing my boots, I raced around the kitchen table, plowing into two wooden chairs as I hustled by. When I reached the phone, I stretched out my arms, grabbed the receiver out of Maggie's hand, and cut off her call. Offering no explanation, I dialed Sarah's number and waited impatiently. **"Come on! . . . Answer the phone!"** The only sounds I heard were the distant ringing of the phone and me, trying to catch my breath. Maggie stood by, obviously upset but silent and very curious.

Finally!

"Hello," a pleasant voice answered. It was Sarah's mom.

"This is Catcher! Is Sarah there? I need to talk to Sarah right away! It's urgent!" I almost shouted, talking very quickly.

"Slow down," Mrs. Jenkins replied. "Sarah is warming up the car in the driveway so she can drive the two of us to a friend's house to deliver a birthday treat. Is something wrong?"

"I really need to talk to her!" I pleaded. "Please don't go!"

I heard the phone being set down and footsteps running. I held my breath as I listened to Mrs. Jenkins open the front door and shout, "Sarah, turn the car off, and come back in! Catcher is on the phone, and it sounds like something is wrong!"

I waited forever.

"She's coming in. She'll be right here. Are you all right?" Mrs. Jenkins asked.

"Yeah," I replied, "but I have to talk to Sarah. Thanks for calling her to the phone."

Again I waited forever, and while I stood there holding on to the phone my heartbeat began to slow down, and I could breathe almost normally again. I began to think about what I had just done. How was I going to explain this?

Finally I heard the sound of Sarah's wonderful voice. "Catcher, what's wrong?" she asked, and I could hear the concern as she spoke.

It took a couple moments before I could find the energy to respond.

"I'm so glad I reached you," I managed to reply. "I don't know exactly how to say this. This will be really hard for me to explain. I hope you will trust me and try to understand what I'm about to tell you. Nothing like this has ever happened to me before, and I am worried about what you might think. Do you remember that day when you promised you would never give up on me?"

"I remember. It was that Sunday when we had that problem at The Grill," Sarah replied.

"Is it still true?" I asked.

"Yes! Of course! Nothing has changed. You and me . . . forever! But you are beginning to scare me!" Sarah said. "Tell me what happened!"

I tried to relax my heart rate, and I took one more deep breath. *Please trust me and try to understand, Sarah.*

"I was just finishing up my chores by the granary bin, and I heard the very clear whistle of a train passing through Jeffers," I said as I began my explanation. "At first I didn't pay much attention to it, but it whistled a second and a third time, and I thought it was calling to me. I listened carefully, and I knew it was a warning. It was very clear, and directed to me, and I knew that I had to do something. I ran to the house as fast as I could to call you, to warn you not to drive anywhere in the car . . . because I knew this train was heading toward Madison Lake . . . and there would be trouble. It was just like someone had been standing directly in front of me and shouting to me, . . . 'Stop her! You have to stop her!' That's why I called you now . . . to warn you. I was afraid that you were going to be in an accident with that train."

"You **did** stop me. I came back in from the car," Sarah said. "I'm okay."

"But I need you to understand why I called you," I continued. "This whole thing probably sounds really crazy to you . . . like it does to me, but I could not ignore the warning and let something bad happen. I had to do this. Do you understand?"

"I understand what you are saying . . . but are you okay?" Sarah asked.

I hesitated. "Yeah . . . I am . . . I'm all right. I was just very worried about you," I explained.

"I'd like to talk to you in person," Sarah said. "Please stay on the line. I'll be right back. I need to check on something with Mom. Don't hang up, okay?"

"Okay," I answered, and I waited for Sarah to return to the phone.

"Catcher, are you there?" Sarah asked after being away for just a couple moments.

"I'm here," I said.

"Mom and I want you to come for supper if you haven't eaten yet. We're still waiting for Dad to get home. He's working late today. We're going to have spaghetti," Sarah said. "Will you come?"

"Sure, I'd like that," I replied. "Thanks. It will be good to see you. Maybe you will understand this better if I explain it to you in person. I'll clean up quickly and be there in about half-an-hour."

It took forever to drive the ten miles to Sarah's house. I was very worried about how she might look at me, what she might be thinking, and what her mom might be thinking. I tried to get my mind off this by looking at farmsteads as I drove by. I looked for dairy cows and beef cattle . . . feeder pig operations . . . tried to figure out if any farm families had horses . . . anything to keep from thinking about the phone call I had made less than an hour earlier.

What was I thinking? **Had** *something happened to me? Why did I think that train was calling to me?*

I couldn't dodge these questions, and the same answer kept coming right back at me. *I did what I did because I felt it was* **real** *and* **true** *and* **crucial**.

That's honestly how it was, and I had no choice. I needed to protect Sarah . . . and I would do it again. That last thought scared me a little. *What if I did do this again? Maybe Sarah and her parents will kind of understand it this time, but if there is a next time . . .*

Sarah came out to meet me when I drove up and parked at the curb. I didn't run to her, but I did kind of hurry. Without a word from either of us, we embraced. I held her tightly and lost myself in her warmth and the wonderful smell of her hair. I was not sure what to say to her. I couldn't tell her that I was sorry that I had called. After a few more moments of silence, I quietly whispered, "I am so glad that you are okay."

We held hands as we walked to her door and went inside. We sat quietly in the entryway. *What else can I say to her? I'm afraid she'll never understand . . . no one will. I hope no one else ever finds out about this. Her parents will probably want Sarah to end our friendship. They, and everyone else will think I am an idiot.*

Sarah looked into my eyes and spoke softly, "Thank you for calling me and warning me, Catch. That was very noble and brave and loving of you. I am grateful."

Though she hadn't said she understood, her words melted my heart, and I felt this huge boulder being lifted from my back, and I smiled to her. I couldn't think of anything different she could have said that would have made me feel any better than I did right now. She hadn't laughed at me or questioned me, though she seemed to be very concerned about how **I** was doing. I didn't feel that explaining myself again was going to improve anything so I didn't say any more about it. Sarah knew what I did, even if she couldn't exactly understand it.

We sat mostly in silence, holding hands for what must have been about twenty minutes. I kept looking at Sarah, studying her face, trying to figure out what she was thinking. Sarah asked me only one question. "Have you been worrying a lot about tomorrow night's game?"

"Not really," I replied. "We practiced well again today, and everyone is excited about our chances if we play well."

When Sarah's dad arrived home from work, we moved to the kitchen table. As far as I could tell, he had not been told about my call to Sarah.

"It's good to see you, Catcher. I'm glad you could join us for spaghetti tonight," Mr. Jenkins said. "This should fuel you up for tomorrow night."

"Thank you," I replied. "Sarah invited me." I could think of nothing else I wanted to say.

Sarah and her mom brought the food to the table, and we dished up and began to eat. There was no conversation for the first couple minutes.

Mr. Jenkins broke the silence. "Did anything exciting happen at school today for any of you?"

I looked at Sarah and her mom. Neither face gave any clue about anything. All three of us shook our heads without saying a word. I kept wondering if my phone call would be brought up for discussion. I knew that I would not be saying anything about it, and I hoped that both Sarah and her mother would keep silent, too.

"Well then," Mr. Jenkins continued. "I'll tell you about some excitement that happened at the plant toward the end of my workday. Shirley Brandon walked in at about six-fifteen, and she was a nervous wreck. I asked her what was wrong, and she told me she had just about been hit by a train as she drove across the railroad tracks on her way to work."

I stopped the fork of spaghetti that was halfway to my mouth, and turned my head to look at Sarah. She looked at me, and she set her slice of bread down and calmly folded her hands in her lap. Sarah's mom gave a slight gasp and reached for her napkin.

Mr. Jenkins didn't seem to notice any of our reactions, and after taking another bite of bread and chewing, he continued telling his story. "Shirley said the train came through town without sounding a single warning whistle, and the train's headlight was not even turned on. She could neither see the train nor hear it, and the train almost hit her as she crossed the tracks. She said she drove to the police station to report it, and they got right on it. When I called the station right before leaving work, I found out that railroad personnel had boarded the slowly moving train near the next town and had discovered that the engineer had suffered a stroke. He had tried to stop the train, but he had not succeeded. It could have been disastrous."

Sarah slid her chair back, stood up, and took a step toward me. I quickly stood and wrapped my arms around her shoulders and kissed the top of her head. I could hear her as she quietly started crying, and I felt a tear or two on my face. I could not let go. I held her and wondered if she was crying because **she** was safe, or if she was crying because she knew that **I** was okay. When Sarah stepped back, I looked into her eyes. She smiled at me through her tears, and I smiled back.

"Thank you. Thank you," Mrs. Jenkins said in an almost inaudible voice, and I turned my head toward her and looked at her. She was wiping away tears from her face, and she appeared to be saying a prayer.

Mr. Jenkins, looking a little confused, began to study us, one at a time.

"I think I must have missed out on something by getting home a little late tonight. Someone will need to fill me in," he said.

Mrs. Jenkins almost smiled. "We've had a little excitement of our own," she said. "I'll tell you all about it while you help me with the dishes. Sarah and Catcher, you are excused from the table after I have given each of you a big hug."

Sarah was first. Her hug lasted for several seconds. I could see that Mrs. Jenkins was whispering something to her, and I could sense the love she felt for her daughter.

I wasn't sure what to do next, but Mrs. Jenkins came to me and put her arms around me and said, "You dear, dear boy," and I just stood there help-lessly with my hands down at my sides.

Sarah and I moved to the living room and sat on the couch, and after a couple minutes Sarah put some music on the stereo. Things felt a little awk-ward to me. I didn't know what it was, but something seemed different. I began to worry.

Sarah reached for my hand and spoke almost in a whisper, "Catch, I can't go to your game tomorrow night."

"Because of my call?" I asked, unsure of what to think.

"**NO** . . . no," Sarah replied. "How could you even think that? I have to be at school tomorrow night. Small groups in band and chorus are performing as kind of a practice for the state contests that are coming up. I have to be there. I feel terrible about this because I promised you that I would go to all of your games. I'm really sorry that I can't make it tomorrow night."

"That's okay, Sarah," I replied. I'm really glad you told me. Now I won't keep looking for you like I did in that one game." I smiled to reassure her. "I really do like it when you come to see us play, but I did not expect you to come to all the games. It won't be quite as much fun if you are not there, but I think the J-Hawks will still be able to 'play hard and have fun.'"

"Don't let this be your last game," Sarah pleaded. "I can come for sure on Friday night . . . so you have to win tomorrow."

"That's what we plan on doing. Don't forget, we did manage to win a couple of games without you to start the season. We'll do all right. Don't you worry about the game. I hope your music goes well. I'm sorry that I won't be there to hear **you** sing and play your music."

"Thanks," Sarah replied.

We sat in silence for a short time.

"Would you like to walk to the park?" I asked.

"Sure. Let's go," Sarah replied.

We grabbed our coats, hats, and mittens and walked to the door.

"Mom and Dad," Sarah announced, "Catch and I are going to walk to the park."

The sidewalk was clear of any snow, and patches of grass were beginning to peek through on the lawns. We held hands as we walked.

"What happened today really frightened me, Sarah, but I hope you know that I didn't mean to scare you when I called," I said. "I'm sorry for that."

"You did kind of scare me. I wasn't sure what was happening," Sarah replied.

"I know. I wasn't either," I said. "This whole thing is a big mystery to me, and I'd feel better if we don't tell anyone about this. They probably wouldn't understand and will ask too many questions. I don't think I'll ever figure it out myself. Right now I almost feel lost. I just knew that I had to do something . . . quickly . . . to keep you safe . . . "

Sarah reached for my arm and gently turned me around. A beautiful smile began to appear on her face.

"A very special friend of mine recently showed me how to find the North Star by using the Big Dipper. Look, it's right up there," she said as she pointed to the northern sky. "Follow those two stars on the front of the dipper to that bright star not too far away. See, there it is. Being able to find the North Star means you are **not** lost, and you'll always be able to find your way. You and I are both safe and well. Everything is good."

"You are a pretty good student," I said. "You learned that lesson really well.

"I had a good teacher," Sarah replied.

We arrived at the park and sat down on adjacent swings.

"Did you know that my friend lives out of town, just a couple of miles beyond the railroad tracks?" Sarah asked, almost in a whisper. "Mom and I would have crossed those tracks on our way to and from her house, but your call stopped us. Calling took a lot of courage, and I will never, ever forget what you did."

I looked through the dim light of the park at her face, and I quietly sang the words that had been camping out in my head: "You are my sunshine . . . my only sunshine . . ."

"What is that all about?" Sarah asked with a hint of laughter in her voice. "Are you practicing for a choir tryout?"

I paused for a moment, and then I explained it to her. "You **are** my sunshine, Sarah." I said to her. "Ever since I met you in November, you have brightened my days. Like the sunshine, you make me feel warm inside, and you bring me laughter and happiness. 'Sunshine' is the special name I decided on for you a couple weeks ago, and now I know for sure that it fits you just right."

The warmth of her smile touched my heart.

We pushed back with our legs, and as we gripped the chains with our mittened hands, we leaned our heads way back and started gliding forward and backward, looking through the bare tree branches to the sparkling stars above, and I began to feel like I was floating on a cloud.

This time I didn't yell it . . . but I thought it. *We are . . . J-Hawks."*

I turned my head and stared at Sarah, and in my mind I pictured myself standing next to her on the top of a small hill in bright sunshine on a warm summer day, listening to the voice of Dizzy Dean in the distance as he sang the words to "The Wabash Cannonball." We would hear the whistle of a far-away train, and I would turn to Sarah and say to her, "That's Dizzy's train, rolling through the hills and by the shore," and I would reach for Sarah's hand and assure her that we did not need to be afraid. There was no longer any danger. We would look into each other's eyes and smile, and I would say a quick, silent prayer of thanks as I squeezed Sarah's hand ever so slightly . . . and I knew in my heart that I would hold on to her forever.

Chapter 48

Building Trust

Not since the opening day of the conference basketball season had we held a pep rally on a Tuesday, but I could understand what might have been the thinking behind it. On the day of that first game, the pep rally's purpose was to get us off to a good start, to fire everyone up. Today was another Tuesday, and someone probably decided that we needed some firing up again after last Friday night's extremely narrow two-point victory in the district playoffs. If we lost tonight, our season would be finished, but a win would earn us another game, and J-Hawk Nation did not want our winning streak to end.

Every student in school, from kindergarten through high school, sat in the bleachers during the pep rally, while Coach and the twelve of us players sat in chairs on the gym floor, facing the students. The Supe spoke first, reminding his audience of our accomplishments this season. "These J-Hawks are undefeated in all twenty-two of their games," he said loudly. "They have won the conference championship and the section championship, and tonight they will play their second game in the district playoffs, going against Chambers."

He went on to tell about other things we had done.

I enjoyed sitting there, listening to him talk about our good character and sportsmanship, hearing him praise our service to the community and our teamwork, because I had experienced words from him in the past, in times of trouble, that were not so positive. Today felt good.

Coach introduced each of us, one-by-one, using the only names that many young kids knew us by, and he said to the students, "Remember these names. These boys are champions, and even when the doors of Jeffers High School are someday closed, the town of Jeffers will remember these J-Hawks because of the way they played basketball and brought honor to their community."

The high school kids stood and applauded, and the junior high students and the elementary school kids soon joined them. We sang the school song twice, and we shouted loudly, "We are . . . J-Hawks! . . . We are . . . J-Hawks!"

The Supe gave the high school kids one last reminder. "The bus leaves at 6:15," he said, and we were then dismissed for the day.

I rode the bus home today, something that I had not done often this year because of baseball, the junior class play, basketball, and other school activities. I knew that I needed to get going on homework right away, that I had chores to do, that I had to eat supper and get cleaned up, and that I needed to be back at the school by six. I was on a tight schedule, so I was lucky that our house was the first stop on the bus route.

As I walked the short distance toward the house on the gravel driveway, avoiding the icy patches, I looked at the dozen or so sugar maples my grandpa had planted many years ago. I walk over to the one I considered my favorite . . . the one with the long strong limb that ran parallel to the ground for more than fifteen feet at a height of almost twenty feet above the ground. For several years when I was younger, this perfect arm of the maple had securely held one end of an old barn rope wrapped around it while the other end of the rope was tied to a bag that was about half filled with straw from the barn. This was our "bag swing," one of the excitement centers on the farm, where Bobby and I could test our strength and courage as we jumped the swinging bag and rode it like a pendulum on a grandfather clock as it reached high and far for the tree's branches until its energy ran out . . . and it slowed down . . . and we jumped off.

Dad had leaned an extension ladder against the limb when he wrapped the rope around the branch and knotted it securely. He had tested it by hanging on it with his full weight, and then, with arms and hands made strong from farming, lowered himself slowly to the ground, carefully avoiding any rope burns.

On the ground he knotted the other end of the rope around the bag of straw, under and around the knot of the tied-off bag. I remember watching as Dad pulled on the bag, sat on it and bounced his weight, made sure it was the right height above the ground, and threw it into the air, checking out the path it followed. After the test was completed, we were given permission to build a platform using the barrels and boards and wire from down by the tractor shed.

"I expect you to be smart with this swing," he had told us. "Play hard . . . see what you can do . . . but no recklessness."

He had trusted us to know how to build a platform that was safe, and he had trusted us to know the difference between what we could attempt and what we shouldn't do.

That's what I was remembering now as I thought about the bag swing, and it felt almost like the trust that Coach had shown in us players this year. I knew that neither Dad nor Coach could watch me every minute. I was given opportunities to try things, learn things on my own, and many times I was successful. Other times . . . maybe I didn't do so well . . . but that caused me to think about what I was doing and come up with new ideas. Living on the farm gave me chances to be resourceful and creative, daring . . . and sometimes stupid, and playing on the J-Hawk basketball team was giving me similar experiences.

"May I say something, Coach?" I asked as we sat on the benches in the locker room at Conrad, tying shoestrings and getting mentally prepared to take to the gym floor for our warm-ups and the game against Chambers.

"Listen up, everyone," Coach announced. "Catcher speaks."

There were a few laughs . . . and a couple fake groans.

"I think I figured something out today, Coach," I said. "Maybe I'm the last one on the team to see this, but I listened to what the Supe said and what you told the other students about us at the pep rally, and it struck me. I think that the key to our whole season has been about trust . . . and I think that you began building that trust on the first day we laced up our shoes.

"I don't think we are the same kids, the same players we were before the basketball season started. We've grown a lot . . . maybe matured is a better word. Our skills have really improved, and we have much more confidence now. I also think we have become better people, and I believe it all happened because you, Coach, gave us the room and the time to do some of those extra things . . . like naming honorary captains for our games . . . giving the clinics on Saturdays for the young kids . . . promoting J-Hawk Nation stocking caps . . . organizing Christmas for the Cade family . . . ushering at the home games . . .

"You trusted us to keep our focus on basketball and allowed us to have our fun, and I think those extra activities made our team stronger. Our senior captains followed your example and also gave us more freedom, and that brought us even closer and more determined than ever to make this a great year for J-Hawk basketball.

"During this season I've felt a responsibility to my teammates and to you, Coach, but it hasn't felt heavy . . . like a duty. It has been something I wanted to do . . . chose to do . . . because everyone else here has done the same. Play hard . . . have fun . . . every practice . . . every game. You've trusted us . . . and we've trusted each other.

"I don't think there's another team out there that has everything that we have. Look at our height advantage and our toughness in grabbing rebounds. All of us shoot well, and we make good passes to find open teammates. Our fast break is outstanding, and our quickness and speed allow us to use a variety of presses and traps on defense. Chambers might have good players . . . but I don't think they have a chance against us tonight. J-Hawk basketball has been built on trust . . . and that trust has given us confidence in each other and so much pride in our team. We play for each other, and I know we'll win tonight because of that.

"This has been the most fun I've ever had playing on a team, Coach, and I want the season to continue."

Everyone just sat there for a few seconds, looking at each other. Then heads started nodding . . . and hands starting clapping . . . and voices started shouting. "We are . . . J-Hawks! We are . . . J-Hawks!"

Pickett almost broke the door down as he led us out to the gym for our warm-ups. Coach smiled at me as I rose from the bench, and he said, "Play hard . . . have fun."

During a break after shooting layups, I looked into the bleachers out of habit, and then I remembered that Sarah wouldn't be here tonight. I looked at the location behind and to the right of our team bench area where Sarah usually sat with her parents. Though she wasn't here, I knew she would be thinking about our game during those times when she wasn't singing or playing music tonight. It didn't bother me that she wasn't here. We each had a job to do tonight . . . in different gyms . . . and I pictured her "playing hard and having fun," just like I would be doing.

I looked back at our basket, grabbed a loose ball, and buried a jump shot from almost twenty feet out. *I'm ready! Let's get this game started!*

We played really well in the first quarter. Pickett played strong defense on Chambers' star player, their 6'5" center, forcing him to take several difficult shots. He shouldn't have taken many of them, but maybe he felt he had to shoot because he was their best player. No one on our team would have taken these shots. We would have passed until we found better opportunities. He missed them often, and Abe and Captain Hook grabbed the rebounds and sent quick outlet passes to Laser and me, and we raced down the floor, scoring many points on layups.

When we brought the ball to our end slowly, Laser and I were able to get the ball to Pickett, who was camped out near the free-throw line. If he was open when he caught our passes, he fired up fade-away jumpers that swished through the net on almost every attempt.

"All right," Coach said to us as we gathered by the bench at the end of the first quarter. "You've built a nice eight-point lead. Keep collecting those rebounds. Break out quickly every chance you get. They don't have the speed or the stamina to stay with you. Nice shooting, Pickett. If they start covering you with a second player, get the ball to Abe or Hook as they move toward the bucket. Let's take advantage of everything they give us. Any questions?"

"I've got one . . . for Catcher," Otto said. "Where's Sarah?"

"She's at her school for band and chorus activities," I replied. I shook my head and laughed at Otto. "I guess I should have told you she wouldn't be here tonight. I hope this hasn't affected your game. Try to focus."

Everyone started laughing after I said that. I could tell they all remembered that game when I played so terribly in the first half because Sarah showed up late, and I was so worried about her that I could not concentrate on the game. Now we were laughing about it.

I made sure I patted Otto on the back before I ran out to the center circle for the start of the second quarter. We were loose, playing well, and I was focused.

We did not let down during the second quarter. Laser kept feeding Pickett whenever a single defender was playing him. That resulted in three more scores from perfect jump shots. Twice I bounced a pass to Captain Hook's left when he stood near the lane, and he was able to step to the ball and catch it, pivot, and shoot, all in one motion, and both attempts dropped through the netting.

On defense we kept switching back and forth between a full-court press and a half-court trap, forcing the Cardinals to hurry, and they kept making mistakes while we continued to make steals. The Cardinals began to fall further behind, and we trotted to the locker room at halftime with a twelve-point lead.

We rested and drank lots of water while Coach laid out the second half for us.

"We're going to keep things the same on defense," he told us. "Until they prove they can eliminate their mistakes, we'll keep the pressure on. Laser, I trust you to call out defensive changes whenever you think it is necessary.

"You've played a very good first half, J-Hawks. Keep working and making plays for the team, and I'll keep sending in fresh legs," Coach added.

We hustled out to the floor to take a few shots and warm up our bodies again. We knew we could beat this team if we continued to play like we did in the first half . . . and that's exactly what we did.

Laser and I took some open jump shots in the third quarter, and we didn't miss many of them. When the Cardinals came out to guard us more closely, we went back to passing the ball inside to the big guys. The defenders couldn't play us one-against-one because they were over-matched, so they double-teamed the player who had the ball. With quick passes, we found the open man, and we were able to take shots when we were not closely guarded. Trusting each other and playing as a team allowed us to get these better shots and play tougher defense, and the Cardinals were unable to stop us or find weaknesses to attack.

During the fourth quarter Coach subbed more often, putting in bench players one-at-a-time to give them some experience playing with starters and giving starters some rest. With two minutes left in the game, both

Coaches emptied the benches. When the final buzzer sounded, we had earned a 17-point victory.

This had been one of our best games of the year, and it meant that we would be coming back here on Friday night to play for the district championship.

I dried off after the game and got a chance to talk to a few friends and parents of the other players. Several people asked about Sarah, and I explained about the activities at her school. It felt very different not having Sarah around. Now that the game was over I allowed myself to think about her . . . and I decided I really missed her. She didn't need to be at the game for me to focus and play well, but some fun was missing when the game had ended, even if it was only for five minutes that I was able to talk with her and maybe laugh a little.

Tonight I wasn't the last J-Hawk player to leave the floor and get to the locker room.

I had set my alarm for six so I would have time to call Sarah after doing chores, cleaning up, and eating breakfast. Since I didn't have any idea what time she got up or left for school, I was just hoping that I might catch her if I called at 7:30.

I dialed . . . and waited . . . for seven or eight rings, and I was feeling disappointed and ready to hang up . . . when my call was picked up.

"Hello," a very sweet voice answered.

"Hi, Sarah. It's Catch," I said. "I called because I wanted to find out how it went with your band and chorus groups last night."

"We did quite well," Sarah replied. "Mom and Dad said everything sounded very professional."

"That's great," I said. "I'm very glad to hear that. I'm sorry I missed it. I wish I could have been there. Next time I will be."

"Thank you," Sarah said. "I would like that. Tell me about your game! Did your team win?"

"**You'll** have to call **me** to find that out," I teased. "This call is about **your** activities."

"Catcher!" Sarah almost sounded a little upset. Then she softened her tone. "It sounds to me like you are in a very good mood. I think that is a sign that you won. Please tell me I am right."

"Actually," I continued, "talking to you or seeing you always makes me feel good, so maybe that is not a sure clue as to how our game went. Remember, you are my Sunshine. However . . . if you don't have plans for Friday night . . . there's a basketball game you might want . . ."

"You did win!" Sarah interrupted. "I am so happy for you . . . and for me! I was so disappointed that I couldn't go last night, and I was afraid I might not get to see you play again! This is such great news! Was it close?"

"Everyone played well," I replied, "and we collected a seventeen-point victory. Pickett got us off to a great start with his accurate shooting, and we scored several fast-break baskets. Abe and Hook were outstanding under both baskets, and Laser and I both hit a few jump shots in the second half. This was one of our top-five games of the year."

"This is the best early-morning phone call I've ever received," Sarah said.

We both laughed.

"It almost sounds like you are poking fun at me, but that was a good one, Sarah," I admitted.

"I am **not** making fun of you," Sarah protested quietly. "That's one of the things I really like about you . . . your 'best evers.' I'm always hoping to hear more of them."

"Good," I said. "This is my best ever start to a school day."

Again Sarah laughed, and the sound of her wonderful laugh tickled my ears, just like seeing her pretty smile always fed my soul."

"I have to get going, or I'll be late. I want to stop in Mom's room at school before my first class to tell her the good news. She'll be so excited! Now we'll get to see you play in another game on Friday night," Sarah said. "I'm so glad you called."

"Me, too," I said. "I hope you have a great day in school. I look forward to Friday night."

"I **will** have a great day," Sarah replied, "because of your call. Thank you for winning last night. I am so happy! I gotta run, Catch. Call me tonight. G'bye."

In the Stands – With John Garris

In talking to a couple young friends the other night, I found out that report cards will be handed out at their school in a couple weeks. They told me they were a little nervous about it. I'm wondering if the Jeffers J-Hawks are feeling anxious at this moment because I have decided to grade them on their season thus far.

Because I've watched a number of their games, I feel qualified to assess the players in several categories, but I will **not** be grading individual players. The J-Hawks don't play individually . . . they play as a team . . . so they will be given only team grades.

* **TEAMWORK:** "A" This one is pretty obvious. I have not seen another team play this selflessly. The sum of the whole is greater than the individual parts.
* **CONDITIONING:** "A" "See how they run!" No team has been able to run with them or has been successful at slowing them down.
* **EXPERIENCE:** "B" At the beginning of the season the best I could have given them was a "C-." They still play only two seniors, but the sophomores are performing like juniors, and all twelve J-Hawks have earned and have already received varsity letters for playing this season.
* **SHOOTING ACCURACY:** "B+" Not every player has a great shooting night in every game, but they play smart and find the hot shooters in each game, and most of the shots are taken by someone who "has the touch."
* **DEFENSIVE PRESSURE:** "A" The J-Hawks use a variety of full-court and half-court presses and traps. They are really adept at making opposing teams work extremely hard for their shots every single game. (See TEAMWORK and CONDITIONING above.)
* **SPORTSMANSHIP:** "A" These young men play the game by the rules, and they show respect to their opponents, the officials, and everyone who watches the games, whether they cheer

for the J-Hawks or against them.

* **INGANGIBLES:** "A" This category includes areas such as community service, Saturday basketball clinics that teach and inspire young players, playing with such heart and determination that the entire Jeffers community is behind them, and having the ability at game time to shut out all distractions and put all of their energy into playing hard while having so much fun that I wish I were a member of their team.

* **GOALS FOR THE SEASON:** "Incomplete" There is some work that is not yet finished.

The J-Hawk winning streak now stands at 23 games after their 17-point victory last night over Chambers in the district semi-finals.

Chapter 49
A Test of Stamina

As students started loading into the bus at five, I could sense the excitement as well as some nervousness. Tonight's game was huge! If we won . . . we were going to play in the state tournament . . . but if we lost . . . we're done.

I understood the nervousness because I was feeling some of that myself, just like I did in practice on Wednesday when Abe was accidentally poked in the eye. His eye kept watering because of the irritation, and he sat out for the last half of our practice. Luckily for us he was much better by yesterday's practice, and in the locker room a little earlier today when we were packing our duffle bags, and I asked him how he was feeling, he answered, "Twenty-twenty."

"Good one, Abe," I replied. "I'm glad because you are the key. Your height scares people. Players don't know how to defend you, and how many times have we seen mommas rush out onto the floor to try save their boys from harm when you start slamming the ball through the hoop."

Abe laughed . . . and I laughed with him.

As I walked down the aisle of the bus toward the back, I saw Otto sitting by himself. I leaned over and quietly whispered to him, "Sarah **will** be at the game tonight . . . so I don't want you to worry."

Otto laughed . . . and I also laughed with him.

At about five-fifteen we were on our way, and the noise level dropped as students respected our wishes for a quiet ride to Conrad. Pickett began plucking the strings of his ukulele, and I immediately began to relax.

Coach had told us to prepare for a running game. That was the style that the Payton Pirates preferred. Coach had explained that the Pirates ran toward their basket every time they had the ball, whether they had grabbed a defensive rebound or had inbounded the ball after a score. "They only rest while playing defense," he had said.

I started drooling when I heard Coach's last statement. This game could be interesting, because we prided ourselves on never resting on defense. We used presses and traps to force mistakes, and we kept our hands up and slid our feet quickly to keep opponents from getting open shots. On offence we ran the fast break almost every time we grabbed a defensive rebound. Only if we slowed the ball down and worked set plays on offense did we get a chance to rest on the floor.

We had used this style of play, very successfully, for 23 games, and we had run hard at almost every practice, so we were in really good shape. I expected that we would be ready to challenge the Pirates at their running game because of our great stamina.

As soon as the word "stamina" crossed through the mazes of my brain, I remembered one time when I wasn't in good enough shape to keep up, and it put me in a very difficult situation.

Because I wasn't strong enough or brave enough to stand up to my older sister or to think for myself, she convinced me to join her in an adventure . . . to run away from home. I can't recall the exact reason we ran away, other than she felt that things were unfair at our house, and my sister sought justice. That's why she decided to escape to Grandma's house in Jeffers, and she wanted my company.

Though I did join my sister willingly in her adventure, I had a couple serious disadvantages to deal with. My tricycle was only about half the size of hers, and at three-and-a-half years old, I was a year-and-a-half younger than she was. My legs must already have been kind of strong even at that early age because I managed to ride over half a mile on that gravel road, but I remember that I couldn't keep up with Maggie, and after we had ridden for a long while, she left me in the dust.

Some neighbor passing by must have ratted us out to our parents, because Dad pulled up in the car and put my trike in the trunk and put me in the back seat. I can't recall if he looked angry or relieved. Then he drove on to about the mile marker to capture Maggie. Because I was getting worn out I was glad to have Dad come along and rescue me, but Maggie wasn't ready to give up yet. When Dad grabbed her trike and placed it in the trunk, she started running down the road to Grandma's. She didn't get very far, but I must have been impressed with her effort to still remember this after over 12 years have passed.

I sat quietly next to San Juan and thought about how so many things about my past years seem to connect somehow to this basketball season. Today . . . it was "stamina." I am in really good shape now, and I do not expect to tire out during the game. I'm ready because I've worked hard. Though I didn't make it to Jeffers on my trike that day, I have ridden my bike to Jeffers countless times on that same gravel road, and each time, my legs were strengthened and my stamina was improved.

The gym was almost empty and very quiet when our bus arrived, but it didn't take long for the students of J-Hawk Nation to liven up the place. They grabbed a section of the bleachers that was close to our bench, and all during our warm-up routine, they were shouting out J-Hawk cheers.

As I shot my layups and jump shots, I glanced at the bleachers and saw bunches of people file into the gym and claim seats. With only one game tonight, I didn't expect the place would sell out, but it was filling fast. I decided not to look for Sarah because I knew she would be here. That was enough for me. I reminded myself that I play for my team, not for her. She just adds to the fun . . . a whole lot.

We were ready to take the floor for the opening tip, but Coach had a few last comments to make. "Tonight is a big opportunity for you J-Hawks," he said. "If you play up to your capabilities you will punch your ticket to the state tournament. You are a good team. You play together as a team . . . and you know how to win as a team. We know the Pirates will run at every offensive chance. Tonight they will also get to run every time on defense. Let's use the fast pace to our advantage. All the running that you have done in practices . . . tonight is the payoff. Let's play hard . . . have fun."

The Pirates played as advertised, running every time they touched the ball, but we were just as fast as they were . . . just as determined . . . and we were in better condition. Most of the points that were scored in the first quarter were from layups or short jumpers, and when the buzzer sounded to end the fast-paced quarter, we held a two-point lead.

While we trotted to the bench, the Pirates walked, and while we stood tall as we listened to Coach, they slumped over in their huddle, resting their hands on their knees, showing me that they were already wearing down. We had earned much more than just a two-point lead. We were winning the stamina battle, and those points would be awarded during the second half. What we needed to do was stay with them during the first half . . . mess with their confidence, and then we would put them away in the second half when their energy level hit bottom.

Both teams subbed more often in the second quarter, and the pace slowed only a little. We made sure they had to run on defense, and I could see in their faces that they were tiring out. A couple of their players signaled to their coach that they needed a break, and that gave us motivation to run harder. Our coach always had to drag us off the floor. We never volunteered to take a seat on the bench.

Sometime during the second quarter it dawned on me that the Pirates were kind of a one-dimensional team. Everything they did on offence centered on running. They obviously had been very successful this year, or they never would have made it to the district championship game, but I wondered if most teams they had played against were afraid of the Pirates' speed and tried to slow them down. Maybe teams lost to the Pirates because they tried to take away the Pirate strength of running and playing at a fast pace, and this allowed the Pirates to rest on defense. Maybe these guys had never been challenged to run both directions, like they had to do tonight, and now they were finding out they could not match our stamina . . . and tonight they would lose.

They never slowed the game down against us. Maybe they couldn't . . . maybe they didn't have the skills to play a style other than running. It seemed like their plan was to run us into the ground . . . or die trying. Tonight they were destined to die trying.

Coach always was flexible with our strategy. Run or don't run . . . press and trap or drop back . . . work the ball inside . . . shoot from outside . . .

call set plays . . . We were ready to switch to something else if the game was not going our way. We had several dimensions to our game.

We started pulling away toward the end of the second quarter, and when Tucson scored on a short jump shot just before the buzzer sounded to end the quarter, it gave us a lead of ten points. I trotted toward the locker room knowing we would add to that lead in the next half. The Payton Pirates were a running team that could not match up to our running game. Tonight, ironically, their strength would bring their downfall.

Before we ran out to the center circle for the second half tip, I sneaked a peek into the bleachers and found Sarah. She smiled at me, cheered, and reached for her necklace. That's all it took for me to know that I was important to her. I nodded my head once and smiled back to her, hopefully assuring her that she meant everything to me.

In an uneventful second half, we gradually increased our lead until it stood at twenty, and Coach kept subbing, giving some of the bench players the chance to play in the game with some of the starters. When the clock showed that only two minutes remained in the game, both coaches cleared their bench by putting in the players that usually only played in big wins or big losses, and tonight it was both . . . a big win for us, and a big loss for them.

It was while we were greeting friends and parents near our bench after the traditional post-game handshake with our opponents that word began to spread. For the second time this winter, high school kids were being invited to The Jeffers Teen Center Café for ten-cent burgers, fries, and sodas, and since we wouldn't get back to Jeffers until about 9:45, Coach agreed to let us players stay until the café closed at 11:15. Then we would have to hustle right home.

Kids started talking to parents and making arrangements for rides home. I found Sarah and Becky as soon as I heard the news.

"Your team played great again tonight," Sarah said. "You made the Pirates look like they were not a very good team."

"We were tough, weren't we," I replied. "Hi, Becky. It's good to see you here. Hey, can you girls stay for the party at the teen center? Remember,

Sarah, how much fun we had last time?"

"I don't know if we can stay," Sarah said, "but I'll ask."

"Wait just a minute. I need to check out something with my folks first," I said, and I left the two girls standing by the bench and hustled to find my parents.

They weren't far away, but they were talking with Captain Hook's dad so I stood by . . . not so patiently.

"Good game tonight, Son," Dad said.

"Thanks." I replied. "I think the Pirates now have a better idea of what a total running game looks like."

"Congratulations on making it to state," the Supe said with lots of pride in his voice. Our school and community are very proud of your team."

I nodded thanks, but I had to talk to Mom right away. "Mom would you be willing to invite Sarah's parents to our house for coffee tonight so Sarah and Becky will be able to go to the teen center?" I asked hurriedly.

Mom didn't even have to think about it. "Sure," she replied. "Where are they? I'll invite them right away."

"Can you look for them while I chase down the girls again? I left them by the bench so I could find you," I explained.

Sarah and Becky weren't standing alone when I returned. They were being "bothered" by Tucson, San Juan, and Otto.

"It's not a good idea leaving these pretty girls here by themselves," Tucson advised. "You never know . . ."

" . . . Who might come along," I interrupted. "I know. I messed up. Sorry, girls. I think we're all set," I told Sarah. "Your parents are being invited for coffee out to the farm. Now would be a good time to ask them if you can visit the teen center tonight."

Sarah's parents accepted Mom's invitation, so both San Juan and I would have special company at the café. As soon as I figured out how lucky I was, I began to worry a little. *Will our parents be discussing my Monday telephone call?*

Kids were in the mood for celebrating tonight. I think The Jeffers Teen Center Café was even louder than last time, and sometimes it was hard to hear the songs that were being played on the jukebox.

After sitting for a few minutes, San Juan handed Becky a nickel and tried to convince her to play the pinball machine. After a little persuasion from Sarah and me, she agreed to try one game. She had a crowd watching as she expertly flipped the steel balls toward the targets and racked up bonus points. She made a couple good saves to keep the balls in play, and she won four free games. I saw the pride in San Juan's face. He was maybe even prouder than if he had won the games himself.

Several times cheers were yelled out to honor the basketball team for making it to the state tournament. Pickett and Laser stood up after one of the cheers, and they held up their arms to quiet the crowd. The café became completely silent.

Pickett looked around slowly at everyone in the room. "We're not **done** yet," was all he said, and they both sat down to additional cheering and applause.

It was difficult to hear normal conversation, and I was too tired to work hard at listening, so Sarah and I mainly just ate, stared at each other, and smiled often. We still had loads of fun.

We talked Becky and San Juan into going for a short walk with us on Main Street so we could escape the noise for a short time. We read all the messages that were painted on the windows of the stores as we slowly moved down one side of the street and back on the other, holding hands and breathing in the crisp air of another winning game night in March.

"You did it!" Sarah said excitedly. "You made it to state!"

"Yeah," I replied. "It feels good, but our goal is to win at state, not just get there. That's why you don't see the players celebrating. We're excited, but we're not satisfied.

Closing time at the café came too quickly, and Sarah's parents pulled up to the curb on Main to pick up the girls and drive home to Madison Lake. San Juan and I walked Sarah and Becky to the car. That's when I found out that all four of us were seeing a movie together tomorrow night. I looked forward to this because I knew that my night would be filled with laughter, just like last time.

"Tomorrow morning?" I asked. "It might be our last clinic."

"Really?" Sarah sounded a little sad. "I'll be there, but I hope it's not your last one."

Then I said loudly enough for her dad to hear," We'll have to convince your dad to keep coming to The Jeffers Café for Saturday morning coffee, even after basketball is done. You'll need to ride along, of course, and you and I can study together at the library."

"I'll work on that idea on the way home," Sarah announced loudly. "Good night."

At the conclusion of Saturday's clinic, Laser announced to the kids that we weren't sure about next Saturday. "We hope to be staying overnight in Des Moines," he said. "There'll be an announcement in school on Wednesday. We will hold one final clinic, but we aren't sure when it will be."

West-Side Story isn't the kind of movie that San Juan and I would say is of high interest for us, but we knew that the girls really wanted to see it, so we decided to be "big boys" about it and willingly go to the musical. After all, Sarah had come to my basketball games all season long. Tonight would be about her . . . taking her to a movie she had been looking forward to seeing ever since it came out, and when it comes right down to it, it doesn't matter what kind of movie I see as long as Sarah is sitting in the seat next to me.

Most of the time I listened to the music and watched the action on the big screen, but some of the time I glanced at Sarah out of the corner of my eye, and I saw how much she was enjoying the music and the dancing. I held her hand all through the movie, and during one of the songs that was about "hands and hearts," Sarah squeezed my hand and reached for her heart neck-lace. It was another great movie night.

We were laughing and kind of singing as we walked from the theater to The Grill, and a policeman slowed down in his squad car, pulled up next to the sidewalk, and asked, "Are these boys from Jeffers bothering you girls?"

I was a little shocked at his question.

"No," Sarah answered. "We're friends."

"All right," the policeman said. Then he laughed and added, "Good luck in the state tournament, J-Hawks," and he drove off.

As his car disappeared down the street, I called out to him, "Thanks, Officer Krupke!"

Sarah started laughing, and then she turned silly and began singing phrases similar to what we had heard in *West-Side Story,* only she made these up herself, and she couldn't stop laughing while she sang, "Who can I be in America? I can be me in America . . ."

It was silent for just a couple of seconds, and then I added to the song, "Everyone's free in America . . ."

After just a few more seconds of almost total silence, Becky finished it off by singing the words, "Happy are we in America."

All four of us laughed at our creative song, and then we put it all together and sang it three or four more times as we walked to The Grill.

When the young waitress brought four glasses of water to our booth, she took out her tablet and wrote down our order. It was exactly the same thing we had gotten on our first double date, and as soon as she walked the order back to the kitchen we began to sing again, but now we sang in much softer voices than we had used outside.

"Who can I be in America?

I can be me in America.

Everyone's free in America.

Happy are we in America."

"I think we should write some new lyrics," I said, "for the newly formed J-Hawk Nation Music Team. Since San Juan and I have already been basketball captains for one game this year, you two should share the honor of being the captains of the music team." I winked at Sarah as I thought about the time she suggested that I had been the captain of the ushering squad. Every time I was with her she brought me laughter and sunshine.

San Juan nodded his support.

"That's a great idea," Becky said. "Let's do it."

"Captain . . . Captain . . . ," I said as I looked first at Sarah, then at Becky,

"I have a suggestion."

"Permission to speak is granted," Sarah replied as a beautiful smile decorated her lovely face.

I returned her smile as I tried to speak in a dignified voice. "I've analyzed our song, and I see a four-syllable pattern in each line, followed by the phrase 'in America.' Additionally, the fourth syllable needs to rhyme with 'me,'" I pointed out. "If you captains agree, I think we should make a list of words we could use for new lyrics, and you could write them down."

"Agree," Sarah responded. She grabbed a napkin and asked if she could borrow a pen when the waitress brought our sodas to the booth. Sarah wrote down a word that began the list.

"What did you write?" I asked. "We need to say the words out loud so we know what they are."

"Agree," Sarah repeated, and when she smiled at me I got it.

"Good one, Sarah," I said to her. "How about tree?"

"Ski," San Juan called out.

"Knee works," I added, and Sarah put them on her list.

I started working through the alphabet, and I could see that the others were doing the same.

"Bee," Sarah said as she added to the list.

"Captain," I said without sounded too harsh, "we've already used 'be' in our first line of the original song."

"This one is the insect," Sarah replied.

"That's a good one," San Juan offered, and I agreed.

"Key," Becky almost shouted.

"See," San Juan said with a grin.

"Spell it for me, please?" Sarah asked.

"It's really not too difficult," San Juan replied. "S–E-E."

"Okay, and then I'll add 'sea' as in water," Sarah said.

"You are sharp, Sarah. Twice you've scored with homonyms. I'm glad you're on my music team," I added as all four of us laughed.

When the hamburgers and fries were delivered to us, we took a short break from adding to the list, but every once-in-a-while someone thought of another word. We were having a great time with our song and our word list.

"Flee," I said. "Put that one down."

"Flea," Sarah repeated. "I'll add that one."

"I just gave that one, Captain. You must not have heard me," I said.

"You spell yours, then I'll spell mine," Sarah replied. "Homonyms."

"I'm impressed again. Write them both, Captain," I suggested. I was having fun with Sarah's new title.

Becky offered "he," and San Juan came up with "fee" as we finished our burgers and fries. Next we started taking turns creating new lyrics. Sometimes the words didn't make much sense, but the rhythms and the rhymes were pretty good, and we continued to laugh, sing, and have a really good time.

"I'll climb a tree in America," I sang.

San Juan followed with, "I want to ski in America."

"Live by the sea in America," Becky sang as she chuckled.

Then Sarah finished with, "Search for my key in America."

We made up several lines, laughed often, and probably had more fun than the laws of Madison Lake should have allowed us to have after having watched the musical *West-Side Story*. I knew that I would never question Sarah about a movie choice she made. I would go very willingly to any movie she wished to see, but I was secretly hoping she would never want me to take her to a scary movie.

We sang quietly and talked not so quietly at times until I casually turned around in the booth to glance at the clock that hung above the main entry door. It read eleven-fifteen!

"In trouble are we in America!" I proclaimed. "Look at the time!"

"Ouch!" Sarah said. "You have to get me home right away."

J-Hawk Nation Music Team was silenced for the night, and San Juan and I hustled to the cash register to pay our bill. While we all put on our coats and stuff, I came up with a plan.

"San Juan, drive Becky home," I said. "I'll walk Sarah to her house. We'll be there in seven or eight minutes. Don't forget to swing by and pick me up."

Sarah and I walked quickly. We would only be a few minutes late, so I hoped her parents would understand.

"Thanks for taking me to this movie," Sarah said. "I loved it. I loved the whole night. Everything was fun."

"I thought so, too," I replied. "This was definitely my best musical ever."

Sarah giggled. "We maybe got a little silly, but I enjoyed all the laughter," Sarah said.

"Laughing so much almost wore me out," I admitted. "It's good that I don't have a game to play right now."

As soon as we reached Sarah's house, we went in and Sarah announced, "Mom and Dad, we're home. We're sorry we're a few minutes late, but we lost track of time while we were making up lyrics and singing at The Grill. Catch and I walked here, and San Juan is coming by for Catch in a couple minutes."

"Did you enjoy the movie?" Sarah's mom asked from the living room.

"We both loved it," Sarah answered, "and afterwards we made up rhymes like we heard in the movie, and we sang them. All four of us had a great time."

I knew I only had a minute or two before I had to leave. I gently wrapped my arms around Sarah and smiled as I looked deeply into her pretty eyes. "Thank you for another wonderful evening," I said quietly, and then I kissed her.

I heard the car pull up, and I hugged Sarah one last time before stepping outside.

I ran down the sidewalk to the car and paused before opening the door. I turned back to look at the house, and I saw Sarah standing behind the glass, smiling and waving to me.

I raised my arms and shouted, "We are . . . J-Hawks! We play 'bb' in America!"

In the Stands – With John Garris

They certainly weren't on my radar as a state-tournament caliber basketball team when I made my preseason predictions back in November, but with steady improvement, great determination, unselfish play, and a commitment to leaving their school and their community something of which to be proud, the J-Hawks of Jeffers have played their way to the small school state basketball tournament which begins next week with a round of substate games at four different sites around the state.

With their 17-point victory over Chambers on Tuesday and a 22-point demolition of Payton last night, the J-Hawks appear to be peaking just as they begin to face the best teams in the state. They have now won twenty-four games without dropping a single contest, and their community is solidly behind them, as I witnessed in Conrad last night, sitting in packed bleachers behind the J-Hawk bench. I have no idea who was left behind in Jeffers to mind the store.

The J-Hawk fast break was running on all eight cylinders against the Pirates, as each J-Hawk starter, supported by three bench players, sprinted down court continually, tossing perfect passes that led players to the bucket and allowed them to score several easy layups. They continued their hustle with defensive pressure, forcing the Pirates into making bad decisions and poor passes. Giving short rest breaks to the starters by freely using substitutes, the J-Hawks put their excellent conditioning on display.

If I were the coach of one of the other seven teams that has made it to the state basketball tournament in Class B, I would be devising a game plan that did not involve playing a running game with the J-Hawks.

Chapter 50
There Is a Season

When I sat down in the pew I looked quickly through the church bulletin to see what songs we would be singing today and what the minister would be preaching about. Upon reading the title of his sermon, "There Is a Season," I wondered if he would be talking about J-Hawk basketball.

I wasn't even close to being right.

Like I usually did on Sunday mornings, I let my mind wander, and it wove between basketball and Sarah Jenkins. I was lost in thought. Part way through the sermon I was awakened by Mom's elbow, and I started listening. It only took a couple of minutes before I started feeling uncomfortable. I didn't like what I heard.

I almost felt like standing up and excusing myself because I was afraid of where this part of the minister's sermon was headed. One-after-another the minister rattled off pairs of words or phrases that were opposites, and I became more and more nervous as I listened.

"There is a time for war and a time for peace," he said loudly. "There is a time to dance and a time to mourn . . . a time to rip open and a time to mend."

I understood what he was saying . . . that there was a time for everything . . . a beginning and an ending . . . a time for the good and the bad to happen.

He continued with other pairs. "A time for disagreeing and a time for embracing . . . a time for love and a time for hate . . . a time for laughter and a time for tears."

I began to squirm in the pew. I was worried that he was going to say the pair of words that I would not allow my ears to hear today.

Please don't jinx our basketball team. Don't say anything about a time to win and a time to lose. I can't hear anything like that today. Maybe you could say something about a time to win and a time to keep on winning. That would work.

The minister went on to say that there is a season for everything, and I thought to myself, "You are absolutely right . . . and now is the season for basketball. It's been a really good season, and all we want is for it to last one more week. That's it . . . ONE . . . MORE . . . WEEK."

I heard nothing about win or lose, so either I had slept through that part of his sermon, or it wasn't in his sermon notes to begin with. At any rate, I didn't hear anything about it, and that was a relief to me.

At the close of the service the minister said that he had been asked to make an announcement about a special event that was happening this afternoon.

"For everything there is a season, and though this may not seem like the proper season for it, there is an outdoor picnic scheduled for this afternoon at the park and in the fire station," he said. "This winter picnic will feature grilled hot dogs, hot chocolate and coffee, potato chips and baked beans, and lots of dessert bars. A huge bonfire will provide extra warmth, and you'll have a chance to talk to the basketball-playing J-Hawks and wish them well as they head to the state tournament this week with hopes of stretching their fine season out three more games.

"The business people of Jeffers have organized this event to honor the team and our community and to raise a little money to help support the basketball team. Donations will be accepted, and a huge bake sale will be set up in the fire station. Starting time is about one o'clock, and the picnic will last until about three. You are advised to dress warmly. Please bring your entire families, and tell your friends to join us."

On the ride home from church I sat in the back seat and stared out at the farming landscape that was still mostly covered by snow. I thought of a few ideas that could have been added to the minister's sermon.

There's a time to mow the hay, rake it into rows and bale it, gather all the bales with the flatbed and the tractor, drive the loads to the barn and raise the bales, ten-at-a-time, into the haymow for storage by using a pulley-and-rope system . . . and a time for me to drop several bales down the chute to the cows at evening feeding time after unraveling the twine, day after day, eventually clearing the floor of hay bales on the south end of the haymow so I could finally shoot baskets again.

There's a time to feed the cows . . . and a time for the cows to feed us. "More *milk, please."*

There's also a time to feed the chickens . . . and a time for the chickens to feed us . . . sometimes at great sacrifice. "These scrambled eggs are delicious. Great job on the fried chicken, Mom."

There's a time to plant the soybeans . . . and a time to walk those long rows in the hot sun with a machete to chop down the weeds and the stalks of corn that grew from last year's seed, while getting stung by numerous bees and bitten by hordes of mosquitoes, and collecting a bad sunburn and an occasional rash from itchweed . . . and a time to get the combine out and harvest the crop and truck the soybeans to the grain elevator in town and sell them so we can all get new shoes.

I guess that these ideas were living proof that I had listened to and understood the minister's sermon.

As soon as I got home I called Sarah to tell her about the winter picnic. Even though I had spent time with her on Friday night at The Jeffers Teen Center Café and on Saturday morning at the clinic and library, followed by Saturday night on our movie date, I was hoping she could convince her parents that they should come to the picnic. Seeing Sarah on three successive days of a weekend might make this my best weekend ever. *There I go again.*

"Though it's really short notice, I bet your home-made brownies would be a big hit at the bake sale," I said.

"Let me talk to Mom and Dad. I'll call you back in a few minutes," Sarah replied.

Sarah called back right away. "We're coming, and we're bringing plates of brownies for the bake sale," she said.

"Did you have to twist some arms pretty hard?" I asked.

"Not at all," Sarah answered. "Mom and Dad got kind of silly right away and said they would **never** want to miss out on a winter picnic. They said they've had such a great winter following your basketball team, and they don't want to miss a single chance to talk with the parents and players. Mom is already gathering the ingredients for baking."

"Good," I said. "I'll watch for you."

I helped Mom by carrying a couple of her plates of chocolate chip cookies into the fire station for the bake sale. There must have been well over 50 plates of bars and cookies, each priced to sell at one dollar, spread out on four tables.

On the east wall of the fire station I saw that a long piece of butcher paper had been taped just a couple of feet above the floor. It read, "J-Hawks — State Tournament Bound." Kids and grownups were writing messages and good luck wishes on the paper. I knew that I would come back later to read some of the messages.

When I walked over by the picnic tables that had been removed from their storage area and had been spread out in one area of the park, I easily located Abe, San Juan, Otto, and Tucson. They stood out in the crowd because of their black-and-white letter jackets. The J-Hawk Nation stocking caps they wore weren't a big clue in finding them because almost everyone, kids and adults, were wearing those black caps. Seeing all those caps drove home to me that the people of Jeffers were really rooting for us.

We can't let them down. Community pride is at stake. I wonder how many caps have been sold?

We sat on the two benches at one table and watched all the young kids running around and chasing each other while parents were drinking coffee and engaging in conversation. Several people came over and spoke with us about our basketball season and about making it to state. Everyone wished us good luck for our Tuesday night game.

After sitting for about ten minutes, I saw Sarah walking in our direction from the fire station. She was carrying a plate.

I quickly jumped to my feet and walked toward her. "Hi, Sarah," I said. "I'm glad you could come to the picnic. What's that you're carrying?"

"You said I could bake for you anytime," Sarah replied. "I chose today. Here are some brownies . . . just for you," and she handed me the plate.

"Thank you! I will savor these," I said as I studied the chocolate-frosted brownies that had numerous chunks of walnuts attempting to escape out through the sides of each of the freshly cut pieces, and I smacked my lips.

Out of the corner of my eye I observed my four teammates get up from the picnic table and walk toward us. As soon as they saw the plate of brownies I was holding, their eyes became enlarged, and they held out begging "paws" and stuck out pink panting tongues.

"Not the puppies again!" I moaned.

Sarah started laughing.

"This looks just like the litter that **hounded** me on the gym bleachers when I tried to read your valentine, Sarah," I protested.

Sarah laughed again. "That was pretty good, Catch," Sarah said. Then she added, "They look pretty hungry. I think you should feed them."

"My brownies?" I asked. "Not my brownies!"

"Man's best friend . . . and these guys **are** your best friends," she added. "I'll bake you some more."

I reluctantly held out the plate, and my friends courteously each took one brownie, leaving just two for me.

"Wow, Sarah, these are really good," Abe said after taking one huge bite. "Thanks for feeding us, Catcher."

"Yeah. Woof! Woof!" Tucson barked. "Thanks."

Sarah and I walked over to the food line. I only had one dollar to donate, but Sarah rescued us because she had a dollar, also. I would not have felt right for two of us to eat for just one dollar. Several of the food servers told us, "Go J-Hawks!" I felt pretty good about all the attention I was receiving today, and Sarah really contributed to that.

It took quite a while for us to eat because Sarah and I did a lot of talking. As we finished I could tell that Sarah was getting chilled, so I suggested that we go over and stand near the bonfire. Seeing and hearing the roaring fire . . . and feeling the heat, I was reminded of the times we had sat on the floor at her house and had watched the flames dance in the fireplace, and I leaned over, gently put my arm around her, and whisper-sang into her ear, "Chances are . . ."

Sarah squeezed my hand and looked at me tenderly, and I stared into her sparkling eyes and smiled. *I hope you understand how much you mean to me.* Today was the third day in a row that we were able to be together, and I was grateful.

"Let's go check out the banner in the fire station," Sarah suggested after we had warmed up by the fire.

We walked past the dessert tables, and Sarah observed that all three plates of brownies she had brought to the bake sale were already sold. "Those buyers are in for a treat," I said, "unless there are some puppies in the neighborhood."

After scanning the banner for a couple minutes I noticed a drawing of a small heart that had written inside it, "SJ + C." I looked at Sarah and saw that she was blushing a little. That was a dead give-away for me.

"I like that," I told her. I picked up a pen, found a small open space, and drew my own heart. It wasn't shaped as nicely as the other one, but inside it I printed "C + SJ." I stepped back to check it out and admire it a little. I nodded approval and said, "Although I am not much of an artist, I like this one, too."

At three o'clock Sarah's parents were ready to leave, so I walked with them to their car. I said to Sarah along the way, "This was my best winter picnic ever." I wasn't surprised that Sarah laughed, but I wasn't expecting her mom to laugh, too.

I was ready to say my good-bye with carefully chosen words when we reached their car. I said, "Thank you, Mr. and Mrs. Jenkins, for coming to this winter picnic . . . and for driving to our basketball games and cheering for the J-Hawks all season . . . and for allowing me to date your wonderful daughter."

Sarah's good-bye hug was accompanied by a few words that she whispered into my ear. "You are my very special friend . . . forever," she said.

I waved as they drove off down Main Street, and I thought back to how this day had started in church. I reflected on picnics that are held out of season and important basketball games that are played at the end of the season. I noticed patches of grass peeking up through dirty snow, and I knew that the season of spring was just around the corner, and that would mean I'd be spending more time on the tractor preparing the earth for planting season.

For everything there is a season, and I have hopes that the end of our basketball season will find us winning . . . and laughing . . . and singing . . . and embracing.

Chapter 51

Distracted

When I walked into the locker room, I saw that only six of my teammates were busy packing their gear. I knew the others would be coming soon because the bus was scheduled to leave at 4:30 for our two-hour ride to Waterloo.

I was bummed about having to play a basketball game in Waterloo. I had been to this city a few years back when the J-Hawks suffered the misfortune of losing in the first round of the state basketball tournament, and I had read in my history class about the French Revolution and Napoleon meeting his "Waterloo."

Why couldn't this game be held somewhere else? Who chose Waterloo? There's nothing positive about Waterloo.

Everyone was kind of quiet. I sensed a little nervousness from Abe and Captain Hook, from San Juan, Otto, Tucson, and Treason, but the atmosphere changed quickly when Pickett and Laser walked in like they owned the place, talking loudly, acting very cheerful.

"All right, J-Hawks!" Laser said confidently. "Tonight we begin working on our third and final goal of the season. Fire Up!"

"It's been great winning the conference championship and making it to the state tournament," Pickett added, "but let's not settle for that. Let's win the whole thing . . . starting with tonight's game."

"We are . . . J-Hawks!" I shouted, trying to do my part to relieve any nervous tension, but my words came out a little hollow.

The other members of the team, Go Forth Son, Nicholson, and Half-Dozen, entered the locker room and added to the noise as they put their stuff in their duffle bags. The sophomores were busy organizing and packing team gear because they were responsible for carrying our uniforms, warm-ups, and both bags of basketballs out to the bus, just like San Juan and I had been two years ago when, as freshmen, we were the youngest on the team.

This year San Juan and I decided we would help these guys, and we each picked up a bag of balls like we had done for most of the games this season, and we headed to the bus.

I didn't feel right about the sophomores carrying everything. We were teammates. We were all equals on the basketball floor. I thought we should share in the burdens . . . just like we all shared in the glory when we won. The sophomores never refused our help. I think it was another one of those little things that helped connect us.

Our high school classmates formed into two lines that stretched out from the bus door, like a tunnel, and they patted us on the back, cheered, and called our names as we walked through. Only after all twelve of us had stepped onto the bus and were seated did they board. I liked the enthusiasm and the spirit that the students had added to our ride. The decision to allow students to ride the player bus had been a good one.

With all passengers seated and my watch reading 4:30, Coach closed the door, and as the bus began rolling forward from the school toward the first of several highways that would take us to our big game, every-one shouted out, "We are . . . J-Hawks! We are . . . J-Hawks! We are . . . J-Hawks!"

As soon as Pickett began strumming chords on his ukulele the bus quiet-ed down, allowing my teammates and me to relax and think about the game.

I followed my usual routine of visualizing myself making good passes and shooting perfect jump shots that always dropped through the center of the net, causing the net to celebrate each time with a little dance as the bas-ketball passed through, tickling its cords. I pictured myself dribbling hard to the basket and laying the ball gently against the backboard into the hoop, and on defense I saw myself aggressively shutting down the kid I was guarding so he could not get off any easy shots. I always played well in my mind games, and tonight was no exception.

I was totally focused . . . but very relaxed . . . almost drowsy.

Then, without any kind of warning, I lost my concentration, and my mind transported me away from basketball, and I began to remember wonderful times I had shared with Sarah Jenkins. Here Sarah and I were, starring in a mental movie, similar to the newsreel highlights that preceded the main feature in the theater. The first "story," complete with instrumental music, was about Sarah and me sitting in a movie theater watching *Swiss Family Robinson* on our first real date back in January. That led to a second movie, and I began to sing in my head some of the lyrics we had created after seeing *West-Side Story*. The newsreel then moved ahead and showed me looking at all the colorful drawings that Sarah had created in the valentine she had made for me, and that connected to dancing with Sarah at the Sweetheart Dance. This was followed by memories of the "Forever Heart" necklace that I had given Sarah as a gift on Valentine's Day, and then I thought about how she had captivated my heart on that Tuesday when she surprisingly showed up at our painting party with a pan of freshly baked brownies. The brownies then triggered memories of the winter picnic. Each story seemed to connect to the next one like the links on a chain.

All these memories passed through my mind so quickly, and I tried to slow everything down so I could enjoy more of the details and linger with the wonderful emotions I was feeling. I took a deep breath and held the air inside me for a few seconds before I exhaled slowly, allowing it to escape, and the newsreel slowed its pace and matched the rhythm of Sarah and me . . . swinging . . . in the park . . . by ourselves, . . . and no one else was near, because we were on our own little island that was completely surrounded by crusty old snow. Soon we were walking in the snow-covered alfalfa field on a winter hike, discovering tracks that had been left behind by small animals . . . then standing under a starlit sky on a cold winter night, listening to a distant hooting owl while holding hands and exhaling small foggy clouds into the air as we searched for the Big Dipper and the North Star amongst the thousands and thousands of twinkling stars that watched us from the heavens . . . and I thought about how absolutely wonderful this winter had been.

This may have been my best movie ever, and I had lost myself in it. I wanted it to continue, to start again at the beginning and replay everything, but I was awakened when the bus hit a bump in the road, and I bounced in my seat. Upon coming to, I looked around and saw that I was sitting inside a bus, and then I remembered that I was on my way to a basketball game.

My mental movie had come to a sudden end, and it was time to concentrate on the upcoming game again . . . but first I needed to adjust the focus on one more picture of Sarah that I would carry in my mind. I chose the night of the Sweetheart Dance, and I pictured how beautiful she was . . . radiant actually, and I prayed that the road of friendship upon which Sarah and I were traveling together . . . would never have any bumps in the road.

Tonight we would need to play our best game of the season, because we were going against Logan, a team that made it to the semi-finals in Des Moines last year, and they graduated only one player from that team. They had state tournament experience, and on our report card Garris had only given us a "B" in experience. We expected that we would be in for a tough game. We were definite underdogs, and we heard that many people, including a few from J-Hawk Nation, didn't give us much of a chance, kind of like David going against Goliath.

"How did David do?" I asked myself, and I managed a small grin. It could happen again tonight. We carry a good-sized bag of stones that we are very capable of slinging at Logan. The bigger they are . . .

We arrived with time to spare so we went into the gym and looked around. This place was huge! A large section of the Main Street business area of Jeffers could fit in here. The basketball court itself seemed small compared to the size of all the seating areas that surrounded it, and I hoped that having people sitting behind the baskets would not affect my shot by messing with my depth perception. I needed to have a great shooting night. All of us needed to play well if we wanted a chance to defeat the Lions.

I could tell we were a little tight during warm-ups. The senior captains became a little more vocal than usual, trying to loosen us up and replace some of our nervousness and blank expressions with smiles. Soon more of us were talking, and we added some spirit and a little laughter as we shot layups and jump shots. We weren't exactly fooling around, but we were now bordering on having fun.

"Just another game," Pickett said as he swished a fade-away jumper.

"The width of the lane . . . the height of the hoop . . . the distance from the top of the key to the basket . . . these are the same exact dimensions as in our gym in Jeffers," Laser pointed out loudly, trying to minimize the impact that the size of the gym may have had on many of us. "Isn't **that** a coincidence?"

As we stood by the bench awaiting introductions, I found Sarah in the bleachers, not too far from our player bench. She was sitting at the edge of the student section, right next to her parents. *The Jenkins family must have struck a compromise.*

Sarah smiled, gave me a slight wave, and touched her necklace . . . and I gave a single nod and returned a quick smile. With our coded messages completed, I looked away. We had talked about this before. I had told her that I was so glad that she came to our games, but while I played, I had to focus on the game itself, so I would not be thinking about her. I knew she understood. I did not play well if I couldn't concentrate, so I could not allow her to be a distraction. Tonight I would play the game . . . and she would watch . . . and when the game ended, the two of us would find each other, and we would laugh and talk about all sorts of things. Then . . . only after the game had ended . . . I would give her all of my attention.

After the introductions were made and Coach gave us our final instructions, we trotted out to the center circle for the opening tip. I shook hands with the two opponents who stood next to me as I took up a position at the circle.

This is it. You don't get to Des Moines without winning tonight. Play hard . . . have fun.

It didn't take long in the first quarter to discover that this was the best team we had faced all year. They could really shoot! In spite of our solid defense, they hardly ever missed a shot.

Every time we took possession of the ball, all five Lions sprinted down court. This limited our success on fast breaks, but we continued to run the ball. I could see in the faces of two or three Lions that they were not enjoying this run-back-every-time strategy, but they kept it up during the entire first quarter.

We mixed the full-court press with a half-court trap, pressuring the Lions each time after we scored. This resulted in two steals for us, and Logan threw one pass away, so we kept at it.

We learned quickly that the Lions couldn't cover our three tall guys very effectively with only two guys that were taller than six feet. They fronted Pickett with a six-footer, so we countered that by making quick passes into Abe and Hook, and they bounced the ball to Pickett. He did much of our scoring by working himself free for short-range jumpers. Laser and I each took some shots from out front to spread the defense, but Abe and Hook were quiet on offence, as each was closely covered by a six-four Lion, mirror twins, one right-handed and the other left-handed. Though on the slim side, each was a decent rebounder, but neither guy did much shooting. The three guards for Logan kept firing long jump shots, and they were so hot they sizzled. They hardly every missed, and they kept shooting and didn't work the ball inside.

Because there weren't many rebounds available, we weren't able to run much of a fast break. This meant we didn't get many easy baskets. We had to work hard for our shots, but after inbounding the ball after a Logan score, we pushed the ball down the court, forcing the Lions to either run with us or give up some easy layups. They chose to run.

When the buzzer sounded to end the first quarter, although we had played solidly and scored eighteen points, we were down by six, because the Lions had shot "lights out."

"Listen up, everyone," Coach said as we stood by the bench. "You played that first quarter very well. I'm pleased with your effort. The only problem is that our opponents are hitting all their shots. We need to keep running, find the open guy, and bury more of **our** shots. I don't think the Lions can keep shooting this well. Let's wear them down and make up the deficit two points at a time. We've got three quarters to catch them, so hang in there. Don't panic. Play hard . . . have fun."

Logan's shooters did begin to cool off a little in the second quarter, but they maintained their lead. We cut it to four points a couple times, but twice they stretched it to eight.

A couple minutes into the quarter, Coach moved Pickett to a low post and brought Abe and Captain Hook out higher. This gave Pickett lots of room under the bucket, and he carried our offence. It also pulled their two tall guys farther out from the basket than they wanted to be, so some times Abe and Hook were open to receive passes and take shots. Getting everyone involved in our offence gave us more ways to score, and with the Lions starting to miss shots occasionally, we played them pretty evenly during most of the second quarter.

Though we had continued to play well, we trotted to the locker room for our half-time break, still down by six points, and I wasn't sure we could play much better than we had. *How are we going to beat this team?*

We drank water and moved about the locker room, talking to each other about playing tighter defense.

I thought about how J-Hawk Nation was counting on us, and I remembered how great it felt to see all the black stocking caps at the winter picnic last Sunday in the park.

Then an idea came to me . . . all at once . . . not in pieces.

"Coach," I said, "do you remember that home game when I had trouble concentrating in the first half?"

"Yes, I do. I believe I sat you on the bench for most of that half," he replied. "You were of no use to us. You were lost on the floor."

"That's the night that Sarah came late, and you kept looking for her," Otto added. "You weren't able to focus on the game."

"Yeah," I said. "That was it exactly. My mind was on something other than basketball, and I didn't play well. I stunk it up in that half. I just thought of something that might cause the same thing to happen to the Lions . . . to mess up their focus and confidence."

"You're going to ask their girlfriends to leave the gym?" Tucson asked as everyone laughed.

"That might work, too," I replied, smiling, "but my idea is a little different. This should not affect anything that we do, but it might change the way that the Lions are playing."

"I'm listening," Coach said, "but we only have about five minutes before we head back out to the floor."

"We need to send for three sisters," I said quickly. "We need San Juan's sister, Otto's sister, and Maggie. They'll be an important part of this."

Coach nodded to Tucson who took off running.

"Sunday at the picnic I noticed all the J-Hawk Nation black stocking caps in the park," I said as we waited for Tucson to return. "Those caps were everywhere. My idea is about using those caps."

Tucson returned with the three girls.

"Hi," I said as the girls sat on a bench we had cleared for them. "Thanks for coming back with Tucson. I have a plan for how you can help us in the second half. Everyone here is hearing this for the first time, and I only have a few minutes. It's a very simple idea that might sidetrack the Lions a little. It involves having all the students wear their black stocking caps. Here goes.

"One of you needs to sit in the bleachers across the gym from our bench and student section," I continued. "You will need to keep your eyes on Treason because he will send you a signal each time we go back on defense in the third quarter, and your job will be to relay the signal to you other two who will be sitting in the student section."

"I'll watch for Treason's signal and pass it on," San Juan's sister volunteered.

"Good. Thanks," I said.

"Treason will give the signal with a white towel," I continued. "If he **holds** the towel in either or both hands, you need to put on your stocking cap as a signal to you other two sisters who will be sitting in the student section. Your job will be to organize the students and ask them to follow your cues with your J-Hawk Nation stocking caps. They need to put on their caps whenever you put yours on. They don't even need to know why. They just need to do it. When we players see all those caps on the heads of the students, we will fast break and run the ball hard. If Treason **rests** the towel anywhere . . . on the floor, his leg, or on the back of his neck, do not wear the black caps, and that will be our signal to rest the ball, to **not** run the ball. We'll slow everything down and work our plays."

"Coach, before we move back to defend our basket each time, tell Treason whether or not you want us to run when we next get possession of the ball," I said. "Treason can give his signal, and we'll know what to do by making a quick glance at the student section."

"The Lions will figure this out," Laser said. "It'll be too obvious. They'll know what we're doing. It won't work."

"We want them to figure it out," I replied. "We want them to think they are smarter than we are. During the third quarter I'm hoping they will focus some of their attention on those black caps, rely on our signal, and learn to trust it. They'll get to walk back on defense once in a while, so I'm thinking it will catch their interest. Meanwhile, we need to keep playing hard so they do not increase their lead."

"What about the fourth quarter?" Captain Hook asked.

"That's when the fun starts," I replied, and I quickly explained what we would change in the last quarter and how everything would hopefully play out.

"This just might work," Pickett said, "and it shouldn't hurt us in any way."

"Let's do it then," Coach said. "We were going to slow the ball down once in a while anyway just to make us more unpredictable. The black stocking caps might do the trick. Let's call on the power of J-Hawk Nation. You **can** win this game. You **can** defeat these Lions. The only reason they have a lead is because of their unconscious shooting percentage in the first quarter. We are now going to play our dominant half, and I believe we will catch them. Let's go."

"We are . . . J-Hawks!" we shouted as we rose to run out to the floor.

Abe mistimed his jump for the third quarter tipoff, and Number 30 for Logan tapped the ball toward his teammate, Number 20. He grabbed the basketball, and while he dribbled into his offensive end, I stole a quick glance toward the student section and saw no one wearing a black cap. *We'll be walking the ball down court when we get possession of the ball.*

Number 20 wasted no time. He launched a long jump shot, probably thinking he'd be just as hot as he was in the first half, but the ball hit the left side of the rim, and after bouncing a few feet into the air, landed in Abe's outstretched arms.

The five Lions immediately raced down-court to defend, but we J-Hawks took our time with the ball, dribbling slowly and making a couple passes. We were in no hurry this time. Though we had a chance to cut the deficit to four, we missed our opportunity when Pickett's 10-footer hit the back of the rim and bounced out.

Number 30 retrieved the rebound, pivoted, and dribbled to safety as we hustled back to cover. Again I looked at the student section, and just like last time, I saw bare heads. *We won't be running our fast break this time either.*

Number 20 was left open for a second, and upon receiving a teammate's pass, took one dribble and shot another jumper from way out. This time Captain Hook collected the rebound on the missed shot, and all five of the Lions sprinted down-court. Hook passed the ball to me, and I dribbled it as all five us walked to our end of the floor.

After several passes, Captain Hook was open just a few feet from the basket, and he banked in a hook shot, cutting the Lion lead to four.

As I ran back to defend, I noticed a whole bunch of black caps being worn by the students in the student section behind out bench. *Next possession we will be running the ball.*

We trapped at half-court, but it was tough for us to cover all five players in this huge gym, and by spreading out, the Lions were able to pass and dribble the ball into their end.

I was hoping that Number 20 would shoot another long one, but this time he passed the ball off. We kept shifting our zone, but after several passes, Number 11 caught a quick pass, found himself open, and banked in a short jump shot.

Pickett quickly grabbed the ball after it dropped through the hoop, and he stepped across the black line and tossed the basketball to Laser as Hook, Abe, and I raced the Lions down the court.

For the next few minutes of clock time, we traded baskets with the Lions, and we were unable to make up any ground. Whenever we gained possession of the basketball, we used the "caps on or caps off" signal to know whether Coach wanted us to run the ball down-court or walk it. By the time the quarter was about half gone, the Lions had figured out our signal, and after testing it to make sure they had it right, they began to trust it. Now they knew they could sometimes walk back to their end, and they took advantage of that knowledge. It was so obvious to me how all of the Logan players, including some of the bench players, looked at the J-Hawk Nation student section, and I saw a couple of the Lions sporting grins. I had to keep myself from grinning back, because this was working just as I hoped it would. The black caps had given the Lions something else to think about, something else to focus their attention on, and my teammates and I just kept on playing. I'm sure that our opponents were feeling confident about how smart they were . . . maybe even a little smug . . . and about how dumb we appeared to be.

When the third quarter ended, we trotted back to our bench, still down by six points, and as soon as we formed into our huddle, I said, "Don't give them any clues by what you say or what you show on your face. This is where we make up the deficit and take the lead. Just play our brand of J-Hawk basketball, and pay attention to the one change in the signal for the fourth quarter."

Coach said calmly, "All right, men, do not panic. Find the open man, and hit your shots. We'll be doing some running and some walking, and this may get a little confusing to the Lions if they continue watching for the black caps in the student section. Play tough defense, and take advantage of every-thing they give us. This fourth quarter . . . this is why we play basketball. We need one more quarter of playing hard and having fun."

"We are . . . J-Hawks!" we shouted as we departed our huddle, and the bareheaded student section's echo rocked the bleachers.

We now had only eight more clock minutes left in our season unless we could overcome this six-point deficit.

Abe stretched his right arm high as he leaped and tapped the center jump to Captain Hook who shoveled it off to Laser. We moved into our of-fensive positions and passed the ball around the perimeter. When the ball came back to me for a second time, I was wide open, having space and time to dribble once and set up my shot. As I jumped, I lifted the ball above my head and pushed it toward the hoop. The shot felt good. My eyes followed the flight of the spinning basketball as it sought out and found the center of the rim and dropped through, touching only the net. The J-Hawk bleachers erupted, and we moved back to set up our half-court trap.

Though we hadn't been able to make very many steals tonight, our trap was forcing them to work harder on offence, and we continued with our strategy.

I glanced quickly in the direction of our bench and student section, and I saw the signal. The students were now standing . . . with their arms crossed in front of them . . . black caps on their heads. I was prepared to run when we took possession of the ball.

The Lions made several passes after dribbling into their own end. This time they didn't appear to be satisfied with taking a long shot. They kept moving the ball around, and finally they found Number 30 free for a shot from about ten feet out. He banked it softly off the backboard into the basket, restoring their six-point lead.

Pickett quickly grabbed the ball, stepped across the end line with his left foot, lifted his right foot off the floor, and passed the ball in to Laser. All five of us sprinted down the floor, and the Lions ran with us. Captain Hook sneaked behind his defender after a couple of passes, and when I lobbed the ball to him, he shot a soft, short hook shot through the hoop, reducing the deficit again to just four points.

Laser called out for us to drop back into our end, and as we set up our zone defense, I looked toward the bench and spotted the signal. The students were seated, arms crossed, heads bare, and I knew we would run the ball when we next gained possession of it.

The Lion guards passed the ball back and forth as they looked inside, searching for an open man closer to the basket. Number 40 crossed the lane, collected a bounce pass, turned, and shot a twelve-footer that hit the front of the rim and fell into Pickett's hands. He pivoted and passed the ball sharply ahead to me near the sideline, and I tossed it down the floor, leading Laser to the basket for a layup, as the confused Lions were walking back to defend. They looked around at each other, and I could see puzzled expressions on their faces. It seems that they had expected us to walk the ball this time, and they had been surprised.

We were now behind by only one basket, and the Lion coach called for a timeout.

"Good job, men," Coach said as we arrived at the bench. "They were fooled that time. Now they are dealing with a little doubt for the first time in this game. Let's throw our full-court press at them as they inbound the ball,"

"We are . . . J-Hawks!" we shouted, and the students repeated, "J-Hawks!"

We pressed tightly, and this time Laser stepped in and made a steal when the ball was passed toward Number 22 who happened to be looking at our student section and did not see the ball being thrown to him.

Pickett set up near the foul line while Abe and Captain Hook took up positions closer to the basket. We made several quick careful passes . . . Laser to Pickett . . . to me . . . bounce pass to Hook . . . back to Pickett. Then Abe crossed the lane in front of his defender and grabbed Pickett's soft pass and laid the ball against the backboard, into the basket, tying the score at 72 all.

As I ran back toward our basket to defend, I saw that we would be running next time. Black caps were sitting on the heads of standing students whose arms were down at their sides. I was enjoying this.

The Lions began looking a little confused as they dribbled and passed the ball around, but they managed to break our press and moved the ball to their end. That look of confidence that they had worn earlier wasn't evident any longer.

We tightened everything up, not allowing the Lions much time to hold the ball. They had to do a lot of pivoting to find open teammates, and sometimes they panicked and rushed their passes, realizing that we would be blanketing them with our pressure defense. Number 20 attempted a cross-court pass that Pickett was able to deflect. The ball hit a Lion player on the leg and bounced out of bounds. Now we had a chance to take the lead.

Logan's players were in no hurry to shift back into their defensive end this time as they looked again toward our student section, and Laser threw the ball in to me. I slowly dribbled the ball into our own end, and watched as a grin formed on Number 33's face. The Lions had gotten this one right.

After four or five passes around the perimeter, Laser bounced the ball to Pickett at the free throw-line. Without any hesitation Pickett lifted his body into the air and launched his fade-away shot, and I started backing up as I watched the ball drop through the net for our first lead of the game.

J-Hawk Nation went wild.

As all five of us hustled back, I looked for the signal. *I got it.* The students were sitting, arms at their sides, heads bare. *I hope the Logan players keep trying to figure out our signal code.*

The confusion that I saw earlier on the faces of the Lions began to look more like fear now. They were behind in the score for the first time in the game, and it was affecting them. They looked unsure of themselves. Their passes were a little off, and the three guards who were so hot in the first half had cooled off and were more hesitant to shoot, especially since we were covering them so closely. The Lions kept passing, eventually getting the ball inside to the tall lefty, but Abe was on him like flies on flypaper, and when Number 30 attempted a shot, Abe's tough defense and great arm length forced the shooter to alter his shot, and it hit only air.

Captain Hook was in great position, and he grabbed the basketball before it hit the floor. He dribbled twice to get outside and fired a pass up-court to me. I dribbled another three or four times, then threw the ball ahead to Laser who had to beat one defender as he drove to the basket for a perfect layup, extending our lead to four.

"C'mon, you guys!" Number 33 yelled out. "Coach said to forget the black caps! We have to run back every time! Pay no attention to the black caps!"

The coach of the Lions called for a timeout, and we hustled over to our bench to huddle up.

"Those are mighty powerful J-Hawk Nation black stocking caps!" Coach said as he looked at me and smiled. "This did give the Lions something else to think about. This shows that the ability to focus is the key to playing your best. Now let's keep up the intensity for these last four minutes. We'll continue to switch between running the fast break and slowing things down, so keep checking for the signal. The student section has played well this second half, and we aren't going to change things, whether or not the Lions continue to be interested in our black stocking caps."

Momentum was now on our side. Logan's shooters turned cold, and we rebounded their missed shots. Our confidence was building, and I could feel the J-Hawk spirit driving our team.

With an eye on the clock, we kept passing the ball around the outside, only looking inside if it was wide open. We weren't comfortable with just a four-point lead. I expected the game would come down to free throws if we did not continue to score.

As I passed off to Laser, I saw Captain Hook move into the lane. Laser quickly returned my pass, and I bounced the basketball outside to Hook as he stepped from the lane and moved toward my sideline. He was immediately double-covered when my defender left me to assist in keeping Hook from getting off a ten-foot hook shot, and Captain Hook responded by bouncing a pass back to me.

For a split second I was open, and I was well within my range. I was so sure that my shot would fall that I considered closing my eyes, just like I had done on the bus on the way to the game when I had taken this same shot numerous times in my mind, and I had never missed, but I kept my eyes open, and I saw the basketball float toward the hoop in slow motion. The gym had turned perfectly silent, and I watched the backward spin of the ball as it arced, and then I heard the snap of the net's cords as the basketball dove through the center of the net, increasing our lead to six, and J-Hawk Nation jumped to their feet and filled our side of the bleachers with applause and cheers.

We were feeling it now . . . the chance to extend our season for at least one more game . . . and the trip to Des Moines where that semi-final game would be played. With about three-and-a-half minutes left . . . and with us holding a six-point lead . . . we knew **we** would not be the team that might panic.

Laser called for full-court pressure. With Lion confidence dwindling and ours on the rise, this was a great call. Number 30 ran around, completely out of control, trying to get open for the inbound pass. After he caught the ball and almost stepped out of bounds, he dribbled as fast as he could toward Logan's basket, as if he were determined to win this game by himself, but Laser and I trapped him at the center line. Looking very frustrated, Number 30 jumped and tossed the ball down-court, but Captain Hook happened to be patrolling that area and he had no trouble reaching out like a wide receiver, snatching the ball out of the air. After protecting the ball, he dribbled toward me and delivered the basketball into my hands.

"Nice grab," I said to him. "That looked a lot like one of those touchdown catches at recess from a few years back. I wish **I** had thrown that ball."

Hook flashed one of his infrequent smiles.

We weren't in any hurry now, but we made quick passes . . . careful passes. For the remainder of the game we would keep the ball away from Logan, and we would shoot the ball only if the result would be a guaranteed two points.

Four of us stood like we were at the corners of a big square, and Pickett stood inside, moving quickly toward the player who held the ball, and our passes burned almost a minute off the clock. Pickett's movement meant that we always had three options for making passes . . . to the left, to the right, or to the inside. Number 40 fell asleep for an instant, and Captain Hook sprinted behind him to the basket. Pickett saw his run and bounced him a perfect pass that Hook collected and laid softly against the backboard for an easy layup. It was a good trade. We scored two points, and the Lions were given the ball. This was a trade that any team would make at any time.

About two minutes remained in the game. As I hustled back on defense I saw that we would run on our next possession. As the Logan dribbler reached the centerline, Laser and I moved out with our hands up, trying to stall their offence. Number 30 was able to pass the ball off to Number 20, and he took a very long jump shot that swished through the net.

Oh, no. I hope he's not heating up again.

Laser quickly dribbled the ball to our end, and we formed the square again, passing and dribbling the basketball, keeping it away from Logan's defenders. This time Pickett made another great play. After catching Laser's pass, he set up to pass off to Abe, but instead, he pivoted left and drove to the basket past an unsuspecting Number 40 and scored on a clean layup that built our lead to eight.

As I sprinted back on defense, I caught the signal that told me we would not be running the ball next time. The students were standing, arms crossed, black caps sitting very visibly atop their heads, and this time I grinned.

I stepped out and closely covered Number 20. I was determined to keep him from getting a good look at the basket. With the seconds on the clock

ticking away and desperation setting in, the Lion launched a bad shot, showing none of the rhythmical shooting touch he had displayed in the first half,
and the ball fell well short of the rim and into Captain Hook's sure hands.

We now held the ball and an eight-point lead, and the clock was winding
down. With sure, quick passes we kept the ball away from Logan's players
who were seeing their season slip away from them as they chased around in
pursuit of the basketball.

As I suspected would happen, Logan began to foul us, hoping to trade
missed free-throw attempts for possession of the ball, but the strategy did
not work for them. Laser and I each hit both shots of a one-and-one, and
Number 30 made one jump shot and missed another, and when the buzzer
sounded to end the game, the scoreboard showed in its bright lights that
we had earned a ten-point victory. The last quarter had changed the game
completely.

We didn't over-react at the buzzer. All five of us just trotted to the
bench like we had expected to win this game, giving a few back slaps on the
way, but there were some smiling faces in the huddle before we returned
to the floor for the handshakes. When we arrived back at the bench, Laser
and Pickett led us over to the student section, and we stood in our line and
applauded all these friends of ours who were also standing and clapping and
cheering, and I noticed the huge smiles that were decorating their faces as
well as the black stocking caps that crowned their heads.

I looked at Sarah and saw her wipe her eyes. All I could do was smile to
her and nod my head. Later I would thank her with a hug.

The student section had done well in helping us win this game, and
their reward would be the same as ours. All of us would be traveling to Des
Moines this weekend for the final games of the state tournament.

Tonight's second game would be starting soon, so we had to clear the
bench area and head for the showers. I knew I would hustle because there
would be members of J-Hawk Nation waiting for us in the lobby . . . and I
would be sure to wear my black stocking cap.

I was the first one into the shower, the first to dry off and dress, and the
first to have my duffle bag packed with all my wet gear. I wanted to get out

of the locker room and go to the lobby area where all the people of J-Hawk Nation would be waiting . . . where Sarah would be waiting, . . . but I wasn't going to walk out there alone like some kind of hero.

"Come on you guys," I prodded. "The people from Jeffers have a long drive ahead of them. They won't wait forever. Hurry up!"

"Have a little patience, Catch," Laser replied. "She'll be standing there with the others when we come out."

It must have been about five more minutes until everyone was ready . . . a long five minutes. Laser and Pickett stepped to the door, paused to make sure everyone and everything was packed up and nothing was being left behind, then they led us out. We exited in a controlled single file, walking the sideline of the gym as the two Class A teams were warming up for the next game, and we entered the packed lobby to all kinds of cheering and applause.

The spontaneous celebration was very loud. Grownups and classmates and young kids congratulated us and shook our hands and patted us on our backs. I know I was beaming, and I kept saying "Thank you" and "Thanks for coming to the game and cheering for us." This went on for a couple minutes, and all that time I was looking around for Sarah.

When Bobby came up to me, I asked him, " Have you seen her?"

"Seen who?" he asked, smiling.

"Sarah!" I replied, and I'm sure he could tell I was a little exasperated at his attempt at humor.

"She's with her parents, right over there in the back," he said, pointing over to my right. "Mom and Dad are talking with them about going to Des Moines."

I worked my way through the crowd, talking to several more people on the way, and I finally found Sarah. As soon as she saw me she reached out and gave me a quick hug. "You did it!" she said excitedly. "You won! Now you get to play in Des Moines! Congratulations! I am so happy for you!"

"Thanks," I replied. "This was a tough one tonight. After the way Logan came out shooting early in the game, I didn't think we stood much of a chance, but we hung in there and did all right."

"Tell me about the black stocking caps," Sarah said. Your sister told me that this was all your idea . . . a way to make the Lions lose some of their focus."

"Yeah, I did come up with this plan at halftime. It just came to me, and I know it was because I have had experience knowing what can happen to a player who is not able to concentrate . . . a player who is too concerned about something else and then loses his focus on the game," I said smiling. "Logan's players got caught up in the black caps, kept looking to see what you guys were doing in the student section, continued trying to figure out what your actions meant, and it caused them to make mistakes. That's all it was. You and the other kids of J-Hawk Nation helped us win tonight, Sarah. It took all of us tonight."

"I got this paper from your coach. It tells when you play and where people can stay," Sarah continued. "I saw Dad talking to Coach, and he took a paper, too. Maybe we'll be talking about this on the drive home."

"I really hope you can come to our next game. You've earned a trip to Des Moines because of all the other games you've watched," I suggested. "Do you remember when you told your family that maybe you were our good luck charms? I think you are. We've never lost a game that you've attended."

"You've not lost a game, period," Sarah said as she laughed.

"That's true," I responded, "but you don't have to remind your folks about that part. Let me know if you need my help in convincing your parents to travel to Des Moines for the weekend, or is it maybe better if I don't talk to them at all about this?"

Sarah smiled, and I wasn't sure what that meant.

"I'll call you tomorrow morning at 7:30 to tell you what I know," Sarah said.

"I'll keep my fingers crossed," I said as I crossed fingers on both hands.

Coach called for attention, and the crowd quieted. "We've got a two-hour drive ahead of us . . . and we have school tomorrow," he announced. "It's time to board the bus and sing our way home."

I moved closer to Sarah, reached for her hand, and whispered to her, "I'm really glad you came to the game tonight. I'll be sitting by the phone tomorrow morning, awaiting your call."

"Good night," Sarah said as she squeezed my hand, and I looked deeply into her sparkling eyes. Then I turned around and noticed that the high school kids and my teammates were already out the door. I had to hustle or I would be the last one to get on the bus.

Somehow I had been distracted.

In the Stands – With John Garris

There were times during the fourth quarter that I wasn't even watching the action on the floor in the basketball game between the Logan Lions and the Jeffers J-Hawks. I was too distracted. I was so busy trying to figure something out, writing down all the possible combinations in my notebook and analyzing my list, that I missed part of the game being played between two fine teams.

In the third quarter it had been obvious to me what was happening in the student section of J-Hawk Nation, and the Lions figured it out also. When the students from Jeffers wore their black J-Hawk Nation stocking caps, the J-Hawks would race the basketball to their basket at top speed, and when the caps were off their heads, the team would slow the ball down and play a more controlled half-court offence.

The Lions broke the code and learned that they didn't have to run back at full speed to defend when the caps were in hands rather than on heads. I could tell by their smiles that they appreciated being told exactly when they could merely trot back on defense and not be burned on a fast break. Things were working well, and the Lions maintained their six-point lead.

In the fourth quarter, however, the game began to change. The actions in the bleachers became more complex, and I could not understand what everything meant: cap on or cap off, standing up or sitting down, arms folded across the chest or hanging by their sides. When exactly do the J-Hawks run? When do they slow the offence down? It appeared that the Lions were as confused as I was, and the focused J-Hawks began cutting into the deficit. A couple of times the Lions were caught off guard when they casually turned to defend their basket, and they were beaten down-court by J-Hawk fast breaks. Twice the Lions threw the ball away because a player was paying more attention to the J-Hawk Nation student section than he was to the action on the floor.

While I kept studying the various combinations of actions

I had written down in my notebook, the distracted Lions began to panic and started to fall apart ... and the J-Hawks continued to play disciplined basketball. With about four minutes left to play in the game, the boys from Jeffers took the lead for the first time.

I never did figure out the fourth-quarter code, but I did observe its effect: the Lions became more concerned about understanding the J-Hawk Nation actions in the bleachers than the game itself, and the game got away from them. They lost by ten points.

I sought out a reliable source after the game had ended, but all I was told was that none of the students' actions in the fourth quarter had meant anything. All of the calls for running or slowing things down had been made from the bench by the coach.

Come on! Really? It was nothing more than a distraction? I can understand how the Lions had gotten caught up in it because the same thing had happened to me. I had become sidetracked, and I lost focus . . . and so had the team from Logan. There was one huge difference concerning outcomes, however. I still got to write my column, but the basketball season came to an end for the Lions.

With this win, the J-Hawks have extended their winning streak to 25 games, and they have earned an invitation to play for the Class B State Championship in Des Moines this weekend.

Chapter 52
Making Good Decisions

I hustled with my chores on Wednesday morning so I would be cleaned up, fed, and ready for Sarah's call. At exactly 7:30 the phone rang, and I quickly picked up the receiver and sat down at the desk.

'Hello," I said.

"Hi," Sarah said. "Good morning."

"Yes, it is. Getting an early morning call from you makes this a **very** good morning," I replied. "I hope you know how much I enjoy talking with you on the phone. Maybe we should stay home from school and talk all day. Do you think anyone would miss us at school?"

"I know you are not serious, and you would definitely be missed at school," Sarah answered. "I would probably be missed, too, and my parents would ground me for a long time . . . and I might not ever get to see you again."

"Whoa! Then that's a very bad idea," I admitted, "but someday I want to be with you the whole day and not share you with anyone. I'll just admire your beautiful smile and listen to your wonderful laugh, and we'll take a long walk and talk about everything."

"That would be a great day," Sarah said. "I look forward to that time."

"What did you find out last night?" I asked.

"We discussed the possibility of going to Des Moines on Friday and staying for two nights in a hotel, but we still have several things to work out," Sarah explained. "For one thing, Mom and I need to check with Mr. Weston to see if I can get the day off from school, and Mom would need to get a substitute teacher for Friday. We hope that Mr. Weston will understand how important this is to our family. He knows that we've gone to almost all your games this year. I'm really glad you talked with him on the phone last month, and that he had a chance to meet you in person at the Sweetheart Dance."

"Hopefully his second impression of me was better than his first," I said laughing.

Sarah joined in my laughter. "Are you as tired as I am this morning?" Sarah asked. "I had a hard time falling asleep last night because I was still so excited about your big win. This morning I didn't even hear my alarm, so Mom had to come in to wake me."

"My brain wouldn't shut down last night when I tried to fall asleep," I replied. "I kept replaying the fourth quarter in my head, and I started thinking about playing for the championship in Des Moines. I hope I can stay awake in class today."

"I'll be going to bed early tonight, as soon as I finish my homework," Sarah said. "Will you call me tonight and tell me everything you find out in school? Then I can tell you how our plans are working out. Please call early, okay? I'll be waiting."

"All right. Stay awake today," I said. "Thanks for calling. Good-bye."

Talking to Sarah got my day off to a great start, but the day really dragged on in school. Besides being really tired, I was very restless. I had a hard time sitting still when Coach met with the team in the locker room immediately after attendance, when he explained the schedule for the week and talked to us about appropriate behaviors and making good choices while we are staying in Des Moines. He said the expected things about being smart about getting our sleep this week and eating well, and that he didn't want anyone going off by himself in the city. Coach reminded us that everything was about basketball, and that he and the Supe would not allow boys and girls to be in hotel rooms together at any time unless parents were present.

Later in the morning the Supe addressed all the high school kids who had signed up to ride the bus and stay in Des Moines for the two nights, so we players had to hear everything again. I understood everything the first time . . . I didn't need to hear this lecture twice. I was feeling so sleepy that I almost stood up and walked to the back of the assembly room in order to make sure I didn't doze off.

The teachers didn't work us too hard on Wednesday, and we did have time in study hall to complete most of our homework. I'm guessing that

Coach and the Supe explained to the teachers that the team needed lots of rest over the next two days, and it appeared that everyone was cooperating.

Before we were excused to basketball practice at the end of the day, the Supe reminded all the high school kids that they needed to bring in a parent signature and their money tomorrow in order to ride the player bus to the game on Friday and have a place in the hotel arranged for them. Then he gave a pretty stern warning to all of us.

"Don't even bother with any of this if you plan to use tobacco or alcohol on this trip," he announced. "If you ignore this rule your parents will be called, and you will be sent home. You will also lose all school privileges for the remainder of the year. All of you are intelligent kids. Use common sense, and make good decisions.

Coach didn't run us too hard at practice. He treated this more like a recovery day, just like we players had used our extra practice time on Saturday mornings as we were preparing for our clinics. After running easy layup drills and full-court grapevine weaving, we worked on our shooting. It was a pretty quiet gym, and all of us appeared to be a little worn out, but we were still quite focused.

We partnered up for a few minutes so Laser, Tucson, San Juan, and I could work on making good passes inside to Captain Hook, Abe, Pickett, and Otto. We concentrated on the timing of the passes so the ball would be in the player's hands exactly at that moment when he became free, and he could immediately step into shooting with perfect rhythm.

Four times during practice Coach called a timeout and sent us to the free-throw line to take some foul shots. He wanted us shooting while we were sweaty and maybe breathing harder, like we probably would be when we went to the line during a game.

As I rebounded for San Juan, I wished Garris had been here to watch our practice. Early in the year he had been very critical of Coach's inexperience, but I think Garris would have seen today that Coach had really grown into this job. Coach was smart, and he understood the game and all of us players. Except for that one game when he had benched several of us, he had been an outstanding leader, and I don't think we could have come this far without him. He was in charge, but he listened to us, gave us opportunities to suggest ideas, and allowed us to play a style of basketball that excited us and used our strengths. I don't think this would have happened with our previous coach or anyone else. A different coach probably would not have allowed us to have fun with all our extra stuff, and that might have kept us from developing the spirit that really contributed to our success this season.

After completing my chores, eating supper, and finishing my small amount of homework, I called Sarah. It was still early in the evening so I expected that Sarah would still be working on her school stuff. She answered after just a couple rings.

"Hello," she said.

"May I please speak with Sarah Jenkins?" I asked.

She started laughing. "Are you feeling goofy from lack of sleep?" she asked.

"No, I'm actually okay," I replied. "I just wanted to hear some laughter . . . and it worked. How are you doing?"

"Great," Sarah replied. "Things are falling into place, and we're going to Des Moines for the weekend. We'll be there for the afternoon game on Friday, and we're staying two nights . . . in the same hotel as your family, your team, and all the kids from Jeffers."

"Outstanding!" I said excitedly. "Will Mr. Weston excuse you for missing school on Friday?"

"Not exactly," Sarah answered. "He explained to Mom and me that because of school policy, I would have to make up some hours that I will be missing on Friday if I don't want my grades to be affected."

"What exactly does that mean?" I asked.

"Next week, from Monday through Thursday, I need to stay after school for an extra hour each day," Sarah replied.

"That doesn't sound fair," I said. "I don't like this. Staying after school is for kids who mess up. You shouldn't have to do this."

"I don't mind," Sarah replied. "It'll be just like an extra study hall, and it means that I will get to see your game. It's worth it, and teachers won't lower my grades."

"Hopefully you'll still make the "A" Honor Roll, or I'll be in serious trouble with your parents," I said.

Sarah laughed again. "Everything will be fine. Don't worry about it. What did you find out in school today?" she asked.

"Quite a few things," I replied. "Most of the high school kids are riding the player bus with us and staying in the hotel. We're leaving at eight o'clock Friday morning. All of us high school students are invited to a spaghetti dinner at the church on Thursday night. The town merchants are feeding us as a thank you for bringing attention to Jeffers.

"Let's see . . . what else?" I continued. "Oh, yes . . . Coach told us that we'll be four players to a room in the hotel, and that the school was given money for our meals. We'll eat together most of the time, but each of us will be given some meal money for the times we eat on our own."

"Sounds great!" Sarah said.

"I think so, too, but to make sure we don't have too much fun, we were given some rules to follow," I said. "They are just common sense things . . . and they don't bother me."

"My parents gave me a few rules to follow, too," Sarah said.

"I expected they would," I added. "I know I'll also hear a few things from my folks. No one wants any trouble. I'll call again tomorrow night if your parents don't mind. I'm really glad you're going to make it to the game . . . but I still don't like it that you have to stay after school next week."

Sarah laughed. "It's okay. I'm making a choice," she explained. "Yes, call tomorrow and tell me about anything that's changed, and maybe I'll know more, too. Thanks for calling early tonight. This is so exciting! I can't wait! Good-bye."

School was great on Thursday. All the talk was about the state tournament. The Supe told us that he was closing Jeffers School on Friday, like a "Snow Day," but this one would be called a "Basketball Day." It would be the first . . . and the last in the history of our school.

I felt really good at practice. Our spirit was great, and Coach ran us hard but not too long. We took lots of shots, and everyone wore smiles as well as the new T-shirts that Laser and Pickett had given us this morning. The black shirts had the statement "NOT DONE YET!" printed on the front in white letters. We believed what the shirts said.

The spaghetti dinner was good, and when Maggie and I returned home, I called Sarah. Neither of us had any new information to share so it was a short phone call. Then I listened to some music and read for an hour. Bedtime came early.

On Friday morning we started loading into the bus at about a quarter-to-eight. All the bags and small suitcases, including the two duffle bags I had with me, were tucked under the seats. Right at eight, the bus pulled out with Coach behind the wheel and the Supe sitting right behind him. As Coach turned the corner onto Main Street and headed east out of town, we noticed lots of people standing on the sidewalks in front of the stores. They all waved as we passed by. Many students lowered bus windows, and we shouted, "We are . . . J-Hawks! We are . . . J-Hawks! We are . . . J-Hawks!"

I heard someone yell, "Bring back a big trophy!"

We cheered as we drove out of town, and then the windows were pushed back up to shut out the cold air. I quickly closed my letter jacket tightly around me and tried to warm up.

It would be a long three-hour ride, and I knew I would not be able to visualize about the game for this whole trip. I would prepare myself with my mental pictures toward the end of the ride. For now I would think . . . and maybe sleep.

The bus quieted down as it rolled along toward Mason City and the high-ways beyond. Pickett's ukulele remained in a bag under his seat, and students settled into their seats and either slept or engaged in quiet conversations.

Of course I thought about Sarah right away. I was very pleased that she was coming to the game, but it still bothered me that she would have to pay for missing a day of school by having to make up hours after school next week. I tried to think of something I could do to help her. All I could come up with was for us to win. Maybe that would make it worth it . . . but I felt like I was really the person who was responsible for Sarah missing school. I couldn't find any fairness in her penalty.

I reflected on what Coach had told us about making good decisions, and I realized that that's what the game of basketball is all about. You have to decide when to pass and when to shoot . . . when to drive to the hoop. You need to make good choices about when you should try to take the charge or when you should let the dribbler go by and get picked up by a teammate. Everything is about decisions. When should you run the fast break all the way to the basket . . . and when should you pull up and wait for help? Who should be taking the shots? All of these situations involved making good decisions.

My mind wandered to the farm, and it struck me that while growing up, I had made many decisions every day. I think I mostly had made good choices because, though I had played hard, I had never broken any bones. Sure I had stepped on a nail or two . . . had been cut by barbed wire a few times . . . had scratched up my arms and legs while running in the woods, and sometimes I even got scraped up when I tipped over on my bike or fell out of a tree, but these were all normal injuries that happened to most active kids.

I remembered the day that the low black clouds rushed toward me as I was out plowing in the south field. I had decided that I could make one more round with the tractor before the storm would hit, but I was wrong, and as I was driving back, darkness and strong winds surrounded me. Quickly I killed the tractor and jumped down and lay on the ground, as low as I could get in the furrow, and I dug my arms into the moist black dirt around the tractor tire, and I held on with all my strength while the wind shook me and the rain pelted me. I was terrified.

Time seemed to stand still as I held on, but eventually the strong storm passed over me, and I stood up, shaking from fear and the cold, and I looked at all the dirt and mud that clung to me, and I managed to laugh a little at myself as I recovered. It had not been wise to attempt one more round with the plow, but at least I had been smart enough to shelter myself a little by digging in under the tractor instead of trying to run for it. I had rescued myself. That's what I took from that experience. My good decision had saved me.

Then I thought of another time, later that same fall, when I was again plowing, but this time it was in the field with the deep ditch. I had driven the tractor too close to the edge of the ditch before I should have raised the plow and made my turn, so I slammed on the brakes. I had put myself in quite a predicament. I didn't think I had enough distance ahead of me and enough time to move forward, raise the plow, and make a safe turn, so I shut the tractor down.

I saw that I had two choices here, and neither one was a good one. I could quit for the day without getting much done, walk back to the house, wait for Dad to return from his job, and explain the situation with the tractor and the ditch. There would not be a happy ending to this. Dad would probably yell at me, ground me for a few days, and maybe even penalize me by withholding some of my meager allowance. Then we'd both walk to the ditch where Dad would rescue the tractor and plow as I watched. I knew he had the skill to do this.

The second choice had a limited potential for success on my part, but if my effort failed, it would be a disaster. Maybe I could make it. Maybe I could coax the plow to rise out of the black earth as I slowly drove the tractor forward, then once the plow was out of the ground I could quickly slam on the left brake and spin the steering wheel to the left and make the turn. There was a chance I could do it, but if I didn't make it, the tractor and I would plummet to the bottom of the ditch, and quite possibly the tractor would roll over. Dad would certainly yell at me (unless he found me trapped under the tractor), I would be grounded, and allowance would be withheld. This choice could damage the tractor, cause great bodily injury, and delay our work in the field . . . but I just might be able to pull it off.

I considered the two choices and made my decision.

When Dad returned home after work, I told him what had happened with the tractor, and he and I walked silently down to the end of the field where the tractor and the ditch were waiting. I watched as Dad mounted the Allis, jockeyed it back and forth while the plow slowly lifted itself above the black earth, and then he cranked the steering wheel hard left while stomping on the left brake, making a successful ninety-degree turn with about a foot to spare. I almost cheered. I knew he could do it.

Dad called to me to jump up on the tractor and sit on the left fender, and as he drove home, he gave me the unnecessary advice about not getting so close to the ditch next time. I nodded in agreement, just out of respect. He surprised me when he told me I had made a good decision in not attempting to make the turn myself. I managed to smile this time. A wise decision had rescued me a second time while plowing, and . . . for the record . . . there was no yelling, no grounding, and no loss of allowance.

Life on a farm . . . and basketball . . . it was all about making good decisions, and in this afternoon's State Tournament game, I would be making many decisions that I hoped would help our team win this game and put us into the championship game tomorrow night.

Chapter 53
Not Done Yet

The bus rolled along, and the rhythmical sound of the tires on the pavement caused me to close my eyes, and I guess I fell asleep. I don't know how long I was out, but I woke up when San Juan nudged me and told me that we were closing in on Des Moines.

I sat up straighter and began looking out the partially frosted windows to my right and to my left. I noticed that the farms that were once here had been replaced over the years by warehouses, trucking companies, and other businesses, and I knew that soon I would be seeing many houses and apartment buildings . . . and eventually the core of the city. I tried to picture in my mind how different this city would appear from our small town of Jeffers, with its population of 340 people, and its total area of about 12 square blocks worth of old houses and small family businesses.

I had been watching the passing landscape for only a few minutes when the Supe turned around in his seat right behind Coach and announced to everyone on the bus, "In about twenty-five or thirty minutes we'll reach Veterans Auditorium. Coach and the team will go check out the basketball floor when we arrive, while the rest of us will remain in or near the bus. Players . . . you might want to eat your bag lunch now, but the rest of you can wait until Coach parks the bus. After the team checks out the auditorium, we'll drive to the hotel, do an early check-in, and drop off our bags. At two o'clock we'll head back to Veterans Auditorium for the game, leaving us plenty of time to find our way around and to prepare for the biggest game that the Jeffers J-Hawks have ever played."

"We are . . . J-Hawks!" someone shouted from one of the bus's middle seats.

As I ate my sandwich, cold chicken on Mom's homemade bread, lightly salted, I began to think about our upcoming game. I was able to picture myself taking jump shots with perfect rhythm from my favorite spots on the floor, and the basketball always found the center of the hoop, snapping the net as the ball dived through toward the floor. I reviewed my defensive stance, seeing myself sliding my feet quickly as I crouched low and held my arms up and out, waving them often in an attempt to confuse the player I was guarding and limit his options. I visualized making perfect passes to Laser, leading him to the bucket for layups, and then I reversed the picture . . . Laser passed to me, and I kissed the ball off the backboard into the net. Everything was clear in my mind, and I felt very confident.

Veterans Auditorium was huge, much bigger than where we had played in Waterloo on Tuesday night and earned our way here, and the hotel looked to me to be a palace. We got checked in, and we found our rooms. I played the role of Goldilocks, trying out all four of the beds until I found the best one for me. Then I lay down for a short resting period.

The Supe came around to the players' room with some apples, oranges, and cookies just before two o'clock, so we ate a light snack before leaving for our game.

By now the excitement was really building. In a little more than two hours the biggest game of our lives would begin, and I sensed that we were ready. Everyone appeared to be relaxed . . . not one of us was throwing up or looking nervous. All of my teammates looked confident, as did Coach, who moved around to the three of our rooms, checking on us and joking with us, making sure we were feeling loose. He visited my room for a few minutes, and he told San Juan, Otto, Tucson, and me, "We'll need all four of you to play your best game today. Give everything you've got. Run hard, and make good choices. We'll leave for the game in just a few minutes."

Coach parked the bus in a lot right next to Veterans Auditorium, and the students exited the bus first and formed another tunnel. They kept repeating, "We are . . . J-hawks!" as all twelve of us players walked through, carrying our duffle bags and the other gear. Coach led our team to the back entry door where a security guard checked us in, and the Supe directed the students to the main doors where he would pick up the tickets and hand them out.

The early game was at the midpoint of the first quarter when we walked in, so we sat down in the bleachers and watched until halftime. I knew we would be playing one of these teams tomorrow afternoon in the 3rd-place game, or we would face the other team in the evening's championship, but I couldn't focus on how either team was playing. We had our own game to win first. There was no reason to get ahead of ourselves.

I did notice, however, that one of the teams had a really tall player. Dressed in the team's green uniforms, he looked like a redwood standing among a small forest of pine trees. He didn't impress me as far as being very athletic . . . but I guess that's the way it is for most redwood trees. He did manage to grab some rebounds without much of a jumping effort, and he banged in a few shots off the backboard, all because he was so tall. *It could be interesting if we play against him.*

As we stripped off our clothes in the locker room, I saw that all twelve players had worn their "NOT DONE YET!" black T-shirts as undershirts today, just like Laser had ordered us to do. I laughed when I saw Coach unbutton his dress shirt to show that he also was wearing the black T-shirt. I'm guessing that Laser gave that order, too.

All of us started moving around the locker room, shaking hands and patting backs, and we repeated the words we read on the shirts. "NOT DONE YET!" could be heard across the entire room, and everyone spoke with pride and certainty.

We dressed in our gold T-shirt style jerseys that said "J-Hawks" across the front, and then after slipping on the gold shorts and the gold socks, I put on my warm-up pants and my "ushering jacket." I could feel the smile forming on my face as I thought of the first night I had laid eyes on Sarah . . . and now we are at season's end, and Sarah and I have become best friends. Much of that credit goes to my warm-up jacket . . . and a clean pair of sweat socks. It's a funny world out there.

After pulling on my tennis shoes and double knotting the laces, I was ready. One-by-one my teammates finished up and sat down on one of the four long benches.

"All right," Coach announced when he saw that all us were dressed and ready. "I've invited a guest to come into the locker room to share some basketball wisdom with you before we run out for warm-ups. Otto, please check to see if he's outside the door."

"Who am I looking for, Coach?" Otto asked.

"You'll know when you see him," Coach replied.

I immediately turned my head and watched as Otto opened the door, and I heard Otto say in surprise, "Mr. Garris . . . come in."

It was John Garris, and he walked in and shook hands with Coach. I smiled when I noticed his black T-shirt that read "NOT DONE YET!" I wondered if that meant that he hadn't finished his column for tomorrow.

"As a favor to me . . . to us . . . John did a little checking on our today's opponent," Coach began. "He informed me yesterday that the Compton Comets, in a direct contradiction to their name, like to slow the game down. They have three front-court players that stand 6'2" or 6'3," and they are accustomed to grabbing most of the missed shots in a game. They often rely on their second or third shots to score points. The Comets struggled early in the season as they searched for their identity, first as a running team, later as a more deliberate team, and they have been defeated eight times this year. Most of those losses happened early in the season. To get to today's game, they've had to build a winning streak of at least seven games so do not take them lightly.

"I'm afraid I've got some bad new for the Comets," Coach continued. "They won't be collecting most of the rebounds today, and they won't be walking much on that gym floor out there either. We'll be pressuring them on defense and running them to death with our fast break. We'll dictate the pace of the game, and I don't believe they'll take much comfort in the speed at which we'll play. This may not be a fun afternoon for them. John, what would you like to say to these young men?"

"Thanks for this opportunity, Coach," Mr. Garris said. He looked into our eyes, nodding and smiling, and then he began to speak. "As you know, I've watched many of your games this year, and over the course of the season, I've become a believer. Because of your speed and your shooting touch . . . your tight defense with presses and traps . . . your toughness in establishing your position under the basket which has allowed you to harvest all those rebounds . . . your never-give-up attitude . . . the unselfish way you men play as a team . . . because of all these attributes, I knew several games ago, that there was a very good chance that I would get to watch you play for the championship here in Des Moines."

Garris continued. "The opportunity you have today may never come your way again. Make the most of it. Play this game like you have played all the others. Show people in the crowd who have not yet had a chance to see one of your games what J-Hawk spirit means. Play with all of your skills, all of your speed, your determination and confidence . . . and your pride. Play **your** game. You've been a great story this year. I've really enjoyed following you and writing about your success. You have more people pulling for you than you can ever imagine. Thousands of kids and grownups in the gym and around the state of Iowa will be cheering for you today and hoping that you add another game onto that impressive winning streak. Play your hearts out . . . and win this game for J-Hawk Nation."

As Garris's words sank in, all of us began applauding. I stood up, walked over to Garris, and extended my hand. "Thanks for believing in us," I told him, and then I watched as my teammates followed my path and also shook Garris's hand. I heard several players thank him for his words today, and many said we'd play our best.

"Well, men," Coach said as everyone took a seat again, "it's time to go out, sweat up those bodies, and add another game to your winning streak. Play your game. Trust your teammates, and give everything you've got. Play with confidence . . . and remember . . . play hard, have fun."

"We are . . . J-Hawks!" everyone shouted, and we ran out to warm up.

The auditorium was packed. I looked at the student section behind our bench as we ran by to our end, and I did catch a quick glimpse of Sarah and her parents. *I'm glad she's here.* I also heard Mom and Dad shout encouragement, and I saw lots of familiar faces I knew from Jeffers. *It looks like the whole town turned out.*

As we warmed up with layups from the right side, then the left, I discovered that this floor was kind to a dribbled basketball, and both the rim and the backboard seemed to be friendly to my soft shots. When we switched to shooting jump shots, I found the hoop to be a great target as most of my shots found the center of the net and dropped through. The seating area behind the backboard did not distract me, and I had hopes that I would have a great shooting afternoon.

After the rosters for both teams were introduced, we met at the bench for Coach's final instructions. As I stood in the huddle, preparing to listen to Coach, I looked into the eyes of Pickett and Laser, Captain Hook and Abe, and I didn't see even a hint of worry. It looked to me like a quiet kind of confidence . . . exactly like I was feeling. If we played well, I knew we would win this game because we were a team . . . a really good team . . . and our school and our town were counting on us.

"You can do this," Coach stated confidently. "Play hard, and have fun. Use your speed and defensive pressure . . . make the good passes and take your open shots . . . box out, and grab all the rebounds. This is your day. We've had a great season, but we're not done yet. Let's go!"

All of J-Hawk Nation shouted out, "We are . . . J-Hawks!" and I glanced quickly in Sarah's direction so I could see the smile that I knew would be accenting her beautiful face. We were both ready.

When I trotted out to the center circle for the opening tip, I shook hands with three Comets who were near me. I saw that their two guards matched Laser and me for height, but their big guys were all a little shorter than the rebounders that I called teammates. I knew that we would give the Compton Comets their money's worth of basketball today. Like Coach said in the locker room earlier, we'll make them run harder and work harder than usual . . . see how much they are willing to commit toward winning this game . . . see what they're willing to pay in effort . . . and then we'd give more . . . much more.

As the ref prepared to throw the ball up for the center jump, I saw all of J-Hawk Nation rise up out of their seats, and they shouted out three times, "We are . . . J-Hawks! We are . . . J-Hawks! We are . . . J-Hawks!"

The ref looked to the scoreboard clock operator, blew his whistle, tossed the ball softly upward into the air, and the game was on.

Abe controlled the tap, sending it to Laser. He protected the ball as the Comets moved back to defend, and Pickett, Captain Hook, and I trotted toward Laser, and each of us touched the basketball that he held in his hands. Then we moved into our offensive positions and began making quick passes around the perimeter, checking out how the Comets responded.

Laser bounced a pass to me as Pickett moved left in my direction, and I didn't hesitate. I sent a firm chest pass to Pickett, and without taking a single dribble, he lifted the ball over his head as he jumped into the air, and he softly shot his silent, deadly fade-away jumper, directing the basketball through the center of the hoop for the first two points of the game. This was a very positive omen for the team. All of us gained even more confidence because of his perfect shot, and I had the feeling that most of our shots would end with that same result.

Laser called for full-court pressure so we hustled into our assigned areas. Pickett challenged the inbound pass, Laser and I prepared to move in aggressively, and Abe and Hook backpedaled to center court. Everything was automatic for us. As the action moved toward Laser's side, Pickett rushed in to double team the dribbler. This frustrated Number 12, and he lost the ball when Laser reached in and tapped it away. Pickett grabbed the basketball and tossed it toward our basket as I sprinted forward. Without breaking my stride, I gathered the ball, stepped into my running jump, and, using my left hand, skipped the basketball off the backboard into the hoop.

Less than thirty seconds had passed, and we already led by four.

During the rest of the first quarter we kept the Comets off balance by switching our defenses around. In addition to our full-court press, we sometimes trapped at half-court, and we alternated between playing a zone and covering man-to-man in defending our basket. All of these strategies kept the Comets from finding a good rhythm, and they lost the ball a few times and missed several shots. Our big guys outrebounded theirs, so they didn't get second or third chances, and we gradually built up a small lead.

It appeared that the Comets were more afraid of our inside game than they were of our outside shooting, and they kept sagging back, leaving both Laser and me open for jumpers. When I buried my first two shots, Laser began to pass up his own shot and fed me the ball. I kept shooting, and I was hot. Almost all of my shots went in cleanly. Between jump shots and fast break layups, I was scorching the net.

When the buzzer signaled the end of the first quarter, the scoreboard showed that we led by a score of 20-12.

Coach spoke in the huddle. "Good work, men. Since Catch has the hot hand today, let's keep feeding him the ball. After grabbing those defensive rebounds, hustle that ball down court. Make the Comets work harder than they are used to. When the Comets start covering Catch more closely, pass the ball around . . . find the open man."

"We are . . . J-Hawks!" sounded from the student section as we ran back onto the court.

Coach subbed frequently in the second quarter, using four guys off the bench, and we kept up the defensive pressure. Many of our fast breaks found me catching the ball near the basket, and I scored on several easy layups. Captain Hook heated up his short hook shots, and he seldom missed. Abe and Pickett established good rebounding positions on both ends of the floor. Everything was working on our offensive end, and we didn't hold anything back.

Our tight defense continued to cause problems for the Comets, and at halftime, we trotted to the locker room with a fourteen-point advantage.

"Everyone, drink water and rest your legs," Coach advised. "During the third quarter we're going to run hard and throw everything we've got at them, including the kitchen sink. Let's build that lead to twenty. These next few minutes will determine how this game goes, so be ready. Don't let the Comets get a rhythm going, and don't give them a chance to build their confidence. Your tough defense has frustrated them and made this game too difficult for them today. That's the key. Keep up the pressure."

I was guarded more closely in the third quarter, but that meant that Pickett and Captain Hook had more room, could move around easier, receive passes, and put up shots from close range. That's what they did, and it was good for our team. We began to work the ball inside, capitalizing on short-range shots, and we added on to our lead. The Comets never figured out a good way to defend us.

We took a twenty-one-point lead into the fourth quarter, and Coach kept rotating us, sometimes leaving only three starters in the game at a time. The Comets never got closer than seventeen points despite all of our subbing, and the net result was that we not only earned a good victory, we all had a chance to rest during some of the game. With another game tomorrow night, it was really important that we had not drained ourselves completely.

All aspects of our game worked well today. It was another huge confidence builder. Everyone had shot well, our passes were on target, we had established great rebounding position, we had run a very effective fast break, and our pressure defense had been outstanding. I don't know how we could have played any better than we had.

All we needed to do was play another game like this in the championship game tomorrow night, and maybe that would get the job done.

Chapter 54
Quiet Time

As we left the gym and entered the lobby of the auditorium, we ran into about a small town's-worth of people waiting for us. J-Hawk Nation was very loud and excited.

We accepted congratulations for tonight's win as we walked around, but I knew we wouldn't let this game be enough. Under our letter jackets each of us was again wearing our black T-shirts that read "NOT DONE YET!" and that's what I kept thinking about. One more game remained on our schedule . . . just one more game, . . . but that game was for all the marbles. We had to win this last one tomorrow night, or it would almost feel like our season was a failure. That's not really the way it was, though. Our season had been outstanding, and as the winning streak kept growing and we kept playing better and better, people began to expect even more from us. We now had a chance to win the championship . . . a good chance, . . . and I knew that we would not have a difficult time keeping our focus on the big prize.

After walking around in the lobby for a short time, I ran into Bobby, Debbie, and my parents. Like the others, they also were pretty excited.

I kept working my way around to the corners of the lobby, looking for Sarah, but it was slow going. Everyone wanted to talk about the game we had just won. Since these people had driven a long way to see us play and cheer for us, I didn't brush anyone off, but my eyes continued to search for Sarah.

It was while I was shaking hands with Bob from The Jeffers Café that I was captured in a bear hug as Sarah surprised me by walking up from behind me. Her wonderful laugh gave her away. I released Bob's handshake, turned around to face Sarah, stared deeply into her beautiful blue eyes, and returned her embrace.

"That was another great game, Catch!" she said excitedly. "You were fantastic again!"

"Thanks," I replied. "However . . ." I backed one step away from Sarah and ripped open my letter jacket to reveal my black T-shirt, and I pointed to its message. "We're not done yet. We have one more game ahead of us."

Sarah smiled and gently pulled me back toward her. "I know you'll play well tomorrow, too," she added.

"I'm so glad you came to the game," I said. "It means a lot to me that you and your family are here, and I'll get to spend lots of time with you this weekend, starting with tonight after Coach and the Supe take us out for a spaghetti dinner. Laser told Coach in the locker room that we needed a team meal at an Italian restaurant so we could replenish our energy level with huge plates of spaghetti. No one spoke against this idea because spaghetti has been good to us this season. Coach told us that he expects that we'll be back at the hotel by eight o'clock, and then we are in for the night. He even gave us a 10:30 bedtime."

"That sounds about right to me," Sarah said. "Isn't that close to normal for you?"

"Yeah, it is," I replied. "You and I can meet in the hotel lobby at eight tonight . . . and we can sit and talk or play cards or something. It doesn't matter to me what we do, but I really want to be with you. Then tomorrow we'll have almost the whole day together . . . unless your parents have other plans for you. Would you like to take an early-morning city-walk with me at about seven-thirty? I know that I have to be back for our team breakfast at 8:30, but after that I have the whole day free until the team meets again for our late-afternoon pre-game meal."

The spaghetti was very tasty, and all of us were plenty hungry, but everyone ate quickly. I could sense that the team wanted to get back to the hotel to relax and meet up with friends and family members.

I didn't even go up to my room when I got back to the hotel. I found a comfortable stuffed chair in a quiet part of the lobby and sat down. The big clock that was hanging behind the registration desk showed that it was not quite eight o'clock, so I wasn't worried about Sarah not being here yet. I expected that she would be down in a few minutes, unless dinner with her parents slowed her down.

The faint light in the room, the softness of the huge chair that cradled my tired body, and the very quiet rhythmical sounds of cars driving past on the street outside all contributed to my being able to relax so easily that I guess I closed my eyes and dozed off.

I think I had just begun dreaming, and I kept hearing a quiet, soothing voice call out to me. "Catcher . . . are you asleep?" the voice asked. "Catch . . . are you all right?"

Just when I was preparing to answer the voice in my dream, I felt someone touch my hand. I was startled. I opened my eyes and saw someone crouching down next to my chair, and for a brief moment I couldn't figure out who it was or where I was.

When I came to, my confusion disappeared, but embarrassment took over.

"Sorry, Sarah," I said. "I think I was lost for a moment. Have you been here long?"

"I just got here . . . eight o'clock . . . like we planned," she replied.

"I've only been here a few minutes myself," I said. "I must have really needed a nap, and I was already caught up in a dream."

For over two hours we talked about the game and our dinners, our rides to Des Moines and our rooms in the hotel, the city itself and our plans for tomorrow. We smiled often and laughed about several funny things we each had noticed today. This was a great way to relax. Being with Sarah was so easy. This is the longest we had ever been together where we just talked to each other. Usually there was a movie or a walk or a game or a church service so we didn't do much talking, but tonight was different. We never ran out of things to talk about, and there were no uncomfortable quiet times where I felt awkward. I wanted to sit here all night . . . until the entire city retired for the night, but I had a curfew.

When I walked Sarah to her room, I stood with her in the hallway for just a couple of minutes. I held her in my arms without saying a word because I knew there were many pairs of ears lurking behind all the hallway doors, and this was private time for the two of us.

I whispered to her, "I'll be in the lobby downstairs at seven-thirty if you'd like to take an early-morning city hike with me. We'll be back before eight-thirty."

"Wait for me," Sarah replied. "I'll go with you."

I kissed her and looked into her eyes. I gently touched my hands to the sides of her beautiful face, and I very tenderly kissed her perfect lips.

"I don't want to say goodnight," I whispered as I reached for her hands, "but Coach says it's my bedtime."

Sarah laughed quietly. "You have a big game tomorrow," she said, "so you do need your sleep. I'll be with you the whole day tomorrow if I can. I look forward to the hike and your game . . . and any other adventures that we can find."

I could not let go of Sarah's hands. I kissed her again. Then I heard Sarah's dad say from inside the room, "Sarah, it's time. Say goodnight to Catcher."

I cringed, and then both Sarah and I started laughing. We both said, "Goodnight," without making any attempt to be quiet this time.

I hugged her one more time before turning to walk to the elevator.

When I returned to my room I found my roommates already in bed, but some lights were still on, and they were talking about tonight's game. I prepared for bed quickly, and I lay down on my bed and found that perfect position for my head on the pillow. The lights were turned off after a round of "good nights," and I drew in deep breaths of air and relaxed by exhaling completely. I closed my eyes and tried to stop thinking about things, but I lay there and discovered that I could not fall asleep. I had napped easily in the lobby a couple of hours ago, but now that I wanted to sleep, it didn't happen.

Even with my eyelids closed, I was bothered by the city's lights that found their way through the windows and around the curtains and invaded the peaceful darkness of our room. I wasn't used to city lights. On the farm it is always totally black at night. All lights are off, including the yard light that hangs from the top of the pole near the garage. Even the twinkling stars and the moon have no chance of sneaking their faint light past the heavy dark curtains that protect the small high window that rests above the dresser in the room that Bobby and I share.

Then there was the noise. The wind creates the only sounds on the farm at night, and I can deal with that, but tonight I kept hearing cars go past the hotel on the street below. It also seemed like someone out in the hallway was opening and closing all the doors, and there were other noises that I could not identify, though I tried . . . because I couldn't fall asleep.

I stared at the ceiling and at the window, and I said some long rambling prayers. I had so much to be thankful for. The basketball season and Sarah's friendship were at the top of my list. I knew it wasn't right to pray for help in winning tomorrow night's game because I didn't think God would favor a team in a basketball game, just like I wasn't sure he would choose sides in a war, but I did ask him to watch over all the players on both teams and protect us from injury, and I felt it was all right to ask him to help me play my best.

Sarah was really on my mind, and I kept wandering in and out of prayer as I thought about her. I would give up anything to be able to hold on to our friendship. If I had to choose between a basketball championship and Sarah . . . I would not hesitate at all. It would be an easy decision for me to make, but I knew that I would never tell my teammates about how I felt. Maybe they already knew.

I thought about the great journey that our team had taken this season, and I did not want it to end. Honestly, I would trade this final championship game for a chance to play four or five more games with my team instead. When the final buzzer sounds to end our game tomorrow night, the season will be over. Basketball will be silenced, and everything will seem dark and cold, and I know that I will be depressed. I'm afraid I won't be very good company tomorrow night, whether we win or whether we lose. I'm fortunate that I'll have Sarah there to provide laughter, and that will help me work through those feelings that may cause problems for me.

But I can't worry about something like this tonight. I need to fall asleep . . . to shut down my brain . . . to trust that tomorrow will be a good day for me . . . for us.

This winter has been the absolute best time of my life, and I want everything to stay the way it is. The snow and the cold weather can move on, of course, and basketball will be replaced by baseball, but I need to make sure that I don't mess things up with Sarah. My prayers have been mostly about her these last couple months, and I don't see anything wrong with that. I keep reminding myself not to do anything stupid that will upset Sarah and her parents, and I also know that I don't want to suffocate Sarah with too much attention. We each have to live our own lives . . . have our own friends . . . do things with our own families . . . continue with our own hobbies and activities, but I know for sure that I will put a lot of energy and thought into taking care of the friendship we share. I will tend it . . . like we do the garden and the field crops, the livestock and the farm pets. Everyone knows that you have to take care of things that are important to you . . . and Sarah means everything to me.

I may have exhausted myself with all of the thinking I had done while trying to fall asleep. All of a sudden my mind seemed to let go . . . gave up trying to be in control of everything . . . and a sense of peacefulness came over me. The noises seemed to disappear, and I didn't even notice any light in the room.

I remember saying "Amen," and then it felt like I was drifting off to sleep.

In the Stands- With John Garris

It sounds like an oxymoron to say that the Jeffers J-Hawks ran a "patient fast break" in their big win over Compton yesterday in the semifinals of the small school state basketball championships, but that's exactly what they did.

Whenever they grabbed a defensive rebound, the J-Hawks rushed the ball down court quickly, and they often scored on uncontested layups, but if an easy basket was not available to them, Laser and Catcher pulled the ball back outside, waited for their teammates, and passed the ball around the perimeter until they found a good opportunity to score.

In the first half, that good opportunity to score resided in the shooting touch of Catcher. He blistered the net with perfect jump shots, and the J-Hawks were content to feed him, let him take his shot, and tally up the points on the scoreboard.

By halftime, the boys from Jeffers had built a fourteen-point lead, and in the second half they extended that lead by taking advantage of their inside game, finding Captain Hook, Abe, and Pickett open near the basket for shorter range shots that usually hit the target.

The Comets played a decent game, but they were up against a formidable opponent who might have played its best game of the playoffs. The J-Hawks were an inspired basketball team, and I heard a rumor that a pre-game talk given in the locker room by one of their supporters may have been the catalyst for their outstanding play.

Tonight in the championship game, the J-Hawks will face the Downey Dragons who feature the tallest center in the state.

Will height or speed prevail in the title game?

Chapter 55

Serendipity

Morning came quickly . . . for a couple of reasons. I remember having had trouble falling asleep last night, so that shortened the number of actual sleeping hours I had, and the second reason comes from living on a farm. There are early morning chores to be done. Every day, including weekends, I am up early to care for the livestock and the chickens. Sleeping late is never an option for me unless I am ill, and that is never a good trade-off. I don't even need an alarm clock. I just wake up at the same time every day.

I looked at my watch that I had set on the nightstand next to my side of the bed last night, and I was not surprised to see that it was just past six o'clock. Normally I would hop out of bed and get moving, but two neighbor kids were doing my chores at home today and tomorrow, so for these two days I could relax in bed in the city. Besides, Tucson, Otto, and San Juan were still asleep so I needed to be quiet. I lay there for about half an hour, eyes wide open.

There was no need for me to shower this morning because I had showered after my game yesterday, but I quietly washed up, got dressed in the dark, and brushed my teeth. Having white teeth and fresh breath had become extremely important to me since sometime early in the basketball season.

I grabbed my letter jacket, cap, and gloves and took the elevator down to the lobby where I waited for Sarah. I found a copy of *The Des Moines Register* and looked at the front page to see what was going on in the world, but I honored Coach's request that we not read the sports pages. He didn't want any of us players to be influenced by any city writers, so he said we could not read anything that anyone had written about the games, and that included Garris who was covering our team for *The Register*. The newspapers would be saved for us, and we could read them later. I didn't have a problem with that.

I sat for about thirty minutes, reading the paper and thinking about to-night's game. Exactly at seven-thirty, Sarah joined me. I saw how beautiful she was, even in the early hours of the morning. She looked perfect.

"Good morning," I said to her as I smiled. "You look great. Are you ready for our city hike?"

"Yes, I am. This will be my first city hike ever," Sarah replied. "Lead the way."

"You do understand that I have no idea what's out there," I said. "We'll be exploring the city together . . . finding our way together. I hope you are not expecting a guided tour."

Sarah's laughter filled my heart, and I had to hold myself back from wrapping my arms around her and kissing her. I held my arm out to her, and we walked confidently out the door, arm in arm.

The sidewalks were clear of snow, but the temperature was a little brisk. I definitely could see my breath . . . my fresh breath, . . . and we walked at a quick pace so we could try to stay warm.

I made mental notes of buildings and stores and other landmarks that we walked past because we would be coming back after breakfast, when things were open, and then we could explore inside. I would guide Sarah back to the music store, the quaint old bookstore, the Five and Dime, and the huge stone church. I had no plans for what we would do at any of these places, but the word that we had discussed in English class last week, "serendipity," came to mind. Maybe we'd come across a happy accident or pleasant surprise.

Because of the cold, we returned to the hotel in about forty-five minutes. It had been a great walk, but we both had felt the stinging cold through our bodies.

"I'm sorry if you got too cold," I said. "It'll be a little warmer at ten, and then we can go inside some of those places we saw. Will you be ready for another adventure at ten?" I asked.

Sarah smiled and nodded. She was a trooper.

I walked Sarah to her room and then returned to mine. I found that the guys were almost ready to go to breakfast.

"Where did you go so early?" Tucson asked.

"I'm a farm boy. I have chores to do every day," I answered.

"Good one. I happen to know that you were on a walk with Sarah, and I am going to tell her what you said about chores," Otto threatened kiddingly. "I don't think she'll like that. You made it sound like it was a job to be with her. What do you guys think?"

"Otto's right," San Juan said. "You'll be in big trouble, Catch."

"How about asking me the question again?" I asked. "Give me another shot at coming up with a good response."

"All right," Tucson said. "Hey, Farm Boy, where have you been so early in the morning?"

"I've been on a wonderful walk with Sarah, and boy did she look beautiful this morning. We had a great time," I replied.

"Much better," Otto said. "We'll go with your second answer."

"Whew! Thanks," I said as I faked a sigh of relief, and we all laughed.

We walked to a nearby diner with Coach and the rest of the team, and we feasted on eggs, breakfast potatoes, pancakes, and sausages. This took the edge off my hunger, and after we returned to the hotel, I lay on my bed for about thirty minutes, waiting for my ten-o'clock walk with Sarah.

When the elevator stopped at my floor and the door opened, there stood Sarah . . . alone . . . on her way down to the lobby. I got in, stood close to her, and waited for the door to close. When we started our descent, I leaned over and kissed her. I knew I would remember this elevator ride forever.

I was still grinning when we reached the main floor and the doors of the elevator opened. I looked at Sarah and saw that she was blushing. We both started laughing as we walked through the lobby and headed for the hotel's main doors

Serendipity. Finding Sarah alone in the elevator . . . a wonderful unexpected "accident" . . . and me taking advantage of the situation.

I felt pretty proud of myself . . . for understanding serendipity.

Our first stop on the walk was the music store where I noticed several pianos spread among all the other musical instruments that were scattered everywhere. An idea came to me immediately, and I walked up to a young man who was organizing sheet music behind the counter, and I said, "My friend and I are in town for the basketball tournament . . . and we aren't looking to buy a piano, but I was wondering if she could sit at one of your pianos and play for awhile. She's really good."

"Sure," he replied. "Have her try the one near the drum set. That's our best one."

"Sarah," I said as returned to her and pointed to the piano. Will you play for me?"

"I don't have any music," she answered as she shrugged.

"It's lucky for us that we are in a music store," I said as I laughed and pointed at everything.

We found a book full of popular songs, and I took it to the clerk and bought it for Sarah. I handed it to her and said, "Meal money paid for this. Music provides food for the spirit."

Sarah played amazingly well, and she started attracting a small crowd in the store, especially when she added her wonderful voice to some of the songs while she played. I recognized two songs from *West-Side Story* and several others I had heard on the radio. I felt very proud of her, and I almost wanted to yell out to those who were listening to her that Sarah was my girlfriend.

She sat at that piano for about forty minutes, and it looked like she was really enjoying herself. When she stopped playing, people applauded, and when she stood up and began to walk away from the piano, the store manager rushed over to her and asked, "Could you please stay for another hour or so? Several people have expressed interest in buying a piano while they listened to your beautiful music. You made everything look so easy. Would you like a job?"

Sarah thanked him for the compliments. "My friend and I are taking a walking tour of your city, and I believe we have several more stops to make, so I really need to be going," Sarah said as she looked at me. "Thank you so much for letting me play. I had fun, and I really like that piano."

"Come back any time," the manager said as we walked out onto the street to continue our adventure.

Three stores down on the same side of the street sat the Five and Dime. When we entered the store I was overwhelmed by all the stuff I saw everywhere. A whole bunch of young kids were gathered at some side display areas, so I led Sarah in that direction. I started drooling when I saw every kind of candy imaginable.

I pulled two nickels out from my pocket and said to Sarah, "Let's have a contest. We each get five cents to spend. The winner of the contest is the person who is able to buy the greatest number of things with the money."

"You're on. I'll spend your money wisely," Sarah boasted. "Good luck to you."

I checked over all the candy. Some things were two for a penny. There were things that I had eaten before, and they had tasted pretty good, but I found an unfamiliar kind of candy that was priced at three pieces for a penny, so I bought fifteen pieces of that candy for my nickel. I stood confidently as I waited for Sarah.

When she walked over to where I was standing, she was smiling. She carried a small paper sack, even smaller than mine.

"How did you do?" I asked.

"You go first," she suggested.

I opened my sack and showed her the contents. I said proudly, "I bought fifteen pieces of candy for my nickel."

"Well done, Catch," Sarah said, and she stood there looking at me.

"What did you get?" I asked.

Sarah's face broke into a beautiful smile. "I spent my nickel on all the buttons I could scoop up in one small cup," she said. "I counted them. There are sixty-two buttons. I'm sorry, Catch, but your sweet tooth cost you this time. This really was no contest."

On the way out of the store I offered Sarah one piece of my candy, and I took one myself. After just a few steps, we both spit the candy out into a wastebasket near the door. I had not done very well in the Five and Dime.

We continued walking a couple more blocks, and we arrived at the huge Catholic church that we had spied earlier this morning. There were a few cars parked in the small parking lot, and several well-dressed people were standing at the large doors at the top of the wide cement steps. Sarah and I decided to look inside.

I approached a nervous looking woman who was pacing near the door.

"My friend and I are in town for the basketball tournament," I said, "and we were wondering if we could take a quick peek inside. We're both from small towns that don't have churches like this, and we are kind of curious what it looks like inside."

"Of course you can," the woman replied. "Come in. We're almost ready to begin a small wedding, but we can't start until we can figure out what to do about the soloist. She showed up with laryngitis, and she can't sing. No one in the wedding party is confident enough to replace her, so I don't know what we'll do. Will you please excuse me?"

Sarah and I looked at each other as the woman walked away. I smiled at Sarah and said quietly, "You can do it. I know you can. You can save this wedding. You have already warmed up your voice this morning. This would be serendipity, another wonderful accident with a happy ending."

"I'll talk to her," Sarah said.

"Good for you. I'll call her over," I added.

"I have sung at a few weddings," Sarah said. "If it's a song that I'm familiar with I would be happy to be your soloist."

"You would?" The woman was astonished. "'Ave Maria' . . . Do you know that one?" she asked.

"I really like that song," Sarah replied. "I'll sing 'Ave Maria' for you."

"Wonderful!" The woman was very relieved. "The bride and groom will be forever grateful."

Sarah sang better than I had ever heard anyone sing before, and it was the highlight of the small wedding. When she completed her song everyone applauded, included me, and the wedding couple left the altar area and walked over to Sarah and thanked her.

After the wedding had been concluded, Sarah and I walked through the reception line, shaking hands with the new couple and their parents. The bride's mother asked Sarah, "Can you and your friend come with us to a restaurant just down the street where we will eat and celebrate?"

Sarah looked at me, and I nodded. "We have about an hour before we should be back at the hotel," I said.

I was careful not to eat too much from the delicious buffet, but I did have a good-sized piece of wedding cake. Several people came over to talk with us while we ate, and they complimented Sarah on her solo. I heard two people say that they had to dry their eyes during the song, and I believed them because I had done the same, but maybe I had done it for a different reason.

The parents of the bride sat with us for a few minutes and asked us several questions. They seemed curious about who we were and what had brought us to the church for this wedding. I explained about the basketball tournament and our city walk.

"I read about your game in this morning's *Register*. You won your game yesterday, and you play for the championship tonight, right?" the dad asked.

"Yes, we do," I replied.

"Catcher?" the man asked. "I saw the name 'Catcher' on your letter jacket. The article I read in the paper told about how well you played yesterday. Good luck in your game, and thanks to both of you for attending the wedding and celebrating with us. You have a beautiful voice, Sarah."

I took a quick look at my watch. It was getting late. We had to be back to the hotel in fifteen minutes, or we would miss the opportunity to ride the school bus to the movie with the other kids.

"Sarah, we have to leave right away, and we still might not make it back on time," I said.

The bride's mother asked, "Where do you need to be?"

I explained about the movie, the hotel, and the bus ride to the movie theater.

"We'll give you a ride back to your hotel right away," the dad said. "We have rented a limo for the day."

We accepted the offer, and we rushed out to the parking lot. The bride's father explained everything to the driver, and we were on our way.

Sitting in the plush roomy limo with Sarah reminded me a little of catching her alone in the elevator earlier this morning, and I created another lasting memory for me by kissing her. Serendipity had scored again. First was the elevator . . . now there was the limo. I would be looking for a third.

As we pulled up to the curb in front of our hotel, I noticed a big crowd of our friends milling about, probably waiting for the bus. A quick glance of my watch showed that we had made it here with about seven or eight minutes to spare.

When the driver came around to open the limo's door, I stepped out onto to the sidewalk and assisted Sarah. I noticed everyone looking at us.

"We were expecting celebrities," Tucson said, and I could hear the disappointment in his voice. "Are congratulations in order?" he asked as he pointed at the limo.

I looked back at the limo and noticed the sign in the window. I caught the smile on Sarah's face.

"No, that sign is not for us. It's for the bride and groom from the wedding we attended," I explained. "The father of the bride offered us a ride back to our hotel from the reception at the restaurant in this limo he had rented for the occasion."

"Sarah? . . . Catcher? What's going on?"

It was Sarah's dad. He and Sarah's mom had also been standing outside by the hotel's front door when we pulled up in the limo, and he had some questions for us. He wasn't exactly smiling, and I could hear the concern in his voice.

Sarah explained everything. She told her parents about the church, the wedding, subbing for the soloist, being invited to the restaurant, and accepting the offer of a ride in the limo. I could see that both her parents were amazed by her story, and I could also sense the relief that her father must have felt.

I wanted to tell Sarah's parents that they didn't need to worry about us. Sure we were just kids, but we were smart kids . . . kids you could trust, but I chose not to say anything. Maybe my comments would have caused additional trouble that I didn't need. Sarah was doing fine in telling about our adventure. I stood there hoping that Sarah's overprotective parents wouldn't overreact about the limo ride and the sign in the window of the limo. We hadn't done anything wrong, but I was worried that I would somehow be paying for the scare we had maybe given Sarah's dad.

Sarah added more details about the wedding, and Mr. Jenkins began to relax. Finally he smiled and patted me on the back. I said to him, "Sarah can tell you later about playing the piano at the music store and the contest she won at the Five and Dime. We've had a great morning."

Coach pulled up in the school bus, and the Supe shouted out, "Load up everyone. This bus is headed for the theater and the matinee showing of *The Guns of Navarone*. We'll be back at about four o'clock, and then the players can rest for a short time before we go for our pregame meal."

The World War II movie was filled with action, and I certainly didn't think about my upcoming basketball game while I was sitting there watching. I did reflect on my adventure with Sarah. We held hands during the entire movie, and I spoke to her once.

"Thanks for the serendipity today," I whispered. "You played the piano really well, and you sang beautifully at the wedding. I am very proud of you. I will remember this day forever."

"Thanks. I'll remember this day, too," Sarah whispered back. "It was my turn to entertain you. Tonight will be your turn again."

"Someday maybe we should rent a limo," I added.

Sarah laughed quietly. "If there is going to be a sign in the window, we'd better tell my dad about it ahead of time," she said.

I squeezed Sarah's hand and watched the big screen as another Nazi bad guy fell off a cliff to his death. It had been an accident, but it wasn't a wonderful accident like the several that I had experienced today. I'll take serendipity every time.

When the movie ended, the theater was very dark for just a second. This was the "third" I had been looking for, and I leaned over and quickly kissed Sarah on the top of her head.

We were bussed back to the hotel, and I lay down on my bed and rested for about an hour.

After eating our pregame meal at a nearby restaurant, we boarded the bus again and Coach drove us to the auditorium for our final basketball game of the season. This is why we came to Des Moines. We would be ready to play.

Chapter 56

The Last Hurrah

As Coach maneuvered the bus into the parking lot next to the auditorium, it suddenly hit me. This is it . . . the championship game. Back in January we had pledged to work hard so we would have a chance to reach this game. We're here now . . . all we need to do is to win it.

I know that I am ready. While lying on my bed at the hotel after the movie, I had prepared myself mentally. I visualized shooting my jump shots so cleanly through the net that the only sound I heard was the net whispering "swish" as the ball dropped through. I saw myself racing down the floor with the ball, sometimes making leading passes to Laser that took him all the way to the hoop for a lay-up, and other times I took the ball to the basket myself after receiving Laser's pass. I pictured myself crouching in my defensive stance, and I had been able to slide my feet quickly enough to smother my responsibility whenever he had the ball. I was ready. My preparation had gone well.

While lying on that bed I had also taken a few minutes to reflect on my day with Sarah. The word "perfect" came to mind . . . several times. Today had been a perfect day. Everything about it had been perfect, especially the way Sarah had played the piano at the music store and had sung at the wedding. She had been so poised and confident. Her perfect smile had constantly reached into my soul, and we had been able to talk so easily as friends for several hours. I love that girl with all my heart, and this feels perfect, too.

I could tell that something was going on with me tonight. I had trouble keeping my focus. Knowing that this was the last basketball game I would play as a J-Hawk had a lot to do with this. I didn't feel scared about the game, but maybe some sadness was creeping in because of the finality of everything. My thoughts bounced from one thing to another like the steel ball in the pinball machine, and nothing seemed to be connected.

"Well, J-Hawks," Coach said after parking the bus and standing up to face his passengers. "What do you say? Let's go into this friendly auditorium . . . play our best game of the year in front of thousands of basketball fans . . . and complete our perfect season."

The bus erupted with cheers, and I wondered if it was because Coach had said "perfect."

We ran into a few strangers as we silently walked our route through a maze of hallways to our locker room, but once we stepped through the doorway and set down our duffle bags and the equipment bags, the silence was chased away. It was the captains that initiated that. It felt to me like our confidence was erupting.

"All right, J-Hawks!" Laser shouted. "It's time to finish this. Let's put on these lucky gold J-Hawk jerseys one more time. Then let's go sweat them up and run the Downey Dragons to death."

"We can do this," Pickett added. "We've put in the work to get into great shape. There's no way the Dragons can run with us, and run is what we'll do. We'll run them into the ground."

It shocked me when Go Forth Son added, "Slay them! Death to the Dragons!" I started laughing a little, and so did a few of the others. We were loose, motivated, and confident. There was no room for fear or doubt, even if the Dragons breathed fire.

During our pregame warm-ups I took a quick glance down at the other basket to see just how tall their center was. He definitely stood out among the Dragons. I saw that he wasn't doing much jumping when he shot or when he rebounded. I guess he didn't need to. He also wasn't moving very quickly or athletically. That's where we will try to take advantage of him. I think we'll try to wear him out by making him play faster than he is used to playing. Tired shooters often become inaccurate shooters.

My shots were dropping during the warm-ups, and I got a good sweat going. I was ready. When Coach called us to the bench for final instructions, I looked into the bleachers and found Sarah. She smiled and reached for her necklace. I smiled back and nodded confidently.

I knew that we needed to win this game because that's all that we knew how to do. We didn't know how to lose. During the entire season no one had taught us how to lose. *We probably wouldn't handle losing very well, and we are really good at winning . . . so I think we should take the easier route . . . play our best and win this one, too.*

As I stood there on the gym floor with the other starters, waiting for player introductions, I started daydreaming, and the announcer's voice became only a muffled sound in the background. I heard him say something about this being the final Class B basketball game of the season, but I heard little else, and it didn't seem to mean anything to me as he began to introduce the starting lineup for Downey. I wasn't very attentive as I struggled to corral my scattered thoughts together. This game was huge, and I needed to be focused, but right now I wasn't being too successful at it.

My mind broke from my body and started wandering, and I followed wherever it took me without resisting. All kinds of mental images flashed quickly through my mind, mostly in black and white like on our first television set a few years back. I made an attempt to figure out what all of these images were so I could put a name to them, but sometimes the pictures passed by too rapidly.

The haymow . . . the hog yard . . . a school bus . . . an orange tractor . . . Santa Claus . . . a freight train . . . a snowy hill . . . three bicycles . . . the gym roof . . . French fries . . . a pair of sweat socks . . . a catcher's mask . . . a school classroom . . . can't see this one clearly . . . a huge fancy tree house . . . a bag of basketballs . . . a piano . . . crack in the ceiling . . . a bag swing . . . a shiny silver heart . . . I don't know this one, it's too blurry . . .

"Could you slow these down, please?" I'm having a hard time making out some of these." I didn't know to whom I was directing my silent plea because I really didn't have any idea what was going on. I shouldn't be thinking about these things right now, but I recognize these pictures as being things from my life. "Hey, it feels as if my life is flashing before my eyes. I'm not dying, am I?"

. . . mosquitoes in the woods . . . Grandma's house in town . . . an aluminum grain shovel . . . a movie theater . . . a basketball hoop . . . light blue paint dripping from a paint brush . . . a study table in the library . . . a Johnny Mathis album . . . can't make this one out . . . a fire in the fireplace . . . the cow pasture . . . a valentine

. . . sand at a swimming beach . . . a pinball machine . . . a black stocking cap . . . a hooked walleye . . .

I was enjoying this fast-paced slide show. I felt so free, so detached from everything. It was all very peaceful and quiet . . . but then I snapped out of it when I heard the announcer say, "And now the starting lineup for the J-Hawks from Jeffers." I shook my head a little to clear away the cobwebs, and I quickly reeled my mind back in.

"At center, Number 44, Pickett!"

The PA system carried this name to all the corners and all the levels of the auditorium, and thousands of voices cheered while countless pairs of hands clapped together.

He's honoring our special names, just like the other announcers have done. Good. This almost feels like a dream. I can see this happening, but I'm just farm kid from a small town. Should I really be out here on the gym floor?

"At forward, Number 33, Abe!"

I wonder how many times my brother and I have ridden our bikes to town to play funball with Abe and his brother. We certainly trampled a bunch of flowers and beat up the grass while making plays on hot summer days.

"At the other forward, Number 22, Captain Hook!"

He always plays hard. I hope his hook shot finds the net tonight. Maybe he should shoot one from center court. I bet his dad is proud of him.

"At guard, Number 20, Laser!"

Pin-point accuracy . . . silent and deadly. We need those jump shots to be on target. Run the break!

"And at the other guard, Number 30, Catcher!"

That's me. He called my name. I'm a J-Hawk, and I'm ready to make this the absolute best day of my life. I'm ready to help frost the cake. This day has been perfect. There's no good reason to mess up a perfect day.

"We are . . . J-Hawks!" I shouted as I trotted back to the bench.

As we stood silently in the huddle, waiting for Coach's final words, I looked around into the eyes of my friends in the gold jerseys. I liked what I saw. There was confidence . . . no fear.

"We have an advantage in this game," Coach said. "Though Number 31 is really tall . . . he doesn't run very well. I noticed yesterday while we watched for a few minutes . . . he struggled going up and down the court . . . and they weren't playing nearly as fast as we'll play tonight. We can wear him down. By pressing full court and trapping at the centerline, we can make the tall kid work so hard that he'll probably want to watch most of this game from the bench. I don't think he would get much playing time if he were on our team. It will be a challenge for us to stop his shot when he's close to the basket, so let's not let the Dragons get the ball to him when he's close in."

"I'll play in front of him near the line," Pickett said, "so I'll need some help behind him."

"Abe and I will be there," Captain Hook replied.

"I think all of Jeffers showed up to watch you win this," Coach continued. "J-Hawk Nation is proud of you. Let's finish this."

I glanced one more time at Sarah, and I read her lips. "You can do this," she whispered.

"We are J-Hawks!" we shouted as we broke the huddle, and five of us turned to run out to the center circle for the jump ball as J-Hawk Nation continued the chant.

In almost every game this season, we had controlled the center jump, but this didn't look possible tonight. *Abe doesn't have the height or reach to compete against the tall kid and his long arms. We'll have to be really aggressive and grab all the loose balls.*

The ref gathered us to the center circle and prepared to toss the ball into the air.

Here we go!

The tall kid tapped the ball to one of his guards, and the Dragons dribbled and passed the ball toward their end as the tall kid walked to a location near his basket. After a few passes around the outside, Number 20 lobbed a high pass over everyone into the outstretched arms of Number 31. He hardly even jumped to get it. He pivoted while holding the ball high above all of us, and he awkwardly banked a shot off the backboard, through the net, for the game's first two points.

Coach was right. We can't let him do that. This game won't be much fun if he gets to put up shots from that close in.

Pickett grabbed the ball before it hit the floor, passed it in to Laser, and we were off and running to the other end. We raced. When we reached our basket the tall kid hadn't even made it to the half line. After two strong passes on the outside, Hook found Pickett inside by the basket. Pickett collected the ball, jumped up, and laid the ball against the backboard, into the net, just before Number 31 arrived to defend. He was too late. We had made a great counter attack.

Immediately we set up our full-court press. Number 31 jogged to a position just short of the half line as Laser, Pickett, and I pressured his teammates into hurrying their passes and dribbles. We needed to force mistakes.

Number 21 dribbled free from me on the sideline, and he lobbed a high pass to the tall kid who was standing near the center of the court. After catching the ball, Number 31 pivoted while holding the ball high above his head, and he passed to a teammate who ran by. This time they had broken our press, but now we knew what their strategy would be, and we would play them even tighter next time.

Number 31 caught another high lob after setting up close to the basket on the right side of the lane, and again he banked in an awkward shot off the backboard. Two shots . . . two scores.

Captain Hook quickly inbounded the ball to Laser, and he dribbled the ball while all five of us sprinted to our basket, hoping we could get off a good shot before Number 31 arrived to help defend.

We used our height advantage against the four Dragon defenders this trip down the floor. Laser tossed a high pass to Abe near the rim, and Abe jumped up and reached high, caught the ball, and banked it into the basket. This play never would have worked for us if the tall kid had hustled down and had been standing in the lane. He would have been able to block the pass or the shot. Our quickness had taken advantage of his inability or unwillingness to run.

We applied tight full-court pressure against the Dragon ball handlers as they moved the ball down-court and passed to their tall center. Pickett challenged the high pass as it came floating through the air in his direction, but he couldn't quite reach it, and he accidentally slapped Number 31 on his arms and was whistled for a foul.

Number 31 went to the foul line, breathing heavily and holding up his body by resting his hands on his knees. He prepared to shoot his "one-and-one." He eyed the basket and, without even bending his knees slightly, without even a hint of rhythm, sent a very flat shot toward the rim. It clanged loudly off the left side of the rim and the backboard and started dropping to the floor like a pheasant that had been shot out of the air. Abe reached high to secure the rebound, spun to the outside, and ripped off a powerful pass to Laser. Anticipating that pass, I raced down-court and caught Laser's long leading pass and stepped into an easy left-handed layup that gave us our first lead of the game. By fouling the tall kid, we had essentially taken the ball away from Downey without giving the kid a shot at the basket, and we had turned the play into two points for us.

Each team had three possessions in the next two minutes. The Dragons managed to score on only one of their three shots when Number 40 scored on a short jumper. Number 31 took the other two shots, and both of them were very flat, and they had bounced off the rim.

Abe grabbed the rebound on the first missed shot, and Captain Hook snatched the other out of the air. Both times we hustled the ball down the court before the Dragons could set up their defense, and Laser and I each scored on a fast break. On our other possession Pickett missed on a ten-footer that rolled around the rim and spun out into the hands of the tall kid. In these two minutes we had been able to increase our lead to four points, and our confidence was on the rise.

The Downey coach called for a timeout.

We drank water and rested at the bench as Coach explained how we were going to play the next couple minutes. "Laser and Pickett will sit, and Otto and San Juan are in," he said. "Apply pressure on defense and run the fast break every time we get the ball. San Juan, you will guard the tall kid, and I expect you to foul him when he gets the ball. Make sure you foul him before he attempts his shot. It needs to be a one-and-one foul, not a two-shot. We'll take a chance that the tall kid will continue to miss those free throws."

"His name is Paul," I said.

"What did you say?" Coach asked.

"Number 31's name is Paul, 'Paul as in Tall,'" I added smiling. "That's what his teammates call him."

"All right, San Juan," Coach repeated. "You cover 'Paul as in Tall,' but we'll just call him 'Tall' for short."

I shook my head and laughed at Coach's comment. Others soon joined me in the laughter.

When the ref called us back out to the floor, we joined hands and shouted, "We are . . . J-Hawks!"

I was still laughing to myself as I trotted onto the floor, and I sneaked a quick glance in Sarah's direction. I could tell by the expression on her face that I would be explaining to her later exactly why I had laughed while running out onto the floor. She would want to know all about it.

San Juan drew a quick foul, and "Tall" missed his first free throw. Hook collected the rebound, pivoted to the outside, and rifled a pass to me. After the catching the ball and taking two quick dribbles as I ran, I passed ahead to Otto, and he took the ball all the way to the basket for an uncontested layup.

The Dragons broke our press just as their ten seconds was running out. They set up their offence with the center near the free-throw line. When Number 40 lobbed a high pass to "Tall," San Juan slapped him on the arms while going for the ball and was called for his second foul. Again the Dragons were held without a shot.

Number 31 made his free throw, but he missed on his bonus shot. Abe leaped high and grabbed the ball off the rim, but we messed up our outlet pass and had to slow things down. Coach yelled out to us, "Pass the ball around the perimeter! Otto, keep moving and trying to get free! Run quickly, back and forth, from the baseline to the free-throw line!"

"Tall" kept following Otto, but he was always a step or two behind him, and I could tell he was not having much fun doing this. We burned a solid minute off the clock with our passes and movement and, except for Otto, we managed to catch our breath. With about three minutes left in the first quarter, Coach called for a timeout.

"San Juan and Otto," he said, "great job. Take a seat. Laser and Pickett are back in. Keep running the ball and pressuring on defense. You'll wear them down eventually, and we've taken a small lead. You are playing great ball. Keep it up."

During the next couple minutes of clock time, both teams missed on a couple attempts and made two baskets. "Tall" scored twice on bank shots, and Captain Hook hit two short hook shots.

In the last minute of play in the first quarter, Laser hit on a wide-open jump shot, and the Dragons countered when Number 40 drove around me and hit on a short jumper. That ended the scoring in the first quarter, and when the buzzer sounded, we trotted to the bench leading by a score of 18-13.

Treason entered the lineup for Captain Hook to start the second quarter. Coach shifted Pickett to forward, and Treason's job was to guard "Tall" and foul him as soon as the Dragons passed him the basketball.

Treason did his job, fouling immediately after a pass was lobbed to the tall kid. Hook reentered the game, and Treason smiled as he returned to the bench. Number 31 walked to the line to shoot his free throw. Only ten seconds had passed in the quarter. Coach had figured out a great way to counter for Downey controlling the center jump. Again "Tall Paul" missed his free throw, and Pickett was in perfect position to grab the rebound after blocking out his man. The Dragons hustled down-court to prevent us from using our fast break, so we slowed the pace by walking the ball to our basket.

Pickett continued to cross the lane near the free-throw line, and both Abe and Hook ran the baseline, switching sides constantly. Laser and I passed the ball back and forth to each other as we looked for chances to feed the ball inside. When Number 40 sagged off me toward Pickett, Laser fired the ball to me, and I was wide open. I took one dribble to set up my rhythm, and I launched a perfect jump shot that snapped the cords on the net as the basketball dove through the hoop, adding to our lead.

Before the Dragons could inbound the ball, we set up our full-court press. I had learned Number 40's tendencies during the first quarter. He always faked going left with his dribble, but he never went that direction. Every time he dribbled to his right. His fake had caused me to lose a step on him twice, but I concluded that he could not dribble with his left hand, and I would not fall for that move again. On this possession I stepped in front of him and trapped him against the right sideline because I knew what he would do. He panicked, and threw a high pass in the tall kid's direction, but it missed its mark completely. Captain Hook intercepted the pass, holding the Dragons without a shot at the basket for the second straight time, and we set up our offence.

While four of us kept passing the ball on the perimeter, Pickett moved on the inside, and we were able to find him open and reach him with bounce passes a couple of times. The tall kid needed to cover Pickett so that meant that he, too, had to keep moving, and this caused him to expend valuable energy.

We didn't score on this possession because Laser's shot was short, hitting the front of the rim, but we had kept the ball from the Dragons for about a minute, forcing them to play defense, and as long as they did not control the ball, they could not score.

During the balance of the second quarter both teams hit some good shots and missed on a few. Number 31 found the hoop several times, but he also shot badly on a few attempts. He was the main shooter and the top scorer for the Dragons, but his teammates didn't do much besides passing the ball to him. Only about five baskets had been scored by someone other than "Tall," and it didn't look to me like this was a fun way to play.

All five of us J-Hawks were involved in the second-quarter scoring. Our movement and quick passes found both Abe and Hook open near the basket because the tall kid was slow to cover defensively. Pickett hit twice on fadeaway shots from near the foul line. Both times the ball barely cleared the mountain-high fingertips of the approaching tall kid. Laser drilled a jump shot from the top of the key, and he and I each scored on a fast-break layup. It was a good quarter for us, and when the buzzer signaled the end of the first half, we hustled to the locker room with a nine-point lead.

"Rest up, and drink water," Coach advised.

I strolled over to the water fountain and took a long, cool drink. Then I took a short side-trip to the locker where I had hung up my clothes, pulled out my black T-shirt, and carried it back to one of the benches and sat down. I laid the shirt over my knees with its message exposed.

Captain Hook and Otto noticed it right away and nodded their approval.

Tucson walked by and read it aloud. "Not done yet," he said.

"That's absolutely right," Laser piped in. "We have two more quarters of basketball ahead of us. We are not done yet. Let's make this last half our best of the year."

"This is where we wear them down," Coach added. "Exhaustion and discouragement are right around the corner for the Dragons, so don't let up."

"I was wondering. Is it my turn, Coach?" Go Forth Son asked.

Coach smiled at him and replied, "As a matter of fact it is. Report in. Abe, join me on the bench and check in after the center jump so you will be ready to go in immediately after the foul is called."

After a spirited warm-up and last minute instructions at the bench, five of us trotted to the center of the floor for the jump ball. It looked really strange to see Go Forth Son, not Abe, standing in the center circle, preparing himself to jump for a ball that he had no chance to touch. I'm sure that most people knew what we would do, and about fifteen seconds into the third quarter, Go Forth Son committed his foul against "Tall" and returned to the bench with a smile on his face.

"Tall" made his free throw, but the second one was wide right and didn't even hit the rim. So far he had made two out of about ten tries, which told me that fouling him was a good strategy for us.

During the first part of the quarter we ran hard on offence and pressured the Dragons on defense, playing really well. Play was pretty even for both teams, and the Dragons and we J-Hawks each scored four times. Number 31 banged in two out of the six shots he took, Number 30 drove the lane and hit a layup, catching us in a defensive shift, and Number 20 hit a long jump shot that bounced in off the backboard.

We made several good plays when we had the ball. Captain Hook sneaked inside and caught a great pass from Pickett, then kissed a short, soft shot off the backboard into the basket for two of our points. Laser and I each scored on fast breaks, causing the Dragon guards to yell at their teammates to hustle back and help out on defense. Pickett hit on his signature fade-away jumper from ten feet out. The tall kid was caught out of position, and he didn't even bother to challenge the shot.

When Coach called for a timeout we ran to the bench, hopefully sending the Dragons the message that we weren't even close to being tired.

"Tucson, San Juan, and Otto, report in and give us your top speed on the fast break and press the Dragons aggressively," Coach said. "You can foul "Tall" if he's in position for a clear shot. No one here is in foul trouble. I want you to wear their players down. I'll give you about three minutes, then I expect to put Laser, Abe, and Catcher back in. Number 31 is wearing out, and when Downey's coach rests him, we'll go back to the starting five and work the ball inside to get some easy baskets from Abe and Captain Hook. Don't let up. Let's go!"

"We are . . . J-Hawks!" we shouted, and all the J-Hawks in the bleacher seats behind our bench shouted out the echo.

Tucson, San Juan, and Otto pestered the Dragon ball handlers like swarms of gnats at sundown. They kept up their great effort and speed because they knew that they didn't need to pace themselves to play the whole game. Their constant running and jumping and waving their arms caused some frustration on the part of Downey's guards. The Dragons were wearing down, and now they had to compete against fresh legs. Otto intercepted a pass, but we weren't able to score this time because San Juan's shot bounced off the rim. Then Tucson stole the ball and fed Otto for an easy layup.

Number 31 clanked a shot off the rim, and Pickett leaped high for the rebound. His outlet pass led Tucson too far, and we lost the ball out of bounds, but that didn't hurt us. The pace at which we were playing was really paying off. It appeared that the Dragons could not catch their breath, that their fire had gone out, and their coach called for a timeout with about three minutes left in the third quarter. Our lead stood at ten.

"I'll give you another minute out there," Coach said as he looked at Otto, Tucson, and San Juan. Give all you've got. Wear 'em down."

When Downey took the floor to resume play, it was without their tall center. He had taken a seat on the bench. The Dragons had put in a third guard into the lineup instead to help handle the pressure that our "gnats" were applying.

Tucson made another great steal, and we set up the offence on our end. After a few passes on the outside, Otto bounced the basketball to Captain

Hook, and he lofted a soft hook shot that hit the rim, bounced straight up, and then dropped down through the net. He had been bumped during his shot, but no foul had been called.

The Dragons brought the ball down, breaking our press this time, but it looked like they had no plan on how they were going to try to score. They kept making passes, but without "Tall" in the lineup, they didn't seem to have an offence. Number 40 grew impatient and shot a long jumper that hit nothing except the floor as it landed out of bounds.

San Juan inbounded the ball, and Coach quickly called a timeout.

"Catcher, Laser, and Abe . . . report back in," Coach said. "Keep working the fast break, but if you can't take it all the way to the basket, pull it back out and wait for your friends. We'll make some passes to our tall kid, and we'll let him show them that we can play that game, too, and we can do it better than they can. If they return "Tall" to the floor, just run him until he's completely out of gas. It didn't look like he had much left in his tank when he went to the bench. Play smart."

Before running out to the floor all of us patted Otto, San Juan, and Tucson on their backs. They had given us a great effort, and three of us had gotten a chance to catch some rest.

After Laser inbounded the ball, I dribbled slowly toward our basket. We set up our offence with Pickett at a high post and with both Abe and Captain Hook moving back and forth from the lane to the outside perimeter. It only took a few passes before Laser connected with Abe on a high toss near the rim. Abe easily out-jumped the Dragon who attempted to guard him, caught the ball, and shot it softly into the net for another two points, extending our lead to twelve, and Downey's coach jumped to his feet and yelled for a timeout.

"That was a great play," Coach said as we met at the bench. "I expect we'll see 'Tall' back in the lineup because of the ease with which we scored. However, we've got two kinds of poison we can use against the Dragons, and if their coach wants to play 'Tall,' we'll run them to death and foul the tall kid. Nicholson, get ready to report in for Captain Hook if we see Number 31 take the floor when we're called back out. Pickett will go to forward, and your job, Nicholson, is to foul before the kid attempts a shot. Hook will report in before the free throw, and then we'll run until the Dragons' fire is completely extinguished.

When the refs whistled us back to the court, "Tall" walked out toward center court, and Nicholson sprinted to the scorer's table and checked in.

Nicholson took up his position in "Tall's" shadow, and when the lob pass came in, Nicholson jumped and tried to bat the ball away, but all he was able to reach was the tall kid's shoulder and arm. I could hear the sound of Nicholson's hand slapping bare skin, and Nicholson was whistled for a foul.

The buzzer signaled that a sub was coming in as we walked toward the Dragon basket for the free-throw attempt, and when Hook ran out to the floor, Nicholson trotted to the bench with satisfaction showing on his face.

So far in this game the Dragons had built their offence around their tall center. He was the biggest factor in this game. He took most of their shots and scored most of their points. Though he was their leading scorer by far, he was also their greatest liability. Because he was unable to make free throws or run with any speed on defense, fouling him and running our fast break were great ways to neutralize his effect on the game.

His flat free-throw attempt drew some groans from the people sitting behind the Dragon bench when it barely hit the rim and fell into Abe's hands. While a couple Downey players were shaking their heads, Abe fired the ball outside to Laser, and I sprinted toward our basket. Laser's pass led me perfectly, and I drove to the basket, kissed the ball off the backboard, and watched as it fell through the hoop, stretching our lead to fourteen points.

Downey scored four points to our two points in the last two minutes of the third quarter, but while we ran to the bench at the buzzer, I saw that "Tall" was breathing heavily, and he was nearly exhausted.

Eight more minutes . . . twelve-point lead . . . not done yet . . .

Half-Dozen's face really lit up when Coach told him to report in for the center jump, and we were all happy for him. He was the last player on our team to get into the game, and it felt good to me that every member of the team got a chance to play and contribute.

The ref tossed the ball into the air to begin the fourth quarter, and Half-Dozen jumped and reached as high as he could, but he had no chance. He stuck to "Tall" like glue as the Dragons moved toward their basket, and when

Number 20 lobbed a high pass to Number 31, Half-Dozen committed his foul and ran to the bench as Pickett replaced him. His grin made him look like the Cheshire cat, and all six players at the bench stood and welcomed him back.

We continued our fast-paced running game during the last quarter, and we did not allow Downey to get back into the game. Otto and San Juan subbed in, giving Laser and Abe a little rest, and we gradually built our lead to eighteen points, using our outstanding fast break and full-court press. The Dragons appeared to be spent.

With two minutes left in the game, Downey's coach called for a time-out, and I watched as he congratulated his tired players for their effort. He motioned to his bench, and five new guys pulled off their warm-ups and reported in at the scorer's table.

I expected Coach to sit the five of us starters down, but he didn't.

"All right, guys," he said. "Outstanding game! Sons Two through Six will report in as soon as we return to the floor. At the first stoppage of play, you'll run out, one-at-a-time, when you are buzzed in, and we'll let J-Hawk Nation show their appreciation as Pickett and Laser hustle off first . . . then Catcher . . . followed by Abe and Hook. I am really proud of all of you guys. This has been a perfect basketball season.

When Number 15 of the Dragons dribbled the ball out of bounds off his own leg after only five seconds had elapsed, the buzzer sounded, and Sons Two and Three ran out onto the court as Pickett and Laser trotted to the bench. All of J-Hawk Nation stood and yelled and applauded. When Go Forth Son ran onto the floor, I hustled to the bench. I looked at Sarah as I reached Coach, and I saw her wipe her eyes. Mine weren't exactly dry either. Five and Six sprinted out, and the noise continued as Captain Hook and Abe joined us at the bench.

Almost two minutes still remained on the clock, but the game was really over. We cheered for our guys from the bench as the clock wound down. People in the bleachers were treated to some energetic but sloppy play as these ten reserves tried to make the most of their time in the sun.

We ended up with a twenty-point victory and, for the record, Tucson scored the last two points in the history of J-Hawk basketball.

After shaking hands with the tamed Dragons, we stood at the bench and waited for the presentation of the trophies.

Downey's captains were called out to the floor first. Everyone applauded as the two captains went out and carried the second-place trophy back to their team bench.

Laser and Pickett quickly called us into a huddle at the bench. "We're all walking out together," Laser said, "Coach included. Keep your composure. No jumping around and yelling. Act like champions. Remember, we are not surprised that we won. We expected this. Be humble . . . and by the way, everyone played a great game. Wow! . . . We completed the entire season perfectly!"

We did that . . . walked out quietly and slowly . . . still the same team we had been all season. Laser and Pickett carried the trophy as we returned to the bench. They lifted the trophy high into the air, and J-Hawk Nation, taking their cue from us players, applauded respectfully, but they did not go overboard with yelling and other noises.

It had been a great victory!

In the privacy of our locker room, we did celebrate with some shouting and singing. Laughter soon joined in. I sat down on a bench after a couple of minutes of shaking hands and slapping backs, . . . and I felt kind of empty. It wasn't just that I was tired and hungry. I realized that this basketball season's wonderful journey had come to an end. I looked around and watched as my friends congratulated each other and whooped it up. I didn't know it was possible to feel so happy . . . so excited . . . but yet be sad at the same time.

We showered, dressed, and packed up our gear, and when everyone was ready, we walked out to the lobby together. J-Hawk Nation greeted us with some shouts and lots of applause. Sarah greeted me with a warm hug.

"You did it . . . and you were fantastic!" Sarah said excitedly.

"We played pretty well didn't we," I replied. "We didn't care how tall that kid was . . . and we knew Coach would come up with a good plan. We were determined to win this game, this championship, and end with a perfect record."

"I'm so proud of you and so happy for you," Sarah added.

"Thanks," I replied. "I hope you understand how much it has meant to me that you have come to our games. You have added so much fun to this whole season."

Coach came by right at that moment and said, "Sarah, we're taking the bus to a hamburger and soda shop where the Jeffers merchants are treating all the high school kids to a celebration. You are one of us, and I'm sure Catcher wouldn't mind if you came with us. Ask your parents. We're leaving in a couple minutes, and we plan to be back at the hotel by about nine-thirty."

Sarah grabbed my hand, and we went looking for her parents. They both gave their permission without even a slight debate. I thanked them, and we headed toward the exit and the bus.

As I stepped out of the auditorium, I raised both arms toward the city-lit sky and shouted, "We are . . . J-Hawks!

Sarah raised her arms also, and she shouted out, "Hurrah!"

We held hands as we walked to the bus.

Chapter 57
Lobbying

When Sarah and I returned to the hotel from the hamburger and soda shop we found some big stuffed chairs off to a corner of the lobby, and after removing our mittens, stocking caps, and coats, we sank down into the softness of the chairs. These comfortable chairs neither faced each other nor were positioned side-by-side. They formed a kind of right angle, and between them stood a square table, upon which sat a short, stubby lamp that produced a very small amount of light.

We both sat quietly at first, a sign of our exhaustion, and I could not take my eyes off Sarah. When she looked at me and smiled, I felt so comfortable with her that I decided it was time to ask the question that had been knocking around in my head for a couple weeks. I spoke in my most serious voice.

"Sarah . . . what do you want to do with your life? Who do you want to be?" I asked. Then I prepared myself for hearing an answer that possibly wouldn't fit into the picture that I was hoping to see.

Sarah sat there for a while, looking at the high ceiling above. She appeared to be organizing her thoughts. Then she turned her head toward me, and I focused my eyes on her beautiful face, and I listened as she answered clearly and confidently. "I want to do something with music," she said. "I really enjoy playing the piano and the flute, and I love to sing. Whenever something bothers me, I head to the piano . . . because it fixes everything for me . . . makes everything right . . . brings me peace and happiness. I want music to continue to be a big part of my life, but I don't think I want it to be my job. It needs to be my hobby . . . something extra so I can relax and enjoy it without worrying if it will be enough to live off. For my job . . . I think I want to teach young children."

Sarah continued, and I listened intently, smiling as I heard her words, hoping that she would say something . . . anything . . . that suggested that she had room in her future for me.

"I want to have a job, but I don't want it to feel like work. I've watched Mom at school, and I've listened to her at home, and I think that seeing how happy she is in her work has influenced me, and I want to be a teacher, too," Sarah explained. "She says that some days seem long and tiring and difficult, but she almost always tells about how much fun she's had working with her young students, helping them learn to become readers and writers and guiding them to an understanding about how numbers work. Mom says that that she feels like she is making a difference, and that's something that I want to do . . . make a difference. I've experienced this feeling when I've read to kids and talked with them on Saturday mornings at the library, and it has felt good . . . so that's what I think I want to be . . . want to do. What about you?"

I didn't pause very long before I answered because I had prepared my thoughts before I had asked Sarah the question. "As you may have already figured out, I definitely want to do something with sports," I replied. "I know I'm not good enough to earn money as an athlete, but I think I might make a good coach . . . for baseball and basketball. Like with your music . . . I don't want it to be my main job, however. I want to coach as something extra . . . something to do that will always be fun for me . . . something that will allow me to be physically active while I teach young kids skills and let them enjoy playing hard and seeing how being a member of a team can be rewarding and can help them learn lessons about life."

I looked into Sarah's eyes, and I stared at the smile on her face. Then I continued. "For my job . . . I want to do something that works well with coaching . . . and I think that would be teaching high school. I think I would like being a teacher. During our Saturday clinics and at the library, I've felt like a teacher and a coach. I've seen how the kids have responded to me and, like you said, it has been a good feeling to think that maybe I've made a small difference. I'm not sure what I would teach . . . maybe biology and science . . . maybe English . . . I guess I would figure that out in college . . . but I'm pretty sure that I want to be a teacher, and I know that this means I'll never become rich."

Sarah's smile broadened when I made my last statement. "I know you'd be a good teacher," she said. "I've watched you."

We both sat silently for a couple minutes. I was thinking about what Sarah had told me and what I had shared with her, and it looked like she was reflecting on things, too.

There was one more thing that I needed to know, so I gathered all of my courage . . . and I asked quietly, "Do you see **us** together in your picture?"

Sarah again hesitated a moment . . . then answered with a question. "Do you?"

I smiled back. She had just put me in a position where I would have to answer first.

I didn't hesitate at all. "That's what I hope . . . that's what I want," I said, trying to sound confident, but hearing my words come out sounding less confident than what I had wanted.

"Me, too," Sarah said immediately. "I know that's what I want . . . **forever** for us. I've hoped for that since our first date . . . and when you gave me the Forever Heart I knew that's what you wanted, too."

I reached across the table for her hand, and at that moment I heard my inner soul cheering, and I saw how her smile lit up the room far better than the stubby lamp was doing.

"I'm just a kid . . . and there are lots of things that I don't understand . . . and I certainly don't have all the answers . . . but I am absolutely sure about two things," I said . . . and then I waited for Sarah's question.

"C'mon," she said, "you can't say that there are two things you are sure about and then not tell me what they are. That's not fair. I really need to know them. Please, what are they?"

"I'll tell you," I replied. I took a deep breath, then looked directly into Sarah's eyes. "The first thing I am absolutely sure about is that I love you very, very much. I love everything about you . . . your energetic personality and all your great talents . . . your intelligence and your beauty . . . your sense of humor and the kindness you show to people . . . the sparkle in your eyes and your contagious laughter . . . everything . . . absolutely everything."

Sarah's response was a quiet smile accompanied by an almost inaudible "Wow!" She stared at me, and I did not know what to do next. I sat there, thinking that she probably would not let me get by with mentioning only one of my "sure things," but maybe that first one was enough.

"And the other?" she asked, breaking the silence.

After another deep breath, I answered, "I am also absolutely sure that I need to start saving money immediately so that someday . . . we can buy a really good piano."

Sarah started laughing, and I soon was laughing with her.

We joined our hands again above the table, sitting quietly for several minutes as we looked at each other . . . and I thought about how fortunate I had been this winter to have Sarah in my life.

At about ten, Bobby and Debbie came down to the lobby looking for us. They had just returned to the hotel with Mom and Dad, and they were looking for something to do.

"Why don't you go up to your room and get your deck of cards? The four of us can play Hearts," I suggested.

Both of them walked to the elevators.

"I hope you're okay with this," I said to Sarah.

"Of course. It'll be fun," Sarah replied.

"You are supposed to watch us until Mom and Dad come back," Debbie said to me when she and Bobby returned. "They are going out for coffee with your parents, Sarah, and they'll be back in about an hour."

The four of us sat around a coffee table on a big colorful rug, and we began playing Hearts. It wasn't long before I saw Coach and his wife enter the lobby, and when they saw us, they walked over.

"If Catcher plays cards like he played basketball tonight, you three have no chance of beating him," Coach said as he looked at me. "You played another great game tonight, like you have all season, and now you have been crowned a champion."

"Thanks, Coach," I replied. "We couldn't have done it without you. You knew just how to handle us, and you were the best coach we could possible have had."

"Your words are too generous," Coach said as he smiled.

"Since we have played our final game of the basketball season, I think we should be able to stay up until midnight," I said. "How about it, Coach? Midnight?"

"That sounds fair," he replied. "Midnight it is."

"Will you explain this to Sarah's parents?" I asked. "Then you could ask them if Sarah could stay up until midnight, too."

Coach laughed. "You're on your own for that. See you down here at eight-thirty tomorrow morning for breakfast. Good night, kids," he said, and they walked to the elevators.

When our parents returned from coffee, Sarah and I talked them into sitting with us. Bobby and Debbie were getting tired and wanted to stop playing cards, so Sarah asked our parents to play, and she dealt out six hands.

"Coach told me that the team could stay up until midnight tonight because our season has ended," I said casually, "and I think he was including Sarah, too."

All four parents laughed and looked at their watches.

"So Coach is relaxing Sarah's curfew for tonight," Mr. Jenkins said as he winked at his wife. "I guess that will work if she stays here to play cards with us."

"I haven't told Sarah about this yet," I began, "but I talked with both Coach and the Supe at the restaurant after the game. I asked them if they would consider allowing Sarah to ride the school bus home with the team and the other high school kids. The Supe said that he had been expecting me to ask him, and Coach said he didn't have any problem with that. They both agreed that Sarah could ride the bus if you allowed her to. I had already checked with my sister and a couple of her friends, and I asked San Juan, Tucson, and Otto earlier in the day how they felt about it, and everyone told me that it was a great idea. So, Sarah, what do you think? Would you like to ride the bus home with us?"

"I've been hoping for this chance," Sarah replied. She looked at her mom . . . then her dad. "May I?"

"You can talk to the Supe in the morning if you need to," I said to Sarah's parents.

"The Supe already told us about your request, Catcher, when we were out for coffee," Mrs. Jenkins replied. "You have our permission, Sarah."

"We are . . . J-Hawks!" Sarah cheered.

Just before midnight the game of Hearts ended, and I walked Sarah up to her room, with her parents following closely behind us.

"I'll be down in the lobby at seven-thirty," I said, "if you want to take an early morning walk."

"I'll be there," Sarah replied.

The evening had been perfect. We had won the championship game . . . Sarah and I had been together for several hours . . . Coach had let the team stay up late . . . and I had arranged for Sarah to ride the school bus home tomorrow. I had done well. This may have been my best night ever in Des Moines.

In the Stands – With John Garris

I'm wondering how the Jeffers J-Hawks are feeling today after having completed their epic journey that officially began back in November but actually was kicked off many years earlier when each of these players began racing in his neighborhood, began playing hard at the park and on the schoolyard, and began dribbling a basketball in the gym for the first time. No one could have envisioned where this would take them or how it would conclude, but in a fairy-tale ending, the J-Hawks crowned their perfect season last night by soundly defeating the Downey Dragons and claiming the trophy for being this year's best Class B basketball team in the state of Iowa.

I was a stowaway on this adventure, and I was there to observe the great effort that the J-Hawks produced game-after-game, and I saw the signature teamwork that allowed them to be so successful in winning all twenty-seven of their basketball games this season. High levels of trust were developed along the way, expectations were raised, and bumps that were encountered were smoothed out and overcome. It was a classic journey.

Now these young men will awaken this morning and will have to face the fact that the games have all been played, and their season has come to an end. Though that trophy that will be on display at Jeffers Public School is a fine prize, the young J-Hawks will soon discover that the assembled collection of shiny wood and shaped metal doesn't hold much value as it sits and collects dust.

I have some advice for this team of victorious basketball players who entertained me and countless others during this harsh winter. When you stand at the trophy case and admire your prize, reflect on the journey itself. Think back to all the hard work you put in and the great effort you put forth on your quest. Remember the sacrifices you made willingly because you understood that you could achieve far greater success by striving for team goals instead of individual desires. Consider all the good will and inspiration you have passed on to the children in your school and to the members of your community.

You have in your possession something that has a far greater value than that of your trophy. You have all that you have internalized . . . the memories that you can always carry with you . . . the insight and knowledge about how to deal with people and problems . . . and the understanding you have gained about the importance that respect plays in our world.

Walk proudly because you have done your best, and you have given J-Hawk Nation something to cherish forever.

Congratulations . . . and thanks for the ride.

Chapter 58
Best Bus Ride Ever

I had planned ahead by giving one of my duffle bags to Bobby to take home in the family car, so as I stood outside the hotel with all the other players and students, waiting for Coach to pull up in the school bus, I only had one bag to deal with, the one that contained my uniforms and my other gym stuff. Our chaperone for the ride home would again be the Supe, and he was counting how many of us there were while he was talking with several of the students and some parents. I think he had enjoyed the ride to Des Moines, and I think he was probably looking forward to the trip home, but I expected that he would be working a little harder today, keeping order on this leg of the trip. We were an excited and energetic bunch of kids, and we had a rather large trophy with us.

When I saw Sarah and her parents exit the hotel and approach our group, I met them with a suggestion. "It would probably be a good idea if you told the Supe that Sarah will be riding the bus," I said.

"Good morning," Mr. Jenkins said as he walked over and extended his hand to the Supe.

"Good morning," the Supe replied. He nodded to Sarah's mom. "Sarah, will you be joining us for the ride home to Jeffers?"

"Yes I will," Sarah replied. "I really appreciate being able to do this. I hear there may be live music."

"Live music . . . and probably lots of live noise," the Supe added. "It should be a great bus ride home."

Instead of the back seats being saved for the players as they usually were, there were a few girls already sitting with some of my teammates. I was glad to see this because I had already decided, that of course, I would be sitting with Sarah. There was an empty seat that was about five from the back, and after Sarah slid in, I placed my duffle bag under the seat and sat down next to her, on the aisle side. I felt very fortunate that Sarah had been allowed to ride our bus. Now she would be able to experience, first hand, the laughter and the music that had become trademarks of each of our rides to and from the games all season long . . . all **perfect** season long.

We were champions, and it wasn't just us players . . . it was our entire school and our small town. Every member of J-Hawk Nation was part of this, and I knew there would be a big celebration when we returned to Jeffers. Sarah had been one of those members since early in the season. It was right that she would be able to celebrate with us.

I had a hard time taking my eyes off Sarah as she looked around at her Jeffers friends and greeted many of them. I noticed surprised looks on the faces of a few kids when they saw her sitting next to me, and a couple girls nodded to me and said, "Good job, Catch."

It was just about ten o'clock when the Supe boarded the bus and said to Coach, loudly enough for all of us to hear, "Let's get this championship trophy back to Jeffers where we can show it off."

Coach shouted out, "We are . . . J-Hawks!" and then everyone on the bus joined in for a couple more rounds of our J-Hawk shout.

We'd been on the road only about fifteen minutes when Pickett started strumming chords on his ukulele and singing. His was not a solo effort today, as many other voices joined him in singing repeated choruses. Sarah and I sang with the others as I held her hand that had been resting on the bench seat between us. Several times I stopped singing so I could hear Sarah as she harmonized with the other voices, and I thought about how, when I am with her, there always is "harmony." I could tell by Sarah's smile that she was enjoying this bus ride.

A few of the kids shouted out requests to Pickett for songs they wished to hear, and again I thought of "Chances Are." I leaned over and whispered to Sarah, "I considered requesting our song, but I don't think there's enough room in the aisle for the two of us to dance."

Sarah's smile gave me confidence that she appreciated my sense of humor, and I certainly enjoyed hearing her laughter. I made a promise to myself that I would make sure that there would always be laughter for us, because laughing was something we were good at, and it connected us.

After we'd been on the road about an hour, there was a break in the music. "There's something I would like to show you," I said as I pulled out an envelope from my jacket pocket. I handed it to Sarah.

She read aloud what I had written on the outside of the envelope. "The Piano Fund – March 17th, 1962 – one dollar – leftover meal money." Her smile melted me.

I grinned back and said to her, "I know I've got a few years to work on this, but I thought this would be a good time to start. I'll give you a report on how I'm doing from time-to-time, and then someday in the future . . . you and I will go shopping," I explained.

Sarah's blue eyes sparkled more than ever. "I could kiss you," she whispered.

"You might get kicked off the bus if you do that," I replied with a grin. "but am I expecting too much if I ask to collect on that kiss at another time?"

"Like a rain check?" she asked.

"Yes, just like a rain check," I replied, "and I intend to use it sometime today."

I read her lips as they formed three short powerful words . . . and I silently returned the same three words to her.

"Are you warm enough to do without your letter jacket for about ten minutes?" Sarah asked. "There's something I need to do."

"Sure," I replied, though I had no idea what she was up to. I took off the jacket and handed it to her.

Sarah reached into her purse and took out a small sewing kit. "Mom always carries this, and sometimes it really comes in handy. This morning I asked her if I could borrow it," she explained. "I have a souvenir for you from this wonderful weekend. It will help you remember our adventures in Des Moines including the music store, your basketball championship, the wedding we attended, and the Five and Dime."

As I watched, Sarah removed a needle and thread from the kit, and she retrieved a dime-sized white button from her coat pocket. She turned my jacket inside out. After threading the needle, she chose an area near where my gold "J" had been stitched on, and she began to sew the button to the lining of my jacket.

"I really like that," I said. "That button will always remind me of you because, just like you have done, it will touch my heart. It's perfect. I'll remember this weekend forever, and this will be my 'forever button.'"

Sarah smiled and nodded her approval. In just a few minutes she had completed her task, and I put my jacket back on. I warmed back up immediately. A special button worn near the heart can do that for you.

There was much more music and singing and laughter as the bus continued it journey toward Jeffers. As we approached Mason City, the Supe stood, got everyone's attention, and announced, "We'll be making a thirty-minute stop up ahead so you can use the bathrooms and get a quick bite to eat. Don't get lost or lose track of time."

Sarah and I each ate a hamburger, and we shared some fries and a soda. If I had ordered more that this, I would have had to dip into The Piano Fund, and I was not about to do that. Seeing the two straws in the same soda looked really great to me. More than once our heads met over the soda, and we started laughing. On one of those times I collected on my rain check.

"This has been . . . " Sarah began, but I thought I knew what she was about to say so I butted in . . .

" . . . my best bus ride ever," I said. I had guessed correctly. These were the exact same words that she said to me . . . and it sounded like a duet. It was pretty funny. It seemed to me that we were growing closer and closer and that we understood each other really well. It gave me even more confidence. I knew that I could trust what I saw in her beautiful blue eyes.

As Coach prepared to drive out of the parking lot to get back on the road, an Iowa Highway Patrol car pulled up. The officer got out of his vehicle and walked over to our bus. It was Officer Milton. Coach opened the bus door, and Officer Milton climbed the two steps and shook Coach's hand.

"Congratulations J-Hawks!" he said. "I watched your game last night. That was an outstanding effort! I'm here to escort you out of town and the rest of the way to Jeffers. I'll get you home safely . . . and try out my flashing lights again.

The Supe said, "We're not expected back until 2:00."

"Then I guess I'll have to hold down my speed and limit the use of my lights and the siren," Officer Milton replied.

The Highway Patrol car pulled out ahead of the bus, and we continued north through the city.

Though Officer Milton and Coach kept the speed down on the highway, the time passed way too quickly. I didn't want this bus ride to ever end. I knew we needed to get back to Jeffers, but I didn't want it to be today. I realized that a bus ride like this would never happen again for me . . . probably not for any of us. I wanted it to last . . . like a Holloway all-day caramel sucker. I was secretly hoping for bus trouble.

When we reached the top of the hill about two miles east of Jeffers, I spied several cars parked on the side roads and in driveways, and I watched as they pulled in behind us and began following us into town. When we were about a mile from town, the two fire trucks from the Jeffers Volunteer Fire Department pulled onto the road right behind the Highway Patrol car, in the gap in front of our bus, and that's when the celebration began.

Officer Milton started it by turning on his wailing siren. Then the two fire trucks added their blasting sirens and flashing lights, and Coach leaned on the bus's horn. The cars behind us started honking like crazy, and all of us in the bus started yelling loudly, "We are . . . J-Hawks!" as the parade of vehicles slowed to a crawl for the journey's final half-mile into Jeffers. I imagined all the dogs in town howling and adding to the volume of our victory march. Our entry into town was spectacular.

When the bus made its turn onto Main Street, I was shocked when I saw that the sidewalks on the one-block long business section were packed with young kids and grownups that were waving and cheering loudly. I even saw some letter jackets from neighboring schools, and it hit me that J-Hawk Nation had signed up some new recruits.

Suspended high into the air between the bank and the dry goods store hung a banner that read, "Welcome home, J-Hawks! Basketball Champions of Iowa!"

Halfway down the block, the parade halted . . . like we were marching in place, but the noise continued. The Supe left the bus and walked to the patrol car to speak with Officer Milton. Then the Supe shouted to the people on the street, "We'll be at the school in ten minutes!"

During those ten minutes, Officer Milton, with the Supe riding shotgun, took us on a tour of the town, driving on almost every street. I looked out the bus window next to Sarah and another window across to the left, and I saw signs hanging from many trees and porches. The whole town seemed to be decorated with cardboard and butcher paper signs that said things like "J-Hawks Are Champions!" and "J-Hawks . . . Pride of Jeffers!" and "J-Hawks Are Perfect!" and "When is the next clinic?"

Sarah and I read the messages to each other, and I pointed out the simplest sign of all. It read, "27-0."

When the patrol car led us back to the school, the Supe directed the students to exit the bus and enter the school. "Put your bags in the assembly room," he added.

He kept us twelve players and Coach on the bus, and he spoke to us very briefly. "Congratulations, J-Hawks," he said. "You are champions in every sense of the word. I am very proud of all of you. You have certainly given your community something to remember. Now it's time to let J-Hawk Nation honor you. Coach, lead your team into the gym."

We rose very quietly from our seats and grabbed our gear. No one said a word as we grouped together outside by the bus. Coach waited patiently as we organized into two lines behind Pickett and Laser who carried the trophy together, and I saw that almost everyone else was carrying bags of warm-ups or basketballs or someone's duffle bag. We still were a team.

It was Captain Hook who broke the silence. Though he spoke softly, I could hear the emotion in his voice. "We are . . . J-Hawks!" he said. "We are champions, . . . and we are the kings on the hill."

With our gloved and mittened hands we gave muffled applause to Hook as we followed Coach into the packed school gym.

J-Hawk Nation stood and applauded as we walked in and dropped off our gear in the locker room. Then we stood in front of the 13 chairs that had been set up for us at the front of the stage. The applause continued. No one in the gym sat or stopped clapping until the thirteen of us were directed by the Supe to sit down.

"J-Hawk Nation," the Supe announced, "here are your champions."

Everyone stood again, and again the applause and the shouts continued until, this time, Coach motioned for us to stand. Once standing, we waved to the people in all parts of the gym, and when we finally sat down, the others sat, and the applause died out.

I could hear my heart beating, and I felt my eyes beginning to mist up. I started breathing faster, and I looked around at all the faces, trying to locate Sarah amongst all of these people, . . . and then I heard her voice.

"I'm behind you in the bleachers," she whispered.

I quickly turned and looked over my left shoulder. I spotted her smile immediately. Sarah was sitting in the second row. I took a couple deep breaths and began to relax. *Settle down and try to enjoy this.*

"I see you must have gone to the hardware store while you were in Des Moines," the Supe said to Laser and Pickett, and laughter filled the gym as he beckoned them to come forward. "I think if we rearrange some shelves in the trophy case we can find a spot to display this well-earned fine piece of hardware, but it may eventually end up in the Jeffers Public Library as a symbol of the spirit of this community. For now, how about setting the trophy on that small table at the foot of the stage. There may be some members of J-Hawk Nation who would like to see it up close and touch it."

Laser and Pickett carried the trophy to the table, raised it high into the air, and shouted out, "To J-Hawk Nation!" Then they set it down to more wild applause.

There were a few short speeches that were given by the Supe, the school board chairman, Coach, and a representative of the town merchants. Laser and Pickett were the last to step to the microphone, and they thanked everyone for their great support.

"We are proud of our team, our school, and our community," Laser said. "We wanted to bring honor to Jeffers, and I think we have done that."

Wild applause filled the small gym.

Pickett waited until the gym was almost silent again. "Let everyone

remember what can be accomplished when people work together unselfish-
ly. This trophy is a tribute to the spirit shown by our school and our town."

More applause greeted his words.

The Supe stood and shouted out to all corners of the gym, "Now, let us
eat cake!"

For the next hour or so we did eat from the many small cakes that had
recently been baked in Jeffers homes, we devoured cookies that were right
out of the ovens, and we drank chilled J-Hawk Juice and hot coffee.

Sarah and I sat at a lunch table with friends, and we all told stories about
the weekend in Des Moines. I noticed that the quietest kids at our table were
my teammates. Maybe the end of the season was hitting us. Basketball was
done now . . . our journey was over. We had won the state championship,
but that felt like an empty accomplishment as I sat there, realizing that there
were no more basketball games to be played with these guys. I'd be living on
memories now, rather than the excitement of the games. I knew that would
not be enough for me.

"How are you doing?" Sarah asked me. "You are kind of quiet, and I'm
not used to that."

I smiled at her. "I was just thinking about our season. We've had a lot of
excitement, but I guess that ends today. Part of me feels a little sad, but I'm
fortunate that my winter has been filled with a lot more than basketball, and
I don't see an end coming for that. There will be lots of tomorrows."

We got up from the table and moved around the gym, talking to many
kids and grown-ups as we wandered around. Three kids asked me if we were
holding a final clinic, and I reminded them that we had promised them one
more clinic when our season had ended.

Laser must have fielded questions about a clinic also, because he made
an announcement with the microphone that our team's final basketball practice would be held on Saturday at 8:45, and our final clinic would follow at
9:30. When he invited everyone to attend and join in the fun I cheered along
with many others.

Sarah and I sneaked out of the gym and sought out some quiet space by the elementary rooms where we sat on the floor in the hallway and caught our breath. I couldn't stop looking at her, and I couldn't stop smiling either. I felt so lucky to have her as a friend.

"I'm sure you won't be too surprised to hear me say that this has been my best weekend ever," I began.

Sarah lit up the hallway with her smile. "Mine too," she said.

"Winning those two basketball games was great," I explained, "and I really had fun listening to you play the piano and sing in the music store. Your beautiful song at the wedding . . . Wow! The walks, the movie, sitting in the lobby, the contest we had, the bus ride home, and this celebration . . . All of these things made it the best, and it's because you were there with me. You are the reason for my best weekend ever."

"Thank you," Sarah replied. "Wouldn't it be great to have more times like this?"

"Yeah, it would," I said, "and I know we will. I'm counting on it. Forever is a long time, and we'll get lots of chances for more adventures. Every time I'm with you . . . that's my best time ever."

Sarah smiled and touched my hand. "I wish we could sit here longer," she said, "but I think I need to go back to the gym. My parents will be looking for me."

We walked back to the gym and into the lunchroom, and we found Sarah's parents sitting on a bench at a table with my mom and dad. We sat down with them. They wanted to hear more about our city walk and the wedding we attended, so Sarah and I retold the stories, and we all laughed together and were amazed one more time by our adventures. I was enjoying myself so much that I wanted to stay there until we were chased out.

"Sorry, everyone," Sarah's mom apologized after another twenty minutes had passed. "I hate to be the one to end this good time, but I have some lessons to prepare for tomorrow. Catcher, your basketball team has given our family an exciting, wonderful winter, and we thank you for that. I know that Sarah is very pleased to have met you, and Andy and I have made many new friends, including your family. Andy has also found a Saturday morning coffee shop, and I don't think he'll be giving that up. I think Sarah just might want to ride along. Your games might be over, but I expect we'll still be see-ing you often, and we look forward to that."

"Thanks," I said. "I'm really glad that you came to my games, and thanks for dragging Sarah along to Des Moines. This has been a great weekend."

"Best ever?" Sarah's mom asked as everyone laughed.

"Best ever," I replied as I smiled and looked at Sarah.

As I walked Sarah to her car, we made plans for the Saturday morning clinic and a Saturday night movie date. It would be almost a week before I would see her again . . . unless I could pull my plan together.

In the Stands – With John Garris

I've taken some criticism during the course of this basketball season. Some callers and writers have said that I became too biased toward the J-Hawks, that I watched and reported on too many of their games and not enough games of other teams. My response? Maybe so.

This was a season that will stand against all others for these young men from Jeffers. They did what no other team had ever done before, and they did it with style and skill, with grace and humility. I offer no excuse for following the J-Hawks so closely. This team was the best story of the season, and I did my best to relate that story to my readers.

I saw amazing basketball skills: nimble dribbling, precise passing, accurate shooting, strong rebounding, and merciless running and defending. The players worked extremely well together. It didn't matter who scored points as long as someone did. They played like they really care for each other.

NEWS FLASH: The J-Hawks do really care for each other. These players connected as teammates, and they brought families and community members together to honor and assist others who were in need of help. They provided basketball clinics and library sessions for youngsters. Basketball games became such a huge event that no one wanted to leave the gym when the game ended. J-Hawk Juice and cookies, honorary captains, a top-rated ushering crew, community service, support and compassion for veterans and others, J-Hawk Nation stocking caps that were worn everywhere . . . There was so much more than just basketball.

Did I write "just basketball?" The J-Hawks capped their spectacular season by winning the small-school state championship. In their efforts on the gym floor they were unmatched, in their service to the community they were unequaled, in their twenty-seven games they were undefeated, and in the hearts of J-Hawk Nation they were unbelievable. The team was a beacon of light that showed the rest of us how it could and should be done.

So you think I gave them too

much time and too much space in my column? Not by my standards. They earned every inch of ink I dedicated to them. My stocking cap is off to this group of young men who resolved to bring glory to their school in its final year of existence.

I'm sad that the season has ended, and I have one fewer excuse to put miles on my car driving to The Jeffers Café, where the coffee is always hot, the service is excellent, and where I can sit with the resident experts of J-Hawk Nation and talk basketball.

If you've not had enough of J-Hawk basketball, you need to visit the café, particularly on a Saturday morning, and take a seat in a booth or at a table, or find an empty stool at the counter if one is available. Listen to the regulars as they replay the season and acknowledge the accomplishments of their young heroes.

If you do go, I recommend that you get there early, as I do, because the café fills quickly.

Chapter 59

Serving Time

This was one of those ideas I had that I knew no one would agree with, that's why I couldn't tell anyone what I was up to. I was sure Mom would try to talk me out of it, and Dad would simply lay down the law and stop me. Even Sarah would probably tell me not to do it, but I felt responsible. It didn't seem fair to me that Sarah should have to stay after school with the delinquents . . . just because she missed a day of school while she was watching my J-Hawks play basketball in the state tournament in Des Moines.

Yesterday during the community celebration in the gym I had made up my mind and had formed a plan. Now all I had to do was put all the pieces together, but I wasn't sure that I could make it work. That's another reason that I couldn't tell anybody about it, but I did have determination on my side. I guess it was my stubbornness showing.

My school schedule had me spending the last forty-five minutes of my day in study hall, but as soon as my last class ended on Monday, I walked directly up to the Supe's desk in the front of the assembly room. I crossed my fingers that he would listen to me.

"I need to be excused from study hall today because I kind of have an appointment," I said, not totally telling the truth.

"**Kind of** have an appointment?" he repeated. "You'll have to do better than that."

I explained. "I need to get to Madison Lake right away to see someone, but he's not expecting me." That's all I offered.

"So this isn't about Sarah?" he asked.

"It kind of is about Sarah," I continued, as I practiced being more truthful, "but she doesn't know anything about this. I have to talk to her principal. He's making her stay after school today because she missed school on Friday when she went to our basketball game."

"What exactly are you planning to tell him?" the Supe inquired.

"I don't really know for sure," I replied, "but I hope he'll allow me to sit in the detention room where Sarah will be. I feel responsible."

"Do your parents know about this?" he asked.

"No," I answered. "I'm doing this on my own. I think they'd try to talk me out of this."

The Supe shook his head in a way that suggested to me that he thought I had a dumb plan, but he smiled. "How will you get there?" he asked.

"I'll get out on the road and catch a ride," I said, "but I have to leave right away. I don't think I have much time because I'd like to get to their high school before students are dismissed."

"If I let you go, can I count on you not getting yourself in trouble, and you'll tell me tomorrow morning how everything worked out?" the Supe asked.

"Yes, Sir," I replied. "May I go now?"

As soon as I saw him nod his head I grabbed my letter jacket and the novel I had been assigned to read, and I exited the school. I ran up to Main Street and started walking west, knowing that I would need to turn around to face any cars and drivers that were going in my direction. I was lucky that it wasn't too cold or too windy out today, but I also needed some luck with traffic on the road. I didn't want to put my thumb up to catch a ride, so I knew that I needed to get to the edge of town to make it more obvious that a ride was what I was looking for.

It only took about ten minutes for a farmer to stop in his pickup. I didn't know him, but when he asked if I needed a ride, I told him I was headed for the school in Madison Lake.

"Hop in," he said. "I'm going to Madison Lake."

The man knew about our basketball team and that we'd won the small-school championship. We talked about our season during most of the ride, but I didn't tell him why I was going to MLHS. When he dropped me off in front of the school, I thanked him and walked around the busses that were parked next to the curb. I had made good time. School had not yet ended for the day.

When I stepped inside the school I asked a student who was walking in the hallway where the principal's office was located.

"Right around the corner," he told me as he pointed.

I found the office and walked in. "I'd like to see Mr. Weston," I said to the woman at the desk. "My name's Catcher, and I've talked with him before."

"Go right in," she said. "I know he's busy, but maybe he'll have a couple of minutes for you."

He recognized me when I walked in.

"Catcher," he said as he stood and shook my hand. "You completed an outstanding basketball season. Congratulations on your J-Hawk championship. What brings you here today?"

"I came here to serve detention because I'm the one who is responsible for Sarah Jenkins missing school on Friday," I said. "I hope you will let me sit in the classroom where Sarah will be. I won't bother her or anyone else. I have an assignment to work on, a book to read."

"Is Sarah expecting you?" Mr. Weston asked.

"No," I replied. "I didn't tell her anything about this because she told me that going to the game was her choice, and besides, I didn't know if I could make this idea work. It's important to me that I do this. Please let me stay."

"It's quite unusual for a student to ask to serve detention, especially someone who doesn't go to school here, but I think I understand what's going on. I'll take you to the room after the dismissal bell rings in about three minutes," Mr. Weston said. "You can sit in here until then. Tell me about your games in Des Moines."

I told him a quick version about the games, and he seemed very interested in what I said.

"Now might be a good time for me to schedule a visit to your school," Mr. Weston said, thinking aloud. "I'll make a call in a few minutes."

When the bell rang and the halls emptied out, Mr. Weston walked me to Room 205 on the second floor. I waited in the hallway while Mr. Weston entered the room and brought out the supervising teacher. We were introduced, and an explanation was given. Mr. Weston assured the teacher that I was a cooperative and respectful student.

"I'll assign you a desk," the teacher said. "Follow me."

I thanked Mr. Weston and followed the teacher into the room.

Sarah was really surprised when I walked in and sat down. She stared at me at first, then a beautiful smile formed on her face, and I knew that what I was doing was worth it.

I looked at her for just a few seconds, then took out my copy of *To Kill a Mockingbird,* found the place where I had left off, and began reading silently about a conversation between Atticus and Scout.

One quick hour later, the teacher excused us, and I met Sarah outside the room. "You didn't have to do this," she said.

I smiled and replied, "Since you missed school because of me, I felt that I needed to 'suffer' detention, too. It didn't seem fair that you are punished and I am not."

"Let's go to Mom's room," Sarah said. "She's waiting for me."

Sarah asked me some questions as we walked, and I explained some things to her.

"How did you get here?" Sarah asked.

"I caught a ride, and I'll need to catch a ride home, too," I replied.

"Mom, guess who's here?" Sarah said as we entered the kindergarten room.

"Catcher!" Mrs. Jenkins said, looking really surprised. "What are you doing here?"

"Catch came to school at the end of the day to serve detention with me because he felt responsible for my missing school on Friday," Sarah explained.

"Wow! I bet not many kids volunteer for detention," Mrs. Jenkins said.

I accepted a ride to the Jenkins house, but when we got there, I told Sarah that I needed to leave right away.

"I've got chores to do at home," I explained.

"It was good to see you today," Sarah said, "and thank you."

We embraced, and I kissed her on the forehead. Then I turned to walk down the street toward the highway.

"I hope you catch a ride soon," Sarah called out.

"Me too," I replied. "See ya."

At about two o'clock on Tuesday, the Supe entered the assembly room with Mr. Weston. *He must have made his call yesterday.*

When Mr. Weston was passing by my desk, he stopped and shook my hand. "It's good to see you again, Catcher," he said, and then he continued walking toward the big desk in the front of the room. Several students looked at me, and I could see the questions on their faces.

I stood up and followed Mr. Weston. "I'd like permission to serve one more day of detention," I said to him quietly. "I need one more day."

Mr. Weston smiled at me and looked at the big clock that hung on the west wall. "All right," he said, "and I'll try to time this so I can give you a ride today."

"Thanks," I replied.

I asked the Supe, "May I say something to the students before Mr. Weston begins? I think that I can help his visit go better than last time."

He nodded, and I waited until everyone quieted down in their seats.

"When Mr. Weston visited us back in January," I began, "I remember that a lot of us were upset, and I know that I didn't do very well. I've talked with him a few times since then, and I have apologized for how I acted that day. I've found Mr. Weston to be very understanding and very helpful. Yesterday when I talked with him he congratulated our school on winning the basketball championship. Three times I've been inside Madison Lake High School, and I can sense that it's a good school. I think we will do all right there."

Mr. Weston's talk went well, and there were no interruptions or distractions. When he finished his presentation and answered a few questions, he passed out a handout to each student. That's when I approached the Supe and told him that I needed to be excused for another appointment and that Mr. Weston had offered me a ride.

"Go on," he said, "but this is the last day."

When I walked into Room 201, I reported to the supervisor and handed her the note that Mr. Weston had written. I looked at Sarah and smiled, and her return smile reached all the way to my soul. I sat in the desk I was assigned and continued reading my novel until the hour passed, and we were excused. Then I left the room to wait for Sarah in the hallway.

Mr. Weston was standing right outside the door.

"You have now paid your debt to society," he said to Sarah, and he laughed at his own joke.

"No, I have two more hours . . . two more days," she insisted.

"I show on this paper that you have credit for four hours . . . two yesterday and two today. I couldn't ignore the two hours that Catcher contributed for you. You're done, Sarah."

"Thank you, Mr. Weston," Sarah said. Then she turned to me. "Thank you, Catch."

"You are welcome," Mr. Weston and I both replied.

On our walk to her mother's room, Sarah said to me, "You have a very kind heart. Thank you for serving time with me."

"You are welcome, Sarah," I said again. "I really care about you, and I felt that this was the right thing to do."

"These have been my best two days in detention ever," Sarah said, and we both started laughing.

"Mom," Sarah said when we reached the kindergarten room, "Catcher came to detention again today, and Mr. Weston told me at the end of the hour that I was done with detention because he counted the two hours that Catch gave. Isn't that something?"

"Yes, it is," Mrs. Jenkins replied, and she nodded and smiled at me. "What Catcher did is really something."

"May I walk you home, Sarah?' I asked. "Then I need to get out on the road right away."

"Let's go," Sarah replied, "but I'm sad that you have to leave right away."

"It's okay," I said as I smiled. "I made a choice, and everything was worth it."

We held hands during our walk, and I was really glad that I had decided to sit in detention with Sarah for these two days. It did make a difference in how I felt, and I had saved Sarah from having to report on Wednesday and Thursday. Mr. Weston had been generous in counting my two hours.

I walked Sarah up the steps to her door. As I looked into her eyes I put my arms around her and said, "I enjoyed serving time with you."

Sarah laughed at me.

"Would you like to go to a movie with me on Saturday night?" I asked. "Since my basketball season is over I'll be able to stay out a little later. Maybe your dad will let you stay out later, too."

"A movie sounds great," Sarah answered, "and I'll work on Dad."

I held Sarah in my arms and kissed her on the top of her head. Then I said in my best John Wayne voice, "Well, Missy, my work here is done, so Ol' Paint and I will be headin' out of town now." I turned and started walking down the sidewalk.

When I reached the street I looked back, raised both my arms, and shouted out, "We are . . . J-Hawks, and we have served our time!"

I could hear Sarah laughing as I headed down the street, and I knew that all was right with the world.

Chapter 60

A New Season

April was already into its second full week now, and the days were getting visibly longer, the grass and weeds in our yard were greening up, and temperatures were gradually climbing. This was one of my favorite times of the year because I enjoy seeing nature awaken each spring . . . and because I play baseball.

About a week after our basketball season ended Coach had started sending us outside to play catch during the last fifteen minutes of our end-of-the-day study hall. He wanted us to loosen up our arms, but he did not want us throwing too hard, so he sent us out each day without our baseball gloves. The strategy was to build up arm strength and flexibility without the risk of doing damage to our elbows or shoulders. At the same time our hands were being toughened up by catching baseballs barehanded, though we didn't throw very hard.

Some days, instead of throwing, we ran. Coach told us that it was about a mile around the huge block that included the school property and the farm fields that surrounded it on three sides. Since most of us had played basketball, running a mile was not much of a challenge.

Last week we had played our first two games of the spring season. On Tuesday we had beaten Benson 7-1 at home behind Laser's great pitching effort, but on Thursday we had lost to Shelby 6-5. San Juan pitched okay in that game, but we made too many errors that resulted in unearned runs for Shelby, and we never recovered. On the ride home from that second game I thought about the fact that we had already lost more games in baseball (one) than we had lost during our entire basketball season. Different sports . . . different skills . . . different results.

I was excited about today's game because we were taking on Madison Lake at their field, and Sarah had told me on the phone that she planned to watch the game.

"Whom will you be cheering for?" I had asked her.

"I will be hoping in my heart that you play well and that you don't get hurt," she had answered, "but I won't be cheering out loud for one team over the other."

"Fair enough," I had responded. "That's a good plan. You are a very wise fifteen-year-old. By the way, when do you turn sixteen?"

"In about two weeks," Sarah had replied.

"Wow! I guess it's about time that I found that out," I said, and I didn't reveal anything about the perfect gift that I had already decided I would give her on her birthday. All I had to do was find it and borrow some money from Mom. Because of the memory behind it, I knew Sarah would think it was a special gift.

Coach and Pickett both drove to the game, their cars each packed with half of the baseball team and some of the equipment. We certainly didn't have a lot of room in the cars, and there was no singing, but it was just a short drive that I had made many times since I had begun dating Sarah.

Today was a decent day for an April ball game. The sky was a bright blue, with no clouds in sight, and it was warm enough that I didn't need a jacket. There was little wind, so I figured no one would have trouble catching fly balls or making accurate throws.

We arrived at the ball field at about four, and I started playing catch with Laser. I was glad he would be pitching today because he gave us our best chance to win. If he had trouble in this game, Coach would probably put Pickett in to throw, and even I was considered an emergency pitcher. I really didn't care if I ever pitched again because I had discovered how much fun it was to be the catcher . . . and I was good at it.

It was after we completed our infield warm-ups that Sarah arrived with a few of her friends. She smiled warmly and waved to me, then sat in the bleachers behind home plate. Seeing her at my game brought back memories of the basketball season that had ended less than a month ago, and I remembered how wonderful it had been, falling in love with her day-by-day and game-by-game.

As Madison Lake took the field to begin the first inning, I grabbed a couple bats and starting loosening up in the on-deck circle. Coach had chosen me to bat leadoff, as he had in the first two games, and my job would be to get us off to a good start.

The umpire called "Play ball," and as I dropped one of the bats to the ground and walked toward the batter's box, I saw that Mr. Jenkins had arrived at the ballpark, and I watched as he stepped up a couple rows on the bleachers and took a seat behind Sarah and her friends. I was surprised to see him here . . . but I was glad he came. I nodded to him.

My "friend" Joe was behind the plate for Madison Lake, and I wouldn't have been surprised if he had signaled to his pitcher to throw at me, so I didn't dig in too deeply when I stepped into the batter's box to hit. After taking two pitches, including a ball that was in the dirt and an inside fastball that was a called strike, I readied myself for the third pitch. I took a good look at it as it came right toward the heart of the plate. I stepped into the pitch and took a quick level swing. My timing was perfect, and I smashed a line drive out to left field, dropping the bat as I ran quickly to first base for a solid single. I had done the first part of my job. Now I needed to complete the second part by scoring

I didn't even look at Coach for a signal to steal. He had told me before our first game that I had permission to steal second base any time I was sure I could make it. He called this "giving me the green light." I studied the pitcher as he went into his stretch, as he glanced over his left shoulder at me, and as he lifted his left leg up high and delivered his pitch to his catcher. I had learned enough . . . I would run on the next pitch.

I crouched and got a good lead. As soon as the pitcher lifted his leg I took off running, and I slid feet-first into second base, kicking up a small cloud of dust and beating the throw easily.

After Tucson was called out on a pitch that he thought was low, Laser lined one into the gap between left and center, and I rounded third at full speed and scored standing up as Laser slid into second for a double. Pickett followed with a ground-ball single to right, scoring Laser, and after San Juan and Hook both grounded out, we took the field for the bottom of the first, leading 2-0.

The only base runner for Madison Lake in the first inning had reached by taking a walk. Joe had shown that he has a good eye. I called timeout and went out to the mound to talk to Laser.

"I know the runner at first," I said. "I think he'll try to steal on us because I stole on him, and he doesn't like me much. Please keep your first three or four pitches on the outside half of the plate and out of the dirt."

"Hey," Laser replied. "You know that the ball doesn't always go where I want it to, but give me a good target where you want the ball, and I will try to hit it."

"All right," I said. "I'll do that. If I can throw Joe out at second . . . that would be perfect."

On the third pitch Joe took off . . . and I was ready. I caught the ball cleanly, quickly shifted my feet as I cocked my arm behind my ear, and fired a bullet right over Laser's head. He ducked, and the ball continued on its path toward second base. The ball might have hit the base if San Juan had not picked it off and put his glove down in front of the bag in plenty of time to tag Joe on his foot for the third out of the inning. It was a perfect play . . . and it was Joe.

The game went our way. Only one more Madison Lake runner tried to steal, and I threw him out at second, too. Laser limited their batters to only three hits and that one walk, and we had made only one error. Meanwhile we scored eleven runs on about ten hits and maybe five walks, and their infielders had made three errors.

In the second inning I hit a liner down the leftfield line, scoring Abe from third, and I slid into second with a double. After Tucson moved me to third with a bunt single, Laser drove me in with a Texas Leaguer to left. Solid singles by Pickett and San Juan allowed both Tucson and Laser to score, giving us a 6-0 lead.

I reached base one more time in the game when I drew a walk. I didn't care that we had a good lead in the game . . . I took off for second anyway, and Joe's throw wasn't close to getting me. My teammates continued to get hits, so I was able to score my third run of the game, and earned my position in the batting order as the leadoff man.

The umpire stopped the game after five complete innings because of the ten-run rule, and I quickly gathered up my equipment so I would have some time to talk to Sarah and her dad.

"Catcher," Mr. Jenkins said after he walked around the screen and stepped onto the field. "Your name makes a lot more sense to me now after seeing how well you play your position. It appears that you have athletic skills beyond basketball. You played a great game, but I'm not sure it's fair for a catcher to steal bases and then throw out opponents when they attempt to steal on him."

He laughed, patted me on the back, and moved off to talk to Coach and other players he knew from having watched our basketball games.

I walked around to the other side of the backstop and sat next to Sarah on the bleachers. "Did your friends abandon you?" I asked.

"They came to watch our boys play, and they are walking back to the school with them," she answered.

"Thanks for coming to the game," I said.

"You are welcome," Sarah replied. "I enjoyed it. You played really well. I see by the sweat on your face that you play hard in baseball like you did in basketball, and I can see that dirt is now part of your reward." She laughed.

"I'm guessing that my girlfriend is not too impressed with me right now," I said as I smiled and gazed at her beautiful face."

Again Sarah laughed, and she reached for my hand. "You are wrong. I am impressed . . . always. Did it feel good to steal bases against Joe and then throw him out at second when he tried to steal on you?" she asked.

"As a matter of fact it did," I replied. "Now I think I've evened things up with Joe, and I'm ready to forgive him for his behavior on that day at The Grill. Are you okay if I do that?"

"Yes, it's time," Sarah said as she nodded.

I knew I only had a few minutes before we would pack up the cars and drive back to Jeffers, but I secretly held out hope that Mr. Jenkins would do me a big favor by engaging Coach in a long conversation in order to stall our departure.

"It's really good to see you again . . . always is. Would you like to go to a movie with me on Saturday night?" I asked.

"I would," Sarah replied. "If you pick me up early we can walk to the movie theater from my house and then stop at the park on our walk home."

"I really like being with you, Sarah. You've made these last few months my best ever," I said. "I can't imagine my life without you."

At that exact moment I heard the distant whistle of a train coming into Madison Lake on the tracks that were about a quarter-mile north of the baseball field. I looked into Sarah's eyes, and I could tell that she remembered that day when I called to warn her about the train that was heading her way . . . on these same tracks. We both sat silently as the whistle sounded a second time. Then Sarah moved closer, and I put my arm around her.

"You don't have to worry about things, Sarah. I will always be there to keep you safe," I whispered to her.

"I know you will," Sarah replied.

"Catch, are you riding with us or are you walking home?" San Juan shouted from near Pickett's car.

"I'll be right there!" I yelled back. "Just give me a minute."

I turned back to Sarah. "Thanks for being in my life. I will love you forever."

Sarah touched her necklace and smiled as we stepped down off the bleachers, and I walked her to her car where her dad was waiting.

"Will you be stopping by the house on Saturday night?" Mr. Jenkins asked.

I nodded. "We'll be going to a movie," I said.

I stared into Sarah's beautiful blue eyes and smiled. I said confidently, "It looks like our friendship will survive into a new season."

"We'll survive every new season," Sarah replied, and I believed her because I could see truth in her sparkling eyes.

As I walked away, I raised both arms into the air as a salute to April's blue sky, and I shouted out, "We are . . . J-Hawks! . . . Forever!"

I turned my head quickly for one more glance at Sarah, and I saw that she had raised her arms up high, and I heard the echo. "Forever!" she shouted. "Forever!"

CPSIA information can be obtained at www.ICGtesting.com
Printed in the USA
BVOW03s1800250713

326829BV00002B/321/P